MORE PRAISE FOR JOHN SAUL

"Chills and thrills . . . a great hair-raiser."

—*San Diego Union-Tribune*

"Chilling suspense."

—*Library Journal*

"One of the masters of the genre."

—*Atlanta Journal*

"All the right scares in all the right places."

—*Seattle Times*

"Suspense-filled . . . tension and terror."

—*Rocky Mountain News*

JOHN SAUL

Three Complete Novels

JOHN SAUL

Three Complete Novels

BRAINCHILD
NATHANIEL
THE GOD PROJECT

WINGS BOOKS
NEW YORK • AVENEL, NEW JERSEY

This omnibus was originally published in separate volumes under the titles:

This edition contains the complete and unabridged texts of the original editions. They have been completely reset for this volume.

This 1995 edition is published by Wings Books,
distributed by Random House Value Publishing, Inc.,
40 Engelhard Avenue, Avenel, New Jersey 07001,
by arrangement with the author.

Random House
New York • Toronto • London • Sydney • Auckland

Printed and bound in the United States of America

Library of Congress Cataloging-in-Publication Data

Saul, John.
[Novels. Selections]
Three complete novels / John Saul.
p. cm.
Contents: Brain child—Nathaniel—The God project.
ISBN 0-517-12334-7
1. Horror tales, American. I. Title.
PS3569.A787A6 1995
813'.54—dc20 94-42892
CIP

8 7 6 5 4 3 2 1

CONTENTS

BRAINCHILD

To Shirley Osborn, with love, affection and appreciation

PROLOGUE

The late-August sun blazed down on the parched hills with an intensity that was usually felt only much farther south, and south, the sixteen-year-old boy thought as he moved stealthily through the scrub-oak underbrush of his father's vast *rancho,* was where he and his family should have gone long before now.

But his father had insisted on staying.

All year, since the Treaty of Guadalupe Hidalgo had been signed, his parents had been quietly arguing about what to do.

"They will drive us away," his mother had said over and over. She had said it again only this morning, her tall figure held firmly erect as she sat on a ladderback chair in the shade of the eastern wall of the hacienda, dressed, as always, in black, despite the heat of the morning. Her hands, their long slender fingers betraying nothing of what she might be feeling, worked steadily at the needlepoint with which she occupied herself during the few moments of each day that the pressures of the hacienda allowed her. But his father, as he had every other day, only shook his head.

"In Los Angeles they are honoring the Spanish grants. They will honor them here, too."

Doña María's eyes had flashed with impatience, and her mouth had tightened, though when she spoke it was with the respect she always paid her husband, and had taught her daughters to pay to both their father and their brother. "They have not found gold in Los Angeles. There, the land is worthless. Why not honor the grants? But here, even if there is no gold, they will take the land. In San Francisco the ships arrive every day, and the city is full. Where will they go?"

"To the goldfields," Don Roberto de Meléndez y Ruiz had insisted, but Doña María had only shaken her head.

"Most of them will go to the goldfields. But not all of them, Roberto. Some will see into the future, and want the land. And those men will come here. Who will defend us?"

"The presidio at Monterey—"

"The presidio is theirs now. The war is over, and we have lost. Our troops have gone back to Mexico, and we should follow them."

"No!" Don Roberto had replied. "We are not Mexicans. We are Californios, and this is our home. We built this hacienda, and we have a right to stay here! And stay here we shall!"

"Then we shall stay," Doña María had said, her voice suddenly placid. "But the hacienda will not be ours. The *rancho* will be taken from us. New people are coming, Roberto, and there is nothing we can do."

And now, this afternoon, they had come.

From a hilltop two hundred yards away, the boy saw a squadron of United States cavalry appear in the distance, making its leisurely way up the trail toward the whitewashed walls of the hacienda. Nothing in their manner indicated a threat, and yet the boy could feel danger. But instead of mounting his horse and riding home, he tied the animal to a tree beyond the crest of the hill, then crouched down into the brush.

He saw his father waiting at the open gates, and could almost hear him offering the men the hospitality of his home. But the riders did not go inside. The squadron waited while one of the stable boys brought his father's horse. Don Roberto mounted, and the squadron, with his father in its midst, started back down the trail toward the mission village a mile away.

The boy moved as swiftly as he could, but it was slow going. There was only the one trail, and all his instincts told him to stay off it, so he made his way through the tangle of dry brush, hiding himself as best he could in the clumps of oak.

He watched as the squad drew close to the mission, and for a moment his fear eased. Perhaps they were only taking his father to a meeting with the American commandant.

No.

The squadron passed the mission, and continued another hundred yards down the trail to the enormous oak tree around which the village had originally been built. Under its mighty branches, Indians had camped for untold centuries before even the Franciscan *padres* had arrived.

Suddenly the boy knew what the squadron was going to do, and knew there was nothing he could do to prevent it.

Nor could he leave. He had to stay, to watch.

As his father sat straight in the saddle, one of the men threw a rope over the lowest branch of the tree, while another tied Don Roberto's hands behind his back. Then they led the black stallion under the tree and tied the free end of the rope around Don Roberto's neck.

From his hiding place in the brush, the boy tried to see his father's face, but he was too far away, and the shade of the oak was impenetrable.

Then one of the cavalrymen lashed the black stallion's flanks with a riding crop; the horse reared, snorting, and came stamping back to earth. A second later it was over.

The black horse was galloping up the trail toward the hacienda, and Don Roberto de Meléndez y Ruiz's body was swinging under the embracing branches of the oak tree.

The cavalry squadron turned and at the same leisurely pace started back up the trail toward the hacienda.

The boy waited until the soldiers were out of sight before he picked his way the last fifty yards to the floor of the valley. He stared up into his father's face for a long time, trying to read in the eyes of the corpse what might now be expected of him. But there was nothing in the twisted grimace of pain, or the bulging, empty eyes. It was as if, even as he died, Don Roberto still hadn't understood what was happening to him.

But the boy understood.

He turned, and faded away back into the brush.

It was late in the afternoon, and as the sun dropped toward the western horizon, long shadows began their march across the hilltops. Far away, the boy could see the beginnings of a fogbank forming over the ocean.

Below him, the last of his family's servants were drifting out of the open gates of the hacienda, their meager belongings tied up in worn *serapes*, their eyes fixed on the brown earth, as if they, too, might be in danger if they so much as glanced up at the guards who flanked the courtyard gates.

Against the inside of the western wall, still protecting herself from the fading heat, his mother sat calmly on her chair, her daughters flanking her, her fingers still occupied with her needlework. Every now and then, he could see her lips move as she offered words of farewell to the departing *peones,* but none of them replied; only one or two even had the courage to nod toward her.

Finally the last of the servants was gone, and at a signal from their leader, the guards slowly swung the heavy gates closed. The officer turned to face Doña María. His words carried clearly up the hillside.

"Where is your son?"

"Gone," his mother replied. "We sent him away last week."

"Do not lie, Doña María. He was seen yesterday."

His mother's voice rose then, and the boy knew her words were for him, as well as for the man she faced. "He is not here, señor. He is gone to Sonora, where he will be safe with our people."

"We'll find him, Doña María."

"No. You will never find him. But he will find you. We are not afraid to die. But you will not gain by killing us. We will not leave our land, señor. My husband said we will stay, and so we shall. And you will kill us. But it will do you no good. My son will come back, and he will find you."

"Will he?" the squadron leader asked. "Get up, Doña María."

As the boy watched from the hillside, his mother rose to her feet. Drawing their courage from their mother, his sisters, too, rose.

"My son will find you," he heard his mother say. "My son will find you, and he will kill you."

The squadron leader jerked his thumb toward the south wall. "Over there." He stepped forward, the bayonet fixed to the barrel of his rifle jabbing menacingly at Doña María and her daughters.

Doña María stood firm. "We are not afraid to die, but we will not be prodded like cattle." She turned and carefully set her needlework on the chair, then took her daughters' hands in her own. She started across the courtyard, her step firm, her back as rigidly erect as ever.

She reached the south wall, still bathed in the afternoon sunlight, then turned and began to pray. As her lips began to move, the boy on the hillside closed his eyes and silently mouthed the words he knew his mother was speaking.

The first shot jerked his eyes open, and he blinked twice before he could focus on the scene in the courtyard.

His mother still stood, her head up and her eyes open, but her right hand was clutching at her breast. A moment later, blood began to seep from between her fingers, and a crimson stain spread across the bosom of her dress.

Then the quiet of the afternoon was shattered as his sisters' terrified screams mixed with the angry rattle of gunfire, and a cacophony of sound echoed off the hacienda walls to roll over the countryside beyond.

His younger sister was the first to fall. Her knees buckled beneath her, and the motion itself seemed to concentrate the gunfire on her. Her body twitched violently for a moment as the bullets slammed home, then she lay still in the dust.

His older sister screamed and her arms reached out as if to help the fallen child, but she only pitched forward, falling facedown into the dirt as the rifles spoke again.

Doña María stood against the wall alone now. She faced the squadron with open eyes, gazing down the barrels of their rifles with a calm serenity. "It will do you no good," she said again. "My son will find you, and he will kill you. We will never leave our land." Then she, too, sank slowly to the ground. A few seconds later the squad emptied its rifles into her lifeless body.

It was past midnight when the boy crept down from the hillside and slipped through the gates of the hacienda. A strange silence hung over the buildings; the night creatures themselves seemed to honor the dead. No guards patrolled the grounds, nor had anyone covered the corpses. The squadron had left long ago, searching out the families of the overseers to deal with them as they had dealt with the family of Don Roberto.

The moon hung low in the night sky, its silvery light casting strange shadows across the courtyard. The crimson stains of his family's blood were faded by the half-light to nothing more than grayish smears on the whitewashed walls. The pallor of death on his mother and sisters seemed only to be the peace of sleep. For a long time the boy stood silently praying for the souls of his parents and his sisters. And then, with his last prayer, he put his grief aside.

He was changed now, and there was much to be done.

He picked up his mother first, and carried her body out of the courtyard, then up to the top of the hill, where he buried it deep within a tangle of brush.

Beside his mother, he buried his sisters, and then sat through the rest of the night, his mind numb as he relived the horrors of the day that had just passed.

As the first light of dawn began to bleach the darkness of the long night away, he rose to his feet and looked down once more on the hacienda that had been his home.

His memories, and his mother's words, were etched on his soul, as the blood of his family and the marks of the bullets that had killed them were etched on the walls of the hacienda.

Nothing would ever erase the images in his mind, or soften the hatred in his heart.

Nor would he ever leave the village that had been his home.

And forever after, night after endless night, he would awake from the dream, shivering.

Always it was the same. Always he was in the hills above the hacienda, watching the slaughter of his family; always he heard the words of his mother clearly, and understood what it was that he was to do.

Was it real? Had it all happened exactly as he saw it in the dream? The shots. The screams. Crimson stains on whitewashed walls.

Always the dream returned. And he knew what he must do. . . .

PART

I

CHAPTER 1

La Paloma was the kind of town that absorbed change slowly. Tucked up in the hills above Palo Alto, it had grown slowly for more than a hundred years, yet its focus remained as it had always been, the tiny plaza of the old Spanish mission. Unlike most of the California missions, Mission La Paloma had never been converted to a museum or a historical monument, becoming, instead, the village hall, with its adjoining school now serving as a library.

Behind the mission there was a tiny cemetery, and beyond the cemetery was a collection of small run-down houses where the descendants of La Paloma's Californio founders lived, still speaking Spanish among themselves, and eking out meager livings by serving the *gringos* who had taken over the lands of the old hacienda generations ago.

Two blocks from the plaza a smallish, roughly triangular piece of land dominated by an immense oak tree lay at the confluence of the main road through La Paloma and the side roads that wandered through the ravines into which the village had spread over the years. The patch of land had existed undisturbed because the original settlers, starting with the mission priests, had elected to leave the massive oak in place and route the roads away from it.

And so it had remained. There were no sidewalks or curbings along La Paloma's haphazardly meandering streets, and though the village that had grown up around the mission had eventually spilled over into this unnamed, unpopulated area, the plaza had remained the center of town.

Now the area surrounding the oak was known as the Square. And the huge oak under which generations of La Paloma children had grown up, had climbed on, hung swings from, carved their initials into, and generally abused beyond all reasonable horticultural endurance, was neatly fenced off, surrounded by a well-manicured lawn crisscrossed by concrete walks carefully planned to appear random. Discreet signs advised people to stay off the lawns, refrain from picnicking, deposit litter in cans prettily painted in adobe brown to conform to La Paloma's Spanish heritage, and the tree itself had an ominous chain surrounding it, and a sign of its own, proclaiming it the largest and oldest oak in California, and forbidding it to be touched in any manner at all by anyone except an authorized representative of the La Paloma Parks Department. The fact that the Parks Department consisted only of two part-time gardeners was nowhere mentioned.

For now the computer people had finally discovered La Paloma.

At first, the thousands who had flocked to the area known as Silicon Valley had clustered on the flats around Palo Alto and Sunnyvale. But tiny, sleepy La Paloma, hidden away up in the hills, spreading out from the oak into the ravines, a beautiful retreat from the California sun, shaded by towering eucalyptus trees, and lush with undergrowth except up toward the tops of the hills where the pasturelands still remained, was too tempting to ignore for long.

The first to move to La Paloma were the upper echelons of the computer people. Determined to use their new wealth to preserve the town's simple beauty, preserve it they had, spending large sums of their high-tech money to keep La Paloma a rustic retreat from the outside world.

Whether that preservation was a blessing or not depended on whom you talked to.

For the last remnants of the Californios, the influx of newcomers meant more jobs. For the merchants of the village, it meant more money. Both these groups suddenly found themselves earning a decent income rather than struggling for survival.

But for others, the preservation of La Paloma meant a radical change in their entire life-style. Ellen Lonsdale was one of these.

Ellen had grown up in La Paloma, and when she had married, she had convinced her husband that La Paloma was the perfect place in which to settle: a small, quiet town where Marsh could set up his medical practice, and they could raise their family in the ideal environment that Ellen herself had been raised in. And Marsh, after spending many college vacations in La Paloma, had agreed.

During the first ten years after Ellen brought Marsh to La Paloma, her life had been ideal. And then the computer people began coming, and the village began to change. The changes were subtle at first; Ellen had barely noticed them until it was too late.

Now, as she steered her Volvo station wagon through the village traffic on a May afternoon, Ellen found herself reflecting on the fact that the Square and its tree seemed to symbolize all the changes both she and the town had gone through. If the truth were known, she thought, La Paloma would not seem as attractive as it looked.

There were, for example, the old houses—the large, rambling mansions built by the Californio overseers in the style of the once-grand hacienda up in the hills. These were finally being restored to their original splendor. But no one ever talked about the fact that often the splendor of the houses failed to alleviate the unhappiness within, and that, as often as not, the homes were sold almost as soon as the restorations were complete, because the families they housed were breaking up, victims of high-tech, high-tension lives.

And now, Ellen was afraid, the same thing might be about to happen to her and her family.

She passed the Square, drove up La Paloma Drive two blocks, and pulled into the parking lot of the Medical Center.

The Medical Center, like the fence around the Square and the chain around the tree, was something Ellen had never expected to see in La Paloma.

She had been wrong.

As La Paloma grew, so had Marsh's practice, and his tiny office had finally become the La Paloma Medical Center, a small but completely equipped hospital. Ellen had long since stopped counting how many people were on staff, as she had also long since given up trying to keep books for Marsh as she had when they'd first married. Marsh, as well as being its director, owned fifty percent of its stock. The Lonsdales, like the village, had prospered. In two more weeks they would be moving out of their cottage on Santa Clara Avenue and into the big old house halfway up Hacienda Drive whose previous owners had filed for a divorce before even beginning the restorations they had planned.

Ellen half-suspected that one of the reasons she had wanted the house—and she had to admit she'd wanted it far more than Marsh or their son, Alex—was to give her something to do to keep her mind off the fact that her own marriage seemed to be failing, as so many in La Paloma seemed to be, not only among the newcomers but those of her childhood friends as well, unions that had started out with such high expectations, had seemed to flourish for a while, and now were ending for reasons that most of them didn't really understand.

Valerie Benson, who had simply thrown her husband out one day, and announced to her friends that she no longer had the energy to put up with George's bad habits, though she'd never really told anyone what those bad habits had been. Now she lived alone in the house George had helped her restore.

Martha Lewis, who still lived with her husband, even though the marriage seemed to have ended years ago. Marty's husband, who had flown high with the computer people for a while as a sales manager, had finally descended into alcoholism. For Marty, life had become a struggle to make the monthly payments on the house she could no longer really afford.

Cynthia Evans, who, like Marty, still lived with her husband, but had long ago lost him to the eighteen-hours-a-day, seven-days-a-week schedule the Silicon Valley people thrived on, and got rich on. Cynthia had finally decided that if she couldn't spend time with her husband, she could at least enjoy spending his money, and had convinced him to buy the old ruin at the top of Hacienda Drive and give her free rein to restore it as she saw fit.

And now, the Lonsdales too were involving themselves in one of the old houses. In the next two weeks, Ellen had to see to it that the floors were refinished, the replumbing and rewiring completed, and the interior of the house painted, activity that she hoped would take her mind off the fact that Marsh seemed to be working longer hours than ever before, and that, more and more, the two of them seemed to be disagreeing on practically everything. But maybe, just maybe, the new house would capture his interest, and they would be able to repair the marriage that, like so many others, had been damaged by the demands of too much to do in too little time.

As she slid the Volvo wagon in between a Mercedes and a BMW, and walked into the receiving room, she put a bright smile on her face and steeled herself to avoid a quarrel.

There had been too many recently, over too many things, and they had to stop. They were hurting her, they were hurting Marsh, and they were hurting Alex, who, at sixteen, was far more sensitive to his parents' moods than Ellen would have thought possible. If she and Marsh quarreled now, Alex would sense it as soon as he came home that afternoon.

Barbara Fannon, who had started with Marsh as his nurse when he'd opened his practice almost twenty years ago, smiled at her. "He just finished a staff meeting and went to his office. Shall I tell him you're here?"

Ellen shook her head. "I'll surprise him. It'll be good for him."

Barbara frowned. "He doesn't like surprises . . ."

"That's why it'll be good for him," Ellen retorted with a forced wink, wishing she didn't sometimes feel that Barbara knew Marsh better than she did herself. "Mustn't let Doctor start feeling too important, must we?" she asked as she started toward her husband's office.

He was at his desk, and when he glanced up, Ellen thought she saw a flash of annoyance in his eyes, but if it was there, he quickly banished it.

"Hi! What drags you down here? I thought you'd be up at the new place driving everyone crazy and spending the last of our money." Though he was smiling broadly, Ellen felt the sting of criticism, then told herself she was imagining it.

"I'm meeting Cynthia Evans," she replied, and immediately regretted her words. To Marsh, Cynthia and Bill Evans represented all the changes that had taken place in La Paloma. Of the fortunes that were being made, Bill's was one of the largest. "Don't worry," she added. "I'm not buying, just looking." She offered Marsh a kiss, and when it was not returned, went to perch uneasily on the sofa that sat against one wall. "Although we *are* going to have to do something about the tile in the patio," she added. "Most of it's broken, and it's impossible to match what isn't."

Marsh shook his head. "Later," he pronounced. "We agreed that for now, we'd only do what we have to to make the place livable."

"I know," Ellen sighed. "But every time Cynthia tells me what she's doing with the hacienda, I get absolutely green with envy."

Marsh set his pen down on the desk and faced her. "Then maybe you should have married a programming genius, not a country doctor," he suggested in a tone Ellen couldn't read.

While she tried to decide how to respond, her eyes surveyed the office. Despite Marsh's objections, she'd insisted on decorating it with rosewood furniture. "This isn't exactly what I'd call shabby," she finally ventured, and was relieved to see Marsh's smile return.

"No, it isn't," he agreed. "And even I have to admit that I kind of like it, even though I flinch every time I think of what it cost. Anyway, is that why you came down here? Just to terrify me with the idea of your shopping with Cynthia Evans?"

Ellen shook her head and tried to match his bantering tone. "Worse. I didn't even come down to see you. I came down to pick up the corsage for Alex." Marsh looked blank. "The prom," she reminded him. "Our son? Sixteen years old? Junior prom? Remember?"

Marsh groaned. "I'm sorry. It's just that there's so damned much to keep track of around here."

"Marsh," Ellen began, "I just wish . . . Oh, never mind."

"You wish I'd spend less time here and more at home," Marsh finished. "I will," he added. "Anyway, I'll try."

Their eyes met, and the office seemed suddenly to fill with the words that both of them had spoken so often they knew them by heart. The argument was old, and there was, both of them knew, no resolution for it. Besides, Marsh wasn't that different from most of the husbands and fathers of La Paloma. They all worked too many hours a day, and all of them were more interested in their careers than in their families.

"I know you'll try," she said. Then she went on, her voice rueful in spite of her intentions. "And I know you'll fail, and I keep telling myself that it doesn't really matter and that everything will be all right." Once again Ellen regretted her words, but this time, instead of looking irritated, Marsh got up and came to her, pulling her to her feet.

"It will be all right," he told her. "We're just caught up in a life we never expected, with more money than we ever thought we'd have, and more demands on my time than we ever planned for. But we love each other, and whatever happens, we'll deal with it." He kissed her. "Okay?"

Ellen nodded, as relief flowed through her. Over the last years, and particularly the last months, there had been so few moments like this, when she knew that she and Marsh did, despite the problems, still belong together. She returned his kiss, then drew away, smiling. "And now I'm going to get Alex his flowers."

Marsh's expression, soft a moment before, hardened slightly. "Alex can't get them himself?"

"Times have changed," Ellen replied, ignoring the look on her husband's face and trying to keep her voice light. "And I don't have time to listen to you recite the litany of the good old days. Let's face it—when you were Alex's age, you didn't have nearly as much to do after school as he does, and since I was going to be in the village anyway, I might as well pick up the flowers."

Marsh's eyes narrowed, and the last trace of his smile disappeared. "And when I was a kid, my school wasn't as good as his is, and there was no accelerated education program for me like there is for Alex. Except he's probably not going to get into it."

"Oh, God," Ellen said, as the last of their moment of peace evaporated. Did he really have to convert something as simple as picking up a corsage into another lecture on his perception of Alex as an underachiever? Which, of course, he wasn't, no matter what Marsh thought. And then, just as she was about to defend Alex, she checked herself, and forced a smile. "Let's not start that, Marsh. Not right now. Please?"

Marsh hesitated, then returned her smile, though it was as forced as her own. Still, he kissed her good-bye, and when she left his office, she hoped perhaps they might have had their last argument of the day. But when she was gone, instead of going back to the work that was stacked up on his desk, Marsh sat for a few minutes, letting his mind drift.

He, too, was aware of the strains that were threatening to pull his marriage apart, but he had no idea of what to do about them. The problems just seemed to pile up. As far as he could see, the only solution was to leave La Paloma, though he and Ellen had agreed a year ago that leaving was no solution at all. Leaving was not solving problems, it was only running away from them.

Nor was Alex's performance in school the real problem, though Marsh was convinced that if Alex only applied himself, he could easily be a straight-A student.

The problem, Marsh thought, was that he was beginning to wonder if his wife, like so many other people in La Paloma, had come to think that money would solve everything.

Then he relented. What was going wrong wasn't Ellen's fault. In fact, it was no one's fault. It was just that the world was changing, and both of them had to work harder to adjust to those changes before their marriage was torn apart.

He made up his mind to get home early that evening and see to it that nothing spoiled his wife's pleasure in their son's first prom.

Alex Lonsdale leaned forward across the bathroom sink and peered closely at the blemish on his right cheek, then decided that it wasn't a pimple at all—merely a slight redness from the pressure he'd put on his father's electric razor while he'd shaved. He ran the razor over his face one last time, then opened it to clean it out the way his father had shown him. Not that there was much to clean—Alex's beard, a month after his sixteenth birthday, was still more a matter of optimism than reality. Still, when he tapped the shaver head against the sink, a few specks appeared, and they were the black of his own hair rather than the sandy brown of his father's. Grinning with satisfaction, he put the razor back together, left the bathroom, and hurried down the hall to his room, doing his best to ignore the sound of his parents' argument as their raised voices drifted in from the kitchen.

The argument had been going on for an hour now, ever since he'd left the dinner table to begin getting ready for the prom. It was a familiar argument, and as Alex began wrestling with the studs of his rented dress shirt, he wondered how far it would go.

He hated it when his parents started arguing, hated the fact that as hard as he tried not to listen, he could hear every word. That, at least, would be something he wouldn't have to worry about when they moved into the new house. Its walls were thick, and from his room on the second floor he wouldn't be able to hear anything that was going on in the rest of the house. So when the shouting matches began, he could just go to his room and shut it all out. Every angry word they spoke hurt him. All he could do was try not to hear.

He finished mounting the studs, shrugged into the shirt, then began working on the cufflinks, finally taking the shirt off again, folding the cuffs, maneuvering the links halfway through, then putting the shirt on once more. The left link was easy, but the right one gave him more trouble. At last it popped through the buttonholes, and he snapped it into position.

He glanced at the clock on his desk. He still had five minutes before he had to leave if he wasn't going to be late. He pulled on his pants, hooked up the suspenders, then eyed the cummerbund that lay on the bed. Which way was it supposed to go? Pleats up, or pleats down? He couldn't remember. He picked up his hairbrush and ran it through the thick shock of hair that always seemed to fall across his forehead, then grabbed the offending maroon cummerbund and matching dinner jacket. As he'd hoped they would, his parents fell silent as he appeared in the kitchen.

"I can't remember which way it goes," he said, holding up the garment.

"Pleats down," Ellen Lonsdale replied. "Otherwise it'll wind up full of crumbs. Turn around." Taking the cummerbund from Alex's hands, she fastened it neatly around his waist, then held his coat while he slid his arms into its sleeves. When he turned to face her once more, she reached up to put her arms around his neck and give him a hug. "You look terrific," she said. She squeezed him once more, then stepped back. "Now, you have a wonderful time, and drive carefully." She shot a warning look toward Marsh, then relaxed as she saw that he was apparently as willing as she to drop their argument.

"Gotta go," Alex was saying. "If I'm late, Lisa will kill me."

"If you're late, you'll kill yourself," Ellen observed, her smile returning. "But don't rush off and forget these." She opened the refrigerator and took out Lisa's corsage, along with the white carnation for Alex's lapel.

"You should've gotten red," Alex groused as he let his mother pin the flower onto his dinner jacket.

"If you wanted a red carnation, you should have gotten a white jacket," Ellen retorted. She stepped back and gazed proudly at Alex. Somehow, he had managed to inherit both their looks, and the combination was startling. His dark eyes and black wavy hair were hers; his fair complexion and even features, his father's. The combination lent his face a sensitive handsomeness that had earned him admiring remarks since he was a baby, and, in the last few months, an unending string of phone calls from girls who hoped he might be tiring of Lisa Cochran. "Don't be surprised if you and Lisa don't wind up the king and queen of the prom," she added, stretching upward to kiss him.

"Aw, Mom—"

"They still have the king and queen of the prom, don't they?" Ellen asked.

Blushing, Alex nodded his head, checked his pockets for his keys and wallet, and started for the door.

"And remember," Ellen called after him. "Don't stay out past one, and don't get into any trouble."

"You mean, don't drink," Alex corrected her. "I won't. I promise. Okay?"

"Okay," Marsh Lonsdale replied. He handed Alex a twenty-dollar bill. "Take some of the kids out and buy them a Coke after the dance."

"Thanks, Dad." Alex disappeared out the back door. A moment later Ellen and Marsh heard his car start. Marsh arched his brows. "I don't believe he's actually going to drive all the way next door," he said, unable to suppress a smile, despite the fact that it was Alex's car that he and Ellen had been arguing about all evening.

"Well, of course he is," Ellen replied. "Do you really think he's going to pick up Lisa, then walk her down our driveway? Not our Alex."

"He could have walked her all the way to the prom," Marsh suggested.

"No, he couldn't," Ellen said, her voice suddenly tired. "He needs a car, Marsh. After we move, I just can't spend all my time ferrying him up and down the ravine. And besides, he's a responsible boy—"

"I'm not saying he isn't," Marsh agreed, "All I'm saying is that I think he should have earned the car. And I'm not saying he should have earned the money, either. But couldn't we have used the car as an incentive for him to pick up his grades?"

Ellen shrugged, and began clearing the dinner dishes off the table. "He's doing just fine."

"He's not doing as well as he could be, and you know it as well as I do."

"I know," Ellen sighed. "But I just think it's two separate issues, that's all." Suddenly she smiled. "I'll tell you what. Why don't we compromise? Let's wait until his grades come out, and see what happens. If they get worse, I'll agree that getting him the car was a mistake, and you can take it away from him. I'll cope with the transportation problem some way. If they stay the same, or improve, he keeps the car. But either way, we stop fighting about it, all right?"

Marsh hesitated only a second, then grinned. "Deal," he said. "Now, what say I help you with the dishes, and we try to put together something with the Cochrans?" He offered his wife a mischievous wink. "I'll even drive over next door and pick them up."

The last of the tension that had been vibrating between them all afternoon suddenly dissipated, and together Ellen and Marsh began clearing away the dinner dishes.

Alex carefully backed his shiny red Mustang down the driveway, then parked it by the curb in front of the Cochran's house next door. He picked up Lisa's corsage, crossed the lawn, and walked into the house without knocking. "Anybody here?" he called. Lisa's six-year-old sister, Kim, hurtled down the stairs and threw herself onto Alex.

"Is that for me?" she demanded, grabbing for the corsage box.

"If Lisa isn't ready, maybe I'll take you to the dance," Alex replied, peeling Kim loose as her father's bulky frame appeared from the living room. "Hi, Mr. Cochran."

Jim Cochran raised one eyebrow and surveyed Alex. "Ah, Prince Charming descends from the castle on the mountain to take Cinderella to the ball."

Alex tried to cover his feelings of embarrassment with a grin. "Aw, come on. We're not moving for two more weeks. And it's not a castle anyway."

"True, true," Cochran agreed. "On the other hand, I haven't noticed you asking if you can rent Kim's room. We'll happily throw her out."

"You will not," Kim yelled, aiming a punch at her father's belly.

"Will too," her father told her. "Want a Coke, Alex? Lisa's still upstairs trying to make herself look human." He dropped his booming voice only slightly, still leaving it loud enough to fill the house. "Actually, she's been ready for an hour, but she doesn't want you to think she's too eager."

"That's a big lie!" Lisa said from the top of the stairs. "He always lies, Alex. Don't believe a word he says." Lisa, unlike Alex, had inherited all her looks from her mother. She was small, with short blond hair swept back from her face so that her green eyes became her dominant feature. And, being not only Lisa, but her father's daughter as well, she had chosen a dress in brilliant emerald rather than the more subdued pastels the other girls would be wearing. Alex's grin widened as she came down the stairs. "Hey, you look gorgeous."

Lisa smiled appreciatively and gave him a mock-seductive wink. "You don't look so bad yourself." She stood waiting for a moment; then: "Aren't you going to pin the corsage on?" Alex stared at the box in his hands, his face reddening as he handed it to Carol Cochran, who had appeared from the direction of the kitchen.

"M-maybe you'd better do it, Mrs. Cochran. I . . . I might slip or something."

"You won't slip, Alex," Lisa told him. "Now, come on. Just pin it on, and let's go. Otherwise we'll be here all night while Mom takes pictures."

Alex fumbled clumsily with the corsage for a moment, but finally succeeded in getting it fastened to Lisa's dress. Then, true to Lisa's words, Carol Cochran began herding them into the living room, camera in hand.

"Mom, we don't have time—" Lisa pleaded, but Carol was adamant.

"You only go to your first prom once, and you only wear your first formal once. And I'm going to have pictures of it. Besides, you both look so—"

"Oh, God, Alex," Lisa moaned. "She's going to say it. Cover your ears."

"Well, I don't care," Carol laughed as Alex and Lisa clapped their hands over their ears. "You *do* look cute!"

Twenty-four pictures later, Alex and Lisa were on their way to the prom.

* * *

"I don't see why we have to stand in the receiving line," Alex complained as he carefully slid the Mustang into a space between an Alfa Romeo and a Porsche. Before Lisa could answer, he was out of the car and opening the passenger door for her.

From a few yards away, a voice came out of the dusk. "Scratch that paint, and your ass is grass, Lonsdale."

Alex grinned and waved to Bob Carey, who was holding hands with Kate Lewis, but paying more attention to his Porsche than his girlfriend. "You tore the side off it last month!" Alex taunted him.

"And my dad nearly tore the side off me," Bob replied. "From now on, I have to pay for all the repairs myself." He waited until Lisa was out of the car and Alex had closed the door, then relaxed. "See you inside." He and Kate turned and started toward the gym, where the dance was being held.

"We have to stand in line because you're going to be student-body president next year," Lisa told Alex. "If you didn't want to do that kind of thing, you shouldn't have run."

"No one told me I had to. I thought all I had to do was have my picture taken for the annual."

"Come on, it won't be that bad. You know everybody in school already. All you have to do is say hello to them."

"And introduce them to you, which is stupid, because you know them all just as well as I do."

Lisa giggled. "It's all supposed to improve our social graces. Don't you want your graces improved?"

"What if I forget someone's name? I'll die."

"Stop worrying. You'll be fine. And we're late, so hurry up."

They hurried up the steps into the foyer of the gym and took their places in the receiving line. The first couple to approach them were Bob Carey and Kate Lewis, and Alex was pleased to see that Bob seemed as nervous about moving down the line as Alex was about standing in it. The two of them stood for a moment, wondering what to say to each other. Finally it was Kate who spoke.

"Isn't this wonderful?" she asked. "All year I've been looking forward to tonight, and I'm never going to forget a minute of it."

"None of us will," Lisa assured her.

And none of them ever did. For none of their lives was ever quite the same again.

CHAPTER 2

The last thundering rock chord was abruptly cut off, and Alex, gasping, glanced around the gym in search of Lisa. The last time he'd seen her—at least fifteen minutes ago—she'd been dancing with Bob Carey, and he'd been dancing with Kate Lewis. Since then, he'd danced with three other girls, and now Bob was standing near the wall shouting in Jennifer Lang's ear. He started outside, certain that he'd find Lisa out on the lawn catching her breath. As he reached the door, a hand closed on his arm. He turned to see Carolyn Evans smiling at him.

"Hey," Carolyn said, "if you're looking for Lisa, she's in the rest room with Kate and Jenny."

"Then I guess I'll have a glass of punch, if there's any left."

"There's loads left," Carolyn told him in the slightly mocking voice Alex knew she always used when she was trying to seem more sophisticated than the rest of the kids. "Hardly anybody's drinking it except you and Lisa. Come on out to my car—I've got some beer."

Alex shook his head.

"Oh, come on," Carolyn urged. "What's one beer gonna do to you? I've had four, and I'm not drunk."

"I'm driving. If I'm driving, I don't drink."

Carolyn's head tipped back, and a throaty laugh that Alex was sure she practiced for hours emerged from her glistening lips. "You're just too good to be true, aren't you? Not even one little tiny beer? Come on, Alex—get human."

"It's not that," Alex replied, forcing a grin. "It's just that my dad'll take my car away from me if I come home with beer on my breath."

"Too bad for you," Carolyn purred. "Then I guess you can't come to my party." When she saw a slight flicker of interest in Alex's eyes, she decided to press her advantage. "Everybody's going to be there—sort of a housewarming."

Alex stared at Carolyn in disbelief. Was she really talking about the hacienda? But his mother told him the Evanses weren't letting anyone see it for another month, until it was completely refurbished.

And everyone in La Paloma, no matter what he thought of the Evanses, wanted to see what Cynthia Evans had done with Bill Evans's money.

At first, when the rumors began circulating that the Evanses had bought the enormous old mansion on top of Hacienda Drive, the assumption had been that they would tear it down. It had stood vacant for too many years, was far too big for a family to keep up without servants, and was far too decayed for anyone to seriously consider restoring it.

But then the project had begun.

First to be repaired was the outer wall. Much of it had long since collapsed; only a few yards of its southern expanse were still standing. But it had been rebuilt, its old wooden gates replaced by new ones whose designs had been copied from faded sketches of the hacienda as it had looked a hundred and fifty years earlier. Except that the new gates were wired with alarms and swung smoothly open on electrically controlled rollers. And then, after the wall was complete, Cynthia had begun the restoration of the mansion and the outbuildings.

Almost everybody in La Paloma had gone up to the top of Hacienda Drive once or twice, but the gates were always closed, and no one had succeeded in getting inside the walls. Alex, along with some of his friends, had climbed the hills a few times to peer down into the courtyard, but all they'd been able to see was the exterior work—the new plaster and the whitewashing, and the replacement of the red tiles on the roof.

What everyone was truly waiting for was a glimpse of the interior, and now Carolyn was saying her friends could see it that very night.

Alex eyed her skeptically. "I thought your mother wasn't letting anyone in until next month."

"Mom and Dad are in San Francisco for the weekend," Carolyn said.

"I don't know—" Alex began, remembering his promise not to go to any parties after the dance.

"Don't know about what?" Lisa asked, slipping her arm through his.

"He doesn't want to come to my party," Carolyn replied before Alex could say anything.

Lisa's eyes widened. "There's a party? At the hacienda?"

Carolyn nodded with elaborate casualness. "Bob and Kate are coming, and Jenny Lang, and everybody."

Lisa turned to Alex. "Well, let's go!" Alex flushed and looked uncomfortable, but said nothing. The band struck up the last dance and Lisa led Alex onto the floor. "What's wrong?" she asked a moment later. "Why can't we go to Carolyn's party?"

" 'Cause I don't want to."

"You just don't like Carolyn," Lisa argued. "But you won't even have to talk to her. Everybody else will be there too."

"It isn't that."

"Then what is it?"

"I promised my folks we wouldn't go to any parties. Dad gave me some money to take some of the kids out for a hamburger, and I promised we'd come home right after that."

Lisa fell silent for a few seconds; then: "We don't have to tell them where we were."

"They'd find out."

"But don't you even want to see the place?"

"Sure, but—"

"Then let's go. Besides, it's not where we go that your mom and dad are worried about—they're afraid you'll drink. So we'll go to the party, but we won't even have a beer. And we won't stay very long."

"Come on, Lisa. I promised them I wouldn't—"

But Lisa suddenly broke away from him and started pulling him off the dance floor. "Let's find Kate and Bob. Maybe we can convince them to go up to Carolyn's with us for just a few minutes, then the four of us can go out for hamburgers. That way we can see the place, and you won't have to lie to your folks."

As Lisa led him out of the gym, Alex knew he'd give in, even though he shouldn't. With Lisa, it was hard not to give in—she always managed to make everything sound perfectly logical, even when Alex was sure it wasn't.

The headlights of Alex's Mustang picked up the open gates of the hacienda, and he braked the car to a stop. "Are we supposed to park out here, or go inside?"

Lisa shrugged. "Search me. Carolyn didn't say." Suddenly a horn sounded, and Bob Carey's Porsche pulled up beside them, its window rolled down.

"Over there," Bob called. He was pointing off to the left, where a small group of cars already stood parked in the shadow of the wall. Following Bob, Alex maneuvered the Mustang into a spot next to a Camaro, shut off the engine, then turned to Lisa.

"Maybe we oughta just go on home," he suggested, but Lisa grinned and shook her head.

"I want to see it. Come on—just for a little while." She got out of the car, and after a second's hesitation, Alex joined her. A moment later Kate and Bob appeared out of the darkness, and the four of them started toward the lights flooding from the gateway.

"I don't believe this," Kate said a moment later. They were standing just inside the gate, trying to absorb the transformation that had come over what had been, only a year earlier, a crumbling ruin.

To the left, the old stables had been rebuilt into garages, and in the bright whiteness of the floodlights, the new plaster was indistinguishable from the old. The only change was that the stable roofs, originally thatched, were now of the same red tile as the house and the servants' quarters.

"It's weird," Alex said. "It looks like it's a couple of hundred years old."

"Except for that," Lisa breathed. "Have you ever seen anything like it?"

Dominating the courtyard, which until recently had been nothing more than an overgrown weed patch, was a glistening swimming pool fed by a cascade of tumbling water that made its way down five intricately tiled tiers before finally splashing into the immense oval of the pool.

Bob Carey whistled softly. "How big do you s'pose it is?"

"Big enough," Alex replied. Then his eyes wandered to what had once been the servants' quarters. "Wanta bet that's a pool house now?"

Before anyone could venture an answer, Carolyn Evans's voice rang out over the rock music that was throbbing from the huge main house. "Hey! Come on in!"

Glancing at each other uneasily, the four of them slowly crossed the courtyard, then stepped up onto the broad loggia that ran the entire length of the house. Carolyn, grinning happily, waited for them at the elaborately carved oaken front door. "Isn't it neat? Come on in—everybody's already here."

They went through the front door into a massive tile-floored entry hall that was dominated by a staircase curving up to the second floor. To the right there was a large dining room, and beyond it they could see through another room into the kitchen. "That's a butler's pantry between the dining room and kitchen," Carolyn explained, then raised her voice as someone turned up the volume on the stereo. "Mom wasn't really sure it was supposed to be there, but she put it in anyway."

"You going to have a butler?" Kate Lewis asked.

Carolyn shrugged with elaborate unconcern. "I don't know. I guess so. Mom says the house is too big for María to take care of by herself."

"María *Torres?*" Bob Carey groaned. "That old witch can't even take care of her own house. My mom fired her after the first day!"

"She's okay—" Alex began, but was immediately drowned out by the others' laughter. Even Lisa joined in.

"Come on, Alex, she's a loony-bin case. Everybody knows that." Then she glanced guiltily toward Carolyn. "She isn't here, is she?"

Carolyn giggled maliciously. "If she is, she just got an earful."

At the top of the stairs, María Torres faded back into the darkness of the second-floor hallway, her black dress making her nearly invisible.

She had been sitting quietly in the large bedroom at the end of the corridor —the bedroom that, by rights, should have been hers—when the first of the cars had arrived.

No one, she knew, should have come back to the hacienda for hours, and she should have had the house to herself and her ghosts from the past. But now her reverie was shattered, and the pounding din of the *gringo* music, and the children of the *gringos* she had spent her life hating, filled the ancient rooms.

She had been in the house since seven o'clock, having let herself in with her own key as soon as Carolyn had left. She had spent the last four hours drifting through the house, imagining that it was hers, that she was not the cleaning woman—no more than a *peón*—but the mistress of the hacienda: Doña María Ruiz de Torres. And one day it would happen; one day, sometime in the vague future, it would happen. The *gringos* would be driven away, and finally the hacienda would be hers.

But for now she could only pretend, and be careful. The *gringos* were strict and never wanted her to be alone in their homes. She must leave the hacienda without being seen, and make her way back down the canyon to her little house behind the mission, and when she came back tomorrow, she must give no hint that she had been here at all tonight.

She glanced once more around the gloom of the bedroom that should have been hers, then slipped away, down the back stairs, the stairs that her ancestors never would have used, and out into the night. Then, as the *gringo* revelry went on—a desecration!—she kept watch, her ancient anger burning inside her. . . .

"Jeez," Bob whispered. "Last time I saw this, it looked like the place had burned. Now look at it."

The living room, across the entry hall from the dining room, was sixty feet long, and was dominated by an immense fireplace on the far wall.

The oak floor gleamed a polished brown that was nearly black, but the white walls picked up the light from sconces that had been wired into them at regular intervals to fill the room with an even brightness that made it seem even larger than it was. Twenty feet above, huge peeled logs supported a cathedral ceiling.

"This is incredible," Lisa breathed.

"This is just the beginning," Carolyn replied. "Just wander around anywhere, and make sure you don't miss the basement. That's Daddy's part of the house, and Mom just hates it." Then she was gone, disappearing into the mass of teenagers who were dancing to the rhythms of a reggae album.

It took them nearly an hour to go through the house, and even then they weren't sure they'd seen it all. Upstairs there was a maze of rooms, and they'd counted seven bedrooms, each with its own bathroom, in addition to a library and a couple of small sitting rooms. All of it looked as if it had been built and furnished nearly two hundred years ago, then somehow frozen in time.

"Can you imagine living here?" Lisa asked as they finally started down toward the basement.

"It's not like a house at all," Alex replied. "It feels more like a museum. Hey," he added, suddenly stopping halfway down the stairs. "I don't remember this place ever having a basement."

"It didn't," Kate told him. "Carolyn says her dad wanted his own space, but her mom wouldn't let him have any of the old rooms. So he dug out a basement. Do you believe it?"

"Holy shit," Bob Carey muttered. "Didn't he think the house was big enough already?"

At the bottom of the stairs they found a laundry room to the left, and beyond that a big empty space that looked as though it was intended for storage.

Under the living room, occupying nearly the same amount of space as the room above, they found Mr. Evans's private space. For a long time they stared at it in silence.

"Well, I think it's tacky," Lisa said when she'd taken it all in.

Bob Carey shrugged. "And I think you're just jealous. I bet you wouldn't think it was tacky if it was your house."

Kate Lewis raked Bob with what she hoped was a scathing glare. "My mother always says the Evanses have more money than taste, and she's right. I mean, just look at it, Bob. It's gross!"

It was a media room. The far wall was nearly covered by an immense screen, which could be used either for movies or projection television. Along one wall was a complex of electronic components that none of them could completely identify. They were, however, apparently the source of the rock music, and they could barely hear Carolyn demanding that it be turned down for fear the neighbors would call the police. Nobody, however, was paying any attention to her, and much of the party seemed to have gravitated downstairs.

What had elicited Lisa Cochran's criticism, though, was not the electronics, but the bar opposite them. Not a typical home bar, with three stools and a rack for glasses, the Evanses' bar ran the entire length of the wall. Behind the counter itself, the wall was covered with shelves of liquor and glasses, and each shelf was edged with a neon tube, which provided a rainbow effect that was reflected throughout the room by the mirrors that covered the wall behind the shelves and the bar itself. The bar, by now, was covered with bottles, and several of the kids were happily filling glasses with various kinds of liquor.

"Want something?" Bob asked, eyeing the array.

Kate hesitated, then shrugged. "Why not? Is there any gin?"

Bob poured them each a tumbler, added a little ginger ale, and handed one of the glasses to Kate, then turned to ask Alex and Lisa what they wanted. But while he'd been mixing the drinks, Alex and Lisa had disappeared. "Hey—where'd they go?"

Kate shrugged. "I don't know. Come on, let's dance." She finished her drink and pulled Bob out onto the floor, but when the record ended, both she and Bob scanned the crowd, looking for Alex and Lisa.

"You think they got mad 'cause we had a drink?" Kate finally asked.

"Who cares? It's not as if we need a ride home or anything. Forget about them."

"No! Come on."

They found Alex and Lisa in the courtyard, staring up at the stars. "Hey," Bob yelled, holding up his glass, "aren't you two gonna join the party?"

"We weren't going to drink, remember?" Alex asked, staring at the glass. "We were going out for hamburgers."

"Who wants hamburgers when you can drink?" Bob replied. He reached down and pulled a bottle of beer out of a tub of ice and thrust it into Alex's hands. Alex looked at it for a moment, then glanced at Lisa, who frowned and shook her head. Alex hesitated, then defiantly twisted the cap loose and took a swig.

Lisa glared accusingly at him. "Alex!"

"I didn't even want to come to this party," Alex told her, his voice taking on a defensive edge. "But since we're here, we might as well enjoy it."

"But we said—"

"I know what we said. And I said I wasn't going to any parties, either. But I'm here. Why shouldn't I do what everybody else is doing?" Deliberately he tipped the beer bottle up and chugalugged it, then reached for another. Lisa's eyes narrowed angrily, but before she could say anything else, Carolyn

Evans's voice suddenly rose over the din of the party as she came out of the front door with her arms full of towels.

"Who wants to go in the pool?"

There was a momentary silence, then someone replied that no one had suits. "Who needs suits?" Carolyn squealed. "Let's go skinny-dipping!" Suddenly she reached behind her, pulled down the zipper of her dress, and let it drop to the patio. Stripping off her panties and strapless bra, she dived into the pool, swam underwater for a few strokes, then broke the surface. "Come on," she yelled. "It's great!"

There was a moment of hesitation, then two more kids stripped and plunged into the water. Three more followed, and suddenly the patio was filling up with discarded clothes and the pool with naked teenagers. Once more, Alex glanced at Lisa.

"No!" she said, reading his eyes. "We were only coming for a few minutes, and we weren't going to drink. And we're certainly not going into the pool."

"Chicken," Alex teased, shrugging out of his dinner jacket. Then he drained the second beer, put the bottle down, and began untying his shoelaces.

"Alex, don't," Lisa begged. "Please?"

"Aw, come on. What's the big deal? Haven't you ever skinny-dipped before?"

"It's not a big deal," Lisa argued. "I just don't think we ought to do it. I think we ought to go home."

"Well, I think we ought to go swimming," Alex crowed. He stripped off his pants and shirt. "I didn't think we ought to come here, but I came, didn't I? Well, now I think we ought to go skinny-dipping, and I think you ought to go along with it." Peeling off his Jockey shorts, he plunged into the water. A moment later he came to the surface and turned around to grin at Lisa.

She was gone.

The effects of the two fast beers suddenly neutralized by the cold water, Alex scanned the crowd, sure that Lisa must be among the kids still on the pool deck. Then he was equally sure she was not. If she'd made up her mind not to come into the pool, she wouldn't change it.

And Alex suddenly felt like a fool.

He hadn't wanted to come to the party, he hadn't really wanted the two beers he'd drunk, and he certainly didn't want Lisa mad at him. He scrambled out of the water, grabbed a towel, then dried himself off and dressed as fast as he could. As he started into the house, he asked Bob Carey if he'd seen Lisa anywhere. Bob hadn't.

Nor had anyone else.

Ten minutes later, Alex left the house, praying that his car wasn't blocked in.

* * *

A quarter of a mile down Hacienda Drive, Lisa Cochran's quick pace slowed, and she wondered if maybe she shouldn't turn around and go back to the party. What, after all, was so horrible about skinny-dipping? And who was she to be so prissy about it? In a way, Alex was right—it *had* been her idea that they go to the party. He'd even argued with her, but she'd insisted. Still, he *had* drunk a couple of beers, and by now he might be working on a third. And if he was, she certainly didn't want to drive home with him.

She stopped walking entirely, and wondered what to do. Perhaps she should walk all the way into the village and wait for Alex at home.

Except that her parents would be up and would want to know what had happened.

Maybe the best thing to do was go back to the party, find Alex, and convince him that it was time for them to go home. She would do the driving.

But that would be giving in, and she wouldn't give in. She had been right, and Alex had been wrong, and it served him right that she'd walked out on him.

She made up her mind, and continued down the road.

Alex jockeyed the Mustang around Bob Carey's Porsche, then put it in drive and gunned the engine. The rear wheels spun on the loose gravel for a moment, then caught, and the car shot forward, down the Evanses' driveway and into Hacienda Drive.

Alex wasn't sure how long Lisa had been walking—it seemed as though it had taken him forever to get dressed and search the house. She could be almost home by now.

He pressed the accelerator, and the car picked up speed. He hugged the wall of the ravine on the first curve, but the car fishtailed slightly, and he had to steer into the skid to regain control. Then he hit a straight stretch and pushed his speed up to seventy. Coming up fast was an S curve that was posted at thirty miles an hour, but he knew they always left a big margin for safety. He slowed to sixty as he started into the first turn.

And then he saw her.

She was standing on the side of the road, her green dress glowing brightly in his headlights, staring at him with terrified eyes.

Or did he just imagine that? Was he already that close to her?

Time suddenly slowed down, and he slammed his foot on the brake.

Too late. He was going to hit her.

It would have been all right if she'd been on the inside of the curve. He'd have swept around her, and she'd have been safe. But now he was skidding right toward her . . .

Turn into it. He had to turn into it!

Taking his foot off the brake, he steered to the right, and suddenly felt the tires grab the pavement.

Lisa was only a few yards away.

And beyond Lisa, almost lost in the darkness, something else.

A face, old and wrinkled, framed with white hair. And the eyes in the face were glaring at him with an intensity he could almost feel.

It was the face that finally made him lose all control of the car.

An ancient, weathered face, a face filled with an unspeakable loathing, looming in the darkness.

At the last possible moment, he wrenched the wheel to the left, and the Mustang responded, slewing around Lisa, charging across the pavement, heading for the ditch and the wall of the ravine beyond.

Straighten it out!

He spun the wheel the other way.

Too far.

The car burst through the guardrail and hurtled over the edge of the ravine.

"Lisaaaa . . ."

CHAPTER 3

It was nearly two A.M. when Ellen Lonsdale heard the first faint wailing of a siren. She hadn't been asleep—indeed she'd been sitting in the living room ever since the Cochrans had left an hour earlier, growing increasingly restless as the minutes ticked by. It wasn't like Alex to be late, and for the last half-hour she'd been fighting a growing feeling that something had happened to him. The siren grew louder. A few seconds later it was joined by another, then a third. As she listened, the mournful wailings grew into shrill screams that tore the last vestiges of calmness from her mind.

It was Alex. Deep in her soul, she knew that the sirens were for her son.

Then, inside the house, the phone began to ring.

That's it, she thought. They're calling to tell me he's dead. Her feet leaden, she forced herself to go to the phone, hesitated a moment, then picked it up.

"H-hello?"

"Ellen?"

"Yes."

"This is Barbara, at the Center?"

The hesitancy in Barbara Fannon's voice told Ellen that something had gone wrong. "What is it? What's happened?"

Barbara's voice remained professionally neutral. "May I speak to Dr. Lonsdale please?"

"What's happened?" Ellen demanded again. Then, hearing the note of hysteria in her voice, she took a deep breath and reminded herself that Marsh was on call that night. "I'm sorry," she said. "Just a moment, Barbara."

Her hand shaking in spite of herself, she laid the receiver on the table next to the phone and turned toward the hall. Marsh, his eyes still bleary with sleep, stood in the doorway. "What's happening? Something woke me up."

"Sirens," Ellen breathed. "Something's happened, and the hospital wants to talk to you."

His eyes immediately clearing, Marsh strode into the room and picked up the phone. "This is Dr. Lonsdale."

"Marsh? It's Barbara. I'm in the emergency room. I hate to call you in this late, but there's been some kind of an accident, and we don't know how bad it is yet. Since you're on call . . ." Her voice trailed off uncertainly.

"You did right. I'll be right there. Does anybody have any details at all?"

"Not really. Apparently at least one car went off the road, and we don't know how many people were in it—"

"Maybe I'd better go up there."

There was a hesitation; then: "The EMT's are with the ambulance, Doctor. . . ."

Now it was Marsh who hesitated, then grimaced slightly. Even after five years, he found it hard to accept that the emergency medical technicians were, indeed, better trained to handle such situations than he himself was. "I get the picture, Barb. Say no more. See you in a few minutes." He hung up the phone, then turned to Ellen, who stood behind a chair, both hands gripping its back.

"It's Alex, isn't it?" she breathed.

"Alex?" Marsh repeated. What could have put that idea into Ellen's head? "Why on earth should it have anything to do with Alex?"

Ellen did her best to steady herself. "I just have a feeling, that's all. I've had it for about half an hour. It *is* Alex, isn't it?"

"No one knows who it is yet," Marsh replied. "It's an automobile accident, but that doesn't mean it's Alex." His words, though, did nothing to dissipate the fear in her eyes, and despite the tension that still hung between them, he took her in his arms. "Honey, don't do this to yourself." When Ellen made no reply, he reluctantly released her and started toward their bedroom, but Ellen held onto his arm, and when she spoke, her eyes, as well as her words, were pleading.

"If it isn't Alex, why did they call you? There's an intern on duty, isn't there?"

Marsh nodded. "But they don't know how many people might have been hurt. They might need me, and I *am* on call." He gently disengaged her hand, but Ellen followed him into the bedroom.

"I want to go with you," she said while he began dressing.

Marsh shook his head. "Ellen, there's no reason—"

"There *is* a reason," Ellen protested, struggling to keep her voice level, but not succeeding. "I have a feeling, and—"

"And it's only a feeling," Marsh insisted, and Ellen flinched at the dismissive tone of his words. He relented, and once more put his arms around his wife. "Honey, please. Think about it. Automobile accidents happen all the time. The odds of this one involving Alex are next to nothing. And I can't deal with whatever's happening if I have to take care of you too."

His words hurt her, but Ellen knew he was right. Deliberately she made herself stop shaking and stepped away from him. "I'm sorry," she said. "It's just that . . . Oh, never mind. Go."

Marsh offered her a smile. "Now, that's my girl."

Though her husband's smile did nothing to alleviate her pain, Ellen picked up his wallet and keys from the dresser and handed them to him. "Marsh?" she asked, then waited until he met her eyes before going on. "As soon as you know what's happened, have someone call me. I don't need details —I just need to know it's not Alex."

"By the time I know what's happened, Alex will probably be home," Marsh replied. Then he relented. "But I'll have someone call. With any luck, I'll be back in an hour myself."

Then he was gone, and Ellen sank slowly onto the sofa to wait.

"Jesus Christ," Sergeant Roscoe Finnerty whispered as the spotlight on his patrol car illuminated the wreckage at the bottom of the ravine. "Why the fuck didn't it burn?" Grabbing his flashlight, he got out of the car and started clambering down the slope, with his partner, Thomas Jefferson Jackson, right behind him. A few yards away, Finnerty saw a shape move, and trained his light on the frightened face of a teenage boy.

"Far enough, son," Finnerty said quietly. "Whatever's happened, we'll take care of it."

"But—" the boy began.

"You heard him," Jackson broke in. "Get back up on the road, and stay out of the way." He flashed his light on the knot of teenagers who were clustered together. Most of them had wet hair, and their clothes were in disarray. "Those your friends?"

The boy nodded.

"Musta been some party. Now, get up there with them, and we'll talk to you later."

Silently the boy turned and started back up the hill, and Jackson followed Finnerty down toward the wreckage. Behind him, he heard car doors slamming, and the sound of voices issuing orders. Vaguely he became aware of other people beginning to move down the slope of the ravine.

The car lay on its side, so battered its make was no longer recognizable. It appeared to have turned end for end at least twice, then rolled until it came to rest against a large boulder.

"The driver's still in it," Jackson heard Finnerty say, and his stomach lurched the way it always did when he had to deal with the victims of automobile accidents. Stoically he moved forward.

"Still alive?"

"Dunno," Finnerty grunted. "Don't hardly see how he can be, though." He paused then, well aware of his partner's weak stomach. "You okay?"

"I'll throw up later," Jackson muttered. "Anybody else in the car?"

"Nope. But if someone wasn't wearing a seat belt, they'd have gone out on the first flip." He shone his light briefly on Jackson's sweating face. "You wanna help out here, or look around for another victim?"

"I'll help. 'Least till the medics get here." He approached the car and stared in at the body that was pitched forward against the steering wheel. The head was covered with blood, and it looked to Jackson as if Finnerty was right —if the smashup itself hadn't killed the driver, he must have bled to death by now. Still, he had his job to do, and clenching his teeth, Jackson began helping his partner cut through the seat belt that held the inert body into what was left of the car.

"Don't move him," one of the emergency technicians warned a moment later. He and his partner began unfolding a stretcher as the two cops finished cutting away the seat belt.

"You think we haven't done this before?" Finnerty rasped. "Anyway, I don't think it'll make much difference with this one."

"We'll decide that," the EMT replied, moving forward and edging Jackson aside. "Anybody know who he is?"

"Not yet," Jackson told him. "We'll run a make on the plate as soon as we get him up to the road."

The two EMT's slowly and carefully began working Alex's body out of the wreckage, and, what seemed to Jackson to be an eternity later, eased him onto the stretcher.

"He's not dead yet," one of the EMT's muttered. "But he will be if we don't get him out of here fast. Come on."

With a man at each corner of the stretcher, the two EMT's and the two cops began making their way up the hill.

* * *

The crowd of teenagers on the road stood silently watching as the stretcher was borne upward. In the midst of them, Lisa Cochran leaned heavily on Kate Lewis, who did her best to keep Lisa from looking at the bloodied shape of Alex Lonsdale.

"He must still be alive," Bob Carey whispered. "They've got something wrapped around his head, but his face isn't covered."

Then the medics were on the road, sliding the stretcher into the ambulance. A second later, its lights flashing and its siren screaming, it roared off into the night.

In the emergency room of the Medical Center, a bell shattered the tense silence, and a scratchy voice emanated from a speaker on the wall.

"This is Unit One. We've got a white male, teenage, with multiple lacerations of the face, a broken arm, damage to the rib cage, and head injuries. Also extensive bleeding."

Marshall Lonsdale reached across the desk and pressed the transmission key himself. "Any identification yet?"

"Negative. We're too busy keeping him alive to check his I.D."

"Will he make it?"

There was a slight hesitation; then: "We'll know in two minutes. We're at the bottom of Hacienda, turning into La Paloma Drive."

Thomas Jefferson Jackson sat in the passenger seat of the patrol car, waiting for the identification of the car that lay at the bottom of the ravine. He glanced out the window and saw Roscoe Finnerty talking to the group of kids whose party had just ended in tragedy. He was glad he didn't have to talk to them—he doubted whether he would have been able to control the rage that seethed in him. Why couldn't they have just had a dance and let it go at that? Why did they have to get drunk and start wrecking cars? He wasn't sure he'd ever understand what motivated them. All he'd do was go on getting sick when they piled themselves up.

"It was Alex Lonsdale," Bob Carey said, unable to meet Sergeant Finnerty's eyes.

"Dr. Lonsdale's kid?"

"Yes."

"You sure he was driving it?"

"Lisa Cochran saw it happen."

"Who's she?"

"Alex's girlfriend. She's over there."

Finnerty followed Bob's eyes and saw a pretty blond in a dirt-smeared green formal sobbing in the arms of another girl. He knew he should go over and talk to her, but decided it could wait—from what he could see, she didn't look too coherent.

"You know where she lives?" he asked Bob Carey. Numbly Bob recited Lisa's address, which Finnerty wrote in his notebook. "Wait here a minute." He strode to the car just as Jackson was opening the door.

"Got a make on the car," Jackson said. "Belongs to Alexander Lonsdale. That's Dr. Lonsdale's son, isn't it?"

Finnerty nodded grimly. "That's what the kids say, too, and apparently the boy was driving it. We got a witness, but I haven't talked to her yet." He tore the sheet with Lisa's address on it out of his notebook and handed it to Jackson. "Here's her name and address. Get hold of her parents and tell them we'll take the girl down to the Center. We'll meet them there."

Jackson looked at his partner uncertainly. "Shouldn't we take her to the station and get a statement?"

"This is La Paloma, Tom, not San Francisco. The kid in the car was her boyfriend, and she's pretty broken up. We're not gonna make things worse by dragging her into the station. Now, get hold of the Center and tell them who's coming in, then get hold of these Cochran people. Okay?"

Jackson nodded and got back in the car.

Lisa sat on the ground, trying to accept what had happened. It all had a dreamlike quality to it, and there seemed to be only bits and pieces left in her memory.

Standing in the road, trying to make up her mind whether or not to go back to the party and find Alex.

And then the sound of a car.

Instinctively, she'd known whose car it was, and her anger had suddenly evaporated.

And then she'd realized the car was coming too fast. She'd turned around to try to wave Alex down.

And then the blur.

The car rushing toward her, swerving away at the last minute, then only a series of sounds.

A shriek of skidding tires—

A scraping noise—

A crash—

And then the awful sound of Alex screaming her name, cut off by the horrible crunching of the car hurtling into the ravine.

Then nothing—just a blank, until suddenly she was back at Carolyn Evans's, and all the kids were staring at her, their faces blank and confused.

She hadn't even been able to tell them what had happened. She'd only been able to scream Alex's name, and point toward the road.

It had been Bob Carey who had finally understood and called the police.

And then there had been more confusion.

People scrambling out of the pool, grabbing clothes, streaming out of the house.

Most of them running down the road.

A few cars starting.

And Carolyn Evans, her eyes more furious than frightened, glaring at her.

"It's your fault," Carolyn had accused. "It's all your fault, and now I'm going to be in trouble."

Lisa had gazed at her: what was she talking about?

"My *parents,*" Carolyn had wailed. "They'll find out, and ground me for the rest of the summer."

And then Kate Lewis was beside her, pulling her away.

Suddenly she was back on Hacienda Drive, and the night was filled with sirens, and flashing lights, and people everywhere, asking her questions, staring down into the ravine. . . .

It had seemed to go on forever.

Finally there was that awful moment when the stretcher had appeared, and she'd seen Alex—

Except it hadn't been Alex.

It had only been a shape covered by a blanket.

She'd only been able to look for a second, then Kate had twisted her around, and she hadn't seen any more.

Now a voice penetrated the haze.

"Lisa? Lisa Cochran?"

She looked up, nodding mutely. A policeman was looking at her, but he didn't seem to be mad at her.

"We need to get you out of here," the policeman said. "We have to take you down to the Medical Center." He held out a hand. "Can you stand up?"

"I . . . I . . ." Lisa struggled to rise, then sank back to the ground. Strong hands slid under her arms and lifted her up. A minute later she was in the back seat of a police car. A few yards away she saw another police car, and a policeman talking to some of her friends.

But they didn't know what had happened. Only she knew.

Lisa buried her face in her hands, sobbing.

* * *

The speaker on the wall of the emergency room crackled to life once again.

"This is Unit One," the anonymous voice droned. "We'll be there in another thirty seconds. And we have an identification on the victim." Suddenly the voice cracked, losing its professional tone. "It's Alex . . . Alex Lonsdale."

Marsh stared at the speaker, willing himself to have heard the words wrong. Then he gazed around the room, and knew by the shock on everyone's face, and by the way they were returning his gaze, that he had not heard wrong. He groped behind him for a chair, found one, and lowered himself into it.

"No," he whispered. "Not Alex. Anyone but Alex . . ."

"Call Frank Mallory," Barbara Fannon told one of the orderlies, immediately taking charge. "He's next on call. His number's on the Rolodex." She moved around the desk and put a hand on Marshall Lonsdale's shoulder. "Maybe it's a mistake, Marsh," she said, though she knew that the ambulance crew wouldn't have identified Alex if they weren't absolutely sure.

Marsh shook his head and then raised his agonized eyes. "How am I going to tell her?" he asked, his voice dazed. "How am I going to tell Ellen? She . . . she had a feeling . . . she told me . . . she wanted to come with me tonight—"

"Come on." Barbara assumed her most authoritative tone, the one she always used with people she knew were close to breaking. Outside, the sound of the approaching ambulance disturbed the night. "We're getting you out of here." When Marsh failed to respond, she took him by the hand and drew him to his feet. "I'm taking you to your office."

"No!" Marsh protested as the approaching siren grew louder. "Alex is my son—"

"Which is exactly why you won't be here when they bring him in. We'll have Frank Mallory here as soon as possible, and until he gets here, Benny Cohen knows what to do."

Marsh looked dazed. "Benny's only an intern—"

Barbara began steering him out of the emergency room as the siren fell silent and headlights glared momentarily through the glass doors of the emergency entrance. "Benny's the best intern we've ever had. You told me so yourself."

Then, as the emergency-room doors opened and the gurney bearing Alex Lonsdale's nearly lifeless body was pushed inside, she forced Marsh Lonsdale into the corridor.

"Go to your office," she told him. "Go to your office and mix yourself a drink from the bottle you and Frank nip at every time you deliver a baby. I can take care of everything else, but right now I can't take care of you. Understand?"

Marsh swallowed, then nodded. "I'll call Ellen—"

"You'll do no such thing," Barbara cut in. "You'll fix a drink, drink it, and wait. I'll be there in five minutes, and by then we'll know something about how he is. Now, go!" She gave Marsh a gentle shove, then disappeared back into the emergency room.

Marsh paused a moment, trying to sort out his thoughts.

He knew that Barbara was right.

With a shambling gait, feeling suddenly helpless, he started down the hall toward his office.

In the little house behind the old mission, across the street from the graveyard, María Torres dropped the blind on the front window back into place, then shuffled slowly into the bedroom and eased her aged body into bed.

She was tired from the long walk home, and tonight it had been particularly exhausting.

Unwilling to be seen by anyone that night, María had been forced to make her way down the canyon by way of the path that wound through the underbrush a few feet below the level of the road. Each time she had heard the wailing of a siren and seen headlights flashing on the road above, she had huddled close to the ground, waiting until the car had passed before once more making her slow progress toward home.

But now it was all right.

She was home, and no one had seen her, and her job was safe.

Tonight she had no trouble. Tonight it was the *gringos* who had the trouble.

To María Torres, what had happened on the road near the hacienda tonight was nothing less than a blessing from the saints. All her life, she had spent many hours each week praying that destruction would come to the *gringos.* Tonight, she knew, was one of the nights the saints had chosen to answer those prayers.

Tomorrow, or the next day, she would find out who had been in the car that had plunged over the edge of the ravine, and remember to go to church and light a candle to whichever saint had, in answer to her prayers, abandoned one of his namesakes this evening. Her candles were not much, she knew, but they were something, and the souls of her ancestors would appreciate them.

Silence finally fell over La Paloma. For the rest of the night, María Torres slept in peace.

Benny Cohen carefully peeled away the towel that had been wrapped around Alex Lonsdale's head, and stared at the gaping wound on the boy's skull.

He's dead, Benny thought. He may still be breathing, but he's dead.

CHAPTER 4

Ellen Lonsdale knew her premonition had come true as soon as she opened the front door and saw Carol Cochran standing on the porch, a handkerchief clutched in her left hand, her eyes rimmed with red.

"It happened, didn't it?" she whispered.

Carol's head moved in a barely perceptible nod. "It's Alex," she whispered. "He . . . he was alone in the car . . ."

"Alone?" Ellen echoed. Where had Lisa been? Hadn't she been with Alex? But her questions went unspoken as she tried to concentrate on what Carol was saying.

"He's at the Center," Carol told her, stepping into the house and closing the door behind her. "I'll take you."

For a moment Ellen felt as if she might collapse. Then, with an oddly detached calmness, she picked her purse up from the table in the entry hall and automatically opened it to check its contents. Satisfied that everything was there, she walked past Carol and opened the front door. "Is he dead?" she asked.

"No," Carol replied, her voice catching. "He's not dead, Ellen."

"But it's bad, isn't it?"

"I don't know. I don't think anyone does."

Silently the two women got into the Cochrans' car and Carol started the engine. As she was backing down the Lonsdales' driveway, Ellen asked the question that was still lurking in her mind. "Why wasn't Lisa with him?"

"I don't know that. We got a call from the police. They said to meet them at the Center, that they were taking Lisa there. I thought . . . Oh, God, never mind what I thought. Anyway, Lisa's all right, but Alex—his car went off the road up near the old hacienda. Carolyn was having a party."

"He said he wouldn't go to any parties," Ellen said numbly, her body slumped against the car door. "He promised—" She broke off her own thought, and remained silent for several seconds as her mind suddenly began to shift gears. *I can't fall apart. I can't give in to what I'm feeling. I have to be strong. For Alex, I have to be strong.* She consciously straightened herself in the car seat. "Well, it doesn't matter what he promised, does it?" she asked. "The only thing that matters is that he be all right." She turned to gaze searchingly at Carol, and when she spoke, her voice was stronger. "If you knew how bad it was, you'd tell me, wouldn't you?"

Carol moved her hand off the steering wheel to give Ellen's arm a quick squeeze. "Of course I would. And I'm not going to tell you not to worry, either."

As Carol drove, Ellen tried to make herself concentrate on anything but what might have happened to Alex. She gazed out the window, forcing her mind to focus only on what her eyes were taking in.

"It's a pretty town," she said suddenly.

"What?" Carol Cochran asked, taken aback by Ellen's odd statement.

"I was just looking at it," Ellen went on. "I haven't really done that for a long time. I drive around it all the time, but it's been years since I really paid attention to what it looks like. And a lot of it hasn't really changed since we were children."

"No," Carol said slowly, still not sure where Ellen's thoughts were leading. "I don't suppose it has."

Ellen uttered a sound that was partly a hollow chuckle, partly a sob. "Do you think I'm crazy, talking about how pretty La Paloma is? Well, I'm not. Anyway, I don't think I am. But I'm having a feeling, and if I let myself think about *that,* then I *will* go crazy."

"Do you want to tell me what it is?"

There was another long silence, and when she spoke again, Ellen's voice had gone strangely flat. "He's dead," she stated. "I have the most awful feeling that Alex is dead. But he isn't dead. I . . . I won't *let* him be dead!"

* * *

Ellen stared at the knot of people in the emergency waiting room. She recognized most of the faces, though for some reason her mind refused to put names to them. Except for a few.

Lisa Cochran.

She was sitting on a couch, huddled close to her father, and a policeman was talking to her. Lisa saw her and immediately stood up and started toward her.

"I'm sorry," she blurted. "Oh, Mrs. Lonsdale, I'm so sorry. I didn't mean to—"

"What happened?" Ellen asked, her voice dull.

"I . . . I'm not sure," Lisa stammered. "We had a fight—well, sort of a fight, and I decided to walk home. And Alex must have been coming after me. But he was driving too fast, and . . ." She went on, blurting out the story of what had happened, while Ellen listened, but only half-heard. Around them, the rest of the people in the waiting room fell silent.

"It was my fault," Lisa finished. "It was all my fault."

Ellen laid a gentle hand on Lisa's cheek, then kissed her. "No," she said quietly. "It wasn't your fault. You weren't in the car, and it wasn't your fault."

She turned away to find Barbara Fannon at her elbow. "Where is he?" she asked. "Where's Alex?"

"He's in the O.R. Frank and Benny are working on him. Marsh is in his office." She took Ellen's arm and began guiding her out of the waiting room.

When she came into his office, Marsh was sitting behind his desk, a glass in front of him, staring at nothing. His gaze shifted, and he stood up, came around the desk, and put his arms around her.

"You were right," he whispered, his voice strangling on the words. "Oh, God, Ellen, you were right."

"Is he dead?" Ellen asked.

Marsh drew back sharply, as if the words had been a physical blow. "Who told you that?"

Ellen's face paled. "No one. I just . . . I just have a feeling, that's all."

"Well, that one isn't true," Marsh told her. "He's alive."

Ellen hesitated; then: "If he's alive, why don't I feel it?"

Marsh shook his head. "I don't know. But he's not dead. He's seriously injured, but he's not dead."

Time seemed to stand still as Ellen gazed deep into her husband's eyes. At last she quietly repeated Marsh's words. "He's not dead. He's not dead. He won't die." Then, despite her determination to be strong, her tears began to flow.

* * *

In the operating room, Frank Mallory carefully withdrew the last visible fragment of shattered skull from the tissue of Alex's brain. He glanced up at the monitors.

By rights, the boy should be dead.

And yet, there on the monitors was the evidence that he was not.

There was a pulse—weak and erratic, but there.

And he was breathing, albeit with the aid of a respirator.

His broken left arm was in a temporary splint, and the worst of his facial lacerations had been stitched just enough to stop the bleeding.

That had been the easy part.

It was his head that was the problem.

From what Mallory could see, as the car tumbled down the ravine, Alex's head must have smashed against a rock, crushing the left parietal plate and damaging the frontal plate. Pieces of both bones had broken away, embedding themselves in Alex's brain, and it was these splinters that Mallory had been carefully removing. Then, with all the skill he could muster, he had worked the fractured pieces as nearly into their normal positions as possible. Now he was applying what could only be temporary bandages—bandages intended to bind Alex's wounds only until the electroencephalogram went totally flat and the boy would be declared dead.

"What do you think?" Benny Cohen asked.

"Right now, I'm trying not to think," Mallory replied. "All I'm doing is putting the pieces back together, and I'm sorry to say I'm not at all sure I can do it."

"He's not gonna make it?"

"I'm not saying that, either," Mallory rasped, unable to admit his true thoughts. "He's made it this far, hasn't he?"

Benny nodded. "With a lot of help. But without the respirator, he'd be gone."

"A lot of people need respirators. That's why they were invented."

"But most people only need them temporarily. He's going to need it the rest of his life."

Frank Mallory glowered at the young intern, then softened. Cohen, after all, hadn't known Alex Lonsdale since the day the boy was born, nor had Cohen yet lost a patient. When he did, maybe he'd realize how much it hurt to see someone die and know there's nothing you can do about it. But Alex had survived the first emergency procedures, and there was still the possibility that he might live. "Let's get him into the ICU, then start setting up for X rays and a CAT scan."

Ten minutes later, still drying his hands with a white towel, Mallory walked into Marshall Lonsdale's office. Both Marsh and Ellen struggled wearily to their feet.

"He's still alive, and in the ICU," Mallory told them, gesturing for them both to sit down again. "But it's bad, Marsh. Real bad."

"Tell me," Marsh replied, his voice toneless.

Mallory shrugged. "I can't tell you all of it yet—you know that. But there's brain damage, and it looks extensive."

Ellen stiffened, but said nothing.

"We're setting up right now for every test we can give him. But it's going to be tough, because he's on a respirator and a cardiostimulator." Then, as Marsh and Ellen listened, he described Alex's injuries, using the dispassionate, factual tone he had learned in medical school, in order to keep himself under control. When he was done, it was Ellen who spoke.

"What can we do?"

Mallory shook his head. "Nothing, for the moment. Try to stabilize him, and try to find out how bad the damage is. We should know sometime early in the morning. Maybe by six."

"I see," Ellen murmured. Then: "Can I see him?"

Frank Mallory's eyes flicked toward Marsh, who nodded. "Of course you can," Mallory said. "You can sit with him all night, if you want to. It can't hurt, and it might help. You never know what people in his condition know or don't know, but if somehow he knows you're there . . . well, it can't hurt, can it?"

Barbara Fannon glanced up at the clock on the wall and was surprised to see that it was nearly five in the morning. To her, it seemed as if it couldn't have been more than an hour since the ambulance arrived with Alex.

There had been so much to do.

There had been all the tests that needed to be set up, and it had fallen to Barbara to coordinate the testing so that Alex was subjected to the least amount of movement possible. Not only had she coordinated the X rays and CAT scan, but everything else Frank Mallory had requested. And, as far as Barbara could determine, he hadn't forgotten anything: he'd ordered ultrasound imaging and a cerebrospinal tap, as well as an arteriograph and an EEG. The only thing he'd left out was a pneumoencephalograph, and Barbara knew the only reason he'd skipped it was that Alex would have had to be put in a vertical position to carry it out. In his present condition, that simply wasn't feasible. It had taken Barbara nearly an hour simply to contact all the technicians necessary and get them to the Center. And then, of course, there had been the people in the waiting room.

They had thinned out after the first couple of hours, when Barbara had finally told them that there would be no more news that night—Alex was undergoing a series of tests, but the results would be unavailable for an indefinite period.

Now, at five o'clock, she could at last go home. Everything that needed to be done, or could be done, was finished, and she realized she was bone weary. All she had to do was check the waiting room, and she could go. She pushed the door open, expecting the room to be empty.

It wasn't.

Sitting on the couch in the far corner was Lisa Cochran, her parents flanking her. She was dry-eyed now, and sitting straight up, her hands folded quietly in her lap. Barbara hesitated, then went into the waiting room, letting the door swing shut behind her.

"Can I get you anything?" she asked. "Some coffee, maybe?"

Lisa shook her head, but said nothing.

"If you can think of a way to convince her to come home with us, that might help," Carol said, rising to her feet, stretching, and offering the tired nurse a resigned smile.

"I can't, Mama," Lisa whispered. "What if he wakes up and asks for me?"

Barbara crossed the room and sat next to the girl. "He's not going to wake up tonight, Lisa."

Lisa regarded her with bloodshot eyes. "Is . . . is he going to wake up at all?"

Barbara knew it wasn't her place to talk to anyone about Alex Lonsdale's condition, but she also knew exactly who Lisa was, and how Alex felt about her. God knew he'd spent enough time perched on the edge of Barbara's desk telling her how wonderful Lisa was. And after watching her through the last several hours, Barbara was convinced that Alex was right. She sighed heavily. "I don't know," she said carefully; then, when Lisa's eyes turned suddenly frightened, she went on: "I said I don't know. That doesn't mean he's not going to wake up. All it means is that I don't know, and no one else does either."

"If he wakes up, will that mean he's going to be all right?"

Barbara shrugged. "We don't know that, either. All we can do is wait and see."

"Then I'll wait," Lisa said.

"You could go home and try to get some sleep," Barbara suggested. "I promise I'll arrange for someone to call you if anything happens. Anything at all."

Lisa rubbed at her eyes, then shook her head. "No," she said. "I want to be here. Just in case." She looked at the nurse beseechingly. "He *might* wake up."

Barbara started to speak, then changed her mind. She's right, she decided. He damned well might wake up. And as she absorbed the thought, she realized that she, like most of the staff at the clinic, had only been going through the motions of administering to Alex.

For all of them, all the trained medical people who had seen injuries like Alex's before, it was a hopeless case. You did what you could, tried not to overlook any measure, no matter how drastic, that might save the life, but deep inside you prepared yourself for the fact that the patient wasn't going to make it.

And at the end of your shift, you went home.

But Lisa Cochran wasn't going home, and Barbara Fannon decided she wasn't going home either, even though her shift had ended long ago. Coming to that decision, she stood up. "Come on," she said.

The Cochrans looked at her uncertainly, but followed her down the hall. Without knocking, she opened the door to Marshall Lonsdale's office and led them inside. "If we're all going to stay, we might as well be as comfortable as possible."

"This is Marsh's office," Jim Cochran said.

"Nobody else's."

"Should we be here?"

"You're his friends, aren't you? It's been a long night, and it's going to be an even longer one. I was going home, but if you can stick this out, so can I. But not out there." She lowered the lights a little, and closed the blinds to the windows. "Make yourselves comfortable while I go find some coffee. If you want something stronger, you might poke around the office while I'm gone. I've heard rumors that sometimes there's a bottle in here."

Jim eyed the nurse. "Any rumors about just where it might be?"

"No," Barbara replied. Then, as she left the office, she spoke once more. "But if I were you, I'd start looking in the credenza. Bottom right."

Ellen Lonsdale sat in a straight-backed chair that had been pulled close to Alex's bed, her right hand resting gently on his. He lay as he had been placed, on his back, the cast on his left arm suspended slightly above the mattress, his limp right arm extended parallel to his body. His face, covered with the respirator mask and a mass of bandages, was barely visible, and totally unrecognizable. Around him was an array of equipment that Ellen couldn't begin to comprehend. All she knew was that the monitors and machinery were somehow keeping her son alive.

She had been there for nearly five hours now. The sky outside the window was beginning to brighten, and she shifted slightly in her chair, not as a reaction to the stiffness that had long ago taken over her body, but so that she could get a clearer look at Alex's eyes.

For some reason, she kept thinking they should be open.

The night had been filled with odd thoughts like that.

Several times she had found herself feeling surprise that the respirator was still operating.

Once, when they brought Alex back from one of the tests—she couldn't remember which one—she had been shocked at the warmth of his hand when she touched it.

She knew what the odd feelings were about.

Despite what she had been told—despite her own inner resolve—she still had the horrible feeling that Alex was dead.

Several times she had found herself studying the monitors, wondering why they were still registering life signs in Alex.

Since he was dead, the graphic displays of his heartbeat and breathing should be flat.

She kept reminding herself that he wasn't dead, that he was only asleep.

Except he wasn't asleep.

He was in a coma, and despite what everyone kept saying, he wasn't going to come out of it.

Abstractly she already understood that it wasn't a matter of waiting to see what would happen. It was a matter of deciding when to remove the respirator and let Alex go.

She didn't know how long that thought had been in her mind, but she knew she was beginning to get used to the reality of it. Sometime today, or perhaps tomorrow, after all the test results had been studied and analyzed, she and Marsh were going to have to make the most difficult decision of their lives, and she wasn't at all sure either of them would be up to it.

If Alex's brain was, indeed, dead, they were going to have to accept that keeping Alex alive the way he was was cruel.

Cruel to Alex.

She stared again at all the machinery, and momentarily wondered why it had ever been invented.

Why couldn't they just let people die?

And yet, she realized with sudden clarity, even though she understood the reality of Alex's situation, she would never simply let him die.

If she were going to, she would have done it already. During the last two hours there had been plenty of opportunities. All she would have had to do was turn off the respirator. Alarms would have gone off, but she could have dealt with that. And it wouldn't have taken long—only a minute or two.

But she hadn't done it. Instead, she'd simply sat there battling her feelings of despair, strengthening her resolve not to let him die, and whispering encouraging words to Alex as she held his hand.

And even though part of her still insisted that Alex was already dead, the other part of her, the part that was determined that he should live, was growing stronger by the hour.

Suddenly the door opened, and Barbara Fannon stepped into the room, closing the door behind her.

"Ellen? It's eight o'clock—you've been here all night."

Ellen turned her head. "I know."

"Marsh is in Frank's office. They have the test results. They're waiting for you."

Ellen thought about it for a moment, then slowly shook her head. "No," she said at last. "I'll stay here with Alex. Marsh will tell me what I need to know."

Barbara hesitated, then nodded. "I'll tell them," she said, then let herself out of the room, leaving Ellen alone with her son.

"It's bad," Frank Mallory said. "About as bad as it can get, I'm afraid."

"Let's see." Marsh's whole body felt drained from the shock and exhaustion of the last hours, but for some reason his mind was perfectly clear. Slowly and deliberately he began going over the results of all the tests and examinations that had been administered to Alex during the long night.

Mallory was right—it was very bad.

The damage to Alex's brain was extensive. Bone fragments seemed to be everywhere, driven deep into the cortex. The cerebrum showed the heaviest damage, much of it apparently centered in the temporal lobe. But nothing seemed to have escaped injury—the parietal and frontal lobes showed extensive injury as well.

"I'm not an expert at this," Marsh said, though both he and Mallory were well aware that many of the ramifications of Alex's injuries were obvious.

Mallory decided to take the direct approach. "If he lives at all, he won't be able to walk or talk, and it's doubtful that he'll be able to hear. He may be able to see—the occipital lobe seems to have suffered the least amount of damage. But all that's almost beside the point. It's highly doubtful if he'll be aware of anything going on around him, or even be aware of himself. And that's if he wakes up."

"I don't believe that," Marsh replied, fixing Mallory with cold eyes.

"Don't, or won't?" Mallory countered gently.

"It doesn't make any difference," Marsh replied. "Everything's going to be done for Alex that is humanly possible."

"That goes without saying, Marsh," Frank Mallory said, his voice reflecting the pain Marsh's words had caused. "You know there isn't anyone here who wouldn't do his best for Alex."

If Marshall heard him, he ignored him. "I want you to start by getting hold of Torres, down in Palo Alto."

"Torres?" Mallory repeated. "Raymond Torres?"

"Is there anyone else who can help Alex?"

Mallory fell silent as he thought about the man to whom Marsh was considering turning over his son.

Raymond Torres had grown up in La Paloma, and though there was little question in anyone's mind of the man's brilliance, there were, and always had been, many questions about the man himself. He had left La Paloma long ago, remaining in Palo Alto after medical school, returning to La Paloma only to see his mother—old María Torres. And even his visits to her were rare. There was a feeling in La Paloma that Torres resented his mother, that she was little more to him than a constant reminder of his past, and that, if there was one thing Torres would like to ignore, it was his past. In La Paloma he was primarily regarded as a curiosity: the boy from behind the mission who had somehow made good.

Beyond La Paloma, he had become, over the years, something of an enigma within the medical community. To his supporters, his aloofness was a result only of the fact that he devoted nearly every waking hour to his research into the functioning of the human brain, while his detractors attributed that same aloofness to intellectual arrogance.

But for all the questions about him, Raymond Torres had succeeded in becoming one of the country's foremost authorities on the structure and functioning of the human brain. In recent years, the thrust of his research had changed slightly, and his primary interest had become reconstructive brain surgery.

"But isn't most of his work experimental?" Mallory asked now. "I don't think a lot of it has even been tried on human beings yet."

Marshall Lonsdale's desperation was reflected in his eyes. "Raymond Torres knows more about the human brain than anybody else alive. And some of the reconstruction work he's done is just this side of incredible. I'd say it *was* incredible if I hadn't seen the results myself. I want him to work on Alex."

"Marsh—"

But Marsh was on his feet, his eyes fixed on the pile of X rays, CAT scans, lab results, graphs, and other documentation pertaining to the damage his son's brain had sustained. "He's still alive, Frank," he said. "And as long as he's alive, I have to try to help him. I can't just leave him alone—you can see what he'll be like as well as I can. He'll be a vegetable, Frank. My God, you told me so yourself just now. Nothing can hurt him anymore, Frank. All Torres can do is help. Call him for me. Tell him what's happened, and that I want to talk to him. Just talk to him, that's all. Just get me in to see him."

When Frank Mallory still hesitated, Marshall Lonsdale spoke once more. "Alex is all I have, Frank. I can't just let him die."

When he was alone, Frank Mallory picked up the phone and dialed the number of Raymond Torres's office in Palo Alto, twenty miles away. After talking to him for thirty minutes, he finally convinced Torres to see Marsh Lonsdale and look at Alex's case.

The doctor made no promises, but he agreed to talk, and to look.

Privately, Frank half-hoped Torres would turn Marsh down.

CHAPTER 5

Exhaustion was overtaking Marsh, and he was beginning to feel that the situation was hopeless. He'd been in Raymond Torres's offices for most of the day, and for most of the day he'd been by himself. Not that it hadn't been interesting; it had, despite the overriding fear for his son's life that had never left his consciousness since the moment he had arrived that morning.

He'd stared at the Institute through bleary eyes. The building itself was a bastard—it had obviously started out as a home, and an imposing one. But from the central core of the mansion—for a mansion it had been—two wings had spread, and no attempt had been made to make them architecturally compatible with the original structure. Instead, they were sleekly functional, in stark contrast with the Georgian massiveness of the core. The buildings were surrounded by a sprawling lawn dotted with trees, and only a neat brass plaque mounted on the face of a large rock near the street identified the structure: INSTITUTE FOR THE HUMAN BRAIN.

Inside, a receptionist had led him immediately to Raymond Torres's office, where he'd turned all of Alex's records over to the surgeon himself, who, without so much as glancing at them, had given them to an assistant. When the assistant had disappeared, Torres had offered him a chair, then spent what Marsh thought was an unnecessarily long time lighting his pipe.

It took Marsh only a few seconds to decide that there was nothing of Torres's scientific reputation in either his manner or his bearing. He was tall, and his chiseled features were carefully framed by prematurely graying hair in a manner that seemed to Marsh more suitable for a movie star than a scientist. The star image was further enhanced by the perfectly cut tan silk suit Torres wore, and the cool casualness of his posture. For all his fine credentials, the first impression Raymond Torres gave his visitor was that of a society doctor more interested in the practice of golf than in the practice of medicine.

Nor was Marsh's instinctive dislike of the man alleviated by the fact that once the pipe was lit, the meeting had lasted only long enough for Torres to tell him that there would be no decision made until his staff had been able to analyze Alex's case, and that the analysis would take most of the day.

"I'll wait," Marsh had said. From behind his desk, Raymond Torres had shrugged with apparent disinterest. "As you wish, but I could just as easily call you when I've come to a decision."

Marsh had shaken his head. "No. I have to be here. Alex is my only child. There's . . . well, there's just nowhere else for me to go."

Torres had risen from his chair in a manner that Marsh found almost offensively dismissive. "As I said, as you wish. But you'll have to excuse me—I have a great deal to do this morning."

Marsh had stared at the man in stunned disbelief. "You're not even interested in hearing about the case?"

"It's all in the records, isn't it?" Torres had countered.

"*Alex* isn't in the records, Dr. Torres," Marsh had replied, his voice trembling with the effort to control his anger. Torres seemed to consider his words for a moment, but didn't reseat himself, and when he finally replied, his voice was cool.

"I'm a research man, Dr. Lonsdale. I'm a research man because, as I discovered long ago, I don't have much of a bedside manner. There are those, I know, who don't think I relate to people very well. Frankly, I don't care. I'm interested in helping people, not in coddling them. And I don't have to know the details of your son's life in order to help him. I don't care who he is, or what he's like, or what the details of his accident were. All I care about are the details of his injuries, so that I can make a reasonable judgment about whether or not I can help him. In other words, everything I need to know about your boy should be in his records. If there is anything missing, I—or someone on my staff—will know, and do whatever has to be done to rectify the matter. If you want to spend the rest of the day here, just in case we need you, I have no objection. Frankly, I doubt we'll need you. If we need anybody, it will be the patient's attending physician."

"Frank Mallory."

"Whoever." Torres shrugged disinterestedly. "But feel free to stay. We have a comfortable lounge, and you'll certainly find plenty to read." Suddenly he smiled. "All of it, of course, having to do with our work. One thing I insist on is that the lounge be well stocked with every article and monograph I've ever written."

Offended as he was by the man's open pride in himself, Marsh managed to keep silent, for without Torres, he knew there was no hope for Alex at all. And by two o'clock that afternoon he'd become totally convinced that whatever Raymond Torres lacked in personal warmth, he more than made up for in professional expertise.

The articles he'd read—and he'd read at least thirty of them, forcing himself to maintain his concentration through the interminable hours—covered a wide field of interest. Torres had not only made himself an expert on the structure of the brain, but he had also become a leading theorist on the functioning of the brain as well. In dozens of articles, Torres had described cases in which he'd found methods with which to circumvent damaged areas of a brain, and utilize other, healthy areas to take over the functions of the traumatized tissue. And through it all ran one constant theme—that the mysteries of the human brain were, indeed, solvable, but that the potentialities of the brain were only just being discovered. Indeed, he'd summed it up in a few sentences that had particularly intrigued Marsh:

> The backup systems of the brain appear to me to be almost limitless. Long ago, we discovered that if a portion of the brain fails, another portion of the same brain can sometimes take over the function of the failed portion. It is almost as if each area of the brain not only knows what every other area does, but can perform that work itself if it really has to. The problem, then, seems to be one of convincing a damaged brain not to give up, and, further, of making it aware of its own problems so that it may redistribute its work load among its healthy components.

Marsh had read and reread that article several times when the receptionist suddenly appeared, smiling warmly at him.

"Dr. Lonsdale? Dr. Torres will see you now." He put the journal aside and followed the neat young woman back to Torres's office. Nodding a greeting, Torres beckoned him to a chair near his desk. In another chair, already seated, was Frank Mallory.

"Frank? What are you doing here?"

"I asked him to come," Torres replied. "There are some things I have to review with him."

"But Alex—"

"He's stable, Marsh," Frank told him. "There haven't been any changes in his condition for several hours. Benny's there, and a nurse is always in the room."

"If we may proceed," Torres interrupted. He turned toward a television screen on a table next to his desk. The screen displayed a high-resolution photograph of a human brain.

"It's not what you think it is," Torres said. Startled, both Marsh Lonsdale and Frank Mallory glanced toward Torres.

"I beg your pardon?" Frank asked.

"It's not a photograph. It's a computer-generated graphic representation of Alexander Lonsdale's brain." He paused a beat; then: "Before the accident."

Mallory's gaze shifted back to the screen. "Here's what happened," he heard Torres's voice say. "Or, more exactly, here's a reconstruction of what happened." He typed some instructions into the keyboard in front of him, and suddenly the image on the monitor began to move, turning upside down. Then, at the bottom of the screen, another shape came into view. As the three of them watched, the image of the brain came into contact with the other object, and suddenly began to distort. It was, Marsh realized, just like watching a movie of someone's head being smashed against a sharp rock.

In slow motion, he could see the skull crack, then splinter and begin to cave in.

Beneath the skull, brain tissue gave way, part of it crushed, part of it torn. Fragments of skull broke away, lacerating the brain further. Frank Mallory and Raymond Torres watched in silence, but Marsh was unable to stifle a groan of empathic pain. Suddenly it was over, and the brain was once again right-side-up. And then, as Torres tapped more instructions into the computer, the image changed again.

"Christ," Mallory whispered. "That's not possible."

"What is it?" Torres demanded.

"It's Alex's head," Mallory breathed. Marsh, his face ashen, gazed at Mallory, but the other man's eyes remained fixed on the screen. "It's his head," Mallory breathed. "And it looks just the way it did when they brought him into the hospital. But . . . how?"

"We'll get to that," Torres replied. Then: "Dr. Mallory, I want you to concentrate on that image very hard. This is very important. How close is that picture to what you saw when they brought the patient in?" He held up a cautioning hand. "Don't answer right away, please. Examine it carefully. If you need me to, I can rotate the image so you can see it from other angles. But I need to know how exact it is."

For two long minutes, as Marsh looked on in agonized silence, Mallory examined the image, asking Torres to turn it first in one direction, then in another. At last he nodded. "As far as I can tell, it's perfect. If there are any flaws, I can't see them."

"All right. Now, the next part should be easier for you. Don't say anything, just watch, and if there's anything that doesn't look as you remember it, tell me."

As they watched, the image came to life once more. A forceps appeared and began removing fragments of bone from the brain. Then the forceps was gone, and a probe appeared. The probe moved, and a small bit of brain tissue tore loose. Mallory winced.

It went on and on, in agonizing detail. For each fragment of bone that was removed from the wound, a new wound was inflicted on Alex's brain. And then, after what seemed an aeon, it was over.

Frank Mallory was staring at an exact image of Alex's brain after he'd finished cleaning his wounds.

"Well?" Torres's voice asked.

Mallory heard his own voice shake as he spoke. "Why did you show me that? Just to prove my incompetence?"

"Don't be ridiculous," Torres snapped. "Aside from the fact that I don't need to waste my time with such a thing, you're not an incompetent. In fact, you did as good a job under the circumstances as could have been expected. What I need to know is whether that reconstruction was accurate."

Mallory chewed his lip, then nodded. "I'm afraid so. I'm sorry—I was doing my best."

"Don't be sorry," Torres remarked coldly. "Just think about it."

"It's accurate," Mallory assured him. "Now, can you tell us how you did it?"

"*I* didn't do it," Torres replied. "A computer did it all. For the last"—he glanced at the clock on his desk—"six hours, we've been feeding the computer information. Much of it the results of the CAT scan your lab did in La Paloma. Fortunately, that was a good job too. But our computer goes a lot further than yours. Your machinery can display any aspect of the brain, from any angle, in two dimensions. Ours is much more sophisticated," he went on, and suddenly his eyes, so cool and aloof until now, took on a glowing intensity. "Once it had all the data, it was able to reconstruct everything that happened to Alexander Lonsdale's brain from the first impact to the time of the CAT scan. For ourselves, an educated guess would have been the best we could do. We would have been able to extrapolate the approximate shape of the traumatizing instrument, and the probable angle from which it struck. And that would have been about all. But the wounds are extensive, and the computer is designed to handle a great many variables simultaneously. According to the computer, what you just saw is 99.624 percent accurate, given that the input was accurate. That's why I wanted you to look at the reconstruction. If there were any basic errors in the data, they would have been magnified by the extrapolation process to the point where you'd have seen something significantly in error. But you didn't, so we can assume that what we saw is what happened."

While Mallory sat in silence, Marsh voiced the question that was in both their minds. "Why is that important? It seems to me that what comes next is what we should be concerned with."

"Exactly," Torres agreed. "Now, watch carefully. What you're about to see is going to be at high speed, but it's what we think we can do for Alexander."

"Everyone calls him Alex," Marsh interjected.

Torres's brows arched slightly. "Very well. Alex. It makes no difference what we call him." He ignored the flash of anger in Marsh's eyes, and his fingers once more flew over the keyboard. The picture began to change again. As the two doctors from La Paloma watched in fascination, layers of brain tissue were peeled back. Certain tissue was removed entirely; some was simply maneuvered back into place. The chaos of the wound began to take on a semblance of order, and then, slowly, the mending process began, beginning deep within the medulla and proceeding outward through the various lobes of the brain. At last it was over, and the image on the screen was once again filled with the recognizable shape of a human brain. Certain areas, however, had taken on various shades of red, and Marsh's frown reflected his puzzlement.

"Those are the areas that are no longer functional," Torres told him before he could ask his question. "The pale pink ones are deep within the brain, the bright red ones on the surface. The gradations, I think, are obvious."

Mallory glanced at Marsh, whose attention seemed totally absorbed by the image on the screen. Finally he turned to Torres, his fingers interlaced beneath his chin. "What you've shown us is pure science fiction, Dr. Torres," he said. "You can't cut that deep, and make repairs that extensive, without killing the patient. Beyond that, it appears to me that what you're proposing to do is to reconstruct Alex's brain, even to the extent of repairing nerve cells. Frankly, I don't believe you or anyone else can do that."

Torres chuckled. "And, of course, you're right. I can't do that, nor can anybody else. Unfortunately, I'm much too large, and my hands are much too clumsy. Which is why Alexan—*Alex,*" he corrected himself, "is going to have to be brought here." He switched off the monitor and rose from his chair. "Come with me. I want to show you something."

They left Torres's office and walked down a corridor that led to the west wing of the building. A security guard looked up at them as they passed, then, recognizing Torres, went back to gazing at the television monitor at his desk. Finally they turned into a scrub room, beyond which was an operating room. Wordlessly Torres stood aside and let the two others precede him through the double doors.

In the center of the room was an operating table, and against one wall was the customary array of O.R. equipment—all the support systems and monitors that both Marsh and Frank Mallory were used to. The rest of the room was taken up with an array of equipment the likes of which neither of them had ever seen before.

"It's a computerized microsurgical robot," Torres explained. "In the simplest terms possible, all it does is reduce the actions of the surgeon—in this case, me—down from increments of millimeters into increments of millimicrons. It incorporates an electron microscope, and a computer program that makes the program you just saw look like simple addition in comparison to advanced calculus. In a way," he went on, the pride in his voice belying his words, "with the development of this machine, I've reduced myself from being a brain surgeon to being little more than a technician. The microscope looks at the problems, and then the computer analyzes them and determines the solutions. Finally it tells me what to attach to what, and I make the movements relative to an enlarged model of the tissue. The robot reduces my motions and performs the procedures on the real tissue. And it works. Physically, that machine and I can repair much of the damage done to Alex Lonsdale's brain."

Marsh studied the equipment for several minutes, then turned to face Torres once again. When he spoke, his voice clearly reflected the uncertainty he was feeling. "What are the chances of Alex surviving the operation?"

Torres's expression turned grim. "Let's go back to my office. The computer can tell us that, too."

No one spoke again until they were back in the old core building, with the door to Torres's office closed behind them. Marsh and Frank Mallory took their seats, and Torres switched the computer back on. Quickly he began entering a series of instructions, and then the monitor flashed into life:

	SURGERY PERFORMED	SURGERY NOT PERFORMED
PROBABILITY OF SURVIVAL PAST ONE WEEK	90%	10%
PROBABILITY OF REGAINING CONSCIOUSNESS	50%	.02%
PROBABILITY OF PARTIAL RECOVERY	20%	0%
PROBABILITY OF TOTAL RECOVERY	0%	0%

Marsh and Mallory studied the chart, then, still staring at the screen, Marsh asked the first question that came to mind.

"What does partial recovery mean, exactly?"

"For starters, that he'll be able to breathe on his own, and that he'll be both cognizant of what is going on around him and able to communicate with the world beyond his own body. To me, anything less is no recovery at all. Though such a patient may be technically conscious, I still consider him to be in a state of coma. I find it inhuman to keep people alive under such circumstances, and I don't believe that simply because such people can't communicate their suffering, they are therefore *not* suffering. For me, such a life would be unbearable, even for a few days."

Marsh struggled to control the inner rage he was feeling at this cool man who was able to discuss Alex so dispassionately. And yet, deep down, he wasn't at all sure he disagreed with Torres. Then he heard Frank Mallory asking another question.

"And full recovery?"

"Exactly what the words say," Torres replied. "In this case, full recovery is simply not possible. Too much tissue has been destroyed. No matter how successful the surgery might be, there will never be total healing. He might, however—and I want to stress the word 'might'—recover what anyone would consider a remarkable number of his faculties. He might walk, talk, think, see, hear, and feel. Or he could recover any combination of those abilities."

"And you, I assume, are willing to perform the surgery?"

Torres shrugged. "I'm afraid I don't like the odds," he said. "I'm a man who doesn't like to fail."

Marsh felt a knot forming in his stomach. "Fail?" he whispered. "Dr. Torres, you're talking about my son. Without you, he'll die. We're not talking success or failure. We're talking life or death."

"I didn't say I wouldn't do it," Torres replied. "In fact, under certain conditions, I will do it."

Marsh's relief was apparent in his sigh, and he allowed himself to slump in his chair. "Anything," he whispered. "Anything at all."

But Frank Mallory was suddenly uneasy. "What are those circumstances?" he asked.

"Very simple. That I be given complete control over the case for as long as I deem necessary, and that I be absolved of any responsibility for any of the consequences of either the surgery or the convalescent period." Marsh started to interrupt, but Torres pressed on. "And by convalescent period, I mean until such time as I—and only I—discharge the patient." He reached into a drawer of his desk and withdrew a multipage document, which he handed to Marsh. "This is the agreement that you and the boy's mother will sign. You may read it if you want to—in fact I think you should—but not so much as a comma of it can be changed. Either you sign it or you don't. If you do, and your wife does, bring the boy here as soon as possible. The longer you wait, the riskier the surgery will be. As I'm sure you know, patients in your son's condition rarely get stronger—if anything, they get weaker." He rose from his chair, indicating his dismissal. "I'm sorry this has taken so long, but I'm afraid there was no choice. Even my computers need time to work."

Mallory rose to his feet. "If the Lonsdales decide to go ahead, when will you do the surgery, and how long will it take?"

"I'll do it tomorrow," Torres replied. "And it will take at least eighteen hours, with fifteen people working. And don't forget," he added, turning to Marsh. "The odds are eighty percent that we'll fail, at least to some extent. I'm sorry, but I don't believe in lying to people."

He opened the door, held it for Marsh and Frank, then closed it as soon as they had stepped through.

Raymond Torres sat alone for a long time after showing the two doctors from La Paloma out of his office.

La Paloma.

Odd that this case—the most challenging case he'd ever been given the opportunity to work on—should not only come from the town he'd grown up in but also involve someone he'd known all his life.

He wondered if Ellen Lonsdale would even remember who he was. Or, more to the point, who he'd been.

Probably not.

In La Paloma, as in most of California during those years of his childhood, he and all the other descendants of the old Californios had been regarded as just more Mexicans, to be ignored at best, and despised at worst.

And in return, his friends had despised the *gringos* even more than they were despised themselves.

Raymond Torres could still remember the long nights in the little kitchen, when his grandmother listened to the indignities his mother and her sisters had suffered at the hands of their various employers, then talked, as she always did, of the old days before even she had been born, when the Meléndez y Ruiz family had owned the hacienda, and the Californios were preeminent. Back then, it had been the families of Torres and Ortiz, Rodríguez and Flores who had lived in the big white houses on the trail up to the hacienda. Over and over, his grandmother had told the legend of the massacre at the hacienda, and the carnage that followed as one by one the old families were driven from their homes, and slowly reduced to the level of *peones*. But things would change, his grandmother had insisted. All they and their friends had to do was maintain their hatred and wait for the day when the son of Don Roberto de Meléndez y

Ruiz would return and drive the *gringos* away from the lands and homes they had stolen.

Raymond had listened to it all, and known it was all useless. His grandmother's tales were no more than legends, and her certainty of future vengeance no more solid than the ghost on which her hopes depended. When she had finally died, he'd thought it might end, but instead, his mother had taken up the litany. Even now, the old legends and hatreds seemed to be all she lived for.

But there would be no revenge, and there would be no driving away of the *gringos,* at least not for Raymond Torres. For himself, he had taken another path, ignoring the slights of the *gringos* and closing his ears to the hatreds of his friends and their plans for someday avenging their ancestors.

For Raymond Torres, vengeance would be simple. He would acquire a *gringo* education and become as superior to the *gringos* as they thought they were to him. But his superiority would be real, not imagined.

Now, finally, the day had come when *they* needed *him.*

And he would help them, despite the fury he would face from his mother.

He would help them, because he had long ago decided that all the years of having been dismissed as being unworthy of the *gringos'* attention would best be avenged by the simple act of forcing them to realize that they had been wrong; that he had always been their equal. He'd always been their equal, though he'd never had their power.

Now, because of an accident on the very site of the ancient massacre, that power had come into his hands.

The skill he would need he had acquired over long years of hard work. Now he would combine that skill with the power they would give him to rebuild Alex Lonsdale into something far more than he had been before his accident.

Slowly and carefully he began making the preparations to rebuild Alex Lonsdale's mind.

In the demonstration of his own genius, he would have his own revenge.

"But why can't he do it here?" Ellen asked. Several hours of fitful sleep had eased the exhaustion she had felt that morning, but she still found it impossible to absorb every word Marsh had spoken. Patiently Marsh explained it once again.

"It's the equipment. It's extensive, and it's all built into his O.R. It simply can't be moved, at least not quickly, and not into our facility. We just don't have the space."

"But can Alex survive it?"

This time it was Frank who answered her question. "We don't know," he said. "I think he can. His pulse is weak, but it's steady, and the respirator can go in the ambulance with him. There's a mobile ICU in Palo Alto, and we can use that."

There was a silence, then Marsh spoke, his voice quiet but urgent. "You have to decide, Ellen. This waiver needs both our signatures."

Ellen gazed at her husband a moment, her thoughts suddenly far in the past.

Raymond Torres. Tall and good-looking, with dark, burning eyes, but no one anyone would ever consider going out with. And he'd been smart, too. In fact, he'd been the smartest person in her class. But strange, in a way she'd never quite understood, nor even, for that matter, cared about understanding. He'd always acted as though he was better than anyone, and never had any friends, either of his own race or of hers. And now, suddenly, the life of her son depended on him.

"What's he like?" she suddenly asked.

Marsh looked at her curiously. "Does it matter?"

Ellen hesitated, then slowly shook her head. "I don't suppose so," she replied. "But I used to know him, and he was always . . . well, I guess he seemed arrogant, and sometimes he was almost scary. None of us ever liked him."

Marsh smiled tightly. "Well, he hasn't changed. He's still arrogant, and I don't like him at all. But he might be able to save Alex."

Once more Ellen hesitated. In times past, she and Marsh used to spend hours discussing their problems, listening to each other, balancing their thoughts and feelings, weighing what was best for them. But in the last few months—or had it become years?—that easy communication had been lost. They had been too busy—Marsh with the expanding Medical Center, herself with the expanding social life that had accompanied the building of the Center. What had been sacrificed, finally, was their ability to communicate with each other. Now, with Alex's life hanging in the balance, she had to come to a decision.

She made up her mind. "We don't have a choice, do we?" she asked. "We have to try." She picked up the pen and signed the waiver, which she had not bothered to read, then handed it back to Marsh. A sudden thought flashed through her mind.

If Raymond Torres thinks it will work, why won't he take responsibility for it?

Then she decided that she didn't want to know the answer to that question.

CHAPTER 6

Carol Cochran covered the telephone's mouthpiece with her right hand and called up the stairs, "Lisa? It's for you." She waited a few seconds, and when there was no answer, she called out again: "Lisa?"

"Tell whoever it is I'm not here." Lisa's voice was muffled, and Carol paused a moment, wondering if she ought to go upstairs and insist that Lisa take the call. Then she sighed. "She says she isn't here, Kate. I'm sorry, but she just doesn't want to talk to anyone right now. I'll have her call you back, all right?"

Hanging up the phone, Carol mounted the stairs, and found Kim standing in the hall.

"Her door's locked, and she won't come out," the six-year-old reported.

"I'll take care of it, dear. Why don't you go find your father?"

"Is he lost?" Kim replied with the same look of innocence Jim always wore when he tortured her with the same kind of response.

"Just go, all right? I need to talk to your sister."

"Do I have to?" Kim begged. "I could talk to her too."

"I'm sure you could," Carol observed. "But right now I want to talk to her alone."

Kim cocked her head, her eyes narrowing inquisitively. "Are you gonna talk about Alex?"

"Possibly," Carol parried.

"Is Alex going to die?"

"I don't know," Carol replied, sticking to the policy of total honesty she'd always followed in raising her children. "But that's something we won't talk about until it happens. I hope it won't. Now, run along and find your father."

Kim, who had long since learned when she'd pushed her luck as far as it would go, headed down the stairs as Carol tapped at Lisa's door.

"Lisa? May I come in?"

There was no answer, but a moment later Carol heard a click as Lisa turned the key from the inside. The door opened a few inches, and Carol saw Lisa's retreating back as the girl returned to her bed, sprawled out on her back, and fixed her gaze on the ceiling. Carol stepped into the room and closed the door behind her.

"Do you want to talk about it?" she asked. When there was no reply, Carol crossed to the bed and sat down on the edge of it. Lisa moved slightly to one side to make more room. "Well, I want to talk about it," Carol went on. "I know what you're thinking, and you're wrong."

Lisa's tear-streaked face turned slowly toward her mother, who reached out to brush a stray hair from her brow. "It was my fault, Mom," she said, her voice bleak. "It was all my fault."

"We're not going to go over it all again," Carol told her. "I've heard the whole story too many times already. If you want to feel guilty, you can feel guilty about talking Alex into going to that party. But that's *all* you can feel guilty about. It was Alex who drank the beer, and it was Alex who was driving the car."

"But he had to swerve—"

"Only because he was driving too fast. *He* caused the accident, Lisa. Not you."

"But . . . but what if he dies?"

Carol bit her lip, then took a deep breath. "If he dies, then we will all feel very badly for a while. Ellen and Marsh will feel badly for a long time. But the world won't end, Lisa. And if Alex does die, that won't be your fault any more than the accident was your fault."

"But Carolyn Evans said—"

"Carolyn Evans is a selfish, spoiled brat, and you weren't the only one who heard her say it was all your fault. I've talked to Bob Carey and Kate Lewis tonight, and they both told me exactly what Carolyn meant. She meant that if you hadn't left the party, then Alex wouldn't have either, and that the accident might not have happened. And do you know what she was worried about? Not you, and not Alex. The only thing that concerned darling Carolyn was the fact that her party was no longer going to be her little secret. Also, as far as I know, Carolyn was the only person at the party who didn't bother to go to the Center last night. All she did was go home and try to clean up the house."

"It doesn't make any difference what she meant," Lisa said, rolling over to face the wall. "It still doesn't change the way I feel."

Carol sat silently for a few seconds, then reached out and pulled Lisa close. "I know, honey. And I suppose you're going to have to get over that feeling your own way. In the meantime, what about Alex?"

Lisa stirred suddenly, and sat up. "Alex? What about him?"

"Suppose he wakes up?"

"He *will* wake up," Lisa said. "He *has* to."

"Why? So you can stop feeling sorry for yourself? Is that why you want him to wake up? So it will make you feel better?"

Lisa's eyes widened with shock. "Mom! That's an awful thing to say—"

Carol shrugged. "Well, what else can I think?" She took Lisa's hands in her own. "Lisa, I want you to listen very carefully. There's a chance that Alex may survive all this, and there's a chance he may wake up. But if he does, he's going to be in bad shape, and he's going to need all the help he can get. His parents won't be enough. He's going to need his friends, too, and he's going to need you. But if you're spending all your energy feeling guilty and sorry for yourself, you're not going to be much good to him, are you?"

Lisa looked dazed. "But what can I do?"

"None of us will know that till the time comes. But for starters, you could try pulling yourself together." She hesitated for a moment, then went on. "Alex is going to be operated on tomorrow." Lisa's eyes reflected her surprise, but before she could say anything, Carol went on. "I know you're going to want to be there—we all want to be there—but you're not going to sit on a sofa and cry. If anyone's going to do that, it's going to be Ellen, and I suspect *she* won't do that either. It's going to be a long operation, and Alex might not make it through. But if you want to be there, both your father and I expect you to behave like the girl we hope we raised."

There was a long silence; then the slightest trace of a smile appeared at the corners of Lisa's mouth. "You mean keep my chin up?" she asked in a tiny voice.

Carol nodded. "And remember that it's Alex who's in trouble, not you. Whatever happens tomorrow, or next week, or whenever, your life will go on. If Alex comes through this, he's not going to have a lot of time to spend cheering you up." She stood up, and forced a grin she didn't truly feel. "The ball's in your court, kid. Play it."

* * *

Forty minutes later, Lisa Cochran came downstairs. She was wearing one of her father's old white shirts and a pair of jeans, and her hair, still wet from the shower, was wrapped in a towel. "Who all called?" she asked. Her father lowered his paper and opened his mouth. "I mean *besides* Prince Andrew and John Travolta, Dad. I already talked to them and told them it's definitely over."

"All the messages are by the phone," her mother told her. "Anything going on you want to tell us about, or shall we read it in the papers?"

"Nothing much," Lisa said. "I just thought I'd get the kids organized for tomorrow. Do you know what time they're operating on Alex?"

Jim put his paper aside, looking curiously at his older daughter. "Early," he said. "They want to start by six, I think." As Lisa started out of the room, he called her back. "Mind telling me just what you're organizing?"

"Well, everyone's going to want to go down there, but there's no point in having everyone show up at once. I'm just going to sort of get them spaced out."

"Most of them already are," Jim commented.

Lisa ignored him. "Tomorrow's Sunday, so nobody has to go to school or anything. We might as well all help out."

Carol frowned uncertainly. "I hope there's not going to be a mob like there was last night—"

"I'll tell them not to stay very long. And I'm going to ask Kate if she'll just sort of hang around, in case anybody needs anything."

Now Jim was shaking his head. "Lisa, honey, I know you want to do the right thing, but—"

"It's all right," Carol interrupted. "But, Lisa? Can I make a suggestion? Why don't you call Ellen and see what she thinks? She might prefer it if you just kept everybody away, at least until we know what's happening."

Lisa's face fell, and she groaned. "Why didn't I think of that?"

" 'Cause you're an idiot," Kim said, abandoning the drawing she'd been working on to scramble into her father's lap. "Isn't she an idiot, Daddy?"

"It takes one to know one."

"Daddy! You're s'posed to be on my side."

"I guess I forgot." Jim snuggled the little girl in, then turned back to Lisa. "Got any plans for your sister?" he asked mildly. "If you really want to do some organizing, why don't you line up your friends to take care of Kim?"

"I want to go with you!" Kim immediately objected.

"That's what you say now," Jim told her. "That's not what you'll say tomorrow. And don't argue with me—I'm bigger than you are, and can pound you into the ground." Kim giggled, but closed her mouth. "Maybe someone could take her to a movie or something. And we'll need a baby-sitter after dinner."

Lisa's eyes clouded. "Won't it be all over by then?"

Carol and Jim exchanged a glance, then Jim spoke. "I talked to Marsh earlier," he said. "He told me the operation will take at least eighteen hours. It's not going to be any party, honey."

Lisa paled slightly, and fought down the tears that were welling in her eyes. When she spoke, though, her voice was steady. "I know it's not a party, Dad," she said softly. "I just want to do whatever I can to help."

"Your mother can—"

"No! *I* can, and I will. I'll take care of Kim, and see to it that there's no mob scene. I'll be all right, Dad. Just let me do this my way, all right?"

When she was gone, and they could hear her murmuring into the telephone, Jim turned to Carol. "What happened up there?" he asked.

"I think she just grew up, Jim. Anyway, she's sure trying."

There was a silence, then Kim squirmed in her father's lap, twisting around to look up at him. "Do I have to go to the movies with her dumb old friends?" she demanded.

"If you do, I'll bet they'll let you choose the movie," Jim replied. Somewhat mollified, Kim settled down again.

"I hope Alex gets better soon," she said. "I *like* Alex."

"We all do," Carol told her. "And he *will* get better, if we all pray a lot."

And, she added to herself, if Raymond Torres really knows what he's doing.

As Carol Cochran entertained that thought, Raymond Torres himself was making his final rounds of the evening.

Not, of course, that they were really rounds, for Alex Lonsdale was his only patient. He stopped first in Alex's room, just across the hall from the operating complex. The night nurse glanced up from the book she was reading. "Nothing, doctor," she said as Torres scanned the monitors that were tracking Alex's vital functions. "No change from an hour ago."

Torres nodded, and gazed thoughtfully at the boy in the bed.

Looks like his mother. The thought drifted through his mind, followed by a sudden flood of unbidden memories from a past he thought could no longer hurt him. Along with his memories of Ellen Lonsdale came memories of three other girls, and as their faces came into focus in his mind's eye, he felt himself begin to tremble.

Forget it, he told himself. *It was long ago, and it's all over now. It doesn't matter.* With an effort of will, he forced himself to concentrate on the motionless form of Alex Lonsdale. He leaned over and carefully opened one of the boy's eyes, checked the pupil, then closed the eye again. There had been no reaction to the sudden incursion of light. Not a good sign.

"All right," he said. "I'm sleeping here tonight, in the room over my office. If anything happens—anything at all—I want to be awakened at once."

"Of course, doctor," the nurse replied. Not that he need have said anything—the first rule for staff working under Torres was made very clear at the time they were hired: "If anything happens, let Dr. Torres know at once." And everyone at the Institute adhered to the rule, quickly learning to suspend his own judgment. So tonight, if Alex Lonsdale so much as twitched, an instrument would record it, and Raymond Torres would be notified immediately. As Torres left the room, the nurse went back to her book.

Torres crossed the corridor and went into the scrub room, his eyes noting instantly that everything necessary for tomorrow's scrub was already there—gowns, gloves, masks, everything. And it would all be checked at least twice more during the night. He proceeded into the O.R. itself, where six technicians were going over every piece of equipment in the room, running test after test, rechecking their own work, then having it verified by two other technicians. They would continue working throughout the night, searching for anything that could possibly fail, and replacing it. They would leave only when it was time for the sterilization process to begin, an hour before the operation was scheduled.

Satisfied, he moved on down the corridor to what had long ago become known as the Rehearsal Hall. It was a large room, housing several desks, each of which held a computer terminal. It was here that every operation carried out at the Institute was rehearsed.

Tonight, all the desks were occupied, and all the terminals glowed brightly in the soft light of the Rehearsal Hall. The technicians at the monitors, using the model of Alex's brain that had been generated earlier that day, were going over the operation step by step, searching for bugs in the program that the computer itself, using its own model, had generated.

They didn't expect to find any bugs, for they had long ago discovered that programs generated by computers are much more accurate than programs written by men.

Except that there was also the possibility that somewhere in the system there was a sleeper.

"Sleeper" was their term for a bug that had never been found. The defect might not even be in the program they were using. It could have been in a program that had been used to write another program, that had, in turn, been used to generate still a third program. They all knew, from bitter experience, that the bug could suddenly pop up and destroy everything.

Or, worse, it could simply inject a tiny error into the program, creating a new sleeper.

In this case, that would be a wrong connection in Alex Lonsdale's mind, which could lead to anything.

Or nothing.

Or Alex's death.

Torres moved silently through the room, concentrating first on one monitor, then on another. All of what he saw was familiar; he would see it all again tomorrow.

Except that tomorrow wouldn't be a rehearsal. Tomorrow his fingers would be on the robot's controls, and as he followed the program, making the connections inside Alex's brain, there would be no turning back. Whatever he did tomorrow, Alex Lonsdale would live with for the rest of his life.

Or die with.

One of the technicians leaned back and stretched.

"Problems?" Torres asked.

The technician shook his head. "Looks perfect so far."

"How many times have you been through it?"

"Five."

"It's a beginning," Torres said. He wished they had months to keep rerunning the program, but they didn't. So even in the morning, they wouldn't be sure there were no bugs. That, indeed, was the worst thing about bugs—sometimes they didn't show up for years. The only way to find them was to keep running and rerunning a program, hoping that if something was going to go wrong it would go wrong early on. But this time, they simply didn't have time—they would have to trust that the program was perfect.

Yet as he moved toward the little bedroom above his office that was always kept ready for him, one thought kept going through Torres's mind: Nothing is ever perfect.

Something always goes wrong.

He pushed the thought away. Not this time. This time, everything had to be perfect. And only he would ever know what that perfection really was.

At five o'clock the next morning, Ellen and Marshall Lonsdale arrived in Palo Alto. It was still dark, but all over the Institute for the Human Brain, lights glowed brightly, and people seemed to be everywhere. They were shown into the same lounge where Marsh had spent most of the previous day, and offered coffee and Danishes.

"Can we see Alex?" Ellen asked.

The receptionist smiled sympathetically. "I'm sorry. He's already being prepped." Ellen carefully kept her expression impassive, but the other woman could clearly see the pain in her eyes. "I really am sorry, Mrs. Lonsdale, but it's one of Doctor's rules. Once the prepping starts, we always keep the patient totally isolated. Doctor's a fanatic about keeping everything sterile."

Suddenly the door opened, and a friendly voice filled the room. "Why do they always have to have operations at dawn?" Valerie Benson asked of no one in particular. "Do they think it's a war or something?" She crossed the room and gave Ellen a quick hug. "It's going to be all right," she whispered. "I don't get up this early unless I know nothing can possibly go wrong, and here I am. So you might as well stop worrying right now. Alex is going to be fine."

Ellen couldn't resist smiling at Valerie, who was a notorious late-riser. Indeed, Valerie sometimes claimed that the real reason she'd divorced her husband was that demanding breakfast by nine A.M. was the worst sort of mental cruelty. But here she was, as always, coming through in the pinch, and looking as if she'd been up for hours.

"You didn't have to come," Ellen told her.

"Of course I did," Valerie said. "If I hadn't, everybody would have talked about it for years. Is Marty here yet?"

"I don't know if she's even coming. And it's so early—"

"Nonsense," Valerie snorted. "Must be nearly noon." She gave Marsh a quick kiss on the cheek. "Everything okay?" she asked, her voice dropping.

"They won't even let us see Alex before the operation," Marsh replied, making no attempt to hide the anger he was feeling. Valerie nodded knowingly.

"I've always said Raymond Torres is impossible. Brilliant, yes. But impossible."

Ellen's eyes clouded. "If he can save Alex, I don't care how impossible he is."

"Of course you don't, darling," Valerie assured her. "None of us does. Besides, maybe he's changed over the last twenty years. My God, if I had any brains, I'd marry him! This is some place, isn't it? Is it all his?"

"Val," Ellen interrupted. "You can slow down. You don't have to distract us—we're going to get through this."

Valerie's bright smile faded, and she sat down abruptly, reaching into her purse and pulling out a handkerchief. She sniffled, wiped her eyes, then determinedly put the handkerchief away. "I'm sorry," she said. "It's just that the thought of anything happening to Alex . . . Oh, Ellen, I'm just so sorry about all of this. Is there anything I can do?"

Ellen shook her head. "Nothing. Just stay with me, Val. Having you and Marty Lewis and Carol here is going to be the most important thing." To know that her friends would be here to support her, to try to comfort her, would help.

The longest day of her life had just begun.

CHAPTER 7

When the lounge door opened just after ten-thirty that evening, neither Ellen nor Marsh paid much attention. People had been in and out all day, some staying only a few minutes, others remaining for an hour or two. But now only her closest friends were still there: the Cochrans, Marty Lewis, and Valerie Benson. Only Cynthia Evans had not come.

Slowly she realized that someone was standing in front of her, had spoken to her. She looked up into the face of a stranger.

"Mrs. Lonsdale? I'm Susan Parker—the night person. Dr. Torres wants to see you and your husband in his office."

Ellen glanced at Marsh, who was already on his feet, his hand extended to her. Suddenly she felt disoriented—she'd thought it was going to take until midnight. Unless . . . She closed her mind to the thought that Alex must, at last, have died. "It's over?" she managed. "He's finished?"

Then she was in Torres's office, and the doctor was gazing at her from the chair behind his desk. He stood up, and came around to offer her his hand. "Hello, Ellen," he said quietly.

Her first fleeting thought was that he was even more handsome than she'd remembered him. Hesitantly she took his hand and squeezed it briefly, then, still clutching his hand, she gazed into his eyes. "Alex," she whispered. "Is he—?"

"He's alive," Torres said, his voice reflecting the exhaustion he was feeling, while his eyes revealed his triumph. "He's out of the O.R., and he's off the respirator. He's breathing by himself, and his pulse is strong."

Ellen's legs buckled, and Marsh eased her into a chair. "Is he awake?" she heard her husband ask. When Torres's head shook negatively, her heart sank.

"But it doesn't mean much," Torres said. "The soonest we want him to wake up is tomorrow morning."

"Then you don't know if the operation is a success." Marsh Lonsdale's voice was flat.

Again Torres shook his head, and rubbed his eyes with his fists. "We'll know tomorrow morning, when—if—he wakes up. But things look good." He offered them a twisted smile. "Coming from me, that's something. You know what I consider success and what I consider failure. And I can tell you right now that if Alex dies in the next week, it won't be from his brain problems. It will be from complications—pneumonia, some kind of viral infection, that sort of thing. I intend to see that that doesn't happen."

"Can . . . can we see him?" Ellen asked.

Torres nodded. "But only for a minute, and only through the window. For the time being, I don't want anyone in that room except members of my staff." Marsh seemed about to say something, but Torres ignored him. "I'm sorry, but that includes you. What you can do is take a look at him—Susan will take you over there—and then go home and get some sleep. Tomorrow morning's going to tell the tale, and I want you to be here. If he wakes up, I'm going to want to try to determine if he can recognize people."

"Us," Ellen breathed.

"Exactly." Torres stood up. "Now, if you'll excuse me, I'm going up to bed."

Ellen struggled to her feet, and reached out to grasp Torres's hand once again. "Thank you, Raymond," she whispered. "I . . . I don't know what to say. I didn't believe . . . I couldn't—"

Torres abruptly withdrew his hand from hers. "Don't thank me, Ellen," he said. "Not yet. There's still a good chance that your son will never wake up." Then he was gone, leaving Ellen to stare after him, her face ashen.

"It's just him," Marsh told her. "It's just his way of telling us not to get our hopes too high."

"But he said—"

"He said Alex is alive, and breathing by himself. And that's all he said." He began guiding her toward the door. "Let's go take a look at him, then go home."

Silently Susan Parker led them into the west wing and down the long corridor past the O.R. She stopped at a window, and the Lonsdales gazed through the glass into a large room. In its center stood a hospital bed, its guardrails up. Around the bed was an array of monitors, each of them attached to some part of Alex's body.

His head, though swathed with bandages, seemed to bristle with tiny wires.

But there was no respirator, and even from beyond the window they could see his chest rising and falling in the deep, even rhythm of sleep. A glance at one of the monitors told Marsh that Alex's pulse was now as strong and regular as his breathing.

"He's going to come out of it," he said softly. Next to him, Ellen squeezed his hand tightly.

"I know," she replied. "I can feel it. He did it, Marsh. Raymond gave us back our son." Then: "But what's he going to be like? He won't be the same, will he?"

"No," Marsh said slowly, "he won't be. But he'll still be Alex."

There was a soft beeping sound, and the nurse whose sole duty was to watch Alex Lonsdale glanced quickly up, scanning the monitors with a practiced eye, then noting the exact time.

Nine-forty-six A.M.

She pressed the buzzer on the control panel, then went to the bed to lean over Alex, concentrating on his eyes.

The beeping sounded again, and this time she saw its cause. She picked up the phone and pressed two buttons. On the first ring, someone picked it up.

"Torres. What is it?"

"Rapid-eye movement, doctor. He may be dreaming, or—"

"Or he may be waking up. I'll be right down." The phone went dead in her hand and the nurse's attention went back to Alex.

Once more, the beeping began, and the occasional faint twitching in Alex Lonsdale's eyelids increased to an erratic flutter.

Hazily he became vaguely aware of himself. Things were happening around him.

There were sounds, and faint images, but none of it meant anything.

Like watching a movie, but run so fast you couldn't see any of it.

And darkness. Darkness all around him, and no sense of being at all. Then, slowly, he began to feel himself. There was more than the darkness, more than the indistinct sounds and images.

A dream.

He was having a dream.

But what was it about? He tried to focus his mind. If it was a dream, where was he? Why wasn't he part of it?

The darkness began to recede a little, and the sounds and images faded away.

Not a dream. Real. He was real.

He.

What did "he" mean?

"He" was a word, and he should know what it meant. There should be a name attached to it, but there wasn't.

The word had no meaning.

Then slowly "he" faded into "me."

"Me." "Me" became "I."

I am me. He is me.

Who?

Alexander James Lonsdale.

The meaning of those little words came back into his mind.

He began to remember.

But there were only fragments, and most of them didn't make any sense. He was going somewhere. Where? A dance. There had been a dance. Picture it.

If you want to remember something, picture it.

Nothing.

Going somewhere.

Car. He was in a car, and he was driving. But where?

Nothing. No image came to mind, no street name.

Picture something—anything.

But nothing came, and for a moment he was sure that all he would ever know was his name. There was nothing else in his mind. Nothing but that great dark void. Then more names came into his mind.

Marshall Lonsdale.

Ellen Smith Lonsdale.

Parents. They were his parents. Then, very slowly, the blackness surrounding him faded into a faint glow.

He opened his eyes to blinding brightness, then closed them again.

"He's awake." The words meant something, and he understood what they meant.

He opened his eyes again. The brightness faded, and blurred images began to form. Then, slowly, his eyes focused.

Certain images clicked in his mind, things he'd seen before, and suddenly he knew where he was. He was in a hospital.

A hospital was where his father worked. His father was a doctor. His eyes moved again, and he saw a face.

His father?

He didn't know. He opened his mouth.

"Wh-who . . . are . . . you?"

"Dr. Torres," a voice said. "Dr. Raymond Torres." There was a silence, then the voice spoke again. "Who are you?"

He lay quiet for a few seconds, then, once more, spoke, the words distorted, but clear enough to be understood. "Lonsdale. Alexander James Lonsdale."

"Good," the man whose name was Dr. Torres told him. "That's very good. Now, do you know where you are?"

"H-hob . . ." Alex fell silent, then carefully tried it again. "Hos . . . pi . . . tal," he said.

"That's right. Do you know why you're in the hospital?"

Alex lapsed into silence again, his mind trying to grasp the meaning of the question. Then, in a rush, it came to him.

"Ha-hacienda," he whispered. "Car."

"Good," Dr. Torres said softly. "Don't try to say anything else right now. Just lie there. Everything's going to be all right. Do you understand?"

"Y-yes."

The image of the doctor disappeared from his vision, and was replaced by another face that he didn't recognize. He closed his eyes.

Ellen and Marsh rose anxiously to their feet as Torres walked into his office a few minutes later.

"He's awake," he told them. "And he can speak."

"He . . . he actually said something?" Ellen asked, her voice alive with hope for the first time since the accident. "It wasn't just sounds?"

Torres seated himself at his desk, his demeanor, as always, perfectly composed. "Better than just saying something. The first thing he did was ask me who I was. Then he told me his name. And he knows what happened."

Marshall Lonsdale felt his heart pounding, and suddenly a vision leapt into his mind. It was the chart of probabilities he'd seen two days earlier. Partial recovery had been only a twenty-percent chance. Full recovery had been zero percent. But Alex could hear, and he could speak, and apparently he could think. Then he realized that Torres was still speaking, and forced himself to concentrate on the doctor's words.

". . . but you have to realize that he might not recognize you."

"Why not?" Ellen asked. Then: "Oh, God. He . . . he isn't blind, is he?"

"Absolutely not," Torres assured her. His eyes fixed on her, and Ellen felt a small shiver run through her. There was a quality of strength in his eyes that had not been there twenty years ago. Where once his eyes had smoldered in a way that she used to find frightening, now they burned with a reassuring self-confidence. Whatever Raymond Torres told her, she was suddenly certain, would be the absolute truth. And if Alex could be healed, Raymond Torres was the one man who could heal him. In his presence, the overriding fear she had fallen victim to since the moment she heard of Alex's accident began to ebb away. She found herself concentrating on his words with an intensity she had never felt before.

"At this point there's no way of knowing what he will remember and what he won't. He could remember your names, but have no memory at all of what you look like. Or just the opposite. You might be familiar to him, but he won't remember exactly who you are. So when you see him, be very careful. If he doesn't recognize you, don't be upset, or at least try not to let him know that you're upset."

"The fact that he's alive, and that he's conscious, is enough," Ellen breathed. Then, though she knew she could never truly express what she was feeling, she went on. "How can I thank you?" she asked. "How can I ever thank you for what you've done?"

"By accepting Alex in whatever condition he is now in," Torres replied, ignoring the emotion in Ellen's words.

"But you said—"

"I know what I said. You must understand that Alex will undoubtedly have a lot of limitations from now on, and you must learn to deal with them. That may not be a simple task."

"I know," Ellen said. "I don't expect it to be. But whatever Alex's needs are, I know we'll be able to meet them. You've given us back Alex's life, Raymond. You . . . well, you've worked a miracle."

Torres rose to his feet. "Let's go see him. I'll take you in myself, and I'd like to do it one at a time. I don't want to give him too much to cope with."

"Of course," Marsh agreed. They started toward the west wing and paused outside Alex's room. Through the window, nothing seemed to have changed. "Does it matter which of us goes in first?" he asked.

"I'd rather you went first," Torres replied. "You're a doctor, and you'll be less likely to have any kind of reaction to whatever might happen."

The Lonsdales exchanged a glance, and Ellen managed to conceal her disappointment. "Go on," she said. "I'll be fine."

Torres opened the door, and the two men stepped inside. Ellen watched as Marsh approached the bed, stopping when he was next to Alex.

* * *

Alex's eyes opened again, and he recognized Dr. Torres. On the other side of him was someone else.

"Who . . . are . . . you?"

There was a slight pause, and then the stranger spoke. "I'm your father, Alex."

"Father?" Alex echoed. His eyes fixed on the man, and he searched his memory. Suddenly the face that had been strange was familiar. "Dad," he said. Then, again: "Dad."

He saw his father's eyes fill with tears, then heard him say, "How are you, son?"

Alex searched his mind for the right word. "H-hurt," he whispered. "I hurt, but not . . . not too bad." A phrase leapt into his mind. "Looks like we're going to live after all."

He watched as his father and Dr. Torres glanced at each other, then back down at him. His father was smiling now. "Of course you are, son," he heard his father say in an oddly choked voice. "Of course you are."

Alex closed his eyes and listened to the sound of footsteps moving away from the bed. The room was silent; then there were more footsteps, and he knew people were once again standing by the bed. Dr. Torres, and someone else. He opened his eyes and peered upward. A face seemed to hang in the air, framed by dark wavy hair.

"Hello . . . Mom," he whispered.

"Alex," she whispered back. "Oh, Alex, you're going to be fine. You're going to be just fine."

"Fine," he echoed. "Just fine." Then, exhausted, he let himself drift back into sleep.

"You can spend the day here if you want to," Torres told them when they were back in his office. "But you won't be allowed to see Alex again until tomorrow."

"Tomorrow?" Marsh asked. "But why? What if he wakes up? What if he asks for us?"

"He won't wake up again," Torres replied. "I'm going to look at him once more, and then give him a sedative."

Marsh's eyes suddenly clouded. "A sedative? He just came out of a coma. You don't give that kind of patient a sedative—you try to keep them awake."

Torres's face seemed cut from stone. "I don't believe I asked for your advice or your opinions, Dr. Lonsdale," he said.

"But—"

"Nor am I interested in hearing them," Torres went on, ignoring the interruption. "Frankly, I don't have time to listen to what you have to say, and I'd just as soon you kept whatever thoughts you might have to yourself. Alex is my patient, and I have my own methods. I made that clear day before yesterday. Now, if you'll excuse me." He opened the door in his habitual gesture of dismissal.

"But he's our son," Marsh protested. "Surely we can—"

"No, Marsh," Ellen interrupted. "We'll do whatever Raymond wants us to do."

Marsh gazed at his wife in silence for a moment, his jaw tightening with anger. But her obvious anguish washed his rage away, and when he turned back to Torres, he had regained his composure. "I'm sorry—I was out of line." He offered Raymond Torres a crooked smile. "From now on I'll try to remember that I'm not the doctor here. I've dealt with enough worried parents to know how difficult they can be."

Torres's demeanor thawed only slightly. "Thank you," he replied. "I'm afraid I have few patients, and no patience, but I do know what I'm doing. Now, if you'll excuse me, I want to get back to Alex."

But as Ellen led him toward the lounge, Marsh's anger surged back. "I've never heard of such a thing—he as much as told us he doesn't want us around!"

"Apparently he doesn't," Ellen agreed.

"But I'm Alex's father, dammit!"

Exhaustion threatening to overwhelm her, Ellen regarded her husband with oddly detached curiosity. Wasn't he even pleased with what Raymond Torres had accomplished? "He's Alex's doctor," she said. "And without him, we wouldn't even have Alex anymore. We owe Raymond Alex's life, Marsh, and I don't intend to forget that."

"Raymond," Marsh repeated. "Since when are you on a first-name basis with him?"

Ellen gazed at him in puzzlement. "Why wouldn't I be?"

"I'm not," Marsh countered.

Her confusion deepened. What on earth was the matter with him? And suddenly the answer came to her. "Marsh, are you jealous of him?"

"Of course not," Marsh replied, too quickly. "I just don't like the man, that's all."

"Well, I'm sorry," Ellen said, a distinct chill in her voice. "But he did save our son's life, and even if you don't like him, you should be grateful to him."

Her words struck home, and once again Marsh's anger evaporated. "I am," he said quietly. "And you were right back there. He *did* perform a miracle, and it's one I couldn't have performed myself. Maybe I *am* a little jealous." He slipped his arms around her. "Promise me you won't fall in love with him?"

For just a moment, Ellen wasn't sure if he was joking or not, but then she smiled and gave him a quick kiss. "I promise. Now, let's tell everyone the good news."

They stepped into the lounge to find Carol and Lisa Cochran pacing anxiously. "Is it true?" Lisa asked eagerly. "Is he really awake?"

Ellen gathered Lisa into her arms and hugged her. "It's true," she said. "He woke up, and he can talk, and he recognized me."

"Thank God," Carol breathed. "The girl at the desk told us, but we could hardly believe it."

"And," Marsh told her, "we've just been thrown out. Don't ask me why, but Torres wants to put him to sleep again, and says we can't see him until tomorrow."

Carol stared at him with incredulous eyes. "You're kidding, of course."

"I wish I were," Marsh replied. "I think it's crazy, but around here, I'm not the doctor. Let's get out of here and go home. I don't know about you, but I didn't get much sleep last night, and I don't think Ellen got any."

As they stepped out into the bright sunlight of the May morning, Ellen paused and looked around as if seeing her surroundings for the first time. "It's beautiful, isn't it?" she asked. "The grounds, and the building—it's just lovely!"

Carol Cochran grinned at her. "This morning, anything would look lovely to you!"

For the first time since Alex's accident, a truly happy smile covered Ellen's face. "And why shouldn't it?" she asked. "Everything's going to be fine. I just know it!" Impulsively she hugged Lisa close. "We've got him back!" she cried. "We've got him back, and he's going to be all right."

"Alex?" Raymond Torres waited for a moment, then spoke again. "Alex, can you hear me?"

Alex's eyes fluttered for a second, then opened, but he said nothing.

"Alex, do you think you can answer a couple of questions?"

Alex struggled for the right words, then spoke carefully: "I don't know. I'll try."

"Good. That's all I want you to do. Now, try to think, Alex. Do you know why you didn't recognize your father?"

There was a long silence; then: "After he told me he was my father, I knew who he was."

"But when you first saw him, Alex, did he look familiar?"

"No."

"Not at all?"

"I . . . I don't know."

"But you recognized your mother, didn't you?"

"Yes."

"So she *did* look familiar?"

"No."

Torres frowned. "Then how did you recognize her?"

Alex fell silent for a moment, then spoke again, his words strained, as if he weren't sure he was using the right ones.

"I . . . I thought she had to be my mother if he was my father. I thought about it, and decided that if my father was here, then my mother was here too. After I decided she was my mother, she started to look familiar."

"So you didn't recognize either of them until you knew who they were?"

"No."

"All right. Now, I'm going to give you something that's going to put you to sleep, and when you wake up again, I'll come to see you." He slid a hypodermic needle under the skin of Alex's right arm and pressed the plunger. As he swabbed the puncture with a wad of cotton soaked with alcohol, he asked Alex if the needle had hurt.

"No."

"Did you feel it at all?"

"Yes."

"What did it feel like?"

"I . . . I don't know," Alex said.

"All right," Torres told him. "Go to sleep now, Alex, and I'll see you later."

Alex closed his eyes, and Torres watched him for a moment, then stepped to the monitors at the head of the bed and made some adjustments. Before leaving the room, he checked Alex once more.

Alex's eyelids were twitching rapidly. Torres wished there were a way to know exactly what was happening inside the boy's mind.

But there were still some mysteries that even he hadn't yet unraveled.

PART II

CHAPTER

Alex glanced at the clock on Raymond Torres's desk, and, as he always did, Torres took careful note of the action.

"Two more hours," he said. "Getting excited?"

Alex shrugged. "Curious, I guess."

Torres placed his pen on the desk and leaned back in his chair. "If I were you, I think I'd be excited. You're finally going home after three months—it seems to me that should be exciting."

"Except I'm not really going home, am I?" Alex asked, his voice as expressionless as his eyes. "I mean, Mom and Dad have moved, so I'll be going to a house I've never lived in before."

"Do you wish you were going back to the house you grew up in?"

Alex hesitated, then shook his head. "I guess it doesn't matter where I go, since I don't remember the old house anyway."

"You don't have any feelings about it at all?"

"No." Alex uttered the single word with no expression whatsoever.

And that, Torres silently reminded himself, was the crux of the matter. Alex had no feelings, no emotions. That was not to say that Alex's recovery had not been remarkable; indeed, it was very little short of miraculous. The boy could walk and talk, see, hear, and touch. But he seemed not to be able to feel at all.

Even the news that he was being released from the Institute had elicited no emotional response from him. Rather, he'd accepted the news with the same detachment with which he now accepted everything. And that, Torres knew, was the one factor that kept the medical world from viewing the operation as a complete success.

"What about going back to La Paloma?" Torres pressed.

Alex shifted in his chair and started to cross his legs. On the second try, his left ankle came to rest on his right knee.

"I . . . I guess I wonder what it will be like," he finally said. "I keep wondering if I'll recognize anything, or if it's all going to be like it was when I first woke up."

"You've remembered a lot since then," Torres replied.

Alex shrugged indifferently. "But I keep wondering if I really remember anything, or if I'm just learning things all over again."

"Not possible," Torres stated flatly. "It has to be recovery—nobody could learn things as fast as you have. And don't forget that when you first woke up, you spoke. You hadn't forgotten language."

"There were a lot of words I didn't understand," Alex reminded him. "And sometimes there still are." He stood up and took a shaky step, paused, then took another.

"Take it easy, Alex," Torres told him. "Don't demand too much of yourself. It's all going to take time. And speaking of time, I think we'd better get started." He waited while Alex swiveled his chair around so both of them were facing the screen that had been set up in a corner of the large office. When Alex was ready, Torres switched off the lights. A picture flashed on the screen.

"What is it?" Torres asked.

Alex didn't hesitate so much as a second. "An amoeba."

"Right. When did you take biology?"

"Last year. It was Mr. Landry's class."

"Can you tell me what Mr. Landry looked like?"

Alex thought a minute, but nothing came. "No."

"All right. What about your grade?"

"An A. But that was easy—I always got A's in science."

Torres said nothing, and changed the slide.

"That's the *Mona Lisa,*" Alex said promptly. "Leonardo da Vinci."

"Good enough. Is there another name for it?"

"La Gioconda."

The pictures changed again and again, and each time Alex correctly identified the image on the screen. Finally the slide show ended, and Torres turned the lights back on. "Well? What do you think?"

Alex shrugged. "I could have learned most of that stuff since I've been here," he said. "All I've been doing is reading."

"What about your grades? Did you read them here, too?"

"No. But Mom told me. I don't really remember much of anything about any of my classes. Just names of teachers and that kind of thing. But I don't *see* anything. Know what I mean?"

Torres nodded, and rifled through some of his notes. "Having problems visualizing things? No mental images?"

Alex nodded.

"But you don't have problems visualizing things you've seen since the accident?"

"No. That's easy. And sometimes, when I see something, it seems familiar, but I can't quite put it together. Then, when someone tells me what it is, it's almost like I remember it, but not quite. It's hard to describe."

"Sort of like *déjà vu?*"

Alex knit his brows, then shook his head. "Isn't that where you think what's happening now has happened before?"

"Exactly."

"It's not like that at all." Alex searched his mind, trying to find the right words to describe the strange sensations he had sometimes. "They're like half-memories," he finally said. "It's like sometimes I see something, and I think I remember it, but I really don't."

"But that's just it," Torres told him. "I think you *do* remember, but your brain isn't healed yet. You've had a lot of damage to your brain, Alex. I was able to put it back together again, but I couldn't do it perfectly. So there are a lot of connections that aren't there yet. It's as though part of your brain knows where the data it's looking for are stored, but can't get there. But it doesn't stop trying, and sometimes—and I think this will happen more and more—it finds a new route, and gets what it's after. But it's a little different. Not the data itself—just the way you remember it. I think you'll have more and more of those half-memories over the next few months. In time, as your brain finds and establishes new paths through itself, it'll happen less and less. And eventually, everything left in your mind after the accident will become accessible again." A buzzer sounded. Torres picked up the phone and spoke for a moment, then hung up. "Your parents are here," he told Alex. "Why don't you go over to the lab, and I'll have a talk with them? And when you're done, that's it. We check you out, and you only have to come back for a couple of hours a day."

Alex got to his feet and started toward the door in the shambling gait that, most of the time, got him where he wanted to go. He was still unsteady, but he hadn't actually lost his footing for a week, and each day he was doing better. Still, he wasn't allowed to attempt stairs without someone there to help him, and he used a cane whenever he wanted to go more than a few yards. But it was coming back to him.

The door opened just before Alex got to it, and his parents stepped inside. He stopped short, leaning his weight on the cane, and bent his head to kiss his mother's cheek as she gave him a hug. Then he shook his father's hand, and started out of the office.

"Alex?" Ellen asked. "Where are you going?"

"My tests, Mom," Alex replied, his voice flat. "Then we can go home, I guess." He turned away, and shambled out of the room. Ellen, her brows furrowed, watched him go, then stood perfectly still for several long moments. When at last she spoke, she still faced the door.

"I'm not sure I'm going to be able to stand this, Raymond," she said, her voice trembling. "He isn't changing, is he? He doesn't really care if he goes home or not."

"Sit down, Ellen." Torres gestured the Lonsdales toward the sofa, but remained standing himself, preferring to roam the room while he brought them up to date on Alex's progress.

"So that's it," he finished thirty minutes later. "Physically and intellectually, he's doing better than we could possibly have hoped for."

"But still no emotions," Ellen said, her voice dull. Then she sighed, and forced a smile. "I'm sorry," she said. "I've got to learn not to expect miracles, don't I?"

"We've already had the miracle," Torres replied. "And I'm not through yet. But I think you have to face the fact that Alex is probably never going to bc thc same as he was before."

"I don't expect him to be," Marsh said evenly, determined that today he would keep his dislike of Torres under control. "I'll be honest—I never expected him to come as far as he has."

Torres shook his head. "Some of it may be deceiving. There are still enormous gaps in his memory, and when he leaves here, he may become completely disoriented. He says he doesn't remember what La Paloma looks like, or how to get to his house."

"We'll get him there," Marsh said. "Anyway, we'll try," he added, grinning ruefully. "I'm afraid I still go to the old place a couple of times a week. But I'm getting better."

Torres didn't respond to Marsh's grin. "Actually, I think Alex could get you there himself. We gave him a map, and after he studied it, I asked him to tell me how to get home from here. He didn't miss a turn. But he says he doesn't have any idea of what any of it looks like. He simply can't get a mental image of anything he hasn't actually seen since the accident."

"Is that possible?" Ellen asked.

"Possible, but unlikely." He told them what he'd told Alex earlier, then, finally, sat down behind his desk. "Which brings us, finally, to the problem of his personality, or lack of it."

Marsh and Ellen exchanged a glance—it was Alex's altered personality that had, during the last few weeks, become their primary concern. Steadfastly Ellen had insisted that Alex's strange passivity was only temporary, that once he had recovered physically from his injuries, Raymond Torres would begin working to restore his personality. Marsh, on the other hand, had tried to prepare her for the possibility that Alex's personality might never recover, that the emotional center of his brain might very well be irrevocably damaged.

"No," Ellen had insisted over and over again. "It's just a matter of time. Raymond will help him. We just have to trust him, that's all."

Futilely Marsh had pointed out that Torres was a surgeon, not a psychologist, but it had done no good. Through the end of spring and the long summer that followed, Ellen's faith in Torres's abilities had only grown stronger, while at the same time, Marsh's own dislike of the man had increased proportionately. On the surface, Marsh pretended that his animosity toward Torres was based solely on the man's arrogance, but privately he was all too aware that he was, indeed, jealous of Torres. More and more, Torres was taking over the role of father to his son, and adviser and confidant to his wife. And there was nothing he could do about it—he owed the man Alex's very life.

"I'm afraid Alex has what we call a flat personality," he heard Torres saying.

"I know the term," he said, abandoning his previous resolve and making no attempt to keep his voice free of sarcasm.

"I don't doubt it," Torres replied coldly. "But I'm going to explain it anyway." He turned to Ellen. "It's very common in this kind of case," he went on. "Often, when there is brain damage—even much less brain damage than Alex suffered—the emotional structure of the victim is the slowest to recover. Sometimes the damage results in what is called a labile personality, in which the patient tends to exhibit inappropriate emotions—such as laughing uncontrollably at things that don't appear funny to others, or suddenly bursting into tears for no apparent reason. Or, as in Alex's case, the personality simply goes flat. There seems to be little emotional reaction to anything. Over a long period of time, the personality may be partially rebuilt, but there is rarely a full recovery. And that, I'm afraid, may easily be the case with Alex. From what we've seen so far, it appears that the permanent damage in him is going to be to his personality."

There was a silence. Then: "I told you at the outset that there was no chance for a complete recovery."

"But of course he *will* recover," Ellen said, and Marsh felt a slight chill at the determination in her voice, and the faith in her eyes as she gazed at Raymond Torres. "He has you to help him." Torres nodded, but made no reply. "All I have to know," Ellen went on, "is how to help him. Should I go ahead and put my arms around him, even though he just stands there? Should I *try* to elicit emotional responses in him?"

Again Torres nodded. "Of course you should. And frankly, I don't think you'll be able to resist trying. But I've worked with Alex all summer, and I can tell you there are times when it will be very frustrating. You'll want him to be as excited about his progress as you are, and it just won't happen. Or perhaps it's just that he hasn't learned how to express his feelings yet. We'll just have to wait and see."

Ellen nodded, and smiled triumphantly at Marsh. "Is there anything else we should expect?" she asked.

"I don't know. Expect anything and nothing. Just don't be surprised at anything. Alex's mind is still healing, and all kinds of things might happen during that process. The most important thing for you to do is keep track of what happens. I want you to keep notes, and bring them with you every day. I don't care what's in the notes—I want to know when his behavior seems normal, and when it doesn't. I particularly want to know what, if anything, makes him laugh or cry. Or even smile."

"Don't worry," Ellen assured him. "I'll get him smiling again."

"I hope so," Torres replied. "But try not to worry about it too much if it doesn't happen. And keep in mind that while he doesn't smile, he doesn't frown, either."

Marsh silently wondered if Torres had intended that to be a comforting thought. If he had, he'd failed totally.

In the lab, Alex began to come up from the anesthesia that was always administered to him during the daily tests, and, as always, slowly became aware of the strange and fleeting images that filled his mind. As always, the images were unidentifiable; as always, they were accompanied by an incomprehensible stream of something that was almost, but not quite, like sound.

Then he came fully awake, and the images and sounds faded away. He opened his eyes.

"How do you feel?" the technician asked. His name was Peter Bloch, but other than that, Alex didn't know much about him. Nor, for that matter, was he curious to know anything about him. To Alex, Peter was simply one more part of the Institute.

"Okay," he said. Then: "How come I always see and hear things just before I wake up?"

Peter frowned. "What kind of things?"

"I don't know. It's like a flickering I can't quite see, and there's a sort of squeaky, rasping sound."

Peter began disconnecting the monitors from the tiny wires that emerged, almost like hairs, from the metal plate that had replaced part of Alex's left parietal bone, and the scalp that had been drawn across to cover it. "What about pain?"

"No. There's no pain."

"Anything at all? Do you feel anything, or smell anything? Taste anything?"

"No."

"Well, I'm not sure," Peter told him. "I know that during the tests, some of these electrodes are constantly stimulating your brain, then measuring its responses. That's why we have to put you to sleep. We're giving your brain artificial stimuli, and if you were awake, it could be pretty unpleasant. You might feel like we'd burned your hand, or cut your arm, or you might smell or taste something pretty awful. It sounds like you're just waking up too early, and responding to visual and otic stimuli—seeing and hearing things that aren't there at all."

Alex got up from the table and pulled his shirt on, then sat still, waiting for the last of the anesthesia to wear off. "Shall I tell Dr. Torres about it?"

Peter Bloch shrugged. "If you want. I'll make a note of it, and tomorrow we'll hold off on flushing you out with oxygen for a few more minutes."

"That's okay," Alex replied. "It doesn't bother me."

Peter offered him an uncertain grin. "Does *anything* ever bother you?"

Alex thought a moment, then shook his head. "No." He tucked in his shirt and carefully put his feet on the floor, then took his cane in his right hand and began making his slow way to the door.

Peter Bloch watched him go, and his grin faded away. He began closing up the lab, shutting down the equipment that had been in use almost constantly over the last three months. For himself, he was glad Alex Lonsdale was going home. The work load, since Alex had arrived, had been nearly intolerable, and Torres had never let up on the staff for a moment.

Besides, Peter realized as he took off his lab jacket and hunched into his favorite khaki windbreaker, he didn't like Alex Lonsdale.

True, what Torres had accomplished with Alex would probably make some kind of medical history, but Peter wasn't impressed. To him, it didn't matter how well Alex was doing.

The kid was a zombie.

Marsh drove north out of Palo Alto, staying on Middlefield Road until he came to La Paloma Drive, where he turned left to start up into the hills. Every few minutes he glanced over at Alex, who sat impassively in the passenger seat next to him, while from the back seat Ellen kept up a steady stream of chatter:

"Do you remember what's just around the next curve? We're almost to La Paloma, and things will start looking familiar to you."

Alex pictured the map he'd studied. "The county park," he said. "Hillside Park."

"You remember!" Ellen exclaimed.

"It was on the map Dr. Torres gave me," Alex corrected her. They came around the bend in the road, and Marsh slowed the car. "Stop," Alex suddenly said.

Marsh braked the car, and followed Alex's gaze. In the distance, there was a group of children playing on a swing set, while two teenage boys tossed a Frisbee back and forth.

"What is it, Alex?" Marsh asked.

Alex's eyes seemed to be fixed on the children on the swings.

"I always wanted to do that when I was little," he said.

Marsh chuckled. "You not only wanted to, you nearly drove us crazy." His voice took on a singsong tone as he mimicked a child's voice. " 'More! More! Don't want to go home. Want to swing!' That's why I finally hung one in the backyard at the old house. It was either that or spend every free minute I had bringing you out here."

Alex turned and gazed at his father, his eyes steady. "I don't remember that at all," he said.

In the rearview mirror, Marsh saw Ellen's worried eyes, and wondered if either of them would be able to stand seeing their son's memory wiped clean of every experience they had all shared. "Do you want to swing now?" he asked.

Alex hesitated, then shook his head. "Let's go home," he said. "Maybe I'll remember our house when I see it."

They drove into La Paloma, and Alex began examining the town he'd lived in all his life. But it was as if he'd never seen it before. Nothing was familiar, nothing he saw triggered any memories.

And then they came to the Square.

Marsh bore right to follow the traffic pattern three-quarters of the way around before turning right once again into Hacienda Drive. Alex's eyes, he noted, were no longer staring out toward the front of the car. Instead, he was leaning forward slightly, so he could look across Marsh's chest and see into the Square.

"Remembering something?" he asked quietly.

"The tree . . ." Alex said. "There's something about the tree." As he stared at the giant oak that dominated the Square, Alex was certain it looked familiar. And yet, something was wrong. The tree looked right, but nothing else did.

"The chain," he said softly. "I don't remember the chain, or the grass."

In the back seat, Ellen nodded, sure she understood what was happening. "It hasn't been there a long time," she said. "When you were little, the tree was there, but there wasn't anything around it."

"A rope," Alex suddenly said. "There was a rope."

Ellen's heart began to pound. "Yes! There was a rope with a tire on it! You and your friends used to play on it when you were little!"

But the image that had flashed into Alex's mind wasn't of a tire at all.

It was the image of a man, and the man had been hanging at the end of the rope.

He wondered if he ought to tell his parents what he'd remembered, but decided he'd better not. The image was too strange, and if he talked about it, his parents might think he, too, was strange.

For some reason—a reason he didn't understand—it was important that people not think he was strange.

Marsh pulled into the driveway, and Alex gazed at the house.

And suddenly he remembered it.

But it, like the oak tree, didn't look quite right either. He stared at the house for a long time.

From the driveway, all he could see was a long expanse of white stucco, broken at regular intervals by deeply recessed windows, each framed with a pair of heavy shutters. There were two stories, topped by a gently sloping red tile roof, and on the north side there was a garden, enclosed by walls which were entirely covered with vines.

It was the vines that were wrong. The garden wall, like the house itself, should be plain white stucco, with decorative tiles implanted in it every six feet or so. And the vines should be small, and climbing on trellises.

He sat still, trying to remember what the inside looked like, but no matter how he searched his memory, there was nothing.

He stared at the chimney that rose from the roof. If there was a chimney, there was a fireplace. He tried to picture a fireplace, but the only one he could visualize was the one in the lobby of the Institute.

He got out of the car, and with his parents following behind him, approached the house. When he came to the wide steps leading up to the garden gate, he felt his father's hand on his elbow.

"I can do it," he said.

"But Dr. Torres told us—" his mother began. Alex cut her off.

"I know what he said. Just stay behind me, in case I trip. I can do it."

Carefully he put his right foot on the first step, then, supporting himself with the cane, cautiously began to bring his left foot up toward the second step. He swayed for a moment, then felt his father's hands steadying him.

"Thank you," he said. Then: "I have to try again. Help me get back down, please."

"You don't have to try right now, darling," Ellen assured him. "Don't you want to go in?"

Alex shook his head. "I have to go up and down the steps by myself. I have to be able to take care of myself. Dr. Torres says it's important."

"Can't it wait?" Marsh asked. "We could get you settled in, then come back out."

"No," Alex replied. "I have to learn it now."

Fifteen minutes later Alex slowly but steadily ascended the three steps that led up to the gate, then turned to come back down. Ellen tried to put her arms around him, but he turned away, his face impassive. "All right," he said. "Let's go in."

As she followed him into the garden, across the tiled patio and into the house itself, Ellen hoped he'd turned away before he saw the tears that, just for a moment, she had been unable to hold back.

Alex gazed around the room that was filled with all the possessions he'd had since he was a child. Oddly, the room itself seemed vaguely familiar, as if sometime, long ago, he'd been in it. But its furnishings meant nothing to him. Against one wall was a desk, and he opened the top drawer to stare at the contents. Some pens and pencils, and a notebook. He picked up the notebook and glanced at its contents.

Notes for a geometry class.

The name of the teacher came instantly to mind: Mrs. Hendricks.

What did Mrs. Hendricks look like?

No image.

He began reading the notes. At the end of the notebook there was a theorem, but he'd never finished the proof of it. He sat down at the desk and picked up a pencil. Writing slowly, his handwriting still shaky, he began entering a series of premises and corollaries in the notebook. Two minutes later, he'd proved the theorem.

But he still couldn't remember what Mrs. Hendricks looked like.

He began scanning the books on the shelf above the desk, his eyes finally coming to rest on a large volume bound in red Leatherette. When he looked at the cover, he saw that it was emblazoned with a cartoon figure of a bird, and the title: *The Cardinal.* He opened it.

It was his high-school annual from last year. Taking the book with him, he went to his bed, stretched out, and began paging slowly through it.

An hour later, when his mother tapped softly at the door, then stuck her head inside to ask him if he wanted anything, he knew what Mrs. Hendricks looked like, and Mr. Landry. If he saw them, he would recognize them.

He would recognize all his friends, all the people Lisa Cochran had told him about each day when she came to visit him at the Institute.

He would recognize them, and be able to match their names to their faces.

But he wouldn't know anything about them.

All of it was still a blank.

He would have to start all over again. He put the book aside and looked up at his mother.

"I don't remember any of it," he said at last. "I thought I recognized the house, and even this room, but I couldn't have, could I?"

"Why not?" Ellen asked.

"Because I thought I remembered the garden wall without vines. But the vines have always been there, haven't they?"

"Why do you say that?"

"I looked at the roots and the branches. They look like they've been there forever."

Ellen nodded. "They have. The wall's been covered with morning glory as long as I can remember. That's one of the reasons I always wanted this house—I love the vines."

Alex nodded. "So I couldn't have remembered. And this room seemed sort of familiar, but it's just a room. And I don't remember any of my things. None of them at all."

Ellen sat on the bed next to him, and put her arms around him. "I know," she said. "We were all hoping you'd remember, but Raymond told us you probably wouldn't. And you mustn't worry about it."

"I won't," Alex said. "I'll just start over, that's all."

"Yes," Ellen replied. "We'll start over. And you'll remember. It will be slow, but it'll come back."

It won't, Alex thought. It won't ever come back. I'll just have to act like it does.

One thing he had learned in the last three months was that when he pretended to remember things, people seemed to be happy with him.

As he followed his mother out to the family room a few minutes later, he wondered what happiness felt like—or if he'd ever feel it himself.

CHAPTER 9

The Monday after Labor Day was the kind of California September morning that belies any hint of a coming change of season. The morning fog had burned off by seven, and as Marsh Lonsdale dropped Alex off in front of the Cochrans' house, the heat was already building.

"Sure you don't want me to take you both to school?"

"I want to walk," Alex replied. "Dr. Torres says I should walk as much as I can."

"Dr. Torres says a lot about everything," Marsh commented. "That doesn't mean you have to do everything he says."

Alex opened the car door and got out, then put his cane in the back seat. When he looked up, his father was watching him with disapproval. "Did Dr. Torres tell you not to use the cane anymore?"

Alex shook his head. "No. I just think it would be better if I stopped using it, that's all."

His father's hard expression dissolved into a smile. "Good for you," he said. Then: "You okay with going back to school?"

Alex nodded. "I think so."

"It's not too late to change your mind. If you want, we can get a tutor up from Stanford, at least for the first semester . . ."

"No," Alex said. "I want to go to school. I might remember a lot, once I'm there."

"You're already remembering a lot," Marsh replied. "I just don't think you should push yourself too hard. You . . . well, you don't have to remember everything that happened before the accident."

"But I do," Alex replied. "If I'm going to get really well, I have to remember everything." He slammed the car door and started toward the Cochrans' front porch, then turned to wave to his father, who waved back, then pulled away from the curb. Only when the car had disappeared around the corner did Alex start once again toward the house, idly wondering if his father knew he'd lied to him.

Since he'd come home, Alex had learned to lie a lot.

He pressed the doorbell, waited, then pressed it again. Even though the Cochrans had told him over and over again that he should simply let himself into their house as he used to, he hadn't yet done it.

Nor did he have any memory of ever having let himself into their house.

Their house, like the one next door where he knew he'd spent most of his life, had rung no bells in his head, elicited no memories whatsoever. But he'd been careful not to say so. Instead, when he'd walked into the Cochrans' house for the first time after leaving the Institute, he'd scanned the rooms carefully, trying to memorize everything in them. Then, when he was sure he had it all firmly fixed in his mind, he'd said that he thought he remembered a picture upstairs—one of himself and Lisa, when they were five or six years old.

Everyone had been pleased. And since then, after he'd relearned something he was sure he'd known before, and discovered as much as he could about its past, he would experiment with "remembering."

It worked well. Last week, while looking for a pen in his parents' desk, he had found a repair bill for the car. He'd studied it carefully, then, as they were driving to the Cochrans' that evening, and passed the shop where the car had been fixed, he'd turned to his father.

"Didn't they work on the car last year?" he'd asked.

"They sure did," his father had replied. Then: "Do you remember what they did to it?"

Alex pretended to ponder the question. "Transmission?" he asked.

His father had sighed, then smiled at him in the rearview mirror. "Right. It's coming back, isn't it?"

"A little bit," Alex had said. "Maybe a little bit."

But, of course, it wasn't.

The front door opened, and Lisa was smiling at him. He carefully returned the smile. "Ready?"

"Who's ever ready for the first day of school?" Lisa replied. "Do I look all right?"

Alex took in her jeans and white blouse, and nodded gravely. "Did you always wear clothes like that to school?"

"Everybody does." She called a good-bye over her shoulder, and a moment later the two of them set out toward La Paloma High.

As they walked through the town, Alex kept asking Lisa an endless series of questions about who lived in which house, the stores they passed, and the people who spoke to them. Lisa patiently answered his questions, then began testing his memory, even though she knew that Alex never seemed to forget anything she told him.

"Who lives in the blue house on Carmel Street?"

"The Jamesons."

"What about the old house at the corner of Monterey?"

"Miss Thorpe," Alex replied. Then he added, "She used to be a witch."

Lisa glanced at him out of the corner of her eye, wondering if he was teasing her, even though she knew he wasn't. Since he'd come home, Alex never teased anybody. "She wasn't *really* a witch," she said. "We just always *thought* she was when we were little."

Alex stopped walking. "If she wasn't one, why did we think she was?"

Lisa wondered what to tell him. He seemed to have forgotten everything about his childhood, including what it had been like to be a child. How could she explain to him how much fun it used to be to scare themselves half to death with speculations on what old Miss Thorpe might be doing behind her heavily curtained windows, or what she might do to them if she ever caught them in her yard? For Alex never seemed to imagine anything anymore. He always wanted to know what things were, and who was who, but it didn't seem to matter to him, and he didn't seem, really, to care. In fact, though she'd told no one of her feelings, Lisa was glad that school was finally starting and she could legitimately spend less time with Alex.

"I don't know," she said at last. "We just thought she was a witch, that's all. Now, come on, or we'll be late."

Alex moved uncertainly around the campus of La Paloma High School. Deep in the recesses of his mind, he had a faint feeling of having been here before, but nothing seemed to be quite right.

The school was built around a quadrangle, with a fountain at its center, and from the fountain, some of the campus seemed familiar.

And yet, the picture in his mind seemed incomplete. It was as if he could remember only parts of the campus; other areas were totally strange.

Still, it was a memory.

He looked at his program card, and when the first bell sounded, he started toward the building that housed what would be his homeroom that year.

It was in one of the buildings he had no memory of, but he had no problem in locating the room. Just before the second bell rang, he stepped into the classroom, and started toward an empty seat next to Lisa Cochran. Before he could sit down, the teacher, whom he recognized from the picture in the yearbook as Mr. Hamlin, told him that he was to report to the dean of boys. He looked questioningly at Lisa, but she only shook her head and shrugged. Silently he left the classroom and went to the Administration Building.

As soon as he was inside, he knew that he was in familiar territory. As he glanced around, the walnut wainscoting seemed to strike a chord in him, and he stopped for a moment to take in the details of the lobby.

To the left, where it felt as though it should be, was a large glass-fronted office. Through the glass, he could see a long counter, and beyond it, several secretaries sitting at desks, typing.

Straight ahead, and off to the right, two corridors ran at right angles to each other, and without thinking, Alex turned right and went into the second office on the left.

A nurse looked up at him. "May I help you?"

Alex stopped short. "I'm looking for Mr. Eisenberg's office. But this isn't it, is it?"

The nurse smiled and shook her head. "It's in the other wing. First door on the right."

"Thank you," Alex said. He left the nurse's office and started back toward the main foyer.

Something, though, was wrong. When he had come into the building, he had recognized everything, and known exactly where the dean's office was. Yet it wasn't there.

Apparently he hadn't remembered after all.

Still, as he made his way into what really was the dean's office, he had the distinct feeling that he *had* remembered, and when the dean's secretary glanced up and smiled at him, he decided he knew what had happened.

"How do you like the new office?" he asked.

The smile faded from the secretary's face. "New office?" she asked. "What are you talking about, Alex?"

Alex swallowed. "Wasn't Mr. Eisenberg's office where the nurse is this year?"

The secretary hesitated, then shook her head. "It's been right here for as long as I've been here," she said. Then she smiled again. "You can go right in, and don't worry. You're not in any trouble."

He passed the desk and knocked at the inner door, as he had always knocked at Dr. Torres's door before going inside.

"Come in," a voice called from within. He opened the door and stepped through. As with everyone else who had been pictured in the yearbook in his bedroom, he recognized the face and knew the man's name, but had no memory of ever having met him before. Whatever his flash of remembrance had been about, it was over now.

Dan Eisenberg unfolded his large frame from the chair behind his desk to offer Alex his hand. "Alex! It's great to see you again."

"It's nice to see you, too, sir," Alex replied, hesitating only a second before grasping Eisenberg's hand in a firm shake. A moment later, the dean indicated the chair next to his desk.

"Sorry to have to call you in on the first day of school," he said, "but I'm afraid a little problem has come up."

Alex's face remained impassive. "Miss Jennings said I wasn't in trouble—"

"And you aren't," Eisenberg reassured him. "But I did take the liberty of talking to Dr. Torres last week, and he suggested that perhaps we might want to give you a couple of tests." He looked for a reaction from Alex, but saw none. "Do you have any idea what the tests might be for?"

"To see how much I've forgotten," Alex said, and Eisenberg had the distinct feeling that Alex wasn't making a guess, but already knew about the tests.

"Right. I take it Dr. Torres told you about them."

"No. But it makes sense, doesn't it? I mean, you don't know which class I should be in if you don't know how much I remember."

"Exactly." Eisenberg picked up a packet of standard form tests. "Do you remember these?" Alex shook his head. "They're the same tests you took at the beginning of last year, and would have taken again in the spring, except . . ." His voice trailed off, and he looked uncomfortable.

"Except for the accident," Alex finished for him. "I don't mind talking about it, but I don't remember it too well, either. Just that it happened."

Eisenberg nodded. "Dr. Torres tells us there are still a lot of gaps in your memory—"

"I've been studying all summer," Alex broke in. "My dad wants me to be in the accelerated class this year."

Which is certainly not going to happen, Eisenberg thought. From what Torres had told him of Alex's case, he knew it was far more likely that Alex would have to start all over again with the school's most basic courses. "We'll just have to see, won't we?" he asked, trying to keep his pessimism out of his voice. "Anyway, if you feel up to it, I'd like you to take the tests today."

"All right."

Ten minutes later Alex sat in an empty classroom while Eisenberg's secretary explained the testing system and the time limits. "And don't worry if you don't finish them," she said as she set the time clock for the first of the battery of eight tests. "You're not expected to finish all of them. Ready?" Alex nodded. "Begin."

Alex opened the first of the booklets and began marking down his answers.

Dan Eisenberg looked up from the report he was working on, his smile fading when he saw the look of disappointment in his secretary's eyes. A glance at his watch told him Alex had begun the tests only an hour and a half ago. "What's happened, Marge? Couldn't he do it?"

The young woman shook her head sorrowfully. "I don't think he even tried," she said. "He just . . . well, he just started marking answers randomly."

"But you told him how they're scored, didn't you? Right minus wrong?"

Marge nodded. "And I asked him again each time he handed me one of his answer sheets. He said he understood how it was scored, and that he was finished."

"How many did he do?"

Marge hesitated; then: "All of them."

The dean's brows arched skeptically. "All of them?" he repeated. Then, after Marge had nodded once more: "But that's impossible. Those tests are supposed to take all day, and even then, no one's supposed to finish them."

"I know. So he must have simply gone down the sheets, marking in his answers. I'm not really sure there's any point in scoring it." Still, she handed the stack of answer sheets to Dan, and he slid the first one under the template.

Behind each tiny slot in the template, there was a neat black mark. Dan frowned, then shook his head. Wordlessly he matched the rest of the answer sheets to their templates. Finally he leaned back, a smile playing around the corners of his mouth.

"Cute," he said. "Real cute." The smile spread into a grin. "He's still working on them, isn't he?"

Now it was Marge Jennings who frowned. "What are you talking about?"

"I'm talking about you," Dan said, chuckling. "You came in early and dummied up this set of answer sheets, didn't you? Well, you went too far. Did you really expect me to buy this?"

"Buy what?" Marge asked. She stepped around the desk and repeated the process of checking the answer sheets. "My God," she breathed.

Dan looked up at her, fully expecting to see her eyes twinkling as she still tried to get him to fall for her joke. And then, slowly, he began to realize it was not a joke at all.

Alex Lonsdale had completed the tests, and his scores were perfect.

"Get Torres on the phone," Dan told his secretary.

Marge Jennings returned to her office, where Alex sat quietly on a sofa, leafing through a magazine. He looked up at her for a moment, then returned to his reading.

"Alex?"

"Yes?" Alex laid the magazine aside.

"Did you . . . well, did anyone show you a copy of those tests? I mean, since you took them last year?"

Alex thought a moment, then shook his head. "No. At least not since the accident."

"I see," Marge said softly.

But, of course, she didn't see at all.

Ellen glanced nervously at the clock, and once more regretted having allowed Cynthia Evans to set up an appointment for her to interview María Torres. Not, of course, that she didn't need a housekeeper; she did. A few months ago, before the accident, she would have felt no hesitation about hiring María Torres. But now things were different, and despite all of Cynthia's arguments, she still felt strange about asking the mother of Alex's doctor to vacuum her floors and do her laundry. Still, it would only be two days a week, and she knew María was going to need the work: starting next month, Cynthia herself was going to have full-time, live-in help.

But right now, María was late, and Ellen herself was due for what Marsh always referred to, with a hint of what Ellen considered to be slightly sexist overtones, as "lunch with the girls." Of course, part of it was her own fault, for try as she would, she still hadn't been able to train herself to think of her friends as "women": they had known each other since childhood, and they would be, forever, "girls," at least in Ellen's mind.

Except Marty Lewis, who had long since stopped being a girl in any sense of the word. Ellen often wondered if Alan Lewis's alcoholism had anything to do with the changes that had come over Marty in the last few years.

Of course it had. If Alan hadn't turned into a drunk, Marty would have been just like the rest of them—staying home, raising her kids, and taking care of her husband. But for Marty, things had been different. Alan couldn't hold a job, so Marty had taken over the support of the family, and made a success of it, too, while Alan drifted from treatment program to treatment program, sobering up and working for a while, but only a while. Sooner or later, he would begin drinking again, and the spiral would start over again. And Marty, finally, had accepted it. She'd talked of divorce a few years ago, but in the end had simply taken over the burdens of the family. At the fairly regular lunches the four of them—Carol Cochran and Valerie Benson were the other two—enjoyed, Marty's main conversation was about her job, and how much she liked it.

"Working's *fun!*" she would insist. "In fact, it's a lot better this way. I never was much good at the domestic scene, and now that Kate's growing up, I don't even feel I'm robbing her of anything. And I don't have to get terrified every time Alan starts drinking anymore. Do you know what it was like? He'd start drinking, and I'd start saving, because I always knew that it would only be a matter of months before he was going to be out of a job again." Then she'd smile ruefully. "I suppose I should have left him years ago, but I still love him. So I put up with him, and hope that every binge will be the last one."

And, of course, there was Valerie Benson, who, three years ago, actually *had* divorced her husband. "Dumbest thing I ever did," was now Val's characteristically blunt summation of the divorce. "I can't even remember what he used to do that made me think I couldn't stand it anymore. I had this idea that if I only got rid of George, life would be wonderful. So I got rid of him, and you know what? Nothing changed. Not one damn thing. Except now I don't have George to blame things on, so, in a way, I suppose I'm a better person." Then she'd roll her eyes: "Lord, how I loathe those words. I'm sick of being a better person. I'd rather be married and miserable."

Ellen glanced at the clock once more, and realized that if María didn't arrive within the next five minutes, she was going to have to choose between waiting for María and going to lunch. Not that the interview would take long—María had been a fixture in La Paloma all of Ellen's life, and all Ellen really had to do was explain to the old woman what she wanted done, then leave the house in María's hands.

Lunch, however, was something else. This would be the group's first lunch since Alex's accident, and she was sure that Alex would be the main topic of conversation.

Alex, and Raymond Torres.

And, she readily admitted to herself, she was looking forward to the lunch, looking forward to spending even a few hours relaxing with her friends.

It had been a long summer. Once the decision had finally been made that Alex could go back to school, Ellen had begun looking forward to this day. This morning, after Alex and Marsh had left, she had treated herself to a leisurely hour of pure relaxation, and then spent two full hours getting herself ready for today's lunch. She was determined that Alex wasn't going to be the only topic of conversation that day, nor was Raymond Torres. Instead, she was going to encourage the others to talk about themselves rather than the Lonsdales' problems. It would be wonderful to laugh and chat with old friends as if nothing had changed.

The doorbell and the telephone rang simultaneously, and Ellen called out to María to let herself in as she picked up the receiver. Then, when the voice at the other end of the wire identified itself as Dan Eisenberg, her heart sank, and she waved María Torres into the living room as she focused her attention on the telephone.

"What's happened?" she asked, wearily setting her purse back on the table.

"I'm not sure," Eisenberg replied. "But I'd like you to come down to the school this afternoon."

"This afternoon?" Ellen asked, relief flooding through her. "Then it isn't an emergency?"

There was a momentary silence. When Eisenberg spoke again, his voice was apologetic. "I'm sorry," he said. "I should have told you right away that Alex is all right. It's just that we gave him some tests this morning, and I'd like to go over the results with you. Both you and Dr. Lonsdale, actually. Would two o'clock be all right?"

"Fine with me," Ellen told him. "I'll have to call my husband, but I imagine it will be fine with him too." She paused; then: "Where Alex is concerned, he tends to make time, even if he hasn't got it."

"Then I'll see you both at two," Eisenberg replied. He was about to hang up when Ellen stopped him.

"Mr. Eisenberg? The tests. Did Alex do all right on them?"

There was a slight hesitation before Eisenberg spoke. "He did very well, Mrs. Lonsdale," he said. "Very well indeed."

A moment later, as Ellen turned her attention to María Torres, she decided to put Dan Eisenberg's words, and the tone in which he'd spoken them, out of her mind. If she didn't, the feeling she had of something amiss would ruin the lunch for her, and she was determined that that wouldn't happen.

María, dressed as always in black, her skirt reaching almost to the floor, still hovered near the door, a worn shawl wrapped around her stooped shoulders, despite the heat of the summerlike day. Her eyes were fixed on the floor. "I am sorry, *señora,*" she said softly. "I am very late."

The abject sorrow evident in the old woman's entire being dissolved Ellen's impatience. "It's all right," she said gently. "I don't really need to interview you anyway, do I?" Without waiting for a reply, she began giving María hurried instructions. "All the cleaning things are in the laundry room behind the kitchen, but if you'll just try to get some vacuuming done today, that's all I really need. Then we can go over the rest of it on Saturday. All right?"

"Sí, señora," María muttered, and as she started toward the kitchen, Ellen hurriedly threw on a coat, picked up her purse, and left the house.

The moment she was gone, María's back straightened and her glittering old eyes began taking in every detail of the Lonsdales' house. She prowled the rooms slowly, examining every possession of the *gringo* family whose son had been saved by Ramón.

Better if Ramón had let him die, as all the *gringos* should die. And it would happen someday, María was sure. It was all she thought about now, as she spent her days wandering through La Paloma, cleaning the old houses for the *ladrones.*

The thieves.

That's what they all were, and even if Ramón didn't understand it, she did.

But she would go on cleaning for them, go on looking after the houses that rightfully belonged to her people, until Alejandro returned to avenge the death of his parents and sisters, and all his descendants could finally return to their rightful homes.

And the time of vengeance was coming. She could feel it, deep in her old bones.

At last she came into the boy's room, and suddenly she knew. Alejandro was here. Soon, *la venganza* would begin.

For Ellen, the lunch she had so looked forward to had been a disaster. As she'd expected, the conversation had revolved around Raymond Torres and Alex, but she had found herself totally distracted with worry over what the dean might have to tell her after lunch. And now, though she'd listened carefully, it still didn't make sense. "I'm sorry," she said, "but I still don't understand exactly what it all means."

She and Marsh had been in Dan Eisenberg's office for nearly an hour, and thirty minutes ago Raymond Torres, too, had arrived. But Ellen still felt as confused as ever—it all seemed quite impossible.

"It means Alex is finally using his brain," Marsh told her. "It's not so difficult. We've seen the results of the tests. His scores were perfect!"

"But how can that be?" Ellen argued. "I know he's been studying all summer, and I know he has a good memory, but *this*"—she picked up the math-testing booklet—"how could he have even done the calculations? He simply didn't have the time, did he?" She dropped the test back on Eisenberg's desk and turned to Torres. If anyone could make her understand, he could. "Explain it to me again," she said, and as his intense eyes met hers, she began to relax, and concentrate.

Torres spread his hands and pressed his fingers together thoughtfully. "It's very simple," he said in the slightly patronizing tone that never failed to infuriate Marsh. "Alex's brain works differently from the way it did before. It's a matter of compensation. If a person loses one sense, his others become sharper. The same kind of thing has happened to Alex. His brain has compensated for the damage to its emotional centers by sharpening its intellectual centers."

"I understand that," Ellen agreed. "At least, I understand the theory. What I don't understand is what it means. I want to know what it means for Alex."

"I'm not sure anyone can tell you that, Mrs. Lonsdale," Dan Eisenberg replied.

"Nor does it matter," Torres pronounced. "With Alex we are no longer at a point where we can do anything about his abilities, or his responses. I've done what can be done. From now on, all I can do is observe Alex—"

"Like a laboratory animal?" Marsh broke in. Torres regarded him with cold eyes.

"If you wish," he said.

"For God's sake, Torres, Alex is my son." Marsh turned to Ellen. "All this means for Alex is that he is a remarkably intelligent young man. In fact," he went on, his attention now shifting to Dan Eisenberg, "I suspect there probably isn't much this school can do for him anymore. Is that right?"

Eisenberg reluctantly nodded his agreement.

"Then it seems to me that perhaps we should take him down to Stanford next week and see if we can get him into some sort of special program."

"I won't agree to that," Torres interrupted. "Alex is brilliant, yes. But brilliance isn't enough. If he were my son—"

"Which he's not," Marsh replied, his smile gone.

"Which he's not," Torres agreed. "But if he *were*, I would keep him right here in La Paloma, and let him reestablish all his old friendships and old patterns of behavior. Somewhere, there might be a trigger, and when he stumbles across that trigger, his mind may fully reopen, and the past will come back to him."

"And what about his intellect?" Marsh demanded. "Suddenly I have a very brilliant son, Dr. Torres—"

"Which, I gather," Torres interrupted in a voice as cool as Marsh's own, "is something you have always wanted."

"Everyone hopes his children will be brilliant," Marsh countered.

"And Alex *is* brilliant, Dr. Lonsdale," Torres replied. "But keeping him here for another year isn't going to affect that. I should imagine that the school can design a course of study for him that will keep his mind active and challenged. But there is another side to Alex—the emotional side—and if he has any chance to recover in that area, I think we have an obligation to give him that chance."

"Of course we do," Ellen agreed. "And Marsh knows it as well as we do." She turned to her husband. "Don't you?"

Marsh was silent for a long time. Torres's words, he knew, made sense. Alex *should* stay home. But he couldn't just go on letting Torres run his life, and the lives of his wife and son.

"I think," he said at last, "that perhaps we ought to talk to Alex about it."

"I agree," Torres replied, rising to his feet. "But not for at least a week. I want to think about this for a while, and then I'll decide what's best for Alex." He glanced at his watch, then offered Eisenberg his hand. "I'm afraid I have another meeting. If you need me for anything, you have my number." With nothing more than a nod to either Marsh or Ellen, he left the dean's office.

Alex lay on his bed staring at the ceiling.

Something was wrong, but he had no idea what it might be, or what he ought to do about it.

All he knew was that something was wrong with him. He was no longer the same as he had been before the accident, and for some reason his parents were upset about it. At least, his mother was upset. His father seemed pleased.

They had told him about the test results as they drove him home that afternoon, and at first he hadn't understood what all the fuss was about. He could have told them he'd correctly answered all the questions before they even checked. The questions had been easy, and didn't really involve anything like thinking. In fact, he'd thought they must be testing his memory rather than his ability to think, because all the tests had involved were a series of facts and calculations, and if you had a good memory and knew the right equations, there wasn't anything to them.

But now they were saying he was brilliant, and his father wanted him to go into a special program down in Palo Alto. From what he'd heard in the car, though, he didn't think that was going to happen. Dr. Torres would see to it that he stayed home.

And that, he decided, was fine with him. All day, he'd been trying to figure out what had happened at school that morning—why he had remembered some things so clearly, other things incorrectly, and still others not at all.

He was sure it had something to do with the damage his brain had suffered, and yet that didn't make sense to him. He could understand how parts of his memory could have been destroyed, but that wouldn't account for the things he had remembered incorrectly. He should, he was sure, either remember things or not remember them. But memories shouldn't have simply changed, unless there was a reason.

The thing to do, he decided, was start keeping track of the things he remembered, and how he remembered them, and see if there was a pattern to the things he remembered incorrectly.

If there was, he might be able to figure out what was wrong with him.

And then, there was María Torres.

She had been in his room when he got home that afternoon, and when he had first seen her, he'd thought he recognized her. It had only been a fleeting moment, and a sharp pain had shot through his head, and then it was over. A moment later he realized that what he'd recognized was not her face, but her eyes. She had the same eyes that Dr. Torres had: almost black eyes that seemed to peer right inside you.

She'd smiled at him, and nodded her head, then quickly left him alone in his room.

By now he should have forgotten the incident, except for the pain in his head.

The pain itself was gone now, but the memory of it was still etched sharply in his mind.

CHAPTER 10

Lisa Cochran's face set into an expression of stubbornness that Kate Lewis had long ago come to realize meant that the argument was over—Lisa would, in the end, have her way. And, as usual, Kate knew Lisa was right. Still, she didn't want to give in too easily.

"But what if he won't go?" she asked.

"He'll go," Lisa insisted. "I can talk him into it. I've always been able to talk Alex into anything."

"That was before," Kate reminded her. "Ever since he's come home, he's . . . well, he's just different, that's all. Most of the time he acts like he doesn't even like us anymore."

Lisa sighed. Over and over again she'd tried to explain to Kate and Bob that Alex *did* still like them—and all his other friends too—but that right now he was just incapable of showing his feelings. Kate and Bob, however, had remained unconvinced.

"If we're going to go up to San Francisco," Bob repeated for the third time that afternoon, "I want to go with people I can have fun with. All Alex ever does anymore is ask questions. He's like a little kid."

The three of them were sitting in their favorite hangout, Jake's Place, which served pizza and video games. While the games had long since lost their novelty, the kids still came for the pizza, which wasn't very good, but was cheap. And Jake didn't mind if they came in right after school and sat around all afternoon, nursing a Coke and talking. Today, gathered around a table with a Pac-Man unit in its top, they had been talking a long time as Lisa tried to convince Bob and Kate that they should take Alex along to San Francisco day after tomorrow. Jake, they knew, had been listening to them casually, but, as always, hadn't tried to offer them any advice. That, too, was one of the reasons they hung out here. Suddenly, however, he appeared by their table and leaned over.

"Better make up your minds," he told them. "Alex just came in."

Kate and Bob looked up guiltily as Lisa waved to Alex. "Over here!" Alex hesitated only a second before coming over to slide into the seat next to Lisa.

"Hi. I looked for you after school, but you didn't wait. What's going on?"

Lisa glanced at Kate and Bob, then decided to end their argument immediately. "We're talking about going up to the City on Saturday. Want to go with us?"

Alex frowned. "The city? What city?"

"San Francisco," Lisa replied, ignoring the roll of Bob Carey's eyes. "Everybody calls it that. Want to go with us?"

"I'll have to ask my folks."

"No, you don't," Lisa told him. "If you tell your folks, they'll tell my folks and Kate's folks, and they'll all say no. We're just going to go."

Bob Carey suddenly reached into his pocket, pulled out a quarter, and began playing Pac-Man. Lisa, sure he was doing it only to avoid talking to Alex, glared at him, but he ignored her. Alex, however, didn't seem to notice the slight. His eyes were fastened on the little yellow man that scooted through the maze under Bob's control.

"What's it do?" he asked, and Lisa immediately knew it was yet one more thing of which he had no memory. Patiently she began explaining the object of the game as Alex kept watching while Bob played. In less than two minutes, the game was over.

"Want me to show you how to do it?" Alex asked. Bob looked at him with skeptical curiosity.

"You? You're even worse at this than me."

Alex slipped a quarter in the slot, and began playing, maneuvering the little man around the maze, always just out of reach of the hungry goblins that chased him. But when the goblins suddenly turned blue, Alex turned on them, gobbling them up one after the other. He cleared board after board, never losing a man, racking up an array of fruit, and an enormous score.

After ten minutes, he took his hands off the controls. Instantly, Pac-Man was gobbled up, and a new one appeared. Alex ignored it, and in a few seconds it, too, was devoured. "It's easy," he said. "There's a pattern, and all you have to do is remember the pattern. Then you know where all the goblins are going to go."

Bob shifted in his chair. "How come you could never do that before?" he asked.

Alex frowned, then shrugged. "I don't know," he admitted.

"And I don't care," Lisa declared. "What about going to the City? Do you want to go with us, or not?"

Alex considered it a moment, then nodded his head. "Okay. What time?"

"We'll tell our folks we're going to the beach in Santa Cruz," Lisa said. "I'll even pack us a lunch. That way we can leave early, and we won't have to be back until dinnertime."

"What if we get caught?" Kate asked.

"How can we get caught?" Bob countered. Then, his eyes fixed on Alex, he added, "Unless someone tells."

"Don't worry," Lisa assured him. "Nobody's going to tell."

Kate drained the last of the warm Coke that had been sitting in front of her most of the afternoon, and stood up. "I've got to get home. Mom'll kill me if I haven't got dinner started when she gets home from work."

"You want us to come along?" Lisa asked. Though none of the kids talked about it much, they all knew about Mr. Lewis's drinking problem. Kate shook her head. "Dad's still sort of okay, but I think he'll have to go back to the hospital next week. Right now he's at the stage where he just sits in front of the TV all the time, drinking beer. I wish Mom would just kick him out."

"No, you don't," Bob Carey said.

"I do too!" Kate flared. "All he does is talk about what he's going to do, but he never does anything except get drunk. If I could, I'd move out!"

"But he's still your father—"

"So what? He's a drunk, and everybody knows it!"

Her eyes brimming with sudden tears, Kate turned and hurried out of Jake's Place, Bob right behind her. "Pay the check, will you, Alex?" Bob called back over his shoulder.

When they were alone, Lisa grinned at Alex. "Do you have any money?" she asked. "Or do I get stuck with the check again?"

"Why should I pay it?" Alex asked, bewildered. "I didn't eat anything."

"Alex! I was only kidding!"

"Well, why *should* I pay it?" Alex insisted.

Lisa tried to keep the exasperation she was feeling out of her voice. "Alex," she said carefully, "nobody expects you to pay the check. But Bob was in a hurry, and he'll pay you back tomorrow. You and Bob have always done that."

Alex's eyes fixed steadily on her. "I don't remember that."

"You don't remember anything," Lisa replied, her voice edged with anger. "So I'm telling you. Now, why don't you just give Jake some money, and we'll get out of here?" Then, when Alex still hesitated, she sighed. "Oh, never mind. I'll do it myself." She paid the check, and started toward the door. "You coming?"

Alex stood up and followed her out into the afternoon sunshine. They started walking toward the Cochrans', and after a few minutes of silence, Lisa finally took Alex's hand in her own. "I'm sorry," she said. "I shouldn't have gotten mad."

"That's okay." Alex dropped her hand, and kept walking.

"You mad at me?" Lisa asked.

"No."

"Is something else wrong?"

Alex shrugged, then shook his head.

"Then how come you don't want to hold hands?" Lisa ventured.

Alex said nothing, but wondered silently why holding hands seemed so important to her.

Apparently it was yet something else he didn't remember. Feeling nothing, he ignored her outstretched hand.

Carol Cochran climbed the stairs to Lisa's room, and found her daughter stretched out on the bed staring at the ceiling as the thundering music of her favorite rock group seemed to make the walls shake. Carol went to the stereo and turned the volume down, then perched on the edge of the bed.

"Want to tell me what's wrong, or is it too big a secret?"

"Nothing's wrong," Lisa replied. "I was just listening to my records."

"For three solid hours," Carol told her. "And it's been the same record, over and over, which is driving your father crazy."

Lisa rolled over onto her side and propped her head up on one hand. "It's Alex. He's . . . well, he's just so different. Sometimes he's almost spooky. He takes everything so seriously, you can't even joke with him anymore."

Carol nodded. "I know. I guess you just have to be patient. He might get over it."

Lisa sat up. "But what if he doesn't? Mom, what's happening is terrible."

"Terrible?" Carol repeated.

"It's the other kids," Lisa told her. "They're starting to talk about him. They say all he ever does is ask questions like a little kid."

"We know what that's all about," Carol replied.

Lisa nodded. "I know. But it still doesn't make it any easier."

"For whom?"

Lisa seemed startled by the question, then flopped onto her back again. "For me," she whispered. Then: "I just get so tired of trying to explain him to everyone all the time. And it's not just that, anyway," she added, her voice suddenly defiant.

"Then what is it?"

"I'm not sure he likes me anymore. He . . . he never seems to want to hold hands with me, or kiss me, or anything. He's just . . . oh, Mom, he just seems so cold."

"I know about that, too," Carol sighed. "But it's not just you, honey. He's that way with everyone."

"Well, that doesn't make it any easier."

"No, it doesn't." Carol shook her head, considering what to tell her daughter. Lisa sat against the headboard, drawing her knees up to her chest and wrapping her arms around her legs, as her mother continued. "I'm going to go right on treating Alex the way I always have, and try not to let my feelings get hurt if he doesn't respond the way he used to," she said. "And he may never respond the way he used to. It's a function of the accident. In a way, Alex is crippled now. But he's still Alex, and he's still my best friends' son. If they can get through this, and Alex can get through this, so can I."

"And so can I?" Lisa asked, but Carol shook her head.

"I don't know. I don't even know if you should try. You're only sixteen, and there's no reason at all that you should have to spend your time explaining Alex to anyone or trying to deal with his new personality. There are lots of other boys in La Paloma, and there's no reason why you shouldn't date them."

"But I can't just dump Alex," Lisa protested.

"I'm not saying you should," Carol replied. "All I'm saying is that you have to make certain decisions based on what's best for you. If it's too difficult for you to go on spending so much time with Alex, then you shouldn't do it. And you shouldn't feel badly about it, either."

Lisa's eyes filled with tears. "But I *do* feel bad," she said. "And I don't even know why. I don't know if I don't like him anymore, or if I'm just hurt because I'm not sure he still likes me. And I don't know if I'm getting tired of having to defend him all the time, or if I'm mad at everybody else for not understanding him. Mom, I just don't know what to do!"

"Then don't do anything," Carol told her. "Just take it all day by day, and see what happens. In time, it will all work out."

Lisa nodded, then got up from the bed and went to the stereo, where she changed the record. Then, with her back to her mother, she said, "What if it doesn't work out, Mom? What if Alex never changes? What's going to happen to him?"

Carol rose to her feet and pulled her daughter close. "I don't know," she said. "But in the end, it really isn't your problem, is it? It's Alex's problem, and his parents' problem. It's only yours if you make it yours, and you don't have to. Do you understand that?"

Lisa nodded. "I guess so," she said. She wiped her eyes, and forced a smile. "And I'll be all right," she said. "I guess I was just feeling sorry for myself."

"And for Alex," Carol added. "I know how much you want to help him and how bad it feels not to be able to." She started toward the door. "But there is one thing you can do," she added before she left the room. "Turn that awful music down, so at least your sister can get some sleep. Good night."

" 'Night, Mom." As the door closed, Lisa plugged in her headset, and the room fell silent as the music from the stereo poured directly into her ears.

Alex lay awake late into the night, pondering what had happened at Jake's Place and on the way home afterward. He knew he'd made a mistake, but he still couldn't quite figure it out.

Lisa had wanted to hold hands with him, and even though he didn't understand why, he should have gone ahead and done it anyway. And she had been mad at him, which was another thing he didn't understand.

There was so much that just didn't make any sense.

At the beginning of the week, there had been the strange memories, and the odd pain that had gone through his head when he'd first seen María Torres.

And beyond those things, which he was sure he would eventually figure out, there were the other things, the concepts he was beginning to feel certain he would never understand.

Love.

That was something he couldn't get any kind of grasp on. His mother was always telling him that she loved him, and he didn't really doubt that she did.

The trouble was, he didn't understand what love was. He'd looked it up, and read that it was a feeling of affection.

But, as he had slowly come to understand as he read more, apparently he didn't have feelings.

It was something he was only beginning to be aware of, and he didn't know whether he should talk to Dr. Torres about it or not. All he knew so far was that things seemed to happen to other people that didn't happen to him.

Things like anger.

He knew Lisa had been angry at him this afternoon, and he knew it was a feeling that she got when he did something she didn't approve of.

But what did it *feel* like?

He thought, from what he'd read, that it must be like pain, only it affected the mind instead of the body. But what was it like?

He was beginning to suspect he'd never know, for every day he was becoming more and more aware that something had, indeed, gone wrong, and that he was no longer like other people.

But he was supposed to be like other people. That was the whole idea of Dr. Torres's operation—to make him the way he'd been before.

The problem was that he couldn't remember how he'd been before. If he could remember, it would be easy. He could *act* as though he was the same, and then people wouldn't know he was different.

He was already doing some of it.

He'd learned to hug his mother, and kiss her, and whenever he did that, she seemed to like it.

He'd decided not to act on any of the things he seemed to remember until he'd determined if his memory of them was correct.

And after this afternoon, he'd remember to hold Lisa's hand when they were walking together, and to pay a check if Bob Carey asked him to.

But what about other people? Were there other people he used to borrow money from and loan money to?

Tomorrow, when he saw Lisa, he'd ask her.

No, he decided, he wouldn't ask her. He couldn't keep asking everybody questions all the time.

He'd seen the look on Bob Carey's face when he'd asked Lisa what city she was talking about, and he knew what it meant, even though it hadn't bothered him.

Still, Bob Carey thought he was stupid, even though he wasn't. In fact, after the tests on Monday, he knew he was just the opposite. If anything, he was a lot smarter than everybody else.

He got out of bed and went to the family room. In the bookcase next to the fireplace, there was an *Encyclopaedia Britannica.* He switched on a lamp, then pulled Volume VIII of the Micropaedia off the shelf. A few minutes later, he began reading every article in the encyclopedia that referred to San Francisco.

By the time they got there, he would be able to tell them more about the city than they knew themselves. And, he decided, he would know his way around.

Tomorrow—Friday—he would find a map of San Francisco, and memorize it by the next morning.

Memorizing things was easy.

Figuring out what was expected of him, and then doing it, was not so easy.

But he would do it.

He didn't know how long it would take, but he knew that if he watched carefully, and remembered everything he saw, sooner or later he would be able to act just like everybody else.

But he still wouldn't feel anything.

And that, he decided, was all right. If he could learn to act as though he felt things, it would be good enough.

Already he'd learned that it didn't matter what he was or wasn't.

The only thing that really mattered was what people *thought* you were.

He closed the book and put it back on the shelf, then turned around to see his father standing in the doorway.

"Alex? Are you all right?"

"I was just looking something up," Alex replied.

"Do you know what time it is?"

Alex glanced at the big clock in the corner. "Three-thirty."

"How come you're not asleep?"

"I just got to thinking about something, so I decided to look it up. I'll go back to bed now." He started out of the room, but his father stopped him with a hand on his shoulder.

"Is something bothering you, son?"

Alex hesitated, wondering if maybe he should try to explain to his father how different he was from other people, and that he thought something might be wrong with his brain, then decided against it. If anyone would understand, it would be Dr. Torres. "I'm fine, Dad. Really."

Marsh dropped into his favorite chair, and looked at Alex critically. Certainly the boy *looked* fine, except for his too-bland expression. "Then I think maybe you and I ought to talk about your future, before Torres decides it for us," he suggested.

Alex listened in silence while Marsh repeated his idea of sending Alex into an advanced program at Stanford. As he talked, Marsh kept his eyes on his son, trying to see what effect his words might be having on the boy.

Apparently there was none.

Alex's expression never changed, and Marsh suddenly had the uneasy feeling that Alex wasn't even hearing him. "Well?" he asked at last. "What do you think?"

Alex was silent for a moment, then stood up. "I'll have to talk to Dr. Torres about it," he said. He started out of the room. "Good night, Dad."

For a moment, all Marsh could do was stare at his son's retreating back. And then, like a breaking storm, fury swept over him. *"Alex!"* The single word echoed through the house. Instantly Alex stopped and turned around.

"Dad?"

"What the hell is going on with you?" Marsh demanded. He could feel blood pounding in his veins, and his fists clutched into tight knots at his side. "Did you even hear me? Do you have any idea of what I was saying to you?"

Alex nodded silently, then, as his father's furious eyes remained fixed on him, began repeating Marsh's words back to him.

"Stop that!" Marsh roared. "Goddammit, just stop it!"

Obediently Alex fell back into silence.

Marsh stood still, forcing his mind to concentrate on the soft ticking of the grandfather clock in the corner, willing his rage to ease. A moment later he became vaguely aware that Ellen, too, was in the room now, her face pale, her frightened eyes darting from him to Alex, then back again.

"Marsh?" she asked uncertainly. "Marsh, what's going on?" When Marsh, still trembling with anger, made no reply, she turned to her son. "Alex?"

"I don't know," Alex replied. "He was talking about me going to college, and I said I'd talk to Dr. Torres about it. Then he started yelling at me."

"Go to bed," Ellen told him. She gave him a quick hug, then gently eased him toward the hall. "Go on. I'll take care of your father." When Alex was gone, she turned to Marsh, her eyes damp. When she spoke, her voice was a bleak reflection of the pain she was feeling, not just for her son, but for her husband too. "You can't do this," she whispered. "You know he's not well yet. What do you expect from him?"

Marsh, his anger spent, sagged onto the couch and buried his face in his hands.

"I'm sorry, honey," he said softly. "It's only that talking to him just now was like talking to a brick wall. And then all he said was that he'd talk to Torres about it. Torres!" he repeated bitterly, then gazed up at her, his face suddenly haggard. "I'm his father, Ellen," he said in a voice breaking with pain. "But for all the reaction I get from him, I might as well not even exist."

Ellen took a deep breath, then slowly let it out. "I know," she said at last. "A lot of the time I feel exactly the same way. But we have to get him through it, Marsh. We can't just send him off somewhere. He can barely deal with the people he's known all his life—how would he ever be able to deal with total strangers?"

"But he's so bright . . ." Marsh whispered.

Ellen nodded. "I know. But he's not well yet. Raymond—" She broke off suddenly, sensing her husband's animosity toward the man who had saved Alex's life. "Dr. Torres," she began again, "is helping him, and we have to help him too. And we have to be patient with him, no matter how hard it is." She hesitated, then went on. "Sometimes . . . well, sometimes the only way I can deal with it is to remember that whatever I'm going through, what Alex is going through must be ten times worse."

Marsh put his arms around his wife and pulled her close. "I know," he said. "I know you're right, but I just can't help myself sometimes." A rueful smile twisted his face. "I guess there's a good reason why doctors should never treat their own family, isn't there? Lord knows, my bedside manner deserted me tonight." His arms fell away from Ellen as he stood up. "I'd better go apologize to him."

But when he entered Alex's room, his son was sound asleep. As far as he could see, even his rage hadn't affected the boy. Still, he laid his hand gently on Alex's cheek. "I'm sorry, son," he whispered. "I'm sorry about everything."

Alex rolled over, unconsciously brushing his father's hand away.

CHAPTER 11

At a few minutes past nine on Saturday morning, Bob Carey maneuvered his father's Volvo into the left lane of the Bayshore Freeway, and three minutes later they left Palo Alto behind. Alex sat quietly in the back seat next to Lisa, his ears taking in the chatter of his three friends while his eyes remained glued to the world outside the car. None of it looked familiar, but he studied the road signs carefully as they passed through Redwood City, San Carlos, and San Mateo, then began skirting the edge of the bay. His eyes took in everything, and he was sure that on the return trip that afternoon, even though he would be seeing it all from the other direction, all of it would be familiar.

Then, a little north of the airport, Bob veered off the freeway and started inland.

"Where are we going?" Kate Lewis asked. "We want to go all the way into the City!"

"We're going to the BART station in Daly City," Bob told her.

"BART?" Kate groaned. "Who wants to ride the subway?"

"I do," Bob told her. "I *like* the subway, and besides, I'm not going to drive Dad's car in the City. All I need is to have to try to explain how I smashed a fender on Nob Hill when I was supposed to be in Santa Cruz. I'd wind up grounded lower than Carolyn Evans was."

Kate started to protest further, but Lisa backed Bob up. "He's right," she said. "I had to argue with my folks for half an hour to keep from having to bring Kim along, and if we get caught now, we'll all be in trouble. Besides, I like BART too. It'll be fun!"

Forty minutes later, they emerged from the BART station, and Alex gazed around him, knowing immediately where he was. Yesterday he'd found a tour guide to San Francisco in the La Paloma bookstore, then spent last night studying it. The city around him looked exactly like the pictures in the guidebook. "Let's ride the cable car out to Fisherman's Wharf," he suggested.

Lisa stared at him with surprised eyes. "How did you know it goes there?" she asked.

Alex hesitated, then pointed to the cable car that was just coasting onto the turntable at Powell and Market. On its end was a sign that read "Powell & Mason" and, below that, "Fisherman's Wharf."

They wandered around the wharf, then started back toward the downtown area, through North Beach on Columbus, then turning south on Grant to go into Chinatown. People milled around them, and suddenly Alex stopped dead in his tracks. Lisa turned to him, but he seemed unaware of her. His eyes were gazing intently at the faces of the people around him.

"Alex, what is it?" she asked. All morning, he'd seemed fine. He'd asked a few questions, but not nearly as many as usual, and he'd always seemed to know exactly where he was and where they were going. Once, in fact, he'd even told them where a street they were looking for was, then, when asked how he knew, admitted to having memorized all the street signs while they rode the cable car. But now he seemed totally baffled. "Alex, what's wrong?" Lisa asked again.

"These people," Alex said. "What are they? They don't look like us."

"Oh, Jeez," Bob Carey groaned.

"They're Chinese," Lisa said, keeping her voice as low as she could, and silencing Bob with a glare. "And stop staring at them, Alex. You're being rude."

"Chinese," Alex repeated. He started walking again, but his eyes kept wandering over the Oriental faces around him. "The Chinese built the railroads," he suddenly said. Then: "The railroad barons, Collis P. Huntington and Leland Stanford, brought them in by the thousands. Now San Francisco has one of the biggest Chinese populations outside of China."

Lisa stared at Alex for a moment; then suddenly she knew. "A tour book," she said. "You read a tour book, didn't you?"

Alex nodded. "I didn't want to spend all day asking you questions," he said. "I know you don't like that. So I studied."

Bob Carey's eyes narrowed suspiciously. "You studied? You read a whole guidebook just because we were coming up here for a day?"

Again Alex nodded.

"But who can remember all that stuff? Who even cares? For Christ's sake, Alex, all we're doing is messing around."

"Well, I think it's neat," Kate told her boyfriend. Then she turned to Alex. "Did you really memorize all the streets while we were on the cable car?"

"I didn't have to," Alex admitted. "I got a map, too. I memorized it."

"Bullshit!" Bob's eyes were suddenly angry. "Where's the mission?" he demanded.

Alex hesitated a moment; then: "Sixteenth and Dolores. It's on the corner, and there's a park in the same block."

"Well?" Kate asked Bob. "Is he right?"

"I don't know," Bob admitted, his face reddening. "Who even cares where the mission is?"

"I do," Lisa said, reaching out to squeeze Alex's hand. "How do we get there?"

"Go down to Market, then up to Dolores, and left on Dolores."

"Then let's go."

The little mission with its adjoining cemetery and garden was exactly where Alex had said it would be, crouching on the corner almost defensively, as if it knew it was no more than a relic from the city's long-forgotten past. The city, indeed, had even taken away its original name—San Francisco de Asís. Now it was called Mission Dolores, and it seemed to have taken on the very sadness its name implied.

"Want to go in?" Lisa asked of no one in particular.

"What for?" Bob groaned. "Haven't we all seen enough missions? They used to drag us off to one every year!"

"Well, what about Alex?" Lisa argued. "I bet he doesn't remember ever seeing a mission before. And did you ever see *this* mission? Come on."

Following Lisa, they went into the little church, then out into the garden, and suddenly the city beyond the garden walls might as well have disappeared, for within the little space occupied by the mission, there was no trace of the modern world.

The garden, still kept neatly trimmed after nearly two hundred years, was in the last stages of its summer bloom. Here and there dead leaves had already fallen to the ground, dotting the pathways with bright gold. Off in the far corner, they could see the old cemetery. "Over there," Alex said softly. "Let's go over there."

The quietness of his voice caught Lisa's attention, and she turned to look into Alex's eyes. For the first time since the accident, there seemed to be life in them. "What is it, Alex?" she asked. "You're remembering something, aren't you?"

"I don't know," Alex whispered. He was walking slowly along one of the paths now, but his eyes remained fixed on the weathered headstones of the graveyard.

"The graveyard?" Lisa asked. "Do you remember the graveyard?"

Alex's mind was whirling, and he barely heard Lisa's question. Images were flickering, and there were sounds. But nothing was clear, except that the images and sounds were connected with this place. Trembling slightly, he kept walking.

"What's wrong with him?" Kate asked, her voice worried. "He looks weird."

"I think he's remembering something," Lisa replied.

"We'd better go with him," Bob added, but Lisa shook her head.

"I'll go," she told them. "You guys wait for us, okay?"

Kate nodded mutely, and as Alex stepped into the tiny fenced cemetery, Lisa hurried after him.

The images had begun coming into focus as soon as he'd entered the cemetery. His heart was pounding, and he felt out of breath, as if he'd been running for a long time. He scanned the little graveyard, and his eyes came to rest on a small stone near the wall.

In his mind, there were images of people.

Women dressed in black, their faces framed by white cowls, their feet clad in sandals.

Nuns.

In his mind's eye he saw a group of nuns clustering around a boy, and the boy was himself.

But he was different somehow.

His hair was darker, and his skin had an olive complexion to it.

And he was crying.

Unconsciously Alex moved closer to the headstone that had triggered the strange images, and the images seemed to move with him. Then he was standing at the grave, gazing down at the inscription that was still barely legible in the worn granite:

FERNANDO MELÉNDEZ Y RUIZ

1802–1850

A word flashed into his mind, and he repeated it out loud. "*¡Tío!*" As he uttered the word, a stab of pain knifed through his brain, then was gone.

And then voices began whispering to him—the voices of the nuns, though the images of them had already faded away.

"*Él está muerto.*" He is dead.

And then there was another voice—a man's voice—whispering to him out of the depths of his memory. "*¡Venganza . . . venganza!*"

He stood very still, his eyes brimming with unfamiliar tears, his pulse throbbing. The voice went on, whispering to him in Spanish, but only the one word registered on his mind: "*Venganza.*"

His tears overflowed, and a sob choked his throat. Then, as the strange words pounded in his head, he gave in to the sudden unfamiliar rush of emotion.

Time seemed to stand still, and he felt a kind of pain he couldn't remember having ever felt before. Pain of the heart, and of the soul.

The pain seared at him, and then he became aware of a hand tugging at him, slowly penetrating the chaos in his mind.

"Alex?" a voice said. "Alex, what's wrong? What is it?"

Alex pointed to the grave, sobbing brokenly, and Lisa, after a moment of utter confusion, began to understand what must have happened. She had listened carefully that day last month before Alex came home from the hospital, and she could still remember the words.

"He could start laughing or crying at any time," Alex's mother had told her. "Dr. Torres says it won't matter if something is funny or sad. It's just that it's possible that there will be misconnections in his brain, and he could react inappropriately to something. Or he could simply overreact."

And that, Lisa was certain, was exactly what was happening now. Alex was overreacting to an ancient grave.

But why?

He had remembered something, she had been sure of it. And now he was staring at the grave, tears streaming down his face, uncontrollable sobs racking his body. Gently she tried to pull him away as a priest appeared from the back of the church and looked at them quizzically.

"Something wrong?"

"No," Lisa quickly replied. "Everything's all right. It . . ." She floundered for a moment, trying to think of an explanation for Alex's behavior, but her mind had suddenly gone blank. "Come *on,* Alex," she whispered. "Let's get out of here."

Half-dragging Alex, she edged her way past the priest, then out of the graveyard. Once back in the garden, she put her arms around Alex and squeezed him. "It's all right, Alex," she whispered. "It was only an old grave. Nothing to cry about."

Slowly Alex's sobs began to subside, and he made himself listen to Lisa's words.

Only a grave. But it hadn't been only a grave. He had recognized the grave, as he had recognized the cemetery itself. What he had just experienced, he had experienced before.

The memories were clear in his mind now. He could remember having been in that cemetery, having looked down at the grave, having listened to the nuns telling him his uncle was dead.

His uncle.

As far as Alex knew, he had no uncle.

And certainly he wouldn't remember an uncle who had died in 1850.

But it was all so clear, just as clear as the memory he'd had at school last week. Clear, but impossible.

He took a deep breath, and his last sob released its grip on his throat. Lisa found a handkerchief in her bag and handed it to him. He blew his nose. "What happened?" she asked.

Alex shrugged, but his mind was whirling. It didn't make any sense, and if he told her what had happened, she would think he was crazy. But he had to tell her something. "I'm not sure," he said. "I . . . I remembered something, but I'm not sure what. But it was like I was here before, and something terrible happened. But I can't remember what."

Lisa frowned. "*Were* you ever here before? Maybe something did happen here."

Then, before Alex could say anything else, Bob and Kate moved toward them, their expressions a mixture of worry and uneasiness.

"What happened?" Kate asked. "Are you okay, Alex?"

Alex nodded. "I just remembered something, and it made me cry. Dr. Torres said it might happen, but I didn't really think it would." Lisa looked at him sharply, but said nothing. If he didn't want to tell them what had really happened, she wouldn't either. "Maybe it's a good sign," he said, making himself smile. "Maybe it means I'm getting better."

Kate and Lisa exchanged a glance, each of them realizing what might have to happen. Finally Kate voiced the thought.

"Are you going to tell your folks about it?"

"He can't," Bob said. "If he does, then all our folks will find out what we did, and we'll *all* be in trouble."

"But what if it's important?" Lisa asked. "What if it means something?"

"Why can't he just say it happened at the beach?" Bob suggested. "Besides, what's the big deal about crying in a graveyard? Isn't that what you're supposed to do?"

"I didn't say it was a big deal," Lisa replied. "All I said was that it might mean something, and if it does, none of us should worry about getting into trouble. I just think Alex should tell his folks exactly what happened."

"Well, I think we should vote on it," Bob said. "And I vote he doesn't tell." He looked expectantly at Kate Lewis, whose eyes reflected her uncertainty. Finally she made up her mind, looking away from Bob.

"Lisa's right," she said. "He should tell. And I think we should go home right now."

"I don't," Alex suddenly said. The other three looked at him, puzzled. "I think I should call Dr. Torres and tell him what happened. Maybe he'll want me to stay here."

"Stay here?" Lisa asked. "Why?"

"Maybe something else will happen."

Bob Carey stared at him. "What are you, some kind of a nut? I'm not gonna waste the rest of the day waiting for you to freak out again!"

"Bob Carey, that's just gross!" Lisa said, her voice quivering with anger. "Can't you ever think of anybody but yourself? Why don't you just go away? We can get home without you. Come on!" She grabbed Alex by the hand and began walking quickly toward the church door. Kate hesitated, then started after them.

"Kate—" Bob called, but his girlfriend whirled around and cut his words off.

"Can't you ever think about anybody but yourself? Just once?" She turned and ran to catch up with Lisa and Alex.

They found a phone booth half a block away, and Alex studied the instructions carefully before placing his call. On the second try, he managed to get through to the Institute. While Lisa and Kate fidgeted on the sidewalk outside the booth, he tried to explain to Torres exactly what had happened. When he was finished, Torres was silent for a few seconds, then asked, "Alex, are you sure you remembered that cemetery?"

"I think so," Alex said. "Do you think I should stay here? Do you think I might remember something else?"

"No," Torres said immediately. "I think one experience like that is enough for one day. I want you to go home right away. I'll call your mother and explain what happened."

"She's gonna be pretty mad," Alex replied. "I . . . well, I told her we were going to the beach. She thinks I'm in Santa Cruz."

"I see." There was another silence, and then Torres spoke once more. "Alex, when you lied to your parents about where you were going today, did you know you were doing the wrong thing?"

Alex thought for a few seconds. "No," he said finally. "I just knew that if I told them where we were going, they wouldn't let me go. None of our folks would have."

"All right," Torres said. "We'll talk about all this on Monday. In the meantime, I'll fix things with your mother so you don't get into any trouble. But I don't see how I can do anything for your friends."

"That's okay," Alex said. He was about to say good-bye when Torres's voice came over the wire once more.

"Alex, do you care if your friends get into trouble?"

Alex thought about it, and knew that he was supposed to say yes, because part of having friends was caring what happened to them. But he also knew he shouldn't lie to Dr. Torres. "No," he said. Then: "I don't really care about anybody."

"I see," Torres replied, his voice barely audible. Then: "Well, we can talk about that, too. And I'll see you tomorrow, Alex. We won't wait 'til Monday."

Alex hung up the phone and stepped out of the booth. Kate and Lisa were staring anxiously at him, and a few feet away, Bob Carey stood uncertainly watching them all.

"He wants me to go home," Alex said. "He'll call my mom and tell her what happened." He fell silent, then decided what he should say. "I'll try to get my mom to make it all right with your folks too."

Lisa smiled at him, while Kate Lewis looked suddenly worried. "How are we supposed to get home?" she asked.

"I'll take you," Bob Carey offered. He stepped closer, his eyes fixed on the sidewalk at his feet. Then he hesitantly offered Alex his hand. "I'm sorry about what I said back there. It's just that . . . Aw, shit, Alex, you're just different now, and I don't know what to do. So I just get pissed off."

Alex tried to figure out what he should say, but couldn't remember being apologized to before. "That's okay," he finally replied. "I don't know what to do either, most of the time."

"But at least you don't get pissed off about it, and if anybody has a right to get pissed, I guess you do." Bob grinned, and Alex decided he'd chosen the right words.

"Maybe I will sometime," he offered. "Maybe sometime I'll get really pissed off."

There was a moment of startled silence while his three friends wondered what his words meant. Then the four of them started home.

Marsh Lonsdale hung up the phone. "Well, that's done," he said, "even though I still don't approve of it."

"But, Marsh," Ellen argued, "you talked to Raymond yourself."

"I know," Marsh replied, sighing. "But the whole idea of four kids getting off scot-free after going someplace they knew perfectly well they shouldn't go, and lying about it to boot, just rubs me the wrong way."

"Alex didn't know he shouldn't go to San Francisco—"

"But he knew he shouldn't lie," Marsh said, turning to Alex. "Didn't you?" he demanded.

Alex shook his head. "But I know now," he offered. "I won't do it again."

"And Alex is right," Ellen added. "It isn't fair for the other kids to be punished, and him not. And besides, if they hadn't decided to break all the rules and go up to the City, Alex might not have had this breakthrough."

Breakthrough, Marsh thought. Why was bursting into tears in a graveyard a breakthrough? And yet, when he'd talked to Torres that afternoon, the specialist had assured him that it was, even though Marsh had suggested that it might be simply a new symptom of the damage that still existed in Alex's mind. Still, Marsh was not yet ready to accept Torres's assessment. "And what if it's not a breakthrough?" he asked, then held up his hand to forestall Ellen's interruption. "Don't. I know what Torres said. But I also know that I've never been to Mission Dolores, and I don't think Alex has either. Did you ever take him up there?"

"No, I don't think I did," Ellen admitted. Then she sighed heavily. "Oh, all right, I *know* I didn't. I've never been there either. But I think you might consider the possibility that Alex went there with someone else. His grandparents, for instance."

"I've already called my parents," Marsh told her. "Neither of them can remember ever taking Alex there."

"All right, maybe it was my folks who took him there. For that matter, it could have been anybody." She searched her mind, looking for something—anything—that might explain what had happened to Alex. Then she remembered. "One of his school classes went to San Francisco on a field trip once! Maybe *they* went to the mission. But if Alex remembers it, he remembers it. And I don't see why you can't simply accept that."

"Because it just doesn't make sense. Why, of all the places Alex has been—that we *know* he's been—would he remember a place that as far as either one of us knows, he's never been to at all? I'm sorry, but I just don't think it adds up." He turned back to Alex. "Are you *sure* you really remembered being there before?"

Alex nodded. "As soon as I saw it, I knew I'd seen it before."

"That could have been *déjà vu,*" Marsh suggested. "That happens all the time to everyone. We've talked about it with Dr. Torres."

"I know," Alex agreed. "But this was different. When I went in, I didn't even look around. I just went right into the cemetery, to the grave. And then I started crying."

"All right," Marsh said. He reached over and squeezed Alex's shoulder. "I guess the fact that you cried is really what's important anyway, isn't it?"

Alex hesitated, then nodded. But what about the words he'd heard? Were they important too? Should he have told his parents about seeing the nuns and hearing the voices? No, he decided, not until he'd talked to Dr. Torres about it. "Is it okay if I go to bed now?" he asked, slipping away from his father's touch.

Marsh glanced at the clock. It was only a quarter to ten, and he knew Alex was seldom in bed before eleven. "So early?"

"I'm gonna read for a while."

He shrugged helplessly. "If you want to."

Alex hesitated, then leaned down to kiss his mother. "Good night."

" 'Night, darling," Ellen replied. She watched her son leave the family room, then turned her gaze to Marsh, and immediately knew that the discussion of what had happened that day was not yet over. "All right," she said tiredly. "What is it?"

But Marsh shook his head. "No," he said. "I'm not going to talk about it anymore." Suddenly he grinned, though there was no humor in it. "I guess I've just suddenly fallen victim to a feeling, and I don't like it."

Ellen sat down on the couch next to him and slipped her hand into his. "Tell me," she said. "You know I won't laugh at you—I won't even argue with you. I've had too many feelings myself."

Marsh considered for a moment, then made up his mind. "All right," he said. "I just feel that something's wrong. I can't quite put my finger on it, because I keep telling myself that what I'm feeling is a result of the accident, and the brain surgery, and the fact that I'm not too crazy about the eminent Dr. Torres. But no matter how much I tell myself that, I still have a feeling that there's more. That Alex has changed somehow, and that it's *more* than the brain damage."

"But everything that's happened is consistent with the damage and the surgery," Ellen replied, keeping her voice as neutral as possible and choosing her words carefully. "Alex *is* different, but he's still Alex."

Marsh sighed. "That's just it," he said. "He's different, all right, but I keep getting the feeling that he's *not* Alex."

No, Ellen thought to herself. That's not it at all. You just can't stand the idea that Raymond Torres did something you couldn't have done yourself. Aloud, though, she was careful to give Marsh no clue as to what she'd been thinking. Instead, she smiled at him encouragingly.

"Just wait," she said. "We've had several miracles already. Maybe we're about to have another one."

As she went to bed that night, she decided that when she took Alex down for the special meeting Raymond had asked for tomorrow morning, she'd have a private talk with the doctor.

A talk about Marsh, not Alex.

For María Torres, sleep would not come that night. For hours she tossed in her bed, then finally rose tiredly to her feet, put on her frayed bathrobe, and went into her tiny living room to light a candle under the image of the Blessed Mother. She prayed silently for a while—a silent prayer of thanksgiving that at last the saints were listening to her entreaties, and answering her.

She was sure the answers were coming now, for she had been in the Lonsdales' house all afternoon. She had listened as they talked to their son and heard his story of what had happened at the mission in San Francisco, and like all the *gringos,* they had barely been aware of her presence.

To them, she was nobody, only someone who came in now and then to clean up after them.

But they would find out who she was, now that the saints were listening to her, and had sent Alejandro back at last.

And Alejandro knew her now, and he would listen to her when she spoke to him.

She let the little candle burn out, then crept back to her bed, knowing that sleep would finally come.

She hoped the *gringos,* too, would sleep well tonight. Soon there would be no sleep for them at all.

CHAPTER 12

How come Peter isn't here?" Alex asked. He was lying on the examining table, his eyes closed, while Raymond Torres himself began the task of attaching the electrodes to his skull.

"Sunday," Torres replied. "Even *my* staff insists on a day or two off each week."

"But not you?"

"I try, but every now and then I have to make an exception. You qualify as an exception."

Alex nodded, his eyes still closed. "Because of how I scored on the tests."

There was a short silence, and Alex opened his eyes. Torres was at the control panel, adjusting a myriad of dials. Finally he turned back to Alex. "Partly," he said. "But frankly, I'm more interested in what happened in San Francisco yesterday, and at school on Monday morning."

"It seems like I'm getting some of my memory back, doesn't it?"

Torres shrugged. "That's what we're going to try to find out. And we're also going to try to find out if there's any significance to the fact that even what little you have remembered seems to be faulty."

"But the dean's office used to be where the nurse's office is now," Alex protested. "Mom just told us so."

"True. But apparently it was moved long before you ever went to La Paloma High. So why—and how—did you remember where it used to be, instead of where it is? Even more important, why did you remember Mission Dolores, when you apparently have never been there?"

"But I *could* have been there," Alex suggested. "Maybe yesterday wasn't the first day I sneaked off to San Francisco."

"Fine," Torres agreed. "Let's assume that's the case. Now tell me why you remembered a grave that's over a hundred years old, and thought it was your uncle's grave? You have no uncles, let alone one who's been dead since 1850."

"Well, why did I?"

Torres's brows arched. "According to those exams you took last week, you're smart enough to know better than to ask that question before these tests."

"Maybe I'm not smart," Alex suggested. "Maybe I'm just good at remembering things."

"Which would make you some kind of *idiot savant,*" Torres replied. "And the fact that you just suggested it is pretty good proof that you're more than that." He slid a pair of diskettes into the twin drives of the master monitor, then began preparing a hypodermic. "Peter tells me you woke up early a couple of times," he said, his voice studiedly casual. "How come you never mentioned it?"

"It didn't seem important."

"Can you tell me what it was like?"

Carefully Alex explained the sensations he'd had when coming up from the anesthesia that always accompanied the tests. "But it wasn't unpleasant," he finished. "In fact, it was interesting. None of it made any sense, but I always had the feeling that if I could only slow it down, it *would* make sense." He hesitated, then spoke again. "Why do I have to be asleep when you test my brain?"

"Peter already explained that," Torres replied. He swabbed Alex's arm with alcohol, then plunged the needle into his arm.

Alex winced slightly, then relaxed. "But if it got bad—if I started hurting or something—you could stop the tests, couldn't you?"

"I could, but I won't," Torres told him. "Besides, if you were awake, the very fact that you'd be thinking during the examination would have an effect on the results. In order for the tests to be valid, your brain has to be at rest when they're administered."

Thirty seconds later, Alex's eyes closed and his breathing became deep and slow. Checking all the monitors one more time, Torres left the room.

* * *

In his office, Torres leaned back in his desk chair and began methodically packing his pipe with tobacco. As he carried out the ritual of lighting the pipe, his eyes kept flicking toward the monitor that showed what was happening in the examining room. All, as he had expected, was as it should be, and he would have a full hour alone with Ellen Lonsdale. "I presume you're going to tell me why your husband isn't here this morning?"

Ellen shifted in her chair and nervously crossed her legs, unconsciously tugging at her skirt as she did so. "He's . . . well, I'm afraid we're having a little trouble."

"That doesn't surprise me," Torres commented, concentrating on his pipe rather than Ellen. "I don't mean this as anything against your husband, but a lot of doctors have a great deal of difficulty in dealing with me. In fact," he added, his hypnotic eyes fixing directly on her, "a lot of people have always had difficulty dealing with me." The barest hint of a smile crossed Torres's face. "I'm talking about the fact that I was always considered something of an oddball."

Ellen forced a smile, though she knew his words carried a certain truth. "Whatever you might have been in high school is all over now," she offered. "You were just so bright we were all terrified of you!"

"And, apparently, people still are," Torres replied dryly. "At least your husband seems to be."

"I'm not sure terrified is the right word—" Ellen began.

"Then what would you suggest?" Torres countered. "Frightened? Insecure? Jealous?" He brushed the words aside with an impatient gesture, and his voice grew hard. "Whatever it is—and I assure you it's of no consequence to me—it has to stop. For Alex's sake."

So this was what it was all about. Ellen sighed in relief. "I know. In fact, that's exactly what I wanted to talk to you about today. Raymond, I'm starting to worry about Marsh. This thing with Alex's intellect . . . Well, I hate to say I'm afraid he's going to get fixated on it, but I guess that's exactly what I *am* afraid of!"

"And," Torres added, "you're afraid that he might decide that I have served my purpose. Is that correct?"

Ellen nodded unhappily.

"Well, then we'll just have to see that that doesn't happen, won't we?" Torres smiled at her, and suddenly Ellen felt reassured. There was a strength to the man, a determination to do whatever must be done, that made her feel that whatever happened, he would be able to deal with it. She felt herself begin to relax under his steady gaze.

"Is there anything I can do?"

Torres shrugged, seeming unconcerned. "Until he actually suggests removing Alex from my care, I don't see that either you or I need to do anything. But if the time comes, you can be sure that I will deal with your husband."

Your husband. Ellen repeated the words to herself, and tried to remember if Raymond had ever used Marsh's first name. To the best of her memory, he hadn't. Was there a reason for that? Or was it just Raymond's way?

Suddenly she realized how little she actually knew about Raymond Torres. Practically nothing, really. A thought drifted into her mind: did he feel as strange about his mother working for her as she did? "Raymond, may I ask you a question that has nothing to do with Alex at all?"

Torres frowned slightly, then shrugged. "You can ask me anything, but I might not choose to answer."

Ellen felt herself flush red. "Of course," she said. "It . . . well, it's about your mother. You know, she's working for me now, and—"

"For you?" Torres broke in. Suddenly he put his pipe on the desk and leaned forward, his eyes blazing with interest. "When did that start?"

Ellen gasped with embarrassment. "Oh, God, what have I done? I was sure you'd know."

"No," Torres replied, shaking his head. Then he picked up his pipe and drew deeply on it. "And don't worry," he added. "There is a lot about my mother that I don't know. Frankly, we don't see each other that much, and we don't agree on much, either. For instance, we don't agree on her working."

"Oh, Lord," Ellen groaned. "I'm sorry. I should never have hired her, should I? I didn't really think it was right, but when Cynthia absolutely insisted, I . . . well, I . . ." She fell silent, acutely aware that she had begun babbling.

"Cynthia," Torres repeated, his expression darkening. "Well, Cynthia's always had her way, hasn't she? Whatever Cynthia wanted, she always got, and whatever she didn't want, she always managed to keep well away from her."

Himself, Ellen suddenly thought. *He's talking about himself. He always wanted to go out with Cynthia, and she'd never give him the time of day.* But was he still holding an old grudge? Surely he wasn't, not after twenty years. And then he was smiling again, and the awkward moment had passed.

"As for Mother, no, I didn't know she was working for you, but it doesn't matter. I'm quite capable of supporting her, but she'll have none of it. I'm afraid," he added, his brows arching, "that my mother doesn't quite approve of me. She's very much of the old country, despite the fact that she was born here, as were her parents and grandparents. She has yet to forgive me for my own success. So she supports herself by doing what she's always done, and whom she works for is no concern of mine. If it helps, I think I'd rather have her working for you than for someone else. At least I can count on you to treat her decently."

"I can't imagine anyone not—" Ellen began, but Torres cut her off with a wave of his hand.

"I'm sure everyone treats her fine. But she tends to imagine things, and sees slights where none are meant. Now, why don't we get back to Alex?"

Though Ellen would have liked to talk more of María, the force of Raymond Torres's personality engulfed her, and a moment later, as Torres wished, they were once more deeply involved in the possible meanings of Alex's experiences in San Francisco.

Alex opened his eyes and gazed at the monitors that surrounded him. The tests were over, and today, as he came up from the sedative, there had been none of the strange sounds and images that he had experienced before. He started to move, then remembered the restraints that held him in place so that he couldn't accidentally disturb the labyrinth of wires that were attached to his skull.

He heard the door open, and a few seconds later the doctor was gazing down at him. "How do you feel?"

"Okay," Alex replied. Then, as Torres began detaching him from the machinery: "Did you find out anything?"

"Not yet," Torres replied. "I'll have to spend some time analyzing the data. But there's something I want you to do. I want you to start wandering around La Paloma, just looking at things."

"I've done that," Alex said. As the last of the wires came free, Torres released the restraints, and Alex sat up, stretching. "I've done that a lot with Lisa Cochran."

Torres shook his head. "I want you to do it alone," he said. "I want you just to wander around, and let your eyes take things in. Don't study things, don't look for anything in particular. Just let your eyes see, and your mind react. Do you think you can do that?"

"I guess so. But why?"

"Call it an experiment," Torres replied. "Let's just see what happens, shall we? Something, somewhere in La Paloma, might trigger another memory, and maybe a pattern will emerge."

As his mother drove him home, Alex tried to figure out what kind of pattern Torres might be looking for, but could think of nothing.

All he could do, he realized, was follow Torres's instructions and see what happened.

* * *

After Alex and Ellen left, Raymond Torres sat at his desk for a long time, studying the results of the tests Alex had just taken. Today, for the first time, the tests had been only that, and nothing more.

No new data had been fed into Alex's mind, no new attempts had been made to fill his empty memory.

Instead, the electrical impulses that had been sent racing through his brain had been searching for something that Torres knew had to be there.

Somewhere, deep in the recesses of Alex's brain, there had to be a misconnection.

It was, as far as Torres could see, the only explanation for what had happened to Alex in San Francisco: somehow, during the long hours of the surgery, a mistake had been made, and the result was that Alex had had an emotional response.

He had cried.

Raymond Torres had never intended that Alex have an emotional response again.

Emotions—feelings—were not part of his plan.

CHAPTER 13

"Well, I don't give a damn what Ellen Lonsdale and Carol Cochran say, I say that Kate's grounded for the next two weeks!" Alan Lewis rose shakily to his feet, an empty glass in his hand, and started toward the cupboard where he kept his liquor. "Don't you think you've had enough?" Marty Lewis asked, carefully keeping her voice level. "It's not even noon yet."

"Not even noon yet," Alan sneered in the mocking singsong voice he always took on when his drinking was becoming serious. "For Christ's sake, Mart, it's Sunday. Even you don't have to go to work today."

"At least I go to work all week," Marty replied, and then immediately wished she could retrieve her words. But it was too late.

"Oh, back to that, are we?" Alan asked, wheeling around to fix her with eyes bleary from too much liquor and not enough sleep. "Well, for your information, it just happens that the kind of job I'm qualified for doesn't grow on trees. I'm not like you—I can't just wander out someday and come home with a job. 'Course, when I *do* come home with a job, it pays about ten times what yours does, but that doesn't count, does it?"

Marty took a deep breath, then let it out slowly. "Alan, I'm sorry I said that. It wasn't fair. And we're not talking about jobs anyway. We're talking about Kate."

"Thass what I was talking about," Alan agreed, his voice starting to slur. "You're the one who changed the subject." He grinned inanely, and poured several shots of bourbon into his glass, then maneuvered back to the kitchen table. "But I don't give a damn what we talk about. The subject of our darling daughter is closed. She's grounded, and thass that."

"No," Marty said, "that is not that. As long as you're drunk, any decisions about Kate will be made by me."

"Oh, ho, ho! My, aren't we the high-and-mighty one? Well, let me tell you something, wife of mine! As long as I'm in this house, I'll decide what's best for my daughter."

Marty dropped any effort to cover her anger. "At the rate you're going, you won't be in this house in two more hours! And if you don't pull yourself together, we won't even be able to keep this house!"

Alan lurched to his feet and towered over his wife. "Are you threatening me?"

As his hand rose above his head, a third voice filled the kitchen.

"If you hit her, I'll kill you, Daddy."

Both the elder Lewises turned to see Kate standing in the kitchen doorway, her face streaked with tears but her eyes blazing with anger.

"Kate, I told you I'd take care of this—" Marty began, but Alan cut in, his voice quavering.

"Kill me? You'll kill me? Nobody kills their daddy . . ."

"You're not my father," Kate said, struggling to hold back her tears. "My father wouldn't drink like you do."

Alan lurched toward her, but Marty grabbed his arm, holding him back. "Leave us alone, Kate," she said. "Just go over to Bob's or something. Just for a few hours. I'll get all this straightened out."

Kate gazed steadily at her father, but when she spoke, her words were for her mother. "Will you send him back to the hospital?"

"I . . . I don't know . . ." Marty faltered, even though she already knew that the binge had gone on too long, and there was no other choice. Alan had switched from beer to bourbon on Friday afternoon, and all day yesterday, while Kate had been gone, he'd been steadily drinking. All day, and then all night. "I'll do whatever has to be done. Just leave us alone. Please?"

"Mom, let me help you," Kate pleaded, but Marty shook her head.

"No! I'll take care of this! Just give me a few hours, and when you get back, everything will be fine."

Kate started to protest again, then changed her mind. After the last five years, she knew the last thing her mother needed during one of her father's binges was an argument from her. "All right," she said. "I'll go. But I'll call before I come back, and if he's not gone, I won't come home."

"You won't even leave!" Alan Lewis suddenly roared. "You take one step out of this house, young lady, and you'll regret it!"

Kate ignored him, and walked out into the patio, letting the screen door slam behind her. A moment later she slammed the patio gate as well, and hurried away down the street, her hands clenched into fists as she tried to control her churning emotions.

In the kitchen, Alan Lewis glared drunkenly at his wife. "Well, this is a fine fuckin' mess you've made," he muttered. "A man's wife shouldn't turn his little girl against him."

"I didn't," Marty hissed. "And she's not against you. She loves you very much, except when you get like this. And so do I."

"If you loved me—"

"Stop it, Alan!" Marty's voice rose to a shout. "Just stop it! None of this is my fault, and none of it is Kate's. It's your fault, Alan! Do you hear me? Your fault!" She stormed out of the kitchen and upstairs to the bedroom her husband had never appeared in last night, shutting the door behind her and locking it.

She had to get control of herself. Right now, shouting at him would accomplish nothing. She had to calm herself down and deal with the situation.

He'd be upstairs in a minute, pounding on the door and alternately begging her forgiveness and threatening her. And she'd have to get through it all once more, and try to talk him into letting her drive him to the hospital in Palo Alto to check himself into the alcoholism unit. Or, if worse came to worst, call them herself, and have them come for Alan with an ambulance. That, though, had only happened once, and she prayed it wouldn't happen again.

She went into the bathroom and washed her face with cold water. Any second now, he'd be at the door, and the argument would begin. Only this time, it wouldn't be about Kate. Kate, at least, would be out of it. Now it would be the drinking again.

Five minutes went by, and nothing happened.

Finally Marty opened the bedroom door and stepped out to the landing at the top of the stairs. From below, there was only silence. "Alan?" she called.

There was no answer.

She started down the stairs, pausing at the bottom to call her husband once more. When there was still no answer, she headed for the kitchen. Perhaps he'd passed out.

The kitchen was empty.

Oh, God, Marty groaned to herself. Now what? She poured herself a cup of coffee from the pot she always kept hot on the stove in the hopes that Alan would choose it over alcohol, and tried to figure out what to do.

At least he hadn't taken his car. If he had, she'd have heard him pulling out of the garage. Still, she checked the garage anyway. Both cars were still there.

Maybe she should call the police. No. If he'd taken his car, she would have, but as long as he was on foot, he couldn't hurt anyone. In fact, one of the La Paloma police would probably pick him up within the hour anyway.

Would they bring him home, or take him to the hospital? Or maybe even to jail?

Marty decided she didn't really care. Yesterday, last night, and this morning had been just too exhausting. It was time for Alan to clean up his own messes. She'd call no one, and do nothing about finding him, at least until this evening. Then, if he still wasn't home, she'd start looking.

Her decision made, she began cleaning up the kitchen, starting with Alan's liquor. She drained the half tumbler of bourbon into the sink, then began taking the bottles off the cupboard shelf.

One by one, she emptied them, too, into the drain, and threw the bottles in the trash basket by the back door.

Thirty minutes later, when the kitchen was spotless, she started on the rest of the house.

Alex wandered through the village, doing his best to follow Raymond Torres's instructions to keep his eyes open and his mind clear. But so far, nothing had happened. The village seemed familiar now, and everything seemed to be in the right place, and surrounded by the right things. After an hour, he stopped in a complex of little shops that specialized in the expensive items that so intrigued the computer people in town.

In one window there was a small glass sphere that seemed to have nothing in it but water. Then, when he looked closer, he realized that there were tiny shrimp swimming in the water, and a little bit of seaweed. It was, according to the card next to it, a fully balanced and self-contained ecosystem that would live on in the sealed globe for years, needing only light to survive. He watched it for a few minutes, fascinated, and then a thought came into his head.

It's like my brain. Sealed up, with no way to get at what's inside. A moment later he turned away and continued up La Paloma Drive until he came to the Square.

He stopped to gaze at the giant oak, and found himself wondering if he'd ever climbed the tree, or carved his initials in its trunk, or tied a swing to its lower branches. But if he had, the memories were gone now.

And then, very slowly, things began to change. His eyes fixed on the base of the tree, and everything around him seemed to fade away, almost as if the coastal fog had drifted down from the hillsides and swallowed up everything except himself and the tree.

Once again, as at the mission in San Francisco, images began to come into his mind, and something he had only vaguely remembered when he came home from the Institute was suddenly clearly visible.

There was a rope hanging from the lowest limb of the tree, and at the end of the rope, a body hung.

Whose body?

Around the body, men on horseback were laughing.

And then a sudden pain lashed through his brain, and the whispering began, as it had begun in the cemetery at the mission in San Francisco.

The words were in Spanish, but he understood them clearly.

"They take our land and our homes. They take our lives. Venganza . . . venganza . . ."

The words droned on and on in his mind, and then, finally, Alex turned away from the ancient oak.

Standing a few yards away, staring at him, was María Torres. His eyes met hers, and then she turned and began walking toward the tiny plaza a few blocks away.

As the strange mists gathered closer around him, Alex followed the old woman.

The plaza had changed, but as Alex sat on a rough-hewn bench, María Torres whispering beside him in the Spanish he now clearly understood, it seemed to him that the plaza had always looked this way.

The mission church stood forty yards away, its whitewashed walls glistening brightly in the sunlight. Brown-cassocked priests, their feet clad in sandals, made their way in and out of the sanctuary, and in the shade of the building, three Indians lounged on the ground.

Set at right angles to the church, the little mission school stood with its doors and windows open to the fresh air, and in the schoolyard five children were playing while a black-habited nun looked on, her hands modestly concealed under the voluminous material of her sleeves.

On the other side of the plaza there was a small store, its wood construction in odd contrast to the substantial adobe of the mission buildings. As Alex watched, a woman came out, and though she looked directly at him, seemed not to see him.

He began to listen as María whispered to him of the church and of the brightly painted images of the saints that lined its walls.

Then María began whispering to him of La Paloma and of the people who had built the village and loved it.

"But there were others," she went on. "Others came, and took it all away. Go, Alejandro. Go into the church and see how it was. See what once was here."

As if in a dream, he rose from the bench and crossed the plaza, then stepped through the doors of the sanctuary. There was a coolness inside the church, and the light from two stained-glass windows, one above the door, the other above the altar, danced colorfully on the walls. In niches all around the sanctuary stood the saints María had told him of, and he went to one of them and looked up into the martyred eyes of the statue. He lit a candle for the saint, then turned and once more left the church. Across the plaza, still sitting on the bench, María Torres smiled at him and nodded.

Without a word being spoken, Alex turned, left the plaza, and began walking through the dusty paths of the village, the whispering voices in his head guiding his feet.

Marty Lewis woke up and listened for the normal morning sounds of the house. Then, slowly, she came to the realization that it was not morning at all, and that the house was empty.

A nap.

After Alan had left, and she'd cleaned up the house, she'd decided to take a nap.

She rolled over on the bed and stared at the clock. Two-thirty. She had been asleep for almost three hours. Groaning tiredly, she rose to her feet and went to the window, where she stared out for a moment into the hills behind the house, and wondered if Alan were up there somewhere, sleeping off his bender. Possibly so.

Or he might have walked into the village and be sitting right now at one of the bars, adding fuel to the fires of his rage.

But he wasn't at the Medical Center. If he were, she would have heard from them by now.

She slipped into a housecoat and went downstairs, wondering once more if she should call the police, and once more deciding against it. Without a car, there was little harm Alan could do.

She poured the last of the morning's coffee, thick with having been heated too long, down the drain, and began preparing a fresh pot.

When Alan came home—*if* Alan came home—he was going to be in need of coffee.

She was just about to begin measuring the coffee into the filter when she heard the back gate suddenly open, then close again. Relief flooded through her.

He'd come back.

She went on with her measuring, sure that before she was done the door would open and she would hear Alan's voice apologizing once again for his drunkenness and pleading with her for forgiveness.

But nothing happened.

She finished setting up the coffee maker, turned it on, and, as it began to drip, went to the back door.

Two minutes later, her heart pounding in her throat, she knew what was going to happen to her, and knew there was nothing she could do about it.

Alex blinked, and looked around him. He was sitting on a bench in the plaza, staring across at the village hall and at the black-clad figure of María Torres disappearing down the side street toward the little cemetery and her home.

A thought flitted through his mind: *She looks like a nun. An old Spanish nun.*

Suddenly he became aware of someone waving to him from the steps of the library, and though he wasn't quite sure who it was, he waved back.

But how had he gotten to the plaza?

The last thing he remembered, he'd been at the Square looking at the old oak tree and trying to remember if he'd ever played in it when he was a boy.

And now he was in the plaza, two blocks away.

But he was tired, as if he'd walked a couple of miles, much of it uphill.

He glanced at his watch. It was a quarter past three. The last time he had looked, only a few minutes ago, it was one-thirty.

Almost two hours had gone by, and he had no memory of it. As he started home, his mind began working at the problem. Hours, he knew, didn't simply disappear. If he thought about it long enough, he knew, he would figure out what had happened during those hours, and know why he didn't remember them.

The back door slammed, and Marsh looked up from the medical journal he was reading in time to see Alex come in from the kitchen. "Hi!"

Alex stopped, then turned toward Marsh. "Hi," he replied.

"Where you been?"

Alex shrugged. "Nowhere."

Marsh offered his son a smile. "Funny, that's exactly where I always was when I was your age."

Alex made no response, and slowly the smile faded away from Marsh's face as Alex silently left the room, drifting upstairs toward his own room. A few months ago, before the accident, Alex's eyes would have lit up, and he would have asked where, exactly, nowhere was, and then they would have been off, the conversation quickly devolving into total nonsense on the subject of the exact location of nowhere and just precisely what one was doing when one was doing nothing in the middle of nowhere.

Now there was nothing in his eyes.

For Marsh, Alex's eyes had become symbolic of all the changes that had come over him since the accident.

The old Alex had had eyes full of life, and Marsh had always been able to read his son's mood with one glance.

But now his eyes showed nothing. When he looked into them, all he saw was a reflection of himself. And yet, he had no sense that Alex was trying to hide anything. Rather, it was as if there was nothing there; as if the flatness of his personality had become visible in his eyes.

The eyes, Marsh remembered, had sometimes been referred to as the windows to the soul. And if that was true, then Alex had no soul. Marsh felt chilled by the thought, then tried to banish it from his mind.

But all afternoon, the thought kept coming back to him.

Perhaps Ellen's feeling on that awful night in May had been right after all. Perhaps Raymond Torres had not saved him at all.

Perhaps in a way Alex was truly dead.

CHAPTER 14

Kate Lewis listened to the hollow ringing of the phone long past the time when she knew it was going to go unanswered. For the fourth time in the last hour, she told herself that her mother must have taken her father to the hospital. But if she had, why hadn't she left a message on the answering machine? Why hadn't the answering machine even been turned on? Worried, she hung up the phone at the back of Jake's and returned to the table she and Bob Carey had been occupying throughout the long Sunday afternoon.

"Still nothing?" Bob asked as Kate slid back into the booth.

Kate tried to force a casual shrug, but failed. "I don't know what to do. I want to go home, but Mom said to call first."

"You've been calling all afternoon," Bob pointed out. "Why don't we go up there, and if they're still fighting, we can leave again. We don't even have to go in. But I'll bet she took him to the hospital." He reached across the table and squeezed Kate's hand reassuringly. "Look, if he was as drunk as you said he was, she was probably so busy getting him out of the house and into the car that she didn't have time to turn on the machine."

Kate nodded reluctantly, though she was still unconvinced. Always before, her mother had left a message for her, or if her father was really bad, not even tried to take him to the hospital. Instead, she'd called an ambulance.

And this morning, her father had been really bad. Still, she couldn't just go on sitting around Jake's. "Okay," she said at last.

Ten minutes later they pulled into the Lewises' driveway, and Bob shut off the engine of his Porsche. They stared first at the open garage door and the two cars that still sat inside it. Then they turned their attention toward the house.

"Well, at least they're not fighting," Kate said, but made no move to get out of the car.

"Maybe she called an ambulance, and went with it," Bob suggested.

Kate shook her head. "She would have followed it, so she wouldn't have to call someone for a ride home."

"You want to stay here while I go see if they're home?" Bob asked.

Kate considered a moment, then shook her head. Her hand trembling, she opened the door of the Porsche and got out. With Bob behind her, she started up the walk to the front door.

When she found it unlocked, she breathed a sigh of relief. One thing she was absolutely certain of—her mother would never leave the house unlocked. She pushed the door open and stepped inside.

"Mom? I'm home!" she called out. An empty silence hung over the house, and Kate's heart began beating faster. "Mom?" she called again, louder this time. She glanced nervously at Bob. "Something's wrong," she whispered. "If the door's unlocked, Mom should be here."

"Maybe she's upstairs," Bob suggested. "You want me to go look?"

Kate nodded silently, and Bob started up the stairs. A moment later he was back. "Nobody up there," he told her. "Let's look in the kitchen."

"No," Kate said. Then, her voice quavering, she spoke again. "Let's call the police."

"The police?" Bob echoed. "Why?"

"Because I'm scared," Kate said, no longer trying to control the fear in her voice. "Something's wrong, and I don't want to go into the kitchen!"

"Aw, come on, Kate," Bob told her, starting down the hall toward the closed kitchen door. "Nothing's wrong at all. She probably just called an ambulance and—" He fell silent as he pushed open the kitchen door. "Oh, God," he whispered. For just a moment he stood perfectly still. Then he stepped back and let the door swing closed. He turned unsteadily around, his face ashen. "Kate," he whispered. "Your mom—I think . . . She looks like she's dead."

Kate stared at him for a moment while the words slowly registered in her mind. Then, without thinking, she started down the hall, pushing her way past

Bob and into the kitchen. Wildly, she scanned the room, and then found what she was looking for.

Her knees buckled, and she sank sobbing to the floor.

Roscoe Finnerty glanced up at Tom Jackson. "You okay?"

Jackson nodded. "I can handle it." He stared at Marty Lewis's body for a moment, trying to get a handle on what he was feeling. It wasn't at all like last spring, when he'd almost fallen apart at the sight of Alex Lonsdale's broken body trapped in the wreckage of the Mustang. No, this was different. Except for the look on her face, and the pallor of her skin, this woman could be sleeping. He knelt and pressed his finger to her neck.

She wasn't sleeping.

"What do you think?" he asked, getting to his feet once more.

"Until I talk to the kids, I don't think anything." A siren sounded, and a few seconds later an ambulance pulled into the driveway. Two medics came into the room and repeated the procedure Finnerty and Jackson had gone through when they'd arrived a few minutes earlier. "Don't move her," Finnerty told them. "Just make sure she's dead, then don't do anything till the detectives get up here. Tom, you get outside and make sure none of the rubberneckers try to come inside, and I'll have a talk with the kids."

Finnerty left the kitchen and went back to the living room, where he found Kate Lewis and Bob Carey still sitting on the sofa where he'd left them, Kate sobbing softly while Bob tried to comfort her.

"How's she doing?" Finnerty asked. Bob looked dazedly up at him.

"How do you *think* she's doing?" he demanded, his voice cracking. "Her mom's . . . her mom's . . ." And then he fell silent as his own emotions overcame him and he choked back a sob.

"It's all right," Finnerty told him. "Just try to take it easy." He searched his memory; then it came to him. "You're Bob Carey, aren't you?"

Bob nodded, and seemed to calm down a little.

"Have you called your folks yet? Do they know what's happened?" Bob shook his head. "Okay. I'll call them and have them come over here. Then I'd like to talk to you. Will that be okay?"

"Nothing happened," Bob said. "We just came over here, found her, and called the cops."

Finnerty patted the boy on the shoulder. "Okay. We'll get the details in a little while." He found the phone and the phone book, and spent the next five minutes assuring Dave Carey that his son was all right. Then he went back to the living room.

Slowly he pieced together the story. The longer he listened, the more he was sure he knew what had happened. It was a story he'd heard over and over during his years as a cop, but this was the first time in his experience that the story had ever ended in death. Only when Dave Carey arrived did Finnerty return to the kitchen.

Two detectives were there, and Finnerty watched in silence as they went over the room, methodically looking for clues as to what might have happened there.

"How's it look?" he asked when Bill Ryan finally nodded to him.

Ryan shrugged. "Without talking to anybody, I'd say it was premeditated, and pretty cold. No signs of a fight, no signs of forced entry, no signs of rape."

"If what the kids say is true, it was the husband. He was drunk, and they were having an argument when the girl left this morning. In fact, that's why she left—her father was pissed at her, and her mother was trying to get him to lay off. The girl thinks her mother was going to try to get her father into detox today."

"And he didn't want to go."

"Right."

Suddenly the back door opened, and Tom Jackson appeared, his right arm supporting a bleary-eyed man whose hands were trembling and whose face was drawn. Without being told, Finnerty knew immediately who he was.

"Mr. Lewis?"

Alan Lewis nodded mutely, his eyes fastened on the sheet-covered form on the floor. "Oh, God," he whispered.

"Read him his rights," Ryan said. "Let's see if we can get a confession right now."

"I still can't believe it," Carol Cochran sighed. "I just can't believe that Alan would have killed Marty, no matter how drunk he was."

It was a little after nine, and the Cochrans had been at the Lonsdales' since six-thirty. All through a dispirited dinner which had gone all but untouched, the Cochrans and the Lonsdales had been discussing what had happened in La Paloma that day. Now, as they sat in the still only partially furnished living room, with Lisa and Alex upstairs and Kim asleep in the guest room, the discussion threatened to go on right through the evening.

"Can't we talk about something else?" Ellen wondered, although she knew the answer. All over La Paloma, there was only one thing being talked about tonight: did Alan Lewis kill his wife, or did someone else?

"Don't ever underestimate what a drunk can do," Marsh Lonsdale told Carol, ignoring his wife's question.

"But Alan was always a harmless drunk. My God, Marsh, Alan's not very effectual when he's sober. And when he's drunk, all he does is pass out."

"Hardly," Jim Cochran observed. "Last time I played golf with him, he wrapped his putter around a tree, and took a swing at me when I suggested maybe he ought to lay off the sauce."

"That's still a far cry from killing your wife," Carol insisted.

"But there weren't any signs of a struggle," Marsh reminded her. "As far as the police can tell, Marty knew whoever killed her."

Carol shook her head dismissively. "Marty knew everybody in town, just like all the rest of us. Besides, she always felt safe in that house, although God alone knows why." Her eyes scanned the Lonsdales' living room, and she shuddered slightly. "I'm sorry, but these old places always give me the willies."

"Carol!"

"Honey, Ellen and I have been friends long enough so I don't have to lie to her. Besides, I told her when she first started looking at this place that if she didn't do something drastic to it within six months, I'd never visit her again. I mean, just look at it—it looks like some kind of monastery or something. I always feel that there ought to be chanting going on in the background. And what about the windows? All covered up with wrought iron—like a prison!" Suddenly running out of steam, she fell into a slightly embarrassed silence, then grinned crookedly at Ellen. "Well, it's what I think."

"And in a way, you're right," Ellen agreed. "Except that I happen to like all those things you hate. But I don't see what it has to do with Marty."

"It's just that she always said that old fortress made her feel safe, and look what happened to her."

"Honey," Jim protested, "murders can happen anywhere. It didn't matter where the house was, or what it looked like."

Once more, Carol sighed. "I know. And I also know it looks as though Alan must have done it. But I don't care. I just don't think that's the way it happened at all."

Suddenly Lisa appeared in the wide archway that separated the living room from the foyer, and the four adults fell guiltily silent.

"Are you still talking about Mrs. Lewis?" Lisa asked uncertainly. Her mother hesitated, then nodded. "Can I . . . well, is it all right if I sit down here and listen?"

"I thought you and Alex were listening to some records—"

"I don't want to," Lisa said, and the sharpness in her voice made the Lonsdales and the Cochrans exchange a curious glance. It was Ellen who finally spoke.

"Lisa, did something happen up there? Did you and Alex have a fight about something?" Lisa hesitated, then shook her head, but it seemed to Ellen the girl was holding something back. "Tell us what happened," she urged. "Whatever it is, it can't be so bad that you can't tell us about it. *Did* you two have a fight?"

"With Alex?" Lisa suddenly blurted. "How can you have a fight with Alex? He doesn't care about anything, so he won't fight about anything!" Suddenly she was crying. "Oh, I'm sorry. I shouldn't say that but—"

"But it's true," Marsh said softly. He got up and went to Lisa, putting his arms around her. "It's okay, Lisa. We all know what Alex is like, and how frustrating it is. Now, tell us what happened."

Somewhat mollified, Lisa sat down and dabbed at her eyes with her father's handkerchief. "We were listening to records, and I wanted to talk about Mrs. Lewis, but Alex wouldn't. I mean, he'd talk, but all he'd say were weird things. It's like he doesn't care what happened to her, or who did it. He . . . he doesn't even care that she's dead." Her eyes fixed on her mother. "Mom, he said he never even met Mrs. Lewis, and even if he had, it wouldn't matter. He said everybody dies, and it doesn't make any difference how." Burying her face in her handkerchief, she began sobbing quietly.

There was a long silence in the room. Carol Cochran moved over to sit next to her daughter, while Marsh, his expression cold, gave his wife a long look. "It . . . it doesn't mean anything—" Ellen began, but he cut her off.

"No matter what it means, he doesn't need to say things like that. He's smart enough to keep his mouth shut sometimes." He turned and started toward the foyer and the stairs.

"Marsh, leave him alone," Ellen protested, but it was too late. All of them could hear the echo of his feet tramping up the stairs. Ellen, her voice trembling, turned back to Lisa. "Really, Lisa," she said again, "it doesn't mean anything. . . ."

Marsh walked into Alex's room without knocking, his breath coming in short, angry rasps, and found his son lying on the bed, a book propped against his drawn-up knees. From the stereo, the precise notes of *Eine Kleine Nachtmusik* echoed off the bare walls. Alex glanced up at his father, then put the book aside.

"Are the Cochrans gone?"

"No, they're not," Marsh grated. "No thanks to you. What the hell did you say to Lisa?" Then, before Alex could answer, he went on, his voice icily cold. "Never mind. I know what you said. What I want to know is why you said it. She's down there crying, and I can't say that I blame her."

"Crying? How come?"

Marsh stared at Alex's serene face. Was it possible the boy really didn't know? And then, as he made a conscious effort to bring his breath under control, he realized that it was, indeed, quite possible that Alex didn't know what effect his words would have on Lisa.

"Because of what you said," he replied. "About Mrs. Lewis, and about dying."

Alex shrugged. "I didn't know Mrs. Lewis. Lisa wanted to talk about her, but how could I? If you don't know someone, you can't talk about them, can you?"

"It wasn't just that, Alex," Marsh said. "It was what you said about dying. That everybody dies, and that it doesn't matter how they die."

"But it's true, isn't it?" Alex countered. "Everybody does die. And if everybody dies, why should it be a big deal?"

"Alex, Marty Lewis was murdered."

Alex nodded, but then said, "But she's still dead, isn't she?"

Marsh took a deep breath, and when he spoke, he chose his words carefully. "Alex, there are some things you have to understand, even though they don't have any meaning to you right now. They have to do with feelings and emotions."

"I know about emotions," Alex replied. "I just don't know what they feel like."

"Exactly. But other people do know, and you used to know. And someday, when you're all well again, you'll feel them too. But in the meantime, you have to be careful, because you can hurt people's feelings by what you say."

"Even if you tell them the truth?" Alex asked.

"Even if you tell them the truth. You have to remember that right now, you don't know the full truth about everything. For instance, you don't know that you can hurt people mentally as well as physically. And that's how you hurt Lisa. You hurt her feelings. She cares a great deal about you, and you made her feel as though you don't care about anything."

Alex said nothing. Watching him, Marsh couldn't see whether the boy was thinking about his words or not. And then, once again, Alex spoke.

"Dad, I don't think I do care about anything. Not the way other people do, anyway. Isn't that what's still wrong with me? Isn't that why Dr. Torres says I'll never get well? Because I don't have all those feelings and emotions that other people have, and I never will?"

The hopelessness of Alex's words was only reinforced by the tonelessness of his voice. Suddenly Marsh wanted to reach out and hold Alex as he'd held him when he was a baby. And yet he knew it would do no good. It wouldn't make Alex feel more secure or more loved, for Alex didn't feel insecure, and didn't feel unloved.

He felt nothing. And there was nothing Marsh could do about it.

"That's right," he said quietly. "That's exactly what's wrong, and I don't know how to fix it." He reached out and squeezed Alex's shoulder, though he knew the gesture was much more for himself than for Alex. "I wish I could fix it, son. I wish I could help you be the way you used to be, but I can't."

"It's all right, Dad," Alex replied. "I don't hurt, and I don't remember what I used to be like."

Marsh tried to swallow the lump that had formed in his throat. "It's okay, son," he managed to say. "I know how hard everything is for you, and I know how hard you're trying. And we'll get you through all this. I promise. Some way, we'll get you through." Then, unwilling to let Alex see him cry, Marsh left the room, pulling the door closed behind him.

Ten minutes later, when he had his emotions back under control, he went downstairs.

"He's sorry," he told Lisa and her parents. "He says he's sorry about what he said, and he didn't really mean it." But a few minutes later, as the Cochrans left, he wondered if anyone had believed his words.

Alex woke up, and for a moment didn't realize where he was. And then, as the walls of his room came into focus, so also did the dream that had awakened him.

He remembered the details, which were as clear in his mind as if he had just experienced them, yet there was no beginning to the dream.

He was just there, in a house very much like the one he lived in, with white plaster walls and a tile floor in the kitchen. He was talking to a woman, and even though he didn't know the woman, did not recognize her face, he knew it was Martha Lewis.

And then there was a sound outside, and Mrs. Lewis went to the back door, where she spoke to someone. She opened the door and let the other person in.

For a moment Alex thought the other person was himself, but then he realized that although the boy resembled him, his skin was darker, and his eyes were almost as black as his hair. And he was angry, though he was trying not to show it.

Mrs. Lewis, too, seemed to think the other boy was Alex, and she was ignoring Alex now, talking only to the other boy, and calling him Alex.

She offered the boy a Coke, and the boy took it. But then, after he'd taken only a couple sips of the Coke, he set it down on the table and abruptly stood up.

Muttering softly, his eyes blazing with fury, he started toward Mrs. Lewis, and began killing her.

Alex remained still in the corner of the kitchen, his eyes glued to the scene that was being played out a few feet away.

He could feel the pain in Mrs. Lewis's neck as the dark-skinned boy's fingers tightened around it.

And he could feel the terror in her soul as she began to realize she was going to die.

But he could do nothing except stand where he was, helplessly watching, for as he endured the pain Mrs. Lewis was feeling, he was also enduring the pain of the thought that kept repeating itself in his brain.

It's me. The boy who is killing her is me.

And now, fully awake, the thought stayed with him, as did the memory of the feelings he'd had during the killing he'd watched.

Feelings. Emotions.

Pity for Mrs. Lewis, anger toward the boy, fear of what might happen after the murder was done.

Then, just as Mrs. Lewis died and Alex woke up, the emotions were gone. But the memory of them remained. The memory, and the image of the killing, and the words the boy had spoken as he killed.

Alex got out of bed and went downstairs. In the back of the third volume of the dictionary, he found the translation of the words the boy had repeated over and over again.

Venganza . . . vengeance.

Ladrones . . . thieves.

Asesinos . . . murderers.

But vengeance for what?

Who were the thieves and murderers?

None of it made any sense to him, and even though he'd recognized her in his dream, Alex still couldn't remember ever meeting Martha Lewis.

Nor did he know Spanish.

Then the boy in the dream couldn't have been him.

It was just a dream.

He put the dictionary back on the shelf, then took himself back to bed.

But the next morning, when he opened up the La Paloma *Herald*, he stared at the picture of Martha Lewis for a long time.

It was, without any question, the woman he had seen in his dream.

CHAPTER 15

On the morning of Martha Lewis's funeral, Ellen Lonsdale woke early. She lay in bed staring out the window at the cloudless California sky. It was not, she decided, the right kind of day for a funeral. On this, of all mornings, the coastal fog should have been hanging over the hills above La Paloma, reaching with damp fingers down into the village below. Beside her, Marsh stirred, then opened one eye.

"You don't have to get up yet," Ellen told him. "It's still early, but I couldn't sleep."

Marsh came fully awake, and propped himself up on one elbow. He reached out a tentative finger to touch the flesh of Ellen's arm, but she shrank away from him, threw back the covers, and got out of bed.

"Do you want to talk about it?" he asked, though he knew full well that she didn't. If she wanted to talk to anybody, it would be Raymond Torres. Increasingly he was feeling more and more cut off from both his wife and his son.

As Marsh had expected, Ellen shook her head. "I'm just not sure how much more I can cope with," she said, then forced a smile. "But I will," she went on.

"Maybe you shouldn't," Marsh suggested. "Maybe you and I should just take off for a while, and see if we can find each other again."

Ellen stopped dressing to face Marsh with incredulous eyes. "Go away? How on earth can we do that? What about Alex? What about Kate Lewis? Who's going to take care of them?"

Marsh shrugged; then he, too, got out of bed. "Valerie Benson's been taking care of Kate, and she can go right on doing it. Hell, at least it gives her something better to do than whine about how she never should have gotten a divorce."

"That's a cruel thing to say—"

"It's not cruel, honey," Marsh interrupted. "It's true, and you know it. As for Alex, he's quite capable of taking care of himself, even if he isn't like he used to be. But you and I are having a problem, whether we want to face it or not." For a split second Marsh wondered why it was all going to come out now, and if he should try to hold his feelings in. But he knew he couldn't. "Did you know you don't talk to me anymore? For three days now, you've barely said a word, and before that, all you were doing was telling me what Raymond Torres had to say about how we should run our lives. Not just Alex's life, but ours too."

"There's no difference," Ellen said. "Right now, Alex's life *is* our life, and Raymond knows what's best."

"Raymond Torres is a brain surgeon, and a damned fine one. But he's not a shrink or a minister—or even God Almighty—even though he's trying to act as though he is."

"He saved Alex's life—"

"Did he?" Marsh asked. He shook his head sadly. "Sometimes I wonder if he saved Alex, or if he stole him. Can't you see what's happening, Ellen? Alex isn't ours anymore, and neither are you. You both belong to Raymond Torres now, and I'm not sure that isn't exactly what he wants."

Ellen sank onto the foot of the bed and put her hands over her ears, as if by shutting out the sound of Marsh's voice she could shut out the words he'd spoken as well. She looked up at him beseechingly. "Don't do this to me, Marsh," she pleaded. "I have to do what I think is best, don't I?"

She looked so close to tears, so defeated, that Marsh felt his bitterness drain away. He knelt beside his wife and took her hands, cold and limp, in his own. "I don't know," he said quietly. "I don't know what any of us has to do anymore. All I know is that I love you, and I love Alex, and I want us to be a family again."

Ellen was silent for a moment, then slowly nodded. "I know," she said at last. "But I just keep wondering what's coming next."

"Nothing's next," Marsh replied. "There's no connection between Alex and Marty Lewis. What happened to Alex was an accident. Marty Lewis was murdered, and unless Alan can come up with something better than 'I don't remember anything,' I'd say he's going to be tried for it, and found guilty."

Ellen nodded glumly. "But I keep having a feeling that there's more to it than that. I keep getting this strange feeling that there's some kind of curse hanging over us."

"That," Marsh told her, "is the silliest thing I've heard in months. There's no such thing as curses, Ellen. What's happening to us is life. It's as simple as that."

But it's not, Ellen thought as she finished dressing, then went downstairs to begin fixing breakfast. In life, you raise your family and enjoy your friends. Everything is ordinary. But Alex isn't ordinary, and someone killing Marty isn't ordinary, and getting up every morning and wondering if you're going to get through the day isn't ordinary.

She glanced at the clock. In another five minutes Marsh would be down, and a few minutes later, Alex, too, would appear. That, at least, was ordinary, and she would concentrate on that. In her mind, she began to make a list of things she could do that would make her life seem as unexceptional and routine as it once had been, but by the time Marsh and Alex appeared, she had come up with nothing. She poured them each a cup of coffee, and kissed Alex on the cheek.

He made no response, and, as always, a pang of disappointment twisted at her stomach.

She mixed up a can of frozen orange juice and poured a glass for her husband and one for her son. It was then that she noticed that Alex was dressed for school, not for Marty Lewis's funeral.

"Honey, you're going to have to change your clothes. You can't wear those to the funeral."

"I decided I'm not going," Alex said, draining his glass of orange juice in one long gulp.

Marsh glanced up from the front page of the paper. "Of course you're going," he said.

"Alex, you *have* to go," Ellen protested. "Marty was one of my best friends, and Kate's always been a friend of yours."

"But it's stupid. I didn't even know Kate's mother. Why should I go to her funeral? It doesn't mean anything to me."

Ellen, too stunned by Alex's words to respond, slid the muffins under the broiler, and reminded herself of what Raymond Torres had told her over and over again: Don't get upset. Deal with Alex on his own level, a level that has nothing to do with feelings. She searched her mind, trying to find something that would reach him.

There was so little, now.

More and more, she was realizing that relationships—Alex's as well as her own and everyone else's—were based on feelings: on love, on anger, on pity, on all the emotions that she'd always taken for granted, and that Alex no longer had. And slowly, all his relationships were disappearing. But how could she stop it? Her thoughts were interrupted by Marsh's voice. She turned to see him staring angrily at Alex.

"Does it make any difference that we'd like you to go?" she heard him ask. "That it would mean a lot to us for you to be there with us?" He sat back, his arms folded across his chest, and Ellen knew he was going to say no more until Alex came up with some kind of answer to his question.

Alex sat still at the table, analyzing what his father had just said.

He'd made a mistake, just as he'd made a mistake with Lisa the other night. He could see from the look on his father's face that he was angry, and now he had to figure out why.

And yet, in his mind, he knew why.

He'd hurt his mother's feelings, so his father was angry.

He was starting to understand feelings, ever since the dream he'd had about Mrs. Lewis. He could still remember how he'd felt in the dream, even though he'd felt nothing since. At least he now had the memory of a feeling. It was a beginning.

"I'm sorry," he said quietly, knowing the words were what his father wanted to hear. "I guess I wasn't thinking."

"I guess you weren't," his father agreed. "Now, I suggest you get yourself upstairs and into your suit, and when you go to that funeral—which you will do—I will expect you to act as if you care about what happened to Marty Lewis. Clear?"

"Yes, sir," Alex said. He rose from the table and left the kitchen. But as he started up the stairs, he could hear his parents' raised voices, and though the words were indistinct, he knew what they were talking about.

They were talking about him, about how strange he was.

That, he knew, was what a lot of people talked about now.

He knew what happened when he came into a room.

People who had been talking suddenly stopped, and their eyes fixed on him.

Other people simply looked away.

Not, of course, that it bothered him. The only thing that bothered him was the dream he'd had, but he still hadn't figured out what it meant, except that it seemed that if he had feelings in his dreams, he should, sooner or later, have them when he was awake, too. And when he did, he'd be like everyone else.

Unless, of course, he really had killed Mrs. Lewis.

Maybe, after all, there was a reason to go to the funeral. Maybe if he actually saw her body, he'd remember whether or not he had killed her.

Alex stepped through the gate of the little cemetery, and immediately knew that something was wrong.

It was happening again.

He had a clear memory of this place, and now it no longer looked as it should have.

The walls were old and worn, and the lawn—the soft grass that the priests always tended so well—was gone. In its place was barren earth, covered only in small patches by tiny clumps of crabgrass.

The tombstones, too, didn't look right. There were too many of them, and they, like the walls, seemed to have worn away so he could barely read the names on them. Nor were there flowers on the graves, as there always had been before.

He gazed at the faces of the people around him. None of them were familiar.

All of them were strangers, and none of them belonged here.

Then the now-familiar pain slashed through his brain, and the voices started, whispering in his ears.

"*Ladrones . . . asesinos . . .*"

Suddenly he had an urge to turn around and run away. Run from the pain in his head, and the voices, and the memories.

He felt a hand on his arm, and tried to pull away, but the grip tightened, and the touch of strong fingers gouging into his flesh suddenly cut through the voices.

"Alex," he heard his father whisper. "Alex, what's wrong?"

Alex shook his head, and glanced around. His mother was looking at him worriedly. A few feet away he recognized Lisa Cochran with her parents. He scanned the rest of the crowd: Kate Lewis stood next to the flower-covered coffin, with Valerie Benson at her side. Over by the wall, he recognized the Evanses.

"Alex?" he heard his father say again.

"Nothing, Dad," Alex whispered back. "I'm okay."

"You're sure?"

Alex nodded. "I just . . . I just thought I remembered something, that's all. But it's gone now."

His father's grip relaxed, and once more Alex let his eyes wander over the cemetery.

The voices were silent now, and the cemetery suddenly seemed right again.

And why had he thought about priests?

He gazed up at the village hall that had once been a mission, and wondered how long it had been since there had been priests here. Certainly there hadn't been any since he was born.

Then why had he remembered priests tending the cemetery?

And why had all the faces of the people looked strange to him?

The words that had been whispered in the depths of his mind came back to him.

"Thieves . . . murderers . . ."

The words from his dream. All that was happening was that he was remembering the words from his dream. But deep in his mind, he knew that it was more. The words had meaning, and the dream had meaning, and all of it was more than dreams and false memories.

All of it, some way, was real, but he couldn't think about it now. There were too many people here, and he could feel them watching him. He had to act as if nothing was wrong.

He forced himself to concentrate on the funeral then, focusing on the coffin next to the grave.

And then, once more, he heard his father's voice.

"What the hell is that son of a bitch doing here?"

He followed his father's eyes. A few yards away, standing alone, he saw Raymond Torres.

He nodded, and Torres nodded back.

He's watching me, Alex suddenly thought. He didn't come here for the funeral at all. He came here to watch me.

Deep in his mind, at the very edges of his consciousness, Alex felt a sudden flicker of emotion.

It was so quick, and so unfamiliar, that he almost didn't recognize it. But it was there, and it wasn't a dream. Something deep inside him was coming alive again—and it was fear.

"How are you, Alex?" Raymond Torres's hand extended. Alex took it, as he knew he was expected to. The funeral had ended an hour ago, and most of the people who had been there were gathered in Valerie Benson's patio, talking quietly, and searching for the right words to say to Kate. Alex had been sitting alone, staring at a small fishpond and the waterfall that fed it, when Torres had approached.

"Okay," he said, feeling the doctor's sharp eyes on him.

"Something happened at the cemetery, didn't it?"

Alex hesitated, then nodded. "It . . . well, it was sort of like what happened up in San Francisco."

Torres nodded. "I see. And something happened here, too." A statement, not a question.

Alex hesitated, then nodded. "The same thing. I came in, and for a minute I thought I recognized the house, but it's different than I remember it. It's the fishpond. The whole patio looked familiar, except the fishpond. I just don't remember it at all."

"Maybe it's new."

"It doesn't look new," Alex replied. "Besides, I asked Mrs. Benson about it, and she said it's always been here."

Again Torres nodded. "I think you'd better come down tomorrow, and we'll talk about it."

Suddenly his father appeared at his side. Alex felt his father's arm fall over his shoulders, but made no move to pull away. "He'll be going to school tomorrow," he heard his father say.

Torres shrugged. "After school's fine."

Marsh hesitated. Every instinct in him was telling him to inform Torres that he wouldn't be bringing Alex to him at all anymore.

But not here. He nodded curtly, making a mental note to clear his schedule tomorrow so that he could take Alex to Palo Alto himself. "That will be fine." And tomorrow afternoon, he added to himself, you and I will have our last conversation. Keeping his arm around Alex's shoulder, he started to draw his son away from Torres, but Torres spoke again.

"Before you make any decisions, I'd like to suggest that you read the waiver you signed very carefully." Then Torres himself turned and strode out of the patio. A moment later, a car engine roared to life, and tires squealed as Torres shot down the road.

As he drove out of La Paloma, Raymond Torres wondered if it had been a mistake to go to Martha Lewis's funeral after all. He hadn't really intended to go. It had been years since he was part of La Paloma, and he knew that he would be something of an intruder there.

And that, of course, was exactly what had happened. He'd arrived, and recognized many of the faces, but most of the people hadn't even acknowledged his presence. It was just as his mother had told him it would be when he stopped to see her before going into the cemetery.

"*Loco,*" she had said. "You are my son, but you are *loco.* You think they want you there? Just because you have a fancy degree, and a fancy hospital all your own, you think they will accept you? Then go! Go let them treat you the way they always did. You think they've changed? *Gringos* never change. Oh, they won't say anything! They'll be polite. But see if any of them invite you to their homes." Her eyes had flashed with fury, and her body had quivered with the pent-up anger of the years. "Their homes!" she had spit. "The homes they stole from our ancestors!"

"That was generations ago, Mama," he had protested. "It's all forgotten. None of these people had anything to do with what happened a hundred years ago. And I grew up with Marty."

"Grew up with her," the old woman had scoffed. "*Sí,* you grew up with her, and went to school with her. But did she ever speak to you? Did she ever treat you like a human being?" María Torres's eyes had narrowed shrewdly. "It's not for her you go to the funeral. It's something else. What, Ramón?"

Under his mother's penetrating gaze, Raymond Torres found his carefully maintained self-confidence slipping away. How did she know? How did she know that his interest in the funeral went beyond the mere paying of respects to the memory of someone he'd known long ago? Did she know that deep in his heart he wanted to see the pain in the eyes of Martha Lewis's friends, see the bewilderment on Cynthia Evans's face, see all of them suffering as he'd suffered so many years ago? No, he decided, she couldn't know all that, and he would never admit it to her.

"It's Alex," he had finally told her. "I want to see what happens to him at the funeral." He told her about Alex's experience in San Francisco, and the old woman nodded knowingly.

"You don't know whose grave that was?" she asked. "Don Roberto had a brother. His name was Fernando, and he was a priest."

"Are you suggesting that Alex Lonsdale saw a ghost?" he asked, his voice betraying his disbelief in his mother's faith.

The old woman's eyes glittered. "Do not be so quick to scoff. There are legends about Don Roberto's family."

"Among our people, there are legends about everything," Torres replied dryly. "In fact, that's about all we've got left."

"No," María had replied. "We have something else. We have our pride, too. Except for you. For you, pride was never enough. You wanted more—you wanted what the *gringos* have, even if it meant becoming one of them to get it. And now you have tried, and you have failed. Look at you, with your fancy cars, and your fancy clothes, and *gringo* education. But do they accept you? No. And they never will."

And so he had left the little house he had been born in. His mother had been right. He had felt out of place at the funeral, even though he knew almost everyone there.

But he was right to have gone.

Something *had* happened to Alex Lonsdale. For a few moments, before his father had grasped his arm, Alex's whole demeanor had changed.

His eyes had come to life, and he had seemed to be listening to something.

But what?

Raymond Torres thought about it all the way back to Palo Alto. When he reached the Institute, he went directly to his office and began going over the records of Alex's case once more.

Somewhere, something had gone wrong. Alex was showing more signs of emotional behavior.

If it went too far, it would destroy everything, including Alex himself.

CHAPTER 16

Alex stood in the middle of the plaza, waiting for the pain to strike his brain, and the strange memories that didn't fit with the real world to begin churning through his mind. He gazed intently at the old buildings that fronted on the plaza, searching for the unfamiliar details that he had expected to find in them. But nothing struck a chord. The buildings merely looked as they had always looked—a village hall that had once been a mission church, and a library that had once been a school.

No voices whispered in his head, and no pain racked his mind. It was all as it had been throughout his lifetime.

When he was at last certain that nothing in the plaza or the buildings around it was going to trigger something in his mind, he walked slowly into the library and approached the desk. Arlette Pringle, who had been librarian in La Paloma for thirty years, raised her brows reprovingly.

"Did someone declare a holiday without telling me, Alex?"

Alex shook his head. "I went to Mrs. Lewis's funeral this morning. And this afternoon . . . well, there's some things I need to look up, and the school library can't help me."

"I see." Arlette Pringle tried to figure out whether Alex had just told her a very smooth lie—and after thirty years of dealing with the children of La Paloma as well as their parents, she thought she'd heard them all—or if he really was working on a school project and was here with the blessing of his teachers. Then she decided it really didn't matter at all. So few of the kids came to the library anymore that a young face was welcome under any circumstances. "Can I help you find anything?"

"The town," Alex said. "Are there any books about the history of La Paloma? I mean, all the way back, when the fathers first came?"

Arlette Pringle immediately nodded, and opened the locked case behind her desk. She pulled out a leather-bound volume and handed it to him. "If it's the old history you're after, this is it. But it was printed almost forty years ago. If you need anything more up-to-date, I'm afraid you're out of luck."

Alex glanced at the cover of the thin oversized book, then opened it to study the first page. Superimposed over an ink drawing of the plaza was the title: *La Paloma: The Dove of the Peninsula.* On the next page was a table of contents, and after scanning it, Alex knew he'd found what he was looking for. "Can I check this out?"

Miss Pringle shook her head. "I'm sorry, but it's the only copy we have, and it can't be replaced. I even made Cynthia Evans sit right here every time she had to refer to it for the hacienda." When Alex looked puzzled, Arlette Pringle suddenly remembered what she'd been told about Alex's memory. "For the restoration," she went on. "In fact, after you read about it, you might want to go up to the Evanses' and see what they've done. On the outside, at least, it's exactly as it used to be." The front door opened, and Arlette instinctively glanced toward it. "If you have any questions, I'll be here," she finished, then turned to the new arrival as Alex settled himself at one of the heavy oak tables that graced the single large room of the library.

The book, as he paged through it, proved to be primarily a collection of old pictures of the early days of La Paloma, accompanied by a sketchy narrative of the history of the town, beginning with the arrival of the Franciscan fathers in 1775, the Mexican land grants to the Californios in the 1820's, and the effect of the Treaty of Hidalgo Guadalupe in 1848. An entire chapter dealt with the story of Roberto Meléndez y Ruiz, who was hanged after attempting to assassinate an American major general. After the hanging, his family abandoned their hacienda in the hills above La Paloma and fled back to Mexico, while the rest of the Californios quickly sold their homes to the Americans, and followed.

The rest of the book was devoted to detailed drawings of the mission, the hacienda, and the homes of the Californios. It was the drawings that commanded Alex's attention.

There was page after page of floor plans and elevations of all the old houses that still stood in and around the village. For many of them, there were accompanying photographs as well, showing how the houses had been altered and modified over the years.

Near the end of the book, Alex found his own house, and stared at the old drawings for a long time. Little had changed over the years—of all the houses in La Paloma, the Lonsdales' alone seemed to have survived in its original condition.

Except for the wall around the garden.

In the detailed drawings of the house that had been done by one of the priests shortly after the mission had lost its lands to the Californios, the patio wall was shown in great detail, complete with intricately tiled insets at regular intervals along its main expanse. Between the insets, set with equal precision, were small, well-clipped vines, espaliered on small trellises. Alex studied the picture carefully.

It was exactly as he had thought the wall should look when his parents had first brought him home from the Institute. But in the photograph of the same wall, taken forty-odd years ago, the vines had long since grown wild, covering the wall with a tangle of vegetation that completely obliterated the insets.

On the next page, he found Valerie Benson's house. It bore little resemblance to what it had once been. Over the years, it had twice burned, and both times, during the rebuilding, walls had been moved and roof lines changed. The only thing that had not been altered beyond recognition was the patio, but even that had not completely survived the remodeling.

In 1927, a fishpond, fed by a waterfall, had been added.

Once again Alex studied the old drawing and the more recent photograph.

Once again it was the old drawing that looked right to him, that depicted the patio as he'd thought he remembered it only that morning.

He closed the book, and sat still for several minutes, trying to find an answer to the puzzle that was forming in his mind. At last he stood up and carried the volume over to Arlette Pringle's desk. The librarian took it from him and carefully slid it back into its position in the locked cabinet behind her desk.

"Miss Pringle?" Alex asked. "Is there any way to tell when the last time I looked at that book was?"

Arlette Pringle pursed her lips. "Why, Alex, what on earth would you want to know that for?"

"I . . . well, I don't remember so many things, but some of the things in that book look kind of familiar. And I just thought it might help if I could find out when the last time I looked at it was."

"Well, I don't know," Miss Pringle mused, wondering if it was worth her while to dig through the old records of the locked cabinet. Then, remembering once more what had happened to Alex only a few months ago, she made up her mind. "Of course," she said. "If it were in the open stacks, it would be impossible, but I keep records of every book that goes in and out of that cabinet. Let's have a look." From the bottom drawer of her desk she took a thick ledger and began flipping through its pages. A minute later she smiled bleakly at Alex. "I'm sorry, Alex. According to my records, you've never seen that book before. In fact, nobody but Cynthia Evans has looked at it for the last five years, and before that, you and your friends were all so young I wouldn't have let you touch it anyway."

Alex frowned, then wordlessly turned and left the library. He walked home slowly, lost in thought. As he approached his house he finally made up his mind, and, though he was already tired, trudged on up Hacienda Drive.

He stopped once to rest, at the curve where only a few months ago his car had crashed through the safety barrier and plunged into the canyon below. He stayed there for nearly half an hour, searching his mind for memories of the crash.

He knew what had happened: he'd been told the details many times since he'd awakened in the hospital. There had been a party, and he and Lisa had had a quarrel, and she had left. A few minutes later he'd gone after her, but he'd been driving too fast, and had to swerve to avoid hitting her. And that was when he'd gone off the road.

But something seemed to be missing. Deep in his mind, he was sure there was one more image—a fleeting glimpse of something he couldn't quite grasp—that was the real reason for his accident.

Somehow, he knew that there was more to it than avoiding Lisa. There had been something else—some*one* else—whom he had also swerved to avoid.

But who? He couldn't bring the image into focus, couldn't quite identify it.

Struggling to his feet, he went on toward the Evanses' mansion and the hills beyond.

Marsh Lonsdale sat in the records office of the Medical Center and punched angrily at the keys of the computer. The screen sat like a Cyclops on the desk in front of him. There were times, of course, when he thanked all the various gods he could think of for the computer system that had been put in the Center five years earlier, but there were times—and this was one of them—when he wished that the microprocessor had never been invented.

"You have to have a special degree just to operate this damned thing," he muttered. From the file cabinet, Barbara Fannon smiled sympathetically.

"It doesn't respond to cursing," she told him. "Why don't you tell me what you're looking for, and I'll pull it up for you." Gently nudging him aside, she sat down and put her fingers on the keyboard.

"Alex," Marsh said. "All I want is the medical records for my own son, and this damned machine won't give them to me."

"Don't be silly," Barbara told him. "You just have to ask it politely, in terms it understands." She tapped at the keyboard for a few moments, and the screen came to life. "There you are. Just push this button, and it will scroll right on down, from the day he was born until the last time he was here." She stood up, relinquishing the chair to Marsh once again, and went back to her filing.

Marsh began scrolling through the record, paying little attention to anything until he suddenly came to the end of the file. The last entry was for a routine checkup that Alex had undergone the previous April. He gazed irritably at the screen for a moment, then glared at Barbara Fannon's back. "Are we really five months behind in the records?"

"I beg your pardon?"

"I asked if we're really five months behind in the records," Marsh repeated. "This is September, and the last entry in Alex's file is for his checkup in April. That's five months."

"That's ridiculous," Barbara replied. "We haven't even been twenty-four hours behind in the last three years. Usually everything that happens to a patient is in the records within two or three hours. Let me see." She bent over Marsh's shoulder and began tapping on the keyboard once more, but this time nothing happened. The record simply came to an abrupt end.

"See?"

"I see that something's wrong, and it could be any number of things. Now, why don't you just go back to your office and get back to administering this place, and I'll figure out what's happened to Alex's records. If I can't get them out of the computer, I'll bring you the originals from downstairs, but that will take a while. All right?"

Reluctantly Marsh got up and started out of the office, but Barbara Fannon stopped him. "Marsh, is something wrong? With Alex, I mean?"

"I don't know," Marsh replied. "I just have a bad feeling about him, and I don't like Torres. I want to go over his records and see exactly what was done, that's all."

"All right," Barbara Fannon sighed. "Then at least I know what I'm looking for. I'll have something for you as soon as possible."

But an hour later, when she came into his office, her expression was both puzzled and worried. "I can't find them," she said.

Marsh looked up from the report he was revising. "They're not in the computer?"

"Worse than that," Barbara replied, seating herself in the chair opposite Marsh and handing him a file folder. "They aren't here at all."

Frowning, Marsh opened the folder, which had Alex's name neatly typed at the top. Inside was a single sheet of paper, with one sentence typed on it:

> CONTENTS OF THIS FILE TRANSFERRED TO THE INSTITUTE FOR THE HUMAN BRAIN, BY AUTHORITY OF MARSHALL LONSDALE, M.D., DIRECTOR.

Marsh's frown deepened. "What the hell does this mean?"

Barbara shrugged. "I assume it means that you sent all the records relating to the accident to Palo Alto, and they never came back."

Marsh reached over and pressed a key on the intercom. "Frank, can you come in here?" A moment later Frank Mallory came into the office, and Marsh handed him the sheet of paper. "Do you know anything about this?"

Mallory glanced at it, then shrugged. "Sure. All the records went to Palo Alto. Torres needed them."

"But why didn't they come back? And why didn't we keep copies?"

Now Mallory, too, was frowning. "I . . . well, I guess I thought they had. They should have been here months ago, along with copies of what was done down there. It's all part of Alex's medical history."

"Exactly," Marsh agreed. "But apparently they didn't. Barbara, would you mind getting on the phone and calling down there? Find out what's going on, and why those records never came back."

When they were alone, Frank Mallory studied Marsh for a moment. "Why the sudden upset, Marsh?" he asked. "Is something going on with Alex that I don't know about?"

"I don't know," Marsh admitted. "It's just something I can't quite put my finger on. I'm worried about him."

"And you don't like Raymond Torres."

"I've never said I did," Marsh replied, unable to keep a defensive tone out of his voice. "But it's more than that. Torres is acting more and more as though he owns Alex, and Alex . . . well, I guess I'm just worried about him."

"What about Ellen? Is she worried too?"

Marsh shrugged helplessly. "I wish she were. Unfortunately, she thinks Torres is the miracle man of the century. But she also thinks there's a curse on La Paloma, or some such thing."

Mallory's eyes widened in disbelief. "A curse? Oh, come on, Marsh, not Ellen—"

"I know," Marsh sighed. "And I don't think she really believes it herself. She was just upset this morning. What with Marty Lewis being killed so soon after Alex's accident—"

"Which events have no connection whatsoever," Mallory pointed out.

"I told her that," Marsh agreed. "And when she thinks about it, I'm sure she'll realize it's true. But what's really bugging me is Torres's attitude." He told Mallory about the conversation he'd had with Torres after the funeral. "And all he did was suggest that I read the release we signed."

"And have you? I mean, since the night you signed it?"

Before Marsh could reply, the door opened, and Barbara Fannon stepped into the office, another file folder in her hand. One look at her face told Marsh that something was wrong.

"What is it? What did they say?"

Barbara shook her head, as if even she couldn't believe what she'd been told. "They said they have all the records and that they won't be returning them. They won't even be returning *our* records, let alone forwarding copies of their own!"

"That's impossible," Marsh said. "They can't do that—"

"They . . . they said they can, Marsh," Barbara replied, her voice so low the two men had to strain to hear her. "They said the instructions and authorizations are very clear in the release you signed before the operation."

"I don't believe it," Marsh declared. "Let's take a look at that release."

Silently Barbara handed him the folder. "I thought you'd want to see it," she said. "I . . . well, I already read it."

Marsh scanned the document, then went back and reread the whole thing very carefully. When he was done, he handed it to Frank Mallory.

"It won't hold up," Mallory said when he, too, had read every word of the agreement Marsh and Ellen had made with the Institute for the Human Brain. "There isn't a court in the country that would uphold all this. My God, according to this, the man isn't accountable to anybody. He doesn't have to release any records, describe any procedures—nothing. And he can do anything he wants with Alex for as long as he wants. According to this, you've even given him custody of Alex. Why the hell did you sign it in the first place?" At the look on Marsh's face, he immediately regretted his words. "Sorry, Marsh," he mumbled, "that was out of line."

"Was it?" Marsh asked, his voice hollow. "I wonder. I should have read it —Lord knows Torres told me to enough times. But I guess I thought it was a standard release."

"It's about as far from standard as anything I've ever seen," Mallory said. "I think we'd better get a lawyer on this right away."

Marsh nodded. "But I'm not sure what good it'll do. Even if a lawyer can get it broken, it'll take months, if not years. Besides," he added, "even if I'd read it thoroughly, I would have signed it."

"But it seems to me the circumstances constitute duress of the worst kind," Mallory said. "It was either sign or let Alex die, for God's sake! What else could you do?"

"More to the point, what do I do now?" Marsh asked.

An uncomfortable silence fell over the room, as all three of its occupants realized the position Marsh was in. Without the records, they had no idea of what had been done to Alex, but that was the least of it.

The first thought that had flashed through all their minds was simply to remove Alex from the area. But that, of course, was impossible now.

Besides not knowing what procedures had been used to save Alex's life, they also had no idea of what treatment might still be in progress, and what the ramifications of ending that treatment might be.

It was a trap, and there seemed to be no way out.

Alex sat on the hillside, the afternoon sun warming his back even though the offshore breeze was already starting to bring the cool sea air inland. He was staring down at the hacienda, and in his memory, images were once again beginning to flash.

He seemed to remember horses filling the courtyard, then riding away toward the village.

He remembered people—his people—walking slowly away from the hacienda, carrying small bundles.

And he remembered three people who remained in the courtyard long after all the others were gone. In his memory, he couldn't see their faces clearly, but he knew who they were.

They were his family.

Then the faintly remembered voices began in his head, one voice standing out from all the others.

"We are not afraid to die . . . we will not leave our land . . ."

But they *had* left. The book had said they fled to Mexico.

"It will do you no good to kill us . . . my son will find you, and he will kill you . . ."

The words echoed in Alex's head. He stood up and began walking up the hillside, and then, when he was near the top, he plunged into a tangle of scrub oak, and a moment later began digging. The earth, packed hard after nearly a century and a half, resisted, but in the end gave way.

Two feet below the surface, Alex found the ancient skeletons. He hunched low to the ground, staring at the three skulls, their hollow eye sockets seeming to plead with him; then he slowly reburied them. When the job was finished, he began walking once again, staying high on the hillside, but always keeping the hacienda in his view. The memories were coming clearer now, and images of what had happened there flashed brightly in his mind.

The walls—the whitewashed walls—were stained with crimson, and the bodies, crumpled and torn, lay still in the dust.

And then, as he moved around to the east, the images began to fade, and soon were gone altogether.

The images were gone, but the memories remained.

Finally he came back down into the village.

Lisa Cochran looked up when the bell on Jake's door clattered noisily, and waved to Alex as he walked into the pizza parlor. He hesitated, then joined Lisa and Bob Carey at the table they were sharing.

"How come you weren't in school this afternoon?"

"I went to the library," Alex replied. "There was some stuff I wanted to look up."

"So you just went?" Bob asked. "Jeez, Alex, didn't you even ask anyone if it was all right? They'll mark you down for a cut."

Alex shrugged. "It doesn't matter."

Lisa looked at Alex sharply. "Alex, is something wrong?"

Again Alex shrugged, then glanced from Lisa to Bob. "Can I . . . well, can I ask you guys a question without you thinking I'm nuts?"

Bob Carey rolled his eyes and stood up. "Ask Lisa," he said. "I gotta get out of here—I promised Kate I'd come by on my way home and give her the homework assignments."

"When's she coming back to school?" Lisa asked.

"Search me," Bob replied. Then he lowered his voice. "Did you hear anything about her not coming back at all?"

Lisa shook her head. "Who'd you hear that from?"

"Carolyn Evans. She said she didn't think Kate would come back to school until after they try her dad, and if he gets convicted, she doesn't think Kate will come back at all."

Lisa groaned. "And you believed her? Carolyn Evans? Oh, come on, Bob. Even if Mr. Lewis did do it, nobody's going to hold it against Kate!"

"I don't know," Bob replied. "Sometimes people can get really weird." Then, after shooting a meaningful look toward Alex, he left.

"I don't believe it!" Lisa cried when he was gone. "I swear to God, Alex, sometimes people make me so mad. Carolyn Evans spreading gossip like that, and Bob looking at you like you're some kind of nut—"

"Maybe I am," Alex said, and Lisa, her mouth still open, stared at him for a moment.

"What?"

"I said, maybe I am a nut."

"Oh, come on, Alex. You're not crazy—you just don't remember a lot of things."

"I know," Alex replied. "But I'm starting to remember some things, and they're really strange. I mean, they're things I couldn't possibly remember, because they happened before I was even born."

"Like what?" Lisa asked. She started to fidget with a straw that lay dripping Coke on the Formica tabletop. She wasn't at all sure she wanted to know.

"I'm not sure," Alex said. "It's just images, and words, and things that don't look quite right. But I don't know what it all means."

"Maybe it doesn't mean anything. Maybe it's just all in your brain. You know, from the accident?"

Alex hesitated, then nodded. "Maybe you're right." But in his own mind, he wasn't so sure. The memories had seemed too real to be figments of his imagination.

Suddenly Lisa looked up at him. "Alex, do you think Mr. Lewis killed Mrs. Lewis?"

Alex hesitated, then shrugged. "How should I know?"

"Well, none of us *knows,*" Lisa replied. "But what do you think?"

Suddenly Alex remembered his dream from the night Kate's mother had died.

"I don't think he did it," he said. "I think someone else did it." He hesitated. "And I think it's going to happen again."

Lisa stared at him, then stood up. "That's an awful thing to say," she whispered, her eyes furious. "If you're trying to convince me you're nuts, you've just done it. Nobody but a crazy person would say something like that!" Picking up her books and her bag, she hurried out into the street, letting the door slam shut behind her.

Alex, his eyes empty, watched her go.

CHAPTER 17

Ellen listened quietly as her husband once again recited the terms of the release they'd signed before Alex's operation. Even after more than an hour's discussion, she was still certain he was overreacting. "Marsh, you're being absolutely paranoid," she said when he at last fell silent. "I don't care what you think Raymond Torres is up to, because you're wrong. Raymond isn't up to anything. He's Alex's doctor, and whatever he's doing is in Alex's best interests."

"Then why won't he let us see the records?" Marsh demanded, and Ellen could only shake her head wearily.

"I don't know. But I'm sure there's an explanation, and it seems to me the person you should be talking to is Raymond, not me."

Marsh had been standing next to the fireplace, leaning on the mantel, but now he wheeled around to face his wife. He hadn't gotten through to her at all. No matter what he told her—about the wall of secrecy Torres had erected around Alex's case, about the terms of the release, in which they'd given Torres full legal custody of Alex—she still remained steadfast in her defense of the man. To her, it came down to only one thing—Torres had saved Alex's life.

"Besides, what does it matter?" he heard her asking. "Why are the records so important? The point is that whatever he did, it worked!" Suddenly the calm façade she had been maintaining slipped, and her voice took on a bitter edge. "I should think you'd be grateful! You always said Alex was brilliant—gifted, even—and now Raymond's proved it."

"But there's more to it than that. For Christ's sake, Ellen. Don't you even *see* Alex anymore? He's like a machine! He doesn't feel anything. Not for any*one* or any*thing*. He's . . . well, in some ways he's just like your precious Raymond Torres. And it's not changing."

Ellen's eyes flashed with sudden anger. Though she knew that what she was about to say would only widen the chasm between them, she didn't try to hold the words back. "So that's what it's all about! I knew it! I knew when this whole thing started that it had nothing to do with the release. It's Raymond, isn't it? In the end, it all comes down to the same thing. You're jealous, Marsh. He did what you couldn't do, and you can't stand it."

Marsh stood silently for a moment, then nodded briefly. "It started out that way," he admitted, moving away from the fireplace to flop into his favorite easy chair. "I'm not going to pretend it didn't. But something's wrong, Ellen. The more I think about it, the less I understand it. How is it possible that Alex could have made such a phenomenal recovery intellectually, and physically, and show no progress at all emotionally?"

"I'm sure there's an explanation—" Ellen began.

"Oh, there is!" Marsh interrupted. He rose to his feet again and began nervously pacing the room. "And it's all in the records that Torres won't let us see."

Ellen sighed and stood up. "This is getting us nowhere. All we're doing is going in circles. I'm sure Raymond has his reasons for keeping the records closed, and I'm sure they're valid. As for the rest of it—the terms of the release . . ." She hesitated, then plunged on. "Well, I'm afraid that's a problem you're going to have to deal with yourself."

"You mean you can accept those terms?" Marsh asked, his voice heavy with disbelief.

Ellen nodded. "I'm sure they're there to protect Alex, and I'm sure Raymond will explain them to me. In fact, he started to the other day."

"The other day?" Marsh asked. "What are you talking about?"

"I talked to him," Ellen replied. "When you were going to pull Alex out of school and send him down to Stanford, I talked to Raymond about it. I was . . . well, I was afraid you might ignore his advice. At any rate, he assured me that I had nothing to worry about. He said . . . well, he said that if you tried to do something, he could deal with you."

Marsh felt dazed. "*Deal* with me? He actually said that?"

Ellen nodded, but said nothing.

"And that didn't faze you at all, that as far as he's concerned, I'm simply someone to be *dealt* with?"

Ellen was silent for several long seconds. "No," she said at last. "In fact, it made me feel relieved."

The words struck Marsh with the force of a physical blow. He sank back into his chair as Ellen rose and quietly left the room.

Alex had long since stopped listening to the argument that was going on downstairs, tuning out his parents' voices as he immersed himself in the book he'd picked up at the library after he left Jake's.

When he'd come in for the second time, Arlette Pringle had immediately turned to the locked case, but Alex had stopped her.

"I need some medical books," he'd told her.

"Medical books? But doesn't your father have any?"

"I need new ones," Alex went on. "I need something about the brain."

"The human brain?"

Alex nodded. "Do you have anything?"

Arlette Pringle removed her glasses and thoughtfully chewed on an earpiece while she ran over the library's medical collection in her mind. "Not much that's really technical," she said at last. "But there's one new one we just got in." She rose from her desk and went to the small shelf labeled "Current Nonfiction." "Here it is. *The Brain.* Think that's specialized enough for you?"

Alex thumbed through the book, nodding. "I think so," he replied. "I'll tell you tomorrow. Can I check this out?"

Arlette led him back to the desk and showed him the process of checking out a book. "If this doesn't seem familiar," she said dryly, "I can tell you why. You were never much of a one for books."

"Then I guess that's something different about me, too," Alex replied, thinking: And maybe the reason why is in here.

Since dinner, while his parents had been arguing, he'd scanned the entire book, and reread Chapter 7, the chapter dealing with learning and memory, two more times. And the more he read, the more puzzled he became.

From what he'd read, what was happening to him seemed to be impossible.

He was about to begin the chapter for the third time, sure that he must have missed something, when there was a soft tap at the door. A second later his mother stuck her head in.

"Hi."

"Hi, Mom." He glanced up from the book. "You and Dad still fighting?"

Ellen studied her son carefully, searching for any sign that the angry words she and Marsh had just exchanged might have upset Alex, but his expression was as bland as always, and his question had been asked in the same tone he might have used had he been interested in the time of day. "No," she said. "But it wasn't really a fight, honey. We were just discussing Dr. Torres, that's all."

Alex frowned thoughtfully; then: "Dad doesn't like him, does he?"

"No," Ellen agreed, "he doesn't. But it doesn't matter. The only thing that matters is that you keep getting better."

"But what if I'm not getting better?"

Ellen stepped into the room and closed Alex's door behind her, then came to sit on the end of the bed. "But you are getting better."

"Am I?"

"Of course you are. You're starting to remember things, aren't you?"

"I don't know," Alex replied. "Sometimes I think I am, but the memories don't always make sense. It's like . . . I remember things that I couldn't possibly remember."

"What do you mean?"

Alex tried to explain some of the things that had happened, but carefully made no mention of the voices that sometimes whispered inside his head. He wouldn't mention those until he understood them. Ellen listened carefully as he talked, and when he was done, she smiled reassuringly.

"But it's all very simple. Obviously you saw the book before."

"Miss Pringle says I didn't."

"Arlette Pringle's memory isn't as good as she likes people to think it is," Ellen replied. "And anyway, even if you didn't ever see that copy of the book, you certainly might have seen it somewhere else. At your grandparents', for instance."

"My grandparents? But I don't even remember them. How could I remember something I saw at their house, without remembering them or their house either?"

"We'll ask Dr. Torres. But it seems to me that your memory must be coming back, even if it's just scraps. Instead of worrying about what you're remembering, I think you ought to be trying to remember more." For the first time her eyes fell on the book Alex had been reading, and she picked it up, studying the immensely enlarged brain cell on the cover for a moment. "Why are you reading this?"

"I thought maybe if I knew more about the brain, I might be able to figure out what's happening to me," Alex replied.

"And are you?"

"I don't know yet. I'm going to have to do a lot more studying."

Ellen put the book down and took Alex's hands. Though he made no response, neither did he immediately draw away from her. "Honey, the only thing that matters is that you're getting better. It doesn't matter why or how. Don't you see that?"

Alex shook his head. "The thing is, I'm not sure I *am* getting better, and I want to know. It just seems . . . well, I just think it's important that I know what's happening in my brain."

Ellen squeezed his hands, then let them go and stood up. "Well, I'm not going to tell you not to study, and Lord knows your father won't either. But don't stay up all night, okay?" Alex nodded and picked up his book. When Ellen leaned down to kiss him good night, he returned the gesture.

But as his mother left the room, Alex wondered why she always kissed him, and what she felt when she did. For his own part, he felt nothing. . . .

Marsh was still in his easy chair, staring morosely into the cold fireplace, when Alex came into the living room an hour later. "Dad?"

Marsh looked up, blinking tiredly. "I thought you'd gone to bed."

"I've been studying, but I need to talk to you. I've been reading about the brain," Alex began, "and there's some things I don't understand."

"So you thought you'd ask the family doctor?" He gestured toward the sofa. "I'm not sure I can help you, but I'll try. What's the problem?"

"I need to know how bad the damage was to my brain," Alex said. Then he shook his head. "No, that's not really it. I guess what I need to know is how deep the damage went. I'm not too worried about the cortex itself. I think that's all right."

The tiredness suddenly drained out of Marsh as he stared at Alex. "You think that's all right?" he echoed. "After reading for a couple of hours, you think the cortex is all right?"

Alex nodded, and if his father's skeptical tone affected him at all, he gave no sign. "It seems as though there must have been damage a lot deeper, but there are some things that don't seem to make any sense."

"For instance?" Marsh asked.

"The amygdala," Alex said, and Marsh stared at him. He searched his mind, and eventually associated the word with a small almond-shaped organ deep within the brain, nearly surrounded by the hippocampus. If he'd ever known its exact function, he'd long since forgotten.

"I know where it is," he said. "But what about it?"

"It seems like mine must have been damaged, but I don't see how that's possible."

Marsh leaned forward, his elbows resting on his knees. "I'm not following you," he said. "Why do you say the amygdala must have been injured?"

"Well, according to this book, what's been happening to me seems like it must be associated with the amygdala. I don't seem to have any emotions, and we know what happened to my memory. But now I'm starting to remember things, except that the way I remember them isn't the way they are, but the way they used to be."

Marsh nodded, though he wasn't exactly sure where Alex was going. "All right. And what do you think that means?"

"Well, it seems that I'm having imaginary memories. I'm remembering things that I couldn't remember."

"Maybe," Marsh cautioned him. "Or maybe your memories are just twisted a bit."

"I've thought of that," Alex said. "But I don't think so. I keep remembering things as they were long before I was even born, so I must only be imagining that I'm remembering them."

"And what does that have to do with the amygdala?"

"Well, it says in the book I read that the amygdala may be the part of the brain that mediates rearrangement of memory images, and that seems to be what's happening to me. As though the images are getting rearranged, and then coming out as real memories when they're not."

Marsh's brows arched skeptically. "And it seems to *me* as though you're jumping to a pretty farfetched conclusion."

"But there's something else," Alex went on. "According to this book, the amygdala also handles emotional memories. And I don't have any of those at all. No emotions, and no memories of emotions."

With a force of will, Marsh kept his expression impassive. "Go on."

Alex shrugged. "That's it. Given the combination of no emotions or memories of emotions, and the imaginary memories, the conclusion is that my amygdala must have been damaged."

"If you read that book right, and if its information is correct—which is a big if, considering how little is actually known about the brain—then I suppose your conclusion is probably right."

"Then I should be dead," Alex stated.

Marsh said nothing, knowing all too well that what his son was positing was absolutely true.

"It's too deep," Alex went on, his voice as steady as if he were discussing the weather. "In order to damage the amygdala, practically everything else would have to be destroyed first: the frontal lobe, the parietal lobe, the hippocampus, the corpus callosum, the cingulate gyrus, and probably the thalamus and the pineal gland too. Dad, if all that happened to me, I should be dead, or at least a vegetable. I shouldn't be conscious, let alone walking, talking, seeing, hearing, and everything else I'm doing."

Marsh nodded, but still said nothing. Again, everything Alex had said was true.

"I want to know what happened, Dad. I want to know how badly my brain was damaged, and how Dr. Torres fixed it. And I want to know why part of my brain is doing so well, and other parts aren't working at all."

Marsh leaned back in his chair, closing his eyes for a moment as he tried to decide what to say to his son. At last, though, he made his decision. Alex might as well know the truth. "I can't tell you," he said. "In fact, I got curious about the same things, and today I tried to pull your records out of our computer. They aren't there anymore. Dr. Torres has all the information pertaining to what happened to you in his own files, and for some reason he doesn't want me or anyone else to see it."

Now it was Alex who fell silent as he turned his father's words over in his mind. When he finally spoke, his eyes met his father's squarely. "It means something's wrong, doesn't it?"

Marsh kept his voice deliberately neutral. "Your mother doesn't think so. She thinks everything is fine, and Torres is simply protecting the privacy of his records."

Alex shook his head. "If that's what she thinks, then she's wrong."

"Or maybe we're wrong," Marsh suggested. He kept his eyes on Alex, searching for any sort of emotional reaction from the boy. So far, there was none. Alex was only shaking his head.

"No, we're not wrong. If I'm alive, then what's happening to me shouldn't be happening. And I *am* alive. So something's wrong, and I have to find out what."

"*We* have to find out," Marsh said softly. He rose to his feet and went to put his hand on Alex's shoulder. "Alex?" he said quietly. The boy looked up at him. "Alex, are you scared?"

Alex was silent for a moment, then shook his head. "No. I'm not scared. I'm just curious."

"Well, *I'm* scared," Marsh admitted.

"Then you're lucky," Alex said quietly. "I keep wishing I was scared, not just curious . . . I wish I was terrified."

Alex sat alone in his first class the next morning. He had known something was wrong from the moment he had stopped by the Cochrans' to walk to school with Lisa, and discovered that she had already left. It was Kim who had told him.

"She thinks you're crazy," the little girl had said, gazing up at Alex with her large and trusting blue eyes. "She says she doesn't want to go out with you anymore. But she's dumb." And then Carol Cochran had appeared, and sent Kim back into the house.

"I'm sorry, Alex," she told him. "She'll get over it. It's just that you scared her yesterday when you told her you thought whoever killed Marty Lewis was still loose."

"I didn't mean to scare her," Alex said. "All she did was ask me if I thought Mr. Lewis did it, and I said I didn't."

"I know what you said," Carol sighed. "And I'm sure Lisa will get over it. But this morning she just wanted to go to school by herself. I'm sorry."

"It's okay," Alex had replied. He'd said good-bye to Lisa's mother, then continued on his way to school. But he wasn't surprised when no one spoke to him, and he wasn't surprised when the classroom fell silent when he came in.

Nor was he surprised to see that there was no empty seat next to Lisa.

He wasn't surprised, but neither was he hurt.

He simply made up his mind that in the future he would be more careful what he said to people, so they wouldn't think he was crazy.

He listened to the first few words of the teacher's history lecture, but then tuned him out, as he had tuned his parents out the night before. All the material the teacher was talking about was in the textbook, and Alex had read it three days earlier.

The entire contents of the history text were now imprinted on his memory. If he'd been asked to, he could have written the book down word for word.

Besides, what concerned Alex that morning was not the history text, but the book about the brain that he had borrowed from the library. In his mind he began going over the problem he had discussed with his father the night before, looking for the answer. Somewhere, he was certain, he had made a mistake. Either he had misread the book, or the book was wrong.

Or there was a third possibility, and it was that third possibility that he spent the rest of the day considering.

The idea came to him late in the afternoon.

His last class had been a study hall, and he'd decided not to bother with it. Instead, he'd wandered around the campus, trying once more to find something that jogged one of his dormant memories to life. But it was useless. Nothing jarred his memory, and more and more, everything he saw was now familiar. Each day, there was less and less in La Paloma that he had not refamiliarized himself with.

He was wandering through the science wing when someone called his name. He stopped and glanced through the open door of one of the labs. At the desk, he recognized Paul Landry.

"Hello, Mr. Landry."

"Come on in, Alex."

Alex stepped into the lab and glanced around.

"Recognize any of it?" Landry asked. Alex hesitated, then shook his head. "Not even that?"

Landry was pointing toward a wooden box with a glass top covering a table near the blackboard. "What is it?" Alex asked.

"Take a look. You don't remember it at all?"

Alex gazed at the crude construction. "Should I?"

"You built it," Landry said. "Last year. It was your project, and you finished it just before the accident."

Alex walked over to examine the plywood construction. It was a simple maze, but apparently he'd made each piece separately, so that the maze could be easily and quickly changed into a myriad of different patterns. "What was I doing?"

"Figure it out," Landry challenged. "From what Eisenberg tells me, it shouldn't take you more than a minute."

Alex glanced at his watch, then went back to the box. At one end was a runway leading to a cage containing three rats, and at the other was a food dispenser. Built into the front of the box was a timer. Forty-five seconds later, Alex nodded. "It must have been a retraining project. I must have wanted to be able to time the rate at which the rats learned each new configuration of the maze. But it looks pretty simpleminded."

"That's not what you thought last year. You thought it was pretty sophisticated."

Alex shrugged disinterestedly, then lifted the gate that allowed the rats to run into the maze. One by one, with no mistakes, they made their way directly to the food and began eating. "How come it's still here?"

Landry shrugged. "I guess I just thought you might want it. And since I was teaching summer school this year, it wasn't any trouble to keep it."

It was then, as he watched the rats, that the idea suddenly came into Alex's mind. "What about the rats?" he asked. "Are they mine too?"

When Landry nodded, Alex removed the glass and picked up one of the large white rats. It wriggled for a moment, then relaxed when Alex put it back in its cage. A minute later, the other two had joined the first. "Can I take them home?" Alex asked.

"Just the rats? What about the box?"

"I don't need it," Alex replied. "It doesn't look like it's worth anything. But I'll take the rats home."

Landry hesitated. "Mind telling me why?"

"I have an idea," Alex said. "I want to try an experiment with them, that's all."

There was something in Alex's tone that struck Landry as strange, and then he realized what it was. There was nothing about Alex of his former openness and eagerness to please. Now he was cold, and, though he hated to use the word, arrogant.

"It's fine with me," he finally said. "Like I said, they're your rats. But if you don't want the box, leave it there. You may think it's pretty simpleminded—which, incidentally, it is—but it still demonstrates a few things. I've been using it for my class." He grinned. "And I've also been telling my kids that this project would have earned the brilliant Alex Lonsdale a genuine C-minus. Even last year, you could have done better work than that, Alex."

"Maybe so," Alex replied, picking up the rat cage and heading toward the door. "And maybe I would have, if you'd been a better teacher."

Then he was gone, and Paul Landry was left alone, trying to reconcile the Alex he'd just talked to with the Alex he'd known the year before. He couldn't, for there was simply no comparison. The Alex he'd known last year had disappeared without a trace. In his place was someone else, and Landry was grateful that whoever he was, he wasn't in his class this year. Before he left that day, he took Alex's project and threw it into the dumpster.

CHAPTER 18

The kitchen door slammed, and despite herself, Ellen jumped. "Alex?" she called. "Is that you? Do you know what time it—" And then, as Alex came into the living room, she fell silent, her eyes fixed on the cage he held in his right hand. "What on earth have you got there?"

"Rats," Alex told her. "The ones from my science project last year. Mr. Landry still had them."

Ellen eyed the little creatures with revulsion. "You're not going to keep them, are you?"

"I've figured out an experiment," Alex told her. "They'll be gone in a couple of days."

"Good. Now, let's go, or we'll be late. In fact," she added, her eyes moving to the clock, "we already are. And you know how Dr. Torres feels about punctuality."

Alex started toward the stairs. "Dad and I aren't sure I ought to keep going to Dr. Torres."

Ellen, in the midst of struggling into a light coat, froze. "Alex, what are you talking about?"

Alex's face remained impassive as he regarded her. "Dad and I had a talk last night, and we think maybe something's wrong with me."

"I don't understand," Ellen breathed, although she was afraid she understood all too well. She and Marsh had barely spoken to each other this morning, and today he had, for the first time in her memory, failed to call her even once. And now, apparently, he was going to use Alex as a pawn in their battle. Except that she wasn't going to tolerate it, particularly when she knew that in the end, the loser would not be her, but Alex himself.

"I've been doing some reading," she heard Alex saying.

"Stop!" Ellen said, her voice sharper than she'd intended. "I don't care what you've been reading, and I don't care what your father and you have decided. You're still a patient of Raymond Torres's, and you have an appointment for this afternoon, which you're going to keep, whether you want to or not."

Alex hesitated only a split second before he nodded. "Can I at least take this up to my room?" he asked, raising the cage.

"No. Leave it outside on the patio."

As they drove down to Palo Alto, neither of them spoke.

"I thought your husband was coming today, Ellen." Raymond Torres remained seated behind his desk, but gestured to the two chairs that Ellen and Alex normally occupied.

"He's not," Ellen replied. "And I think we'd better talk about it." Her eyes shifted slightly toward Alex. Torres immediately picked up her message.

"I don't think the lab's quite ready for you yet," he told Alex. "Why don't you wait in Peter's office while he sets up?"

Wordlessly Alex left Torres's office, and when he was gone, Ellen finally sat down and began telling the doctor what had happened between herself and her husband the night before. "And now," she finished, "he's apparently convinced Alex that something's wrong, too."

Torres's fingers drummed on the desktop for a moment, then began the elaborate ritual of packing and lighting his pipe. Only when the first thick cloud of smoke had begun drifting toward the ceiling did he speak.

"The problem, of course, is that he's right," he finally observed. "In fact, today I was going to tell him that I want to check Alex back into the Institute."

Ellen suddenly felt numb. "What . . . what do you mean?" she stammered. "I thought . . . well, I thought everything was going very well."

"Of course you would," Torres said. "And for the most part, it is. But there's something going on that I don't quite understand." His head turned slightly, and his gaze fixed on Ellen. "So Alex will come back here until I know what's happening, and have decided what to do about it."

Ellen closed her eyes for a moment, as if by the action she could shut out the thoughts that were suddenly crowding in on her. How could she handle Marsh now? If she left Alex at the Institute, as she knew Raymond was going to insist upon, what could she say to Marsh? That he'd been right, that something was, indeed, wrong with Alex, and that she'd left him with a doctor who had apparently made a mistake? But then she realized that that wasn't what Torres had said. All he'd said was that something was wrong.

"Can you tell me just exactly what's wrong?" she asked, unable to control the trembling in her voice.

"Nothing too serious," Torres assured her, his voice soothing while his eyes remained locked to hers. "In fact, perhaps nothing at all. But until I know just what it is, I'll want Alex here."

Ellen found herself nervously twisting her wedding ring, knowing that if he insisted, she would inevitably give in. "I don't know if Alex will agree to that," she said so softly the words were almost whispered.

"But Alex doesn't have anything to say about it, does he?" Torres pointed out. "Nor, for that matter, does your husband." Then, when Ellen still hesitated, he spoke once more. "Ellen, you know that what I'm doing is in Alex's best interests."

Ellen hesitated only slightly before nodding. "But can't it wait a day?" she pleaded. "Can't I at least have a day to try to convince Marsh? If I go home without Alex this afternoon, I hate even to think what he might do."

Raymond Torres turned it over in his mind, briefly reviewing once again what his lawyer had told him only that morning: "Yes, in the long run the release will probably hold up. But don't forget that Marshall Lonsdale is not only the boy's father, but a doctor as well. He'll be able to get an injunction, and keep the boy until the issue is decided in the courts. And by then, it'll be too late. I know you hate it, Raymond, but in this instance, I suggest you try to negotiate. If you don't try to take the boy, perhaps they'll give him to you."

"All right," he said. "For today, I'll just take some tests, but tomorrow I want you to bring Alex back. You have twenty-four hours to convince your husband."

Alex had been in Peter Bloch's office next door to the test lab for almost five minutes before he saw the stack of orders on the technician's desk.

On the top of the stack, he found Torres's neatly typed orders relating to himself. He scanned the single page, trying to translate the various abbreviations in his mind, but none of it meant anything to him.

And then his eyes fell onto a line near the bottom of the page: "Anesthesia: SPTL."

He stared at the four letters for several seconds, then his eyes moved to the old IBM Selectric II that sat on the desk's return. The idea formed in his head instantly, and almost as quickly, he made up his mind. He inserted the page into the carriage, and carefully lined up the letters with the red guidemarks on the cardholder. Thirty seconds later he was finished, and the line near the bottom of the page was changed.

"Anesthesia: NONE."

When Peter Bloch came in a few minutes later, Alex was sitting in a chair next to the door, thumbing through a catalog of lab equipment. Out of the corner of his eye, he watched the technician go to the desk and pick up the thin stack of orders.

"Hunh," Bloch grunted. "Finally talked him into it, did you?"

Alex looked up, laying the catalog aside. "Talked him into what?"

Bloch made a sour face, then shrugged. "Never mind. But if you don't like what happens today, don't blame me. Blame yourself and Dr. Brilliant. Come on, let's get started."

Twenty minutes later Alex was strapped securely to the table, and the electrodes had all been connected to his skull. "Hope you don't decide you want to change your mind," Bloch said. "I don't have any idea what's going to happen to you, but I can practically guarantee you it isn't going to be pleasant." Leaving Alex's side, he stepped to the panel and began adjusting its myriad controls.

The first thing Alex noticed was a strange odor in the room. At first it was like vanilla, sweet and pleasant, but slowly it began mutating into something else. The sweetness faded away, and was replaced by an acrid odor, and Alex's first thought was that something in the lab must be burning. Then the smoky scent turned sour, and Alex's nostrils suddenly seemed to fill with the stench of rotting garbage.

It's in my mind, Alex told himself. It's all in my mind, and I'm not really smelling anything.

And then the sounds began, and with them the physical sensations.

The room was heating up, and he could feel himself beginning to sweat as a shrill screaming noise cut through his eardrums and slashed into his mind.

The heat increased, and suddenly centered in his groin.

A hot poker.

Someone was pressing into his genitalia with a white-hot poker.

He could smell the sickly sweetness of burning flesh, and he writhed helplessly against the bonds that held him to the table.

The sound in his mind was his own voice screaming in agony.

The burning stopped, and he was suddenly cold. Slowly, reluctantly, he opened his eyes, but saw nothing except the blinding whiteness of snowflakes swirling around him, while the wind whistled and moaned in his ears.

Suddenly there was pressure on his left leg.

It was gentle at first, as if something were there, touching him every few seconds.

Then, its yellow eyes glaring at him through the blizzard, its fangs dripping saliva, he saw the face of the wolf.

The image disappeared, and as the beast's hungry snarl drifted high over the wailings of the wind, he felt its jaws close on his leg.

His flesh was being torn to shreds, and in the strength of the wolf's jaws, his bones gave way. His lower leg went numb, but he could sense his blood spurting from the severed artery below his knee.

All around him, the blizzard shrieked.

Suddenly the sounds began fading away, and with it the pain. The blinding whiteness of the blizzard began taking on tinges of color, and soon he was surrounded by a sea of soft blue. He felt the warm waters laving his skin, and a cool breeze wafted over his face.

He floated peacefully, rocked gently by the motion of the water, and then began to feel something else in the back reaches of his mind.

It was indistinct at first, but as he began to focus on it, it became clearer.

Energy.

It was as if pure energy were flowing directly into his mind.

And then it stopped, and the cool breezes died out. The waters around him were no longer moving, and the blueness in front of his eyes gave way slowly until he was once more staring at the ceiling of the laboratory. Peter Bloch loomed over him.

"I almost shut you down," the technician said. "You started screaming, and twisting around until I was afraid you were going to hurt yourself."

Alex said nothing for a moment, but kept his eyes anchored steadily on the lamp above his head as he fixed everything that had happened in his memory.

"Nothing happened," he said at last.

"Horseshit," Peter Bloch replied. "You damned near went crazy! What the hell's Torres trying to prove now?"

"Nothing," Alex repeated. "Nothing happened to me, and he's not trying to prove anything."

Bloch shook his head doubtfully. "Maybe nothing happened, but I'll bet you thought something was happening. Want to tell me about it?"

Alex's eyes finally shifted to the lab technician. "Don't you know?"

"You think Torres tells me anything?" Peter countered. "I know we're stimulating your brain. But what it's all about, I don't know."

"But that *is* what it's about," Alex said quietly. "It's about what gets into my brain, and how my brain reacts." Then his expression twisted into a strange smile. "Except that it's not my brain anymore, is it?" When Peter Bloch made no answer, Alex answered his own question.

"It's not my brain anymore. Ever since I woke up from the operation, it's been Dr. Torres's brain."

Raymond Torres wordlessly took Alex's test reports from Peter Bloch's hands and began flipping through them. He frowned slightly, then the frown deepened into a scowl.

"You must have made a mistake," he said finally, tossing the thin sheaf of papers onto the desk as he faced his head technician. "None of these results make any sense at all. These are what you'd get from a brain that was awake, not asleep."

"Then there's no mistake," Bloch replied, his face set into a mask of forced unconcern. As always when dealing with Raymond Torres, he would have preferred to roll the test results up tight and shove them down the man's arrogant throat. But the money was too good and the work too light to throw it away over something as trivial as his dislike of his employer, who, he noticed, was now glowering at him.

"What do you mean, no mistake? Are you telling me that Alex Lonsdale was awake during this?"

Peter Bloch felt as if the floor had just tilted. "Of course he was," he said as forcefully as he could, though he was suddenly certain he knew exactly what had happened. "You wrote the order yourself."

"Indeed I did," Torres replied. "And I have a copy of it right here." He opened his bottom desk drawer and pulled out a sheet of pink paper, which he silently handed to Bloch. There, near the bottom of the page, were the words: "Anesthesia: SPTL."

Once more, Peter pictured Alex Lonsdale, his face impassive, sitting thumbing through a catalog.

And watching him.

How long had he been there? Apparently, long enough.

"I thought . . . I thought it was highly unusual, sir," he mumbled.

"Unusual?" Torres demanded, his voice crackling with harsh sarcasm. "You thought it was unusual to put a patient out with Sodium Pentothal while inducing hallucinations in his brain?"

"No, sir," the technician muttered, thoroughly cowed. "I thought it was unusual *not* to. I should . . . well, I should have called."

Torres was fairly trembling with rage now. "What, exactly, are you talking about?"

Exactly three minutes and twenty-two seconds later, when Bloch had returned to his office, Torres knew. His eyes fixed on the altered anesthesia prescription for several long seconds, then shifted slowly to the technician.

"And you didn't think you ought to call me about this?" he asked, his voice deceptively low.

"I . . . well, the kid told me a long time ago he wanted to take the test without the Pentothal. I thought he'd finally talked you into letting him try."

Raymond Torres rose to his feet, and leaned across the desk so that his face was close to Peter Bloch's. When he spoke, he made no attempt to keep his fury under control. "Talked me into it?" he shouted. "We never even discussed such a thing! Do you have any idea of exactly what goes on in those tests?"

"Yes, sir," Peter Bloch managed.

"Yes, sir," Torres mimicked, his tone icy. "We deliberately induce pain, Mr. Bloch. We induce physical pain, and mental pain, and of the worst sort. The only thing that makes it tolerable at all is that the patient is unconscious. Without the anesthetic, we are at risk of driving a patient insane."

"He's . . . he seems to be all right," Bloch stammered, but Torres froze him with a look.

"And perhaps he is," Torres agreed. "But *if* he is, it is only because the boy has no emotions. Or, as you have so inelegantly put it in the past, because he's a 'zombie.' "

Bloch flinched, but stood his ground. "I was going to shut it off," he insisted. "I was watching him carefully, and if it looked like it was getting too bad, I was going to shut it off in spite of your orders."

"Not good enough," Torres replied. "If you had any questions about those orders, you should have called me immediately. You didn't. Well, perhaps you will do this: go to your lab and begin packing anything that is personally yours. Then you will wait there for a security guard to come and escort you out of the building. Your check will be sent to you. Is that clear?"

"Sir—"

"Is that clear?" Torres repeated, his voice rising to drown out the other man.

"Yes, sir," Bloch whispered. A moment later he was gone, and Raymond Torres seated himself once more, then waited until his breathing had returned to its normal rhythm before picking up the sheaf of test results.

Perhaps, he reflected, it will be all right after all. The boy hadn't cracked under the battering his brain had absorbed. With any luck at all, Alex's brain had been so busy dealing with the chaos of stimulation that he hadn't consciously noticed what else had been happening.

Or had he?

CHAPTER 19

"But he didn't say what was wrong, did he?" Marsh asked. He folded his napkin precisely—a gesture Ellen immediately recognized as a sign that his mind was irrevocably made up—and placed it on the table next to his coffee cup.

"That's why he wants Alex back," Ellen said for the third time. Why, she wondered, couldn't Marsh understand that there was nothing sinister in Raymond's wanting Alex to come back to the Institute for a few days? "Besides," she went on, "if he thought it was anything serious, he wouldn't have let Alex come home with me this afternoon. He could have just kept him there."

"And I would have had an injunction by tomorrow morning," Marsh pointed out. "Which I'm sure he knows. In spite of that release, I'm still his father, and unless he tells us the details of the surgery, and tells us exactly what he thinks has gone wrong, Alex doesn't go back there again." He pushed his chair back and stood up, and though Ellen wanted to argue with him further, she knew it was useless. She would just have to do what she knew was best for Alex, and deal with Marsh after she'd done it. As Marsh left the dining room, she began clearing the dishes from the table and loading them into the dishwasher.

Marsh found Alex in his room. He was at his desk, one of Marsh's medical texts in front of him, opened to the anatomy of the human brain, while one of the white rats poked inquisitively around among the clutter that surrounded the book.

"Anything I can help you with?"

Alex looked up. "I don't think so."

"Try me," Marsh challenged. When Alex still hesitated, he picked up the rat and scratched it around its ears. The little animal wriggled with pleasure. "Mind telling me what you're going to use to dissect this little fellow's brain with?"

Alex's eyes met his father's. "How did you know?"

"I may not be a genius," Marsh replied, "but last night you told me that considering the damage that was done to your brain, you ought to be dead. Now I find you studying the anatomy of the brain, and white rats are not exactly unheard of as subjects for dissection."

"All right," Alex said. "I want to see what happens to the rat if I cut as far into its brain as Dr. Torres had to cut into mine."

"You mean you want to see if it dies," Marsh replied. His son nodded. "Then I think we'd better go down to the Center, and I think you'd better let me help you."

"You mean you will?" Alex asked.

"If I don't, your rats won't survive the first cut."

When they came downstairs a few minutes later, Ellen glanced at them from her place at the kitchen sink, then, seeing the rat cage, smiled appreciatively. "Well, at least we agree that the house is no place for those things," she offered, hoping to break the tension that had spoiled dinner.

"We're taking them down to the lab," Marsh told her. "And we may hang around awhile, if anything interesting's going on."

Ellen frowned. "Interesting? What could be interesting in the lab at this hour? There won't even be anyone there."

"We'll be there," Marsh replied. Then, while Ellen wondered what was going on, her husband and son disappeared into the patio. A moment later she heard the gate slam closed.

The fluorescent lamps over the lab table cast a shadowless light, and as Marsh prepared to inject the anesthesia into the rat's vein, he suddenly wondered if the creature somehow knew what was about to happen. Its little eyes seemed wary, and he could feel it trembling in his hand. He glanced at Alex, who stood at the other side of the table, looking on impassively. "It won't survive this, you know," Marsh told his son.

"I know," Alex replied in the emotionless voice Marsh knew he would never get used to. "Go ahead."

Marsh slid the needle under the rat's skin and pressed the plunger. The rat struggled for a few seconds, then gradually went limp, and Marsh began fastening it to the dissecting board. When he was done, he studied the illustration he'd found in one of the lab books, then deftly used a scalpel to cut the skin away from the rat's skull, starting just behind the left eye and slicing neatly around to the opposite position behind the right eye, then folding the loose flap of skin forward. Then, using a tiny saw, he began removing the top of the skull itself. He worked slowly. When he was done, the rat's brain lay exposed to the light, but its heartbeat and breathing were still unaffected.

"This probably isn't going to work," Marsh said. "We should have much smaller tools, and proportionally, much more of a rat's brain than a human's is used to keep its vital functions going."

"Then let's just cut away a little bit at a time, and see how deep we can go."

Marsh hesitated, then nodded. Using the smallest scalpel he had been able to find, he began peeling away the cortex of the rat's brain.

An hour later, all three of the rats were dead. In none of them had Marsh succeeded in reaching the inner structures of the brain before their heartbeats had ceased.

"But they didn't have to die," he pointed out. "I could have gone in with a probe, and destroyed part of the limbic system without doing much damage to anything else."

Alex shook his head. "It wouldn't have meant anything, Dad. When you cut away their brains the way Torres had to cut away mine, the rats died. So why didn't I?"

"I don't know," Marsh confessed. "All I know is that you didn't die."

Alex was silent for a long time, staring at the three small corpses on the lab table. "Maybe I did," he said at last. "Maybe I'm really dead."

Valerie Benson looked up from her knitting. Across the room, Kate Lewis was curled up on the sofa, her eyes on the television set, but Valerie was almost sure she wasn't watching the program.

"Want to talk about it?" she asked. Kate's eyes remained on the television.

"Talk about what?"

"Everything that's bothering you."

"Nothing's bothering me," Kate replied. "I'm okay."

"No," Valerie replied, "you're not okay." She put her knitting aside, then got up and turned off the television set. "Are you planning to go back to school tomorrow?"

"I . . . I don't know."

I should have had children, Valerie thought. If I'd had children of my own, I'd know what to do. Or would she? Would she really know what to say to a teenage girl whose father had killed her mother? What was there to say? And yet, Kate couldn't just go on sitting in front of the television set all day and all evening, moping.

"Well, I think it's time you went back," Valerie ventured. Then, sure she knew what was really going on in Kate's mind, she went on: "What happened wasn't your fault, Kate, and none of the kids are going to hold it against you."

Kate turned to stare at Valerie. "Is that what you think?" she asked. "That I'm afraid of what the kids might think?"

"Isn't it?"

Kate slowly shook her head. "Everybody knew all about Dad," she said so quietly Valerie had to strain to hear her. "I always talked about what a drunk he is so no one else could do it first."

Valerie went to the sofa and sat close to Kate. "That couldn't have been easy."

"It was better than having everybody gossip." Her eyes met Valerie's for the first time. "But he didn't kill Mom," she said. "I don't care how it looks, and I don't care if he doesn't remember what happened after I left. All I know is they used to fight every time he got drunk, but he never hit her. He yelled at her, and sometimes he threatened her, but he never hit her. In the end, he always let her take him to the hospital."

"Then you should be out with your friends, letting them know exactly what you think."

Kate shook her head silently, and her eyes filled with tears. "I . . . I'm scared," she whispered.

"Scared? Scared of what?"

"I'm afraid of what might happen if I leave. I'm afraid I might come back and find you . . . find you . . ." Unable to say the words, Kate began sobbing softly, and Valerie held her close.

"Oh, honey, you don't have to worry about me. What on earth could happen to me?"

"But someone killed Mom," Kate sobbed. "She was by herself, and someone came in and . . . and . . ."

Your father killed her, Valerie thought, but she knew she wouldn't say it out loud. If Kate didn't want to believe the evidence, she wouldn't try to force her to, at least not yet. But after the trial, after Alan Lewis was convicted . . . She cut the thought off, telling herself that she should at least try to keep an open mind. "No one's going to do anything to me," she said. "I've been living by myself in this house for five years now, and there's never been any trouble at all. And I'm not going to let you become a prisoner here." She stood up briskly, went to pick up the telephone that sat on the table next to her chair, and brought it to the coffee table in front of the sofa. "Now you call Bob Carey and tell him you want to go out for a pizza or something."

Kate hesitated. "I can't do that—"

"Of course you can," Valerie told her. "He comes by every day and drops off your homework, doesn't he? So why wouldn't he want to take you out?" She picked up the phone. "What's his number?"

Kate blurted it out before she could think, and Valerie promptly punched the numbers. When Bob himself answered, she said only, "I have someone here who wants to talk to you," and handed the phone to Kate. Kate sniffled, but took the phone.

Forty-five minutes later, Valerie stood at the front door. "And no matter what she says, I don't want her back a minute before eleven," she told Bob Carey. "She's been cooped up too long, and she needs a good time." When Bob's car had disappeared down the hill, she closed the door, then went back to her knitting.

Ellen was about to call the Medical Center when she heard the patio gate slam once more. Then the door opened, and her husband and son came in. She dropped the receiver back on the hook just as the dial tone switched over to the angry whine of a forgotten phone, and didn't try to conceal the irritation she was feeling. "You might have told me how long you were going to be gone. What on earth have you been doing?"

"Killing rats," Alex said.

Ellen paled slightly, and her eyes moved to her husband. "Marsh, what's he talking about?"

"I'll tell you later," Marsh replied, but the look on Ellen's face told him that she was going to demand an explanation right now. He sighed, and hung his jacket in the armoire that stood opposite the front door. "We were dissecting their brains, to see how much damage they could sustain before they died."

Ellen's stomach turned queasy, and she had to struggle to keep her voice steady. "You killed them?" she asked. "You killed those three helpless creatures?"

Marsh nodded. "Honey, you know perfectly well that rats die in laboratories every day. And there was something both Alex and I wanted to know." He stepped past Ellen and moved into the living room, then glanced at Alex.

"Why don't you make yourself scarce?" he asked. Then he smiled tiredly. "I have a feeling your mother and I are about to have another fight." Alex started toward the stairs, but Marsh stopped him, fishing in his pocket for his car keys. "Why don't you go find some of your friends?" he asked, tossing the keys to his son.

Ellen, watching, felt a chill go through her. Something had happened between her husband and her son. She was certain that an alliance had somehow formed between them that she was not a part of. A moment later, when Alex spoke again, she knew she was right.

"You mean do what we were talking about?" he asked, and Marsh nodded. And then something happened that Ellen hadn't seen since the night of the prom last spring.

Alex smiled.

It was a tentative smile, and it didn't last long, but it was still a smile. And then he was gone.

Ellen stared after him, then slowly turned to Marsh, her anger evaporating.

"Did you see that?" she breathed. "Marsh, he smiled. He actually smiled!"

Marsh nodded. "But it doesn't mean anything," he said. "At least it doesn't mean anything yet." Slowly he tried to explain the conversation he and Alex had had on the way home, and what they had decided Alex should do.

"So you see, the smile didn't really mean anything at all," he finished fifteen minutes later. "He doesn't feel anything, Ellen, and he knows it, which is making it even worse. He told me he's starting to wonder if he's even human anymore. But he said he can mimic emotions if he wants to, or at least mimic emotional reactions. And that's what he did. He intellectually figured out that he should be happy that he gets to go out for the evening and use my car, and he knows that when people are happy, they smile. So he smiled. He didn't feel the smile, and there was nothing spontaneous about it. It was like an actor performing a role."

The growing chill Ellen had been feeling as Marsh talked turned into a shudder. "Why?" she whispered. "Why should he want to do such a thing?"

"He said people are beginning to think he's crazy," Marsh replied. "And he doesn't want that to happen. He said he doesn't want to be locked up until he knows what's wrong with him."

"Locked up?" The room seemed to be spinning, and for a moment Ellen thought she might faint. "Who would lock him up?"

"But isn't that what happens to crazy people?" Marsh asked. "You have to look at it from his point of view. He knows we love him, and he knows we care for him, but he doesn't know what that means. All he knows is what he's read, and he's read about mental institutions." His voice suddenly broke. "Hell," he muttered. "He reads damned near everything, and remembers it all. But he just doesn't know what anything means."

María Torres shifted the heavy weight of her shopping bag from her right hand to her left, then sighed and lowered it to the sidewalk for a moment.

Ramón had promised to come that evening and take her shopping, but then he'd telephoned and said he wasn't coming. Something had come up with his patient, and he had to stay in his office. His patient, she thought bitterly. His patient was Alejandro, and there was nothing wrong with the boy. But Ramón couldn't see that, not for all his schooling. Ramón had forgotten. Forgotten so much. But someday he would understand. Someday soon, Ramón would know that all the hatreds she had carefully nursed in him were still there. But for now, he still pretended to be a *gringo.*

And tonight, the shopping still had to be done, even though she was tired after working all day, so she'd walked the five blocks to the store, which wasn't too bad. It was the five blocks home, with the full shopping bag, that was the hard part. Her arms aching with arthritis, she picked up the bag and was about to continue on her way when a car pulled up to the curb next to her. She glanced at it with little interest, then looked again as she recognized the driver.

It was the boy.

And he was returning her gaze, his eyes studying her. He knew who she was, and the saints—her saints—had sent him. It was an omen: though Ramón had not come to her tonight, Alejandro had. She stepped forward, and bent down to put her head through the open window of the car.

"Vámos," she whispered, her rheumy eyes glowing. *"Vámos a matar."*

The words echoed in Alex's ears, and he understood them. *We go to kill.* Deep in his mind, a memory stirred and the mists began gathering around him once again. He reached across the front seat and pushed the door open. María Torres settled herself into the seat beside him, and pulled the door closed. As the old woman whispered to him, he put the car in gear and started slowly up into the hills above the town.

Fifteen minutes later, he parked the car, still listening to the words María was whispering in his ears. And then he was alone, and María Torres was walking slowly away from the car, her bag of groceries clutched close to her breast.

Only when she had finally disappeared around a bend in the road did Alex, too, leave the car, and step through the gate into Valerie Benson's patio.

In the dark recesses of his throbbing brain, the familiar voices took up María's ancient litany . . .

Venganza . . . venganza . . .

Vaguely he became aware of another sound, and turned to see a woman standing framed in the light of an open doorway.

"Alex?" Valerie Benson asked. "Alex, are you all right?"

She'd heard the gate open, and waited for the doorbell to ring. When it hadn't, she'd gone to the door and pressed her eye to the peephole. There, standing in the patio, she'd seen Alex Lonsdale, and opened the door. But when she'd spoken, he hadn't replied, so she'd stepped outside and called to him.

Now he was looking at her, but she still wasn't sure he'd heard her words.

"Alex, what is it? Has something happened?"

"Ladrones," Alex whispered. *"Asesinos . . ."*

Valerie frowned, and stepped back, uneasy. What was he talking about? Thieves? Murderers? It sounded like the ravings of a paranoiac.

"K-Kate's not here," she stammered, backing toward the front door. "If you're looking for her, she's gone out."

She was inside and the door was halfway closed when Alex hurled himself forward, his weight slamming into the door, sending Valerie sprawling to the floor while the door itself smashed back against the wall.

Valerie tried to scramble away across the red quarry tile of the foyer, but it was too late.

Alex's fingers closed around her neck, and he began to squeeze.

"Venganza . . ." he muttered once more. And then again, as Valerie Benson died: *"Venganza . . ."*

Alex stepped through the door of Jake's and glanced around. In the booth in the far corner, he saw Kate Lewis and Bob Carey sitting with Lisa Cochran and a couple of other kids. Carefully composing his features into a smile, he crossed the room.

"Hi. Is it a private party, or can anybody join?"

The six occupants of the booth fell silent. Alex saw the uneasy glances that passed between them, but he kept his smile carefully in place. Finally Bob Carey shrugged and squeezed closer to Kate to make room at the end of the booth. Still no one said anything. When the silence was finally broken, it was Lisa, announcing that she had to go home.

Alex carefully changed his expression, letting his smile dissolve into a look of disappointment. "But I just got here," he said.

Lisa hesitated, her eyes fixing suspiciously on Alex. "I didn't think you'd care if I stayed or not," she said. "In fact, none of us thought you cared about anything anymore."

Alex nodded, and hoped that when he spoke his voice would have the right inflection. "I know," he said. "But I think things are starting to change. I think . . ." He dropped his eyes to the table, as he'd seen other people do when they seemed to be having trouble saying something. "I think I'm starting to feel things again." Then, making himself stammer slightly, he went on. "I . . . well, I really like you guys, and I'm sorry if I hurt your feelings."

Once again the rest of the kids glanced at each other, their self-consciousness only worsening at Alex's words.

It was Bob Carey who broke the embarrassed silence. "Hey, come on. Don't go all weird on us the other way now."

And suddenly everything was all right again, and Alex knew he'd won.

They'd believed his performance.

But slowly, as the conversation went on, he began to wonder, for Lisa Cochran still seemed to be avoiding talking to him.

Lisa herself was not about to tell him that she was wondering exactly what he was up to.

Long ago, before the accident, she'd heard Alex stammer and seen him look away when he was talking about his feelings.

And always, when he did that, he'd blushed.

This time, everything had been fine except for that one thing.

This time, Alex hadn't blushed.

CHAPTER 20

"Come in with me."

Bob Carey couldn't see Kate's face in the darkness, but the tremor in her voice revealed that she was frightened. His eyes moved past her silhouette, focusing on the house beyond. Everything, he thought, looked normal. Except for the gate.

The patio gate stood open, and both he and Kate clearly remembered closing it when they had left earlier in the evening.

"Nothing's wrong," he assured her, trying to make his voice sound more confident than he was actually feeling. "Maybe we didn't really latch it."

"We did," Kate breathed. "I know we did."

Bob got out of the car and went around to open the other door for Kate, but instead of getting out, she only gazed past him at the ominously open gate. "Maybe . . . maybe we ought to call the police," she whispered.

"Just because the gate's open?" Bob asked with a bravado he wasn't feeling. "They'd think we were nuts."

"No they wouldn't," Kate argued. "Not after . . ." She fell silent, unable to finish the thought.

Bob wavered, telling himself once more that the open gate meant nothing.

The wind could have done it, or Mrs. Benson might have gone out herself and left the gate open. In fact, she might not even be home.

He made up his mind.

"Stay here," he told Kate. "I'll go see."

He went through the open gate into the patio and looked around. The lights flanking the front door were on, and the white walls of the patio reflected their glow so that even the shadowed areas of the little garden were clearly visible. Nothing seemed to be amiss, and yet as he stood in the patio, he sensed that something was wrong.

Bob told himself the growing uneasiness he felt was only in his imagination. As soon as he rang the bell, Mrs. Benson would come to the door and everything would be all right.

But when he rang the bell, Mrs. Benson did not come to the door. Bob rang the bell once more, waited, then tried the door. It was locked. Slowly he backed away from the door, then hurried to the car.

"She's not here," he told Kate a few seconds later. "She must have gone somewhere." But even as he spoke the words, he knew they weren't true. He started the car.

"Where are we going?"

"We're going to call the police, just like you wanted to. It doesn't feel right in there."

Fifteen minutes later they were back. Bob parked his Porsche behind the squad car, then got out and went to the patio gate.

"Stay in your car," one of the cops at the front door told him. "If there's a creep in here, I don't want to have to worry about you." Only when Bob had disappeared did Roscoe Finnerty reach out and press the bell a second time, as Bob himself had done only a few minutes earlier. "She probably just took off somewhere," he told Tom Jackson, "but with these two, I guess we can't blame them for being nervous." When there was still no answer, Finnerty moved to a window and shone his flashlight through into the foyer. "Shit," he said softly, and Tom Jackson immediately felt his stomach knot.

"She there?" he asked.

Finnerty nodded. "On the floor, just like the other one. And if there's any blood, I don't see it. Take a look."

Tom Jackson dutifully stepped to the window and peered into the foyer. "Maybe she's just unconscious," he suggested.

"Maybe she is," Finnerty replied, but both men knew that neither of them believed it. "Go ask the Lewis girl if she's got a key, but don't tell her what we've seen. And when you ask for the key, see how she reacts."

Jackson frowned. "You don't think—"

"I don't know what I think," Finnerty growled. "But I sure as hell know Alan Lewis didn't do this one, and I keep thinking about the shit that came down in Marin a few years back when that girl and her boyfriend killed her folks, then went out and partied all night. So you just go see if she has a key, and keep your eyes open."

"Is she all right?" Kate asked when Jackson approached the car.

"Don't even know if she's here," Jackson lied. "Do you have a key? We want to take a look around."

Kate fumbled in her purse for a moment, then silently handed Jackson a single key on a ring. "Stay here," Jackson ordered. He started back to the house, wondering what he was supposed to have been looking for. Whatever it was, he hadn't seen it—all he'd seen were two kids who'd had a horrible experience only a few days ago, and were now very frightened.

"Well?"

Jackson shrugged. "She just gave me the key when I asked for it. Asked if the Benson woman's okay."

"What'd you say?"

"I lied. Figured we should both be there when we tell them."

Finnerty nodded, and slid the key into the lock, then pushed the door open and led his partner into the silent house. One look at Valerie Benson's open eyes and grimace of frozen terror told him she was dead. He called the station and told the duty officer what had happened, then rejoined Jackson. "Might as well tell them."

From then on, the long night took on a feeling of eerie familiarity, as Finnerty replayed the scene he'd gone through less than a week earlier when the same two kids had found the body of Martha Lewis.

The dusty road wound steadily up the hill, and Alex looked neither to the left nor to the right. He knew every inch of these hills, for he'd ridden over them with his father ever since he was a little boy. Now, though, he walked, for along with his father's land, the *gringos* had taken the horses as well. Indeed, they'd taken everything, even his name.

Still, he hadn't left La Paloma—would never leave La Paloma until finally the *gringos* had paid with their lives for the lives they had taken.

He came to a house, opened the gate, and stepped through into the patio. Not too long ago he'd been in this patio as an honored guest, with his parents and his sisters, attending a *fiesta.* Now he was here for another reason.

For a few *centavos,* the new owners would let him take care of the plants in their patio. Idly he wondered what they would do if they knew who he really was.

As he worked, he kept a watchful eye on the house, and one by one the people left, until he knew that the woman was alone. Then he went to the front door, lifted the heavy knocker, and let it fall back against its plate. The door opened, and the woman stood in the cool gloom of the foyer, looking at him uncertainly.

He reached out and put his hands around her neck.

As he began squeezing her life away, he felt her terror, felt all the emotions that racked her spirit. He felt her die, and began to sweat. . . .

He woke up with a start, and sat up. The dream ended, but Alex could still see the face of the woman he'd strangled, and his body was damp with the memory of fear.

And he knew the woman in the dream.

It was Valerie Benson.

But who was he?

The memory of the dream was clear in his mind, and he went over it piece by piece.

The road hadn't been paved. It had been a dirt road, and yet it hadn't seemed strange to him.

And he didn't have a name.

They'd stolen his name.

He knew who "they" were, just as he knew why he'd strangled Valerie Benson.

His parents were dead, and he was taking vengeance on the people who had killed them.

But it still made no sense, for his parents were asleep in their room down the hall.

Or were they?

More and more, the line between what was real and what was not was becoming indistinct.

More and more the odd memories of things that couldn't be were becoming more real than the unfamiliar world he lived in.

Perhaps, that very night, he had killed his parents, and now had no memory of it. He glanced at the clock by the bed; the fluorescent hands read eleven-thirty. He had been in bed only half an hour. There hadn't been enough time for him to go to sleep, then wake up, kill his parents, go back to sleep, then dream about it.

He went back over the evening, step by step, and all of it was perfectly clear in his memory, except for one brief moment. He'd parked across the street from Jake's when María Torres had spoken to him.

Spoken to him in Spanish.

The next thing he remembered was going into Jake's, and that, too, was very clear: he'd gotten out of the car, locked it, and walked from the parking lot into the pizza place.

The parking lot.

He distinctly remembered parking his car on the street across from the pizza parlor, but he also remembered entering Jake's from the parking lot, which was next to the restaurant.

The two memories were in direct conflict, but were equally as strong. There must, therefore, have been two events involved. He must have gone to Jake's twice.

He was still trying to make sense out of his memories, and tie them to the dream, when he heard the wailing of a siren in the distance. Then there was another sound, as the telephone began to ring.

Alex got out of bed and put on his robe, then went down the hall to his parents' room. Though their voices were muffled by the closed door, he could still make out the words.

"They don't know," he heard his father say. "All they know is that they're bringing her in, and that they think she's a DOA."

"If you're going down there, I'm going with you," his mother replied. "And don't try to argue with me. Valerie and I have been friends all our lives. I want to be there."

"Honey, neither of us is going anywhere. I'm not on call tonight, remember? They called because they knew Valerie was a friend of ours."

Slowly Alex backed away from the closed door and returned to his own room.

Valerie. He searched his memory, hoping there was another Valerie there, but there wasn't. It had to be Valerie Benson, and she was dead.

Then, though he had no conscious memory of it at all, he knew why he had arrived at Jake's twice.

He'd gone there once, and then left. After María Torres had spoken to him in Spanish, he'd driven away and gone to Valerie Benson's house, and he'd killed her. Then he'd gone back to Jake's, and sat down at the table with Kate and Bob and Lisa, and talked for a while.

And then he'd come home and gone to bed and dreamed about what he'd done.

But he still didn't know why.

His parents were still alive, and he'd hardly even known Valerie Benson. He had no reason to kill her.

And yet he had.

He got back in bed, and lay for a while staring up at the ceiling in the darkness. Somewhere in his mind he was sure there were answers, and if he thought about the problem long enough, he would figure out what those answers were.

He heard a door open and close, then footsteps in the hall. It was his mother. He heard her going downstairs, then, a little later, he heard his father following her.

For a few minutes he toyed with the idea of going downstairs himself, and telling them about his dream, and that he was sure he'd killed Valerie Benson, and probably Mrs. Lewis too. But then he rejected the whole idea. Unless he could tell them why he'd killed the two women, they surely wouldn't believe he'd done it.

Instead, they'd just think he was crazy.

Alex turned over and pulled the covers snugly around him. He let his mind run free.

And, as he was sure they would, the connections began to come together, and he began to understand what was happening to him.

A few minutes later, he was sound asleep. Through the rest of the night his sleep was undisturbed.

"I'm telling you, Tom, the kids did it," Roscoe Finnerty said as he and Jackson sat in the police station the next morning.

Neither of them had had any sleep, and all Tom Jackson really wanted to do was go home and go to bed, but if Finnerty wanted to talk—and Finnerty usually did—the least he could do was listen. In fact, with Finnerty, listening was all he really had to do, since Finnerty was as capable of posing the questions as he was of coming up with the answers.

"Lookit," Finnerty was saying now. "We got two killings, same M.O. And we got the same two kids discovering both bodies. What could be simpler? And don't tell me there's no previous record of trouble with these kids. They were both up at that bash last spring, when the Lonsdale kid smashed up his car, and they were both drunk—"

"Now, wait a minute, Roscoe," Jackson interrupted. "Let's at least be fair. Did you give any of those kids a test?"

"Well, no, but—"

"Then don't tell me you're going to stand up in court and tell a judge they were drunk, 'cause you ain't! Now, why don't we just go home and let the plainclothes guys do their job?"

Finnerty stared at his partner over the edge of his coffee cup for several long seconds. "You think we ought to just forget it?"

Jackson sighed, and stretched his tired muscles. "I'm not saying to forget it. I'm just saying we've got a job to do, and I think we oughta do it, and not butt in where we aren't invited."

"And leave that poor drunken slob locked up for something he obviously didn't do."

"Whoa up, buddy!" Jackson said, deciding that enough was enough. "You forgetting that the two events might not be connected at all? That we just might have two different perps here?"

"Oh, sure. Both of them apparently let into the house by the victims, and both of them strangled. And both of them discovered by the same girl, who happens to live in the houses where the crimes are committed. You ask me, that's just a bit too much."

"So what are you suggesting?" Jackson asked, knowing full well that whatever it was, it wasn't going to involve going home and going to bed.

"For openers, I think we might have a talk with the other kids that were down at Jake's last night, and see if they noticed anything funny about their friends."

Her eyes puffy from lack of sleep, Carol Cochran stared at the two policemen on the front porch, then glanced at her watch. Though it was a few minutes past seven, it felt much earlier. But despite her exhaustion, she was sure she knew why they were here.

"It's about Valerie Benson, isn't it?" she asked.

The two officers exchanged a glance, then Finnerty nodded. "I'm afraid so. We . . . well, we'd like to talk to your daughter."

Carol blinked. What on earth were they talking about? What could Lisa have to do with what had happened to Valerie? "I . . . I'm sorry," she stammered, "but I don't know what you're talking about." Jim, she thought. Call Jim. He'll know what to do. As if he'd heard her thought, her husband emerged from the kitchen.

"Something wrong, honey?" she heard him ask, and managed to nod her head.

"They . . . they want to talk to Lisa . . ."

Jim Cochran stepped out onto the porch, pulling the door closed behind him. "Now, what's this all about?" he asked. As briefly as they could, Finnerty and Jackson explained why they were there.

Reluctantly Jim invited them into the living room and asked them to sit down. "If she wants to talk to you, it's all right," he said. "But she doesn't have to, you know."

"I know," Finnerty replied. "Believe me, Mr. Cochran, we don't suspect her of anything. All we want to know is if she noticed anything last night."

"I find it impossible to believe that Kate Lewis and Bob Carey would kill anyone," Jim said, his voice tight. "Let alone two people."

"I know, sir," Finnerty said. "But I'd still like to talk to your daughter, if you don't mind."

"What is it?" Carol asked when Jim came into the kitchen a moment later. Jim glanced around the room, but only his wife and older daughter were there. Kim was nowhere to be seen. "I sent Kim up to her room and told her not to come down again until I came up for her. Now, what do they want?"

"It's crazy, if you ask me," Jim replied. "For some reason, they think maybe Kate and Bob killed Valerie, and they want to talk to Lisa about what happened last night. They want to know if she noticed anything strange about either one of them."

"Oh, God," Carol groaned. She sank into a chair, her fingers suddenly twisting at the tie of her bathrobe. Lisa, her eyes wide, was shaking her head in disbelief.

"They think Kate killed Mrs. Benson?" she asked. "That's the dumbest thing I ever heard."

"I know, sweetheart," Jim said. "It doesn't seem possible, but apparently that's what they think. And you don't have to talk to them if you don't want to."

But Lisa stood up. "No," she said. "It's all right. I'll talk to them. And I'll tell them just what a dumb idea they've come up with."

She went into the living room, and the two officers rose to their feet, but before they could speak, Lisa began talking.

"Kate and Bob didn't do anything," she said. "And if you want me to say they were acting funny last night, I won't. They were acting just like they always act, except that Kate was a little quieter than usual."

"Nobody's saying anyone did anything, Lisa," Finnerty interjected. "We're just trying to find out what happened, and if the kids could have had any part in it at all."

"Well, they couldn't," Lisa replied. "And I know why you're asking questions about them. It's those kids in Marin, isn't it?"

Finnerty swallowed, and nodded.

"Well, they were creeps. They were doing drugs all the time, and drinking, and all that kind of stuff. And Bob and Kate aren't like that at all."

"Honey, take it easy," Jim Cochran said, stepping into the room and putting his arm around his daughter. "They just want to ask some questions. If you don't want to answer them, you don't have to, but don't try to keep them from doing their job."

As Lisa turned to gaze into her father's eyes, her indignation dissolved into tears. "But, Daddy, it's so awful. Why would they think Kate and Bob would do such a thing?"

"I don't know," Jim admitted. "And maybe they don't. Now, do you want to talk to them, or not?"

Lisa hesitated, then nodded, and dabbed at her eyes with the handkerchief her father handed her. "I'm sorry," she apologized. "But nothing happened last night."

"All right," Finnerty said, taking out his notebook. "Let's start with that."

Slowly Lisa reconstructed the events of the evening before. She'd gone to Jake's by herself, and, as usual, a lot of the kids had been there. Then, when Bob and Kate came in, the three of them had taken a table together, and sat sipping Cokes and talking about nothing in particular. Then Alex Lonsdale had joined them for a while, and eventually they had all left.

"And there wasn't anything odd about Kate or Bob? They didn't seem nervous, or worried, or anything?"

Lisa's eyes narrowed. "If you mean did they act like they'd just killed someone, no, they didn't. In fact, when they left, Kate even wondered if they ought to call Mrs. Benson and tell her they were on their way." Then, when she saw the two policemen exchange a glance, she spoke again. "And don't try to make anything out of that, either. Kate always called her mom if she was going to be late. She always said her mom had enough to worry about with her dad being a drunk and shouldn't have to worry about her, too."

Finnerty closed his notebook and stood up. "All right," he said. "I guess that's it, if you can't think of anything else—anything out of the ordinary at all."

Lisa hesitated, and once more Finnerty and Jackson exchanged a glance.

"Is there something?" Jim asked.

"I . . . I don't know," Lisa replied.

"It doesn't matter what it is," Finnerty told her, reopening his notepad.

"But it doesn't have anything to do with Kate and Bob," Lisa said.

Jackson frowned. "Then what does it have to do with? One of the other kids?"

Again Lisa hesitated, then nodded. "With . . . with Alex Lonsdale," she said.

"What about Alex?" Jim asked. "It's all right, honey. Just tell us what happened with Alex."

"Well, nothing, really," Lisa said. "Ever since the accident, he's so strange, but last night he said he was getting better, and for a while I thought he was. I mean, he was smiling, and he laughed at jokes, and he seemed almost . . . well, almost like he used to be." She fell silent, and Finnerty finally asked her what, exactly, had happened.

"I don't know," Lisa confessed. "But finally Bob started teasing Alex about something, and Alex didn't blush."

"That's all?" Finnerty asked. "The strange thing was that he *didn't blush?*"

Lisa nodded. "Alex always used to blush. In fact, some of the kids used to say things to him just to watch him get embarrassed. But last night, even though he was smiling, and laughing, and all that, he still wasn't blushing."

"I see," Finnerty said. He closed his notebook for the last time and slid his pencil back in his pocket. A few minutes later, when they were outside, he turned to Jackson. "Well, what do you think?"

"I still think we're barking up the wrong tree," Jackson replied. "But I guess we might as well have a talk with the Lonsdale boy."

"Yeah," Finnerty agreed. Then he rolled his eyes. "Kids amaze me," he said. "They spend a whole evening together, and the only odd thing the girl can remember is that her boyfriend didn't blush. Isn't that something?"

Jackson frowned. "Maybe it *is* important," he said. "Maybe it's very important."

CHAPTER 21

Marsh Lonsdale sat listening as the two officers interviewed Alex about the events of the night before, but found himself concentrating much more on the manner in which his son spoke than on the words themselves. They were in the living room, gathered around the fireplace, and at the far end—huddled alone in a chair as if she wanted to divorce herself from everything—Ellen seemed not to be listening at all.

"Everything," Finnerty had said an hour ago. "We want you to tell us everything you remember about last night, just the way you remember it."

And ever since, Alex had been speaking, his voice steady and expressionless, recounting what he remembered of his activities the night before, from the time he left the house to go to Jake's, to the moment he returned. It was, Marsh realized, almost like listening to a tape recorder. Alex remembered what everyone had said, and repeated it verbatim. After the first twenty minutes, both Finnerty and Jackson had stopped taking notes, and were now simply sitting, listening. When, at last, Alex's recitation was over, there was a long silence, then Roscoe Finnerty got to his feet and went to the mantel. Resting most of his weight on the heavy oak beam that ran the width of the fireplace, he gazed curiously at Alex.

"You really remember all that?" he asked at last.

Alex nodded.

"In that kind of detail?" Finnerty mused aloud.

"His memory is remarkable," Marsh said, speaking for the first time since the interview had begun. "It seems to be a function of the brain surgery that was done after his accident. If he says he remembers all of what he just told you, then you can believe he does."

Finnerty nodded. "I'm not doubting it," he said. "I'm just amazed at the detail, that's all." He turned back to Alex. "You've told us everything that happened at Jake's, and you've told us everything everyone said. But what I want to know is if you noticed anything about Kate Lewis and Bob Carey. Did they act . . . well, *normal?*"

Alex gazed steadily at Finnerty. "I don't know," he said. "I don't really know what normal is anymore. What you're asking me to do is describe how they appeared to be feeling, but I can't do that, since I don't have feelings anymore. I had them before the accident—or at least everyone says I did—but since the accident I don't. But they acted just like they always have." Suddenly he grinned uncomfortably. "Bob was teasing me a little."

"I know," Tom Jackson said. "Your girlfriend told us about that. And she said you didn't blush."

"I don't think I can blush. I might be able to learn how, but I haven't yet."

"Learn how?" Jackson echoed blankly. "But you just *smiled.*"

Alex glanced at his father, and Marsh nodded. "I've been practicing. I'm not like other people, so I'm practicing being like other people. It seemed like I ought to grin before I admitted that Bob was teasing me, so I did."

"Okay," Finnerty said, staring at the boy and feeling chilled. "Is there anything else you remember? Anything at all?"

Alex hesitated, then shook his head. A few minutes later, Finnerty and Jackson were gone.

"Alex?" Marsh asked. "Is there something else you remember about last night that you didn't tell them?"

Once again, Alex shook his head. Everything he remembered, he'd told them about. But they hadn't asked him if he knew who killed Valerie Benson. If they had, he would have told them, though he wouldn't have been able to tell them why she died, or why Mrs. Lewis died, either. But when he'd awakened this morning, the last pieces had fallen into place, and it had all come together in his mind. He understood his brain now, and soon he would understand exactly what had happened.

He would understand what had happened, and he would know who he was.

* * *

"Why, Alex," Arlette Pringle said, her plain features lighting up with a smile, "you're becoming quite a regular here, aren't you?"

"I need some more information, Miss Pringle," Alex replied. "I need to know more about the town."

"La Paloma?" Miss Pringle asked, her voice doubtful. "I'm afraid I just don't have much. I have the book I showed you a couple of days ago, but that's about it." She shrugged ruefully. "I'm afraid not much ever happened here. Nothing worth writing about, anyway."

"But there has to be something," Alex pressed. "Something about the old days, when the town was mostly Mexican."

"Mexican," Arlette repeated, her lips pursing thoughtfully as her fingers tapped on her desktop. "I'm afraid I just don't know exactly what you want. I have some information about the Franciscan fathers, and the missions, but I'm not sure there's much that's specifically about *our* mission. La Paloma just wasn't that important."

"What about when the Americans came?"

Again Arlette shrugged. "Not that I know of. Of course, there are the old stories, but I don't pay any attention to them, and I don't think they're written down anywhere."

"What stories?"

"Oh, some of the older Chicanos in town still talk about the old days, when Don Roberto de Meléndez y Ruiz still had the hacienda, and about what happened after the treaty was signed." She leaned forward, and her voice dropped confidentially. "Supposedly there was a massacre up there."

Alex frowned slightly, as a vague memory stirred on the edges of his consciousness. "At the hacienda?"

"That's what they say. But of course, the stories have been passed down through the generations, and I don't suppose there's much truth to any of them, really. But if you really want to know about them, why don't you go see Mrs. Torres?"

"María?" Alex asked, his voice suddenly hollow. For the first time since his operation, a pang of genuine fear crashed through the barriers in his mind, and he felt himself tremble. It fit. It fit perfectly with the idea that had begun forming in his mind last night, then come to fruition this morning.

Arlette Pringle nodded. "That's right. She still lives around the corner in a little house behind the mission. You tell her I sent you, but I warn you, once she starts talking, she won't stop." She wrote an address on a slip of paper and handed it to Alex. "Now, don't believe everything she says," she cautioned as Alex was about to leave the library. "Don't forget, she's old, and she's always been very bitter. I can't say I blame her, really, but still, it's best not to put too much stock in her stories. I'm afraid a lot of them have been terribly exaggerated."

Alex left the library, and glanced at the address on the scrap of paper, then crumpled it and threw it into a trash bin. A few minutes later he was a block and a half away, his eyes fixed on a tiny frame house that seemed on the verge of falling in on itself.

Home.

The word flashed into his mind, and images of the little house tumbled over one another. He knew, with all the certainty of a lifetime of memories, that he had come home. He pushed his way through the broken gate and made his way up onto the sagging porch. He knocked at the front door, then waited. As he was about to knock again, the door opened a crack, and the ancient eyes of María Torres peered out at him.

A sigh drifted from her throat, and she opened the door wider.

"M-Mama?" Alex stammered uncertainly.

María gazed at him for a moment, then slowly shook her head. "No," she said softly. "You are not my son. You are someone else. What do you want?"

"M-Miss Pringle sent me." Alex faltered. "She said you might be able to tell me what happened here a long time ago."

There was a long silence while she seemed to consider his words. "You want to know?" she asked at last, her eyes narrowing to slits. "But you already know. You are Alejandro."

Alex frowned, suddenly certain that the familiar searing pain was about to rip through his mind and that the voices were about to start whispering to him. He could almost feel them, niggling around the edges of his consciousness. Doggedly he fought against them. "I . . . I just want to know what happened a long time ago," he managed to repeat.

María Torres fell silent once more, regarding him thoughtfully. At last she nodded. "You are Alejandro," she said again. "You should know what happened." She held the door wide, and Alex stepped through into the eerily familiar confines of a tiny living room furnished only with a threadbare couch, a sagging easy chair, and a Formica-topped table surrounded by four worn dining chairs.

All of it was exactly as it had been in his memories a few moments before.

The shades were drawn, but from one corner a color television suffused the room with an eerie light. Its sound was muted.

"For company," the old woman muttered. "I don't listen, but I watch." She lowered herself carefully into the easy chair, and Alex sat gingerly on the edge of the sofa. "What stories you want to hear?"

"The thieves," Alex said quietly. "Tell me about the thieves and the murderers."

María Torres's eyes flashed darkly in the dim light. *"Por qué?"* she demanded. "Why do you want to know now?"

"I remember things," Alex said. "I remember things that happened, and I want to know more about them."

"What things?" The old woman was leaning forward now, her eyes fixed intently on Alex.

"Fernando," Alex said. "Tío Fernando. He's buried in San Francisco, at the mission."

María's eyes widened momentarily, then she nodded, and let herself sag back in the chair once again. *"Su tío,"* she muttered. *"Sí, es la verdad . . ."*

"The truth?" Alex asked. "What's the truth?"

Once again the old woman's eyes brightened. *"Habla usted español?"*

"I . . . I don't know," Alex said. "But I understood what you said."

The old lady fell silent again, and examined Alex closely through her bleary eyes. In the light of the television set, his features were indistinct, and yet, she realized, the coloring was right. His hair was dark, and his eyes were blue, just as her grandfather had told her Don Roberto's had been, and as his own had been. Making up her mind, she nodded emphatically. *"Sí,"* she muttered. *"Es la verdad. Don Alejando ha regresado . . ."*

"Tell me the stories," Alex said again. "Please just tell me the stories."

"They stole," María said finally. "They came and they stole our lands, and murdered our people. They went up into the canyons first, and murdered the wives of the overseers while the men were out on the land. Then they went to the hacienda and took Don Roberto away and hanged him."

Alex frowned. "The tree," he said. "They hanged him from the big tree."

"Sí," María agreed. "And then they went back to the hacienda, and they killed his family. They killed Doña María, and Isabella, and Estellita. And they would have killed Alejandro, too, if they had found him."

"Alejandro?" Alex asked.

"El hijo," María Torres said softly. "The son of Don Roberto de Meléndez y Ruiz. Doña María told them she had sent him to Sonora, and they believed her. But he stayed. He hid in the mission with his uncle, who was the priest, and they fled to San Francisco. And then, when Padre Fernando died, Alejandro returned to La Paloma."

"Why?" Alex asked. "Why did he come back?"

María Torres stared at him for a long time. When she spoke, her voice was barely audible, but nonetheless her words seemed to fill the room. *"Venganza,"* she said. "He came for vengeance on the thieves and the murderers. Even when he was dying, he said he would never leave. From beyond the grave, he said. From beyond the grave, *venganza.*"

Alex emerged from the little house into the blazing sun of the September morning. He began walking through the village, pausing here and there, turning over the bits and pieces of the story María Torres had told him, examining them carefully, searching for the flaw. His mind told him that the answer he had come up with was impossible, but still the pieces of the story matched his strange memories too well. He knew, though, where he would find the ultimate truth, and what he would do once he found it.

The phone on his desk jangled loudly. For a moment Marsh was tempted to let it ring. Then he realized the call was coming in on his private line. Only a few people knew that number, and even they used it only when it was an emergency.

"I trust you aren't going to force me to implement the provisions of the release," Raymond Torres's cold voice said.

"How did you get this number?"

"I've had this number since the moment I took on your son's case, Dr. Lonsdale. Not that it matters. The only thing that matters is that your wife was to bring Alex to me today."

"I'm afraid that won't be possible, Dr. Torres," Marsh replied. "We've discussed the matter, and it's my decision that you can do Alex no more good. I'm afraid he won't be coming back there anymore."

There was a long silence, and when Torres's voice finally came over the line again, its tone had hardened even further. "And I'm afraid that's not your decision to make, Dr. Lonsdale."

"Nonetheless," Marsh replied, "that's the decision I've made. And I wouldn't advise you to try to come and get him, or have anyone else try to come and get him either. I'm his father, Dr. Torres, and despite your release, I have some rights."

"I see," Torres said, and Marsh thought he heard a sigh come through the phone. "Very well, I'm willing to strike a compromise with you. Bring Alex down this afternoon, and I will explain to you exactly what my procedures have been up until now, and why I think it's necessary that he come back to the Institute."

"Not a chance. Until I know exactly what you've done, you won't see Alex again."

In the privacy of his office, Raymond Torres slumped tiredly behind his desk. Too many hours of too little sleep had finally taken their toll, and he knew he was no longer thinking clearly. But he also knew that letting Alex leave the Institute yesterday had been a mistake. Whatever the consequences, he had to get him back. "Very well," he said. "What time can I expect you?"

Marsh glanced at his appointment book. "A couple of hours?"

"Fine. And after you've heard what I have to say, I'm sure you'll agree that Alex should be back here." The line went dead in Marsh's hand.

* * *

Alex paused at the garden gate, and stared at the high vine-covered wall that separated the patio from the street. Then, making up his mind, he went into the patio, then into the house. The house, as he had hoped it would be, was empty. He went to the garage and began searching through the mound of boxes that still sat, unpacked, against the back wall. Each of them was neatly marked with its contents, and it didn't take him long to find the two he was looking for.

The hedge clippers were at the bottom of the first box. As Alex worked them loose from the tangle of other tools, he wondered if he was doing the right thing. And yet, he had to know. The vines covering the garden wall were part of the pattern, and he had to see for himself if he was right.

The book, after all, might have been wrong.

The clippers in hand, he left the garage and walked down the driveway to the sidewalk. Then, working slowly and deliberately, he began cutting the vines off as close to the ground as the strength in his arms and the thickness of the trunks would allow. He worked his way slowly up the hill until the last stems had been cut; then, going the other way, he tore the thickly matted vegetation loose, letting it pile on the sidewalk at his feet. When he was done, he stepped back and looked at the wall once more.

Though it was covered with the collected dust and dirt of the years, and its whitewash had long since disappeared, the tiles remained.

The wall looked exactly as he had thought it should look when he had first come home from the Institute.

He went back into the garage and opened the second box. His father's shotgun was on top, neatly packed away in its case. He opened the case and methodically began putting the pieces together. When the gun was fully assembled, he took five shells from a half-full box of ammunition and put them in his pocket. Carrying the gun easily in the crook of his right arm, he left the garage and walked once more down the driveway, then turned to the right and started the long climb up toward the hacienda. . . .

It had been a bad morning for Ellen, and as she started up Hacienda Drive she was beginning to wonder if she was going to get through the next few days at all.

She'd spent most of the morning with Carol Cochran, and none of it had been easy. Part of the time they'd simply cried, and part of the time they'd tried to make plans for Valerie Benson's funeral. And over it all hung the question of who had killed Valerie.

And then there had been Carol's oddly phrased question about Alex:

"But is he really getting better? I mean, Lisa keeps telling me about strange things he says."

"No, I don't really remember what"—though Ellen was quite sure she did, and simply didn't want to tell her. "But Lisa really seems very worried. In fact, I think she's just a little frightened of Alex."

Ellen had become increasingly certain that after Valerie's funeral, the Cochrans and the Lonsdales would be seeing a lot less of each other.

She came around the last curve, swinging wide to pull into the driveway, when she suddenly slammed on the brakes. Piled on the sidewalk, nearly blocking the driveway itself, lay the ruins of the masses of morning glory that had covered the patio wall only two hours ago.

"I don't believe it," she whispered aloud, though she was alone in the car. Suddenly the sound of a horn yanked her attention away from the tangle of vines, and she jerkily pulled into the driveway to make room for the car that was coming down the hill. She sat numbly behind the wheel for a moment, then got out of the car and walked back down the drive to stare once more at the mess on the sidewalk.

Who would do such a thing? It made no sense—no sense whatever. It would take years for the vines to grow back. She surveyed the wall, slowly taking in the streaked and stained expanse of plaster, and the intricate patterns of tile that were now all that broke its forbidding expanse. And then, behind her, a voice spoke. Startled, she turned to see one of the neighbors standing on the sidewalk looking glumly at the vines. Ellen's mind suddenly blanked and she had to grope for the woman's name. Then it came back to her. Sheila. Sheila Rosenberg.

"Sheila," she said. Then, her bewilderment showing in her voice: "Look at this. Just look at it!"

Sheila smiled ruefully. "That's kids," she said.

Ellen's expression suddenly hardened. "Kids? Kids did this?"

Now it was Sheila Rosenberg who seemed at a loss. "I meant leave the job half-done." She sighed. "Well, I suppose you know what you're doing, but I'm going to miss the vines, especially in the summer. The colors were always so incredible—"

"What *I'm* doing?" Ellen asked. "Sheila, what on earth are you talking about?"

Finally the smile faded from Sheila's face. "Alex," she said. "Didn't you ask him to cut the vines down?"

Alex? Ellen thought. Alex did this? But . . . but why? Once again she surveyed the wall, and this time her eyes came to rest on the tiles. "Sheila," she asked, "did you know that wall had tiles inlaid in it?"

The other woman shook her head. "Who could know? Those vines were two feet thick, at least. No one's seen the wall itself for years." Her eyes scanned the wall, and her brows furrowed speculatively. "But you know, maybe you did the right thing. If you put in smaller plants, and maybe some trellises, it could be very pretty."

"Sheila, I didn't ask Alex to cut down those vines. Are you sure it was him?"

Sheila stared at her for a moment, then nodded her head firmly. "Absolutely. Do you think I would have let a stranger do it? I saw him a couple of hours ago, and then I got busy with something else. The next time I looked, the vines were all down, and Alex was gone. I thought he must be having lunch or something."

Ellen's gaze shifted to the house. "Maybe that's what he's doing," she said, though she didn't believe it. For some reason, she was sure that Alex was not in the house. "Thanks, Sheila," she said abstractedly. "I . . . well, I guess I'd better find out what's going on." Leaving Sheila Rosenberg standing on the sidewalk, she went through the patio into the house. "Alex? Alex, are you here?"

She was still listening to the silence of the house when the phone began ringing, and she snatched the receiver off the hook and spoke without thinking. "Alex? Alex, is that you?"

There was a moment of silence, and then Marsh's voice came over the line. "Ellen, has something else happened?"

Something else? Ellen thought. My best friends are being murdered, and I don't know what's happening to my son, and you want to know if something else is wrong? At that particular moment, she decided, she hated her husband. When she spoke, though, her voice was eerily calm. "Not really," she said. "It's just that for some reason Alex cut all the vines off the patio wall."

Again there was a silence; then: "Alex is supposed to be at school."

"I know that," Ellen replied. "But apparently he isn't. Apparently he left school—if he even went—and came home and cut down the vines. And now he's gone. Don't ask me where, because I don't know."

In his office, Marsh listened more to the tone of his wife's voice than to her words, and knew that she was on the edge of coming apart.

"Take it easy," he said. "Just sit down and take it easy. I'm on my way home to get you, and then we're going down to Palo Alto."

"Palo Alto?" Ellen asked vacantly. "Why?"

"Torres has agreed to talk to us," Marsh replied. "He'll tell us what's happening to Alex."

Ellen nodded to herself. "But what about Alex?" she asked. "Shouldn't we try to find him?"

"We will," Marsh assured her. "By the time we get back from Palo Alto, he'll probably be home."

"What . . . what if he's not?"

"Then we'll find him."

Now, Ellen thought. We should find him now. But the words wouldn't come. Too much was happening, and too much was closing in on her.

And maybe, she thought, as she sat waiting for Marsh to come for her, maybe finally Raymond would be able to convince Marsh to let him help Alex.

Half a mile away, on the hill above the hacienda, Alex, too, was waiting.

He wasn't yet sure what he was waiting for, but he knew that whatever it was, he was prepared for it.

In his arms, cradled carefully against his chest, was the now loaded shotgun.

CHAPTER 22

Cynthia Evans glanced nervously at her watch. She was running late, and she hated to run late. But if she hurried, she could get the shopping done, swing by the school and pick up Carolyn, and still be home in time for her three-thirty appointment with the gardener. She pulled the front door closed behind her, and moved quickly toward the BMW that stood just inside the gates to the courtyard. As she was about to get into the car, a flash of reflected sunlight caught her eyes, and she looked up onto the hillside that rose beyond the hacienda walls.

He was still sitting there, as he had been since a little past noon.

She knew who it was—it was Alex Lonsdale. She'd determined that much when she'd first seen him, then gotten her husband's binoculars to take a better look. If it had been a stranger, she would have called the police immediately, especially after what had happened to Valerie Benson last night. But to call the police on Alex was another matter. Alex—and Ellen as well—had had enough troubles lately, without her adding to them. If he wanted to sit in the hills, he probably had his reasons.

Even so, she was starting to get annoyed. When they bought the hacienda, why had they not bought the surrounding acreage as well? It was far too easy for people to climb up the hillside and gaze down over the walls, as Alex had done today, invading the privacy they had spent so much money to achieve. For a moment Cynthia was tempted to call the police anyway, and to hell with the Lonsdales' feelings. The only reason she didn't, in fact, was the time.

She was running late, and she hated to run late.

She started the BMW, put it in gear, and raced out of the courtyard and down Hacienda Drive, not even taking the time to make sure the security gates had closed behind her.

Alex watched the car disappear from sight, and knew the house was empty now. He rose to his feet and began scrambling down the hill, holding the shotgun in his left hand, using his right to steady himself on the steep slope. Five minutes later he was at the gates, staring into the courtyard.

The gates were wrong.

They should have been wooden. He remembered them as being made of massive oaken planks, held together by wide wrought-iron straps ending in immense hinges.

And the courtyard itself wasn't right, either. There should be no pool, and instead of the flagstone paving, there should only be packed earth, swept of its dust by the *peones* each day. Silently, his memories coming clearer, Alex moved through the gates, across the courtyard, and into the house.

Here, things were better. The rooms looked as he remembered them, and there was a comforting familiarity. He wandered through them slowly, until he came to the room that had been his. He had been happy when he had lived in this room, and the house had been filled with his parents and his sisters, and everyone else who lived on the hacienda.

Before the *gringos* came.

Los ladrones. Los ladrones y los asesinos.

The pain that always filled him when the memories came surged through him now, and he left the room on the second floor and continued moving through the house.

In the kitchen, nothing was right. The old fireplace was there, but the cooking kettle was gone, and there were new things that had never been there in the old days. He left the kitchen and went back to the foyer.

He stopped, frowning.

There was a new door, a door he had never seen before. He hesitated, then opened it.

There were stairs down into a cellar.

His house had never had a cellar.

Clutching the gun tighter, he descended the stairs, and gazed around him.

All along the wall, there was a mirror, and in front of the mirror, on glass shelves, were masses of bottles and glasses.

All of it wrong, all of it belonging to the thieves.

Raising the shotgun, Alex fired into the mirror.

The mirror exploded, and shards of glass flew everywhere, then the shelves of glasses and bottles collapsed on themselves. A moment later, all that was left was wreckage.

Alex turned away, and started back up the stairs. He would wait in the courtyard for the murderers, as his mother and sisters had waited before.

Now, at last, he would have his vengeance. . . .

"Darling, how would I know why Alex was up there? All he was doing was sitting, looking down at the house."

"Well, you should have called the police," Carolyn complained. "Everybody knows Alex is crazy."

Cynthia shot her daughter a reproving glance. "Carolyn, that's unkind."

"It's true," Carolyn replied. "Mom, I'm telling you—he's acting weirder and weirder all the time. And Lisa says he told her he didn't think Mr. Lewis killed Mrs. Lewis and that he thought someone else was going to get killed. And look what happened to Mrs. Benson last night."

Cynthia turned left up Hacienda Drive. "If you're trying to tell me you think Alex killed them, I don't want to hear it. Ellen Lonsdale is a friend of mine—"

"What's that got to do with anything? I don't care if she's the nicest person in the world—Alex is a fruitcake!"

"That's enough, Carolyn!"

"Aw, come on, Mom—"

"No! I'm tired of the way you talk about people, and I won't hear any more of it." Then, remembering her own impulse just before she'd left the house an hour ago, she softened. "Tell you what. You promise not to talk about him like that anymore, and I promise to call the police if he's still there when we get back. Okay?"

Carolyn shrugged elaborately, and they drove on up the ravine in silence. They came around the last curve, and as Cynthia scanned the hillside, she heard Carolyn groaning.

"Now what's wrong?"

"The gates," Carolyn said. "If I'd left them open, you'd ground me for a week."

Cynthia swore under her breath, then reminded herself that she'd only been gone an hour, and it was the middle of the afternoon. Besides, the courtyard was empty. She drove inside and got out of the car. "Well, at least we don't have to call the police," she observed, her eyes scanning the hills once more. "He's gone."

"Thieves," a soft voice hissed from the shadows of the wide loggia in front of the house. "Murderers."

Cynthia froze.

"Who . . . who's there?" she asked.

"Oh, God," she heard Carolyn whimper. "It's Alex. Mama, it's Alex."

"Quiet," Cynthia said softly. "Just don't say anything, Carolyn. Everything will be all right." Then, her voice louder: "Alex? Is that you?"

Alex stepped out of the shadows, the shotgun held firmly in his hands. "I am Alejandro," he whispered.

His face was dripping blood from a cut above his left eye, and his shirt was stained darkly from another on his shoulder, but if he felt any pain, he gave no sign. Instead he walked slowly forward.

"There," he said, gesturing with the gun toward the south wall. "Over there."

"Do as he says, Carolyn," Cynthia said softly. "Just do as he says, and everything will be all right."

"But he's crazy, Mama!"

"Hush! Just be quiet, and do as he says." She waited for what seemed like an aeon, praying that Carolyn wouldn't try to get back in the car or bolt toward the gates. Then, out of the corner of her eye, she saw her daughter begin to move slowly around the end of the car until she was standing at her side. Cynthia took the girl's hand in her own. "We'll do exactly as he says," she said again. "If we do as he says, he won't hurt us."

Slowly, keeping her eyes fixed on Alex, she began backing around, pulling Carolyn with her. "What is it, Alex?" she asked. "What do you want?"

"Venganza," Alex whispered. *"Venganza para mi familia."*

"Your family, Alex?"

Alex nodded. *"Sí."* Again he began moving forward, backing Cynthia and Carolyn Evans slowly toward the wall.

He could see the wall as it had been that day, even though they'd plastered over the damage and tried to wash away the blood of his family. But the pits from the bullets were still there, and the red stains were as bright as they had been on the day he'd watched his family die.

And now, the moment was finally at hand.

He wondered if the *gringa* woman would face death with the bravery of his mother, crying out her defiance even as the bullets cut the life out of her.

He knew she wouldn't.

She would die a *gringa's* death, begging for mercy. Even now, he could hear her.

"Why?" she was saying. "Why are you doing this? What have we done to you?"

What did my mother and my sisters do to deserve to die at the hands of your men? he thought, but it was not the time for questions.

It was the time for vengeance.

He squeezed the trigger, and the quiet of the afternoon exploded with the roar of the shotgun.

The *gringa's* face exploded before his eyes, and new blood was added to the courtyard wall. Then, as with his mother before her, the woman's knees gave way, and she sank slowly to the ground as her daughter watched, screaming.

As Alex squeezed the trigger a second time, his only wish was that the courtyard was as it should have been, and he could have watched as the blood of the *gringas* disappeared into the dust of the hacienda.

José Carillo turned up Hacienda Drive, and shifted his battered pickup truck into low gear. Listening to the transmission's angry grinding, he hoped the truck would last long enough for him to begin the job at the hacienda. With the amount of money that one job would produce, he would be able to afford a new truck. But he was already late, and worried that he might lose the job before he ever got it. He pressed on the gas pedal, and the old truck coughed, then reluctantly surged forward.

It was on the second curve that he saw the boy coming down the road, a shotgun cradled in his arms, his face and shirt covered with blood. He braked to a stop and called out to the boy. At first the boy hadn't seemed to hear him. Only when José called out a second time did the boy look up.

"You okay?" José asked. "Need some help?"

The boy stared at him for a moment, then shook his head and continued down the road. José watched him until he disappeared through the gate in the wall whose vines had just been torn down—something José's gardener's eyes had noticed as he'd come up the hill. Then he forced the truck back in gear.

He was already inside the courtyard before he saw the carnage that lay against the south wall.

"Jesús, José, y María," he muttered. He crossed himself, then fought down the nausea in his gut as he hurried into the house to find a telephone.

Alex stared at himself in the mirror. Blood still oozed from the cut over his eye, and his shirt was growing stiff.

He'd already examined the shotgun, and knew that he'd fired three shells. The last two were now in the chambers.

And though he had no conscious memory of it, he knew where he'd been when the voices began whispering to him and the images from the past began to flood his mind. He also knew where he'd been when it had ended.

When it began, he'd been on the hillside overlooking the hacienda, remembering María Torres's stories of the past.

And when it ended, he'd been walking away from the hacienda, and the smell of gunpowder was strong, and he was bleeding, and though his body was in pain, in his soul he felt nothing.

Nothing.

But tonight, he was sure, he would dream again, and see what he had done, and feel the pain in his soul.

But it was the last time it would happen, for now he knew why it had happened, and how to end it.

And he also knew that he, Alex, had done none of it.

Everything that had been done, had been done by Alejandro de Meléndez y Ruiz. Now all that was left was to kill Alejandro.

He changed his shirt, but didn't bother to bandage the cut on his forehead.

Picking up the shotgun, he went back downstairs and found the extra set of keys to his mother's car in the kitchen drawer.

He went out to the driveway and started the car. He shifted the gear lever into reverse, then kept his foot on the brake as a police car, its siren screaming, raced up the hill past the house.

He was sure he knew where it was going, and he was sure he knew what its occupants would find when they reached their destination. But instead of following the police car and trying to explain to the officers what he thought had happened, Alex went the other way.

His mind suddenly crystal clear, he drove down the hill, through La Paloma, and out of town. It would take him thirty minutes to reach Palo Alto.

"I'm telling you, something's wrong," Roscoe Finnerty had been saying when the phone on the kitchen wall suddenly rang, and he decided it could damned well ring until he'd finished what he was saying. "The kid said he parked across the street from Jake's. It's right here in my notes."

"And my notes say he parked in the lot next door," Tom Jackson replied. He nodded toward the phone. "And we're in your kitchen, so you can answer the phone."

"Shit," Finnerty muttered, reaching up and grabbing the receiver. "Yeah?" He listened for a few seconds, and Jackson saw the color drain from his face. "Aah, shit," he said again. Then: "Yeah, we'll go up." He hung up the phone and reluctantly met his partner's eyes. "We got two more," he said. "The chief wants us to take a look and see if it looks like the other two. From what he said, though, it doesn't. This time, it's messy."

But he hadn't counted on its being as messy as it actually was. He stood in the courtyard wondering if he should even try to take a pulse from the two corpses that lay against the wall. On one of them, the face was gone, and most of the head as well. Still, he was pretty sure he knew who it was, because the other corpse had taken the shotgun blast in the chest, and the face was still clearly recognizable.

Carolyn Evans.

The other one, judging from what Finnerty could see, had to be her mother. "Call the Center," he muttered to Jackson. "And tell them to bring bags, and not to bother with the sirens." Then he turned his attention to José Carillo, who was sitting by the pool, resolutely looking away from the corpses and the bloodstained wall they rested against.

"You know anything about this, José?" Finnerty asked, though he was almost certain he knew the answer. He'd known José for almost ten years, and the gardener was known only for three things: his industriousness and his honesty and his refusal to involve himself in violence under any circumstances.

José shook his head. "I was coming up for a job. When I got here . . ." His voice broke off, and he shook his head helplessly. "As soon as I found them, I called the police."

"Did you see anything? Anything at all?"

José started to shake his head, then hesitated.

"What is it?" Finnerty urged.

"I forgot," the gardener said. "On the way up, I saw a boy. He looked like he'd been fighting, and he was carrying a gun."

"Do you know who he was?"

The gardener shook his head again. "But I know where he went."

Finnerty stiffened. "Can you show me?"

"Down the road. It's right down the road."

Finnerty glanced toward the squad car, where Jackson was still on the radio. "Let's take your truck, José. You feel good enough to drive?"

José looked uncertain, but then climbed into the cab, and while Finnerty yelled to Jackson that he'd be right back, pressed on the starter and prayed that now, of all times, the truck wouldn't finally give up. The engine sputtered and coughed, then caught.

Half a mile down the hill, José brought the truck to a stop and pointed. "There," he said. "He went in there."

Finnerty stared at the house for several seconds. "Are you sure, José? This could be very serious."

José's head bobbed eagerly. "I'm sure. Look at the mess. They cut the vines off the wall and didn't even clean them up. I don't forget things like that. That's the house the boy went into."

Even with the vines off the wall, Finnerty recognized the Lonsdales' house. After all, it had been little more than eight hours since he'd been there himself.

He got out of the truck, and noted the empty garage. "José, I want you to go back up to the hacienda and send my partner down with the car. Then wait. Okay?"

José nodded, and maneuvered the truck through a clumsy U-turn before disappearing back up the hill. Finnerty stayed where he was, his eyes on the house, though he had a growing feeling that it was empty. A few minutes later, Jackson arrived, and at almost the same time, a woman appeared from the house across the street and a few yards down from the Lonsdales'.

"There isn't anyone there," Sheila Rosenberg volunteered. "Marsh and Ellen left two hours ago, and I saw Alex leave in Ellen's car a few minutes ago."

"Do you know where they went? The parents, I mean?"

"I'm sure I haven't a clue," Sheila replied. "I don't keep track of everything that happens in the neighborhood, you know." Then her voice dropped slightly. "Is something wrong?"

Finnerty glared at the woman, certain that she did, indeed, keep track of everything her neighbors were doing. "No," he said. If he told her the truth, she would be the first one up the hill. "We just want to get some information, that's all."

"Then you'd better call the Center," Sheila Rosenberg replied. "I'm sure they'll know where to find Marsh."

Despite Sheila Rosenberg's assertion that the house was as empty as he thought it was, Finnerty searched it anyway.

In the bedroom he was sure was Alex's, he found the blood-soaked shirt and carefully put it in a plastic bag Jackson brought from the squad car. Then he called the Medical Center.

"I know exactly where he went," Barbara Fannon told him after he'd identified himself. "He and Ellen went down to Palo Alto to talk to Dr. Torres about Alex. Apparently he's having some kind of trouble." And that, Finnerty thought grimly as Barbara Fannon searched for the number of the Institute for the Human Brain, is the understatement of the year.

Marsh felt his patience slipping rapidly away.

They had been at the Institute for almost two hours, and for the first hour and a half they had cooled their heels in the waiting room. This time, Marsh had ignored the journals, in favor of pacing the room. Ellen, however, had hardly moved at all from her place on the sofa, where she sat silently, her face pale, her hands folded in her lap.

And now, as they sat in Torres's office, they were being fed double-talk. The first thing Torres had done when he'd finally deigned to see them was show them a computer reconstruction of the operation.

It had been meaningless, as far as Marsh could tell. It had been speeded up, and the graphics on the monitor were not nearly as clear as they had been when Torres had produced the original depiction of Alex's injured brain.

"This is, of course, an operating program, not a diagnostic one," Torres had said smoothly. "What you're seeing here was never really meant for human eyes. It's a program designed to be read by a computer, and fed to a robot, and the graphics simply aren't important. In fact, they're incidental."

"And they don't mean a damned thing to me, Dr. Torres," Marsh declared. "You told me you'd explain what's happening to Alex, and so far, all you've done is dodge the issue. You now have a choice. Either get to the point, or I'm walking out of here—*with* my wife—and the next time you see us we'll all be in court. Can I make it any clearer than that?"

Before Torres could make any reply, the telephone rang. "I said I wasn't to be disturbed under any circumstances," he said as soon as he'd put the phone to his ear. He listened for a moment, then frowned and held the receiver toward Marsh. "It's for you, and I take it it's some sort of emergency."

"This is Dr. Lonsdale," Marsh said, his voice almost as impatient as Torres's had been. "What is it?"

And then he, too, listened in silence as the other person talked. When he hung up, his face was pale and his hands were trembling.

"Marsh . . ." Ellen breathed. "Marsh, what is it?"

"It's Alex," Marsh said, his voice suddenly dead. "That was Sergeant Finnerty. He says he wants to talk to Alex."

"Again?" Ellen asked, her heart suddenly pounding. "Why?"

When he answered, Marsh kept his eyes on Raymond Torres.

"He says Cynthia and Carolyn Evans are both dead, and he says he has reason to think that Alex killed them."

As Ellen gasped, Raymond Torres rose to his feet.

"If he said that, then he's a fool," Torres rasped, his normally cold eyes glittering angrily.

"But that *is* what he said," Marsh whispered. Then, as Torres sank slowly back into his chair, Marsh spoke again. "Please, Dr. Torres, tell me what you've done to my son."

"I saved him," Torres replied, but for the first time, his icy demeanor had disappeared. He met Marsh's eyes, and for a moment said nothing. Then he nodded almost imperceptibly.

"All right," he said quietly. "I'll tell you what I did. And when I'm done, you'll see why Alex couldn't have killed anyone." He fell silent for a moment, and when he spoke again, Marsh was almost sure he was speaking more to himself than to either Marsh or Ellen. "No, it's impossible. Alex couldn't have killed anyone."

Speaking slowly and carefully, he explained exactly what had been done to Alex Lonsdale.

CHAPTER 23

Ellen tried to still her trembling hands as her eyes searched her husband's face for whatever truth might be written there. But Marsh's face remained stonily impassive, as it had been all through Raymond Torres's long recitation. "But . . . but what does it all mean?" she finally asked. For the last hour, at least, she had no longer been able to follow the details of what Torres had been saying, nor was she sure the details mattered. What was frightening her was the implications of what she had heard.

"It doesn't matter what it means," Marsh said, "because it's medically impossible."

"Think what you like, Dr. Lonsdale," Raymond Torres replied, "but what I've told you is the absolute truth. The fact that your son is still alive is the proof of it." He offered Marsh a smile that was little more than a twisted grimace. "The morning after the operation, I believe you made reference to a miracle. You were, I assume, thinking of a medical miracle, and I chose not to correct you. What it was, though, was a technological miracle."

"If what you're saying is actually true," Marsh said, "what you've done is no miracle at all. It's an obscenity."

Ellen's eyes filled with tears, which she made no attempt to wipe away. "But he's alive, Marsh," she protested, and then shrank back in her chair as Marsh turned to face her.

"Is he? By what criteria? Let's assume that what Torres says is true. That Alex's brain was far too extensively damaged even to attempt repairs." His eyes, flashing with anger, flicked to Torres. "That *is* what you said, isn't it?"

Torres nodded. "There was no brain activity whatever, except on the most primitive level. His heart was beating, but that was all. Without the respirator, he couldn't breathe, and as far as we could tell, he made no response to any sort of stimulation."

"In other words, he was brain dead, with no hope of recovery?"

Again Torres nodded. "Not only was his brain dead, it was physically torn beyond repair. Which is the only reason I went ahead with the techniques I used."

"Without our permission," Marsh grated.

"*With* your permission," Torres corrected. "The release clearly allowed me to use any methods I deemed necessary or fit, whether they were proven or unproven, traditional or experimental. And they worked." He hesitated, then went on. "Perhaps I made a mistake," he said. "Perhaps I should have declared Alex dead, and asked that his body be donated to science."

"But isn't that exactly what you did?" Marsh demanded. "Without, of course, the niceties of telling us what you were doing?"

Torres shook his head. "For the operation to be a complete success, I wanted there to be no question that Alex is still Alex. Had I declared him dead, what I have done would have led to certain questions I was not yet prepared to deal with."

Suddenly Ellen rose to her feet. "Stop it! Just stop it!" Her eyes moved wildly from Marsh to Raymond Torres. "You're talking about Alex as if he no longer exists!"

"In a way, Ellen," Torres replied, "that's exactly the truth. The Alex you knew doesn't exist anymore. The only Alex that is real is the one I created."

There was a sudden silence in the room, broken at last by Marsh's voice, barely more than a whisper. "That you created with *microprocessors?* I still can't believe it. It just isn't possible."

"But it is," Torres said. "And it isn't nearly as complicated as it sounds, except physically. It's the connections that are the most difficult. Finding exactly the right neurons to connect to the leads of the microprocessors themselves. Fortunately, the brain itself is an aid there. Given an opportunity, it will build its own pathways and straighten out most of the human errors by itself."

"But Alex is alive," Ellen insisted. "He's alive."

"His body is alive," Torres agreed. "And it's kept alive by seventeen separate microprocessors, each of which is programmed to maintain and monitor the various physical systems of his body. Three of those microprocessors are concerned with nothing except the endocrine system, and four more handle the nervous system. Some of the systems are less complicated than those two, and could be lumped together in a single chip with a backup. Four of the chips are strictly memory. They were the easy ones."

"Easy ones?" Ellen echoed, her voice weak.

Torres nodded. "This project has been under way for years, ever since I became interested in artificial intelligence—the concept of building a computer that can actually reason on its own, rather than simply make computations at an incredibly rapid speed. And the problem there is that despite all we know about the brain, we still have no real concept of how the process of original thought takes place. It very quickly became obvious to me that until we understood the process in the human brain, we couldn't hope to duplicate it in a machine. And yet, we want machines that can think like people."

"And you found the answer," Marsh said, his voice tight.

Torres ignored his tone. "I found the answer. It seemed to me that since we couldn't make a machine that could think like a man, perhaps we could create a man who could compute like a machine.

"A man with the memory capacity of a computer.

"The implication was obvious, and though the technology was not there ten years ago, it is today. The answer seemed to me to involve installing a high-capacity microprocessor inside the brain itself, giving the brain access to massive amounts of information, and enormous computational abilities, while the brain itself provides the reasoning circuits that are not yet feasible."

"And did you do that?" Marsh asked.

Torres hesitated, then shook his head. "The risks seemed to me to be entirely too great, and the stakes too high. I had no idea what the results might be. That's when I began work on the project of which Alex is the end result." He smiled thinly. "It's no accident that the Institute for the Human Brain is in the heart of Silicon Valley, you know. All our work is highly technical, and extremely expensive. And we have very little to show for it, despite all those articles out in the lobby." Marsh seemed about to interrupt him, but Torres held up a restraining hand. "Let me finish. As I said, my work is highly technical, and very expensive, but this is one area of the country that has an abundance of money available to do just such work. And so I took my proposed solution to the problem to certain companies and venture capitalists, and managed to intrigue them to the point where they have been willing to fund my research. And what my research has been, for the last ten years, is nothing more or less than reducing the monitoring and operation of every system in the human body to language a computer can understand, and then programming that information into microprocessors."

"If it's true," Marsh breathed, "that's quite incredible."

"Not quite as incredible as it is useless," Torres replied. "At first glance, it might seem quite marvelous, with all kinds of applications, but I'm afraid that isn't the case. Usually, when a system goes bad in the human body, the dysfunction is caused by disease, not a failure of the brain. And good as my programs are, they can only function with healthy systems. What they don't need is a healthy brain.

"You see," he said quietly, "I decided years ago that I couldn't experiment on someone who had a normal life ahead of him. I was only willing to work with a hopelessly brain-damaged case—someone who would unquestionably die unless I tried installing my processors—but whose body was basically intact. And that meant that the memory and computation chips wouldn't be enough. So I spent ten years developing all the systems-maintenance programs as well."

Raymond Torres opened the top drawer of his desk and pulled out a Lucite block, which he pushed across the desk to Marsh. "If you're interested," he said, "that block contains duplicates of the processors that are in Alex's brain."

Marsh picked up the block of Lucite—only a couple of inches on a side—and gazed into the transparent plastic. Floating in the apparent emptiness were several tiny specks, each no bigger than the head of a pin. "Those," he heard Torres saying, "are the most powerful microprocessors available today. They're a new technology, which I don't pretend to understand, and they can operate perfectly on the tiny amount of current generated by the human body. Indeed, I'm told they require less electrical energy than the brain itself."

Finally, as he stared at the tiny chips held prisoner in the Lucite, Marsh began to believe what Raymond Torres had been telling him, and when he finally shifted his gaze to the other doctor, his eyes were brimming with tears.

"Then Alex was right," he said, his voice unsteady. "When he told me last night that he thought maybe he hadn't really survived the operation—that maybe he really was dead—he was right."

Torres hesitated, then reluctantly nodded. "Yes," he agreed. "Certainly, in one sense, at least, Alex is dead. His body isn't dead, and his intellect isn't dead, but almost certainly, his personality is dead."

"No!" Ellen was on her feet, and she took a step toward Torres's desk. "You said he was all right! You said he was getting better!"

"And part of him is," Torres replied. "Physically and mentally, he's been getting better every day."

"But there's more," Ellen protested. "You know there's more. He . . . he's starting to remember things—"

"Which is exactly why I wanted him to come back here," Torres said smoothly. Until this moment, he had told them the truth.

Now the lies would begin.

"He's remembering things that he couldn't possibly remember at all. Some of them are things that happened—if they happened at all—long before he was born."

"But he *is* remembering things," Ellen insisted.

Torres only shook his head. "No, he's not," he said flatly. "Please listen to me, Ellen. It's very important that you understand what I'm about to tell you." Ellen looked uncertain, then lowered herself back into her chair. "There are some things you still aren't accepting, and although I know it's difficult, you have to accept them. First, Alex has no memories of what happened before his accident. All he knows is what was programmed into the memory banks I installed during the operation, together with whatever experiences he's had since then. Basically, when he woke up he had a certain amount of data that were readily accessible to him. Vocabulary, recognition of certain images—that sort of thing. Since then, he has been taking in data and processing it at the rate of a very large computer. Which is why," he went on, turning to Marsh, "he appears to have the intelligence of a genius." Torres picked up the little block of Lucite and began toying with it. "What he actually has is total recall of everything he's come in contact with since the operation, plus the ability to do calculations in his head at an astonishing rate, with total accuracy, plus the very human ability to reason. Whether that makes him a genius, I don't know. Frankly, what Alex is or is not is for other people to decide, not me.

"But he has limitations, as well. The most obvious one is his lack of emotional response." For the first time that afternoon, Torres picked up his pipe, and began stuffing it with tobacco. "We know a great deal about emotions. We even know from which areas of the brain certain of them spring. Indeed, we can create some of them by stimulating certain areas of the brain. But in the end, they aren't anything I've been able to write programs for, which is why Alex is totally lacking them. And that," he added, almost incidentally, "brings us back to the reason why I've told you all this at all." As he lit his pipe, his eyes met Marsh's, and held them steadily. "If you accept the truth of what I've been telling you, then I think you'll agree that Alex is quite incapable of murder."

"I'm afraid I don't see that at all," Marsh replied. "From what you've said, it would seem to me that Alex would make the most ideal killer in the world, since he has no feelings."

"And he would," Torres agreed. "Except that murder is not part of his programming, and he's only capable of doing what he's programmed to do. Murder, as I'm sure you're aware, is most often motivated by emotions. Anger, jealousy, fear—any number of things. But they are all things of which Alex has no knowledge or experience. He's aware that emotions exist, but he's never experienced them. And without emotions, he would never find himself prey to the urge to kill."

"Unless," Marsh replied, "he were programmed to kill."

"Exactly. But even then, he would analyze the order, and unless the killing made intellectual sense to him, he would refuse the order."

Marsh tried to digest Torres's words, but found himself unable to. His mind was too filled with conflicting emotions and thoughts. He felt a numbness of the spirit that he abstractedly identified as shock. And why not? he thought. He's dead. My son is dead, and yet he's not. He's somewhere right now, walking and talking and thinking, while I sit here being told that he doesn't really exist at all, that he's nothing more than . . . He rejected the word that came to mind, then accepted it: nothing more than some kind of a machine. His eyes moved to Ellen, and he could see that she, too, was struggling with her emotions. He got to his feet and went to her, kneeling by her chair.

"He's dead, sweetheart," he whispered softly.

"No," Ellen moaned, burying her face in her hands as her body was finally racked by the sobs she had been holding back so long. "No, Marsh, he can't be dead. He can't be. . . ." He put his arms around her and held her close, gently stroking her hair. When he spoke again, it was to Raymond Torres, and his words were choked with anger and grief.

"Why?" he asked. "Why did you do this to us?"

"Because you asked me to," Torres replied. "You asked me to save his life, any way I could, and that's what I did, to the best of my ability." Then he sighed heavily, and carefully placed his pipe back on his desk. "But I did it for myself, too," he said. "I won't deny that. I had the technology, and I had the skill." His eyes met Marsh's. "Let me ask you something. If you had been in my position, would you have done what I did?"

Marsh was silent for a full minute, and he knew that Torres had asked a question for which he had no answer. When he at last spoke, his voice reflected nothing except the exhaustion he was feeling. "I don't know," he said. "I wish I could say that I wouldn't have, but I don't know." Shakily he rose to his feet, but kept his hand protectively on Ellen's shoulder. "What do we do now?"

"Find Alex," Torres replied. "We have to find him, and get him back here. Something happened yesterday, and I don't know what effect it might have had on Alex. There was . . . well, there was an error in the lab, and Alex underwent some tests without anesthesia." Briefly he described the tests, and what Alex must have experienced. "He didn't show any effects afterward, which indicates that there was no damage done, but I'd like to be sure. And there's still the problem of the memories he thinks he's having."

Marsh stiffened as he suddenly realized that for all his carefully worded explanations, Torres was still holding something back. "But he *is* having them," he said. "How can that be?"

"I don't know," Torres admitted. "And that's why I want him back here. Somewhere in his memory banks there is an error, and that error has to be corrected. What seems to be happening is that Alex is becoming increasingly involved in finding the source of those memories. *There is no source,*" Torres said, and paused as his words penetrated the Lonsdales like daggers of ice. "When he discovers that, I'm not sure what might happen to him."

Marsh's voice hardened once more. "It sounds to me, Dr. Torres, as if you're implying that Alex might go insane. If that has indeed happened, isn't it possible that you're entirely wrong, and Alex could, after all, have committed murder?"

"No," Torres insisted. "The word doesn't apply. Computers don't go insane. But they do stop functioning."

"A systems crash, I believe they call it," Marsh said coldly, and Torres nodded. "And in Alex's case, may I assume that would be fatal?"

Again Torres nodded, this time with obvious reluctance. "I have to agree that that is quite possible, yes." Then, seeing the look of fear and confusion on Ellen's face, he went on: "Believe me, Ellen, Alex has done nothing wrong. In all likelihood, I'll be able to help him. He'll be all right."

"But he won't," Marsh said quietly, drawing Ellen to her feet. "Dr. Torres, please don't try to hold out any more false hope to my wife. The best thing she can do right now is try to accept the fact that Alex died last May. As of this moment, I do not know exactly who the person is who looks like my son and has been living in my house, but I do know that it is not Alex." As Ellen began quietly sobbing once more, he led her toward the door. "I don't know what to do now, Dr. Torres, but you may rest assured that should Alex come home, I will call the police and explain to them that Alex—or whoever he is—is legally in your custody, and that any questions they have should be directed to you. He is not my son anymore, Dr. Torres. He hasn't been since the day I brought him to you." He turned away, and led Ellen out of the office.

They were halfway back to La Paloma before Ellen finally spoke. Her voice was hoarse from her crying. "Is he really dead, Marsh?" she asked. "Was he telling us the truth?"

"I don't know," Marsh replied. It was the same question he'd been grappling with ever since they'd left the Institute, and he still had no answer. "He was telling us the truth, yes. I believe he did exactly what he says he did. But as for Alex, I wish I could tell you. Who knows what death really is? Legally, Alex could have been declared dead before we ever took him down to Palo

Alto. According to the brain scans, there was no activity, and that's a legal criterion for death."

"But he was still breathing—"

"No, he wasn't. Not really. Our machines were breathing for him. And now Raymond Torres has invented new machines, and Alex is walking and talking. But I don't know if he's Alex. He doesn't act like Alex, and he doesn't think like Alex, and he doesn't respond like Alex. For weeks now, I've had this strange feeling that Alex wasn't there, and apparently I was right. Alex *isn't* there. All that's there is whatever Raymond Torres constructed in Alex's body."

"But it *is* Alex's body," Ellen insisted.

"But isn't that all it is?" Marsh asked, his voice reflecting the pain he was feeling. "Isn't it the part we bury when the spirit's gone? And Alex's spirit is gone, Ellen. Or if it isn't, then it's trapped so deep inside the wreckage of his brain that it will never escape."

Ellen said nothing for a long time, staring out into the gathering gloom of the evening. "Then why do I still love him?" she asked at last. "Why do I still feel that he's my son?"

"I don't know," Marsh replied. Then: "But I'm afraid I lied back there. I was angry, and I was hurt, and I didn't want to believe what I was hearing, and for a little while, I wanted Alex to be dead. And part of me is absolutely certain that he is." He fell silent, but Ellen was certain he had more to say, so she sat quietly waiting. After a few moments, as if there had been no lapse of time, Marsh went on. "But part of me says that as long as he's living and breathing, he's alive, and he's my son. I love him too, Ellen."

For the first time in months, Ellen slid across the seat and pressed close to her husband. "Oh, God, Marsh," she whispered. "What are we going to do?"

"I don't know," he confessed. "In fact, I'm not sure there's anything we can do, except wait for Alex to come home."

He didn't tell Ellen that he wasn't at all sure Alex would ever come home again.

CHAPTER 24

It was not a large house, but it was set well back from the street. Though he couldn't read the address, Alex knew he was at the right place. It had been simple, really. When he'd come into Palo Alto, he'd shut all images of La Paloma out of his mind, then concentrated on the idea of going home. After that, he'd merely followed the impulses his brain sent him at each intersection until he'd finally come to a stop in front of the Moorish-style house he was now absolutely certain belonged to Dr. Raymond Torres. He studied it for a few moments, then turned into the driveway, parking the car on the concrete apron that widened out behind the house.

From the street, the car was no longer visible.

Alex got out of the car, closed the driver's door, then opened the trunk.

He picked up the shotgun, holding it in his right hand while he used his left to slam the trunk lid. Carrying the gun almost casually, he crossed to the back door of the house and tried the knob. It was locked.

He glanced around the patio behind the house, uncertain of what he was looking for, but sure that he would recognize it when he saw it.

It was a large earthenware planter, exploding with the vivid colors of impatiens in full bloom. In the center of the planter, wrapped neatly in aluminum foil and well-hidden by the profuse foliage, he found the spare key to the house. Letting himself inside, he moved confidently through the kitchen and dining room, then down a short hall to the den.

This, he was sure, was the room in which Dr. Torres spent most of his time. There was a fireplace in one corner, and a battered desk that was in stark contrast to the gleaming sleekness of the desk Torres used at the Brain Institute. And in equal contrast to the Institute office was the clutter of the den. Everywhere were books and journals, stacked high on the desk and shoved untidily onto the shelves that lined the walls. Most were medical books and technical journals relating to Torres's work, but some were not. Resting the gun on its butt in the corner behind the door, Alex began a closer examination of the library, knowing already what he was looking for, and knowing that he would find it.

There were several old histories of California, detailing the settling of the area by the Spanish-Mexicans, and the subsequent ceding of the territory to the United States. Tucked between two thick tomes was the thin leather-bound volume, its spine intricately tooled in gold, that Alex was looking for. Handling the book carefully, he removed it from the shelf, then sat down in the worn leather chair that stood between the fireplace and the desk. He opened it to the first page, and examined the details of the illuminations that had been painstakingly worked around the ornate lettering.

It was a family tree, detailing the history of the family of Don Roberto de Meléndez y Ruiz, his antecedents, and his descendants. Alex scanned the pages quickly until he came to the end.

The last entry was Raymond Torres, son of María and Carlos Torres.

It was through his mother, María Ruiz, that Raymond Torres traced his lineage back to Don Roberto, through Don Roberto's only surviving son, Alejandro. Below the box containing Raymond Torres's name, there was another box.

It was empty.

Alex closed the book and laid it on the hearth in front of the fireplace, then moved on to Torres's desk. Without hesitation, he pulled the bottom-right-hand drawer open, reached into its depths, and pulled out a nondescript notebook.

In the notebook, neatly penned in a precise hand, was Raymond Torres's plan for creating the son he had never fathered.

It was getting dark when Alex heard the car pull up. He retrieved the gun from the corner behind the door. When Raymond Torres entered the den a few moments later, it lay almost carelessly in Alex's lap, though his right forefinger was curled around the trigger. Torres paused in the doorway, frowning thoughtfully, then smiled.

"I don't think you'll kill me," he said. "Nor, for that matter, do I think you have killed anyone else. So why don't you put that gun down, and let us talk about what's happening to you."

"There's no need to talk," Alex replied. "I already know what happened to me. You've put computers in my brain, and you've been programming me."

"You found the notebook."

"I didn't need to find it. I knew where it was. I knew where this house was, and I knew what I'd find here."

Torres's smile faded into a slight frown. "I don't think you could have known those things."

"Of course I could," Alex replied. "Don't you understand what you've done?"

Torres closed the door, then, ignoring the gun, moved around his desk and eased himself into his chair. He regarded Alex carefully, and wondered briefly if, indeed, something had gone awry. But he rejected the idea; it was impossible. "Of course I understand," he finally said. "But I'm not sure you do. What, exactly, do you think I've done?"

"Turned me into you," Alex said softly. "Did you think I wouldn't figure it out?"

Torres ignored the question. "And how, exactly, did I do that?"

"The testing," Alex replied. "Only you weren't testing me, really. You were programming me."

"I'll agree to that," Torres replied, "since it happens to be absolutely true. Incidentally, I explained it all to your parents this afternoon."

"Did you? Did you really tell them all of it?" Alex asked. "Did you tell them that it wasn't just data you programmed in?"

Torres frowned. "But it was."

Alex shook his head. "Then you don't understand, do you?"

"I don't understand what you're talking about, no," Torres said, though he understood perfectly. For the first time, he began to feel afraid.

"Then I'll tell you. After the operation, my brain was a blank. I had the capacity to learn, because of the computers you put in my brain, but I didn't have the capacity to think."

"That's not true—"

"It *is* true," Alex insisted. "And I think you knew it, which is why you had to give me a personality as well as just enough data to look like I was . . . What? Suffering from amnesia? Was I supposed to remember things slowly, so it would look like I was recovering? But I couldn't remember anything, could

I? My brain—Alex Lonsdale's brain—was dead. So you gave me things to remember, but they were the wrong things."

"I haven't the vaguest idea what you're talking about, Alex, and neither have you," Torres declared icily.

"It's strange, really," Alex went on, ignoring Torres's words. "Some of the mistakes were so small, and yet they set me to wondering. If it had only been the oldest stuff—"

"The 'oldest stuff'?" Torres echoed archly.

"The oldest memories. The memories of the stories your mother used to tell you."

"My mother is an old woman. Sometimes she gets confused."

"No," Alex replied. "She's not confused, and neither are you. The memories served their purpose, and all the people died. You used me to kill them, and I did. And, as you wished, I had no memory of what I'd done. As soon as the killings were over, they were wiped out of my memory banks. But even if I had remembered them, I wouldn't have been able to say why I was killing. All I would have been able to do is talk about Alejandro de Meléndez y Ruiz and *venganza.* Revenge. I would have sounded crazy, wouldn't I?"

"You're sounding crazy right now," Torres said, rising to his feet.

Alex's hands tightened on the shotgun. "Sit down," he said. Torres hesitated, then sank back into his chair. "But it *was* revenge you wanted," Alex went on. "Only not revenge for what happened in 1848. Revenge for what happened twenty years ago."

"Alex, what you're saying makes no sense."

"But it does," Alex insisted. "The school. That was one of your mistakes, but only a small one. I remembered the dean's office being in the wrong place. But it wasn't the wrong place—I was just twenty years too late. When *you* were at La Paloma High, the dean's office was where the nurse's office is now."

"Which means nothing."

"True. I could have seen the same pictures of the school in my mother's yearbook that I saw in yours."

Torres's eyes flickered over the room, first to the bookshelf where his family tree rested, then to the notebook that still lay on top of his desk where Alex had left it.

Next to it, lying open, was the annual from his senior year at La Paloma High. It was open to a picture he had studied many times over the years. As he looked at it now, he felt once more the pain the people it depicted had caused him.

All four of them: Marty and Valerie and Cynthia and Ellen.

The Four Musketeers, who had inflicted wounds on him that he had nursed over the years—never allowing them to heal—until finally they had festered.

And as the wounds festered, the planning had begun, and then, when the opportunity finally came, he had executed his plan.

The memories had been carefully constructed in Alex—the memories of things he couldn't possibly remember—so that when he finally got caught, as Torres knew he eventually would, all he would be able to do was talk of ancient wrongs and the spirit of a long-dead man who had taken possession of him.

The truth would be carefully shielded, for Torres had programmed no memories in Alex of the hatred he felt toward the four women who had looked down on him so many years ago, ignored him as if he didn't exist.

Even now, he could hear his mother's voice talking about them:

"You think they even look at you, Ramón? They are *gringos* who would spit on you. They are no different than the ones who killed our family, and they will kill you too. You wait, Ramón. Pretend all you want, but in the end you will know the truth. They hate you, Ramón, as you will hate them."

And in the end, she had been right, and he had hated them as much as she did.

And now it was over. Because Raymond Torres had created Alex, he knew what Alex was going to do. Oddly, he could even accept it. "How did you figure it out?"

"With the tools you gave me," Alex replied. "I processed data. The facts were simple. From the damage done to my brain, I should have died.

"But I wasn't dead.

"The two facts didn't match, until I realized that there was one way I could make them match. I could still be alive, if something had been done to keep my body functioning in spite of the damage to my brain. And the only thing capable of doing that was a system of microprocessors performing the functions of my brain.

"But then I had to fit the memories in.

"Alex Lonsdale has no memories. None at all, because he's dead. But I was remembering things, and the answer had to be the same. What I was remembering had to have been programmed into me too, along with all the rest of the data. From there, it wasn't hard to figure out who I really am."

"My son," Torres said softly. "The son I never had."

"No," Alex replied. "I am not your son, Dr. Torres. I am you. Inside my head are all the memories you grew up with. They're not my memories, Dr. Torres. They're yours. Don't you understand?"

"It's the same thing," Torres said, but Alex shook his head.

"No. It's not the same thing, because if it were, I would be about to kill my father. But I'm you, Dr. Torres, so I guess you are about to kill yourself."

His hands steady, Alex raised the shotgun, leveled it at Raymond Torres, and squeezed the trigger. Alex watched as Raymond Torres's head was nearly torn from his body by the force of the buckshot that exploded from the gun's barrel.

As he left Torres's house, the phone began ringing, but Alex ignored it.

Getting into Torres's car—his own car, now—he started back toward La Paloma.

All of them were dead—Valerie Benson, Marty Lewis, and Cynthia Evans. All of them dead, except one.

Ellen Lonsdale was still alive.

Roscoe Finnerty carefully replaced the phone on its hook, and turned to face the Lonsdales once more.

Ellen, as she had been since they got home, was sitting on the sofa, her face pale, her hands trembling. Her eyes, reddened from weeping, blinked nervously, and she seemed to have become incapable of speech.

Marsh, on the other hand, wore a demeanor of calm that belied the inner turmoil he was feeling. Before beginning to answer Finnerty's questions, he had tried to think carefully about what he should say, but in the end he'd decided to tell the officers the truth.

First, they had asked about the gun, and Marsh had led them to the garage, and the box where he was sure his shotgun was still stored.

It was gone.

Once more, he remembered Torres's words: "Alex is totally incapable of killing anyone."

But up the street, Cynthia and Carolyn Evans had both been cut down by a shotgun, and someone matching Alex's description had been seen carrying a shotgun into this house.

Torres had been wrong.

Slowly Marsh began telling the two officers, Finnerty and Jackson, what Torres had told him only an hour or so earlier. They'd listened politely, then insisted on checking Marsh's story with Raymond Torres. When they'd called his office, they'd been told the director of the Institute had left for the day. Only after identifying themselves had they been able to obtain Torres's home phone number.

"Well, he's not there either," Finnerty said. Then: "Dr. Lonsdale, I don't want to seem to be pushing you, but I think the most important thing right now is to find Alex. Do you have any idea where he might have gone?"

Marsh shook his head. "If he didn't go to Torres, I haven't any idea at all."

"What about friends?" Jackson asked, and again Marsh shook his head.

"He . . . well, since the accident, he doesn't really have any friends anymore." His eyes filled with tears. "I'm afraid—I'm afraid that the longer time went on, the more the kids decided that there was something wrong with Alex. Besides the obvious problems, I mean," he added.

"Okay. We're going to put a stakeout on the house," Finnerty told him. "I've already got an APB out on your wife's car, but frankly, that doesn't mean much. The odds of someone spotting it are next to none. And it seems to me that eventually, your son will come home. So we'll be out there in an unmarked car. Or, at least, someone will. Anyway, we'll be keeping an eye on this place."

Marsh nodded, but Finnerty wasn't sure he'd been listening. "Dr. Lonsdale?" he asked, and Marsh met his eyes. "I can't tell you how sorry I am about this," Finnerty went on. "I keep hoping that there's been a mistake, and that maybe your boy didn't have anything to do with this."

Marsh's head came up, and he used his handkerchief to blot away the last of the tears on his cheeks.

"It's all right, Sergeant," he said. "You're just doing your job, and I understand it." He hesitated, then went on. "And there's something else I should tell you. I . . . well, I don't think there's been a mistake. I think you should be aware that Alex may be very dangerous. Ever since the operation, he hasn't felt anything—no love, no hate, no anger, nothing. If he's started killing, for whatever reason, he probably won't stop. Nor will he care what he does."

There was a short silence while Finnerty tried to assess Marsh Lonsdale's words. "Dr. Lonsdale," he finally asked, "would you mind telling me exactly what you're trying to say?"

"I'm trying to say that if you find Alex, I think you'd better kill him. If you don't, I suspect he won't hesitate to kill you."

Jackson and Finnerty glanced at each other. Finally, it was Jackson who spoke for both of them. "We can't do that, Dr. Lonsdale," he said quietly. "So far, it hasn't been proven that your son has done anything. For all we know, he might have been up in the hills shooting rabbits, and hurt himself some way."

"No," Marsh said, his voice almost a whisper. "No, that's not it. He did it."

"If he did, that will be for a court to decide," Jackson went on. "We'll find your son, Dr. Lonsdale. But we won't kill him."

Marsh shook his head wearily. "You don't understand, do you? That boy out there—he's not Alex. I don't know who he is, but he's not Alex. . . ."

"Okay," Finnerty said, in the gently soothing voice he'd long ago developed for situations in which he found himself dealing with someone who was less than rational. "You just take it easy for a while, Dr. Lonsdale, and we'll take care of it." He waited until Marsh had settled himself onto the sofa next to Ellen, then led Jackson out of the house. "Well? What do you think?"

"I don't know what to think."

"Neither do I," Finnerty sighed. "Neither do I."

* * *

"I don't believe any of this," Jim Cochran declared. His glance alternated between his wife and his elder daughter, neither of whom seemed willing to meet his gaze. Only Kim seemed to agree with him, and Carol had insisted she be sent up to her room five minutes ago, when it became obvious a fight was brewing. "Ellen and Marsh and Alex have been friends of ours for most of our lives. And now you don't even want me to call them?"

"I didn't say that," Carol protested, though she knew that even if she hadn't said the words, certainly that was what she had meant. "I just think we should leave them alone until we know what's happened."

"That's not you talking," Jim replied. "It's someone else."

"No!" Carol exclaimed. "After today, I just can't stand any more."

"And what about Marsh and Ellen? How do you think they feel? They're the ones whose lives are falling apart, Carol, not us."

Carol tried to close her ears to the words that were so much an echo of what she herself had said to Lisa only weeks ago. But weeks ago, no one had died.

"And what if Alex comes home?" Carol demanded. "No one knows where he is, or what he's doing, but according to Sheila Rosenberg, he murdered Cynthia and Carolyn Evans this morning, and probably murdered Marty and Valerie as well."

"We don't know that," Jim insisted. "And you both know that Sheila is the worst gossip in this town."

"Daddy!" Lisa said. "Alex didn't care about what happened to Mrs. Lewis, and he didn't think Mr. Lewis killed her. He told me so. He even said he thought someone else might get killed."

"That doesn't mean—"

"And he's been acting weirder and weirder ever since he came home. Are you going to tell me that's not true, too?"

"It's not the point," Jim insisted. "The point is that people stick by their friends, no matter what happens. And I don't accept that Alex has killed anyone."

"Then I'm afraid you're burying your head in the sand," Carol replied. "If he hasn't done anything, then where is he?"

"Anywhere," Jim said. "Who knows? He could have gone up into the hills, and had another accident."

"Daddy—"

"No," Jim said. "I've heard enough. I'm calling Marsh, and finding out what's going on. And if they need me, I'm going up there." He left the kitchen, and a few seconds later, Carol and Lisa heard him talking on the phone.

"I don't want to go up there, Mom," Lisa said quietly, her eyes beseeching. "I'm scared of Alex."

Carol patted Lisa's hand reassuringly. "It's all right, honey. We're not going anywhere. I'm . . . well, I'm just as frightened as you are." Suddenly Jim appeared in the doorway, and Carol's attention was diverted from her daughter to her husband.

"I just talked to Marsh," Jim told them, "and he wasn't making much sense. And Ellen's not talking at all. He says she's just sitting on the sofa, and he's not sure she's even hearing what anyone says."

"Anyone?" Carol asked. "Is someone else there?"

"The police were there. They just left."

There was a silence. Carol sighed as she came to a decision. "All right," she said quietly. "If you think you have to go, we'll all go. I guess you're right—we can't just sit here and do nothing." She stood up, but Lisa remained seated where she was.

"No," she said, her eyes flooding. "I can't go."

And finally, seeing the extent of his daughter's fear, Jim relented. "It's okay, princess," he said softly. "I guess I can understand how you're feeling." His eyes moved to his wife, and he offered her a tight smile. "I guess that lets you off the hook, too."

Carol hesitated, then nodded. "I'll stay here." Guiltily, she hoped the relief she was feeling didn't show, but she was sure it did.

"I won't stay long," Jim promised. "I'll just see if there's anything I can do, and let them know they're not alone. Then I'll be back. Okay?"

Again Carol nodded, and walked with her husband to the front door, where she kissed him good-bye. "I'm sorry," she whispered. "I'm sorry I've lost my nerve, but I just have. Forgive me?"

"Always," Jim told her. Then, before he closed the door, he spoke again. "Until I get back, don't open the door for anyone."

Then he was gone, and Carol went back to the kitchen, to wait.

CHAPTER 25

Darkness was falling as Alex made the turn off Middlefield Road, and as he started up into the hills on La Paloma Drive, he reached down and turned on the headlights of Raymond Torres's car. He wondered if he would dream about Dr. Torres tonight—if he chose to live that long—and wondered if, in whatever dreams he might have, he would feel the same emotional pain again, as he had when he dreamed about Mrs. Lewis and Mrs. Benson. With Dr. Torres, he decided, he wouldn't. Torres's death was very clear in his memory, and he felt no pain when he thought about it.

But he would dream about Mrs. Evans, and Carolyn, too, and then the pain would come.

There was, he had finally come to believe, still some little fragment of Alex Lonsdale still alive, deep within the recesses of his central brain core. It was that fragment of Alex who was having the dreams, and feeling the pain of what he had done. But when he was awake, there was none of Alex left. Only . . . who?

Did he even have a name?

Alejandro.

That was the name Dr. Torres had chosen for him, and then carefully built the memories of Alejandro into him. But the emotions that went with Alejandro's memories were Raymond Torres's, and those he had carefully left out.

It had, Alex realized, avoided confusion. When he saw the women—the women Torres hated—in the environment of Alejandro's memory, they had become other people from other times, and Alejandro had killed them.

And why not? To Alejandro, they were the wives of thieves and murderers, and as guilty of those crimes as their husbands.

But in the darkness of night, in the visions generated by the remnants of Alex Lonsdale's subconscious, they were old friends, people he had known all his life, and he mourned them.

And that had been Torres's mistake.

For his creation to have been perfect, there should have been none of Alex Lonsdale left.

Ahead of him, the headlights picked up the sign for the park that lay on the outskirts of the village. Alex pulled into the parking lot and shut off the engine.

His father had told him that when he was a boy, he'd played here often, yet he still had no memory of it. *His* only memory was Raymond Torres's memory of standing on the street, pleading with his mother to take him to the swings and push him as the other mothers were pushing their children.

"No," María Torres would mutter. "The park is not for us. It is for *los gringos.* Mira!" And she would point to the sign dedicating the park to the first American settlers who had come to La Paloma after the Treaty of Guadalupe Hidalgo had been signed. Then she would take Ramón by the hand and drag him away.

Alex got out of the car and began making his way across the empty lawn toward the swings. Tentatively he settled himself into one of them, and gave an experimental kick with his foot.

The movement had the vaguest feeling of familiarity to it, and Alex began pumping himself higher and higher. As the air rushed over his face and he felt the slight lurch in his stomach at the apex of each arc, Alex realized that this must have been what he'd done as a boy, this must be what he'd loved so much.

He stopped pumping, and let the swing slowly die until he was sitting still once again.

Then, knowing he had much to do before he went to the house on Hacienda Drive where the people who thought they were his parents lived, he left the swing and returned to his car.

He drove on into La Paloma, and turned left before he got to the Square. Two blocks further on, he came to the plaza. In the flickering lights of the gas lamps, the memories of Alejandro began creeping back to him, but Alex forced them out of his consciousness, keeping himself in the present. Only when he drove around the village hall to the mission graveyard did he let the memories come back.

Was this where they would bury him, or would they take him up into the hills above the hacienda and bury him with his mother and his sisters?

No.

They would bury him here, for they would be burying Alex, not Alejandro. Again he got out of the car, and slipped into the little graveyard. Tucked away in a dusty corner, he found the grave he was looking for.

ALEJANDRO DE MELÉNDEZ Y RUIZ
1832–1926

His own grave, in a way, and already sixty years old. There were flowers on the grave, though, and Alex knew who had put them there. Old María Torres, still honoring her grandfather's memory. Alex reached down and picked one of the flowers, breathing in its fragrance. Then, taking the flower with him, he went back to the car.

In the Square, he stepped over the chain around the tree, and stood for a long time under the spreading branches. Alejandro's memories were strong again, and Alex let them spread through his mind.

Once more he saw his father's body swinging limply from the hempen noose knotted around his neck, and felt the unfamiliar sensation of tears dampening his cheeks. He took the flower from Alejandro's grave and laid it gently on the ground above his father's grave. Then he turned away, knowing he'd seen the great oak tree for the last time.

Lisa and Carol Cochran were still sitting in the friendly brightness of the kitchen when they heard the car pull up outside, and a door slam. Carol hesitated, then pulled the drawn shades just far enough back to allow her to peer out into the street. A car she didn't recognize sat by the curb, and it was too dark to see who had gotten out of it. She dropped the shade back into position, and went to the stove, where she nervously poured herself yet another cup of coffee. As soon as Jim had left the house, she had given up any idea of sleeping that night.

"Who was it, Mom?" Lisa whispered, and Carol forced a grin that held much more confidence than she was feeling.

"It's no one. I've never seen the car before, and I don't think anyone's in it. Whoever it was must have gone across the street." But even as she spoke, she had the uncanny feeling that she was wrong, and that whoever had arrived in the car was still outside.

At that moment, the doorbell rang, its normally friendly chime taking on an ominous tone.

"What shall we do?" Lisa asked, her voice barely audible.

"Nothing," Carol whispered back. "We'll just sit here, and whoever it is will go away."

The doorbell sounded again, and Lisa seemed to shrink away from the sound.

"He'll go away," Carol repeated. "If we don't answer it, he'll go away."

And then, as the bell rang for the third time, there was a pounding of feet on the stairs, and through the dining room Carol could see Kim, apparently having leapt from the third step, catching herself before crashing headlong into the door. Knowing what was about to happen, she rose to her feet. "Kim!"

But it was too late. Over her own cry, she heard Kim's exuberant voice demanding to know who was outside before she opened the door.

"Don't open it, Kim," she cried, but Kim only turned to give her an exasperated glare.

"Don't be dumb, Mommy," Kim called. "It's only Alex." She reached up and turned the knob, then pulled the door open wide.

Carrying the shotgun in his right hand, Alex stepped into the Cochrans' foyer.

"How long we going to sit here?" Jackson asked. He reached into his pocket and pulled out a cigarette, then cupped his hand over his lighter as a brief flame illuminated the dark interior of the car they had parked fifty feet up the hill from the Lonsdales'.

"As long as it takes," Finnerty growled, shifting in the seat in a vain attempt to ease the cramps in his legs. He'd been up too many hours, and exhaustion was beginning to take its toll.

"What makes you so sure the kid's going to come back here at all?"

Finnerty shrugged stiffly. "Instincts. He doesn't really have any place else to go. Besides, why shouldn't he come back here?"

Jackson glanced across at his partner, and took a deep drag on his cigarette, hoping perhaps the smoke might drive away the sleepiness that was threatening to overwhelm him. "Seems to me that if I were in his shoes, this is the last place I'd come. I think I'd be heading for Mexico right about now."

"Except for one thing," Finnerty growled. "According to the kid's dad, the kid couldn't have done anything, remember?"

"You believe that shit?"

"We saw Alex Lonsdale the night he wrecked himself, remember? By rights, that kid should have been dead. Jesus, Tom, half his head was caved in. But he's not dead. So who am I to say how they saved him? Maybe they did exactly what Doc Lonsdale says they did."

"All right," Jackson replied. Though he still wasn't accepting the strange tale they'd heard, he was willing to go along with it for the sake of conversation. "So what's your idea?"

"That maybe the kid was programmed to kill after all, and was also programmed to forget what he'd done, after he'd done it."

"Now you're reaching," Jackson replied.

"Except it accounts for the discrepancy in our notes. Remember how you wrote down that Alex said he parked across from Jake's last night, and I wrote down that he said he parked in the lot next door?"

"So? One of us heard wrong."

"What if we didn't? What if we both heard it right, and we both wrote it down right? What if he told us both things?"

Jackson frowned in the darkness. "Then he was lying."

"Maybe not," Finnerty mused. "What if he went down to Jake's, parked across the street, then changed his mind and went up to Mrs. Benson's? He kills her, then goes back to Jake's, and parks in the lot. But he forgets what he did in between the two arrivals, because that's what he's been programmed to do. When he tells us everything he remembers about last night, he remembers parking both places, so that's what he tells us. We didn't make any mistakes, and he didn't lie. He just doesn't remember what he did."

"That's crazy—"

"What's happening in this town is crazy," Finnerty rasped. "But at least that theory fits the facts. Or at least what we think are the facts."

"So he'll come home, because he doesn't remember what he's done?"

"Right. Why shouldn't he come home? As far as he knows, nothing's wrong."

"But what if he does remember?" Jackson asked. "What if he knows exactly what he's doing, and just doesn't care?"

"Then," Finnerty said, his voice grim, "we might have to do exactly what his father suggested. We might have to kill him."

Jackson took two more nervous drags on his cigarette, then stubbed it out in the ashtray. "Roscoe? I don't think I could do it," he said finally. "If it comes down to it, I'm just not sure I could shoot anyone."

"Well, let's hope it won't come down to that," Roscoe Finnerty replied. Then, giving in to his exhaustion, he slid deeper in his seat and closed his eyes. "Wake me up if anything happens."

"Kim!"

Carol Cochran tried to make the word commanding, but her voice cracked with fear. Nonetheless, Kim turned to gaze at her curiously. "Come here,

Kim," she pleaded. Still Kim hesitated, and gazed up at Alex, her face screwed into a worried frown.

"Did you hurt yourself, Alex?" she asked, her eyes fixing on the cut over his eye.

Alex nodded.

"How?"

"I . . . I don't know," Alex admitted, then turned to look into the kitchen, where Carol and Lisa seemed frozen in place. "It's all right," Alex said. "I'm not going to hurt you."

As he spoke the words, Carol took a step forward. "Kim, I told you to come here!"

Kim glanced uncertainly from her mother to Alex, then back to her mother. She backed slowly into the dining room, then turned and dashed on into the kitchen.

When her younger daughter was in her arms, Carol's strength seemed to come back to her. "Go away, Alex," she said, the steadiness in her voice surprising even herself. "Just go away and leave us alone."

Alex nodded, but moved slowly through the dining room until he came to the kitchen door, the gun still clutched in his right hand.

From her chair, Lisa watched Alex's eyes, and her fear, instead of easing, only grew. There was an emptiness to his eyes that she'd never seen before. It was far beyond the strange blankness she'd almost grown used to over the last few months. Now his eyes looked as if they might be the eyes of a dead man. "Go away," she whispered. "Please, Alex, just go away."

"I will," Alex replied. "I just . . . I just wanted to tell you I'm sorry for what's happened."

"Sorry?" Lisa echoed. "How can you be—" And then she broke off her own words, as her eyes suddenly fell on the shotgun. Alex followed her gaze with his own eyes, and his expression became almost puzzled.

"I didn't kill anyone," he said softly. "I mean . . . Alex didn't kill anyone. It was the other."

Lisa and Carol glanced nervously at each other, and Carol shook her head almost imperceptibly.

"I'm not Alex," he went on. "That's what I came to tell you. Alex is dead."

"Dead?" Lisa echoed. "Alex, what are you talking about?"

"He's dead," Alex said again. "He died in the wreck. That's all I came to tell you, so you wouldn't think he'd done anything." His eyes fixed on Lisa, and when he spoke again, his voice was strangled, as if the very act of speaking the words was painful for him. "He loved you," he whispered. "Alex loved you very much. I . . . I don't understand what that means, but I know it's true. Don't blame Alex for what I've done. He couldn't stop it."

Suddenly his eyes filled with tears once again. "He would have stopped it," he whispered. "If so much of him hadn't died—if just a little more of him had lived—I know he would have stopped it."

Carol Cochran shakily rose to her feet. "What, Alex?" she whispered. "What would you have stopped?"

"Not me," Alex breathed. "Him. Alex would have stopped what Dr. Torres did. But I didn't know. He wouldn't let me remember, so I didn't know. But Alex found out. What was left of him found out, and he's trying to stop it. He's still trying, but he might not be able to, because he's dead." His eyes suddenly took on a wildness as they focused on Lisa once more. "Don't you understand?" he begged. "Alex is dead, Lisa!" Then he turned, and shambled back through the dining room and out into the night. A moment later, Carol heard a car door slam and an engine start. And then she heard Kim, and felt the little girl tugging at her arms.

"What's wrong with him?" she asked. "What's wrong with Alex?"

Carol swallowed hard, then held Kim close. "He's sick, honey," she whispered. "He's very sick in his head, that's all." Then she released Kim, and started toward the phone. "I'd better call the police," she said.

"No!" Carol turned back to see Lisa standing up, her expression suddenly clear. "Let him go, Mama," she said softly. "He won't hurt anyone else now. Don't you understand? That's what he was trying to tell us. All he wants to do now is die, and we have to let him." She knelt down, and pulled Kim close. "That wasn't Alex that was just here, Kim," she said softly. "That was someone else. Alex is dead. That's what he was telling us. That he's dead, and we should remember him the way he used to be. The way he was the night he took me to the dance." She hesitated, as her eyes flooded with tears. "Do you remember that night, Kim?"

Kim nodded, but said nothing.

"Then let's remember him that way, sweetheart. Let's remember how he looked all dressed up in his dinner jacket, and let's remember how good he was. All right?"

Kim hesitated, then nodded, and Lisa's gaze shifted to her mother. "Let him go, Mama. Please?" she begged. "He won't hurt anyone. I know he won't."

Carol stood silently watching her daughter for several long seconds, then, at last, moved toward her and embraced her.

"All right," she said softly. Then: "I'm sorry."

"I am too," Lisa replied. "And so is Alex."

"You're sure there's nothing I can do?" Jim Cochran asked.

Marsh opened the front door, and gazed out into the night as if expecting Alex to appear, but there was nothing. "No," he sighed. "Go on back to Carol and the girls. And tell them I understand why they didn't come," he added.

Jim Cochran regarded his friend shrewdly. "I don't believe I told you why they didn't come."

"You told me," Marsh replied with a tight smile. "Maybe not in words, but I understood." He glanced back over his shoulder to the living room, where Ellen was still sitting on the couch. "I'd better get back in," he went on. "I don't think she can stand to be by herself very long."

During the hour that Jim Cochran had been there, Ellen had finally begun to speak, but she was still confused, as if she wasn't exactly sure what had happened.

"Where's Carol?" she had asked half an hour ago. Then she'd peered vacantly around the room.

"She's home," Jim had told her. "Home with the girls. Kim's not feeling too well."

"Oh," Ellen had breathed, then fallen silent again before repeating her question five minutes later.

"She'll be all right," Marsh had assured him. "It's a kind of shock, and she'll pull out of it."

But even as he was about to leave, Jim wasn't sure he should be going at all. To him, Marsh didn't look much better than Ellen.

"Maybe I'd better stay—"

"No. If Alex comes home, I don't know what might happen. But I know I'd rather nobody was here. Except them." He gestured past the patio wall and up the road in the direction of the car Jim knew was still parked there, waiting.

"Okay. But if you need me, call me. All right?"

"All right." And then, without saying anything more, Marsh closed the door.

Jim Cochran crossed the patio, and let himself out through the gate. As he got into his car, he waved toward the two policemen, and one of them waved back. Finally he started the engine, put the car in gear, and backed out into the street.

Thirty seconds later, as he neared the bottom of the hill, he passed another car going up, but it was too dark for him to see Alex Lonsdale behind its wheel.

Alex pulled the car off the road just before he rounded the last curve. By now, he was sure, they would be looking for him, and they would be watching the house. He checked the breech of the shotgun.

There was one shell left.

It would be all he needed.

He got out of the car and quietly shut the door, then left the road and worked his way up the hillside, circling around to approach the house from the rear. In the dim light of the moon, the old house looked as it had so many years ago, and deep in his memory, the voices—Alejandro's voices—began whispering to him once more.

He crept down the slope into the shadows of the house itself, and a moment later had scaled the wall and dropped into the patio.

He stood at the front door.

He hesitated, then twisted the handle and pushed the door open. Twenty feet away, in the living room, he saw his father.

Not his father.

Alex Lonsdale's father.

Alex Lonsdale was dead.

But Ellen Lonsdale was still alive.

"Venganza . . . venganza . . ."

Alejandro de Meléndez y Ruiz was dead, as was Raymond Torres.

And yet, they weren't. They were alive, in Alex Lonsdale's body, and the remnants of Alex Lonsdale's brain.

Alex's father was staring at him.

"Alex?"

He heard the name, as he'd heard it at the Cochrans' such a short time ago. But it wasn't his name.

"No. Not Alex," he whispered. "Someone else."

He raised the shotgun, and began walking slowly into the living room, where the last of the four women—Alex's mother—sat on the sofa, staring at him in terror.

Roscoe Finnerty's entire body twitched, and his eyes jerked open. For just a second he felt disoriented, then his mind focused, and he turned to his partner. "What's going on?"

"Nothin'," Jackson replied. "Cochran took off a few minutes ago, and since then, nothing."

"Unh-unh," Finnerty growled. "Something woke me up."

Jackson lifted one eyebrow a fraction of an inch, but he straightened himself in the seat, lit another cigarette, and scanned the scene on Hacienda Drive. Nothing, as far as he could see, had changed.

Still, he'd long since learned that Finnerty sometimes had a sixth sense about things.

And then he remembered.

A few minutes ago, there'd been a glow, as if a car had been coming up the hill, but it had stopped before coming around the last curve.

He'd assumed it had been a neighbor coming home.

"God damn!" he said aloud. He told his partner what had happened, and Finnerty cursed softly, then opened the car door.

"Come on. Let's take a look."

Both the officers got out of the car and started down the street.

Ellen's eyes focused slowly on Alex. It was like a dream, and she was only able to see little bits at a time.

The blood on his forehead, crusting over a deep gash that almost reached his eye.

The eyes themselves, staring at her unblinkingly, empty of all emotion except one.

Deep in his eyes, she thought she could see a smoldering spark of hatred.

The shotgun. Its barrels were enormous—black holes as empty as Alex's eyes—and they seemed to be staring at her with the same hatred as Alex.

Suddenly Ellen Lonsdale knew she was not looking at her son.

She was looking at someone else, someone who was going to kill her.

"Why?" she whispered. "Why?"

Then, as if her senses were turning on one by one, she heard her husband's voice.

"What is it, Alex? What's wrong?"

"Venganza . . ." she heard Alex whisper.

"Vengeance?" Marsh asked. "Vengeance for what?"

"Ladrones . . . asesinos . . ."

"No, Alex," Marsh said softly. "You've got it wrong." Wildly Marsh searched his mind for something to say, something that would get through to Alex.

Except it wasn't Alex. Whoever it was, it wasn't Alex.

Where the hell were the cops?

And then the front door flew open, and Finnerty and Jackson were in the entry hall.

Alex's head swung around toward the foyer, and Marsh used the moment. Lunging forward, he grasped the shotgun by the barrel, then threw himself sideways, twisting the gun out of Alex's hands. The force of his weight knocked Alex off balance, and he staggered toward the fireplace, then caught himself on the mantel. A moment later, his eyes met Marsh's.

"Do it," he whispered. "If you loved your son, do it."

Marsh hesitated. "Who are you?" he asked, his voice choking on the words. "Are you Alex?"

"No. I'm someone else. I'm whoever I was programmed to be, and I'll do what I was programmed to do. Alex tried to stop me, but he can't. Do it . . . Father. Please do it for me."

Marsh raised the gun, and as Ellen and the two policemen looked on, he squeezed the trigger.

The gun roared once more, and Alex's body, torn and bleeding, collapsed slowly onto the hearth.

Time stood still.

Ellen's eyes fixed on the body that lay in front of the fireplace, but what she saw was not her son.

It was someone else—someone she had never known—who had lived in her home for a while, and whom she had tried to love, tried to reach. But whoever he was, he was too far away from her, and she had not been able to reach him.

And he was not Alex.

She turned and faced Marsh.

"Thank you," she said softly. Then she rose and went to hold her husband.

One arm still cradling the shotgun, the other around his wife, Marsh finally tore his eyes away from the body of his son and faced the two policemen who stood as if frozen just inside the front door. "I . . . I'm sorry," he whispered, his voice breaking. "I had to . . ." He seemed about to say something else, but didn't. Instead, he let the gun fall to the floor, and held Ellen close. "I just had to, that's all."

Jackson and Finnerty glanced at each other for a split second, and then Finnerty spoke.

"We saw it all, Dr. Lonsdale," he said, his voice carefully level. "We saw the boy attacking you and your wife—"

"No!" Marsh began, "he didn't attack us—"

But Finnerty ignored him. "He attacked you, and you were struggling for the gun when it went off." When Marsh tried to interrupt him again, he held up his hand. "Please, Dr. Lonsdale. Jackson and I both know what happened." He turned to his partner. "Don't we, Tom?"

Tom Jackson hesitated only a second before nodding his head. "It's like Roscoe says," he said at last. "It was an accident, and we're both witnesses to it. Take your wife upstairs, Dr. Lonsdale."

Without looking again at the body on the hearth, Ellen and Marsh turned away and left the room.

EPILOGUE

María Torres drew her shawl close around her shoulders against the chill of the December morning, then locked the front door of her little house and slowly crossed the street to the cemetery behind the old mission.

The cemetery was bright with flowers, for no one in La Paloma had forgotten what had happened three months earlier. All of them were buried here. Valerie Benson only a few yards from Marty Lewis, and Cynthia and Carolyn Evans, side by side, a little further north. All their graves, as they were every day, were covered with fresh flowers.

In the southeast corner, set apart from the other graves, lay Alex Lonsdale. On his grave only a single flower lay—the white rose delivered each day by the florist. María paused at Alex's grave, and wondered how long the roses would come, how long it would be before the Lonsdales, three months gone from La Paloma, forgot about their son. For them, María was sure, there would be other children, and when those children came, the roses would stop.

Then it would be up to her. Long after his parents had stopped honoring his memory, she would still come and leave a flower for Alejandro.

She moved on into the oldest section of the cemetery, where her parents and grandparents were buried, and where now, finally returned to his family, her son lay as well. She stood at the foot of Ramón's grave for several minutes, and, as she always did, tried to understand what part he had played in what she had come to think of as the days of vengeance. But, as always, it was a mystery to her. Somehow, though, the saints had touched him, and he had fulfilled his destiny, and she honored his memory as she honored the memory of Alejandro de Meléndez y Ruiz. She whispered a prayer for her son, then left the cemetery. For her, there was still work to be done.

She trudged slowly through the village, feeling the burden of her age with every step, pausing once more in the Square, partly to rest, but partly, too, to repeat one more prayer for Don Roberto. Then, when she was rested, she went on.

She turned up Hacienda Drive, and was glad that today, at least, she needn't climb all the way up to the hacienda. It was empty again, and now she only went there once a week to wipe the dust away from its polished oaken floors and wrought-iron sconces. The furniture was gone, but she didn't miss it. In her mind's eye it was still as it had always been. Her ghosts were still there. Soon, she was sure, she would go to join them, and though her body would lie in the cemetery, her spirit would return to the hacienda which had always been her true home.

Today, though, she would not go to the hacienda. Today she would go to one of the other houses—the house where Alejandro had died—to speak to the new people.

They had only come to La Paloma last week, and she had heard that they needed a housekeeper.

She came to the last curve before the house would come into view, and paused to catch her breath. Then she walked on, and a moment later, saw the house.

It was as it should have been. Along the garden wall, neatly spaced between the tile insets, were small vines, well-trimmed and espaliered. From the outside, at least, the house looked as it had looked a century ago.

María stepped through the gate into the little patio, then knocked at the front door and waited. As she was about to knock again, the door opened, and a woman appeared.

A blond woman, with bright blue eyes and a smiling face.

A *gringo* woman.

"Mrs. Torres?" the woman asked, and María nodded. "I'm so glad to meet you," the woman went on. "I'm Donna Ruiz."

María felt her heart skip a beat, and her legs suddenly felt weak. She reached out and steadied herself on the door frame.

"Ruiz . . ." she whispered. "*No es posible . . .*"

The woman's smile widened. "It's all right," she said. "I know I don't look like a Ruiz. And of course I'm not. I was a Riley before I married Paul." She took María's arm and drew her into the house, closing the door behind her. A moment later they were in the living room. "Isn't this wonderful? Paul says it's exactly the kind of house he's always wanted to live in, and that it's really authentic. He says it must be over a hundred years old."

"More," María said softly, her eyes going to the hearth where Alejandro had died so short a time ago. "It was built for one of the overseers."

Donna Ruiz looked puzzled. "Overseers?"

"From the hacienda, before the . . . before the *americanos* came."

"How interesting," Donna replied. "It sounds like you know the house well."

"*Sí*," María said. "I cleaned for Señora Lonsdale."

Donna's smile faded. "Oh, dear. I didn't know . . . Perhaps you'd rather not work here."

María shook her head. "It is all right. I worked here before. I will work here again. And someday, I will go back to the hacienda."

The last of Donna Ruiz's smile disappeared, and she shook her head sadly. "It must have been awful. Just awful. That poor boy." She hesitated; then: "It almost seems like it would have been better if he'd died in the accident, doesn't it? To go through all he went through, and end up . . ." Her voice trailed off; then she took a deep breath and stood up. "Well. Perhaps we should go through the house, and I can tell you what I want done."

María heaved herself to her feet and silently followed Donna Ruiz through the rooms on the first floor, wondering why the *gringo* women always assumed that she couldn't see what needed to be done in a house. Did they think she never cleaned her own house? Or did they just think she was stupid?

The rooms were all as they had been the last time she had been here, and Señora Ruiz wanted the same things done that Señora Lonsdale had wanted.

The cleaning supplies were where they had always been, as were the vacuum cleaner and the dust rags, the mops and the brooms.

And all of it, of course, was explained to her in detail, as if she hadn't heard it all a hundred times before, hadn't known it all long before these women were even born.

At last they went upstairs, and one by one Donna Ruiz showed her all the rooms María Torres already knew. Finally they came to the room at the end of the hall, the room that had been Alejandro's. They paused, and Donna Ruiz knocked at the door.

"It's okay," a voice called from within. "Come on in, Mom."

Donna Ruiz opened the door, and María gazed into the room. All the furniture was still there—Alejandro's desk and bed, the bookshelves and the rug, all as they had been when the Lonsdales left.

Sitting at the desk, working on a model airplane, was a boy who looked to be about thirteen. He grinned at his mother, then, seeing that she wasn't alone, stood up. "Are you the cleaning lady?" he asked.

María nodded, her old eyes studying him. His eyes were dark, and his hair, nearly black, was thick and curly. *"Cómo se llama?"* she asked.

"Roberto," the boy replied. "But everybody calls me Bobby."

"Roberto," María repeated, her heart once again beating faster. "It is a good name."

"And he's fascinated with history," Donna Ruiz said. She turned to her son. "María seems to know all about the house and the town. I'll bet if you asked her, she could tell you everything that's ever happened here."

Bobby Ruiz turned eager eyes toward María. "Could you?" he asked. "Do you really know all about the town?"

María hesitated only an instant, then nodded. *"Sí,"* she said softly. "I know all the old legends, and I will tell them all to you." She smiled gently. "I will tell them to you, and you will understand them. All of them. And someday, you will live in the hacienda. Would you like that?"

The boy's eyes burned brightly. "Yes," he said. "I'd like that very much."

"Then I will take you there," María replied. "I will take you there, and someday it will be yours."

A moment later, María was gone, and Bobby Ruiz was alone in his room. He went to his bed and lay down on his back so that he could gaze at the ceiling, but he saw nothing. Instead, he listened to the sounds in his head, the whisperings in Spanish that he had been hearing since the first time he came into this room. But now, after talking to María Torres, he understood the whisperings.

Soon, he knew, the killings would begin again. . . .

NATHANIEL

For the Bitch and Moan Society

PROLOGUE

The night closed in like something alive, its warm dampness imbuing the house with an oppressive atmosphere that seemed somehow threatening to the child who sat in the small front parlor. There was something in the air she could almost touch, and as she sat waiting, she began to feel her skin crawl with the peculiar itching that always came over her late in the summer. She squirmed on the mohair sofa, but it did no good—her cotton dress still clung to her like wet cellophane.

Outside the wind began to rise, and for a moment the girl felt relief. For the first time in hours, the angry sound of her father's voice was muted, covered by the wind, so that if she concentrated hard, she could almost pretend that that sound was a part of the rising storm, rather than a proof of her father's fury and her mother's terror.

Then her father was looming in the doorway, his eyes hard, his anger suddenly directed toward her. She cringed on the sofa—perhaps if she made herself smaller he wouldn't see her.

"The cellar," her father said, the softness of his voice making it no less threatening. "I told you to go to the cellar."

"Father—"

"Storm's coming. You'll be safe in the cellar. Now go on."

Hesitantly, the child stood up and began edging toward the kitchen door, her eyes flickering once, leaving her father's angry face to focus on the door behind him, the door beyond which her mother lay struggling with the pains of labor. "She'll be all right," he said.

Not reassured, but knowing argument would only increase her father's wrath, the girl pulled a jacket from a hook and struggled to force her arms through its tangled sleeves. Then, shielding her eyes from the driving wind with her right arm, she left the house and scuttled across the yard to the cyclone cellar that had been carved out of the unyielding prairie earth so many years ago. Once she glanced up, squinting her eyes against the stinging dust. In the distance, almost invisible in the roiling clouds, she could barely make out the beginnings of the storm's angry funnel.

More terrified now of the storm than of her father's anger, she grasped the heavy wooden door of the cellar and hauled it partway open, just far enough to slip her body through the gap. She scrambled down the steep steps, letting the door drop into place behind her.

For what seemed like an eternity, she sat in the near-total darkness of the storm cellar, her ears filled with the sounds of the raging winds.

But sometimes, when the howlings of the storm momentarily abated, she thought she could hear something else. Her mother, calling out to her, begging her to come and help her.

The girl tried to ignore those sounds—it was impossible for her mother's voice to carry over the storm. Besides, she knew what was happening to her mother and knew there was nothing for her to do.

When the baby came, and the storm had passed, someone—her father or her brother—would come for her. Until then, she would stay where she was and try to pretend she wasn't frightened.

She curled herself up in a corner of the cellar and squeezed her eyes tight against the darkness and the fear.

She didn't know how much time had passed, knew only that she couldn't stay by herself any longer, couldn't stay alone in the cellar. She listened to the wind, tried to gauge its danger, but in the end she wrapped the jacket close around her thin body, and forced the cellar door open. The wind caught it, jerked it out of her grasp, then tore it loose from its hinges and sent it tumbling across the yard. It caught on the barbed wire fence for a moment; then the wire gave way and the wooden door hurtled on, flipping end over end across the plains, quickly disappearing into the gathering dusk. The girl huddled at the top of the steps for a few moments. There was a light on in the house now, not the bright lights she was used to, but the glow of a lantern, and she knew the power had gone out. The flickering lamplight drew her like a moth, and she braced herself against the driving wind, leaning into it as she began making her way back across the yard. She was disobeying, she knew, but even facing Pa's anger was better than staying alone any longer.

Still, when she reached the house, she couldn't bring herself to go in, for even over the howling wind she could hear her father's voice. His words were unintelligible but his anger was terrifying. The girl crept around the corner of the house, crouched low, until she was beneath the window of the room in which her mother lay.

Slowly, she straightened up, until she could see into the room. On the nightstand stood an oil lantern, its wick turned low, its yellowish light casting odd shadows. Her mother looked almost lifeless, resting against a pillow, damp hair clinging to sallow skin, her eyes wide, staring balefully at the towering figure of her father.

And now she could hear the words.

"You killed him."

"No," her father replied. "He was born dead."

The little girl watched as her mother's head moved, shaking slowly from side to side as her eyes closed tight. "No. My baby was alive. I felt it moving. Right up until the end, I felt it moving. It was alive, and you killed it."

A movement distracted the girl, and her eyes left her mother's tortured face. Someone else stood in the corner of the room, but until he turned, the girl didn't recognize him.

It was the doctor, and in his arms he cradled a tiny bundle wrapped in a blanket. A fold of the blanket dropped away; the girl saw the baby's face, its eyes closed, its wizened features barely visible in the flickering lantern light.

By its stillness, she knew it was dead.

"Give it to me!" she heard her mother demand. Then her voice became pleading. "Please, give it to me . . ."

But the doctor said nothing, only refolding the blanket around the baby's face, then turning away once more. Her mother's screams filled the night then, and a moment later, when the girl looked for the doctor again, he had retreated from the room. Now that they were left alone, her father was regarding her mother with smoldering eyes.

"I warned you," he said. "I warned you God would punish you, and He has."

"It was you," her mother protested, her voice weakened by pain and despair. "It wasn't God punishing me, it was you." Her voice broke, and she began sobbing, making no attempt to wipe her tears away from her streaming eyes. "It was alive, and you killed it. You had no right—you had no right . . ."

Suddenly the girl saw the door open, and her brother appeared. He stood still for a moment, staring at their mother. He started to speak, but before he could utter a word, their father turned on him.

"Get out!" Then, as the girl watched, her father's fist rose into the air, then swung forward, catching the side of her brother's head, slamming him against the wall. Her brother crumpled to the floor. For a time that seemed endless to the watching girl, he lay still. No one spoke. Then, slowly, he rose to face their father.

He opened his mouth to speak, but no words came out. His eyes glowed with hatred as he stared at his father; then he turned away and stumbled out of the little room.

The girl backed away from the window, unconscious now of the wind that still battered at her, her mind filled only with the sights and sounds she instinctively knew she should not have witnessed. She should have obeyed her father and stayed in the storm cellar, waiting for someone to come for her.

She started back toward the storm cellar. Perhaps, if she tried very hard, she could blot all of it out of her mind, pretend that she had seen and heard none of it, convince herself that she had never left the cellar, never witnessed her mother's pain and her father's fury. And then, ahead of her, a few feet away, she saw her brother and cried out to him.

He turned to face her, but she knew he didn't see her. His eyes were blank, and he seemed to be looking past her, looking out into the storm and the night.

"Please," the girl whispered. "Help me. Please help me . . ."

But if her brother heard her, he gave no sign. Instead, he turned away, and as if he was following the call of some other voice the girl couldn't hear, he left the house and the yard, disappearing into the prairie. A moment later he was gone, swallowed up by the storm and the night. Alone, the girl made her way back to the cyclone cellar.

She crept down the steps through the gaping hole where the door had been, and went back to her corner. She drew the jacket tightly around herself, but neither the jacket nor the doorless cellar could protect her.

Through the long night she huddled there, the storm and the scene she had witnessed lashing at her, torturing her, boring deep within her soul.

After that night she never spoke of what she'd seen or what she'd heard. She never spoke of it, but she never quite forgot.

CHAPTER

1

"Are you my grandpa?"

Michael Hall gazed uncertainly up into the weathered face. He had never seen the man before, yet he recognized him as clearly as if he were looking into a mirror. He tried to keep his voice steady, tried not to shrink back against his mother, tried to remember all the things his father had taught him about meeting people for the first time:

Stand up straight, and put your hand out.

Look the person in the eye.

Tell them your name. He'd forgotten that part.

"I—I'm Michael, and this is my mother," he stammered.

He felt his mother's grip tighten on his shoulders, and for just a moment was afraid he'd done something wrong. But then the man he was talking to smiled at him, and he felt his mother's hands relax a little.

He looks like Mark. He looks just like Mark. The thought flashed through Janet Hall's mind, and she had to make a conscious effort to keep from hurling herself into the arms of the stranger who was now moving closer to her, an uneasy smile failing to mask the troubled look in his eyes. Barely conscious of the airport crowd that eddied around her, Janet found herself focusing on the lean angularity of her father-in-law's figure, the strength in his face, the aura of calm control that seemed to hover around him as it had around his son. Unconsciously, her hand moved to her waist and she smoothed her skirt in a nervous gesture.

It's going to be all right, Janet told herself. *He's just like Mark, and he'll take care of us.*

Almost as if he'd heard Janet's private thought, Amos Hall leaned down and swung his eleven-year-old grandson off his feet, his farmer's strength belying his own sixty-seven years. He hugged the boy, but when his eyes met Janet's over Michael's shoulder, there was no joy in them.

"I'm sorry," he said, dropping his voice to a level that would be inaudible to anyone but Janet and Michael. "I don't know what to say. All these years, and we only meet when Mark—" His voice faltered, and Janet could see him struggling against his feelings. "I'm sorry," he repeated, his voice suddenly gruff. "Let's get your baggage and get on out of here. We can talk in the car."

But they didn't talk in the car. They drove out of North Platte and into the vast expanse of the prairie in silence, the three of them huddled in the front seat of Amos Hall's Oldsmobile, Janet and Amos separated by Michael. The numbness that had overcome Janet from the moment the night before when she had been told that her husband was dead still pervaded her, and the reality of where she was—and the why of it—had still not come fully into her consciousness. She had a feeling of being trapped in a nightmare, and every second she was waiting for Mark to awaken her from the dream and assure her that everything was all right, everything was as it had always been.

And yet, that was not to be.

The miles rolled past. Finally, Janet made herself glance across to her father-in-law, who seemed intent on studying the arrow-straight road ahead, his eyes glued to the shimmering pavement as if, by concentration alone, he, too, could deny the reality of what had happened.

Janet cleared her throat, and Amos's eyes left the road for a split second. "Mark's mother—"

"She never leaves Prairie Bend," Amos replied, his gaze returning to the highway. "Rarely leaves the house anymore, if truth be known. She's getting along, and the years—" He paused, and Janet could see a tightness forming in his jaw. "The years haven't been as kind to her as they might," he finished. Then: "Funeral's gonna be tomorrow morning."

Janet nodded mutely, relieved that the decision had been made; then, once more, she let herself fall into silence.

An hour later they arrived at the Halls' farm. The old two-story house was not large, but it seemed to Janet to have a sense of itself, sitting solidly on its foundation, surrounded by a grove of elms and cottonwoods, protected from the vast emptiness of the plains that stretched to the horizon in every direction save one, where a stand of trees marked the route of a river making its way eastward, to flow eventually into the Platte.

"What's the name of the river?" Michael suddenly asked, and the question pulled Janet's attention from her father-in-law.

"The Dismal," Amos replied as he brought the car to a stop in front of the house. A moment later he was taking Janet's baggage out of the trunk. With a suitcase in each hand, he mounted the steps of the front porch, Janet and Michael trailing behind him. Suddenly the door opened and a figure appeared on the threshold, a woman, gaunt and hollow-cheeked, as though her life had been spent in constant battle with the unrelenting prairie.

She was seated in a wheelchair.

Janet felt Michael freeze next to her, and took him by the hand.

"We're back," she heard Amos Hall saying to the woman. "This is Mark's Janet, and this is Michael."

The woman in the wheelchair stared at them in silence for a moment. Her face, worn with age and infirmity, had a haggard look to it, and her eyes, rimmed with red, seemed nearly lifeless. But a moment later she smiled, a soft smile that seemed to wash some of the years away from her countenance. "Come here," she said, spreading her arms wide. "Come and let me hold you."

The numbness Janet had been feeling since last night; the numbness that had insulated her every minute today and allowed her to maintain her self-control as she packed their bags, ordered a cab, and got herself and Michael from Manhattan to the airport; the numbness that had sustained her through the change of planes in Omaha, the arrival in North Platte, and the drive to Prairie Bend, drained away from her now.

"He's dead," she said, her voice breaking as for the first time she truly admitted to herself what had happened. Dropping Michael's hand, she stumbled up the steps and sank to her knees next to Anna Hall's wheelchair. "Oh, God, what happened to him? Why did he die? Why?"

Anna's arms encircled Janet, and she cradled her daughter-in-law's head against her breast. "It's all right, child," she soothed. "Things happen, sometimes, and there's nothing we can do about them. We just have to accept them." Over Janet's head, her gaze met her husband's for a moment, then moved on, coming to rest on Michael, who stood uncertainly at the foot of the steps, his eyes riveted in worried fascination on his mother. "You, too, Michael," Anna gently urged. "Come give Grandma a hug, and let her take the hurt away."

The boy looked up then, and as his eyes met her own, Anna felt a flash of recognition surge over her frail body. In the boy, she saw the father. And as she saw her son in her grandson's eyes, she began to feel fear.

* * *

Amos Hall led Janet and Michael up the narrow staircase to the second floor, where three large bedrooms and a generous bathroom opened off the hallway that bisected the house. He opened the door to the first bedroom, then stood aside to let Janet pass him. "You'll be in here. Used to be Laura's room."

"Laura?" Janet echoed, in a voice that sounded dazed even to herself. "Who's Laura?"

Amos frowned, his eyes clouding. "Mark's sister. Until she got married, this was her room." He paused a moment, then, as if he felt an explanation was necessary, spoke again. "I was going to turn it into a den, or a study. I just never got around to it."

Janet gazed at the room, taking in its details with apparent calm, while she frantically searched the corners of her memory for the information she knew must be there, that had somehow slipped away from her.

The name Laura meant nothing to her.

The whole idea of Mark having had a sister meant nothing to her.

But that was ridiculous. If Mark had had a sister, he *must* have talked about her sometime over the years. She'd simply forgotten. Some kind of amnesia, maybe: somehow, during the last few hours of shock, it must have been driven from her mind.

"It's just fine," she said at last, careful not to let her voice betray her confusion. She glanced around the room once more, this time forcing herself to concentrate. There was nothing special about the room; it was simply a room, with a bed, a chair, a nightstand, and a dresser. A chenille bedspread covered the slightly sagging mattress, and there was a braided rug covering most of the pine floor. Ill-fitting curtains hung at the window, and an image of a Sears catalog suddenly came into Janet's mind. A second later, she made the connection: the curtains were identical to the ones she had had in her own room when she was a little girl, the ones her mother had ordered from the Sears catalog, in a size close to, but not quite right for, the windows. Her mind churned on, and the rest of the memories flooded back, the memories she'd deliberately suppressed, hoped never to look at again:

The fire, when the old house she'd been born in had burned to the ground, consuming everything she loved—her parents and her brother, too—leaving her to be raised by a series of aunts who somehow had always found reasons to pass her on to someone else until, at last, she'd turned eighteen and gone to live by herself in New York. A year later, she'd married Mark.

And now, once again, here were those mail-order curtains, bringing back those memories. She sank onto the bed, one hand reflexively coming up to cover her eyes as she felt them fill with tears.

"Are you all right?" she heard her father-in-law ask. She took a deep breath, then made herself smile.

"I'll be fine. It's just that—that—"

But Amos Hall stopped her. "Lie down for a little while. Just lie down, and try to go to sleep. I'll take care of Michael, and later on we'll talk. But for now, just try to get a little sleep." Taking the boy firmly by the hand, Amos left the room, closing the door behind him.

For a long time, Janet lay on the bed, trying to make herself be calm, trying to put the memories of the past to rest and cope with the problems of the present.

Laura.

She would concentrate on Laura.

Somewhere in her memory, there must be something about Mark's sister, and if she concentrated, it would come back to her. It just wasn't possible that Mark, in their thirteen years together, had never mentioned having a sister. It wasn't possible. . . .

And then the exhaustion of the last hours caught up with her, and she slept.

Michael stared in awe at the room his grandfather had shown him into. It was a boy's room, its walls covered with baseball and football pennants. Suspended from the ceiling were four model airplanes, frozen in flight as if they were involved in a dogfight. Over the bed there was a bookshelf, and Michael could recognize some of the books without reading the titles: identical volumes sat on his own bookshelf back home in New York. "Was this my father's room?" he asked at last.

"This is all the stuff he had when he was a boy," his grandfather replied. "All these years, and here it is. I suppose I should have gotten rid of it, but now I'm glad I didn't. Maybe I was saving it just for you."

Michael frowned, regarding his grandfather with suspicious eyes. "But you didn't know I was coming."

"But you would have, wouldn't you?" Amos countered. "Someday, wouldn't you have come to visit your grandparents?"

Michael shook his head. "I don't think Dad wanted to come here. I don't think he liked it here."

"Now what makes you say a thing like that?" Amos asked, lowering himself onto the studio couch that served as a bed, and drawing Michael down beside him.

" 'Cause every time I asked him if we could come here to visit, he said maybe next year. That's what he always said, and whenever I told him that's what he said last year, he always said he'd only said maybe. So I guess he never really wanted to come, did he?"

"Maybe he could just never find the time," Amos suggested.

Michael shrugged, and drew slightly away from his grandfather. "He always took us on a vacation. One year we went to Florida, and twice we went camping in the mountains." Suddenly he grinned. "That was neat. Do you ever go camping?"

"Not for years. But now that you're here, I don't see why we couldn't go. Would you like that?"

The grin on Michael's face faded. "I don't know. I always went camping with my dad." He fell silent for a moment, then turned to look up into his grandfather's face. "How come my dad died? How come he even came out here without bringing us with him? Or even telling us he was coming?" Anger began to tinge his voice. "He said he was going to Chicago."

"And he went to Chicago," Amos replied. "Then he came here. I don't rightly know exactly why."

Michael's eyes narrowed. "You mean you won't tell me."

"I mean I don't know," Amos said gruffly, standing up. He paused, then reached down and took Michael's chin in his rough hand, forcing the boy to face him. "If you mean I'm not telling you something because I think you're too young to know, then you're wrong. I don't hold with that sort of nonsense. If a boy's old enough to ask a question, he's old enough to hear the answer." His hand dropped away from Michael's face but he continued to regard his grandson with an unbending gaze. "I don't know why your father came out here," he said. "All I can tell you is that he got here yesterday, and last night he died."

Michael stared at his grandfather for a long time, and when he finally spoke, his voice was quavering. "But how come he died? He wasn't sick, was he?"

"It was an accident," Amos said shortly. "He was in the barn, up in the loft. He must have tripped over something."

The suspicion came back into Michael's eyes. "What?" he demanded.

Amos stiffened slightly. "I don't know—nobody does. Anyway, he fell off the edge of the loft, into the haybin."

Michael frowned. "What's a haybin?"

"On a farm, you keep the hay in bales up in a loft. Then, when you want to feed the animals in the barn, you pitch some of the hay down from the loft into the haybin."

"But how far is it?"

"Maybe ten feet."

Michael's frown deepened. "I fell that far once, and all that happened was that I twisted my ankle."

Amos hesitated, then spoke again. "But you didn't fall onto a pitchfork, did you?"

Michael's eyes widened. "A pitchfork?"

Amos nodded. "It's a big fork, with four tines. It's what you use to move hay around with. It was lying in the bin, and your dad fell onto it."

Suddenly Michael was on his feet, his face contorted with fury. "No! That's not what happened!" His voice rose as his angry eyes riveted his grandfather. "My dad didn't fall—he wouldn't have! Somebody must have pushed him. Somebody killed him, didn't they? Somebody killed my father!"

Michael's fists came up, ready to begin pummeling at his grandfather, but Amos reached out, putting one large hand on each of Michael's forearms. As his strong fingers closed, Michael found himself held immobile.

"Now you listen to me, young man," he heard his grandfather say. "What happened to your father was an accident. Nobody pushed him, and nobody killed him. It was an accident, and it's over with. Do you understand?"

Michael stared at his grandfather, then started to speak, but something in the old man's eyes made him remain silent. He swallowed hard, then nodded his head. His grandfather's iron grip eased, and his arms dropped to his side.

"And another thing," Amos added, his voice softer now, but no less commanding. "If I tell you something, you can count on it being the truth. So I don't ever again want to hear you arguing with me. Is that clear?"

"But—"

His grandfather interrupted, "You're not a baby anymore, and you mustn't act like one. You asked me what happened, and I told you." He was silent for a moment, then: "If you don't want an answer, don't ask a question. And don't ever argue with me. I'm older than you, and I'm wiser than you, and I don't hold with children not respecting their elders. All right?"

For several seconds Michael said nothing, but then, from the depths of his subconscious, the right words rose to the surface. "Yes, sir," he said softly. His grandfather smiled.

"Good. We're going to get along just fine, you and I. Now, you get settled in here, and when you're ready, come on downstairs, and I'll show you around the place. And I bet your grandma will have something good in the oven. You like apple pie?"

Michael nodded, but said nothing.

"Well, I'll bet you've never tasted anything like your grandmother's apple pie." He started out of the room, but stopped when Michael suddenly spoke again.

"Grandpa, how come Grandma can't walk?"

Slowly, Amos Hall turned back to face the boy. "I was wrong a couple of minutes ago," he said after a long silence. "I won't answer all your questions, because some questions just don't have answers. And that's one of them. I don't know why your grandma can't walk, Michael. It's just something that happened a long time ago." He turned, and left Michael alone in the room that was filled with all the things that had belonged to his father.

Anna Hall looked up from the kitchen table where she sat in her wheelchair, shelling peas for that evening's dinner. "Well? Are they getting settled in?"

Amos lowered himself into the chair opposite her. "If you can call it that. The girl's taking it hard, I think."

Anna stopped working for a moment, but still avoided her husband's eyes. "We can't expect her not to, can we? For us, it's a little different. We hadn't even seen him for twenty years. It was almost as if he was already dead—"

"He *was,*" Amos replied, his voice bitter. "As far as I'm concerned, he was as good as dead the day he walked out of here."

"Don't say that, Amos," Anna pleaded. "Please don't say that, not anymore. What if Janet hears you? What would she think?"

"What does she think anyway? What do you suppose Mark told her about us? You don't think he didn't talk about us, do you?" When Anna remained silent, his voice rose. "Do you? Do you really think he wouldn't have told her all about that night, and what he thought he saw?"

Anna's eyes narrowed. "If he did, then why is she here? Why didn't she tell us to ship Mark's body back to New York? I don't think he told her anything. Nothing at all."

Amos sighed and stood up. "Well, it doesn't matter. The important thing is that she came back and brought the child with her."

"But that doesn't mean she'll stay, Amos."

"She'll stay," Amos replied grimly. "She needs us right now, and we'll be here for her. She'll stay. I'll see to it."

As Amos strode through the back door, Anna regarded her husband's erect spine with bitterness. It was true, she realized. If Amos wanted Janet and Michael to stay in Prairie Bend, they would. And she, who had never been able to defy her husband in all the years of their marriage, would not defy him now.

Janet Hall awoke from a restless sleep. The nightmare had come back, the one she hadn't had since she'd married Mark. Now, as she came out of the dream, she felt disoriented, and the acrid smell of smoke lingered in her memory. For a moment she listened for the familiar sounds of the city at night, but heard only the silence of the prairie. And then, in the silence, there was something else: a whimpering sound, mixed with soft moanings.

Michael, in the grip of his own nightmare.

Shaking off the last vestiges of sleep, she got out of bed, slipped into the flannel robe Anna had given her, and made her way through the darkness to the room next door, where Michael slept. She found him tangled in the sheets, his arms moving spasmodically, his hands bunched into tight fists.

"Michael—Michael, wake up. You're having a nightmare."

Michael's eyes flew open. He stared at his mother without speaking, then his arms went around her neck, and he buried his face in her breast. She drew his quivering body close, cradling him. "He's not here," he sobbed. "He's gone, Mommy. I saw someone push him, and then he fell off the edge. He fell, and he fell, and then there was a—a pitchfork. I saw it, Mom. I tried to warn him, but I couldn't. And then—and then—"

"Hush," Janet soothed. "It was only a dream, sweetheart. You just had a bad dream." The shaking subsided, and Michael relaxed his grip on her, but Janet hugged him closer. "Would you like to come and sleep with me tonight?"

Now Michael wriggled out of her arms and drew slightly away from her, shaking his head. "I'm too old for that," he said.

"I know," Janet agreed. "But sometimes people get lonely, or frightened, and they need to be close to someone. I just thought maybe tonight you might want—"

"I'm okay," Michael interrupted. He sat up in bed and began straightening out the sheets, and Janet rose uncertainly to her feet.

"If you're sure you're all right—"

Michael nodded vigorously. "I'm fine, Mom." He lay back down, pulling the sheet up to his chin.

Janet leaned down and kissed him on the forehead. "All right. Sleep tight. If you need me, I'm right next door. Okay?"

Michael nodded, turning away from her to curl himself up into a tight ball. Janet watched him for a moment; then, reluctantly, she left him alone and started back to her own room. In the hall, standing at the head of the stairs, she found Amos. Startled, she tripped over the hem of her robe. Instantly, Amos put out a hand to steady her.

"Are you all right?"

"A nightmare. Michael just had a nightmare."

Amos nodded. "I heard something. I was coming up to see what was wrong."

Janet nodded. "I guess I wasn't sleeping very well anyway. I—I just feel all confused. It's as if everything's a dream, and I keep thinking I'll wake up, but then I know I won't."

Wordlessly, Amos led her into her room and guided her back into bed. "It'll take time," he finally said. "You have to give yourself time to get used to it. But you'll be all right, Janet. You and Michael will both be all right. We're here, and we love you, and we'll take care of you for as long as you need us. All right?"

In the dim moonlight that filtered into the darkened room, Janet looked up at her father-in-law. There was so much of Mark in his face, so much of Mark's strength in his eyes. "I—I just feel so helpless—"

"And that's all right, too," Amos assured her. "Just try to go back to sleep, and try not to worry."

He stayed with her, sitting in the chair near her bed, until once more she drifted into sleep.

Michael lay still in bed, listening first to the soft mutterings of his grandfather and his mother talking, then shifting his attention to the sounds of the night. Crickets chirped softly, and the lowing of cattle drifted through the darkness. His eyes searched out the model airplanes, and he began thinking once more about his father.

He couldn't *feel* his father.

That, he decided, was what was strange about this room. Even though it was filled with his father's things, he couldn't feel his father.

That was something he'd never experienced before. Always, for as long as he could remember, he'd been able to sense his father's presence near him, even when Mark wasn't at home. It was as if any place his father had been, he'd left something of himself behind, something for Michael to hold on to. It was something special between himself and his father, and even though they'd never talked about it, Michael was sure his father had felt it too.

And yet, in this room, with all his father's things around him, Michael couldn't feel him.

He'd felt him in the dream, though.

In the dream, he'd seen his father standing in the hayloft, and he'd seen someone else, someone he couldn't quite make out, near his father.

And then there'd been a flash of movement, and suddenly his father was over the edge, falling.

It was as if Michael himself was falling, but even as he felt himself tumbling endlessly toward the haybin, he'd also watched as his father's body plummeted toward the darkness below.

He'd seen the pitchfork, its handle buried in the hay, its four gleaming tines pointed straight upward, waiting for him, waiting for his father.

He'd tried to cry out, tried to scream, but no sound would come from his throat.

And then he could feel the cold, knife-edged steel plunging into his flesh, but even as the pitchfork pierced him, he could see that it wasn't himself falling onto the dangerous tines, but his father. Yet even knowing it was not he who was dying, Michael could still feel the pain, feel the agony shooting through his father's body, feel the death that had come for his father.

And above, watching, there was someone else. . . .

It was only a dream, and yet deep within himself, Michael knew it was more than his mind's imaginings.

It was real.

CHAPTER 2

No matter how hard she tried, Janet Hall couldn't focus her mind on the reality of what was happening. There was a sense of wrongness to everything, and she found herself grasping at inconsequentials. Suddenly, in the warmth of the spring morning, she saw herself as she should have been right now, striding down Madison Avenue, past the Carlyle Hotel toward American Expression, the boutique that was the usual focus of her Wednesday morning shopping expeditions.

And Michael should have been sitting in his classroom at the Manhattan Academy, pretending to be paying attention to his teacher. He wouldn't be, of course. Instead, Michael would be gazing out on the bright and sunny morning and dreaming of spending the weekend camping with Mark in the Berkshires.

And Mark. Mark should be facing his eleven o'clock class, polishing his glasses and filling his pipe while he glanced over his notes on The Effects of the War in Viet Nam on the Middle-class Family.

That was the way it should be. A typical family—if not the almost laughably stereotypical family Mark had once called them—going through the routines of their normal, stereotypical lives. But things were rarely as they should be, and today *nothing* was as it should be.

Everything was wrong; everything was unreal.

Mark was *dead.*

That was the thing she had to accept; when she could understand that, then everything else would fit, and she would be able to orient herself to her surroundings.

She forced herself into reality, yanked herself out of New York and back into Prairie Bend, and fixed her eyes on the coffin that stood next to the open grave. That's Mark, she told herself. That's all that's left of him, and in a few minutes, they are going to put him in the ground, and cover him up, and then he will be gone. *Gone.* She repeated the word to herself, but it still had no real meaning for her. Mark couldn't be gone, not forever. It wasn't fair. And that, she realized in a moment of sudden clarity, was the key to it all. *It wasn't fair.* There hadn't been anything wrong with Mark, except perhaps that odd daredevil streak in him that had never fit with his professorial personality, those sudden, inexplicable urges to thrust himself into danger that had, apparently, finally killed him.

It hadn't always been that way. When they'd first gotten married, he'd been what she'd always dreamed of: a quiet man living a quiet life. And then, a year into the marriage—eleven years ago—two things had happened: Michael had been born, and Mark had bought a motorcycle. Though Mark had denied it, Janet had always been sure there was a connection between the two events. It was as if Mark wanted to prove to his son that he was more than a milquetoast professor, that he was some kind of he-man, or at least his own image of a he-man. The motorcycle had been just the beginning.

Finally, there had been the skydiving. He'd taken that up two years ago, after a year of dragging his family out to the Jersey meadows every weekend to "watch." From the beginning, Janet had been sure that her husband would not be content to stay on the ground, and she had been right. Six months after he started watching, he started jumping. Of course, he'd been careful, as he was careful about everything.

And there, she realized, was the irony. Two years of skydiving, two years of risking his life from thousands of feet in the air, only to die in what couldn't have been more than a ten-foot fall.

It simply wasn't possible—not possible that he was dead, had left her alone to raise Michael—Michael, and the baby. She had not told the Halls yet about the baby, and they hadn't seemed to notice. But soon she would have to face telling them. And telling Michael.

And the guilty, disloyal thought came into her head once more: it was all Mark's own fault. If he'd come straight home from Chicago, as he'd planned to do, none of this would be happening. He hadn't been back to Prairie Bend in years. Not, in fact, in all the years she'd known him. So why had he gone back now?

It didn't make sense.

A wave of nausea swept over her, a twinge of the morning sickness that had plagued her far past the time when it should have ceased. Janet steeled herself against it, refusing to give in to it. *I won't be sick,* she told herself. *I won't be sick at Mark's funeral. I'll get through this.* Suddenly she felt a steadying hand on her elbow, and looked up to see Amos Hall watching her intently, his blue eyes—so like Mark's eyes—filled with concern. Shutting everything else out of her mind, she clutched her father-in-law's hand and forced herself to watch as they lowered her husband's coffin into the ground.

Michael stood quietly next to his mother, doing his best to keep his mind on what the minister was saying about his father. If he listened hard to the words, then maybe his headache would go away. But try as he would, he couldn't concentrate, for what the minister was saying didn't seem to be about his father at all. At least, not the father he had known. The minister kept talking about the importance of being at home and living and dying among your own, and Michael couldn't really see the connection between the words and his dad. Did the minister mean that if his father hadn't ever left Prairie Bend, then he wouldn't have died? But that didn't make sense—he'd been in Prairie Bend when he died.

Died. The word hadn't really had any meaning to Michael before yesterday. People died, but not people you knew, much less your own father. And yet it had happened. He stared at the coffin, knowing this was the last he would ever see of his father, but even as he watched it, he still couldn't believe that his father was really inside that wooden box, was really being buried in the ground, was really gone forever. He couldn't be . . .

He let his eyes wander away from the coffin, to scan over countless unfamiliar faces that all seemed to look alike, and then gaze out toward the horizon. Never in his life had he been able to see so far. The town, more like a village really, was behind him, and beyond the low stone wall of the cemetery, the plains stretched endlessly to the horizon, broken only by the slowly flowing river that curved around the town, giving the community its name, and the farmhouses, scattered here and there in the emptiness, each of them surrounded by a few huddled trees planted as protection against sudden prairie winds. And above it all the enormous sky, not the flat kind of sky he was used to, but a three-dimensional sky that seemed to cover the world like an enormous blue bowl. It was all so much larger than anything at home. At home, the city was always close around you, and even when you were out of the city there was a smallness to the countryside, with the forests crowding in and the profusion of low hills cutting off the view in every direction. But out here, on the plains, everything was open. He felt as though he could breathe more deeply than he ever had before.

He sensed movement next to him and felt his mother's hand squeezing his own. The service was ending. The minister had stooped down to pick up a clod of the black earth, which he was now holding over the open grave. It was all over, and his father was gone.

"Ashes to ashes, dust to dust . . ." Strong fingers squeezed the clump of earth, and as Michael stared, it broke up, dirt drumming onto the casket with a hollow sound that made Michael's throat constrict. A snuffling next to him told him that his mother was crying, and suddenly his eyes, too, filled with tears. Self-consciously, Michael let go of his mother's hand, pulled a handkerchief from his hip pocket, and blew his nose. He felt his mother's hand on his shoulder, pressing gently. Then it was over. He turned away from his father's grave.

And as he turned, something caught his attention. A glint. A movement. At first he wasn't sure what it was, but as his eyes scanned the plains again, he realized it must have been the sun flashing off the weathervane that stood perched high on the ridgepole of a weathered barn about a half mile away. Yet, as he watched it, he realized that there was no wind today. The vane wasn't moving. Then what had flashed? Maybe it was just his imagination. He started to turn away once more, to follow his mother toward his grandfather's car, but once again his attention was caught by the flash. No, not quite a flash. It was something else, something he couldn't quite focus on. He examined the farm and frowned. There was something different about it, something he couldn't quite figure out. He cocked his head, shading his eyes with his hand, and then felt an unfamiliar touch on his shoulder. He looked up to find his grandfather frowning at him.

"You all right?" Amos Hall asked.

Michael nodded. "I thought I saw something. Out there."

The older man followed his gaze, then shrugged. "That's Ben Findley's place. Not much to see out there. Man doesn't keep it up like he should. It comes of living alone."

"Doesn't he have a wife?" Michael asked.

His grandfather hesitated, then shook his head and started leading Michael away. "Had one years ago, but she left. And you'd do well to stay clear of that place."

Michael stopped, turning back to stare once more at the farm which had suddenly become fascinating. "How come?"

His grandfather offered him a faint smile. " 'Cause Ben Findley doesn't like kids," he said. "He doesn't like anybody, but especially, he doesn't like kids." Then his voice softened, and he took Michael's hand. "Now come on, son. Let's get back to the farm. This is all over here, and we've all got to get back to living." He started walking slowly away, and his arm fell across Michael's shoulders. He was silent as they moved through the sunshine, but before they got to the car, he paused and turned to face Michael.

"You sure you're all right?" he asked, and Michael knew that this time Amos was talking about his father.

"I think so," he said uncertainly. "I—I just can't get used to it. I keep thinking he's going to come back, even though I know he's not."

His grandfather glanced back toward the grave, then pulled his handkerchief from his jacket pocket and wiped at his eyes. "He should have come back a long time ago," he said in a voice that made Michael wonder if he was supposed to be listening or if the old man was talking to himself. "All of you should have. But now that you're home, we'll see that you stay here."

Then, once more, he moved toward the car, where Anna, brushing off Janet's attempts to help her, had swung herself out of her wheelchair and into the back seat of the Olds, then folded up the chair and pulled it in after her.

"See?" she asked Janet when she was done. "It's just a matter of deciding what you have to do, then doing it." A few moments later, when Janet had joined her in the back seat, and Amos, with Michael beside him, had pulled away from the little cemetery, she reached out and took Janet's hand. "That's what you're going to have to do now," she said. "Decide what to do, then do it. But don't you fret about it, dear—we're all here, and we'll all help."

Janet lay her head back against the seat, and closed her eyes, offering a small prayer of gratitude for the family Mark had left behind him. He may not have needed them, she thought, but I do. Dear God, how I need them . . .

Janet glanced at the clock in the corner of the living room and wondered how much longer it could go on. It was already four-thirty, and it was becoming harder and harder to fight off the exhaustion of the day. The room was hot and stuffy, and overfilled with people, and Janet was beginning to think the situation, for her, was hopeless. She could remember the names of Mark's sister, Laura, and her husband—Buck Shields—and their son, Ryan, who seemed to be about Michael's age, but that was all. And the introduction to them had been terribly awkward, for she hadn't even been able to utter a polite "I've heard so much about you." She'd hoped that when she saw Laura, she'd recognize her, that something about her would jog her memory, but it hadn't. What *had* struck her immediately, though, was the fact that Laura, like herself, was pregnant, but much further along. Though Janet had not commented on it, and was relieved that Laura had not seemed to guess, the coincidence had made her feel an immediate bond to the delicate-looking woman who was her sister-in-law. Nevertheless, Janet had finally come to the conclusion that in all their years together, Mark had never mentioned his sister to her.

Why?

Each time she saw Laura—an ethereal wisp of a woman whose eyes, even when she smiled, seemed oddly haunted—the question of why Mark had never spoken of her came into Janet's mind. Each time, she rejected it, shifting what was left of her concentration to someone else.

But there was only a sea of nameless faces, people whom she hoped were not offended by her inability to greet them with the same familiarity with which they greeted her:

"So you're Mark's Janet."

Mark's Janet.

Over and over again, the same two words. *"Mark's Janet."* At first it had upset her, the casual reference to herself as if she were nothing more than her husband's possession, but as the afternoon wore on she had grown used to it, discovering that the phrase wasn't truly offensive; indeed, there was a strangely comforting quality to it. It wasn't that she had been owned by Mark, it was simply that she was a part of him. To these people—so different from her New York friends—she and Mark had, upon their marriage, ceased to be individuals. Had these been her family instead of Mark's, had Mark been here instead of herself, the words would simply have been reversed.

This day, Janet was finding comfort in that lack of individuality. It meant that she did not have to put herself out to define herself to these people, did not have to expose herself to them or make them understand her. They already knew who she was.

"Are you all right?"

Startled, Janet looked up. She recognized the man as someone to whom she'd been introduced, but as with all the others, she could not put a name to the face.

"Potter. Dr. Charles Potter."

He was, she judged, in his late fifties—maybe his early sixties—and he looked exactly like what he was, a country GP. His hair was white, and his manner was what would once have been described as courtly. And, though she could hardly believe it, he was wearing an ice-cream suit.

"I beg your pardon?" Janet blurted.

"Are you all right?" Potter repeated. "You look a mite peaked."

"I'm fine," Janet assured him, and then realized that the room was much too warm, and she felt flushed. She tried to stand up, and discovered she couldn't. "Well, I guess I'm not all right after all," she said weakly. "How do I look?"

Potter grinned, losing a bit of what Janet was certain was a carefully cultivated image. "As I said, a mite peaked. Which, around here, covers most conditions not covered by 'right fit.' And you certainly don't look right fit." Then, as he continued speaking, his voice turned serious. "Which isn't remarkable, under the circumstances. I said it at the funeral, and I said it earlier this afternoon, but I'll say it again. I'm sorry about Mark. He was a good man."

Janet nodded automatically, suddenly aware of a strange dizziness and a surge of nausea. "I wonder if maybe I ought to lie down," she suggested, and Potter was immediately on his feet, signaling to Amos Hall, who hurried over.

"I think we'd better get her upstairs," Potter said. "It all seems to have been a bit too much for her."

Suddenly everyone in the room seemed to be staring at her. "No—please —I'll be all right, really I will," Janet protested, but Amos, still powerful despite his years, picked her up and carried her up the stairs, Dr. Potter following close behind.

In her room, Amos laid her gently on the bed, then smiled at her. "Doc will have a look at you, and Mama and I'll get rid of the mob downstairs. They all should have left hours ago anyway, but you know how these things are. Doesn't matter that everyone sees everyone else every day of the year. You put them together for whatever reason, and they just keep on talkin'." Then he was gone, and Potter was sitting on the edge of the bed, taking her pulse. A moment later a thermometer was in her mouth, and Potter was asking her what seemed to be an unending series of questions about the state of her health. Finally he got to his feet, pulled a blanket over her, and instructed her to get some sleep.

Janet looked at him curiously. "But I'm not sleepy," she protested. She paused, then: "I just had a bad moment, because of the heat downstairs."

Potter peered at her over the tops of his glasses, taking in her condition. "Are you sure?" he asked pointedly.

Janet sighed. Though she was barely starting to show, the doctor seemed to have guessed the truth with one shrewd glance. Still, he seemed to be waiting for her to acknowledge it. When she only smiled wanly, he shrugged.

"It's probably the stress of the last few days," he said, adding, "On the other hand, it could be something else, a touch of the flu or some bug or other. I'll tell you what you do. You get some sleep, and tomorrow I want you to come to my office and we'll take a look. All right?"

Janet lowered herself gratefully into the pillows, as Potter closed the door behind him. She *was* tired, she *didn't* feel good, and if she at least feigned sleep, then she would be left alone. Otherwise—

She had a vision of all the women of Prairie Bend, each one just like all the others, parading through her room, clucking over her, fussing at her, offering her homemade soup.

But even that vision, like the phrase "Mark's Janet" a little earlier, was somehow comforting. Totally alien from her life in New York, but nonetheless comforting. Slowly, she let herself drift into sleep.

"When are you going home?" Ryan Shields asked his cousin. After some initial suspicious circling of each other, the two boys had formed an alliance as the day had gone on, and after Michael's mother had been taken upstairs, they had finally escaped from their grandmother's living room. Now Ryan, ignoring the fact that he was wearing his Sunday suit, sprawled on the patchy green beneath the immense elm tree that shaded the yard between the house and the barn. He stared curiously up at Michael. Even though Michael was a year younger than himself, and three inches shorter, Ryan wasn't at all sure he could take him in a fight. Indeed, an hour ago he'd given up even considering the possibilities, after Michael had rescued him from the clutches of his Grandmother Shields, who never failed to treat him as if he were still four years old.

From his perch on the rotting rope swing, Michael gave an experimental kick that barely set the device in motion. "I don't know," he replied. "I guess in a few days."

Ryan frowned. "That's what my dad said you'd do. But I think my mom wishes you'd stay here."

Michael cocked his head. "Why would she want that?"

"Search me," Ryan replied. "All I know is that they got in a big fight about it on the way over here. Well, it started to be a fight, anyway." He paused and looked down, studying a blade of grass he'd plucked from the lawn as if it fascinated him. Not looking at Michael, he said, "Did your mom and dad fight?"

Michael shook his head. "Hunh-unh. At least not when I was around. Do your folks fight a lot?"

Ryan nodded. "Mostly about this place. Mom hates it here. Today, she said your dad was right to leave when he did."

Suddenly Michael brought the swing to a halt, and joined his cousin on the ground. "Did she ever say how come Dad left?"

"Hunh?"

Michael, in unconscious imitation of his cousin, plucked a blade of grass and stuck it between his teeth. "I always thought Dad just didn't want to be a farmer. But that seems kind of stupid. I mean, just because he wasn't a farmer isn't any reason not to come and visit, is it?"

"Nope," Ryan agreed. "My dad doesn't farm. What does that have to do with it?"

Michael rolled over and stared up into the elm tree, and for a long time the two boys were silent. When at last he spoke, Michael's voice trembled. "Did—did you ever think about your dad dying?"

Ryan shifted uncomfortably, then glanced away from Michael. "Sure. Doesn't everybody? Except—"

"Except what?" Michael asked.

"Well, I guess I only thought about it 'cause I knew it wasn't really gonna happen."

Suddenly Michael sat up, and his eyes fixed on his cousin. "I used to think about my dad dying when he went skydiving. That's like falling. Do you think me thinking about it could have made it happen?"

"That's crazy," Ryan replied. "You can't make something happen just by thinking about it. Besides, what happened to your dad was an accident, wasn't it?"

Michael nodded, but his eyes were uncertain.

"Then it wasn't your fault." Suddenly both boys sensed a presence nearby, and looked up to see their grandfather looming over them. They scrambled to their feet, self-consciously brushing the dust and grass from their clothes.

"That'll make your mothers real thrilled with you," Amos Hall commented. "What's going on out here?"

"We were just talking," Ryan told him.

"About what?"

The two boys glanced at each other. "Things," Michael replied.

"Things," Amos repeated. He fixed his eyes on Ryan. "You know what I was just saying to your grandma a couple of minutes ago? I was saying that I'll bet those two boys are sitting out there discussing 'things.' And do you know what she said?"

Ryan regarded his grandfather suspiciously, sure he was about to fall into a trap, but in the end his curiosity got the best of him. "What?" he asked.

Amos grinned at the boy. "Well, why don't you just go find her and ask her yourself? And while she tells you, you can help her with the dishes." Then, when Ryan had disappeared through the back door of the house, he lowered himself to the ground and gestured for Michael to sit down beside him. "Everybody's gone home," he said, "so you can go back in without having to worry about them all poking at you and telling you how cute you are, and how much you look like your father, or your mother, or your Uncle Harry, if you have one. It's all over." He paused, then: "Do you understand?"

Michael hesitated, then nodded unhappily. "The funeral's over."

Amos Hall's head bobbed once. "That's right. The funeral's over, and now we all have to get on with life. Your mother's still in bed—"

"Is she all right?" Michael broke in.

"She's probably just tired. It was hot as blazes in there, so we put her to bed. When you go inside I want you to be quiet so you don't wake her up. Go on in and change your clothes, and then come out to the barn. There's still a lot to be done, and we only have a couple of hours of light left." He stood up, then offered Michael a hand. For a moment, he thought the boy was going to refuse it, but then Michael slipped his small hand into Amos's much larger one, and pulled himself to his feet. Still, instead of heading for the house, Michael hesitated. Amos waited for him to speak, then prompted him.

"What is it, boy?" he asked, his voice gruff, but not unkind.

Michael looked up at his grandfather, his eyes wide. "What—what's going to happen now, Grandpa?"

Amos Hall slipped an arm around his grandson, and started walking him toward the house. "Life goes on," he said, and then in a tone meant to be reassuring, "We'll just take it one step at a time, all right?"

But Michael frowned. "I guess so," he said at last. "But I wish dad were here."

"So do I," Amos Hall replied, but the gentleness had gone out of his voice. "So do I."

Janet awoke to the setting sun, and for the first time since she had been married, did not reach out to touch her husband. The funeral, then, had accomplished that much. Never again, she was sure, would she awaken and reach out for Mark. He was truly gone, and she was truly on her own now.

She sat up and began tentatively to get out of bed. The nausea was gone, and the flushed feeling with it, so she put her feet into a pair of slippers and went into the bathroom, where she splashed her face with cold water. Then she went back to her bedroom, took off the clothes she had been sleeping in, and put on a robe. At the top of the stairs, she listened for a moment.

There was a murmuring of voices from the kitchen but only silence from the living room. Running a hand through her hair, she started down the stairs.

The family was gathered around the kitchen table, and as she came upon them she stopped, startled. It was as if they belonged together, the elderly couple at either end of the table, and Michael, so obviously *theirs*, between them. It must, Janet realized, have been what the family looked like twenty years ago, except that instead of Michael between them, it would have been Mark. And Laura.

Almost abstractly, she noted that there was no place set for her at the table.

Michael saw her first.

"Mom! Are you okay?"

"I'm fine. I was just tired, and it was so hot—well, I'm afraid your old mother had what they call a fainting spell."

"Are you sure you should be up, dear?" Anna Hall asked, her voice anxious. "Why don't you go back up, and I'll fix a plate for you. It's just leftovers from the reception, but we're making do with it. Or I could fix you some soup. There's nothing like good homemade—"

"I'm fine, Anna," Janet insisted. "If I could just sit down, I'll—"

"Get your mother a chair, Michael."

As his grandfather spoke, Michael got up from the table, ducked around his mother, and disappeared into the dining room. A moment later he was back, bearing one of Anna's needlepoint-seated lyre-back "Sunday" chairs.

"Now why can't I ever get action like that at home?" Janet asked as she settled herself at the table. "It would have taken me ages just to get his attention, and then there would have been a chorus of 'Aw, Moms,'—"

"Aw, Mom . . ."

"See what I mean?"

Amos glared at her. "Children do what's expected of them," he stated, his tone indicating that there was no room for discussion.

"Or perhaps it's just novelty," Anna hesitantly suggested. Amos turned, about to speak, but she ignored him, wheeling her chair away from the table. A moment later she handed Michael some silverware and nodded toward Janet. "Set your mother a place." She shifted her attention back to Janet. "It's a known fact that children behave better in other people's houses than they do in their own. As for expectations," she added, turning to her husband, "what about Mark? We expected Mark to stay in Prairie Bend forever, and you certainly made that expectation clear to him. So much for *that* theory."

An odd look came into Amos's eyes, one that could have been either hurt or anger. In the tense silence that followed, Janet reached out to squeeze the old man's hand. "I hadn't known Mark was supposed to come home after college," she said. "What would a sociologist have done here?"

Though she'd directed the question at her father-in-law, it was Anna who answered.

"At first, after he . . . left," she said in a near whisper, choosing her words cautiously, "we didn't even know he'd gone to college. We didn't know where he'd gone. All we knew was that he wasn't here. But we thought he'd come back." She shrugged helplessly, avoiding Amos's silent stare. "By then, we just didn't know him anymore. And you don't need a degree to run a farm. I guess he was never interested in farming. Not this farm, and not his own farm, either."

Janet's fork stopped halfway between her plate and her mouth, and she stared at Anna. "*His* farm? What are you talking about? Mark never had a farm."

"Of course he had a farm," Anna replied, her expression clearly indicating her conviction that Janet must be suffering a momentary lapse of memory. Then, as Janet's demeanor failed to clear, her eyes shifted to her husband, then back to Janet. "You don't mean to tell me he never told you about the farm, do you?"

Janet, feeling a sudden panic, turned to Michael for support. Was the same thing that had happened when she'd heard about Mark's sister about to happen again? "Did daddy ever say anything to you about a farm? About owning a farm, I mean?"

Michael shook his head.

"But that's not possible," Amos interjected. "You must have known. The taxes, the estate—"

"The estate?" Janet asked. What on earth was he talking about? Slowly she put down her fork, then looked from Amos to Anna. At last her eyes came to rest on Michael. "I think perhaps it's time you went up to your room."

"Aw, Mom . . ."

"Do as your mother says," Amos snapped, and after a moment of hesitation, Michael got up and left the table. Only when his footsteps had stopped echoing in the stairwell did Janet speak again. When she did, her voice was quavering.

"Now what is all this about?" she asked. "I thought you meant that Mark owned a farm a long time ago, before I met him. But when you mentioned taxes, and the estate—"

"He's always owned a farm," Amos said. "It was a wedding present, just as half of Laura and Buck's farm was a wedding present to them. Buck's parents gave them the other half. They don't live on it, but they still own it and take the responsibility for it. And if Mark had married a local girl—"

But Janet had stopped listening. "A wedding present," she whispered. "But you sent us silverware—"

"Well, of course there was that, too," Anna replied.

"But that was *all* there was," Janet insisted, her voice growing shrill in spite of herself. "If there'd been anything else, Mark would have told me. Wouldn't he? *Wouldn't he?*"

Amos reached out and took her hand. "You really don't know anything about it, do you?"

Mutely, Janet shook her head.

"It's forty acres," Amos said. "It was deeded to Mark on your wedding day, and he's owned it ever since. I know, because I was afraid he might try to sell it, so I've kept track. I always hoped he'd come and live on it someday, but I guess I always knew that wouldn't happen. Not ever, not the way he felt. But he did pay the taxes on it. As far as I know, he never tried to sell it."

"But what's happened to it?" Janet asked. "And why haven't I ever heard of it before?"

"I don't know why you've never heard of it," Amos replied. "But it's still there. It's yours now."

For a long moment, Janet stared at her husband's parents, her mind churning. When at last she spoke, it was without thinking.

"He hated you very much, didn't he? All of you."

Amos Hall's eyes flashed with anger, but Anna only stared ahead, looking into space.

"Yes, I suppose he did," Amos finally said, the anger in his eyes disappearing as quickly as it had come. "But he's dead, now. All that's behind us, isn't it?"

CHAPTER 3

Though she went to bed early that night, Janet Hall did not go to sleep. She sat up, staring out over the moonlit prairie, her robe drawn tightly around her as if it could protect her from her own thoughts. For a while she tried to concentrate on the stars, laboriously picking out constellations she hadn't seen so clearly since her childhood, but then, as the night wore on, her thoughts bore in on her.

It wasn't just his sister Mark had never mentioned.

There was a farm, too.

All along, there had been a farm.

Painfully, she made herself remember all the talks they'd had, she and Mark, all the nights—nights like this—when they'd sat up talking about the future.

For Janet, the future had always held a farm.

Nothing concrete, nothing real. For Janet, the farm of her dream was something from a child's picture book—a small place, somewhere in New England, with a whitewashed clapboard house, a bright red barn with white trim, an immaculate barnyard populated with hens and tiny fuzzy chicks, the whole thing neatly fenced off with white post-and-rail. There would be stone walls, of course, old stone walls meandering through the pastures, but the borders, the limits of her world, would be edged in white. And there they would live, their small family, released at last from the congestion of the city, their senses no longer dunned by the smells of garbage and exhaust, the sounds of jackhammers and blasting horns, but expanding to the aroma of fresh-mown hay and the crowing of roosters at dawn.

All idyllic, all a dream, and all of it, always, gently derided by Mark. All the reasons why it was impossible, all the excuses that they continually debated: They were city people, though they both had been born in the country, and New Yorkers by choice, Mark would insist; choices could still be made, Janet would counter. Mark was a teacher, not a farmer; there were colleges in New England, everywhere you looked—he could still teach, and they could hire someone to run the farm. Michael was happy in his school, Mark would point out; children change schools all the time, and there's no proof, Janet would argue, that city schools are better than small-town schools.

In the end, however, it had always come down to the one argument for which Janet had no answer.

They couldn't afford a farm, couldn't manage to save enough even for a half-acre in the suburbs, let alone a farm.

Now, Janet realized that it had all been a lie. From the day they were married, the lie had been between them, and she had never felt it, never faintly suspected it. There had even been times when Mark had seemed to join in her dream.

They had been in Millbrook, and they had come around a curve in the road, and there, spread out before them, was Janet's dream. It had been Mark who had noticed it first; Janet had been studying a map, trying to match the route numbers to the street names that seemed to be posted only every five miles and then changed with every village they passed through. Suddenly Mark had stopped the car and said, "Well, there it is, and even I have to admit that it's pretty." She'd looked up, and across a pasture that sloped gently away from the highway, she had seen her farm—white clapboard house, red barn, white post-and-rail fence, even a stream, dammed to form a millpond. And it was for sale.

They'd talked about it all weekend, even going so far as to investigate the possibility of Mark's finding a job in Poughkeepsie. But in the end, on Sunday night as they drove south on the Taconic Parkway, they'd faced reality.

They had no money, and they couldn't buy the farm without money.

But it had been a lie. And Mark had known it was a lie.

What else was there? How much had this stranger with whom she had spent thirteen years of her life kept hidden from her? What else would she find as the days went by and she learned more about the man she had married?

Anna. Had Mark known his mother was confined to a wheelchair? It seemed impossible that he hadn't, and yet it seemed equally impossible that he had never said anything to her about it. But he hadn't.

When Janet had asked her mother-in-law about it just before coming upstairs that night, Anna had only shrugged, a look of philosophical resignation in her eyes. "I suppose he must have known," she'd said. "It happened after he went away, but I think Laura must have told him about it."

"But he never heard from Laura," Janet had protested. "He never even *talked* about her. Until yesterday, I didn't even know Mark had a sister."

Anna's eyes had flickered with pain for a moment. "You have to understand," she'd finally said. "There were some things Mark just wanted to shut out of his mind. He always did that, even when he was little. I remember he had a puppy once—a little black shepherd—but it got sick, and Amos had to put it down. Afterward, I tried to talk to Mark about it, but he wouldn't admit the puppy'd ever even existed. Just shut it out completely." She sighed, weariness spreading across her features. "I suppose that's what he did when he left Prairie Bend. Shut us out, just like that dog."

"But why? Why did he leave?"

And for that, there had been no answer. "It doesn't matter anymore," was all Anna would say. "It's all in the past. There's no use dredging it up now. It would only cause pain." She'd looked beseechingly at Janet. "I've had enough pain, dear. Can't we leave this alone?" Then she'd held out her arms, and Janet, her throat constricting with feeling, had leaned down, clumsily embracing this fragile woman she hardly knew.

As she sat in the darkness that night, trying to concentrate on the stars, Janet felt the props of her life slipping away from her, felt the rock of trust she'd always had in Mark dissolving into sand. Already, it was slipping through her fingers, leaving her with nothing to cling to.

By the time the horizon edged silvery-gray with dawn and she drifted into an uneasy sleep, Janet's grief over the death of her husband had begun to change into something else. An odd fear had begun to pervade her, a fear of what else she might discover about Mark, what other secrets might have lain hidden from her during all the years of her marriage.

When she awoke several hours later, she could feel a difference in herself. It was as if uncertainty had gathered around her, crippling her. She lay still for a long time, unable to make up her mind to get up, unsure whether she could face the day.

She closed her eyes for a few moments, and suddenly she saw an image of Mark's face, but his features were slightly blurred, and there was something in his eyes—a secretiveness—that she'd never seen before. And then the image changed, hardened and sharpened into the visage of Amos.

His eyes were clear, his features strong. And he was smiling at her, offering her the strength she could no longer get from Mark or find within herself.

She rose from her bed and went to the window. Below her, in the barnyard, she watched Michael feeding the chickens. A moment later Amos emerged from the barn, and as if feeling her gaze, looked up; she waved to him; he waved back to her.

And then the nausea hit her. Turning away from the window, she hurried to the bathroom, threw up in the toilet, and waited for the sickness to pass.

What's going to happen to us? she wondered a few minutes later as she began dressing. *What's going to happen to us now?*

Ryan Shields pedaled furiously through the village, then east on the highway toward his grandparents' farm. He didn't slow down until he'd made the turn into the driveway, but by the time he got to the front yard, he was coasting, his feet dragging in the dust as makeshift brakes. He came to a dead stop, expertly dropped the kickstand with one toe, then balanced on the leaning bike, his arms crossed, only his slouching posture preventing the bike from tipping over. It was a technique he'd learned only a month ago, and it had quickly become his favorite pose. He cocked his head, squinting in the brightness of the sun, peering at the house. "Hey! Anybody home?"

A moment later the front door opened, and Michael came out on the porch. "Hi."

"Hi. Whatcha doin'?"

"Nothing. Everybody's gone into town to Dr. Potter's."

Ryan swung his leg over the handlebar, and stepped off the bike, which promptly fell over into the dust of the driveway. "Shit." He picked up the bike, carefully balanced it on the kickstand, then mounted the steps to the porch. "Is your mom still sick?"

Michael shrugged. "I don't know. I guess not. Anyway, it didn't seem like it this morning, and she was okay last night." Then he frowned. "How come you're not in school?"

"School's out."

"At home, we don't get out for another three weeks."

"We always get out early here. Most of the kids have to help their dads with planting. Can I come in?"

Michael's expression became guarded. "There's nobody home."

"You're home."

"But I'm not supposed to let anybody in the house when I'm by myself."

Ryan stared at him in disbelief. "Why not?"

" 'Cause you never know who might come to the door. There's all kinds of crazies in the city. What can you do?"

"Well, I'm not crazy, and this is my grandparents' house, and I can come in if I want to." Then, seeing Michael suddenly tense, he grinned. "Stop worrying. Grandma and Grandpa won't care, and it's their house, not yours. I come out here all the time." He brushed past Michael and went inside, then called back over his shoulder, "You want a Coke?"

Michael hesitated a moment, then decided that Ryan was right. This wasn't New York, and Ryan was his cousin. "There aren't any," he said, following Ryan inside and letting the screen door slam behind him. "I already looked."

"Where'd you look?"

"In the 'fridge."

"Grandma keeps them in the laundry room. Come on."

A moment later, each of them armed with a warm Coke, they wandered out into the backyard. "Hey, have you been down to the river yet?"

Michael shook his head. "I haven't been anywhere."

"Well, come on," Ryan told him. "The river's the best part of Prairie Bend." With Michael following him, Ryan headed around behind the barn, then across the pasture toward the strip of cottonwoods that bordered the river. Five minutes later, the two of them stepped out of the sunshine into the deep shade of the trees. In contrast to the openness of the prairie, the woods were choked with underbrush. The canopied branches overhead created a closed-in feeling that made Michael shiver.

"Where's the river?" he asked.

"Down the trail. Come on."

A couple of minutes later the path made a sharp right, then opened out onto the river. Here the bank was low, and Ryan scrambled down onto the beach that separated the woods from the water. "You should have seen it last month. It was full, and the whole beach was covered. Right here, the water must have been six feet deep."

"How deep is it now?" Michael asked. They'd crossed the beach and stood at the water's edge. The river was moving lazily, the current only rippling the surface near the far bank, but it was murky, its waters stained by the silt it carried.

"Only a couple feet on this side. You could wade almost all the way across, but it gets deep over by the other bank."

"Can we go swimming?" Michael asked.

Ryan looked doubtful. "I don't know. It's still kind of early, and the water's pretty cold."

"Aw, come on," Michael urged. "You said it was shallow."

But Ryan still hesitated. "Nobody ever goes in this early. It's too dangerous. You can't see where the holes are, and the current can grab you."

Michael stared out at the river. "You chicken?" he finally asked.

That did it. Ryan scowled at his cousin. "There's a swimming hole down near the bend. Come on."

They started downstream and in a few minutes came to the point where the river began the first of the curves that would take it around the village. Here, the spring floods had eroded the bank, creating an inlet where the water seemed almost still. A huge cottonwood stood by the inlet, its roots half exposed, one enormous limb reaching out over the water. From that branch, a rope hung, an old tire tied to its free end. Michael knew immediately what it was for.

"How do you get to it?"

"You have to climb the tree, then go down the rope," Ryan explained. "Once you're on it, you get it swinging, then dive off it."

"You wanna go first?"

Ryan stared at him. "Are you crazy? Nobody's been in swimming yet. There could be rocks in there, and it's cold, and you don't know how deep it is. None of the kids go off the tire until someone's been down there to make sure it's safe."

"What could happen?" Michael asked.

"You could break your neck, that's what," Ryan replied.

"Bullshit."

"Bullshit, nothin'! It's happened."

"Well, it won't happen to me," Michael said. He set his half-drunk Coke down and started stripping off his clothes. A moment later, naked, he scrambled up the cottonwood and began making his way out onto the limb that overhung the swimming hole. From the shore, Ryan watched him anxiously.

"Don't start down the rope 'till you check it out. It might be rotten."

Michael nodded. A few seconds later he came to the rope, and straddling the branch, grasped the loop with both hands. He gave it an experimental tug and, when it held, began pulling harder. Satisfied that it wouldn't break, he reached down and took hold of the hanging section. Finally he rolled off the trunk, and began letting himself down the rope until his feet touched the tire. When he was standing on the tire, he grinned at Ryan, then began slowly pumping to get the tire swinging.

"You're supposed to sit on the tire," Ryan yelled.

Michael ignored him. The makeshift swing began to move, with Michael maneuvering it so that soon it was arcing back and forth, over the bank on the backswing, and out over the center of the swimming hole on the forward swing. When he had it going as high as he could, he crouched on top of the tire, waited for the crest of the forward swing, then released his grasp on the rope and sprang away from the tire, flipping himself into a back dive. Just before he hit the water he took a deep breath, and listened with satisfaction to the scream that had burst out of Ryan. Then he plunged into the icy water.

From the shore, Ryan stared at the spot where Michael had disappeared into the murk, unconsciously holding his breath and counting the seconds. Time seemed to stand still as he waited for his cousin's head to reappear.

Ten seconds went by, then fifteen.

Twenty seconds.

Thirty.

His breath bursting out of his lungs, Ryan began to panic. Should he jump in after Michael, or run for help? But run where? No one was home at his grandparents', and the village was too far away.

"Help! Somebody help us!"

And then, just as he was about to jump into the dark water, the surface broke, and Michael's grinning face appeared. With three strong strokes, he made it to the shore and scrambled out.

"It's neat!" he cried. "You want to try it?"

Ryan ignored the question. "What the hell are you doing? I thought you'd hit a rock!"

"I coulda stayed under for a whole minute," Michael said, flopping down on the ground. He was barely even panting, and his eyes were sparkling. "Did I scare you?"

Ryan glared down at his cousin and again ignored the question. "You coulda gotten killed."

"I scared you, didn't I?"

Ryan finally nodded his head. "So what?"

"Betcha thought I wouldn't do it."

Ryan shrugged elaborately. "So you did it. What's that prove, except that you're stupid?"

"It wasn't stupid—it was fun. Go on—try it!"

But instead of peeling off his clothes, Ryan only sat down and reached for his Coke. "I'm not gonna try it, and if you want to think I'm chicken, go ahead. There's rocks down there. You were just lucky you didn't hit one."

Michael took a sip of his Coke and thought about it. He'd known there were rocks beneath the surface—at least, Ryan had told him so, and he hadn't thought Ryan was lying. And yet, while he'd been swinging on the rope, he hadn't felt frightened. He'd felt excited, and knowing he was taking a risk was part of the excitement. But he hadn't really thought about getting hurt. Or had he? He tried to remember, but couldn't. All he could remember was the thrill of swinging out over the river, then letting go and plunging toward the cold water, not knowing exactly what was under the surface.

Suddenly a vision of his father came into his mind, plunging through the air, then slowing as his chute opened. Always, the chute had opened. But what if it hadn't?

Was that what his father had loved about skydiving? The risk? Knowing that each time he tried it, the parachute might not open? And yet, even as he'd dived, Michael had known nothing was going to happen to him. He'd *known* it. But how?

He began pulling his clothes back on, and a few minutes later the two boys started back toward their grandparents' house. It wasn't until they'd emerged from the woods and started across the pasture, though, that Michael finally spoke.

"I wasn't going to hurt myself."

Ryan glanced at him, but kept walking. "How do you know?"

Michael shrugged. "I just know."

Now Ryan came to a halt and stared at Michael. "What are you, some kind of nut?"

"N-no," Michael stammered. "But when I dove, I knew I was going to be all right. I just knew it." Unconsciously, his hand went up and rubbed the back of his neck, and Ryan suddenly grinned.

"If you didn't get hurt, how come you're rubbing your neck?"

Michael dropped his hand to his side. "It's not my neck. I just have a headache, that's all."

"Yeah," Ryan agreed, his voice mocking now. "Just a headache. You *did* hit a rock, didn't you. Lemme see your head."

Bending, Michael let his cousin examine the back of his head. "Is there a cut?" he asked, his voice half curious, half challenging.

"Unh-unh. Is it sore?"

"Not like I hit it. It's just a headache." Suddenly he frowned, wrinkling his nose. There was a strange odor, as if something was burning. "What's that stink?"

"Stink? What stink?" Ryan sniffed at the air, then shook his head. "I don't smell anything."

"It's like something's on fire." He scanned the horizon, sure he would see a plume of smoke nearby, but there was nothing. He turned back to Ryan. "Don't you smell it?"

Ryan scowled. "I don't smell anything, 'cause there's nothing to smell. What are you, some kind of nut?" he said again.

A flash of pain shot through Michael's head. "Don't you call me crazy," he flared.

Ryan's expression darkened. "I'll call you whatever I want to! What are you gonna do about it?"

Michael stood still, sudden fury toward his cousin mounting inside him as his head throbbed with pain. "Drop dead," he heard himself whisper. "Why don't you just drop dead?"

Ryan's eyes began to dance, and the beginnings of a grin spread over his face. But then, as Michael glared at him, the grin faded, and the color drained from Ryan's face as his hands clutched at his stomach. He began backing away from Michael, then turned and began running across the field.

A moment later Michael was alone, and his headache began to ease. As he started walking back toward his grandparents' house, he tried to figure out what had happened. But no matter how hard he thought about it, it still didn't make sense. All he'd done had been to tell his cousin to drop dead. Everybody did that, and everybody knew it was only words. And yet, for a few seconds, it had almost looked like Ryan really *was* going to drop dead.

But they were only words, and they weren't even his words. They'd just sort of tumbled out of his mouth, almost as if someone else had spoken them.

But there was no one else. . . .

Janet emerged from Dr. Potter's small consultation room into the parlor that served as reception area during the day and Potter's living room at night. Amos Hall rose from his position on the Victorian sofa that stood in the bay window, but Anna remained still in her chair, her hands folded in her lap, her posture expressing a calmness that her anxious eyes belied. "Well?" she asked.

Janet's mouth curved into an uncertain smile. Now or never. She had to tell them, and through a sleepless night she had decided that the examination would provide the perfect moment. "Well, I'm pregnant," she said.

A sigh emerged from the older woman, and she slumped in her chair. "So," she said at last, her eyes shifting away from Janet to glance warily at her husband. "I suppose that's some kind of blessing, isn't it?" she said.

"I don't know," Janet replied, too involved in her own emotions to notice her mother-in-law's reaction to the news. "I'm afraid I'm going to have to do some thinking about it."

"Thinking?" Amos Hall strode across the room and took Janet's coat from a hook, holding it for her as she slid her arms into its sleeves. "What's there to think about?"

Janet swallowed, wondering if she should tell them that her first thought on having the pregnancy confirmed was that she should have an abortion as soon as possible. She had known she was pregnant for several weeks and had kept her suspicions to herself, hesitating even to tell Mark. There had been no real notion in her mind then that she would not have the baby—she loved Mark too much to deny him a second child, despite the upheavals it might cause in their lives. After all, Michael was already nearly twelve—almost a teenager—and their small family was settled, comfortable. But now Mark was dead. Everything had changed.

"I'm not at all sure I should have it," she said in a carefully neutral voice. "I'm not as young as I could be—"

"Not have it?" Anna cried. "Not have Mark's baby? Oh, Janet, you can't be serious. Why, that would be—well, to start with, it would be murder!"

"Now, Mama, don't get yourself worked up," Amos Hall cautioned his wife, though his eyes never left Janet. "Things have changed. Not everyone thinks the way you and I do anymore."

"If the baby's healthy, it has a right to live," Anna declared, her eyes flashing with anger. Then, softening a little, she turned to Janet. "I'm not an old-fashioned woman, dear, whatever Amos says. I can certainly see that there might be circumstances where it could be better for a baby not to be born." She eyed Janet's midsection critically, its slight swelling apparent to her now. "Besides, it's too late, isn't it?"

"Almost," Janet conceded. "But what about my feelings? Don't my feelings count?" she added, then wished she hadn't.

"Your feelings?" Anna asked. "What do you mean? Do you mean you don't *want* the baby?"

Janet shook her head. "That's not it at all, Anna. It just seems like—" She stopped short, suddenly realizing she didn't have the slightest idea of how she felt about anything. All she felt was confused. If only she could talk to Mark. . . . But she couldn't, not ever again. And, she remembered with a shudder, the Mark she had thought she'd known was a different man from the one she was discovering since she'd arrived in Prairie Bend. She appealed to Amos. "Would you mind if I walked home?" she asked. "I really think I need to walk a bit. I need to get used to things. There's so much to sort out."

Amos frowned. "Are you sure? I'm not sure how much exercise—"

Janet put up a protesting hand, and made herself smile with a confidence she wasn't feeling. "Times have changed, Amos. And I really do need to be by myself, just for a little while." Without waiting for a response, she opened the door and stepped out of Dr. Potter's office into the bright noontime sun. She glanced around, orienting herself, and then set out for the center of the village.

Prairie Bend, she realized, was truly no more than a village, and it seemed, as she walked the single block from Potter's house to the main street, oddly familiar. It wasn't until she'd walked a bit further, though, that she realized just what it was about the town that she recognized. It was like the country village of her dreams, the picturesque town she'd imagined whenever she'd envisioned the peaceful little farm that would someday be hers.

Prairie Bend was more than a century old, but it appeared that it had reached its full size shortly after it had been founded.

It had been carefully planned in the shape of a half wheel, with four spokelike streets radiating out from the square at the hub, and three more streets, each of them paralleling the curve of the river, sweeping around those spokes. The lots had been carefully laid out, with obvious foresight, but then, apparently, the planned-for population had never materialized, for most of the lots were still empty, though none of them was uncared for, and the wide green lawns, bordered by trees and occasional gardens, created a parklike, spacious feeling.

Nowhere was there a building that looked new, yet nowhere was there a building that was in disrepair. The village was small: a general store, the post office, a drugstore which did double duty as the only café in town, two gas stations—one of which had a garage—a tiny school, and the church. All of it neatly arranged around the little square, all of it shaded by immense old trees, and all of it cradled in the bend of the river.

Janet paused in the square and tried to reconcile what she was seeing with what Mark had told her about Prairie Bend. But slowly, she began to realize that he had never said much about it at all—only that he hoped never to see it again.

But why?

There was nothing threatening about it, nothing out of the ordinary, really, except for its loveliness.

Then what was it that Mark had hated so much?

And why had Prairie Bend never grown?

Why had a place so lovely stayed so small?

She didn't know, and she probably never would know.

Unless she stayed.

It was the first time she'd let herself fully face the idea that had been niggling at her mind all morning, but now, in the quiet and peace of the spring noontime, she began examining the idea, making a mental ledger of its advantages and disadvantages.

She had family, albeit in-laws, in Prairie Bend; none in New York.

She had little money in either place, and nothing much in the way of professional skills.

She would be able to keep her apartment in New York for the moment, but only for the moment. Eventually, she would have to find a cheaper place to live.

In Prairie Bend, she owned a farm.

Mark had hated Prairie Bend, but had never told her why. Perhaps there had been no reason, or at least no good reason.

She thought about her in-laws. Good people, kind people, who wanted to take care of her. But why? Who was she but the widow of the son who had rejected them? Why should they care about her?

Yet, even as she asked herself the question, she was sure she knew the answer. They cared about her because they were warm and loving people who didn't hold their son's actions against her or her child. No—they wanted her, and they wanted Michael. And for a while, at least, she wanted to rest in the refuge of Prairie Bend and the love of Mark's parents.

As she left the square and passed through the rest of the village, then started out toward the Halls', she knew her mind was made up.

Forty minutes later she walked into Anna Hall's kitchen and sat down at the table. Her mother-in-law glanced disapprovingly up from the cake batter she was stirring, then away.

"Did you get your thinking done?" she asked in a voice that implied a sure knowledge of the outcome of that thinking.

"Yes, I did," Janet said quietly. "I'm going to keep my baby, and I'm going to keep my farm. Michael and I are going to live here."

Anna Hall put down the spoon, then held her arms out to Janet, who slipped willingly into her embrace.

"If that's what you want," Anna whispered. "If you're sure that's what you want, then you're welcome here. More than welcome. But I warn you," she suddenly added. "Once you become a part of Prairie Bend, you'll never be able to leave."

A shiver passed through Janet, but a moment later she had forgotten it.

CHAPTER 4

We're not going home at all?" Michael's voice clearly reflected his bewilderment. "But why?"

He was sitting with his mother in Anna Hall's rarely used living room, and while Janet perched nervously on the edge of a sofa, Michael himself rocked furiously on a bentwood chair.

"Lots of reasons, darling," Janet replied, forcing herself to meet Michael's angry eyes. "For one thing, we have a home here—a place to live that's all our own. Wouldn't you rather live in a house than an apartment?"

"I don't know," Michael answered, too promptly. "Dad never wanted to live on a farm. I bet if Dad were here, we'd be back home."

"I know," Janet sighed. "If your father were here, everything would be the way it always was, but he isn't here, and everything has changed. I know it's hard, and it's going to get harder, honey. Now it's up to me to figure out what's best for us, and I think it's best that we stay here."

"But *why?*"

"For one thing, we don't have much money, and living in New York is very expensive."

"Why don't you get a job?" Michael asked with the serene innocence of his years.

"I might be able to," Janet agreed. "But it wouldn't be much of a job. And what would you do? I can't leave you by yourself every day, and we'd never be able to afford someone to come in."

"I can take care of myself," Michael replied. "I'm not a baby anymore."

Janet smiled at her son. "Of course you aren't. And if we weren't living in New York, I wouldn't worry at all. But in the city I'd worry about you all day, every day. Besides, right now, I don't think I could get any kind of a job at all."

Michael stared at her, and suddenly stopped rocking. "Why not?" he asked, the sullenness in his eyes fading slightly.

"Well," Janet said, "it seems our family is going to get a little larger."

There was a silence, and then Michael realized what she was saying. "You mean you're going to have a baby?"

Janet nodded. "So you see, I'd have to leave whatever job I got in a few months. And most people wouldn't hire me to begin with, right now."

"Why tell them?" Michael asked. "You don't look pregnant."

"I don't lie," Janet spoke quietly. "And I don't ever again want to hear you suggest such a thing. Is that clear?"

Michael squirmed and his eyes shifted away from hers. "I didn't mean you should lie . . ." he began, but Janet didn't let him finish.

"Not telling the truth is lying, Michael. It doesn't matter if someone doesn't ask you a question. If you know something that's important to a situation and don't say anything about it, that's lying. And you know it, so let's end it right there." She paused for a moment, and settled herself back into the sofa. "The point of all this is that I can't get anything more than temporary work right now, and won't be able to for at least a year, maybe more. And we can't live in New York without me working. Can you understand that?"

There was a long silence, and then Michael nodded. "I guess so." Then, a moment later: "But what about all my friends?"

"You'll make friends here," Janet assured him.

Michael left the rocking chair, and went to gaze out the window. "What if I don't?" he asked, and in his voice Janet heard all the doubts that she herself had not yet been able to put aside.

"But you *will*," she insisted, and immediately wondered if her reassuring words were for her son or for herself.

For a long time, Michael stared silently out the window, and then abruptly turned to face her with the question she had least expected. "Why didn't Daddy ever tell us we had a farm?"

Janet searched for an answer, but found none. None, at any rate, that wouldn't tarnish Michael's memory of his father, and she wasn't willing to do that. "There was no reason to, really," she said at last. "Daddy wasn't a farmer, and never wanted to be. And there aren't any universities around here where he could have taught." She brightened, as an idea came to her. "Perhaps it was his idea of insurance, in case anything ever happened to him. Something to leave us. Not only a home, but a family, too. What if he'd told me?" she improvised. "I'd have talked him into selling it, and buying something closer to New York, and now, instead of having something we own, we'd have a mortgage to pay, and no family around to help us. Maybe Daddy was smart never to tell us about the farm."

If only, she thought to herself, I could believe that. But I don't. Not a word of it.

Michael, however, seemed to accept her words at face value. "Where is it?" he asked.

Janet stared at her son, then burst into laughter for the first time since Mark had died. Michael looked at her oddly, then glanced uneasily away. "What's so funny?"

"You know what?" Janet gasped. "I don't even *know* where it is! Here I've made up my mind to move us onto a farm, and I never even asked where it was, let alone what it looked like. Let's get your grandparents and go see it."

But the Halls refused to take them.

"Tomorrow," Anna insisted. "We'll show it to you tomorrow."

"But why not today?" Janet asked.

Amos grinned at her. "If you saw it today, you'd never move in. By tomorrow, it'll be cleaned up and at least habitable."

"But I don't care if it's a mess," Janet protested. "You don't have to hire someone to clean it up. Michael and I can do that."

"Hire someone?" Anna asked. "Why would we do that?" Then suddenly she understood what Janet meant. "This isn't like New York," she said. "Out here, everybody knows everybody else and helps them out. It's just like having one huge family. We'll take care of you. That's what we're for."

Janet's eyes flooded with tears, and she leaned down to hug the elderly woman. "Thank you," she whispered. "You've no idea what all this means to me. Ever since Mark died, I've been so . . . so frightened."

Anna gently patted her back. "I know, dear. I know just how you feel. But everything's going to be fine. Just fine," she said, as her eyes met Amos's beyond Janet's shoulder.

"Do you know Mr. Findley?"

The sun was high, and Michael and Ryan, yesterday's fight forgotten, had taken shelter from the heat under the enormous cottonwood in the Shieldses' front yard. Ryan, to Michael's disappointment, hadn't been at all surprised by

Michael's news. In fact, when he'd told his cousin that he and his mother had decided to stay in Prairie Bend, Ryan had only grinned and said that if he thought that was news, he was wrong—there probably wasn't anyone in Prairie Bend who *didn't* know they were staying. Now, however, he looked at Michael curiously.

"He's crazy," he said at last. "How'd you hear about him?"

Michael ignored the question. "Who is he?"

"He's an old guy who lives all by himself. Everybody says he's crazy and ought to be locked up, but nobody ever does anything about it."

"Crazy how?"

"Just crazy. You know. He talks to himself all the time, and never lets anybody near the place, except Dr. Potter. I heard the only reason Dr. Potter ever goes out there is to see if old man Findley's still alive or not."

"Do the kids ever go out there?"

"What for?"

"Just to see what's going on."

Ryan glanced at his cousin with suspicion. "Nothin's going on. And if you go out there, he shoots at you."

"Bullshit," Michael challenged.

"Bullshit, nothin'. Eric Simpson lives out that way, and he *saw* old man Findley shoot at someone."

"Then how come they didn't arrest him?" Michael demanded.

Ryan frowned. "I don't know," he reluctantly admitted.

" 'Cause he didn't do anything, that's why," Michael told him with a certainty he didn't really feel. "I bet he was just shooting at an animal or something. If he'd done anything, they would have arrested him."

"That's not what Eric says, and he saw it."

"What did he see?"

"Why don't you ask him?"

"I don't know him."

"Well, let's go out there," Ryan suggested. "Then you'll know him."

Ten minutes later they were riding out of Prairie Bend and east along the river road, Michael on an old Schwinn that Ryan had dragged up from the Shieldses' basement. He was straining to match his cousin's ease with the machine, but it wasn't easy. Unlike Ryan, Michael had not grown up on a bike, and the one time he had risked Ryan's no-hands technique, he had nearly lost control.

"Whatcha going to do about school?" Ryan suddenly asked, braking his bike so he fell back alongside Michael.

"What do you mean?"

"Aren't you going back?"

Michael shrugged. "I guess not."

"Then what grade will you be in next year? Will they pass you?"

"Why wouldn't they?"

"Don't you have to take tests?"

"Our school doesn't have tests," Michael replied. "It's an experimental school."

Ryan's look was one of disbelief. "No tests? How do they know who to pass?"

"Everybody passes." Suddenly, Michael slowed the bike and called out to Ryan, "Is that Findley's place?" He pointed off to the right, where an old farmhouse, its paint peeling and its porch sagging slightly, huddled in a grove of scraggly elms at the end of a rutted driveway. A barn loomed twenty yards from the house, and between the two buildings some chickens scratched at the dusty surface of the unkempt and unfenced yard. As he looked at the place, a man appeared on the front porch, dressed in overalls, cradling a shotgun in his arms.

"Let's get out of here," Ryan said. Without waiting for a reply, he pumped hard on his bike, spewing a cloud of dust into Michael's face. Michael paused a moment longer, his eyes leaving the figure on the porch and concentrating on the barn. For a second, he thought he'd seen something—something he couldn't really identify—but as he studied the barn there was nothing. And yet, even as he rode after Ryan, something tugged at him, an ill-formed thought—a feeling, really—that made him look back once more. The man on the porch was gone, and the barn looked exactly as it had before.

He pedaled harder, catching up with Ryan, but it wasn't until they'd passed over a slight rise that Michael's uneasy feeling—that feeling of something pulling at him—passed.

A little further on, they came to another drive, overgrown with weeds. A mailbox dangled from a post by a rusted nail—the only sign that anyone had ever lived there. Ryan pulled his bike off the road. Michael had to slam on his brakes to keep from running into him. He finally spotted the house, nearly invisible in the tangle of weeds that surrounded it.

"Is this where Eric lives?" he asked, his voice reflecting his incredulity at the idea that anyone could inhabit such an abandoned-looking place.

Ryan shook his head, grinning. "This is where you live."

Michael's mouth dropped open, and he stared at the house for a long time. "Mom's gonna croak," he said at last.

Ryan nodded. "I wasn't supposed to tell you, but I couldn't resist. Isn't it something?"

"It doesn't look like anybody's ever lived there."

"Who'd want to?"

"Let's go look at it."

Michael started maneuvering his bicycle up the drive, but Ryan stopped him. "I wasn't even supposed to tell you about it, and if we go look, Mom might see us. She's helping clean it up."

"Why don't they just burn it down?"

"Search me." He paused, then: "You won't tell anyone I showed you where it was, will you?"

"Hell, no." Suddenly Michael grinned. "But I can hardly wait to see the look on Mom's face when she sees it." Then, as he gazed at the old house, his voice dropped to a whisper. "No wonder Dad never said anything about it."

"Hunh?"

"My dad never told us about this place. Mom just found out about it the other night, when Grandpa told her." He was silent for a little while, then turned to his cousin. "Ryan?"

"Yeah?"

"How come my dad didn't like it here?"

Ryan glanced impatiently at Michael. "I already told you I don't know."

"Well—didn't anyone ever talk about him?"

"What do you mean by talk?"

"You know—the way people talk about people."

Ryan thought about it for a little while. "My mom talks about him sometimes. Mom always says he was smart to get out of here, and she wishes she'd had a chance to do it, too."

"How come?"

"I don't know. I guess 'cause it's so small." He gave his bike a push. "Come on, let's get over to Eric's. It's the next place."

The Simpsons' farm, in contrast to the place Michael was going to be living, was well tended, its buildings sitting squarely on their foundations, everything except the house painted the traditional barn red. The house itself, green with white trim, was surrounded by a grove of cottonwoods dotting a neatly trimmed lawn. As they pulled their bikes to a stop near the back door of the house, Eric Simpson, a curly-haired, freckle-faced boy of about Ryan's age, spun the small tractor-mower he was riding around to face them, grinned, and gunned the engine. He expertly cut the throttle and applied the brakes just before the machine crushed Michael's bike.

"Hi."

"Hi," Michael replied. "I'm Michael Hall."

"I know," Eric said as he jumped off the little tractor. "You're gonna live next door." Then, remembering what his mother had told him to say, he scuffed self-consciously at the ground. "Sorry about what happened to your dad," he mumbled.

Michael, still not used to the reality of his father's death, searched for a reply, and found none. An awkward silence fell over them.

"He's not supposed to know about the house," Ryan finally said. "But I knew you'd never be able to keep your big mouth shut, so I already told him."

Relieved, Eric grabbed at the topic. "Did you go inside?"

Ryan shook his head.

"Good thing," Eric said, barely suppressing a grin. "Mom said it looked like some raccoons were living there all winter. There's shit all over the place."

Michael swallowed.

Noting the reaction, Eric pushed on. "And rats, too. Big ones. And then, up in the attic, there's the bats, but at least they don't bite. Much."

Michael caught on. "That's okay. I'm gonna live in the attic, and I had pet rats at home. And I bet there aren't any alligators in the sewers here. You know what it's like to have to beat an alligator over the head before you take a crap?"

Eric grinned slyly at Ryan. "Has he been snipe hunting yet?" he asked. Ryan shrugged, but Michael nodded.

"They tried that at camp last summer, but I already knew about it."

"Michael wants to know about old man Findley," Ryan said. "I told him you saw him shoot at someone, but he didn't believe me. Then just now, he came out on his porch, and he had his shotgun."

"But he didn't shoot at us," Michael argued. "He didn't even point it at us."

"Did you go onto his property?"

"No."

"Well, try it sometime. Me and another guy were messing around there last summer, and we were going to sneak into Potter's Field. So just when I was gonna sneak under the fence, old man Findley came out. He didn't even yell at us. Just blasted at us with his shotgun."

"I bet he was shooting up in the air," Michael suggested. "Just tryin' to scare you. What's Potter's Field?"

"It's down near the river, sort of between your place and old man Findley's, except that he owns it—old man Findley, that is. Hey, you guys want to see my mare? She's gonna foal any day now."

Michael and Ryan followed Eric around to the barn, and a moment later the subject of old man Findley was forgotten. The mare, a large bay, stood in her stall, liquid brown eyes regarding the three boys with benign curiosity. Even Michael could see the swelling of her pregnancy. "Wow," he breathed. "She's really big, isn't she?"

"She was even bigger last time." Eric's voice reflected his pride in the animal, and he pointed to a sleek young horse in the next stall. "That's Blackjack. He was foaled two years ago." Eric's face broke into a grin as he remembered. "That was really something. The same night Magic was dropping him, Ma was having my baby sister, and Doc Potter and the vet were both here. Pa kept running back and forth, so I got to help with the foaling."

Magic, nervously eyeing the three boys, suddenly snorted and reared in her stall. Eric moved forward as the other two boys backed away.

"Easy, girl, easy," Eric soothed her. He continued talking to the nervous mare, and waved Michael and Ryan out of the barn. A moment later the horse calmed, and he joined them. "You guys want to come out when she foals? I'm gonna help the vet, but you could watch."

Ryan shrugged, pretending lack of interest. "I've seen lots of colts being foaled."

But Michael was intrigued. "When's it gonna happen?" he asked.

"Maybe over the weekend, or next week. You want me to call you?"

"Sure. But what if I don't get here in time?"

Eric grinned. "You will. Sometimes it takes all night, but it's always at least a couple of hours." He looked at his watch. "Hey, it's almost three, and I gotta clean up the yard before Ma gets home. You guys wanna help?"

"I can't," Ryan replied. "I gotta be back home by three-thirty."

Eric's eyes shifted over to Michael, but Michael, too, shook his head. "I better not. I have to take the bike back to Ryan's, then walk home."

"Keep the bike," Ryan offered. "You can give it back when you get one of your own."

"Won't Aunt Laura be mad?"

"Nah."

"You care if I stay?"

Ryan shrugged. "All I'm gonna do is go down to the store and help my dad."

Michael made up his mind, and a few minutes later, after Ryan had left, he sat happily on the seat of the tractor-mower while Eric showed him how to work the controls. As he put the tractor in gear and began moving across the lawn, he decided that Prairie Bend wasn't going to be so bad after all. Except that the only reason he was here was that his father had died. His good mood suddenly evaporated, and a stab of pain shot through his temples.

As he rode home through the soft lazy light of the spring afternoon, Michael was unaware of the eyes that followed him. First there were the eyes of Laura Shields and Ione Simpson, looking up from the final stages of their cleaning of Janet Hall's old farmhouse, watching as Michael rode by. Then, a little further on, there was Ben Findley, peering out from behind the heavy curtains that kept his rundown house in constant gloom. As Michael slowed and peered at the Findley place through the darkening day, the old man's hand automatically reached out and clutched the shotgun that stood on its butt next to the front door. But Michael passed on, and Ben Findley relaxed.

CHAPTER 5

The first word that came into Janet's mind was "firetrap," but she made herself deny it, even though she knew it accurately described what she was seeing as the Shieldses' Chevy slewed over the bumpy dirt driveway and the house came into view. Then she got a grip on her emotions and reminded herself that any wooden structure can burn, that this house was no different from any other house. What had happened to the house she grew up in would not happen to this house. She would not let it happen.

Her sudden panic checked, she made herself look at the house objectively.

Objectively, she didn't know whether to laugh or cry.

From what she could see, the building had no discernible color whatsoever. The prairie weather had long ago stripped it of its paint, and its siding was a streaked and dirty gray, far from the silvery color of the salt-weathered cedar cottages of the eastern seaboard.

She'd wanted a red barn.

This barn, crouched almost defensively behind the house, bore the same drab color as the house, but was in an even worse state of disrepair. Its shingles were half gone, and the loft door, visible beyond one of the dormers of the house, seemed to be hanging from only one hinge.

"This place," she declared at last, "lends new meaning to the word 'awful.' "

"Are we really going to live here, Mom?" Michael asked, voicing Janet's own thought. He had been tempted to giggle as he watched his mother's reaction until he realized the terrible truth: this . . . *place* was his new home.

"Maybe it's not so bad, once you get inside," she replied doubtfully.

"Actually, it's worse," Laura told her.

Janet turned to gaze at her sister-in-law. "Worse? What could be worse? It doesn't have dirt floors, does it?"

Laura carefully brought the car to a stop in the weed-choked front yard, and Janet fell silent, studying the house once more. There was something about it that didn't fit. And then she realized what it was.

"My God," she breathed. "All the windows are whole."

Laura gave her a puzzled look. "Why wouldn't they be?"

"But the place is abandoned. What about—well, don't kids like to throw rocks anymore?"

Suddenly understanding, Laura laughed. "Amos fixes them when they do get broken. I'm not going to pretend everybody's perfect around here." She opened the car door and eased her bulk out, smiling wryly at Janet. "I hope you carry your babies more gracefully than I carry mine," she said, then turned her attention to the house. "Actually, it isn't nearly as bad as it looks. It's weathered, and it needs a lot of work, but basically, it's sound. And the floors, believe it or not, are hardwood."

Slowly, the three of them went through the house, and to her own amazement Janet discovered that Laura was right. Though the paint and wallpaper were peeling and the floors needed refinishing, the house did seem to be solid. The floors were level, and the doors square. The plaster had no holes in it, and the plumbing worked.

There were four rooms downstairs—a living room, a dining room, a kitchen, and a pantry; four more upstairs—three bedrooms and a bathroom, with an attic tucked under the steeply sloping roof. Each of the upstairs rooms had a dormered window, including the bathroom. A narrow staircase through the center of the house connected the two floors, with a spring-loaded pull-down ladder providing access to the attic.

There was no furniture.

Ten minutes later, Janet and Laura were back in the living room.

"I know it isn't much," Laura sighed, moving out onto the front porch and lowering herself awkwardly onto the top step.

"No, Laura," Janet protested. "You were right. It's much better than it looks from the outside."

"And it's a lot better than it looked yesterday," Laura pointed out, brightening a little. "Ione Simpson and I worked like dogs cleaning out the grime."

"I wish you hadn't," Janet began. "The kids and I could have done it. And in your condition—"

Laura brushed her objections aside. "You'd have taken one look and fled. Ione and I almost gave it up ourselves. But by next week or the week after, you won't know the place. We'll have all the weeds cleaned out, the buildings painted, and the fields plowed."

"But I can't afford—"

"Janet," Laura said quietly, "this was Mark's home. Now it's going to be yours, and we're your family. Let us do for you what we'd do for each other." When Janet still hesitated, she added, "Please?"

"But there's so much that needs to be done—"

"And the whole town can do it," Laura stated. "We'll make a party of it, just like an old-fashioned roof-raising. Except, thank God, the roof's in good shape."

The two women fell silent, gazing out into the prairie. It was a comfortable silence, and Janet could feel the quiet of the plains seeping into her, easing the tension that had been her constant companion over the last several days. "I think I'm going to like it here," she said at last. Next to her, she felt Laura shift her position slightly.

"Really?" the other woman asked. Then she laughed, a brittle laugh that made Janet turn to face her.

"It's so quiet. So different from New York. There's a sense of calm here that I haven't felt since I was a little girl. I'd almost forgotten it."

"That's boredom you're feeling," Laura remarked, her voice tinged with uncharacteristic sarcasm. "Right now it seems like peace, but just wait a year or so."

"Oh, come on," Janet cajoled. "If it's that bad, why do you stay?"

Now Laura turned to face her, her large eyes serious. "You think it's that easy?" she asked. "How do you leave a place like this? When you've grown up here, and your husband's grown up here, and you've never been anywhere else, how do you leave? They don't let you, you know."

"But Mark—"

"Mark ran away," Laura said, her voice suddenly bitter. "Mark fled, and I should have too. Except that when he got out, I was too young to go with him. And by the time I was old enough, it was too late. I was already trapped."

"Trapped? What do you mean, trapped?"

"Just that," Laura told her. "That's what a small town is, you know. A trap. At least that's what Prairie Bend is. I used to dream about getting out. I used to think I'd take Ryan and just run away. But of course, I never did." Suddenly her eyes met Janet's. "You won't either, if you stay. They'll get to you, just like they get to everyone."

"Who? Laura, what are you talking about?"

"Father—all of them."

"Laura—"

But Laura pressed on, her words building into a torrent. "I can't get out, Janet. I'm stuck here, trapped by this whole place. I tried to leave once. I really tried. Do you know what happened? Mother just looked at me. That's all she had to do. Just look at me, with those sad, empty eyes. She didn't have to say a word. Didn't have to tell me that I was all she had left, that Mark was gone, and the baby was dead, and there was no one left but me. It was all right there in her eyes. Ever since that night . . ." Her voice trailed off, and her eyes wandered away from Janet, across the yard, fixing finally on a pair of doors that lay low to the ground, covering what Janet assumed was a root cellar.

"What night?" Janet asked at last. "What are you talking about?"

Laura turned back to her, and when she spoke, her voice was unsteady. "Didn't Mark ever tell you about it?" Then, without waiting for Janet to reply, she sighed heavily. "No, I suppose he didn't. No one ever talks about that night. Not mother or father, not even me. So why would Mark?"

"Do you want to talk about it?" Janet asked, her voice gentle, sure that whatever had happened that night must account for the odd haunted look she had seen in Laura's eyes.

There was a long silence, and then, finally, Laura shook her head. When she spoke, it was in a whisper. "I'm not even sure I know what happened, really. Isn't that strange? I think it was the most important night of my life, and I'm not even sure what happened." Again she fell silent, then finally nodded toward the twin doors she had been staring at a few moments before. "I was in there. Right in there, in the cyclone cellar."

"Here?" Janet asked, her voice reflecting her puzzlement.

Laura's eyes came back to Janet. And then she suddenly understood, and a harsh laugh emerged from her throat. "My God, they didn't even tell you *that*, did they? This was *our* house. This is the house Mark and I were born in."

"But I thought—their farm—"

"*This* was our farm until that night. It was in the summer. I was nine, and Mark must have been sixteen. And mother was pregnant."

"Pregnant?" Janet repeated. "I thought there were only the two of you."

"There were," Laura replied, her voice dropping to a whisper. "The baby —well, mother lost it. At least, that's what they always said." Her eyes clouded for a moment, and she seemed almost to disappear somewhere inside herself, into some dark corner Janet knew she couldn't penetrate. And then Laura's expression cleared again, and she began speaking once more. Something in her voice had changed, though. It was almost as if she was repeating a memorized story, reciting carefully rehearsed words.

"It was hot that day," she said, "and Mother had been trying to do too much, and her labor came on early. Father was furious at her. It was almost as if he blamed her for the early labor. And then a storm came up, and they sent me to the cyclone cellar. And I stayed there. All afternoon, and all night. I stayed there," she repeated. And then, once more, "I stayed there."

Janet wondered what to say. There was more to the story, she was sure. But she was also sure that Laura didn't want to talk about it. Still, she had a certain feeling that she needed to know the whole story of that night, needed to know not only what had happened to Laura, but what had happened to Mark, as well. "And that was the night Mark left home?" she asked.

Laura nodded. "The next morning, Father came for me. He told me the baby had been born dead. I didn't believe him. There was something inside me that didn't believe him, but I don't know what it was." She smiled weakly at Janet. "It's still there," she said. "Even after all these years, I don't believe that baby was born dead, but I don't know why I don't believe it. It's as if there's something in my mind, something I know, but can't remember." She sighed. "Anyway, after that night, Mother was crippled, and Mark was gone."

Janet stared at her, speechless.

"You're still wondering what happened, aren't you?" Laura asked at last. "Well, I can't tell you. I've always wondered, but Mother never spoke about it, and neither did Father. It almost seems as though Mark must have done something, but I know he didn't." Her voice changed, became almost pleading. "I *know* he didn't, Janet. Mark was a wonderful brother, but then, after that night, he was gone." She reached out and took Janet's hand, her eyes taking on the look of a hunted animal. "For a while, I didn't hear from him. Then he wrote to me—he was in college. Just one letter, and then, later, another one, from New York. I wrote back. Oh, I wrote so many letters! No one knew, not even Buck. But he never answered my letters. Maybe he never even got them."

Janet slipped an arm around the distraught woman, cradling Laura's head against her shoulder. "How awful," she whispered. "How horrible for all of you."

Laura nodded. "It was as if our whole family came to an end that night. And I can't remember why. A little while after that, we moved to the other farm, where Mother and Father still live, but it never really made any difference—ever since that night, I've been so terrified. When Ryan was born, I was sure it was all going to happen over again. And now—" Unconsciously, Laura touched her swollen torso.

"It'll be all right," Janet said.

Laura's eyes met Janet's. "If I could only remember what happened that night, what happened to Mother. I—I'm always so scared now, Janet. Every time Buck wants to make love, I'm afraid of getting pregnant. And then, when I do, all I can think of is that horrible night." Suddenly her eyes narrowed. "Did—did Mark ever talk about it?"

Janet shook her head. "Never. Never so much as a word. And you mustn't worry about it, Laura. There's no reason why what happened to Anna should happen to you."

"Isn't there?" Laura whispered. She swallowed once, then spoke again. "Oh, Janet, I wish I could believe that. But I can't. . . . I just can't."

Wordlessly, Janet took her sister-in-law's hand in her own, and for a long moment the two young women sat silently, staring at the innocent-looking doors to the storm cellar, each of them wondering just what of Laura's past had been hidden away in that dark room beneath the earth so many years ago.

Michael stood at the window of the smallest bedroom, his eyes fixed on Ben Findley's barn. If he'd been asked to describe what was happening to him, he wouldn't have been able to. But one thing he knew: he was home.

This house, this room, this view of the limitless prairie from the small dormer window, all of it felt familiar, all of it right. His father was here; he could almost feel his presence in the empty room.

And the barn. Old man Findley's barn, clearly visible from this window. It was almost as if he could see into it, and yet he couldn't, not really. Still, if he'd been asked what was inside that barn, he'd have been able to sketch it out: ten stalls, five on each side, facing each other, none of them occupied. Two of them, though, seemed to have been put together into some kind of workshop. Above the stalls, a hayloft, with a broken ladder its only means of access. At the back, a tack room, still filled with rotting leather, bridles and harnesses long ago stiffened and dried from lack of use and attention. And below the tack room, something else, something Michael could feel as he could feel the rest of the barn.

It was as if there were a presence there, calling out to him, whispering to him in a voice he could feel, but couldn't quite hear. . . .

"Michael? Michael, are you all right?"

Startled, Michael turned. Standing in the doorway, looking at him oddly, were his mother and aunt.

"Didn't you hear me?" he heard his mother say. He frowned.

"Hear what?"

"Hear me calling you. We're ready to go."

"But we just got here." He saw his mother and aunt glance at each other.

"We've been here for an hour and a half," his mother told him. "We called you, and when you didn't answer, we thought you must have gone outside. I looked in the barn, the loft, even the tool shed."

"Why?" Michael asked. His eyes drifted back toward the window, and Findley's barn, but though he could still see it, he could no longer *feel* it. Then, as he heard his mother's voice, tinged with anger now, he forced his attention back into the room where they stood.

"Because we couldn't *find* you," his mother was saying.

"I was right here," Michael explained. Why was she mad at him? He hadn't done anything. "I've been right here all the time." And yet, even as he spoke the words, he wondered. *Had* he been there, or had he gone out, gone over to Mr. Findley's barn? Suddenly he was no longer sure.

"Then why didn't you answer me when I called you?"

"I—I didn't hear you." He felt a throbbing in his left temple. "I must have been daydreaming."

"For an hour?" his mother asked.

"It hasn't been that long—"

"It *has,*" Janet replied. She saw a flicker of what looked like fear in Michael's eyes, and turned to Laura. "Why don't you wait for us in the car? We'll be right out."

Nodding her understanding, Laura smiled encouragingly at Michael, then disappeared down the stairs.

"Are you mad at me?" Michael asked when he and his mother were alone.

"Well, it seems to me—" She stopped, her eyes narrowing slightly as she looked at him. "Michael," she said, her voice gentle now. "Are you all right?"

The throbbing in his head faded away, and Michael nodded. "I'm sorry," he said softly. "I was just daydreaming, I guess." His eyes roamed over the room, and he smiled. "Can this be my room?" he asked.

"This room?" Janet asked. She looked around the tiny room, wondering why Michael would ask for it. Of the three bedrooms, it was the smallest. "I suppose so, if you want it."

"I do," Michael told her.

From his tone, Janet was sure that something had happened in that room, that it had affected Michael in some way. "But why?" she asked.

Because Daddy's here, Michael thought. He opened his mouth to voice the thought, but then changed his mind. Instead, he glanced around the room, and then, as before, his eyes were drawn to the window. "I like the view," he said. Janet crossed the little room in four easy steps and stood in the dormer, her hands resting on Michael's shoulders as she looked past him out over the prairie vista.

"It isn't much different from the view from the other windows, is it?" she asked.

"It's the barn," Michael said quietly. "I like being able to look at the barn."

"But you can't even see the barn from here—" Janet began, and then stopped as she realized he wasn't talking about their barn, but another barn, one she could see in the near distance. There was nothing special about the structure; indeed, if anything, it was remarkable only for its shabbiness.

"It looks like it's going to fall down," she commented.

Michael said nothing.

"Am I missing something?" Janet asked. "Do you see something about it that I don't?"

Michael hesitated, then she felt him shrug under the touch of her hands. "I just like it," he said at last.

"Well, then, I guess that's that."

Michael turned and faced her. "Then I can have it? This room?"

Janet nodded, the odd tension she had been feeling in the room, and in herself and Michael, suddenly evaporating. She smiled. "And it's a good thing you wanted it. I was afraid I was going to have to fight you for the other big one."

"I'd have lost," Michael replied.

"But you'd have argued," Janet observed.

Michael was silent for a few seconds, apparently thinking about it. Finally, he shook his head. "Maybe last week." His voice was quiet, and Janet tensed, certain that he was about to say something she didn't want to hear. "Last week, you'd have had Dad on your side, but now you don't." His dark blue eyes—Mark's eyes—held her own. "I'll try not to fight with you anymore, Mom."

"Fight?" Janet asked, feeling tears form in spite of herself. "We've never fought."

Michael shifted uncomfortably, and his gaze broke away from hers. "You know what I mean. Arguing, trying to get around you. I—well, I'm not gonna do that anymore."

Janet reached out to her son and took him in her arms, holding him tight.

"Thank you, Michael," she whispered. "We're going to be all right here, you and I. I know it. I can just feel it."

Then, as she felt Michael's arms tighten around her, she glanced once more out the window toward the barn that had so captured her son's attention.

There was a bleakness to it, deprivation and neglect that doused the spark of optimism she had just felt.

CHAPTER 6

Janet hung up the phone, then moved pensively into the kitchen, where Anna, expertly maneuvering her chair with one hand, was sweeping the floor with the other. As Janet watched, Anna moved the pile of dust toward the open back door, then gave the chair a quick spin, catching the screen door with one of its handles and knocking it open. At the same time, a last whisk of the broom sent the accumulated dirt flying into the backyard. As the screen door slammed shut, she turned the chair back to face Janet. "It took me two months to learn how to do that," she said in a voice that carried with it no emotion whatsoever.

Janet shook her head. "I wish you'd let me help—"

But Anna had already rolled across the kitchen to put the broom away. "I've been doing it for years." She wheeled herself over to the table, and gestured for Janet to join her. "Well, is it all taken care of?"

Janet nodded. "I guess so, but I'm still not certain I'm doing the right thing."

Anna shrugged. "It's done, anyway, and believe me, it's a lot easier to go along with Amos than to try to do it your way. Besides, I'm afraid he's right—it doesn't make any sense for you to go back to New York just to pack up. All you'd do is wear yourself out, and we don't want you to do that, do we? Carrying a baby always has its risks, you know."

Though there was nothing in Anna's voice to indicate that she was thinking of her own last pregnancy, Janet decided to use her mother-in-law's words as an opening. "Laura told me what happened," she said, softly. When Anna made no response, she pressed a little harder. "The night Mark left—"

Suddenly understanding, Anna's eyes hardened. "Laura had no right to burden you with that," she said. "Besides, she doesn't know the first thing about it. She was just a child."

"But she wasn't burdening me," Janet protested. "She's frightened. We were talking about you, and I asked her what happened. So she told me. At least she told me about you losing your baby, and Mark never coming home again." Janet's voice dropped slightly. "And she said that you never told her exactly what happened that night. I think she's been terrified ever since. Terrified that the same thing might happen to her."

Anna stared at Janet for a few seconds, then shook her head. "She shouldn't worry," she said at last. And then Anna's voice took on the same tone of recitation Janet had heard from Laura. "All that happened to me was that I overworked myself and brought the labor on prematurely. It was a breech birth, and the cord wrapped around the baby's neck." She paused a moment, then: "That's what they told me, and that's what I believe," she finished. The emphasis in her voice, though, only made Janet certain there was something Anna was leaving out, something she was not about to talk about. Indeed, she had already wheeled herself out of the kitchen to the foot of the stairs, and was now calling to her husband and grandson.

"You mean we're not going back to New York *at all?*" Michael asked. He'd sat in silence while Janet had explained to him that she'd decided to arrange for movers to pack them and let an agent handle the subleasing of the apartment. Now he was on his feet, his eyes stormy, a vein throbbing angrily in his forehead.

"It just seems best—" Janet began, but Michael cut her off.

"Best for who?" he demanded. "What about my friends? Don't I even get to say goodbye to them?"

"But you said goodbye when we came out here—"

"That was different!" Michael's voice began to rise. "When we left, we were coming back!"

Amos rose and moved toward the angry boy. "Michael! Don't talk to your mother in that tone of voice."

With no hesitation, Michael swung around to face his grandfather. "Don't tell me what to do," he said. "You're not my father!" Whirling around, his face contorted with fury, he stormed out of the dining room. Amos started to follow him, but Janet blocked his path.

"Let him go, Amos," she pleaded. "He didn't mean it. He's just upset, and he'll come back down to apologize."

"He can't talk that way," Amos said, his voice firm but bearing no trace of anger. "He can't talk that way to you, and he can't talk that way to me. And he'd better understand that right now." Moving around Janet, he, too, left the dining room. The two women watched each other warily, Janet knowing with all her instincts that Anna would back her husband up. But instead, the older woman seemed to sag in her chair.

"I'm sorry," she said. "I suppose I should have stopped him, but he believes children should be respectful, and even though I know that's old-fashioned, that's the way he is."

And he's right.

The thought skittered through Janet's mind, an alien idea long ago rejected by herself and her husband, and most of their friends. They were modern parents, ever-mindful of the tenderness of the young psyche, ever-striving to allow their son the same freedom of expression they themselves enjoyed. Mark, she knew, would not have reacted to Michael's outburst as his father had. Mark would have taken the time to explain the situation to Michael, and listened to Michael's point of view. And in the end he (and she) would have decided that the trauma of Michael having to leave his friends with no final goodbye outweighed the expense of that last trip to New York, even though logic dictated that they stay where they were.

But here, away from the city and its environment of advanced thinking and experimentation, the same thought kept drumming in Janet's head: *Amos is right.*

These people did things as they had always done them, and if they seemed in some ways backward or reactionary, they had other qualities that made up for it. They had a sense of community, of caring, that refugees to the cities had lost. They retained values that people of Janet's own environment had shed long ago and with no remorse.

There was a solidity to Amos, to all the people of Prairie Bend, that Janet was just beginning to realize she had missed in the years of her marriage.

She stood up and moved around to where Anna still sat, and rested one hand on the older woman's shoulder. "Thank you," she said quietly. "Thank you so much for all you're doing."

Anna covered Janet's hand with her own. "Don't be silly, dear. You're family. We're only doing what any family would do. And it's our pleasure. I lost Mark years ago, but at least now I have you and Michael."

Though neither of them could see the other's face, each of them realized the other was weeping, one for a lost son, the other for—

For what? Janet wondered.

If she'd been asked, which she was blessedly not, Janet would not have been able to say exactly why tears had come to her eyes. Partly for Mark, she supposed, though of that she was no longer sure, but partly for something else, something she was only beginning to discover. Mixed with her sense of loss, there was that something else, a sense of something recovered, a sense of values she had once held, but lost along the way, that were now being restored. She squeezed Anna's shoulder gently, then, wanting to be alone with her thoughts, she slipped out into the fading evening light.

Amos Hall stood at the door to the room that should have been Mark's and was now occupied by Michael, about to put his hand on the knob and open it. Then, out of a sense that he owed the boy the same courtesy he intended to demand, he knocked.

"Go away," Michael replied, his voice tight with anger. Ignoring the words, Amos opened the door, stepped inside, and closed the door behind him. He stood still, saying nothing, waiting for Michael to respond. For several long minutes, the room was still. Then, his movement involuntarily exposing the uncertainty he was trying to conceal, Michael rolled over, propped himself up against the cast-iron bedstead, and folded his arms over his chest.

"I didn't say you could come in here," he challenged. "This is my room."

Amos's brows arched. He moved further into the room, seating himself on a wooden chair a few feet from the bed. "If I ever hear you speak that way to me again," he said, in a tone so low Michael had to strain to hear, "or speak to your mother or any other adult the way you did a few minutes ago, I will take you out behind the barn and give you a whipping such as I haven't given anyone since your father was your age. Is that clear?"

"You can't—"

"And when I knock at your door," Amos went implacably on, "I'm not asking for permission to enter. I'm simply warning you that I'm coming in." Michael opened his mouth once more, but Amos still gave him no opportunity to speak. "Now, three things are about to happen. First, you are going to have an experience I'm sure you've never had before. Ever heard of washing your mouth out with soap and water? Nod or shake your head. I'm not interested in anything you might have to say right now."

Michael hesitated, then shook his head.

"I thought not. Well, you won't like it, but it won't kill you. When you're done with that, you and I are going downstairs, and you are going to apologize to your mother."

Again, Michael opened his mouth, but this time he thought better of it. Instead, he clamped his mouth shut, and his eyes narrowed angrily. In his temples, a dull throbbing began.

"Then, after you've apologized," Amos went on, "this is going to be all over, and we're going to fix some cocoa and forget about it. Do you understand? Nod or shake your head."

For a long minute, as the throbbing pain in his head grew, thoughts tumbled through Michael's mind. His father had never talked to him like that, never in his life. He'd always said what he wanted to say, and his parents had always listened to him. And no one, since he was a little boy, had come into his room without his permission, at least not when he was there. Then why was his grandfather so angry with him? Or *was* his grandfather angry with him? Maybe this was something else. He watched Amos, but could see nothing. The old man just sat there, returning his gaze, waiting. Michael began to feel sure that his grandfather was goading him, pushing at him, wanting something from him. But what?

Whatever it was, Michael decided he wouldn't give it to him, not until he understood what was really happening.

His head pounding, but his face set in an expression that revealed nothing of his growing fury, Michael got off the bed and walked out the bedroom door, then down the hall to the bathroom. He could feel more than hear his grandfather following him.

In the bathroom he stood at the sink, stared at the bar of Ivory soap that sat next to the cold water tap. He reached out and turned on the water, then picked up his toothbrush. Finally he took the bar of soap. Holding the soap in his left hand, he dampened the toothbrush, and began.

The sharp bitterness of the soap nearly gagged him at first, but he went doggedly on, scrubbing first his teeth, then his whole mouth. Once he glanced at himself in the mirror, and watched the foam oozing from his lips, but he quickly looked away from the reflection of his humiliation. At last he dropped the toothbrush into the sink and rinsed out his mouth, flushing it with water again and again until the taste of the soap had almost disappeared. He wiped his face and hands, put his toothbrush away, carefully folded the towel before putting it back on the bar, then wordlessly left the bathroom, his grandfather still following him.

Downstairs, he found his grandmother in the kitchen. Her eyes were flashing with anger, but Michael instinctively knew her fury was not directed at him. Indeed, as she glanced at him, he thought he saw a trace of a smile on her lips, as if she were telling him not to worry, that whatever had happened upstairs, she was on his side. Feeling a little better, he looked for his mother, but she was nowhere to be seen. Then, through the window, he saw her sitting under the elm tree. With his grandfather close on his heels, he went outside.

Janet looked up and saw them coming, but her smile of greeting faded as she saw the grim expression on her father-in-law's face, and Michael's own stoic visage of self-control. At last Michael glanced uncertainly back at the tall figure of his grandfather looming behind him, but the old man simply nodded.

Michael turned back to face his mother. "I'm sorry I spoke to you the way I did." He went on, "If you think we ought to stay here and not go back to New York, then we will."

Janet's eyes darted from her son to her father-in-law, then back to Michael again. "Thank y—" she began, then changed her mind. "That is what I think," she said. Then, softening, she reached out to touch Michael, but got no response. She hesitated, stood up and started toward the house, then turned back. "It's going to be all right, Michael," she said. He glanced at her, anger still clouding his eyes, then dropped his gaze to the ground.

"Go inside and give your grandmother a hand, son," Amos said. "And tell me when you're done. We'll make some cocoa."

Knowing better than to do anything except follow his grandfather's instructions, Michael followed his mother into the kitchen and took the dish towel from his grandmother's hands. "I'll do that," he said.

Anna hesitated, then handed him the towel and wheeled herself over to the kitchen table. She busied her hands with some mending, but her eyes, clouded with a combination of love and apprehension, never left her grandson. He was so like his father, she reflected. So like his father—and so unlike his grandfather.

Michael began drying the last of the dishes. His head was still throbbing with pain, and the kitchen seemed filled with the same acrid smell of smoke he'd noticed the other day when he'd been so angry with Ryan. And somewhere, through the fog of pain in his head, he thought he could hear something—or someone—calling to him.

As he worked, he kept hearing his grandfather's words, about how after he had apologized to his mother, it would all be over.

But it wasn't all over.

Instead, he was sure it had just begun.

True to his promise, Amos Hall produced a pot of cocoa that evening, but it failed to serve its intended function. The four of them drank it, but a pall, emanating from Michael, hung over the room, and though Janet and Anna did their best, they couldn't dispel it. By nine-thirty, everyone had gone to bed.

Janet stopped at Michael's room, knocked softly at the door, waited for permission to enter. When there was no response, she hesitated; then, like her father-in-law before her, she opened the door and stepped inside. Michael was on his bed, propped up against the headboard, reading. "May I come in?"

Michael shrugged, his eyes carefully fastened on the book that rested against his drawn-up legs. Janet crossed the small room, sat down on the bed, then picked up the book, closed it, and put it on the nightstand. Only then did Michael look at her.

"Would you like to talk about what happened?" she asked.

Michael's brows knit into a thoughtful frown. He shook his head. "I've got a headache."

Janet frowned. "A bad one?"

"I took some aspirin."

"How many?"

"Only two."

"Okay. About what happened this evening—"

"I don't want to talk about it," Michael interrupted.

"Michael, this afternoon you said you weren't going to argue with me anymore. Do you remember that?"

The boy hesitated, then nodded.

"It didn't last long, did it?"

He shook his head. "I guess not," he admitted.

"Didn't you mean what you said this afternoon?"

"Yes, but—" He faltered, then fell silent.

"But what?"

"But we always talked things over before we decided things. Now it seems like Grandpa is always deciding what we should do."

"*I'm* making the decisions," Janet corrected him. "Grandpa is giving me advice, but I'm making the decisions. And for a while, that's the way it's going to have to be. Once we're settled in our own house we can go back to the old way. But right now, there are too many decisions to be made, and too much to be done, and I just don't have the time to discuss it all with you. And I have to depend on you to understand that."

Michael fidgeted in the bed. "I do. It's just that—"

"That what?"

Michael's eyes fastened self-consciously on the ceiling. "Grandpa made me wash my mouth out with soap."

Janet tried to stifle her laugh, but failed. "Then maybe you won't talk back to him anymore."

"He said it was because of the way I was talking to you."

"Well, maybe it was a little bit of both. Anyway, it's not the end of the world. Lord knows, I survived a lot of mouth soapings."

"When you were eleven?"

And suddenly Janet knew what the real root of the problem was. "I don't think I got one much after I was ten," she said carefully. "But on the other hand, when I was eleven, I'd learned better than to talk back to my elders."

"But you and Dad always let me talk back to you. Even when I was little."

"So we did," Janet said softly. "But who's to say whether we were right or not? Anyway, if I were you, I'd be careful how I talked, at least until we move out of here and into our own place." She stood up, then bent over to kiss Michael goodnight. "How's the headache doing?"

"Still there."

"Well, go to sleep. It'll be gone by morning." She turned off the light on the nightstand, and a moment later was gone.

Michael lay in the darkness, trying to understand what was happening. Brushing his teeth twice had failed to remove the bitter residue of soap in his mouth, and the aspirin had done nothing to alleviate his headache. Furthermore, the smoky odor in the kitchen had followed him upstairs, and as he lay in bed he suddenly felt as if he couldn't breathe.

At last he got up and went to the window. The prairie was lit by a full moon, and as he looked out into the silvery glow of the night, he began to feel trapped by the confines of the house. If only he could go outside. . . .

He knew he shouldn't. He should stay where he was and try to go to sleep. If his grandfather found out he'd snuck out in the middle of the night . . .

That was what made up his mind. There was something about doing what he knew he shouldn't do that made it more fun, that made an adventure out of practically anything. And besides, this wasn't New York. This was Prairie Bend, where no one ever even locked their doors, and the streets weren't filled with strange people. And he wasn't going to be in the streets, because it wasn't the streets that called him.

He pulled his jeans on, and a sweatshirt. Taking his shoes and socks with him, he slipped out of the bedroom and down the stairs, carefully avoiding the third one from the bottom, the one that creaked. He went out the back door, stopping on the porch to put on his socks and shoes. Then, not looking back at the house, he dashed across the yard and around the corner of the barn. He waited there, sure that if anybody'd heard him or seen him, they'd call him or come after him. But after a few seconds that seemed like hours, with the silence of the night still undisturbed, he moved away from the barn, across the freshly plowed field, toward the stand of cottonwoods that bordered the river.

As Janet watched the small figure of her son fade into the gloom of the night, her first instinct was, indeed, to go after him. She put on her robe, hurried down the stairs, and was about to go out the back door when she heard a movement in the depths of the house. A moment later Amos appeared in the kitchen.

"What's wrong?"

Janet shook her head. "It's nothing, really. It's just Michael. He—well, he seems to have decided to go for a walk."

Amos frowned. "In the middle of the night?"

"So it seems. I was just going to go after him—"

"You'll do nothing of the sort," Amos replied, his frown deepening. "In your condition, all you should be thinking about is getting a good night's sleep. I'll go after him myself."

He disappeared back toward his bedroom, and Janet sank down onto one of the kitchen chairs. But as she waited for him to dress, she began to change her mind. A few minutes later Amos returned, dressed in jeans and a flannel shirt. Janet rose once again to her feet as he started out the back door.

"Amos? Maybe—well, maybe we should just leave him alone." The old man swung around, his eyes fixing on her.

"He probably just needs to be by himself and think things over," she said. "Let's give him some time, all right?"

Amos hesitated, his eyes narrowing. "If that's what you want. But he oughtn't to be going out in the middle of the night. It's not right."

"I know," Janet sighed. "And I can't say you're wrong. But just this once, can't we let it go? You go back to bed. Everything will be all right."

"Don't you want me to wait up with you 'til he gets back?"

Janet shook her head. "No."

There was a long silence, and then Amos nodded. "Okay. But I'll have a talk with him in the morning, and I'll see to it that he doesn't do this again."

A moment later he was gone, and Janet started slowly up the stairs to begin her vigil.

Waiting was harder than she'd thought it would be.

The air had shed the cold bite of the month before, but had not yet acquired the soggy heat that would blanket the plains in the days to come, when temperatures of ninety and more would hang over the prairie like a cloying shroud, suffocating people and animals alike with a dank heaviness that was even less bearable than the freeze of winter. Now, at the end of May, there was a briskness to the night air, and the musky odor of fresh-turned earth foretold of the crops that would soon begin to fill the fields. The night was crystal clear, and as he walked, aimlessly at first, Michael gazed up into the sky, picking out the Big Dipper, Orion, and the Little Dipper. Then he came to the stand of cottonwoods bordering the river, and he paused. There was a darkness among the trees, where the moonlight was blocked out by the leaves that had already sprouted from the heavily intertwined branches. No wonder they called it the Dismal, he thought. What little light spilled through from the pasture only lent the woods an eerie look, shadows cast upon shadows, with no easy path apparent.

Shivering, Michael set himself a destination now and began walking along the edges of the pastures, the woods on his right, climbing each fence as he came to it. Sooner than he would have expected, the woods curved away to the right, following the course of the river as it deviated from its southeastern flow to curl around the village. Ahead of him he could see the scattered twinkling lights of Prairie Bend. For a moment, he considered going into the village, but then, as he looked off to the southeast, he changed his mind, for there, seeming almost to glow in the moonlight, was the hulking shape of Findley's barn.

That, Michael knew, was where he was going.

He cut diagonally across the field, then darted across the deserted highway and into another field. He moved quickly now, feeling exposed in the emptiness with the full moon shining down on him. Ten minutes later he had crossed the field and come once more to the highway, this time as it emerged from the village. Across the street, he could see Ben Findley's driveway and, at its end, the little house, and the barn.

He considered trying to go down the driveway and around the house, but quickly abandoned the idea. A light showed dimly from behind a curtained window, and he had a sudden vision of old man Findley, his gun cradled in his arms, standing in silhouette at the front door.

Staying on the north side of the road, he continued moving eastward until he came abreast of his own driveway. He waited a few minutes, wondering whether perhaps he shouldn't go back to his grandparents'. In the end, though, he crossed the road and started down the drive to the abandoned house that was about to become his home. As he came into the overgrown yard, he stopped to stare at the house. Even had he not known that it was empty, he could have sensed that it was. In contrast to the other houses he had passed that night, which all seemed to radiate life from within, this house—his house—gave off only a sense of loneliness that made Michael shiver again in the night and hurry quickly past it.

His progress slowed as he plunged into the weed-choked pastures that lay between the house and the river, but he was determined to stay away from the fence separating Findley's property from their own until the old man's barn could conceal him from the same man's prying eyes. It wasn't until he was near the river that he finally felt safe enough to slip between the strands of barbed wire that fenced off the Findley property and begin doubling back toward the barn that had become his goal.

He could feel it now, feel the strange sense of familiarity he had felt that afternoon, only it was stronger here, pulling him forward through the night. He didn't try to resist it, though there was something vaguely frightening about it.

Frightening but exciting. There was a sense of discovery, almost a sense of memory. And his headache, the throbbing pain that had been with him all evening, was gone.

He came up to the barn and paused. There should be a door just around the corner, a door with a bar on it. He didn't understand how he knew it was there, for he'd never seen that side of the barn, but he *knew.* He started toward the corner of the barn, his steps sure, the uncertainty he'd felt a few minutes ago erased.

Around the corner, just as he knew it would be, he found the door, held securely shut by a heavy wooden beam resting in a pair of wrought-iron brackets. Without hesitation, Michael lifted the bar out of its brackets and propped it carefully against the wall. As he pulled the door open, no squeaking hinges betrayed his presence. Though the barn was nearly pitch dark inside, it wasn't the kind of eerie darkness the woods by the river had held, at least not for Michael. For Michael, it was an inviting darkness.

He stepped into the barn.

He waited, half expectantly, as the darkness seeped into him, enveloping him within its folds. And then something reached out of the darkness and touched him.

Michael started, but stood his ground, oddly unafraid. And then he heard a voice, flat, almost toneless, drifting hollowly from somewhere in the depths of the barn.

"Michael."

Michael froze.

"I knew you'd come." There was a pause, then the voice went on. "I have been calling you. I wasn't sure you heard me."

"Who are you?" Michael asked. His eyes searched the darkness, but could find nothing. Nor could he be certain just where the voice came from. As the silence lengthened, he began backing toward the door. "Tell me who you are," he said, more loudly this time.

And then a dog began barking outside with a sharp, staccato sound, once, twice, three times. And somewhere nearby, a door slammed. Michael darted out of the barn, swung the door closed, and dropped the bar back in the brackets. But just before he ran back into the comparative safety of the fields, he heard the voice once more. Its flat atonality echoed in his mind all the way home.

"I am Nathaniel," the voice said. "I am Nathaniel . . ."

CHAPTER 7

Michael came into the kitchen the next morning to find his grandfather waiting for him, sitting at the kitchen table, his back ramrod straight. The old man's eyes fixed on Michael with a coldness that stopped the boy in his tracks.

"Sleep well?" Amos asked.

Uncertainly, Michael edged toward the refrigerator and began rummaging on the top shelf for the pitcher of orange juice he knew was there, well concealed by the masses of leftovers his grandmother always seemed to have on hand. "I guess," he said, finally locating the pitcher behind a bottle of milk. He edged it out of the refrigerator, picked up a glass from the drainboard, and started toward the table.

"I didn't," Amos replied. "I heard your mother moving around, and came out to see if she was all right. She was. But she was worried because you were gone."

"I—I went for a walk."

"I see." Amos stood up. "And you're about to go for another walk. March."

Michael's eyes widened, and he stared up at his grandfather. "Wh-where?"

"To the barn," Amos told him, and for the first time Michael noticed the razor strop clutched in his right hand.

"But—"

"No buts," Amos cut in. "You worried your mother last night. You worried her very much. You won't do it again. Now start walking."

Michael's eyes darted toward the door to the hallway, but there was no one in sight, no one to rescue him. Reluctantly, but knowing he had no choice, he followed his grandfather out into the morning sunshine. Only when they were behind the barn, out of sight of the house, did Amos speak again.

"Where did you go?"

Michael hesitated. This morning, what had happened the night before seemed almost to have been a dream. Indeed, as he thought about it, he was no longer sure exactly what had happened. He had gone for a walk, and he seemed to remember having started out toward old man Findley's place. But now he was no longer sure. *Had* he gone there? He tried hard, but all he could really remember was the forest by the river, and the pasture. And a voice. There had been a voice. Or had there?

"N—nowhere," he said at last. "Just down to the woods by the river. I—I wasn't gone long."

"Drop your pants and bend over."

Slowly, Michael unbuckled his belt and undid his jeans. He turned around, then dropped his pants and leaned over, clutching his knees. A second later he felt the first lash of the strop sting his buttocks, and a scream burst from him.

"Don't yell," Amos told him. "If you yell, it will only get worse. Now, tell me where you went."

"I didn't go anywhere," Michael wailed. "I told you, I only went down by the river."

"You were gone for over an hour."

Again the leather strop slashed across his buttocks, but this time Michael was able to choke off his scream.

"I—I didn't know," he pleaded. "I thought it was only a few minutes."

"You shouldn't have gone at all, not without telling your mother."

"I don't have to tell her everything I do—"

The strop whistled through the air this time and seemed to wrap itself around Michael's thigh like a snake.

"From now on, you ask your mother or me before you do anything. Do you understand?"

Michael said nothing, steeling himself against the next slash of the leather. In a moment, it came, and immediately afterward, the sound of his grandfather's voice.

"Did you hear me?"

"Y-yes . . ."

Again the strop whistled through the air and burned into his flesh. "Yes, what?"

Michael thought wildly, clenching his teeth against the pain as tears burned in his eyes. "Yes, sir," he finally cried.

And the whipping was suddenly over.

"All right," his grandfather said. Slowly, Michael straightened up and pulled his jeans up to cover his stinging buttocks. Then he turned to face his grandfather, his eyes blazing with fury and his head throbbing with a sudden ache that overpowered even the pain of the thrashing. "Wait 'til I tell my mom—" he began, but Amos knelt down and took him by the shoulders, his hands gripping him like twin vises.

"Stop that, Michael," he said. "What just happened here is between you and me. You're not to speak to your mother of this. She's been through a lot, and you're not to put her through any more. From now on, you behave yourself. If you don't, you know what will happen. And if you take your troubles to your mother, I can guarantee you they'll only get worse. You're a big boy. I expect you to behave like one."

"But—"

"No buts. Things are different now, and you'd better understand that. I don't like having to do this, but so help me, I'm going to teach you some respect, boy, so that next time you feel like going for a walk in the middle of the night, you'll think twice about it. Understand?"

Michael hesitated, then nodded. But as he followed the old man back to the house, his headache grew worse, and his mind whirled with confused thoughts. *It's not fair. I didn't do anything. . . . All I did was go for a walk. . . . It's not fair. . . .*

In the kitchen, Janet was at the table, sipping a cup of coffee and making notes on a spiral pad. She looked up as Michael and Amos came through the back door. "Hi. What have you two been up to this morning?"

"Chores," Amos replied before Michael could say anything. He went to the sink and washed his hands; then, drying them on a dish towel, he went around to peer over Janet's shoulder. "What's all this?"

"Things to be done," Janet sighed. "There's so much, and I haven't any idea of where to start. But here're the colors I want for the farm." She tore off the top sheet and handed it to Amos, who studied it for a moment, then passed it to Michael.

"Some imagination your mother's got, huh?"

Michael stared at the old man. It was as if his grandfather had never been angry at all. He was smiling as if the thrashing behind the barn had never happened. And his voice was calm. He was even trying to make a joke: "White paint for the house, red for the barn, with white trim. Now, how do you suppose she came up with something so radical?" His expression turned serious, and he studied Janet's face. "Any problems this morning?"

"You mean morning sickness? Not a trace." Though her stomach was still queasy from that morning's session in the bathroom, she put on what she hoped was a bright smile and rapped the wooden tabletop a couple of times. "I'm hoping it's over with. It was probably just—well, the last few days." She took a deep breath and emphatically returned to her lists. "The problem's going to be the furniture."

"What's wrong with our furniture?" Michael asked, easing himself carefully onto one of the hard kitchen chairs. "I like it."

"There's nothing wrong with it," Janet tried to explain. "It just doesn't seem practical for a farmhouse in Prairie Bend, that's all."

"Farmhouse furniture is ugly," Michael pronounced; then, realizing what he had said, his eyes filled with fright and shifted to his grandfather.

But the old man only nodded in agreement. "It may be ugly, but it's comfortable," he said just as Anna rolled her chair into the kitchen and brought it to a stop between the sink and the range. Janet started to get up, but Anna waved her back to her chair. She dropped an apron over her lap, then pulled a skillet from a low cupboard and placed it on the stove. "What were you talking about?" she asked of no one in particular. "What's ugly but comfortable?"

"Farmer's furniture," Amos told her.

"According to whom?" Anna demanded, suddenly taking on the look of a ruffled hen.

"According to your grandson."

"Oh," Anna said. She hesitated only a second, then shrugged. "Well, of course he's right. But don't you worry about it," she said, addressing Janet, as she began scrambling a dozen eggs in the enormous cast-iron skillet. "I can furnish that house with a couple of phone calls. Every barn and attic in Prairie Bend is full of furniture, and it won't cost a cent. Besides, you'll spend more money shipping your stuff out here than you'd get if you sold it, so you'll be money ahead even if you have to give it away. Bring me the plates, Michael."

As Michael hesitated, Anna watched him. There was something in his eyes —a hurt—that she had seen before, years ago, in her son's eyes. She had hoped never to see it again. "Michael, are you all right?"

Michael's gaze met his grandmother's, and for a quick moment there was an unspoken communication between the two of them. But then Michael nodded, turning away to move toward the cupboard where the china was kept. Anna's eyes followed the boy, then shifted suspiciously toward her husband. But if Amos noticed the concealed fury in his wife's eyes, he gave no sign.

As Michael began putting the breakfast plates on the table, Janet thought over what her mother-in-law had just said. It did make sense. Still, there was a faint twinge at the feeling that by leaving her belongings behind, she would be shedding still another piece of her old life. But she quickly shook off her misgivings. After all, she had made up her mind to start all over again in Prairie Bend.

The sun was high in the sky as Michael carried the pail of garbage around the corner of the barn. The pigs, milling around in their pen, immediately began grunting and snorting in anticipation of their midmorning snack. Michael climbed the sturdy metal bars of the small enclosure, using only one hand to haul himself up, while he clutched the bucket with his free hand. The pigs clustered around, snuffling at the toes of his sneakers, shoving each other aside in their eagerness to be first at the trough. Finally, when he was perched on the top rail, Michael grinned down at the churning animals.

"Okay," he said. "Here it comes!" He upended the bucket, and the garbage cascaded into the feeding trough. A boar, the largest of the herd, immediately shouldered his way between two sows, one of which promptly nipped him on the ear. The boar squealed in surprise and quickly backed off. The sight of the immense hog giving way to the smaller female struck Michael as funny, and he began to laugh, shouting encouragement to the big pig. "Come on, don't let her get it all. Get in there and fight for it!"

The hog, as if sensing that he was being mocked, suddenly turned toward Michael, his small eyes gleaming. Then, with a speed Michael wouldn't have believed possible from such a clumsy-looking animal, he reared up, grabbed Michael's foot in his mouth, and gave a quick jerk.

Michael tumbled into the pigpen, and his laughter turned to a sudden scream of fright.

The boar backed off for a moment, his front hoof scraping at the ground as his beady eyes fixed upon Michael. Then, grunting angrily, he hurled himself forward.

Michael rolled aside at the last minute and tried to get to his feet, but stumbled over a second pig. Suddenly the whole herd seemed to be on the move, their sharp hooves digging into the ground as they jockeyed for position, half of them attempting to get to the trough, the other half more interested in Michael.

"Help!" Michael screamed. "Someone help me!"

Janet heard Michael's scream and raced out of the kitchen just as Amos emerged from the barn. "What's happened?" she yelled as she dashed across the yard.

"The pigs," Amos shouted back. "He must have fallen into the pigpen." Then he disappeared around the corner of the barn.

By the time Janet reached the hog enclosure, Amos was already using a long pole to poke at the furious animals. "Get up," he yelled to Michael. "Get on your feet boy, or they'll trample you. Get up!"

Suddenly, from around the far corner of the barn, a black dog the size of a large shepherd hurtled into sight, charging straight for the pigpen. With one leap, it was over the top rail, and then it was in the midst of the pigs, snarling and barking, snapping first at one of the sows, then turning its attention to the big boar. The boar, surprised at the sudden attack at its flank, backed off for a moment, giving Michael a chance to scramble to his feet. A moment later, Amos had lifted him up and over the top rail of the enclosure.

As soon as Michael was out of the pigpen, the dog abandoned the fight and leaped out of the pen. A moment later he was next to Michael, who was clinging to his mother, sobbing with fright.

"They were going to kill me," he cried. "They were going to trample me!" The dog, as if trying to comfort the terrified child, licked at his face, his tail wagging. Suddenly one of Michael's arms left his mother to curl around the dog's neck, hugging him close.

Janet stared down at the animal. "Where'd he come from?" she asked. "Whose is he?"

Amos frowned, sure he'd never seen the dog before. If he had, he'd have remembered it. It stood two and a half feet high at the shoulder, with a broad, deep chest and heavily muscled legs. Its coat, coal black without so much as a trace of white markings, was thick, and its eyes, alert and intelligent, seemed to fix on him with a mixture of equal parts of suspicion and hostility. "Don't know," he admitted.

Michael, who had been more frightened than hurt by the pigs, hugged the dog closer. "I bet he followed me home last night," he said. Then he gazed up at his mother. "He saved my life, Mom. Can I keep him? Please?"

Janet felt dazed by what had happened, but when she had assured herself that Michael was, indeed, unhurt, she turned her attention to the dog. The animal seemed to regard her with quizzical eyes, as if awaiting her decision. "I don't know," she said at last. "He must belong to someone," she went on, though she had already seen that the dog wore no collar.

"But what if he doesn't?" Michael asked. "What if he's only a stray? Then can I keep him?"

"We'll see," Janet temporized. "Right now, though, I want you to go in and get yourself cleaned up."

Michael was about to argue, but when he saw the look in his grandfather's eyes, he changed his mind. "All right," he agreed. He started toward the house, and the big dog followed close at his heels. When Michael disappeared into the kitchen, the dog sat by the back porch.

"What do you think?" Janet asked Amos.

Amos shrugged. "I don't know. Never seen him before. But if he's still around when we get back tonight, I don't suppose there's any harm in keeping him."

A moment later, Amos wasn't so sure. As he passed the dog on his way into the house, it lifted its big head and laid back its ears. A snarl rumbled up from the depths of its throat.

Janet and Michael stared in awe at the little farm, barely able to recognize it even though it was not yet noon and the work had been under way for only three hours. Already the weeds had been cleared from the front yard; people swarmed over the house with scrapers, removing the last traces of paint from the weathered siding, and in the backyard, yet another crew was busy piling brush and weeds onto a smoldering bonfire. Still more people were at work on the barn.

The driveway, barely passable yesterday, had been scraped, and now a backhoe was working, digging drainage trenches along the shoulders of the road. Buck Shields, manipulating its controls with expert ease, brought the machine to a halt and jumped to the ground. "Want to try it?" he asked Michael. Michael immediately climbed up the caterpillar tread of the hoe and perched on its steel seat.

"What do I do?"

"Hold on," his uncle replied, climbing up to stand behind Michael, his work-coarsened hands covering Michael's own softer ones. "It's real easy. This lever brings the hoe up and puts it down, and this one moves it back and forth. See?" He demonstrated the hoe's operation, and another foot was added to the drainage ditch. "We can do about three or four feet at a time, then we have to move the whole thing forward. Try it."

Michael moved one of the levers, and the hoe plunged deep into the earth. "Easy," Buck cautioned. "We want a trench, not a pit." He eased the lever back, and the hoe responded. "Now try moving the dirt to the side, and dumping it." Michael hesitated, chose a lever, and pulled. The claw of the hoe dropped downward and the earth was deposited back into the trench.

"I'm messing it up," Michael said by way of apologizing.

"Maybe we better start you out with the tractor and work up to this. Why don't you see if you can lend a hand out back?"

Michael scrambled down and disappeared around the corner of the house, while Janet walked slowly along next to Anna as she wheeled her chair up the drive. At the foot of the porch steps, the old woman came to a halt and stared silently up at the house.

"You must have a lot of memories of this place," Janet said at last. Anna's eyes flickered, then met Janet's.

"I do," she replied. "But that's all past now, isn't it? For you, maybe this house will be a good one."

Janet frowned thoughtfully. "I don't believe in good houses and bad houses. It seems to me a house is happy if the people who live in it are happy."

"I hope you're right." Sighing, Anna approached the porch steps, then came to another halt. This time, when she looked up it was to Janet, not to the house. "There's some people who can manage stairs in these things, but I'm not one of them."

"I put a ramp for you on the top of my list," Janet told her as she began working the wheelchair up the four steps to the porch, "but I don't know when we'll be able to get it built."

"I'll mention it to Amos," Anna replied. Then, as Janet pushed her through the front door, she seemed to shrink into the chair. Her eyes scanned the foyer and the stairs, then shifted to stare almost fearfully at the closed door to the small room in which she'd delivered her last child.

"If you don't want to be here, I'll understand," Janet said, putting a reassuring hand on the old woman's shoulder.

"No. No, it'll be all right. It's just that it's been so many years." A wry smile twisted her mouth, a smile that Janet had a feeling was forced. "I'm afraid we may not have done you a favor with this place. I had no idea how bad it had gotten."

"But it's *not* bad," Janet protested. "It's going to be wonderful. Come on. Let's go on a tour, and I'll tell you everything I'm going to do."

They went from room to room, Anna falling silent as Janet explained her plans for each area. At last they came back to the foot of the stairs. Anna gazed thoughtfully up toward the second floor. "Which rooms are you going to use?" she asked at last.

"I'm taking the big one in front. Michael wants the little one."

"The little one?" Anna frowned. "Why the little one?"

"He likes the view. You can see Mr. Findley's place from there."

Anna's expression darkened. "That place," she said. "Ben Findley should be ashamed of himself, the way he's let it go. I swear, I don't know why that man stays around here. If it wasn't for Charles Potter, he wouldn't have a friend in Prairie Bend."

"But doesn't he have family?"

Anna's eyes clouded, and a sigh escaped her lips. "Ben? Not anymore. He had a wife once—Jenny Potter. For a while they had a good marriage, but then—" She fell silent for a moment, then smiled wanly. "Things happen, I guess. Anyway, Jenny left, and ever since, Ben's just gotten stranger and stranger."

"But surely he must have *some* friends."

Anna shook her head. "He doesn't seem to want friends anymore. In fact,

I've often wondered why he stays here at all. His life must be so lonely. . . ." Her eyes drifted toward the staircase. After a moment, she turned back to Janet. Suddenly, she nodded her head. "Of course Michael would want the little room." A look that might have been sadness, or something else, shadowed her face. Then she said, "It was his father's."

As his mother had asked his grandmother about Ben Findley, so too had Michael asked Ryan Shields again about the man next door. They were in the barn with a third boy—Damon Hollings—whom Michael had met only today.

"How come he's not here?"

"Are you kidding?" Damon replied, though Michael had directed his question to his cousin. "He never goes out of that weird house, and he never speaks to anyone. And he wouldn't help anyone, even if they were dying on the road in front of his driveway." Damon paused, enjoying the effect his words were having on Michael. "And his place is haunted," he added, his voice dropping to a loud whisper. "There's ghosts there."

"There's no such thing as ghosts," Michael protested, but nonetheless his gaze shifted away from Damon toward the loft door. Beyond, only a few hundred yards away, lay the ramshackle buildings of the Findley farm. And in the depths of his consciousness, a memory—or was it a dream?—stirred. "What kind of a ghost?" he asked, his voice noticeably less certain than it had been a moment earlier.

"It's someone who died a long time ago," Damon told him. "And sometimes you can see it, at night, out in Potter's Field. It looks like lights moving around out there."

"Lights?" Michael asked. "What kind of lights?"

"I—I never saw it myself," Damon admitted.

"You never saw it 'cause it doesn't exist. Right, Ryan?" Michael said, turning to his cousin, but Ryan didn't answer.

Damon shrugged with exaggerated indifference and ran a hand through the tangle of blond hair that capped his mischievous face. "Well, who cares what you think?" he said to Michael. "All I'm telling you is what I heard. And what I heard, and what everybody around here knows, is that old man Findley's place is haunted. So there!"

"Well, I don't believe it," Michael shot back. "I don't believe in ghosts, and I bet there's nothing wrong with Mr. Findley. I bet nobody around here likes him 'cause he's not related to anybody," he said with sudden certainty.

"Well, why don't you go find out?" Damon challenged.

"Maybe I will," Michael replied, taking up the challenge. He turned to Ryan again. "Will you go with me?"

Ryan stared at him, then emphatically shook his head. "And you better not go, either," he said.

Michael's expression set stubbornly as the beginnings of a headache shot through his temples. "I'll do what I want," he said in a tight voice. He turned away from the other two boys and concentrated his attention on the old barn in the distance. As he stared at it, the pain in his head began to ease. From somewhere inside his head, he could almost hear a voice whispering to him. The words were unclear, but the tone was somehow familiar. . . .

By six-thirty the heavy work was done, and only the Halls remained at the little farm.

"Doesn't look much like it did this morning, does it?" Anna Hall commented.

Indeed, it did not. Gone was the tangle of weeds that had nearly hidden the house, and the lawn, mown and trimmed, needed only water and some fertilizer to restore it to the luxuriant green that was the norm in Prairie Bend. The driveway, scraped and graveled, formed a graceful curve to the highway, and the buildings, denuded of the last remnants of their faded and peeling paint, seemed almost to be anticipating the morrow, when a coat of fresh white would restore them to their former respectability. Behind the buildings, forty acres of newly plowed earth awaited whatever plantings Amos eventually decided on. Even Michael had to admit that the place had changed.

"Maybe we really *can* live here," he murmured. Then his eyes shifted westward toward the sagging buildings of the Findley farm, and he fell silent.

Misunderstanding Michael's silence, Amos reached out and drew him close, his arm around the boy's shoulders. "You don't like that place?" he asked, then interpreted Michael's continued silence as assent. "Well, that's just as well. If I'd had my way, I'd have bought Ben's place long ago, but he wouldn't hear of it. Said he'd found the place where he was going to die, and he was too old to change his mind. So there he is, and if I were you, I'd leave him alone."

With an effort, Michael tore his eyes away from the old barn and looked up at his grandfather. "Is there really a ghost there?" he asked.

Janet had not been paying much attention to the conversation. Now she turned to look at her son. "A ghost?" she asked, her voice incredulous. "What on earth are you talking about?"

Michael shifted uncomfortably. "Damon Hollings says Mr. Findley's farm is haunted."

"Oh, for heaven's sake. You didn't believe him, did you, honey?" When Michael hesitated, Janet's voice lost some of its lightness. "There's no such thing as ghosts, Michael, and there never have been." She turned to Amos and

Anna, expecting them to support her, but Amos seemed lost in thought, while Anna had turned away and was slowly pushing her chair toward the car. "Amos, tell him there's no such thing as ghosts."

"I'm not going to tell him something I don't know about, Janet," he said at last.

Janet stared at him. "Something you don't know about?" she repeated. "Amos, you aren't going to tell me you believe in ghosts!"

"All I can tell you is that there've been stories," Amos said at last. "So I guess I'll just have to say I don't know."

"What kind of stories?" Michael demanded.

"Things," Amos told him after a long silence. Then he smiled grimly. "Maybe, if you're good, I'll tell you all about them, just before you go to bed tonight."

Michael tried to keep his excitement from showing, tried to keep his expression disinterested. He failed completely.

CHAPTER 8

The prairie was different then; the grass was tall, and in the summer you couldn't even see where you were going. It would grow five, maybe six feet high, and it was like a great sea, green at first, during the spring, and then, in the summer, it would turn brown, and as far as you could see, there it was, waving in the wind just like in the song. Then the cattle came, and the grass started getting more like it is now—still thick, and still tall in the spring, but cut down as the summer goes on. It never used to get cut at all. It would just stand, bloom, go to seed, and die.

And in the winter, the prairie would turn white, and the snow would be so thick no one could go out in it. No one except the Indians, with their travois. And even they didn't travel much in the winter. They'd pitch their tepees, and huddle together, and somehow they'd get through it.

That was what the white people didn't know. They didn't understand the prairie, didn't have any idea of what it could be like. The thing of the prairie is that it just seems to go on and on forever. And there's nothing to measure it by. So what used to happen is that people would lose track out on the prairie. Not of where they were—they always knew that. But they'd lose track of who they were, and what they were.

It would happen slowly, so slowly that most people never knew it was happening to them. They'd come out here from the east, and they'd be looking for land. A lot of them were city people, and what they wanted was to be out of the city. So at first they didn't even have towns. Instead, they'd claim tracts of land—big tracts—and they'd build their houses right in the middle of it, and everything they could see was theirs. And they didn't have any neighbors, not to speak of. Oh, there were other people, but they lived miles away, and the only time you saw your neighbors was during a house-raising or a wedding, a birth or a death. For the rest of the time, you were by yourself, with no one but your family. And sometimes you'd be snowbound for months on end.

It seems like it was the women it got to the most. They'd go on for years, raising their children and taking care of their husbands, and everything would seem to be fine. But inside, they'd start losing their sense of themselves. They'd start feeling like they were disappearing into the prairie. Every day, little by little, getting smaller and smaller, until they'd start to feel like one morning they just wouldn't be there anymore. And then it would happen. One day something would just sort of snap inside their heads.

That's what happened in Prairie Bend. Except that it wasn't called Prairie Bend then, and there was no town yet. Just a few big farms, and the bend in the river. And there was a woman. A woman named Abby Randolph. Her husband had died that fall, and even though she was pregnant, she stayed on, trying to take care of the farm and raise the children.

She seemed fine, the last time anyone saw her, which was in the fall, just before the first snow. And then the snow came, and it kept on coming. The drifts built up, covering everything, and a lot of people died, right in their own houses.

That's not what happened to Abby, though.

Abby started hearing things. At first, she didn't pay any attention to it. She'd wake up in the night, and she'd hear something downstairs, like someone moving around. So she'd get out of bed and go downstairs, but there wouldn't be anyone there. Then she'd check on the children, thinking maybe one of them was playing a joke on her. But they'd be in their beds, sound asleep.

Then one night Abby heard the sound downstairs. It didn't go away. It got louder and louder. Finally, Abby went downstairs.

The noise was coming from the front door. Three knocks, and then a long silence, and then three more knocks. For a long time, Abby just stared at the door, knowing it wasn't possible that anyone could be outside. It was February, and the drifts were ten feet deep, and there was no one else for miles around. But the knocking didn't stop. And then Abby opened the door.

There was a huge man looming in the doorframe, covered with snow, with ice forming on his beard and his eyebrows. Abby stared at him for a long time, and then the man took a step forward and his eyes seemed to flash at Abby. And he spoke.

"I've come for my boy."

The first time it happened, Abby just shut the door, but after that, it happened every night. Every night, she'd wake up and hear the pounding on the door, and every night the man would be there, and every night he'd say the same thing.

"I've come for my boy."

Then one morning, after the man had come the night before, and Abby had shut the door, one of the children was gone. And that night, the man didn't come back. But then, a week later, he came back again, and when Abby opened the door, he smiled at her. "You can have him back in the summer," he said. "You can have him back when the grass is high."

And one by one, that winter, Abby Randolph's children disappeared until there was only one left.

Then spring came, and the snow melted, and people started visiting each other again. When they first came to see Abby, she was sitting on her front porch, with a very strange look in her eyes. And they found one child upstairs—her oldest son—crouched in the corner of his room. They tried to talk to him, but all he'd do was scream whenever anyone went near him. And the rest of the children were gone.

They tried to talk to Abby, but she wouldn't say much. All she'd say was that the children's father had come for them, and that he'd bring them back when the grass was high.

The spring passed, and then the summer came, and one day some neighbors went to visit Abby and found her out in the field, digging. When they asked her what she was looking for, she said she was looking for her children.

"The grass is high," she said. "The grass is high, and it's time for them to come back."

The next day, they found Abby. She was in the barn, pinned up against the wall with a pitchfork. Her son was with her, crouched down on the floor of the barn, watching his mother bleed to death. They didn't talk to the boy, didn't bother to give him anything like a trial. They just hanged him, right there in the barn. They say he died even before his mother did. Abby didn't die for hours. She hung on, trying to save her baby. And in the end, she did. The baby was born just before she died. And later on, in Abby's cyclone cellar, they found some bones. They were the bones of children, and it looked like they'd been boiled.

For years after that, people would disappear around Prairie Bend every now and then, just like people disappear everywhere. But around Prairie Bend, they never found the bodies, and they always say it was because of Abby's last son. They said Abby's boy had gotten hungry, and gone looking for something to eat.

And they said that sometimes, when the weather was stormy and the grass was high, you could still see Abby, late at night, out in the field, looking for her children. . . .

Michael stared up at his grandfather, his blue eyes wide and frightened. "That—that's not a true story, is it Grandpa?"

"Of course it isn't," Janet quickly replied. "It's a horrible story, and I wish we hadn't heard it." She turned to Amos, her face pale. "My God, Amos, how could you tell a story like that to a little boy?"

Amos Hall shrugged. "If he hadn't heard it from me, he'd have heard it from someone else. It's been around for years, and it never changes much."

"But surely no one believes it?"

"About Abby? I don't suppose anybody knows the full truth about her and her kids, but it's probably close to the truth. Things like that used to happen around here. Like I said, the prairie would get to people, and they'd just crack up. It could have happened to Abby that winter—"

"No more," Janet pleaded. "I don't want to hear any more about it. I meant the last part, about her son still wandering around and people still seeing her out in the field. Surely no one believes that, do they?"

"I don't know," Amos replied. "Who knows what people see? But I can tell you, people around here tend to be pretty careful about their kids, particularly during summer. But of course, that's only common sense. We get tornadoes during the summer, and they can be nasty. Get caught out in a tornado, and you just have to trust to luck." He stood up, stretching. "Anyway, that's the story. You can believe it or not, as you see fit." He turned to Michael. "And as for you, it's time you were in bed."

Michael got slowly to his feet and kissed his mother goodnight, then his grandmother. He started out of the little parlor, but then turned back.

"Grandpa? What was the name of Abby's son?"

"Nathaniel," Amos told him. "His name was Nathaniel."

Michael climbed up the stairs and went to his room, then undressed and slid into bed. A few minutes later he turned off the light to lie in the darkness and stare out the window into the night. Far away across the field, he could see a shape moving through the moonlight. He knew it was the dog, the dog who had saved him from the pigs, then waited for him all day, wagging his tail fiercely when he caught sight of Michael, and not seeming to mind when he had not been allowed inside the house. But he was still there, like a shadow in the night, patrolling the fields while Michael slept.

That's what I'll name him, Michael thought. Shadow. His name will be Shadow.

But as he drifted off into sleep, it was another name that kept echoing in his ears.

Nathaniel . . .

CHAPTER 9

You guys ever hear of somebody named Nathaniel?" Michael's voice betrayed none of the tension he had been feeling as he helped with the painting of the house the next day, glancing only occasionally westward toward Findley's barn. Now, in the bright spring sunshine, the crumbling barn's fascination seemed to have lessened, and Michael had begun to wonder if the sensation of its calling to him—or of something inside it calling to him—had been nothing more than his imagination. But that name kept coming back to him. Nathaniel.

The name he had heard whispered in the barn; the name his grandfather had used last night.

So now, as he diligently helped Ryan Shields and Eric Simpson apply an uneven coat of not-quite-white paint to his bedroom walls, he tried to ask his question with a nonchalance he wasn't feeling.

"Nathaniel?" Ryan repeated. "Where'd you hear about him?"

"Grandpa."

"The story about the kid who killed his mother?"

Michael nodded, and put down his brush. "Is it true?"

Ryan shrugged. "I guess so. Except the part about the ghosts of Nathaniel and Abby still hanging around here. That's just a story they told us to keep us from shagging out at night."

"My dad told it to me," Eric offered. "I was only a little kid, but it gave me nightmares."

"How do you know it's not true?"

Ryan gave him a scathing look. "Come on. It's just a ghost story." Then, seeing the look of uncertainty that clouded Michael's expression, he grinned. "You don't believe in ghosts, do you?"

Michael hesitated only a split second. "Hell, no." He picked up the brush once more and began applying more paint to the wall, covering up the thin patches but leaving a series of brush marks. Eric watched him for a moment, then shook his head in disgust.

"You sure don't know much about painting, do you? I bet your mom makes you do that over again." He dipped his roller into the tray of paint, and began going over the area Michael had just done.

"Did Grandpa tell about the knocking at the door, and that weird man all covered with snow?" Ryan asked. "That was the scariest part."

Michael nodded, but Eric looked perplexed. "What man? All I ever heard was that every time Abby ran out of food, she cooked one of her children and fed it to the rest of them."

"Yeah," Ryan agreed. "But Grandpa says she never even knew what she'd done. She always thought a man came for the kids. That's why she's supposed to still be out looking for them."

"Can you believe that?" Eric asked. "Who'd ever believe a story like that?"

"Well, we did," Ryan said, reddening slightly.

"Yeah, but that was when we were little," Eric declared. "I figured out the ghost part of it was just a story when I was ten."

"Sure," Ryan teased. "That's why you're always the one that chickens out when someone wants to sneak into Findley's barn in the middle of the night."

Now it was Eric's turn to redden, but he made an attempt at a recovery. "That place is dangerous. It's gonna fall down any day now."

"You've been saying that since you were ten, too." Ryan deliberately ran a paint roller over Eric's hand. "Oops."

"Cut that out," Eric yelped. "It *is* gonna fall down!" He shook his own roller at Ryan, spattering paint across his friend's face.

Ryan only grinned. "Seems like one of us is still pretty clean, doesn't it?" he said.

Eric nodded, and the two of them turned on Michael.

In seconds the scuffle degenerated into chaos. The sides constantly changed, until all three of them were covered with paint, along with the ceiling, the walls, the floor, and the window. That portion of the window, at any rate, that was closed. Too late, they noticed that the upper section of the casement had been lowered, and the battlefield had not contained the ammunition. And they only noticed that when they became aware of Janet Hall standing in the doorway, her expression of fury carefully masking her urge to laugh.

"What's going on here?"

"Nothing." Though the reply had come from Michael, it was nearly simultaneously echoed by Ryan and Eric.

"Nothing," Janet repeated, her expression darkening.

Michael stooped down to pick up a rag. "I guess we better get it cleaned up before it dries," he mumbled.

"And you'd better get yourselves cleaned up, too," Janet told them. "You can use sandpaper on the floor, and a scraper on the window, but if you don't get that paint out of your hair, it's going to have to be cut off. Now get into the bathroom—all of you—and get those clothes off. Put them in the tub and let them soak. Then get yourselves into the shower—"

"But there's no hot water!" Michael protested.

Janet allowed herself a faintly malicious smile. "You should have thought of that before you started all this. Now get to it. By the time you're done, I'll have some clean clothes for you. Lord knows if they'll fit anyone but Eric, but they'll be here."

Eric's eyes widened apprehensively. "You're not gonna tell my mom—" he began, but Janet cut him off.

"Your mother already knows. She was standing right under that window, helping *your* mother—" she turned her gaze to Ryan, "—paint the shutters downstairs."

Ryan groaned. "Oh, God. She'll kill me, Aunt Janet."

"Quite possibly she will," Janet agreed, keeping her voice implacable, unwilling to let the children see her amusement. "But before she gets the chance, I want an explanation for all this. Otherwise, you can all work naked for the rest of the afternoon, and go home the same way. Is that clear?"

The three boys nodded mutely and headed for the bathroom. Janet Hall waited until she heard their anguished screams as the icy water began sluicing the latex paint from their skins, then went thoughtfully down the stairs.

She, too, had been under the window, and she had heard the conversation that had led to the paint fight.

"You were talking about Nathaniel," she said. Though her eyes were on Michael, Ryan and Eric were clear in the periphery of Janet's vision. Michael nodded, and out of the corner of her eye, she saw Eric echo the gesture. Ryan, however, suddenly looked worried.

"Ryan was teasing Eric about being afraid of ghosts," Michael said. "And then—well, it just sort of happened. It wasn't anyone's fault, Mom. We all started it. I just wanted to find out if anyone else heard the story Grandpa told me last night. What's wrong with that?"

"Nothing," Janet assured him. "Except that I think it's time you understood that it's only a story. All of it."

"Grandpa says—" Ryan began, but Janet didn't let him finish.

"Your grandfather told us a revolting story last night, and I'm sure very little of it is true. The whole idea of that poor woman doing what your grandfather says she did is disgusting, and probably nothing like it ever happened. And as for ghosts, there are no such things, as all of you well know."

"Then why did Grandpa tell it to us?" Michael asked.

"Probably for a couple of reasons. Ghost stories are fun. Furthermore, a good ghost story can keep people off property where they're not wanted." She turned to Ryan and Eric. "When you two were younger, did you believe there were ghosts out here?"

Sheepishly, they both nodded.

"And did it keep you off Mr. Findley's property?" Again, they nodded. "Then it served its purpose, didn't it?" She focused her attention on Michael. "As for why your grandfather decided to tell it to you, I haven't any idea. But it seems to me you're a bit old for that sort of thing. If Mr. Findley doesn't want people on his property, certainly you don't need a ghost story to keep you away, do you?"

"But—but what if it's *not* just a story?" Michael pressed. "What if there really *is* a ghost out here?"

Janet saw the glance that passed between Ryan and Eric, and was sure her son had just lost a part of their respect. Michael himself, however, hadn't seemed to notice it. Instead, his large eyes were fixed seriously on her own. "There are no ghosts," she said. And yet, even as she said the words, she wondered if they were true. What about her own ghosts? What about the ghost of Mark that was beginning to haunt her? The doubts about him, the questions about him that were always nagging at the fringes of her mind, demanding answers? Weren't those ghosts? Wasn't she, herself, beginning to wonder what was real and what was not?

Resolutely, she banished her doubts from her mind, and reached out to squeeze Michael's shoulder. "There are no ghosts," she said once more. "There are ghost stories, but that's all they are. Just stories." Then, pointedly eyeing the paint that was quickly drying on the floor and windows, she left the three boys alone in Michael's room.

When she emerged from the house a few moments later, she found Laura and Anna on the front porch, Laura bent over as if she'd been whispering into her mother's ear. Seeing Janet, she straightened up and smiled, but there was a falseness to her expression that wasn't lost on Janet.

"Has something else gone wrong?" Janet asked, her voice anxious.

"Heavens, no," Anna assured her. "I was just telling Laura not to overdo, that's all. But I'm afraid it doesn't do much good. Sometimes she digs in her heels, and it seems like she's trying to work herself to death. Do you suppose you could find some of that lemonade we had with lunch?"

"I'll look," Janet replied. She went back into the kitchen and found the last of the lemonade, though there was no ice. Still, she rinsed out a glass, filled it with the warm liquid, and started back toward the front porch. Once again, Laura was whispering into Anna's ear, and when Janet made a deliberate sound, there was something furtive in the manner in which Laura looked up. Furtive and frightened. Somehow, Janet had the feeling that it had something to do with the conversation that she and Laura, along with Ione Simpson, had overheard earlier.

The conversation about Nathaniel.

She handed Laura the glass of lemonade.

"You *believe* that crazy ghost story, don't you?" she asked as Laura raised the glass to her lips.

As the color drained from Laura's face, the glass shattered on the floor of the front porch.

Laura Shields was still upset by Janet's accusation. That evening, when she eased her ungainly bulk into the chair that was normally reserved for her husband, she smiled apologetically, hoping Buck wouldn't question her about the nervousness she'd been unable to cover. "I guess maybe I overdid it a little bit today. Women in my condition shouldn't try to paint shutters."

Buck looked up from the paperwork he'd been poring over, and his eyes suddenly hardened. "I told you not to try it. If anything happens to that baby, I guess you know whose fault it will be."

"But I wanted to help Janet with the house," Laura murmured. She settled herself in and sighed.

Buck smiled sourly, and his voice took on a sarcastic edge. "You're just like your mother—if you don't do it yourself, you don't think it'll be done right." He pushed his papers aside. "It never ceases to amaze me that there's a town here at all, considering you weren't even born 'til thirty-one years ago."

"It amazes me, too," Laura said, with careful placidity, determined not to rise to her husband's bait. She reached over to pick up the *TV Guide,* and felt a sudden twinge of pain in her abdomen. Frowning in spite of herself, she waited for the pain to pass, then completed the motion.

"Something wrong?" Buck asked.

"Don't be silly. What could be wrong?" With studied nonchalance, Laura opened the little magazine and began examining the listings. Another pain seized her, and this time she had to bite her lip to keep from crying out. Now Buck rose to his feet, the hardness in his eyes dissolving into concern.

"Something *is* wrong."

"It's nothing," Laura insisted. "It's just something I ate. I've just got a little cramp, that's all."

"Cramp, or contraction?"

"I—I'm sure it's just a—" She jerked spasmodically as another pain shot through her, then, as it eased, she felt a spreading dampness on the chair beneath her. "Damn," she whispered. She looked up at Buck, her expression a mixture of sorrow, pain, and fear. "I'm sorry. I guess I really did overdo it today. You'd better call Dr. Potter." She began to lift herself out of the chair, but another sharp contraction forced her back.

"Ryan? Ryan!" Buck called, the urgency in his voice bringing his son out of the kitchen immediately. "Call Doc Potter, and tell him to get over here right away. The baby's coming."

"But it's not supposed to be—"

"Damn it!" Buck snapped. "Do as I say. Call the Doc while I get your mother upstairs." He slid his large hands under Laura's arms and eased her to her feet. "Can you make it, or shall I carry you?"

Laura took a tentative step, leaning heavily on Buck's arm. "I can make it," she assured him. "But if the baby's going to come tonight, don't you think I ought to go to the hospital?"

Buck ignored the question. "Let's get you upstairs."

"But—"

"Don't argue with me, Laura," Buck told her. "We know what's best for you."

Laura opened her mouth, then closed it again. He was right—argument would be useless; he was just like her father. "All right," she finally whispered. "Just stay with me." She began moving slowly toward the stairs, pausing only to reach out and touch Ryan's hand as she passed him. "Call Dr. Potter, sweetheart. And don't worry. I'm going to be all right, and so is the baby." As Ryan finally started toward the phone, she began climbing the stairs, with Buck beside her.

Three minutes later, she lowered herself gratefully onto the bed, then allowed herself a groan. Another contraction gripped her, and she had to fight not to allow the groan to turn into a scream. She lay still, waited for it to pass, then looked up at Buck, for the first time letting the fear she was feeling show in her eyes.

Ryan appeared at the door, his face pale and his eyes frightened. "Doc'll be here in a few minutes. He said not to worry, that everything's going to be fine."

"Of course everything's going to be fine," Buck said. "You go on back downstairs and wait for Doc. Okay?"

Ryan nodded uncertainly, then opened his mouth to say something, but apparently thought better of it. Laura smiled weakly at him. "What is it?"

"Is—is the baby going to be all right this time?" he asked.

Laura nodded and made herself smile at her son. "This time there isn't going to be any problem at all." But as Ryan left the room, her eyes drifted toward her husband. "There won't, will there? This one will be all right, won't it?" Then, before Buck could answer, another violent contraction seized Laura. This time, she was unable to stifle her scream.

Eric Simpson looked worriedly up at his father.

"Is it time?" he asked. "Is she gonna foal tonight?"

Leif Simpson eyed the mare critically, then nodded. "Looks like it," he said. "Maybe another hour, maybe two. And I bet this one doesn't take all night."

"Should I call the vet?" Eric was standing next to the mare, stroking her head gently. She whinnied softly and pawed at the floor of the stall. "Easy, Magic. Everything's gonna be okay. We'll take care of you."

"You and I can handle this one," Leif told his son. "But if your friends want to watch, you'd better tell them to get on over here." As Eric hesitated, Leif stepped into the stall, gently easing the boy away from the horse. "Go on. You won't miss anything. She's hardly even started to dilate yet."

Moments later, breathless from running from the barn to the house, Eric was on the phone, dialing Ryan Shields's phone number. He listened impatiently as the connection went through, then grumbled to himself as he heard a busy signal. He waited a few seconds, then dialed again. Again, the busy signal.

"Shit," he said softly, but distinctly enough so that Ione Shields, coming through the dining room door, heard him quite clearly.

"Eric!"

"I'm sorry, Ma," Eric automatically apologized. "I gotta call Ryan and Michael, and Ryan's line is busy."

"Then call Michael," Ione suggested.

"I don't know their number."

"Look it up."

"Aw, Ma, I don't have time to do that. Magic's dropping her foal, and I gotta get back out to the barn." As he spoke, he dialed the Shieldses' number for the third time. Still busy. Eric gave his mother an appealing look, one that he was well aware she couldn't resist. "Could you call for me? Please? All you have to do is tell them Magic's foaling, and if they want to watch, they better get out here."

As he was sure she would, his mother nodded. "Run along," she told him. Then, as her son dashed out the kitchen door, she picked up the phone and dialed Anna Hall's number. It, too, was busy.

After four tries, alternating between the Shieldses and the Halls, she finally got through to the latter. The phone rang six times before it was finally picked up.

"Anna? It's Ione. What on earth is going on? Have you been talking to Laura? I've been trying to call them, too, and both your lines have been tied up."

There was a moment's hesitation, then Anna's voice came over the line. "It's Laura," she explained. "It seems as if the baby's decided to come tonight."

Ione paused, the smile fading from her face. "Oh, dear," she said finally. "Poor Laura. Do you think I should go over there?"

This time there was no hesitation from the older woman. "I'm sure if Laura needs any help, Dr. Potter can provide it."

Ione felt a twinge of annoyance at Anna's brusqueness. In truth, she was more than a little hurt. In Prairie Bend, when someone was having a baby, the neighbors gathered around, just as they did when there was illness, or trouble of some sort. It had been that way for as long as Ione could remember—except for the Halls. For some reason Ione had never understood, the Halls tended to keep to themselves.

Oh, they'd accept helping hands to get the crops in, Ione thought, or to fix up that old house for Janet and her son. Ione herself had willingly helped out with that and hadn't begrudged the effort for a minute. But when it came to themselves and their children, the Halls had always been standoffish. Tonight, obviously, was going to be no exception. It occurred to Ione that even with the doctor present, Laura might be able to use the nursing skills Ione had acquired years earlier, before she'd married Leif. But Anna had already made it quite clear that Ione wasn't wanted.

"I see," she said stiffly, making no attempt to mask her feelings. "Well, then, I don't suppose there's much chance of Michael coming over here tonight, is there? Magic's foaling, and Eric promised him he could watch." She paused. "I suppose that'll be out of the question now."

Again there was no hesitation in Anna's reply. "I don't see why. Let me call him," she said.

* * *

As she crossed the yard a few minutes later, Ione Simpson paused halfway to the barn to gaze at the newly painted little house that was silhouetted in the distance against the setting sun. In this light, it looked no different from the way it had ever looked, and for a moment Ione wondered if Janet Hall hadn't made a horrible mistake in deciding to move onto the long-abandoned farm. There had been so many stories over the years, so much speculation. . . .

In the end, though, she decided that what Janet Hall did was her own business.

And yet, she knew that wasn't quite true. In Prairie Bend, everything that happened to anyone affected everyone else. And something, she knew, had happened in that house that Janet Hall was moving into. . . .

Twenty minutes later, Michael skidded his borrowed bicycle to a halt in front of the Shieldses', sure that Ryan would be waiting for him. With Shadow at his heels, he started across the yard to the front door, but suddenly stopped as he noticed his grandfather's big Oldsmobile parked in the driveway behind his Uncle Buck's car. He gazed at the Olds for a moment, trying to figure out what was going on. His grandfather had said he was going to a grange meeting when he'd left the house a half hour earlier.

Now, as Michael thought about it, something seemed odd. Wasn't the grange just for farmers? And if it was, why would it be at the Shieldses' house? Uncle Buck wasn't a farmer. And come to think of it, why hadn't his grandfather said anything about a meeting earlier? In fact, he'd been watching television when the phone rang, and then he'd just left, saying something about the grange as he went out the door. But if he was coming over to the Shieldses, why hadn't he suggested that everyone come along? As Michael turned the matter over in his mind, a pair of headlights glowed from around the bend. Instinctively, he grabbed his bike and eased himself behind the hedge that separated the house from the lot next door.

The car pulled up, and a moment later Dr. Potter got out, carrying his black bag, and hurried across the lawn and up the porch steps. The door opened almost immediately, and Michael saw his grandfather take Dr. Potter by the arm and pull him inside.

For a moment, Michael was tempted to walk across the lawn, climb the steps, and knock on the door. But then, as he stood in the gathering gloom of the evening, his mind was changed. It was almost as if there were a voice inside his head, whispering to him, telling him to leave the house. From beside him, a low growl rumbled from Shadow's throat, and Michael laid a hand on the dog to calm him.

Almost against his will, he wheeled the bicycle out from behind the hedge, mounted it, and started pedaling away, Shadow trotting along behind. Once, Michael glanced back over his shoulder, but from the outside nothing at the Shieldses' seemed amiss. It was just a house, with some kind of a meeting going on inside.

Except the voice in his head told him there was something else.

Something he didn't understand yet, but soon would . . .

As Michael Hall rode away from the house, Laura Shields gazed up at Dr. Potter, her eyes pleading.

"Can't I go to the hospital? Please, can't you take me to the hospital?"

Potter took her hand in his own, stroking it gently. "It's too late, Laura. The baby could come any time, and the hospital is forty miles away."

"I can make it," Laura whispered, even though she knew she couldn't. Another cramp wracked her body, and she felt the tiny form inside her shift its position. "If I'm in the hospital, I know the baby will be all right. I *know* it."

"Hush," Potter soothed. "Hush, Laura. We're all here, and we're all going to take care of you. You'll be fine. In a few hours, it'll all be over, and you'll be fine." He released her hand, then rummaged in his bag. A moment later he handed Laura a small white pill and held a glass of water for her. "Take this," he commanded. "Take this, and try to get some sleep."

"But the baby," Laura moaned. "What about the baby? I have to be awake when my baby comes."

"You will be," Potter promised. "But right now, you mustn't worry about the baby, Laura. You mustn't even think about it. Not yet."

Not think about it? Laura wondered as she felt the pill begin its swift work. How can I not think about my baby?

And then, as Potter sat gently wiping her sweating brow with a cool washcloth, she began drifting into a fitful sleep. But just before she slipped into unconsciousness, she spoke once again.

"He can't have this one," she whispered. "It's not for him. It's not for Nathaniel . . . it's for *me* . . ."

CHAPTER 10

"Easy, Magic, take it easy."

It had been going on for nearly two hours, and Michael was beginning to wonder if anything was ever going to happen. He was perched on the partition between Magic's stall and the one next to it, while Eric stood at the mare's head, a steady stream of soothing words flowing from his mouth into her ear. His hands roamed over the horse's head and neck, gripping her halter whenever she tried to pull away, but never jerking at the leather straps. "How long does it take?" Michael asked, but if Eric heard his words, he ignored them. It was Leif Simpson who replied.

"Won't know for a little while yet. So far, everything looks all right, and if she can do it herself, we might have a foal in another hour. But if things are twisted around, it could take a lot longer."

"Twisted around? Twisted how?"

"If the colt's in the wrong position," Leif explained. "If it comes out head first, we're home free. But sometimes they don't, and you have to lend a hand."

"How?"

Eric's father grinned at him, his eyes twinkling. "You have to climb right in after the colt. Grab it by the legs, or anything else you can get hold of, and start working it out."

Michael wasn't at all sure he believed the man, and the doubt in his eyes was reflected in his words. "But what about wild horses? What happens to them?"

"Wild horses are a different breed of cat, so to speak," Leif told him, "different from domesticated ones. We breed farm animals for traits we want, but sometimes when we breed things in, we breed other things out. So wild horses don't have problems foaling, but on the other hand, they're not as big, and not as strong as old Magic here. Understand?"

As Michael nodded, Magic whinnied loudly, shook herself, and pawed at the floor with her forelegs. "Hang on to her, son," Leif warned unnecessarily, for Eric had a firm grip on the worried mare.

"It's like she doesn't know what's happening," Michael observed.

"Oh, she knows, all right," Leif Simpson replied. "She's been shoving hay around her stall for a couple of days now, getting things ready." He glanced up at Michael. "Sure you don't want to come down here? You can see better."

Michael shook his head. Though he wanted to watch the birth, he also wanted to be safely out of the way if something went wrong. Though he wasn't about to admit it, he had not yet taken on the casual attitude toward horses that the kids in Prairie Bend all seemed to have been born with.

As Michael watched, Leif Simpson frowned, looked closely at the horse, then smiled. "Hang on, Eric," he said quietly. "Here it comes." And as Michael watched, the head of the foal slowly emerged from the mare's womb. "Come on," Leif Simpson urged. "Come on, baby, you're almost there. Easy. Easy . . . eeeeeasy!"

Suddenly the emerging form stopped moving, and Leif Simpson cursed softly. He reached out and began working his hand around the foal, gently pressing with his fingers, feeling his way into the cervical opening.

"What is it, Pa?" Eric asked. Though his hands remained firm on the nervous mare's halter, his anxious eyes were on his father.

"It's a foreleg," Leif replied. "It's not bad. Just got to ease it around so the hoof is loose, and it can slip right out."

Without thinking, Michael slid off the partition and moved closer, staring in fascination at the tiny form that hung suspended, only partially born, its coat matted and damp with the wetness of birth. And then, as he watched, Leif Simpson pulled his hand gently away, exposing a tiny hoof. Almost immediately, the birthing process resumed, and a few moments later the foal dropped from the womb, Leif easing it to the floor of the stall.

"Let her go," he told his son, and Eric released his hold on the mare's halter. Magic, freed, immediately strained her head and neck back, and began licking at the tiny colt. It shivered under its mother's tongue, then struggled uncertainly to its feet, teetered for a few seconds, and dropped back to the floor. It rested; then, once more, it rose to its feet. Instinctively, as Magic still licked at it, it found a teat and began suckling.

"Wow," Michael breathed.

"Neat, isn't it?" Eric asked as proudly as if he himself were the father of the colt. "This one was easier than the last one. Last time, she breeched, and it took most of the night."

"Can I touch it?" Michael asked.

"Not yet," Leif cautioned him. "We want it to get a good fix on Magic. If we start handling it too soon, it could imprint on one of us, and wind up thinking we're its mother. You want to spend the next few months with a colt following you around, trying to get milk?"

Michael cocked his head, gazing in wonder at the tiny form. Unborn only a few minutes ago, the foal was already beginning to take care of itself. "If it were that colt," he eventually said, "I might not mind at all."

"Well, maybe you wouldn't," Leif Simpson replied. "But Magic would be mighty upset." He glanced around the stall, then pointed to the mops and brooms that leaned against one of its walls. "The sooner you two get this mess cleaned up, the sooner you can get back to admiring that little family."

The two boys began working on the stall, cleaning up and disposing of the placenta, removing the soiled straw and replacing it with fresh. But as they worked Michael's eyes kept drifting to the colt.

He wished the colt were his.

Laura Shields woke up, her body wracked with pain. The contractions were coming rapidly now, only a few seconds apart. Dimly, she was aware of people around her: Dr. Potter, standing near the foot of the bed; Buck, next to her, holding her hand. In the far corner, near the door, her father stood, watching her intently. Laura lay still for a moment, waiting for a respite from the pain before she finally spoke, and when it came, her voice sounded distant to her, as if she were far away from herself.

"Go away," she whispered hoarsely. "Go away and leave me alone."

"Hush," Buck told her, his gruff voice distorted with an attempt to be tender. "It's going to be all right. We're all here, and we'll take care of you."

"I don't *want* you," Laura moaned. "Get Mother. I want Mother to help me. Please? If I can't go to the hospital, can't I at least have Mother?"

"Don't, Laura," Buck replied. "Don't talk that way. You know it has to be this way. You know it."

Why? Laura wondered as the pain closed in on her once more. Why does it have to be this way? Why do I have to be alone with the men? Why can't I have my mother with me?

There were no answers to her questions, and all she could do was look up into her husband's eyes. "It's going to be all right, isn't it?" she whispered. "Please, tell me it's going to be perfect, and it's going to be mine, and it isn't going to die. Promise me? Please, Buck, promise me?"

There was silence for a moment as another contraction surged through Laura. Involuntarily, she crushed Buck's hand in her own, but managed to suppress the scream that rose in her throat. "Please," she begged when she could talk once more. "Please promise me."

"I can't," Buck whispered. "You know I can't."

And then the contractions seized her once again, and Laura knew the time had come. Clenching her hands, bracing herself against Buck's strong arms, she bore down, and felt the child within her move, edging slightly downward.

"Good," she heard Dr. Potter say, as if from a great distance. "That's good Laura. I can see the head. Again." Once more, feeling the rhythm of the contractions, she bore down. "Again. Again. Once more . . ."

She bore down hard, and again she felt the baby move. This time, though, the movement was accompanied by a searing pain that sliced through her body, forcing a scream from her throat.

And in her mind, that searing pain cut through her consciousness, peeled away the layers of scar tissue she'd built up over the years, and the memories came flooding back to her. Her brain, muddled with drugs and pain, began garbling memory and reality. As Laura's body delivered her baby into the world, her mind delivered her into the past.

Her father was there, standing at the foot of the bed, staring at her.

"You killed him."

Laura heard the words, but wasn't sure what they meant. And yet, she knew, they were her words, her voice that had spoken them.

Beside her, Potter ignored the tormented words that Laura had uttered, concentrating only on the baby that was slowly emerging from her womb.

Laura's whole body was writhing on the bed now, and her arms flailed at the air, striking out at something that wasn't there. "My baby was alive," she screamed. "I felt it moving. It was alive, and you killed it!"

Amos Hall's eyes fixed on his daughter. "Stop it, Laura," he said. "You don't know what you're saying. The baby isn't born yet."

Laura's agony only increased. She was moaning now, and her hands twisted at the sheets. Her words became indistinguishable, but in her mind she could see it all. It was her baby, and Dr. Potter was holding it, and it was dead, and they were telling her it had been born dead, but she knew they were lying. She knew it had been all right, and that they had killed it. She knew it. She knew . . .

At the foot of the bed, Dr. Potter held the tiny form that had finally slipped free from the strictures of the womb. Its eyes were closed, and there was a bluish cast to its skin.

Potter held the baby deftly in his left hand, its head down, and with his right hand, he delivered a quick slap to its buttocks.

Potter's eyes met Amos's, and a silent message seemed to pass between the two men. Nearby, Buck Shields stood, watching the doctor, watching his father-in-law, waiting.

"Again," Amos Hall said, his impassive eyes fixed on the baby. "Try again."

Potter nodded once, then struck the baby's rump again, harder this time.

"That's it, then," Amos Hall said softly.

Laura Shields began screaming, and her husband quickly gathered her in his arms, holding her head against his chest, muffling her cries as best he could. She struggled in his arms, trying to work herself loose, trying to reach out for her baby, but it was no use. Buck held her immobile, and after a moment she made herself stop screaming, closed her eyes, and lay back on the pillow, sobbing softly.

Potter sighed. "This can't keep happening," he said quietly, as Amos Hall took the tiny body from his hands. Then he moved to the bed, and reached out, tentatively touching Laura's hair. She jerked away from him.

"Go away," she whispered in a broken voice. "Just go away and leave me alone."

"It was born dead, Laura," Dr. Potter told her. "You have to believe that. Your baby was born dead. You've had a miscarriage."

She opened her eyes and tried to reconcile his words to her memories. "Miscarried?" she asked. "It was born dead?"

Potter nodded. "It was premature, and it was born dead. You have to remember that, Laura. Can you do that?"

"I miscarried," Laura repeated in disbelieving tones. "I miscarried, and my baby was born dead."

A few minutes later, as Potter's sedative began easing her into sleep, Laura Shields repeated the words to herself once more, but she knew she didn't believe them.

The baby had been alive. She was sure it had been alive. And she was sure they had killed it. They had killed it, and they had sent it to Nathaniel.

But still, she couldn't be sure. It had all been so strange, and even as it had all been happening, and the baby was being born, she couldn't be sure of what was real and what was memory. And now, she would never really know.

Then, in her last moments of consciousness, she came to a decision. She would try to accept what the doctor had told her. From now on, when she thought of this night, she'd tell herself that all that had happened was that she'd miscarried.

She'd miscarried, and the baby was born dead.

It would be easier that way.

Eric Simpson cocked his head and stared at Michael Hall. He looked as though he was watching something, but Eric couldn't figure out what it was. "Somethin' wrong?" he finally asked.

Michael started, and then his eyes slowly focused on Eric. "I thought I saw something," he said uncertainly. "Or heard something. And I've got a headache."

Eric grinned. "That's the stuff we slopped down the floor with. It'll go away as soon as we're outside. Come on."

It was nearly midnight, and the cleanup from the foaling was finally done. But Michael couldn't quite remember finishing the job. He'd been hosing down the barn floor, and his head had begun to ache, and then he'd seen something. It had only been a flash, and it had seemed to come from inside his head, and yet he was sure he'd recognized some faces.

His grandfather, and Dr. Potter.

And Dr. Potter had been holding something, but Michael hadn't quite been able to make out what it was.

And there had been a sound, high pitched, like the shriek of the wind, or like someone screaming.

Then it was gone.

Now, outside in the cool night air, Michael couldn't even quite remember what it had been like, except for the scream.

The scream was still echoing in his head, and despite what Eric had said, his head still ached.

"It's Nathaniel," he muttered. "I bet it's Nathaniel."

Suddenly the sound of a screen door slamming jarred his reverie, and he heard Eric's mother's voice.

"You boys all done? Want something to eat?"

Michael looked up at Mrs. Simpson. She seemed to be a long way away, and he couldn't really see her very well. He shook his head. "I—I better get back to Grandpa's house."

"Would you like a ride?" Mrs. Simpson asked. "It's past midnight."

Again Michael shook his head. "I can ride my bike. I'll be okay."

His head still pounding with pain and his vision oddly blurry, Michael mounted his bike, whistled to Shadow, and rode off into the night. When he was gone, Ione Simpson put an arm around her son's shoulders and started toward the house. "Is Michael all right?" she asked. "He seemed sort of—odd, just now."

Eric frowned up at his mother. "He was weird," he said emphatically.

"Out in the barn, he started acting funny, and then he said he had a headache." Michael had said something else, too, Eric thought, something about Nathaniel. He considered telling his mother that as well, then changed his mind. No point in getting his mom all riled up over that old ghost story. But it really was weird. And a little scary. Eric felt a shiver start crawling up his spine.

It was as he came around the curve between the Simpsons' farm and his mother's that Michael first became aware of the lights.

Far off to the left, dimmed by the distance, he first thought they were fireflies. He slowed, then stopped the bike, dropping one foot to the ground to maintain his balance. Shadow, his hackles slightly raised, crouched beside him. Michael squinted into the darkness, trying to determine shapes and forms, but there were none. Only a faint glow, broken every now and then as something passed between himself and the source of the lights. Frowning, the pain in his head increasing by the moment, he started the bike moving again, concentrating on the lights until the dark shape of his mother's house cut them off. And then, as he came to the driveway, they reappeared, and he suddenly knew where they were.

Potter's Field.

His mind flashed back twenty-four hours, and he saw what his grandfather had described—a woman, her back bent as she stooped over, wandering in the night, searching, constantly searching for what she would never find.

He remembered the tale, and as his headache worsened, he tried to shake it from his mind. He couldn't.

He dismounted the bicycle, and began walking it up the driveway until he stood in the shelter of the house, concealed from whatever might be lurking in the field. Still, whatever was there was too far away for him to see clearly. He stayed where he was for a moment, indecisive. Then Shadow, whimpering softly, slunk away into the darkness. Michael made up his mind, leaned the bike against the side of the house, and followed the dog.

He came to the fence that separated his mother's property from Mr. Findley's. Barely pausing, he slipped between the strands of barbed wire; then, crouching low in the dim moonlight, he scurried across to Findley's barn. His head was throbbing now, but it seemed to him he could begin to make out forms in the faint light emanating from the field.

And then, as he and Shadow slipped into the darkness next to the barn, he heard the voice, the same voice he'd heard before: flat, toneless.

"Michael."

It wasn't a question, and Michael knew it. The possessor of that voice knew who he was. He pressed closer to the barn.

"Nathaniel?" he whispered.

"Come in," the voice urged him. "Come in."

As if in a trance, Michael moved around the barn and lifted the bar from its brackets. Swinging the door open just enough to let himself through, he slipped inside, then pulled the door closed behind him.

"Over here." The voice drifted eerily out of the darkness, seeming to come from nowhere and everywhere. "Over this way."

And then, though the voice had not told him which way to go, though he could see nothing in the pitch blackness of the barn, Michael began moving through the darkness, knowing with the passage of every second that he was coming closer to Nathaniel. It was as if Nathaniel was reaching out to him, guiding him, showing him the way through the darkness with his own eyes.

And Michael's headache was suddenly gone.

He drifted down the aisle between the rows of stalls, his footsteps echoing in the emptiness. Then he paused. Though he could still see nothing, he reached out a hand, and immediately touched a door handle. Lifting the latch, he pulled the door open and stepped into the tack room that lay beyond. He was close now, very close. He could feel Nathaniel's presence.

"Here," the voice of Nathaniel told him. "You can see from here." Michael crossed the room, his senses vibrating with a strange kind of awareness, a feeling of sharing himself with another, and sharing that other as well. Then he was standing near the outer wall of the barn, and Nathaniel was with him.

"Closer," Nathaniel urged him, his voice no longer filling the little room, but seeming to emanate from inside Michael's own head. "Stand closer, and see with me."

There was a tiny gap in the barn siding, and Michael pressed his eye against it. The moonlight outside seemed to have grown brighter, and suddenly Michael could see clearly across the fields to the cottonwoods along the river.

And near the cottonwoods, he could see the lights. Three of them, oil lanterns, their wicks turned low, set in a triangle. And inside the triangle, the form of a man.

"Who is it?" Michael whispered in the darkness.

"My father."

"What's he doing?" he asked.

"Do not speak," Nathaniel's voice commanded. "If he knows you are with me, he will try to kill you."

Michael fell silent, knowing deep within himself that the words, though incomprehensible, were the truth. He waited. In a moment the strangely toneless voice came to him again. "I have been calling you. Why did you not come before?"

Michael was silent, but his mind was working, remembering.

His father's funeral, when he had seen this barn, seen something here that no one else had seen.

Watching the barn from the window of the room that would be his, knowing what it looked like inside, though he'd never been here.

Night before last, when he'd come to the barn, knowing that there was something waiting for him.

And now, tonight.

When finally he spoke, he spoke only within himself. "I couldn't hear you. Did you call me tonight?"

And the answer came back, also from within. "Yes. I saw him in the field and felt you near. I called you here so he would not see you."

"But what's he doing?"

"Sending one of us away. One of us was born tonight, and he is sending him away. Just as he sent me away. He does that to all of us . . . if he can." And in those words that sounded only in his head, Michael could feel a terrible loneliness. Then the voice came again. "I have been waiting for you a long time."

"Why?"

"I need you. And you need me. We are alone, Michael. There is no one else. Do you never feel the loneliness?"

Michael trembled in the darkness, but then Nathaniel touched him, and he felt calm again.

"Will you take me outside?"

Michael frowned in the darkness. "Now?"

"Yes."

"He'll see us."

"It does not matter. He cannot hurt us, if we are together. He hurt that one, though."

"Who?"

"The one who was born tonight. I felt it coming, and called out to it. It was a little boy."

"There was a foal . . ." Michael whispered, then fell silent. Once again, that strange vision flashed into his head, only now the faces were clear, and he could see what was in Dr. Potter's hands.

"Not a foal," Nathaniel's voice came. "A boy. A little boy. But he knew that the boy was mine so he brought him here. Now he is burying him. Look."

Michael gazed out into the night, but the light seemed to have faded slightly, and he couldn't see exactly what was happening.

"Take me out there," Nathaniel's voice echoed in Michael's head. "Take me out there, so we can kill him."

"K-kill him? Why?"

"Because he kills. It is for us to punish him, Michael. He hates us, and he fears us, and he will kill us. If he finds us, and if we are alone."

"But—"

The oddly disembodied voice seemed not to notice Michael's interruption. "He does not know about you yet, but if he finds out about you, you will die. Unless you stay with me. Stay with me, Michael."

Michael turned and for the first time saw Nathaniel's face, lit softly by the moonlight filtering through the weathered siding of the barn.

It seemed to be his own face—the same dark blue eyes and wavy brown hair, the same angular cheeks and strong jaw. But the blue eyes were without light, and Nathaniel's skin was pale, almost translucent, like his father's had been at the funeral, and his face was as expressionless as the voice Michael had been hearing in his head.

"How long have you been here?" Michael asked.

"A long time," Nathaniel told him, his voice resonating softly through the large, empty barn. "As long as I can remember. Will you take me outside?"

"Why can't you go out by yourself?" Michael asked with no note of challenge in his words.

Nathaniel stared at him for a long time, his dark blue eyes cold and empty. "I cannot do that," he whispered. "I can never go out by myself. Only with you, or with the others if I find them. Not by myself. It would not be safe."

"Why not?" Though the words formed in his mind, Michael didn't utter them. Nevertheless, Nathaniel answered.

"Only together will we be safe, Michael. Alone we have no power. Alone, they can destroy us. If they find out about me, I will die, and you will die. Unless we are together. Remember that, Michael."

Michael frowned in the darkness of the barn, trying to fathom the meaning of the words, the odd, almost chantlike cadence of the flat-toned speech. Then, as he turned away and peered once more through the crack of the siding, Nathaniel spoke again.

"Never speak of what you saw tonight. If they ask you, tell them what they want to hear. But do not speak the truth. If you tell them the truth, if you tell them of me, you will die."

The moonlight seemed to be fading faster now, and in the distance Michael could barely make out the glimmering light of the lanterns. He strained his eyes against the darkness, and became aware once more that his head was aching. "I—I can't see," he said, turning questioningly to Nathaniel.

But Nathaniel was gone.

CHAPTER 11

By the time Michael left the barn, the moon had disappeared below the horizon, and the night had taken on a blackness that made the last of the lanterns gleam with an almost unnatural brilliance. Michael carefully replaced the bar on the barn door, then with Shadow beside him, moved slowly through the darkness, his hands extended, feeling for the barbed wire fence.

He found it. Holding the strands apart as far as he could, he put his left leg through the fence, then bent down to duck under the top wire.

A barb snagged the flannel of his shirt, and Michael reflexively tried to jerk free. The barb worked further into the material. He reached back with his right hand, feeling for the wire. A barb pierced his skin, sinking into the ball of his thumb. Suppressing a cry, he yanked his hand back. Shadow whined sympathetically and tried to lick the injured hand, but Michael brushed him aside and inserted the thumb in his mouth, sucking hard on the wound. As the salty taste of blood filled his mouth, his eyes instinctively went to the single lantern that still glowed in the field. As he watched, it went out. With the disappearance of the light, Shadow's whine turned into a warning growl.

A moment later, Michael heard a car door slam and an engine grind, cough once, then catch, quickly settling into a reluctant hum.

Ignoring the barbs, Michael forced his torso through the fence, pulling his right leg behind him. The sound of the car was louder now, and even though no lights were showing, he knew the car was coming toward him. He twisted frantically against the fence, but several of the barbs were now firmly embedded in the shredding flannel of his shirt, and he was held fast.

And then, as the engine's drone drew ever nearer, he gave a last lunge against the restraining fence, and his shirt tore free. He dashed across the open space between the fence and his mother's house and dove behind a patch of bushes. A second later, the car—unrecognizable in the darkness—cruised slowly by the house, then down the driveway to the road. Only when it was on the highway did its lights go on.

Michael waited until the car was well out of sight before he emerged from the bushes, breathing hard, his torn shirt damp with sweat. Shadow skittered nervously at his feet. He located his bike, but instead of mounting it, he wheeled it along the driveway, then across the road. He paused there for several more minutes, thinking hard. What was he going to tell his mother? How could he explain his torn shirt?

And then Nathaniel's words came back to him.

"Never tell them the truth.

"If you tell them the truth, you will die.

"Tell them what they want to hear."

Even as fear began to grip him, an idea began to take shape in his mind.

"Laura lost her baby?" Janet asked, the words echoing oddly in the Halls' kitchen. "What are you talking about?"

"She miscarried," Amos Hall replied. He peeled off his jacket and hung it on the hook by the back door, then poured himself a cup of coffee from the ever-present pot on the stove. When he finally sat down in his usual position at the kitchen table, Janet stared at him dazedly. Though his expression was impassive, she could see the pain in his eyes. Then, as if sensing the thought that had immediately formed in her mind, he said, "It didn't have anything to do with her overworking this weekend. The—the fetus was malformed, and Dr. Potter said the baby would have been born dead even if Laura'd carried it to term."

Janet released the breath she'd been unconsciously holding, and sank back in her chair. "But why didn't you tell me what was happening?" she asked. "Why that story about the grange? I'd have gone with you. Anna and I both would have." Her eyes shifted to her mother-in-law for confirmation, but

Anna only sat motionless in her chair, her hands folded in her lap, her eyes blank. Janet turned helplessly back to Amos.

"We thought it would be better this way," he said. "We were afraid something like this might happen, and we decided it would be better if you weren't there." His eyes moved toward Janet's torso, and Janet's fingers moved instinctively to touch her abdomen.

"I—I don't understand. . . ."

"This isn't the first child Laura's lost," Amos told her. "She—well, she doesn't have children easily."

"But I should have been there," Janet insisted. "After all she's done for me, the least I could have done was be there."

"No," Anna said, sighing deeply. Janet turned to look at her. A sad, apologetic smile reflected the look in Anna's eyes. "Laura wouldn't have wanted you there," she said. "She wouldn't have wanted either of us there. For me—you know why it would have been painful for me. And for you . . . well, you and Laura are about the same age, and she wouldn't want to frighten you. She wouldn't want you to go through the next few months worrying that what happened to her might happen to you."

"Me?" Janet asked, her bewilderment increasing. "Did she tell you that?"

Anna reached out and took Janet's hand. "She didn't need to. You've been through so much already, dear. And it's not just Laura, you know. We all worry about you. Tonight, Amos decided the best thing to do was wait until it was all over, and hope we'd be able to tell you you had a new niece or nephew." The half smile left her face, and her eyes hardened as they flashed briefly toward her husband. "Things don't always work out the way we want them to," she said.

Oblivious to the look that had passed between Anna and Amos, Janet nodded her head. "It must have been terrible for her," she said at last. "Not even in the hospital, and with nobody there—"

"I was there," Amos Hall corrected her. "And Buck and Dr. Potter."

"I'm sorry," Janet said quickly, immediately contrite. "I didn't mean that. I just meant—"

"Don't worry, dear," Anna assured her. "I know exactly what you meant."

Again, Janet fell silent for a moment, but then she took a deep breath, as a thought struck her. "But what about Ryan? Wasn't he going out to the Simpsons' with Michael?"

Amos shook his head. "He was home all evening."

Janet's eyes darted to the clock on the wall. It was a little past midnight. "But look at the time! Where's Michael?"

"Probably still at the Simpsons'," Anna told her. "A foaling can take all night."

"But what if he's coming home? He's all by himself, and he's only eleven—"

"And he can take care of himself," Amos assured her. "He's like his father—he'll be all right. Just try to take it easy, Janet. Getting yourself into a state won't help."

It was then that they heard the first scream.

Michael had mounted the bike and ridden quickly back toward the Simpsons'. When he was halfway there, he picked the bicycle up and jammed it into the fence between the north side of the road and the field beyond. When the wheels were securely tangled in the wire, Michael climbed the fence and began walking across the field. In the distance, he could see the faint glow which he knew marked his grandparents' house. Sure of his bearings, he began running, stumbling in the darkness every few yards, pitching headlong into the fresh-turned soil. Each time he fell, Shadow was instantly next to him, nosing at him, snuffling and whining until Michael rose once more to his feet. By the time he reached the far side of the field, with his grandparents' house clearly visible, his hands and face were scratched and bleeding, and what was left of his clothing was covered with grime. He climbed carefully through the last fence and paused to catch his breath.

As his breathing slowly settled into an easy rhythm, he watched the house, but if there was any movement inside, he was too far away to see it. Still, even as he crossed the road to the end of the driveway, he was sure that his grandparents, as well as his mother, were waiting for him.

Twenty yards from the house, he gathered his energy together, and began running.

Running, and screaming. Shadow, as if picking up a cue, added his furious barking to the melee.

"Mother! Grandpa! Help! Help me!"

Still running at top speed, he dashed around the house and hurled himself up the steps of the back porch, his fists pounding on the door. "Help me! Mother, help me!" The door flew open, and Michael threw himself into his mother's arms.

Janet's arms closed tightly around her hysterical son, and she sank to her knees to gather him against her. "What is it?" she asked when Michael's terrified screams finally stopped. "Michael, what happened?"

"My bike!" Michael wailed. "I was coming home, and all of a sudden there was a car behind me. I thought it was Mrs. Simpson, but it wasn't. It—it ran me right off the road."

"Where?" Janet asked. "Where did it happen?"

"Right near the Simpsons'. I hadn't even gotten to our house yet."

Her mind spinning, Janet's gaze drifted up to Amos Hall. He was on his feet now, staring at his grandson.

"Tell us exactly what happened."

They were at the kitchen table now, and Michael was sitting huddled close against his mother, his eyes fixed on the face of his grandfather, who finally reached out to pat his hand. Instinctively, Michael pulled his hand away, but the old man ignored the rebuff. "It's all right. You're safe now. Just try to tell us what happened."

"I was coming home from Eric's," Michael began, letting his voice quaver. "I was coming along the road, and I was looking at our place in the moonlight. And then I heard something. It was a car, and it was coming along the road behind me." He fell silent, as if the memory was too frightening to talk about.

"Go on," his mother said gently. "What kind of car was it? Did you recognize it?"

Michael hesitated, then shook his head. "I don't think it was from around here. And it was coming real fast." He stared up at his mother. "It—it was almost like they were trying to hit me."

"Oh, no . . ." Janet protested, but Michael bobbed his head.

"I got way over, as far as I could, and pedaled faster. I thought maybe I could make it to our driveway, but I couldn't. And then, when it was right behind me, they honked their horn, and I skidded off the road."

"You mean they hit you?" Janet asked, the color draining from her face.

Michael swallowed, but shook his head. "Unh-unh. But then the car slowed down, and I got scared. So I climbed over the fence and hid in the field across the street from our house. And when the car came back, I started running."

"But honey, they were probably looking for you to see if you were all right."

"Maybe—maybe they wanted to kidnap me," Michael suggested, his eyes wide. "Anyway, I didn't even try to go back for the bike. I just started running across the field, but I kept falling and got my clothes all messed up." He looked uncertainly from his mother to his grandfather, then back to his mother again. "Are—are you mad at me?"

Janet hugged him close. "Mad at you? Honey, why would I be mad at you? It was just an accident, that's all. I'm sure no one was trying to run over you, or hurt you at all."

"But—"

"Shh," Janet said. "There isn't any reason why anyone would want to hurt you. You just had a bad fright, that's all. And I think the best thing you can do is go upstairs, take a nice hot bath, then go to bed. By morning you'll have forgotten all about this."

"But what about my bike?" Michael protested.

"Your bike?"

"It's still out there. It got all tangled in the fence, and I was so scared, I just left it there."

"We can get it in the morning," Amos told him. "Now, do what your mother says, and get on upstairs."

"But not before you give your grandmother a kiss," Anna suddenly interrupted. All through the conversation, she had sat in silence, her hands folded in her lap, her eyes shifting constantly between her husband and her grandson. But now she held her arms up, and Michael moved to her side. She wrapped her thin arms around him, and drew him close, so close her lips were at his ear, as if she were going to kiss him. "It's all right," she whispered. "I don't know what happened tonight, but I'll make him believe whatever you say." Then she kissed him on the cheek and released him.

As Michael straightened up, he looked at his grandmother in puzzlement. She knew he had lied. Was she going to tell on him? And then he understood the rest of her words. She was not going to tell on him. Instead, she was going to back him up. Without thinking, he smiled at her. "I love you, too, Grandma," he whispered, just loud enough for her to hear. Then he turned to his mother. "Mom? Can Shadow sleep in my room tonight?"

Janet smiled and nodded her head. "All right. But just tonight."

His face wreathed in smiles, Michael dashed to the back door and pulled it open. "Shadow! Come on, boy!" Instantly, the big dog loped into the kitchen, then paused to peer suspiciously at the three people who sat around the table. As Michael left the kitchen to go upstairs, the dog hesitated only a second before following. When the boy was out of earshot, Amos spoke.

"I don't like that, Janet. Dogs belong outside. Particularly that dog."

"Oh, Amos, it's only for one night," Janet replied. "Besides, the dog is crazy about Michael. He never leaves his side."

"But we don't know where it came from. For all we know, it could be sick."

"Shadow?" Janet asked. "Amos, that's one of the healthiest-looking dogs I've ever seen. But if it'll make you feel better, I'll tell Michael to make him sleep on the floor."

"I'll tell him myself," Amos said. "As soon as he's in bed, I'll go up."

"I'm *not* lying," Michael protested. He was in bed, the covers drawn tightly up around his neck as if they could protect him from the anger he could see in his grandfather's eyes.

Amos sat on the edge of the bed, and in the corner, his ears up and his eyes alert, Shadow crouched watchfully, his tail curled around his feet, its tip twitching dangerously.

"No one would try to run you down, and no one would try to kidnap you," Amos said once more. "And you didn't just fall off your bicycle, did you?" He spoke in a low voice, his eyes steady on the frightened boy in the bed. "Tell me the truth, Michael," he went on. "Sooner or later, you'll have to tell me the truth."

"If you tell them the truth, you will die."

Nathaniel's words rang in his head, and Michael squirmed further into the bed. "But that *is* the truth," he whispered. "I wouldn't lie to you, Grandpa. Really, I wouldn't."

Amos's hand came up, and Michael was certain his grandfather was about to strike him. But then, from the corner, came a low snarl. Startled, Amos glanced over at Shadow. The big dog was on his feet now. His ears no longer stood up, but were flat back against his head, and his whole body seemed to be a mass of tension. Only when Amos lowered his upraised hand did the dog begin to relax.

"I'm not lying," Michael said once more.

But Amos seemed to have forgotten everything except the dog. "Where'd he come from?" he asked. From his tone Michael knew the old man wasn't asking him a question, so he didn't try to answer it. Then Amos's eyes shifted back to Michael. "We're going to have to get rid of him, you know. If his owner doesn't turn up, we're going to have to get rid of him."

"Why?" Michael demanded. Suddenly, with Shadow threatened rather than himself, he sat up in the bed, the covers falling away from his chest. "Why can't I keep him?"

"I don't like dogs," Amos told him.

"But he's mine! He saved my life, and he's mine!"

"No, he's not. He's a stray, and he doesn't have a home. And tomorrow, if his owner doesn't show up, I'm going to get rid of him."

"No!" Michael's head was suddenly pounding, and his eyes blazed with fury.

Amos's voice dropped dangerously. "Don't argue with me, boy. You know I won't be argued with."

Shadow, sensing the menace to his master in the old man's voice, rose to his feet again, his fangs bared; his snarl barely audible.

For a moment there was dead silence and then, as the dog and the old man watched each other with wary eyes, the tension in the room was broken by a tapping at the door. A moment later Janet stepped inside. Shadow instantly dropped back to the floor, resting his muzzle on his forepaws.

"Is everything all right?" Janet asked.

Amos rose to his feet. "Everything's fine. I was just saying goodnight." He reached down and patted Michael's shoulder. "See you in the morning. And remember what I said." Then he was gone, and Michael and Janet were alone, except for Shadow, who rose and padded over to the bed. As Janet lowered herself to the spot that Amos had just vacated, the big dog rested his head in her lap, and his large eyes gazed up at her.

"He wants you to scratch his ears," Michael said. Janet tentatively touched the animal's ears, and his tail began wagging. Smiling, Janet scratched harder, and the big dog wriggled with pleasure. As her fingers continued to play over the dog's fur, she turned her attention to Michael.

"Does it hurt?"

Michael shook his head. He looked uncertain for a moment, then once more shook his head. "Grandpa didn't believe me."

Janet frowned. "Didn't believe you? What do you mean?"

"He didn't believe someone almost ran over me. And he wants to kill Shadow."

"Michael, what are you talking about?"

"He says we have to get rid of Shadow. We don't, do we? I can keep him, can't I?"

"But what if his owner shows up?"

"He won't," Michael said. "I think he's a stray. Besides, he saved my life. I can keep him, can't I? You won't let Grandpa hurt him, will you?"

"Of course not," Janet assured him. "And if no one shows up to claim him, you can keep him. You may not be able to keep him in the house until we move into our own place, but he won't mind staying outside. Will you, Shadow?"

Shadow sat down and raised one paw, which he offered to Janet. Solemnly, the dog and the woman shook hands. "See?" Janet asked Michael. "We just made a deal. After tonight, Shadow will sleep outside 'til we get moved. Then all three of us will share the house. Now, what do you mean, Grandpa didn't believe you? You mean he didn't believe someone tried to run over you?"

Michael nodded.

"Well, maybe he's right. In fact, he probably is. I'll bet the car was going much slower than you thought, and when you fell off your bike, they just stopped to make sure you were all right."

"But—"

Janet put a gentle finger to his lips. "Hush." She tucked the covers snugly around him. "Now, why don't you tell me all about the foaling. Was it interesting?"

A few moments later Michael was excitedly talking about the birth of the colt, describing in detail everything that had happened, everything that he and Eric had done.

"Well, it all sounds fascinating," Janet said when he was done. She stood up, then tucked the covers around her son, and leaned down to kiss him goodnight. "Now you just think about all those things you learned tonight, and in a few minutes you'll be sound asleep. By tomorrow morning, you'll have forgotten all about your accident." She started toward the door, but Michael's voice stopped her.

"Mom?"

She turned back.

"Mom, Aunt Laura had her baby tonight, didn't she?"

Janet frowned. "How did you know that?"

"I—I saw Dr. Potter go into Ryan's house. And I saw Grandpa's car there, too." He fell silent for a moment, then his brow furrowed. "Mom, did something happen to the baby?"

Janet returned to the bed, and sat down again. "What makes you ask a question like that?"

"Did it?" Michael pressed.

For a moment Janet wondered how to explain to Michael what had happened, then decided to face the question head on. "It was born dead, honey," she said quietly. "Those things happen sometimes. It's called a miscarriage, and all kinds of things can cause it. For your Aunt Laura, it was probably a blessing in disguise."

"Why?"

"Well, sometimes things go wrong with babies, and they just don't develop right. That's what happened to Aunt Laura's baby. Her miscarriage was just nature's way of correcting a mistake." Suddenly she frowned. "How did you know Aunt Laura had her baby tonight?"

Michael hesitated only a moment before shrugging. "I don't know. I guess Mrs. Simpson must have told me."

"All right." Once again Janet kissed her son goodnight. Then she went to the door of his room, turned to smile at him one last time, and switched off the light.

For a long time, Michael lay in the darkness, thinking.

Aunt Laura's baby hadn't been born dead.

He knew it hadn't, because Nathaniel had told him so. . . .

CHAPTER 12

"What am I supposed to say?" Michael asked anxiously as Janet pulled Amos Hall's Olds into the Shieldses' driveway.

"You probably won't have to say anything at all," Janet replied. "You can talk to Ryan while I talk to Aunt Laura. She's in bed, and you won't even have to go upstairs."

Relieved, Michael got out of the car and started across the lawn, his mother behind him. Then, as they mounted the steps to the porch of the white clapboard house, the front door opened and Buck Shields appeared, weariness etching haggard lines around his eyes. He nodded a greeting to Michael, then turned to Janet.

"Thanks for coming," he said. "She's upstairs in our room, the first one on the left."

Janet slipped her arms around her brother-in-law. "I'm so sorry," she whispered. "I wish I'd been here—"

"There was nothing you could have done." There was a flat lifelessness in Buck's voice that wrenched at Janet, and she had to turn her head away as her eyes flooded with tears. Brusquely, Buck extricated himself from her embrace. "Go on upstairs. She's waiting for you. I've got to get down to the store." An uncharacteristic grin played at the corners of his mouth. "My mother's looking after it. She means well, but she never quite manages to make things add up. Can you stay with Laura 'til I get back?"

"Of course," Janet assured him. "I can stay all day, if you need me." Her eyes fell on Michael, who was fidgeting near the front door. "Where's Ryan?"

"Out back, I think. Somewhere around, anyway." He started down the steps, then turned back. "Janet. Laura's—well, she's taking this hard. Don't upset her." Then, before Janet could reply, he hurried down the steps and across the yard. A moment later, he was gone.

As Michael headed around to the backyard, Janet went directly upstairs. She found Laura propped up against some pillows, her pale face framed by her dark hair, her eyes closed.

"Laura?" Janet whispered. "Are you awake?"

Slowly Laura's eyes came open, and she stared at Janet as if she didn't recognize her. Then a soft smile came over her face. "Janet? Janet, is that really you?"

Janet moved across the room, pulling a small chair close to the bed. "Who were you expecting?"

Laura's smile faded away. "Nobody, really," she said. "I've just been lying here, trying to pretend nothing happened." Her eyes met Janet's. "Did you do that when Mark died? Try to pretend it hadn't happened?"

Janet hesitated, then nodded. "It's shock, I suppose. You can't handle the pain, so you deny the injury. But all it does is postpone it." She paused, then: "Do you want to talk about it?"

A sigh escaped Laura's lips, and she turned her face away from Janet to stare at the wall. "I think they killed my baby, Janet," she whispered as her resolve to believe what she'd been told slipped away. "They said it was born dead, but I think they killed it."

Janet's mouth opened, but no words came out. Then, a moment later, she felt Laura's hand in her own.

"Why do they do that, Janet?" Laura continued. "Why do they kill my babies?"

The agony in Laura's voice wrenched at Janet. "Laura. Oh, Laura, you mustn't even think such a thing."

Laura's head turned once more, and Janet could see the tears that streaked her cheeks. "But it was all right, Janet. I *know* it was all right. They said it was born dead, but right up till the end, I could feel it moving." Her voice began to rise, and her grip on Janet's hand tightened. "I could feel it, Janet. If it had been dead, it wouldn't have moved, would it? Would it?"

Janet wondered what to say, wondered if she ought to call Buck or Dr. Potter. "I—I don't know," she said at last. "But sometimes things happen, Laura. Sometimes things go wrong, and there's nothing anybody can do."

Seeming to calm slightly, Laura let her head fall once more onto the pillows, and now her eyes fixed on the ceiling. When she spoke again, her voice was dull. "They wouldn't let me go to the hospital. They wouldn't take me to the hospital, and they wouldn't let mother come. I begged them, but they wouldn't let her come."

"She wouldn't have been able to do anything," Janet said, trying to soothe the distraught woman. "I know how horrible it must have been for you—"

Suddenly the fire came back into Laura's eyes, and she sat straight up in the bed. "Do you?" she demanded, her voice once more rising toward hysteria. "How can you know? Have you ever lost a baby? Have you ever been through what I went through last night? Have you?"

And once again Janet's childhood memory flashed through her mind. But it hadn't been a baby she had lost. It had been her whole family, burning before her very eyes. But she couldn't tell Laura about that, not now.

"N-no—" she stammered.

"Well, just wait, then. Just wait 'til your baby comes. They'll do it to you, too, Janet. Just like they did it to mother when her last baby came. They didn't let mother go to the hospital, either. And they won't let you! When your time comes, you'll be all alone, and they'll do what they want, and you won't be able to do anything about it. Then you'll know how I feel!"

Exhausted, she fell back onto the pillows, and her breathing became a strangling sob. Janet, on her feet now, glanced frantically around the room, her eyes finally alighting on a small vial of pills on the dresser. She picked them up and read the label, but the complicated name of the drug meant nothing to her. She took them to the bed. "Laura? Laura, do you want one of these?"

For a long time Laura was silent, and Janet began to wonder if she'd fainted. Then, once more, her eyes opened, and she stared at the bottle. Finally she shook her head. "No." She hesitated, then reached out to Janet. "I'm sorry," she said. "I shouldn't have said all those things. I must have sounded crazy. It was all just so terrible last night, Janet. It hurt so much, and I was so frightened and confused, and I knew they were killing the baby but I couldn't stop them. I couldn't stop them, Janet." Quietly, she began to cry. "I saw what happened," she repeated brokenly. "I saw it." Then her sobbing overcame her, and Janet took her in her arms, rocking her gently as if Laura herself were the baby she'd just lost.

Michael found Ryan behind the garage, desultorily stacking a pile of split logs. "Whatcha doing?"

Ryan glanced up, then stared openly at the scratches on Michael's face. "What happened to you?"

"I—I fell off my bike. Whatcha doing with the wood?"

"What's it look like? My dad says I have to get all this wood stacked by tonight. Wanta help?"

Michael shrugged, and picked up a piece of wood. Beneath it, something moved, and he immediately dropped the wood back on the pile. "Something's under there."

"Prob'ly a lizard," Ryan told him. "I caught three so far."

"How do you catch 'em?"

Ryan grinned. "Easy. You just hold real still, and pretty soon they think you're gone, so they come out to lie in the sun. Then you put your hand out real slowly, and sneak up behind them, and grab 'em. Wanta try it?"

"Sure."

Cheerfully abandoning work, Ryan picked a likely-looking spot and lowered himself onto a log, Michael taking up a position beside him. For a few minutes, the two of them sat silently.

"Can we talk?" Michael finally asked.

Ryan gave him a sidelong glance. "What about?"

"I mean, will the noise scare the lizards away?"

"Nah. They're deaf." Then: "How long'd the foaling take last night?"

"A long time," Michael bragged. "I didn't go to bed 'til real late." He hesitated, wanting to tell Ryan what had happened the night before, but Nathaniel's strange words still lingered in his mind: *"Never tell them the truth. Tell them what they want to hear."* But Nathaniel hadn't been talking about Ryan, had he?

Michael decided he had not: in his eleven-year-old mind, "them" meant "adults." It was grown-ups you had to keep secrets from, not other kids. "I—I think I saw Nathaniel last night."

Ryan turned to stare at him. "Nathaniel? The ghost?" His tone clearly betrayed his disbelief.

"I think so." Again Michael hesitated. Then: "If I tell you what happened, will you promise not to tell anyone? Anyone at all?"

Ryan regarded him with scorn. "What do you think I am? Besides, who'll I tell?"

"You can't tell anyone."

Ryan shrugged. "Okay. But what's the big deal? There's no such things as ghosts, so you couldn't have seen Nathaniel anyway."

"I didn't say I saw him," Michael argued. "I said I *thought* I saw him."

"Where?" Ryan demanded.

"In—he was in a building."

"What building?"

"A—a barn," Michael hedged.

Ryan's eyes narrowed suspiciously. "Whose barn?" he asked.

"None of your business," Michael said, but when Ryan turned away with an elaborate show of disdain, Michael retreated. "I don't know whose barn it was," he compromised. "But that's where I saw Nathaniel. At least I think I did."

Ryan's curiosity made him face Michael again. "Well, did you, or didn't you?"

"I don't know," Michael said, still not willing to commit himself to telling Ryan everything that had happened. "It was really weird. He—he wanted me to take him outside."

Suddenly something moved in the woodpile, and Ryan tensed, his eyes locked on a dark gap between two logs. Michael fell silent, and a few seconds later, the movement was repeated. Then, slowly, the pointed scaly nose of a small lizard appeared, its tongue darting out every few seconds.

"Don't move," Ryan warned. "If you move, it'll run away." There was a long silence as both boys concentrated on the lizard, while the wary reptile, as if sensing the danger, stayed where it was. "What do you mean, he wanted you to take him outside?" Ryan finally asked. "If he wanted to go outside, why didn't he just go?"

"How should I know? He said he couldn't. But then he—well, he just disappeared. I was talking to him, or sort of talking to him—"

"What do you mean, 'sort of'?" Ryan asked, turning his attention away from the lizard and focusing it fully on his cousin. "Did you talk to him or not?"

Michael wondered how to explain it. "He . . . he sort of talked to me without saying anything. It was like he was inside my head or something."

"That's crazy," Ryan declared. "People can't talk that way."

"I know," Michael agreed. "That's what I've been thinking about. Last night I was sure I saw him and talked to him, but now I'm not so sure. Do you think—" He broke off, suddenly sure he knew what Ryan would say if he finished the question.

"Think what?" Ryan pressed.

"Do you think I could have seen a ghost?" he asked, his eyes carefully on the woodpile and away from Ryan.

"There's no such thing as ghosts," Ryan repeated, but with a little less assurance than he'd had earlier.

"I know," Michael agreed. "And last night, I was sure he was real. But this morning, I'm not sure. It's weird."

"*You're* weird," Ryan replied. Suddenly he froze. "Wait a minute. Here comes one. Hold still."

Out of one of the gaps in the woodpile, a lizard appeared, moving slowly, almost as if it were under water. As Michael watched in fascination, its legs began to move, one by one. The tongue, flashing out every few seconds, seemed to be sensing the environment. Once, the lizard froze for a moment, and Michael was sure it was about to scurry back into the dark shelter from which it had come. But instead it started moving in a series of short darts, coming finally to rest on the top of a log, basking in the full sun. Its head was pointed away from the two boys. Michael felt Ryan stir.

"I'm gonna try for him," Ryan whispered. "Hold real still."

Moving as slowly as the lizard had, Ryan began bringing his hand forward, keeping it low down, out of the creature's line of sight. Each time the lizard tensed, Ryan froze, waiting until the lizard relaxed once more before resuming his furtive movements toward it. Finally, when he was only a few inches from the lizard, he made his move.

"Gotcha!" he crowed, cupping his hand over the wriggling animal. A second later, he grinned at Michael. "Wanta hold him?"

"Sure." Michael held out his hand, and Ryan carefully transferred the lizard from his fist to Michael's. For a few seconds it wriggled furiously against Michael's confining fingers, then lay still. Michael looked up at Ryan. "It stopped wiggling. Is it dead?"

"Naw. Open your hand real carefully, and take it in your fingers. Grab it right behind the front legs. If you grab it by the tail, it'll just take off, and grow another tail."

While Ryan supervised, Michael slid a finger into his still-closed fist, feeling around until he was sure he had the lizard trapped between his palm and the finger. Then he opened his fist, and picked up the little creature with two fingers. Its scaly back was the color of wood bark, and there were tiny claws at the end of each of its toes. But when he turned it over, its belly flashed an iridescent blue in the sunlight.

"Wanta hypnotize it?" Ryan asked.

Michael looked dubiously at his cousin. "How?"

"Just hold it upside down and rub its belly a couple of times."

Michael hesitated, then did as Ryan had told him. As he watched, the lizard's torso seemed to arch, and its eyes closed.

"Now put him down."

Carefully, Michael laid the lizard on a log, then stroked its belly a few more times. Finally he drew his finger away. The lizard stayed where he'd left it, its eyes closed, only a faint movement in its throat indicating that it was still alive.

"How long'll it stay that way?"

Ryan shrugged. "A few minutes. You can keep it that way forever, if you rub its belly again every time it starts to wake up. Except if you leave it in the sun too long, it'll get too hot and die." The two boys watched the lizard for a few minutes. Then, without warning, its eyes blinked open. It flipped itself over and disappeared back into the safety of the woodpile.

"Ryan?" Michael asked a few minutes later as the two of them once more began stacking the wood neatly against the back wall of the garage. "Do you think I really could have seen a ghost last night?"

Ryan looked at him disgustedly. "No."

"Then what did I see?"

"I don't think you saw anything," Ryan said. "And I don't want to talk about it anymore."

"But I *did* see something!"

"Bull!" Ryan exploded. "You didn't see anything, and you didn't go into any old barn, and you're just making all this up. All you did was fall off your bike, and now you're trying to make it sound like it wasn't your fault, 'cause you saw a ghost. Well, I don't believe you, and none of the other guys will, either. So if you don't shut up, I'm gonna tell my dad you went into old man Findley's barn. Then you'll really be in trouble."

Michael's eyes blazed with sudden anger. "You said you wouldn't tell anyone! You promised. Besides, I never said it was old man Findley's barn."

"So what?" Ryan sneered. "How was I supposed to know you were going to start trying to con me with a bunch of bull? And I can say anything I want to anyone I want to, so you just better watch out."

Michael fell silent. His head was throbbing with pain, and deep within his mind he thought he could hear a voice whispering to him, urging him to strike out at Ryan. Then, vaguely, he remembered the other day, when he'd suddenly told Ryan to drop dead, and for a moment—just for a second, really—he'd actually thought it was going to happen. He struggled to control himself, afraid of what might happen now if he gave in to that voice inside him, and at the same time knowing that if he kept talking about what he had seen the night before, Ryan would only accuse him of being crazy. But as he went on helping his cousin stack the wood, he kept thinking about the night before. And the more he thought about it, the more everything he'd seen and heard in the darkness began to seem like a dream.

And yet, he *had* seen lights in the field, and he *had* gone into Findley's barn.

He had seen a car, and he had seen someone in the light of the lanterns.

But had he seen Nathaniel?

And how could he have seen what was happening in the field? It had been so dark, and he'd been looking through a crack in the wall of a barn.

And that voice, the voice he thought was Nathaniel's.

It had been so strange, so flat. Had he really heard it at all?

He tried to picture it all in his mind: the blackness of the barn and the faint traces of silvery moonlight that had filtered through the wall.

How *could* he have seen anything? And he hadn't, he realized, really heard anything. That voice had been in his head, like the voice he had heard just now. Besides, he'd had a headache that night, and he could never quite remember exactly what happened when he had one of those headaches.

Maybe Ryan was right. Maybe he was crazy.

He decided he wouldn't talk anymore about what had happened last night, not to anybody. Still, he wished he could talk to his dad about it. His father had always been able to help him figure things out, but now he couldn't do that. Nor could he talk to his grandfather. He shuddered as he remembered the beating a couple of days ago—never his grandfather. But maybe his grandmother. Maybe sometime when he was alone with his grandmother, he'd talk to her about it.

Maybe . . .

As soon as Janet and Michael had left the house that morning, Amos had begun calling around Prairie Bend, trying to find Shadow's owner.

No one, however, was missing a dog, nor did anyone respond to Amos's description of Shadow. He hung up the phone after the last call and turned to Anna. "Well, I guess it's a stray. I'm gonna get my gun."

Anna glared at her husband. "You mean you're going to shoot that dog?"

"That's what I mean to do," Amos replied, his voice grim.

"No."

Amos turned baleful eyes on his wife. "What did you say?"

"There's no reason to shoot it. What's it done to you?"

"I don't like dogs."

"Sometimes I don't like you, either," Anna retorted, her voice low but steady. "Does that mean I should shoot you?"

"Anna—"

"It's not your dog, Amos. It's Michael's dog. It may have saved his life, and if you do anything to that animal, Michael will never forgive you. Your daughter hates you, and your son ran away from you. Do you want your grandson to hate you, too?"

"He'll never know," Amos told her. "By the time he gets home, the dog will be dead and buried. We'll tell him it ran away. He'll believe us."

"He might," Anna agreed. "He might believe us if we both told him that, but if you tell him the dog ran off, and I tell him you shot it, who's he going to believe?"

Amos's eyes hardened. "You wouldn't do that, Anna. You've never gone against my wishes, and you won't now."

"I will," Anna told him, folding her hands in her lap. "This time I will. You leave that dog alone."

Amos left the house without another word, but he felt his wife's eyes on him as he crossed the yard to the barn.

His wife's eyes, and Shadow's eyes.

The dog was curled up next to the back porch, his habitual post when Michael either was in the house or had left him behind. When the kitchen door suddenly swung open, and Amos's heavy tread struck the porch, Shadow's body tensed, and a vaguely menacing sound rumbled from his throat. His hackles raised slightly, but he made no move to get up. Amos regarded the dog with angry eyes.

"Get out of here," he said. He drew his right foot back, then swung it forward. Before the kick could land, Shadow had leapt to his feet and moved a few yards from the house. Amos followed him.

A yard at a time, Shadow backed away toward the barn. Amos kept steady pace with him, softly cursing at the dog, constantly trying to land one of his boots on Shadow's flank. But each time he lashed out with his foot, Shadow dodged away from him.

Suddenly the barn was between them and the house, and Shadow stopped backing away. He crouched low to the ground, and his ears lay back flat against his head. His snarl was loud now, and to Amos it appeared that a cunning had come into the animal's eyes.

Amos tried one more kick.

This time, Shadow made no attempt to leap away from Amos's foot. Instead, he seemed to wait until the last possible instant, then whipped his body to one side, at the same time twisting his neck so he could clamp his massive jaws down on Amos's ankle. With a lunge, he threw Amos off balance, and the big man fell heavily to the ground, grunting in a combination of pain and anger. In another second Shadow had abandoned his grip on Amos's ankle, and was at his throat, his fangs bared, saliva glistening on his tongue. For a long moment, Amos stared into the animal's eyes, only inches from his own, sure that those sharp canine teeth were about to begin slashing at him.

But it didn't happen. Instead of attacking Amos, Shadow suddenly moved forward, raising his leg.

A stream of hot yellow fluid spurted over Amos, drenching his shirt front, stinging his eyes, gagging him as some of it penetrated his mouth to trickle down his throat. And then, when he was through, Shadow moved off to sit on the ground a few feet away, his tail curled around his legs, his ears up, his tongue hanging from his open mouth.

Enraged, Amos lay still for a moment, then rose to his feet and started toward the house. But when he emerged a few minutes later, one hand gripping his gun, the yard was empty.

Shadow had disappeared.

CHAPTER 13

The weeks passed quickly. Janet spent her time working on the little farmhouse that she was fast coming to think of as home. Prairie Bend itself was also becoming home, giving Janet a sense of belonging she hadn't felt since her childhood.

The village seemed to be making a project of her little farm. Every day, as she and Michael worked on the house, people dropped by. Some of them came to work, some of them came bearing supplies.

"Found this linoleum out in the shed. Just been sitting there for a couple of years now. Do me a favor and use it before it rots."

"Got an old wood-electric the missus won't use anymore. Think you might be able to find a place for it? It's not much, but it should last a year or two."

"Thought I'd use this lumber to build a new hog-shed, but I found a prefab I couldn't pass up. Maybe you can use it to brace up that old cyclone cellar. Fact is, I've got some time, and I could show you how it's done." That man spent the rest of the day and half of the next rebuilding her storm cellar with his own lumber, and acted as if she was doing him a favor by "getting him away from work for a couple of days."

And so it went. With each day Janet came to feel more a part of the community, came to feel the closeness of the people in Prairie Bend.

For Michael, though, it was a difficult time. He'd searched everywhere for Shadow, but been unable to find even a trace of the dog. The shepherd seemed to have vanished as mysteriously as it had appeared. Every day, Michael asked his grandfather what had happened, and every day, Amos told him the same thing: "That's the way with dogs. They come and they go, and you can't count on them. Be glad that pain-in-the-neck beast's gone." But Michael was not glad, and no matter how Janet tried to cheer him up, his low spirits persisted.

Amos Hall pulled his Olds to a halt just before the driveway and waved the truck past him. That morning, the moving van had arrived from New York. Finally, after much delay and frustration, Janet and Michael were going to move into their own house. From the back seat, Amos heard Janet's sigh of satisfaction.

"Just look at it," she said. "It's perfect—just perfect."

"It did come out nice," Amos agreed. He glanced at Michael, beside him, but the boy remained silent. "We better get on up there before the movers wreck everything," Amos said. He started to put the car in gear, but Janet stopped him.

"No! I want to walk. I want to enjoy every second of it. After all the work, I just want to soak in what we've done. Come on, Michael!"

While the elder Halls drove on up to the house, Janet and Michael strolled slowly, enjoying the crunch of gravel under their feet.

At the top of the newly installed ramp that paralleled the steps to the front porch, Amos and Anna awaited them, and as Janet absorbed the scene, her eyes filled with tears. "I still can't believe it. Last week it was just a poor decaying wreck, and now it's—well, it's everything I ever dreamed of—"

"Except for the fence," Anna interrupted, her brow creasing fretfully as she shifted her gaze from the freshly painted house—white with green trim, just as Janet had wanted—to the remnants of the old fence that still stood as a bleak reminder of what the property had been. "I still think you should have gone ahead and let Buck put it in. Post-and-rail would look perfect here."

"It's not practical," Amos interjected, picking up the argument that he and Anna had been wrangling over for days, and which Janet suspected was about more than a simple fence. "What you need is some barbed wire."

Anna opened her mouth to contradict her husband, but Janet stopped her.

"Let's forget about the fence and go look inside before it gets all cluttered up."

Inside, the dinginess and neglect were gone, replaced everywhere with a bright newness that belied the age of the structure. The off-white paint had, as Janet hoped, given the small rooms a more spacious feeling than had existed before. She moved from room to room slowly, placing furniture in her mind's eye, selecting papers for the walls that would bring the rooms to life while retaining their feeling of coziness.

In the kitchen, a blue-painted table with cane-seated chairs, rescued from someone's attic, sat next to the window, and an old, but serviceable, refrigerator purred next to the wood-electric stove that Janet had already come to love. She patted the imposing hunk of cast iron affectionately.

"I haven't seen one of those since I was a child. I'd have sworn they all wound up in the junkyards years ago."

"Out here we still need them," Anna replied ruefully. "When the power goes, sometimes it seems like it's going to stay gone forever." Then she smiled brightly. "But that's mostly in winter, of course. Until November, it's usually back on in an hour or two."

Suddenly Michael's voice interrupted them, shouting from the backyard. "Mom! Mom, come quick! Look!"

Janet stepped out onto the back porch, with Anna and Amos following behind her. Michael was pointing off into the distance, toward the newly plowed field that stretched away toward the river. Janet's eyes followed her son's gesturing arm, and in a moment she saw it.

It was Shadow, trotting slowly up the field, his tongue hanging out of his mouth, his tail low to the ground.

"Shadow!" Michael yelled. "It's Shadow, Mom! Come on, boy. Come on, Shadow!"

The dog's tail came up and began waving like a banner in the breeze. His trot gave way to a dead run, and he charged up the field, barking wildly. A moment later he'd vaulted the fence separating the field from the barnyard and then was on top of Michael, knocking him off his feet, putting his forepaws firmly on the boy's chest while he licked his face.

As Janet watched the scene in the yard, she heard Anna's voice behind her. "So he ran away, did he? Gone for good, was he?" Then, for the first time, Janet heard her mother-in-law chuckle. "I think I like that dog. Yes, I think I do."

Amos, however, made no reply to his wife's remarks. Instead, he simply turned and wordlessly went back into the house.

A few minutes later, with Shadow on his heels, Michael burst excitedly into the kitchen. "Can I take him upstairs, Mom? I want to show him my room." Then he paused and cocked his head. "Mom? Can we sleep here tonight?"

"Of course," Janet replied. "Where else would we sleep? This is our home now."

"Oh, but how can you, dear?" Anna protested as Michael and Shadow pounded up the stairs. "There's still so much to be done. You don't want to try to live in the middle of all the unpacking, do you?"

Janet stopped her with a gesture. "Anna, if you were in my place, where would you stay tonight?"

Anna hesitated only a moment, then her habitual look of worry gave way to a tiny smile. "If it were me, you couldn't pry me out of here with a crowbar," she agreed. "I'd be up all night, putting things away, and making plans, and driving Amos crazy." She sighed as they reached the bottom of the stairs, and looked wistfully up toward the second floor, but said nothing about the fact that there was, at present, no way for her to get there. Then, after a moment, she smiled again. "It's a nice little house, isn't it?" she asked of no one in particular. "Such a shame, the condition it had gotten into. All those years, just standing here. And we let it go, too, of course."

Janet, who was already halfway up the stairs, paused and turned back to face her mother-in-law. "It wasn't you who let it go," she said, her voice low and her expression serious. "It was Mark."

Anna seemed to recoil from Janet's words, her right hand reflexively coming up to flutter at her bosom, her eyes clouding over. "Why, Janet, what on earth do you mean?"

Janet hesitated, wondering what exactly she *had* meant by her words. Indeed, she hadn't meant to say them at all. They had just slipped out, unbidden and unconsidered. And yet, as she thought about it, she realized she meant the words, realized that during the past weeks, as she'd worked so hard to restore the house to what it had once been, she'd begun to resent Mark's neglect of the place and, more and more, come to resent Mark himself. Mark, who had lied to her. A feeling had grown inside her that the past was not the only thing Mark had hidden from her and that as she began going through his papers—all the files he'd kept locked away in his office at the university, but that were now packed in cardboard cartons in the little parlor at the front of the house—she'd find more hidden things, find another Mark, one he'd kept as well hidden as this farm, whom she'd never known and wasn't at all sure she wanted to meet. And yet for Anna, there was no hidden Mark. There was only a memory of the boy who had been her son and who had run away from her, who had finally come home only to be taken cruelly from her. How could she talk to this woman who had suffered so, about her own dark feelings?

"Nothing," Janet finally said. "Nothing at all, really. It's just that I don't want you to feel bad about the condition the house was in. After all, you gave it to Mark, didn't you? So it wasn't really your responsibility."

"But Mark was our son," Anna replied. "Everything he was or did was our responsibility, wasn't it?"

Janet met the older woman's intense gaze for a moment, wondering what, if anything, to say. Then, at last, she turned silently away, and continued on up to the second floor.

"It's perfect," Janet repeated an hour later when they were all gathered together again in the little parlor. Her eyes moved from Amos to Anna and then back again. "How can I thank you? How can I ever thank you for all you've done?"

"You don't have to," Amos Hall told her. "We did it because we belong to you, and you belong to us. You're ours, Janet. You must never forget that."

Janet returned her father-in-law's smile. "I won't," she whispered. "You can be sure I won't."

And then, with her son, Janet Hall was alone in her house.

It was late in the afternoon when Janet looked out the kitchen window and, for the first time, saw Ben Findley. He was in his barnyard, throwing feed to the chickens, and as Janet watched him he suddenly looked up, as if he'd felt her eyes on him. A moment later, he turned abruptly and disappeared into his house, and Janet heard the slam of his screen door echo like a cannonshot through the stillness of the prairie afternoon.

She stood thoughtfully at the sink for a moment, then made up her mind. "Michael?" she called from the foot of the stairs. "What are you doing?"

"Nothing," Michael called back. "Just sorting out my stuff. Can I use an old blanket for a bed for Shadow?"

"Okay. I'll be back in a few minutes. I just have to run next door."

Without waiting for a reply, she left the house, crossed the yard, and carefully worked her way through the barbed wire fence that separated her property from Findley's. A few minutes later she stood on his collapsing porch, knocking at his front door. When there was no response, she knocked again, more loudly. Again, there was only silence from the interior of the house. Just as she was beginning to think the man had decided to ignore her, the door opened slightly, and Ben Findley peered at her, his face lost in the shadows of his house, his veined eyes cloudy with suspicion.

"Mr. Findley?" Janet asked. "I'm Janet Hall—"

"I know who you are," Ben Findley cut in. "You're Mark Hall's widow."

Janet nodded, feeling faintly foolish. Of course he'd know who she was. She decided to try again. "I live next door, and when I saw you in your yard, I thought it was time we got acquainted."

"Why?"

"Why?" Janet echoed. Of all the possible responses, this was the last she'd expected.

"I didn't ask you to come live there, and where you live is none of my business," Findley said in a harsh, flat voice. "Just because you live next door, don't think that's going to make us neighbors. It's not."

"But I only thought—"

"I don't give a damn what you thought, young woman," Findley growled. "I know how this town is—everybody knowing everybody else's business, and acting real friendly-like. Well, I can tell you, it's bullshit. Pure bullshit, and I don't want no part of it a'tall. Most folks out here have come to respect that, and they leave me alone."

Reflexively, Janet took a step back. "I—I'm sorry you feel that way."

Findley's eyes narrowed, and his lips tightened. "Don't be. I don't want your pity. All I want is to be left alone. That's why I have that fence. It's not only to keep the critters in. It's to keep people out. I notice it didn't stop you, though."

Janet felt the first twinge of anger stab at her. "Mr. Findley, I was just trying to be friendly. We're going to be living next door to each other for a long time, and it just seemed to me that the least we could do is know each other. So I came over to say hello."

"You've said it."

Furious now, Janet glared at the old man. "Yes, I have, haven't I? And though I'm sure it doesn't interest you, Mr. Findley, I already wish I hadn't wasted my time." She turned away and started off the porch, fully expecting to hear the sound of the door slamming behind her. Instead, she was surprised to hear Findley's voice once more.

"Mrs. Hall!"

She turned back. The door was opened wider now. For the first time, she could see the shotgun cradled in Findley's arms. And for the first time, she got a clear look at Ben Findley's face. A shock of recognition surged through her, for what she saw was yet another version of Mark. The deep blue eyes, the strong features, the wavy hair. All of it there, but in Ben Findley, all of it worn and bitter. "My God," Janet breathed. "You're one of us—you're a Hall."

Findley glared at her. "I'm not a Hall," he replied. "We're kin, but I'll not claim to be one of them. I'll not claim to be family with Amos Hall. And if you're smart, you won't, either."

Janet swallowed, determined to control her temper. "Amos has been very good to me, Mr. Findley—"

"Has he, now," Findley growled. "Well, it's none of my business. All I want to tell you is to stay away from here, Mrs. Hall. Stay away from here, and keep that brat of yours away, too."

"Is that a threat, Mr. Findley?" Janet demanded, her voice icy.

"If you want to call it that."

"I do, Mr. Findley. And I can assure you that Michael will not be trespassing on your property. But in the event that he does, I will expect you to confine yourself to sending him home."

"I'll do what I have to do," Findley replied, his voice grim. "I don't like people around this place, and I particularly don't like kids. So you keep your brat to home, and everything will be fine. Is that clear enough for you?"

"Entirely," Janet snapped, boiling with fury at the old man. "I'm sorry to have bothered you. I can assure you it won't happen again."

"I'll count on it," Findley said. The door closed in Janet's face.

Seething with anger, Janet turned away once more, and began walking down Findley's driveway. If he didn't want his fence climbed, then so be it! She would damned well walk all the way down his driveway and along the road, to her own house. Her back held ramrod straight, she marched along, feeling his malevolent eyes boring into her every step of the way. Only when she had reached the road did she pause and turn back to glare once more at the rundown shack the old man was so possessive about. And then, allowing herself the luxury of venting her rage in what she knew was a thoroughly childish way, she raised the middle finger of her right hand in a mock salute.

It was nearly eleven before they decided that the house was finally theirs. Their clothes hung in the closets, what little furniture there was had been placed to Janet's satisfaction, and the kitchenware had been stored away in a manner that, though she insisted it was only temporary, Janet knew would probably never be changed. Their beds, made up with the first bedding that had come to light, awaited them upstairs.

Now the two of them sat at the kitchen table sipping the cocoa Janet had made, while Shadow sprawled contentedly on the floor. "Well, what do you two think?" Janet asked, breaking the comfortable silence that had fallen over them. "Did we do the right thing?"

Shadow's tail thumped appreciatively against the floor, but Michael only glanced up at his mother, then away, his serious eyes roving restlessly over the kitchen. "I guess so," he said at last, but his voice betrayed his uncertainty.

"You don't sound very sure. Is something wrong?"

Michael opened his mouth as if to speak, then closed it abruptly. Puzzled, Janet repeated her question. "*Is* something wrong?"

Michael fidgeted in his chair, suddenly interested in the gummy layer that was forming on the surface of his untouched cocoa. He touched it with his spoon, watching it wrinkle, then reached down and carefully picked it up with his thumb and forefinger. "Ryan's mad at me," he mumbled at last.

Nonplussed, Janet stared at her son for a moment. "Mad at you? But why?"

Suddenly she frowned, as she realized that it had been a while since she had seen Michael with his cousin. On the occasions Janet had been to visit Laura, still weak and bedridden from the stillbirth, Michael had not accompanied her, and she had chosen not to press the point. Now though, her anxiety was aroused. "Did you two have a fight?" she asked.

Michael shrugged. "I—I don't know," he mumbled. Then he looked up at her. "Is it okay if I go to bed now?" Without waiting for a reply, he scurried out of the kitchen, and she heard him hurtling up the stairs to his room. A moment later, Shadow followed his master.

Janet finished her cocoa, then slowly cleaned up the kitchen. At last she wandered through the downstairs rooms of the little house, locking up, and eyeing the mass of boxes that still waited to be unpacked. Finally turning out the lights, she went upstairs, but paused uncertainly outside the closed door to Michael's room. Though no light showed through the crack at the bottom of the door, neither did she hear the regular sound of her son's breath as he slept. She waited a moment, listening carefully, then tapped softly at the door. When there was no answer, she opened the door and peeped in. Michael, still fully dressed, sat on the floor beside the dormer window, staring out into the night. Shadow lay beside him, his big head cradled in the boy's lap.

"May I come in?"

There was no answer, so Janet stepped into the little room, closing the door behind her. She crossed the tiny alcove and joined her son on the floor. She let her eyes follow his and, in the distance, saw the dark outline of Findley's barn silhouetted against the star-filled sky.

She frowned, remembering her conversation with Ben Findley that afternoon, then decided the view had nothing to do with the crotchety old man. "It's beautiful, isn't it?"

"I like it," Michael replied in a neutral voice.

"Would you like to tell me what happened between you and Ryan?"

"He didn't believe me," Michael said. "He said I was crazy."

Janet's frown deepened. "Didn't believe you about what?"

Michael turned, his eyes searching his mother's face in the gloom. "I saw something that night," he said, and Janet knew instantly the night he was referring to.

"You mean something besides the car that almost ran over you?"

Michael nodded.

"I see," Janet said. "Would you like to tell me what you saw?"

Michael shrugged. "You won't believe me either. It sounds crazy."

"Try me," Janet offered, gently stroking Michael's hair.

"Never tell them the truth."

The words resounded through Michael's mind, and though he tried to ignore them, he couldn't. He wanted to tell his mother what he remembered, but he *couldn't.* Twice, he opened his mouth to tell her about Nathaniel. Each time, he felt Shadow stiffen under his hands, and thought he heard the dog growl softly. Twice, he closed his mouth without speaking, and felt the dog relax.

Finally, an idea came to him. "I—I think I saw Abby out in the field that night."

"Abby? You mean the ghost Grandpa told you about?"

Michael nodded uncertainly. "I—I think so. Anyway, I saw *something* out there."

"Maybe you only imagine you saw something," Janet suggested, but Michael shook his head.

"But I can't remember it very well anymore." He looked puzzled. "I can *sort* of remember what happened, and *sort* of remember what I saw, but I can't really remember how it *felt* anymore. You know what I mean?"

"Of course," Janet told him. "It's like a dream. You can remember every detail when you first wake up, but then, a minute later, it's gone, and all you can remember was whether it was a nice dream or a bad dream. Is that how it is?"

Michael nodded. "And I had a headache that night. But when I saw—" He hesitated as Shadow tensed, then: "When I saw her, it went away." Shadow's body relaxed. "Ryan thinks I'm crazy." He stared at her now, his large eyes frightened and appealing. "I'm not crazy, am I, Mom?"

Janet got to her feet, thinking hard. He hadn't mentioned having a headache before. Could that be the explanation? She reached down and touched his head, stroking his hair with her fingertips. "Of course you're not crazy. Don't ever think that. You just thought you saw something that wasn't there, that's all. It was probably the headache. They can do that to you, you know. Was it bad?"

Michael hesitated, then nodded. "It was a throbbing in my temples."

"Did you take anything for it? Did you ask Mrs. Simpson for some aspirin?"

"No. I didn't get it 'til I was on my way back to Grandpa's house."

"Have you had headaches like that before?"

Again Michael hesitated before he said, "A few. But they aren't too bad, and they don't last very long."

"Well, that's good, anyway. But I think tomorrow we'll go have a talk with Dr. Potter. Maybe you're just allergic to something in the air. In the meantime, you just get a good night's sleep tonight. All right?"

Michael stood up and switched on the light that hung suspended from the center of the ceiling. The glare from the naked bulb filled the room with a harsh light that made Janet squint, but as her eyes adjusted to the brightness, she studied Michael's face. For a moment, his eyes met hers, then drifted away, back to the window.

"You don't believe me, do you?" he said quietly. "You don't think I saw anything."

Now it was Janet who hesitated, and when she spoke, she chose her words carefully. "I believe you *think* you saw something, and that's what counts."

Then, in an instant, a searing pain slashed through Michael's head, and his eyes, frightened only a second earlier, suddenly turned furious. "I saw him," he shouted, his face twisting into a visage of anger. "I saw him, and I talked to him, and he's my friend. I don't give a fuck what anybody says."

Without thinking, Janet stepped forward and slapped her son across the face. "Michael! Don't you ever speak to me that way!" From the corner of her eye, Janet saw Shadow's hackles suddenly rise and felt a sudden pang of fear. What would she do if the dog decided to defend his master?

But as quickly as it had come, Michael's fury was gone, and as he calmed down, so also did the dog. Dazed, Michael stared at his mother, his left hand massaging his stinging cheek. "What did you do that for?" he asked. "Why'd you hit me?"

"You know why," Janet replied, her voice coldly controlled. "Now go to bed and go to sleep, and we'll forget all about this. But it won't happen again. Is that clear?" Without waiting for a reply, she turned and left Michael alone in his room, pulling the door shut behind her.

Michael, his cheek still stinging from the slap, undressed and then turned off the light. But instead of getting into bed, he went back to the window, staring out into the night, trying to figure out what had happened.

She'd said she believed him, and then she'd slapped him and told him not to talk that way again.

But he hadn't said anything. There'd just been a sudden pain in his head, and then the slap.

Still not sure what had happened, Michael crept into his bed. When Shadow climbed up to join him a moment later, Michael slipped his arms around the big dog, hugging him close. . . .

H*im.* I saw *him.* I talked to *him.*

The words echoed through Janet's mind as she tried to fall asleep, and as she recalled the words, she pictured his face. Her son's clear features had been distorted with rage, his eyes glazed with a fury she'd never seen before.

What had he been talking about? It was Abby he'd insisted he'd seen that night. So who was *he?*

She turned over and closed her eyes, determined to sleep. And yet, sleep would not come.

It was the house, she decided. The strangeness of it, and the emptiness—that was all; that, and her loneliness.

At last, unable to sleep, Janet left her bed and went back to Michael's room. She found him asleep, his face peaceful, one arm flung carelessly over the edge of the bed, the other encircling Shadow's neck. And yet, as she watched his face, she thought she saw something besides peace.

She thought she saw the same loneliness in Michael's face that she herself was feeling.

Gently easing Shadow aside, Janet crept into the narrow bed and gathered Michael into her arms. And then, with her son's head cradled against her breast, she at last drifted off to sleep.

CHAPTER 14

Charles Potter emerged from his office, wiping his hands on a kitchen towel. He smiled at Janet and Michael Hall, who sat side by side on the sofa in the bay window. "My goodness—the whole family today? We're not having some kind of epidemic, are we? Nobody ever tells me anything around here." Then his eyes came to rest on Janet, and his smile faded into an expression of concern. "It's not you, is it?"

"No, no. I'm fine," Janet assured him. "I haven't even had any morning sickness since Monday. It's Michael. He's been complaining of headaches, and I thought you might have a look at him. I—well, I was thinking of allergies, or something."

Potter sniffed disdainfully. "I don't believe in allergies. It's what incompetent doctors diagnose when they can't find out what's really wrong. An allergy is simply an imbalance in the system, and there are remedies for that. Trace elements, we call 'em. Ever hear of homeopathy?"

Janet shook her head.

"Figured you hadn't. Best kept nonsecret in medicine. It's too cheap, and too easy. No money in homeopathy, which is why I'm so poor, I suppose. Well, come on in." Janet stood up and, with Michael trailing her, followed Potter into his examining room.

"What kind of headaches are these, son?" Potter asked when Michael had stripped off his shirt and perched himself on the edge of the examining table. Janet leaned against Potter's desk.

"I don't know. Kind of like a throbbing, I guess."

Potter frowned. "Where? In the front? The back? All over? Just the temples?"

"The temples mostly, I guess. I don't know."

"Well, let's take a look at a couple of things." He wrapped the sleeve of a sphygmomanometer around Michael's upper arm. A moment later he began pumping air into the sleeve, his eyes on the pressure gauge, his stethoscope plugged into his ears. Finally he nodded, grinning. "Guess what? You're not dead."

"Is his blood pressure normal?" Janet asked.

Potter shrugged. "Within reason. It's a little high, but that's not surprising. Has he had any nosebleeds?"

Janet turned to her son. "Michael?"

"No."

"Well, you might," Potter told him. "If you do, it's nothing to worry about. Just apply a cold compress, and take it easy for a while. Let's have a look at your eyes and ears, then hit your funny bones."

Ten minutes later, Potter finished his examination, and Michael, buttoning up his shirt, went back to the waiting room. Potter seated himself behind his desk and made a few notes, then peeled off his glasses. As he absentmindedly wiped the lenses with his fingers, only worsening their condition, he smiled at Janet, who was now sitting opposite him. "All in all, I'd say there's nothing really wrong with him. The blood pressure's a little high, but as I say, that doesn't surprise me. The stress of his father's death could have brought that on. And it, in turn, could exacerbate a headache. Has he ever complained of headaches before?"

"Nothing serious. The usual. I've always given him aspirin, and that's taken care of it. But these seem to be different, in a strange sort of way."

Potter frowned. "Different? How?"

Janet shifted uncomfortably. "Well, I'm not quite sure how to say it. A while ago he had one of the headaches, and apparently he thinks he saw a ghost that night."

Potter stopped mauling his lenses. "A ghost?" he asked, his voice betraying his skepticism.

Janet's brows arched, and she shrugged her agreement with his doubt. "That's what he told me. And he was quite adamant about it. Except that now he can't quite remember what happened. But he says that while the ghost was around, the headache went away, and after the ghost left, the headache came back. But everything that happened seems to be kind of fuzzy in his mind."

"I'll bet," Potter replied. Then his forehead furrowed in thought. "Where'd all this take place?"

"Near our house," Janet told him. "He was out at the Simpsons', and it happened on his way home."

"Hmmm." Potter leaned back in his chair and folded his hands over his midriff. He gazed at the ceiling for a moment, then his eyes came back to Janet. "Maybe I'd better talk to him," he said at last. "Whatever he thinks happened, I'd like to hear it firsthand. Do you mind?"

"Of course not." Janet stood up. "Shall I call him in?"

Potter gave her a conspiratorial smile and a wink. "Why don't you send him in, and let me talk to him alone? Sometimes kids talk more freely if their parents aren't around."

Michael sat stiffly on the edge of his chair, regarding Dr. Potter with suspicious eyes. The familiar throbbing was beginning to play around his temples, but Michael tried to ignore it, concentrating instead on what the doctor was saying.

"You didn't see Abby in the field, did you? You saw something else, and you know what it was you saw. Isn't that right?"

"No," Michael replied. "It was Abby, and she was looking for her children, just like in the story."

Potter shook his head. "No, Michael. There's no such person as Abby Randolph. She died a hundred years ago, and she isn't still here, wandering around looking for anything. So you saw something else. Now, I want you to concentrate very hard and tell me exactly what you saw and where you were."

"I was at our house—"

"Why?" Potter interrupted. "It was the middle of the night, and no one was there. Why did you go there?"

"I *told* you. I saw a light in the field, and I wanted to see what it was."

"And you *did* see what it was, didn't you?" Potter leaned forward, the knuckles of his right hand white as he clutched his glasses. "Didn't you?" he repeated.

Michael's headache worsened, and suddenly his nostrils filled with the strange smoky odor that was becoming as familiar to him as the headaches. And then, as if from far away, he heard the voice.

"He knows."

Michael's eyes widened slightly, and his eyes darted to the corners of the room, even though he knew the voice had come from within his own head. Then the voice, Nathaniel's voice, came again.

"He knows, and he's going to make you tell."

"What is it, Michael?" Potter asked, his voice low. "Is something wrong?"

"N-no," Michael answered. "I just—I just thought I heard something."

"What? What did you hear?"

Michael's head was pounding now, and something seemed to have happened to his eyes. It was as if the office had suddenly filled with fog, except that it wasn't quite like fog. And then he knew. Smoke. The room seemed to have filled with smoke.

"I—I can't breathe. . . ."

Potter rose from his chair and moved around the desk. "What is it, Michael? Tell me what's happening."

"I can't breathe," Michael replied. "My head hurts, and I can't breathe."

Again, he heard the voice. *"He knows. He's going to make you tell. Don't let him. Stop him, Michael. Stop him now!"*

Michael's mouth opened wide, as if he was about to scream, but all that came out was a desperate whisper. "No. Stop it. Please stop it."

"Stop what, Michael?" Potter asked. "What do you want me to stop?"

"Not you," Michael whispered. "Not you. Him. Make him stop talking to me."

Potter grasped the distraught boy by the shoulders. "Who is talking to you, Michael?" he asked, his eyes fixing on the boy. "Who?"

"Nath—"

"No! Do not speak my name!"

"Leave me alone!" Michael wailed. "Please . . ."

Potter released Michael from his grip, and as the boy slumped in his chair, he returned to his desk. Silence hung over the room for a few minutes, and then, when Michael's breathing had returned to normal, Potter finally spoke.

"The barn," he said softly. "You were in Ben Findley's barn, weren't you?"

Michael said nothing and held himself perfectly still, terrified of what might happen if he so much as nodded his head.

"It was Nathaniel you saw, wasn't it?" Potter pressed, his voice low but nonetheless insistent. "You went into Ben Findley's barn, and you saw Nathaniel, didn't you?"

Michael shook his head fearfully. "No," he whispered. "He's not real. He's only a ghost, and I didn't see him. I didn't see him, and I didn't talk to him."

But now it was Potter who shook his head. "No, Michael. That's not the truth, is it? Don't lie to me. We both know what you saw and what you heard, don't we?" When Michael made no reply, Potter pushed further. "He looked like you, and he looked like your father, didn't he, Michael?"

Michael bit his lip and squirmed deeper into the chair. Then, as he offered an almost imperceptible nod, Nathaniel's voice whispered to him, no longer loud, no longer threatening. Now it was soft and gentle, caressing. *"Kill him."*

And suddenly, as Michael watched Dr. Potter while Nathaniel whispered to him, he knew he could do it. If he wished it right now, with Nathaniel there inside his head, Dr. Potter would die.

"No," he whispered. Then, again, "No."

"But you will," Nathaniel whispered. *"You must, and soon. You will. . . ."* The voice trailed off, and Michael's headache faded away. As his vision cleared, he frowned uncertainly at the doctor. "Can I go now?" he asked shyly.

Potter said nothing for a moment, then finally shrugged. "We both know what happened that night, don't we, Michael?"

Michael hesitated, then nodded.

"But you won't talk about it, will you?"

This time, Michael shook his head.

"Can you tell me why not?"

Again, Michael shook his head.

"All right," Potter told him. "Now, listen to me carefully. I know what you did, and I know what you think you saw. But you didn't see anything. Do you understand? You didn't see anything in Ben Findley's barn, and you didn't see anything in the field. It was the middle of the night, and you were tired, and all that happened was that you imagined you saw some things that weren't there. They weren't there, because they couldn't have been there. Do you understand?"

Michael hesitated, then nodded. "I—I think so."

"All right." Potter stood up and moved toward the door, but before he opened it, he turned back to Michael. "And one more thing. From now on, you stay away from Ben Findley's barn. You stay away from his barn, and stay off his property."

Michael gazed up at the doctor. He knows, he thought. He knows about Nathaniel, and he knows what we saw. And now we're going to have to make him die. He turned the strange thought over in his mind, and wondered why the idea of making Dr. Potter die didn't scare him. Then, while he half listened to the doctor talking to his mother, he began to think about something.

Was making someone die the same as killing them?

He thought it probably was, but somehow, deep inside, it didn't feel the same. Making someone die, he was suddenly sure, was different from killing them. He could never kill anyone.

But he could make someone die.

* * *

Janet gazed questioningly at Michael as he emerged from Potter's office, but when he said nothing, her eyes shifted to Potter.

"I don't know," Potter said thoughtfully. "I don't think anything too serious is wrong, but I'd like to think about it and maybe make a couple of calls. Why don't you bring him back tomorrow afternoon?"

A few moments later, after they'd left Potter's house, Michael finally spoke, a fearful note in his voice. "Why did you tell him about—" He hesitated, then finished the question: "Why did you tell him about the ghost?"

"I—well, I was worried about the headaches, and I thought the doctor ought to know what happened when you got them."

"He thinks I'm crazy."

"I'm sure he doesn't—"

"He does too," Michael insisted, his face beginning to redden. "He told me there's no such things as ghosts, and that I couldn't have seen anything out there. Then he wanted me to tell him everything that happened."

"Did you?"

As Michael hesitated, Janet thought she saw a furtive flicker in his eyes, but then he nodded. "What I remember."

They walked along in silence for a few minutes, and Janet had an uneasy sense that Michael had not told Potter all of what he remembered. But before she could think of a way to draw him out on the subject without making him angrier than he already was, she heard someone calling her name. She looked around to see Ione Simpson beckoning to her from in front of the Shieldses' general store.

"Janet, look at this. Isn't it wonderful?" Ione asked as Janet and Michael approached. "Have you ever seen anything like it?"

In the store window, propped up against a galvanized milk can, was an immense Raggedy Ann doll that seemed, somewhere during its lifetime, to have suffered a minor accident. There were a few buttons missing, and one of its shoulders had a tear in it. Looking at it, Janet couldn't help grinning: it was huge and clumsy, and its flaws appeared almost self-induced, as if it had stumbled over its own feet. It was totally irresistible. "It *is* wonderful," she agreed. "But what on earth would you do with it?"

"Peggy," Ione said decisively. Janet stared at her. Peggy, Eric Simpson's two-year-old sister, was only about a third the size of the doll.

"If it fell on her, she'd suffocate," Janet pointed out, but Ione only shook her head.

"I don't care. She'll grow into it. But do you suppose it's for sale? It doesn't look new."

"Well, let's go in and find out," Janet replied. "I've got a whole list of things to get there anyway." With Michael trailing along, the two women entered the cluttered store.

They were greeted by a large matronly woman with a happy face and wide blue eyes, whom Janet recognized but couldn't put a name to.

"Well, now, don't you worry," the woman told them. "You can't be expected to know everybody's name until at least day after tomorrow. I'm Aunt Lulu—Buck's mother? Isn't that terrible, having a name like Lulu at my age? But what can you do? I've been Lulu since I was a baby, and I'll be Lulu when I die. Now, what can I do for you?"

"I have a whole list—" Janet began, but Ione Simpson immediately interrupted.

"The doll, Lulu. The Raggedy Ann in the window."

Aunt Lulu smiled. "Oh, I didn't put that out there to sell it," she explained. "But it's been in the back room too long, and I thought it might be fun to give it some sunshine, do you know what I mean?"

"You mean it isn't for sale?" Janet asked, feeling Ione's disappointment as keenly as if it were her own.

"Why—well—I don't know, really," Lulu stammered. "It's been here for I don't know how long. It was ordered for little Becky—" She hesitated for just a second, her eyes bulging slightly, and then hurriedly corrected herself. "We ordered it for Ryan, but he didn't want it. I don't see how he could have resisted it, do you? Isn't it wonderful? Just wonderful. And almost as big as a real child—"

"It's bigger than the child I want it for," Ione broke in. "I just have to have it for Peggy. Please?"

Lulu's big eyes blinked. "Well—well, I suppose if it's for Peggy, we'll just have to make sure it's for sale, won't we? I'll have to call Buck and find out what the price is. He's at home, you know, taking care of Laura." Suddenly her happy expression collapsed, and her eyes brimmed with tears. "Isn't it a shame about Laura? So close, and then losing the baby like that." She gazed at Janet, then reached out and took her hand. "But of course, you were there, weren't you? While Laura worked all day in that hot sun? And everything was going along so well for a change. Well, we certainly can't blame you, can we? I mean, if you'd known Laura better, you certainly wouldn't have let her work so hard at your place, would you? I told her she should take it easier, but you know Laura—she won't take anybody's word for anything, and her so small she almost died when Ryan was born, and now this has to happen. I just don't know how much more she can take. I just don't."

As Michael began edging away from the teary woman, and Ione looked on in what appeared to be horrified embarrassment, Janet tried to understand what the woman was really saying. Though she'd denied it, was she blaming her for Laura's miscarriage? At last though, Lulu's tears began to abate, and her warm smile spread once more over her round face. She glanced around distractedly, then lowered her voice, even though there was no one else in the store. "I do run on, don't I? Well, it's just something everyone has to put up with from us older women. I was a good wife to Fred, and I never talked back to him, not once. But ever since he's been gone, I've found I just love to talk. I suppose it was all those years of not saying much at all. It all just bottles up, doesn't it?"

Janet smiled weakly, wondering if there was a graceful way to end Lulu's ramblings, when Ione Simpson came to her rescue.

"The doll?" Ione asked. "Could we find out how much the doll is?"

"Oh, you just take it, and anything else you want. I'll keep track of it all, and Buck can tell you some other time how much it all comes to. I don't usually work here, you know," she said, turning to Janet again. "Fred always thought a woman's place was in the home, and until he died, that's where I stayed. I'm afraid Buck thinks the same way as his father did. He only lets me in here when he absolutely can't be here himself, and that's only when Laura's having one of her—"

And once again Lulu Shields fell silent, the last, unspoken words of her sentence hanging on her tongue like wineglasses teetering on the edge of a shelf. But in the end, they didn't fall. Instead, Lulu stepped back from Janet, though her eyes suddenly went to Ione Simpson. "You girls just prowl around and find what you need. All right?"

"Fine," Janet agreed, then turned away to begin her shopping before Aunt Lulu could wind herself up again. Thirty minutes later she and Ione left the store together, their arms filled with packages. Behind them came Michael, totally occupied with coping with the giant Raggedy Ann.

"Do you have a way to get home, or were you planning to haul all this stuff by hand?" Ione asked as they approached her car.

"Well, we were planning to walk, but I hadn't really realized how much there was going to be."

"Say no more," Ione declared. Then she suppressed a giggle. "That's what I should have told Lulu Shields. Isn't she something else? And don't you believe she never said a word to her husband. There's a lot of people around here, me included, who think she talked him into an early grave, and that he wasn't the least bit sorry to go."

The three of them piled into the front seat of Ione's car. Raggedy Ann and the groceries occupied the rear. "You don't suppose she really thinks Laura's miscarriage was my fault, do you?" Janet asked as they left the village behind and started out toward their farms.

Ione glanced at her over Michael's head. "With Lulu, you can count on her not thinking at all. I can't imagine why she said that." Then: "Yes, I can. She didn't think. But she didn't mean anything by it, either, so don't worry about it. She's just a little batty."

"She's weird," Michael said.

Janet frowned at him. "She's just talkative. And don't you dare start to get in the habit of calling people weird." She turned her attention back to Ione. "Who's Becky?"

"Becky?" Ione repeated. "What are you talking about?"

"The girl they bought the doll for. That's what Lulu said before she said they bought it for Ryan."

"I didn't hear that." Ione shrugged. "I'm afraid I don't hear a lot of what Lulu says. I just tune her out after a while." Then her brow furrowed. "Are you sure she said 'Becky'? As far as I know, there aren't any little girls named Becky in Prairie Bend."

"I bet they killed her," Michael suddenly said as Ione turned into Janet's driveway.

Janet stared at her son. "What a terrible thing to say!"

Michael's eyes narrowed. "I bet that's what happened to her. I bet they buried her in Potter's Field."

And then, as the car came to a halt in front of the house and Janet got out, Michael slid off the seat and jumped to the ground. "Is Eric home, Mrs. Simpson?" he asked.

"He's cleaning out the stable—" Ione faltered, shaken by Michael's strange pronouncement.

"I'm gonna go help him. Okay, Mom?"

Janet, as shaken as Ione, nodded her assent, and Michael ran off. They watched him until he'd scrambled through the fence that separated the two farms and disappeared into the Simpson's stable, then began unloading Janet's packages from the back seat of Ione's car.

"What on earth was Michael talking about just now?" Ione asked when they were in the kitchen.

Though her heart was suddenly pounding, and she hadn't the least idea what the answer to Ione's question might be, Janet feigned nonchalance. "Nothing, really. It's probably just an association with that horrible ghost story Amos told him just after we arrived, and the coincidence of names." She smiled weakly. "They used to bury paupers and unknowns in potter's fields, you know."

"Oh, come on, Janet," Ione protested. "There's got to be more to it than that! When was the last time you heard of a graveyard called a potter's field? The term's obsolete! And even so—something like that in Prairie Bend? As far as I know, we've never even *had* a stranger or a pauper here. And the idea of anybody burying a baby out there—well, it sounds crazy!"

Janet sighed heavily, and sank into one of the chairs at the kitchen table. "I know," she agreed. "And I have to confess I'm a little worried." She glanced up, wryly. "In fact, I took him to Dr. Potter this morning." She hesitated.

"Michael's been having some headaches. But the doctor couldn't find anything wrong. He says it's probably all a reaction to Mark's death."

Ione's eyes reflected her chagrin. "Oh, God, Janet, I'm sorry. It was stupid of me not to think of that. I must have sounded just like Lulu Shields. Forgive me?"

Janet smiled. "There's nothing to forgive. But you could do me a favor—"

"Anything!"

"Help me out with Michael. I think he just needs some time to get used to things. He's lost his father, and he's living in a new place, and he hardly knows anyone. And I know how kids can be. They can gang up on someone and make his life miserable."

"And you think that might happen to Michael?"

"Apparently Michael and Ryan Shields had an argument. Ryan already told him he's crazy."

Ione's eyes narrowed as she remembered the boy's odd behavior the night Magic had foaled. "Well, we'll just see to it it doesn't happen with Eric, okay?" She paused for a moment, then: "Janet, I don't want you to get upset, but if you think you'd like Michael to talk to someone, I know a good psychiatrist in Omaha."

"A psychiatrist? Come on, Ione, Michael's just a little boy. He doesn't need—"

"I didn't say he does," Ione interrupted. "But you said yourself he's been through a lot, and sometimes children can have problems their parents aren't even aware of."

Janet looked quizzically at the other woman. "Why does it seem to me unlikely that a farmer's wife in Prairie Bend would be acquainted with a psychiatrist in Omaha?" she asked.

Ione burst into laughter. "Because I'm a nurse, that's why! Not everybody in this town never got out. I got out for eight years. But then I reverted to type, and married the boy next door. Anyway, I know someone in Omaha in case you ever need someone for Michael. Okay?"

Janet hesitated, then offered Ione a small smile. "Okay," she agreed. "And thanks." Suddenly she brightened. "I have an idea. Why don't you come over for supper tonight? All of you. It'll be my first party in my new house, and I can't think of better people to have than my neighbors."

"What about your family?" Ione asked. "Don't you think maybe your first guests ought to be Amos and Anna or the Shieldses?"

Janet considered it, then shook her head. "I'll have Laura and Buck as soon as Laura's better, and Amos and Anna must be sick and tired of me by now. Besides, if it's just the six of us, who's going to know? Or care?"

Ione shrugged. "Okay, if that's the way you want it, it's fine with me." A wry grin came over her face. "But I can tell you one thing: everybody in town is going to know we were your first guests. Mark my words!"

Michael stepped out of the sunlight into the shadows of the Simpsons' barn. "Eric?" he called out. When there was no reply, he went farther into the barn. A soft whinny came from Magic's stall, and Michael paused to pat the big mare's muzzle. "Where's Eric?" he asked, and Magic, almost as if she'd understood the question, pawed at the floor of the stall, neighed loudly, and tossed her head. Michael grinned, then called out his friend's name once again, more loudly this time.

"Back here." Eric's voice drifted faintly from the far end of the barn, and Michael abandoned Magic for the tack room, where he found Eric working with a tangle of leather straps.

"Whatcha doin'?"

"Trying to make a bridle for Whitesock."

Michael frowned. "Who's Whitesock?"

"Magic's colt. He's got one white stocking, so we named him Whitesock. I found this old bridle, and if I can make it small enough, I can start training him."

"Where is he?"

"Out in the pasture behind the barn."

"Can I go play with him?"

Eric shrugged. "I guess so. But he probably won't play very much. Today's the first time he's been away from Magic, and he's kinda skittish."

A few minutes later, Michael was staring over the pasture fence. Just yards away, the colt stared back at him through large, suspicious eyes.

"Hi, Whitesock," Michael said softly, and the colt's ears twitched interestedly. "Come on, boy. Come over here." He reached down and tore up a fistful of grass, then held it out toward the colt. "Want something to eat?"

The colt took a step forward, then quickly changed its mind and backed away. Michael frowned, and shook the grass. The colt wheeled around and trotted across the pasture, then finally stopped to look back at Michael.

Grinning, Michael scrambled through the barbed wire fence and began walking toward the colt, holding the grass out in front of him. "It's okay, Whitesock. It's good. Come on, boy. I'm not going to hurt you."

But when he was still a few yards away, the colt once more bolted and ran off to the far corner of the pasture.

Michael was about to follow the horse once again when he felt something brush against him. He looked down to see Shadow, his tail wagging happily, crouched eagerly at his feet. "You want to help, Shadow?" The dog let out a joyful yelp and jumped to his feet. "Okay, let's sneak up on him. Come on."

Slowly, the boy and the dog approached the colt, and this time Michael was careful to do nothing that might spook the little horse. He moved only a few feet at a time, pausing often to let the colt get used to him. Shadow, seeming to sense what his master was doing, stayed close to Michael, matching his movements almost perfectly.

Finally, when they were only a few feet away from the horse, Michael began speaking quietly, as he'd heard Eric do when he was calming Magic. "Easy, Whitesock. Easy, boy. No one's going to hurt you. Look." Slowly he raised his hand, offering the colt a taste of the grass. "It's food, Whitesock. Come on. Try it."

Michael inched closer, and Whitesock tensed, his eyes fixed on Michael, his right forepaw nervously scraping the ground. Again Michael moved toward the horse, freezing when the colt's head came up and he seemed to be seeking a means of escape.

At last when he was only a foot from the colt, he reached out and gently brushed the grass against Whitesock's muzzle.

And then, from the other side of the fence, Eric's voice broke the quiet Michael had been maintaining. "Hey! Whatcha doing?"

Startled, the colt reared up, his forelegs striking out at Michael. But before the horse's hooves could come in contact with the boy, Shadow had hurled himself against Michael, knocking him to the ground and out of the way of Whitesock's flailing legs. Michael rolled away from the frightened horse, then got to his feet as Whitesock broke into a gallop and dashed across the field, Shadow behind him.

"Shadow!" Michael yelled, and the dog instantly came to a stop, turning to stare back at Michael. "It's okay, boy. Come on. Come back here!" Obediently, the dog began trotting back.

"What were you tryin' to do?" Eric demanded.

"It was your fault!" Michael shot back. "I was just trying to make friends with him. I was giving him some grass, but you scared him when you yelled."

"Well, you shouldn't've been in there at all!"

Stung, Michael glowered at Eric, and his head began to throb with the familiar pain. "You said I could play with him."

"I thought you'd have enough brains to stay out of the pasture. What do you know about horses?"

"I didn't get hurt, did I? And I wasn't even scared!"

"Just get out of the field, and let me take care of him, all right?" Then, ignoring Michael's protestations, Eric climbed through the fence, and holding the bridle in his left hand, started toward the colt.

His headache growing, Michael watched as Eric began working his way toward the colt, weaving back and forth across the field, countering each of Whitesock's moves with one of his own. Slowly, he began trapping the colt in one corner of the field.

Finally, he moved in on the frightened animal and tried to slip the bridle over the colt's head. Whitesock jerked at the last second and avoided the harness straps.

Once again, Eric made a move to bridle the horse, but again Whitesock ducked away at the last second. But this time, instead of trying to move away from Eric, he reared up and struck out. Eric dodged the flying hooves, but tripped and stumbled to the ground.

Horrified, Michael watched as the colt danced for a moment on his hind legs, then came down to glare angrily at Eric, who was rolling away at the same time he was trying to scramble to his feet.

He's gonna kill him, Michael thought. He's gonna trample him. Suddenly his vision blurred, and Michael's senses filled with the smell of smoke. And he heard a voice in his head.

"Kill him."

Obeying the voice without thinking, Michael focused his mind on the colt.

Die, he thought. *Die. Die. Die. . . .*

The colt seemed to freeze for a moment, then with an anguished whinny, rose up once again on his hind legs, his forelegs flailing as if at an unseen enemy. Finally, as Eric got to his feet and began backing away from the terrified colt, Whitesock crumpled to the ground. He lay still, his eyes open, his breathing stopped.

Michael's vision cleared, and his headache faded away. The smoky odor disappeared, too, and all he could smell now was the sweetness of the fresh grass in the pasture. Shadow sat at his feet, whining softly. Michael gazed across the field, unsure of what had happened.

"Eric?" he called. "You okay?"

There was a moment of silence, then Eric turned around to stare at him. "He's dead," Eric said. "He's just lying there, and he's dead."

Michael's eyes shifted from Eric to the colt, and he knew his friend's words were true.

And he also knew that somehow he had done it.

Somehow, while his head was hurting and his vision was blurred, he'd made Whitesock die.

His eyes filling with tears, he backed slowly away.

CHAPTER 15

Supper was over, a supper during which much of the conversation had centered on what had happened in the Simpsons' pasture that afternoon. In the end, though, Leif Simpson had put an end to the discussion. "The colt just died," he had said. "It doesn't really matter much why it died. The point is that if it hadn't, it might have hurt Eric pretty bad. So I guess we might just as well chalk it up to providence. It was God looking after Eric, and that's that."

Michael, who had taken little part in the discussion, said nothing, though he didn't believe what Eric's father had said. He'd thought about it all afternoon, and no matter what anybody said, he knew that somehow he'd made the colt die. He hadn't wanted to—all he'd wanted to do was help Eric—but still, he'd done it.

And he couldn't tell anybody. For one thing, no one would believe him. And he couldn't say how he'd done it, because he didn't know. Sighing inaudibly, he decided it was one more thing he could never talk about.

As Janet and Ione attacked the dishes, the two boys headed upstairs toward Michael's room. But when they came to the landing, Eric stopped, gazing up at the trapdoor to the attic. "What's up there?"

"I don't know," Michael replied, his mind still on the colt. "Nothing, I guess."

"Why don't we go up and look?"

A moment later Michael had dragged a chair from his room and climbed up on it. He was barely able to reach the folding ladder that gave the attic its only access. It creaked angrily as he pulled it down, but when he tested his weight on it, it seemed secure enough. He climbed up and pushed at the trapdoor. It stuck for a moment, then gave way, dropping a shower of dust on him. Michael poked his head through the trapdoor.

"Go down and ask Mom for a flashlight," he told Eric. "It's too dark to see anything."

Five minutes later Eric crowded up behind Michael, flashlight in hand. "Let me see."

"Give me the light," Michael replied. "It's my attic, and I get to look first."

Reluctantly, Eric passed the light over, and Michael switched it on, throwing a weak beam into the blackness of the attic. "Wow," he breathed. "It's all full of old crates." He scrambled up into the attic, and Eric followed. "What do you think's in 'em?"

Eric shrugged in the gloom. "Let's get my dad and bring them down."

Fifteen minutes later, the contents of the attic had been transferred to the living room. There were five crates: old pine boxes held together with hand-forged nails, their boards dry and brittle, shrunken with age. The last thing they brought down was an ancient trunk, and when Leif Simpson had deposited it, too, in the living room, the six of them gathered around, staring at the strange collection. Peggy Simpson, with the curiosity of her two years, was busily trying to open one of the boxes with her stubby fingers.

"Do you have a hammer and screwdriver?" Leif eventually asked. "We'll never find out what's in them if we count on Peg."

Michael found the tools in the kitchen drawer that had already been established as a catchall. "Which one first? The trunk?"

"Let's save it for last," Janet suggested. "Let's do the boxes first."

"They're crates," Michael corrected. "Boxes are made of cardboard."

"Never mind," Janet replied. "Just open them."

One by one, Michael and Eric began prying the lids off the crates. The first one was filled with old china, thin and delicate, with an ornate floral pattern done in pink against a white background.

Janet picked up one of the plates, examining it carefully. "I know what this is," she said. "It's French. My grandmother had some of this." She flipped it over. On the back, faint but distinct, was the Limoges mark.

"It's ugly," Michael pronounced, already beginning to pry at the second crate.

Janet and Ione exchanged a knowing look. "It may be ugly, but it's valuable," Janet said. Then, as she passed one of the plates to Ione, the lid came off the second crate, revealing a cache of battered cookware.

"That's old, but I don't think I'd call it valuable," Leif Simpson remarked, holding up a badly dented tin coffeepot with a hole in the bottom. "Why would anyone keep this?"

In the third crate there was a wooden toolchest, bereft of its contents, and the fourth produced a mass of old linens, rotted with age, which crumbled in their hands as they tried to pick them up. Finally Michael pried the lid off the fifth crate.

"My God," Janet whispered. "Look at it. Just look at it."

"Wow." Eric reached out and touched an elaborately tooled coffeepot. "Is it real?"

Inside the box, wrapped in disintegrating paper, was a large set of sterling: the coffeepot, a matching teapot, creamer and sugar bowl, and a tray to hold them all. Below the coffee service they found a condiment caster, each of its silver-topped glass cruets and pots carefully wrapped. In a separate box, there was a set of silver flatware, all of it as heavily decorated as the coffee set. The value of the china faded into insignificance as Janet assessed the silver.

Suddenly the sound of Michael's voice echoing Eric penetrated Janet's mind. "*Is* it real?"

"It's real," Janet assured them.

"Maybe it's plate," Ione Simpson suggested.

Janet shook her head. "It's not plate. It's sterling, and it couldn't have been made much after 1820."

"How can you tell?"

Janet smiled wryly. "One of my hobbies over the last few years has been drooling over things like this in stores on Madison Avenue. Believe me, I know what this is."

"But whose is it?" Eric suddenly asked.

Michael threw him a scornful look. "It's ours, stupid. It's our house, isn't it?"

Eric ignored him. "But where'd it come from?"

"I don't know," Janet said softly. One by one, she picked the pieces up, examining them carefully. Though they were heavily tarnished, she could find no dents or scratches, and none of the sets seemed to have pieces missing. "But I think Michael's probably right. If they've been in the attic as long as I think they have, they're probably ours." Suddenly, her anticipation heightened by the discovery of the silver, she turned to the trunk. "Pry it open, Michael. Maybe it's full of gold!"

Five minutes later, with some help from Leif Simpson, the old locks gave way, and the boys lifted the lid. Their first feeling was one of disappointment—the trunk seemed to be filled with nothing but old clothing. Carefully, Janet and Ione lifted out garment after garment, all of it seeming primitive in contrast to the silver and china. The materials were coarse homespuns, and much of the stitching was inexpertly done. Below the clothes—mostly dresses and shirts—there was a tray containing some shoes, a few pairs of rotted cotton hose, and some moth-eaten woolen socks. Below the tray, more clothes.

Buried at the bottom, Janet found a book. She took it out of the trunk and held it under a lamp. It was a small volume, bound in leather, with a leather strap held fast by a small gold clasp. The clasp was locked, but when Janet gently tugged at the strap, it easily tore away.

"Damn," she swore softly, immediately regretting the curiosity that had caused her to damage the volume. Gingerly, she opened the cover. The first page was blank, but starting with the second, the pages were filled with an uncertain script, done mostly in black ink. Janet glanced up, but no one seemed to be paying any attention to her. Instead, they were engrossed in examining the contents of the various boxes. Ione was carefully sorting the silver, while her husband unwrapped the china. Peggy had found a wooden spoon, and was happily beating on the bottom of a rusted pan, while the boys examined the trunk, in search of a secret compartment.

Impulsively, Janet turned to the last page of the diary. The script seemed to her to be particularly shaky, as if the writer had been ill or nervous about something. Slowly, she deciphered the old-fashioned penmanship:

> *14 March, 1884—Spring comes, and it is almost over. Nathaniel and I still live, but when they find out what Nathaniel has done, I am sure they will kill him. In the meantime, though, my baby grows inside me, and it is better that some of us live than that all of us die. I have decided to tell them a man came for the children, and though they will not believe me, and will think me daft, perhaps it will save Nathaniel—all that matters now is that Nathaniel and my unborn child survive.*

Janet reread the passage several times, and then slowly closed the little book. She held it in her lap, staring at it. A moment later her eyes drifted to Michael. As if feeling her gaze, he turned and looked at her, as did Ione Simpson. It was Ione who spoke.

"What is it?"

"It's nothing," Janet replied. "Just an old diary."

Janet let Shadow out the back door, and watched as he disappeared into the darkness, intent on making his evening rounds of the little farm. Then, knowing the dog wouldn't be back for a while, she went upstairs, tapped on Michael's door, and stuck her head into his room. He was in bed, his head propped up on his left hand, reading.

"Where's Shadow?" he asked.

"Prowling," Janet told him. She sat on the edge of Michael's bed and took his hand. "I want to talk to you about something," she said.

Michael looked nervous, but didn't turn away. "A-about what I saw?"

Janet nodded. "And about what you said about that little girl—Becky—today. That you think someone killed her and buried her in Potter's Field. What made you say that, honey?"

Suddenly Michael's eyes filled with terror. "I—I can't tell you. I—I promised not to tell anybody."

"Not even me?"

Michael nervously twisted the bedcovers in his clenched fist.

"Please?"

"You won't tell anyone? Anyone at all?"

Sensing that her son's fright was genuine, Janet promised.

"I—I lied to you," Michael said at last, his voice quavering.

"Why would you want to do that?"

"I was scared."

"Of me?"

Michael shook his head.

"Of Grandpa?"

"I—I'm not sure. I guess so."

Janet reached out and gently removed the bedclothes from Michael's hand. "Why don't you tell me what really happened?"

Slowly, Michael began telling his mother as much as he could remember of what had happened that night.

"And on the way home, I saw something," he finished. "But it wasn't Abby."

"Then what was it?" Janet pressed.

"It was Nathaniel," Michael whispered. "I saw Nathaniel, and I talked to him, and I saw someone else, too, but I'm not sure who it was."

Janet swallowed. A knot of tension had formed in her stomach. "You saw Nathaniel, and you were talking to him," she repeated.

Michael hesitated, then nodded in the darkness.

"But Nathaniel's just like Abby. He doesn't exist, honey. He's only a ghost."

"Maybe—maybe he's not," Michael ventured. In his memory, Dr. Potter's words returned, the words with which he'd described Nathaniel: *'He looked like you, and he looked like your father. . . .'*

"All right," Janet said patiently, still unsure of exactly what Michael was trying to say. "Let's assume Nathaniel isn't a ghost. What did he say that scared you so much?"

Michael racked his brain, trying to remember what Nathaniel had said, the exact words. But they were gone; all that was left were the warnings. And a vague memory.

"He—he said they'd brought us something. A—a baby."

"A *baby?*" Janet repeated, unable to keep her incredulity out of her voice.

Again Michael nodded. "They were burying it out in the field."

Janet's heart began to pound. "What field?"

"The one down near the woods by the river. Potter's Field."

"And you think it was Aunt Laura's baby they were burying?"

Again, Michael's head bobbed.

Janet paused for a long time, then reached out and touched Michael's face, tipping his head so his eyes were clearly visible. "Michael, are you sure you saw any of this?"

"I—I think so."

"You think so. But you're not sure."

"Well—" Michael faltered, then backed off a little. "It was dark, and I couldn't see very well, except when Nathaniel was with me. Then I could see real good."

The knot in Janet's stomach tightened. What was he talking about now? "You could see in the dark when Nathaniel was with you?"

Michael nodded.

"All right," Janet told him. "Now, what about Becky?"

Michael squirmed. "I—I'm not sure. But I bet whoever she is, she's in Potter's Field, too."

"But we don't even know who she is."

Michael swallowed hard, then spoke in a whisper. "I don't care," Michael said, his voice reflecting his misery. "I bet they killed her, too."

Janet gathered her son into her arms. "Oh, Michael," she whispered. "What are you saying? Why are you saying these things?"

Michael met her gaze evenly. "Nathaniel," he said. "I'm only saying what Nathaniel told me."

"But sweetheart, Nathaniel doesn't exist. You only imagined all this."

Michael lay still for a long time, then slowly shook his head. "I didn't," he said softly. Then: "Did I?"

Outside, Shadow began barking.

That night, long after Michael had fallen asleep, Janet remained awake. She read the diary over and over, read all the entries, describing how Abby Randolph and her children had tried to survive the winter of 1884.

How the food had run out, and they had begun to starve.

How one of the children—the youngest—had gotten sick and finally died, and what Abby had done with its remains.

And then, one by one, the other children had died, but never again was there a mention of illness. And in the end, all of them were gone except Nathaniel, who, along with his mother, survived.

". . . *Better that some of us live than that all of us die* . . ."

She went to bed finally, but didn't sleep. Instead she lay staring into the darkness, the words drumming in her mind. Perhaps, she told herself, it didn't mean anything. Perhaps it was nothing but the ravings of a woman driven mad by the loneliness of the long prairie winter. Or perhaps it had been written somewhere else, packed in the trunk for shipment, and never unpacked again.

Finally, near dawn, she drifted into half sleep, but even in her semiconscious state she could hear the name:

Nathaniel . . .

She shivered.

There could be no question of the roots of that terrible ghost story now, for she had found its confirmation. Inscribed on the flyleaf of the diary, barely discernible in faded pencil, was the proof: the name Abigail Randolph.

But why were Abby Randolph's things in this house? Who had put them there?

CHAPTER 16

Michael wasn't sure what had awakened him. It might have been the headache that was playing around his temples—not really painful yet, but nevertheless there—or it might have been something else.

It might have been the dream. Though the dream was already fading from his memory as he lay in the darkness, a few fragments remained. His father. His father had been in the dream, and some of the dream had taken place in this room. It had started here, and it had ended here, but part of it had been in the room downstairs, the living room. But it hadn't looked like it did now, filled with packing crates and a few pieces of furniture. In the dream the furniture had been old-fashioned, and his father had been sitting on a sofa—one of those hard sofas with slippery upholstery like some of his parents' friends had in New York.

And his father had looked different. He'd looked young, like Nathaniel, but even though he'd looked like Nathaniel, Michael had known it was his father. And Michael hadn't been there. At least, he hadn't felt like he'd been there. Instead, he'd just been sort of watching, almost as if he was standing in a corner but nobody could see him.

But it had started in the bedroom, the room that had been his father's and was now his. His father had been in the room, working on one of his model airplanes, when suddenly the door had opened, and his grandfather had come into the room. Michael had known right away that Amos was mad at his father. He'd tried to tell his father, but he couldn't speak. He'd opened his mouth, but when he'd tried to speak, his throat had tightened, and nothing had come out. And the harder he tried, the tighter his throat got, till he could hardly breathe. And then his grandfather had hit his father. Suddenly there'd been a razor strop in his hand, and without saying a word, Amos had raised it up over his head and brought it slashing down onto his father's back. But his father hadn't screamed. Instead, while Michael watched, his father's eyes widened, and his body stiffened and arched away from the pain. His hands, which had been holding one wing of the model, tightened, crushing the balsa wood and tissue paper into a crumpled mass. Twice more the razor strop had lashed down, but still his father had said nothing. And then it was over, and suddenly Michael's father was in the living room, sitting on the old-fashioned sofa, and though he couldn't hear anything, Michael knew that somewhere in the house, someone was screaming.

Then his father was back in the bedroom again, and he was packing a suitcase, and Michael knew he was going away and never coming back.

And then, just before he'd awakened, his father had said something.

"He's alive. I know he's alive."

Now, as he lay in his bed, Michael wondered who his father had been talking about. Could it have been Nathaniel? Had his father known Nathaniel, too?

Michael got out of bed and went to the window. The night was clear, and the moon hung just above the horizon, casting long shadows over the prairie. Old man Findley's barn shimmered in the moonlight, its weathered siding glowing silver in the darkness. Michael stared at the barn for a long time, feeling it, feeling Nathaniel's presence there.

And then Nathaniel was once more inside his head, whispering to him.

"It is time, Michael. If we wait, it will be too late."

The night seemed to darken, the moonlight fade away, and for a moment Michael saw nothing. But then his vision cleared, and he saw a house, a house which he recognized, but couldn't quite place. And once again, he felt the familiar throbbing in his temples.

Then he knew. It was Dr. Potter's house. In one of the downstairs windows, a single light glowed. Outside the house, ranging across the yard, he saw a dark shape that he knew was Shadow. . . .

Charles Potter had been sitting alone in the tiny room that was his private retreat. He had been there for hours now, sitting still in his large easy chair, moving only when the fire burned low and demanded more fuel to keep it going. The room was stiflingly hot, but the flames, Potter thought, were helping him think, helping him decide what he must do.

So far, he had done nothing. So far, he had talked to no one about Michael Hall. Nor had he yet decided exactly what had happened in his office that day.

It had been almost as if there were a third person there, a third person invisible to him, who was whispering to Michael. And yet, there had been something about the strange phenomenon that had told Potter there was more to that third person than an invention of Michael's mind.

It was as if Nathaniel had been there, speaking to the boy.

Of course it was impossible, and Potter knew it was impossible. But still, he had sat through the night, wondering if it could have been true, if Nathaniel could, indeed, have been in his office that day.

A sound disturbed his reverie, and Potter stirred in his chair, shifting his attention to the night.

He heard it again, a snuffling sound, as if some animal were outside. He got up from his chair and went to the window. Outside, he saw nothing but darkness.

The sound came again, and then once more. Frowning, Potter left his tiny den and moved quickly through the house to the front door. He opened it a few inches and looked out.

Suddenly there was a flicker of movement on the porch, and an angry growl. Startled, Potter took a step back, and as his hand fell away from the doorknob, the door itself flew open.

Crouched in the foyer, his fangs bared and his hackles raised, Shadow fixed his glowing eyes on Charles Potter.

Potter stared at the dog, his heart suddenly pounding. He took another step backward, and the dog rose from his crouch, one foreleg slightly raised, his tail slung low.

As he watched the dog, Charles Potter suddenly knew that it had been true.

Nathaniel had been there that day, and Nathaniel was here now.

Charles Potter stared at Shadow, and knew that he was going to die.

Michael stood perfectly still in his room, absorbed only in what he was seeing and hearing within his head.

He was inside Dr. Potter's house now, and Nathaniel was with him. He was watching as Shadow slowly backed the old man through the house until they were in the tiny room where the fire blazed on the hearth.

Michael could smell the smoke of the fire and feel the heat of the room. It was hard to breathe, and the smoke seemed to be drifting out of the fireplace now, filling the room.

"It is time," Nathaniel's voice whispered. *"It is time for him to die. He knows, Michael. He knows about me, and now he knows about you. Help me, Michael. Help me make him die. . . ."*

Michael could see the fear in the old man's eyes, see the growing terror as the man came to know that there was no place to retreat, nowhere else for him to go. Silently, he released Shadow. . . .

Charles Potter sank back into his chair, his eyes still fixed on the threatening visage of the snarling dog. And then, though he knew this, too, couldn't be happening, he began to feel another presence in the room. It was as if there were eyes on him, blue eyes, intense and angry, filled with hatred. He knew whose eyes they were, and knew why they were there.

His heart was pounding harder now, and suddenly there was a pain in his head, an intense pain—as intense as those staring eyes that now seemed to fill his vision—and he knew what was happening to him.

Then the vessel in his head, filled beyond capacity by his pounding heart, gave way, and blood began to spread through his brain. His face turned scarlet, and his head pitched forward to rest on his chest, as his arms went limp.

Only when the last of Charles Potter's life had drained out of his body did the great black dog let the tension go out of his muscles, let his snarl die in his throat, let his coat smooth down. Then, after sniffing once at the body in the chair, he turned away and trotted out of the house into the night.

In his room, Michael turned away from the window. His headache was easing now, and he was once more aware of where he was. In the back of his mind, there was a faint memory, like the memory of a dream, in which he and Nathaniel had made Dr. Potter die.

But it must have been a dream, like the dream he'd had about his father. It couldn't have been real.

And yet, as he went back to bed and pulled the covers close around himself, he wondered.

It had *seemed* real.

All of it, everything Nathaniel had showed him, had seemed real.

He was still thinking about it when he finally drifted back into sleep.

* * *

The sun was well up, promising a beautifully clear day. Janet and Michael, who had been silent that morning, were cleaning up the last of the breakfast dishes when Michael saw the strange truck pull into the driveway.

"Someone's coming, Mom."

Janet glanced out the window, but as the battered old green pickup made its way up the drive, she couldn't place it. And then it came to a stop in front of the house, and Amos Hall climbed out. Seeing Janet watching him from the kitchen window, he smiled and beckoned to her.

"What in the world—?" Janet began, and then suddenly realized she was talking to an empty room. Michael was gone. Assuming he had already headed out to greet his grandfather, she flung her damp dish towel over the back of one of the kitchen chairs, then started toward the front door. But when she reached the front yard, Michael was nowhere to be seen, though Amos still stood by the truck. "Hi," she greeted him, then paused uncertainly. Amos's weathered face wore an uncharacteristic grin. "You look like the cat that swallowed the canary," she said at last.

Amos only shrugged, then stepped back to gaze admiringly at the truck. "What do you think of it."

"Think of what?" Janet replied.

"The truck. Think it'll do?"

Janet stared at it. It was of indeterminate age, though far from new, and it had apparently seen a lot of service. There didn't seem to be a square foot on it anywhere that was free from small dents and scratches, and both the fenders were badly crushed.

"Do for what? It looks like it's ready for the junkheap," she said at last.

Amos nodded. "Inside, though, where it counts, it's sound as a dollar. It ought to give you a good ten, maybe twenty thousand miles yet."

"Me?" Janet took a step forward. "What on earth are you talking about?"

"Well, you can't spend all your time walking to the village, then begging rides home off the neighbors," Amos replied, his eyes shifting pointedly toward the Simpsons' farm next door.

Instantly Janet realized that Ione had been right yesterday. Someone had apparently seen her getting into Ione's car, and the news had gotten back to the Halls. "But I don't need a truck—" she began.

Amos interrupted her.

"How do you know what you need and don't need? All those years in the city—how would you know what you'll need out here? Anyway, I was up to Mulford this morning, and found this thing just sort of sitting around looking for a new home. So I bought it. What do you think?"

Suddenly touched, Janet went to Amos and slipped her arms around him. "I think you're wonderful, but I think you'd better tell me how much you paid for it, so I can pay you."

Amos self-consciously pulled her arms loose and stepped back. "Don't be silly. They practically gave it to me. You keep your money for other things. You know how to drive a stick shift?"

Janet nodded. "I used to have a VW."

"Then you're all set. This thing might take a little getting used to, but you'll catch right on. Get in."

Tentatively, Janet climbed into the driver's seat. The upholstery had long since given up any notion of holding itself together. Someone, though, had installed seat covers, and though she could feel the springs beneath her, there didn't seem to be any sharp points sticking through. She turned on the ignition, and a moment later the engine coughed reluctantly to life. A red light on the dashboard glowed for a second, flickered, then went out. The gas gauge read empty.

"I'd better get it to a filling station," she commented, but Amos only chuckled.

"She's full up. The gauge doesn't work, and neither does the speedometer or the temperature gauge."

Janet gave him an arch look. "Did they knock the price down for any of that?"

"Can't knock down something that's already collapsed," Amos replied. "Want to take her for a spin? You can take me home and say hello to Anna, and Michael can give me a hand with a couple of things."

Janet thought of all the things she had to do that morning, then quickly decided there was nothing that couldn't wait. "Sure. Michael can ride in the—" And suddenly she fell silent for a moment. "Where *is* Michael?"

Amos shrugged. "Isn't he in the house?"

Janet shook her head uncertainly. "I don't think so. I thought he came outside when you got here. We were both in the kitchen, and I just assumed—"

"He didn't come out here," Amos told her.

Janet shut off the truck's engine and jumped to the ground. "Michael?" she called. "Michael!" When there was no reply, she smiled apologetically at Amos. "He must have gone upstairs. I'll get him."

But he wasn't upstairs, or anywhere in the house. A few moments later, she was back in the front yard, alone. "I can't imagine where he's gone. I *know* he saw you—"

"That's kids," Amos replied. "He's probably out back somewhere, pokin' around. Come on."

They went around the corner of the house, then into the barn. Janet called out to her son, but still there was no answer. And then, as they were leaving the barn and heading toward the toolshed, a slight movement caught Janet's eye. She stopped, and turned to stare thoughtfully at the cyclone cellar. Amos, his eyes following hers, frowned.

"What'd he be doing down there?"

"I don't know," Janet replied. "But would you mind waiting here while I go see?" Then, without waiting for an answer, she started purposefully toward the sloping door.

She pulled the door open, letting it fall back so that the sunlight flooded into the dimness of the storm shelter. In the far corner, crouched on the floor with his arms wrapped around Shadow, she saw Michael, his knees drawn up against his chest, his eyes wide with trepidation.

"What—?" she began.

"Are you mad at me?" Michael asked, his voice quavering slightly.

"Mad at you?" Janet repeated. "Honey, why would I be mad at you?"

" 'Cause I didn't say hello to Grandpa."

Janet paused. Up until now, she'd assumed that Michael hadn't realized who was in the truck. "So you *did* see Grandpa?"

Michael nodded.

"Then why didn't you say hello to him?"

Michael shrugged unhappily. "I—I had a dream last night," he said at last.

Sensing his fear, Janet sat down on the bench next to her son and put her arm around him. "A bad dream?"

Michael nodded. "It was about Dad. Grandpa was beating him. He was beating him with a piece of leather."

Janet felt her body react to the image that suddenly formed in her mind, but when she spoke, she managed to keep her voice steady. "But honey, you know dreams are only dreams. It wasn't real. Is that why you didn't say hello to Grandpa this morning?"

Again, Michael nodded. He pulled away from her and pressed himself closer to the big dog. For a moment, Janet wished Mark were there. He would know what to say to Michael, how to explain what was happening to him. But if Mark were here, she realized with stark clarity, none of this would be happening; there would be nothing to explain to Michael. "The next time you have a dream like that, I want you to tell me about it right away, all right? That way, we can talk about it, and you won't have to be afraid."

But Michael didn't seem to hear her. His gaze seemed far away, and when he spoke, there was a hollowness in his voice. "Why did Grandpa beat Dad?" he asked. And then another vision flashed into his mind, a vision that seemed far in the past. It was the dream he'd had of his father falling from the hayloft, falling onto the pitchfork. Only there was someone else in the loft with his father, and suddenly he could see that person, see him clearly. It was his grandfather.

He looked up at his mother. "Mom, why did Grandpa want to kill Dad?"

Janet's thoughts tumbled chaotically in her mind. Amos beating Mark? Killing Mark? It made no sense.

"They were only dreams, honey," she said, her voice taking on a note of desperation. "You have to remember that the dreams you have don't have anything to do with the real world. All they mean is that something is happening in your mind, and you're trying to deal with it. But the things you dream about aren't real—they're only fantasies."

Michael's brow furrowed as he considered his mother's words. But there were too many memories, too many images. His father, his grandfather . . . Dr. Potter. His frown deepened.

Janet nodded. "I know, honey. Dreams are like that. When you're having them, they seem terribly real. Sometimes they still do, even after you wake up. But in a while, you realize they were only dreams, and forget them." She stood up, and drew Michael to his feet. "I want you to come out and say hello to Grandpa now, and then we're going to go over to see Grandma. Okay?"

But Michael drew back. "Do I have to? Can't I stay here?"

Janet frowned. "No, you can't. Grandpa needs you to help him with some things, and after all he's done for us, I can't see that you wouldn't want to help him."

"But—sometimes he scares me!" Michael protested.

Suddenly Janet reached the end of her patience. "Now, that's enough. Your grandfather loves you very much, and he'd never do anything to hurt you, just as he never did anything to hurt your father. So you're going to pull yourself together, and act like a man. Is that clear?"

Michael opened his mouth, then closed it again. Silently, he nodded his head, then started up the short staircase that led out of the storm cellar, his mother behind him.

Just outside, where he must have heard everything they'd said, they found Amos Hall. But if he had heard them, he gave no sign.

Janet leaned over to give her mother-in-law a kiss on the cheek, but for the first time since they'd met, Anna made no response. Instead, she moved her face away, and continued darning one of Amos's gray woolen work socks.

"It was so good of you to get the truck for me," Janet began, but Anna glanced at her with a look that made Janet fall silent.

"We couldn't very well have you begging favors off strangers, could we?" she said in a distinctly cold voice.

"Strangers?" Janet echoed. "You mean Ione Simpson?"

"I'm sure Ione and Leif Simpson are very nice people, but you do have a family, Janet. If you need something, I wish you'd just ask us."

Janet sank into a chair across from the older woman, barely able to believe that Anna was insulted by what had happened yesterday. "Anna, Michael and I walked into town and had every intention of walking back. But we bumped into Ione, and she offered us a ride."

"So you invited her to dinner? It seems to me that you might have thought of having us first. We've worked so hard on the place, and after all, it *was* our home—"

"—And it's still a mess," Janet interrupted, improvising rapidly. "Last night was hardly what you could call a party. Ione brought over some things she had in the 'fridge, and we just sort of had a picnic." She thought Anna's expression softened slightly, so she pressed on. "It was all very impromptu, but if I hurt your feelings, I'm sorry. Of course, I'll fix my first real dinner for you and Amos, but that's not what last night was. Forgive me?"

Anna's eyes narrowed for a moment, but then she smiled. "Of course I do. It's just that—well, you know how people gossip in small towns. I just don't want people to start claiming there's trouble between us. And that's what they'd say, you know."

"Why on earth would they?" Janet asked, now genuinely puzzled by Anna's words. There had to be more to it than simply an imagined slight.

"They've always talked about us around here, even though we've been here longer than anyone else," Anna replied.

"Well, you can believe *I* won't give anyone anything to talk about," Janet declared. Then, before Anna could begin worrying the subject any further, she decided to change it. "I think Michael and I found some of your things last night."

Now it was Anna who was puzzled. "Mine? What do you mean?"

"Late last night, we decided to explore the attic." She waited for a reaction, but there was none. Instead, Anna only looked at her with mild curiosity. "We found all kinds of things. I assumed they must have belonged to you."

Now Anna's brows knit thoughtfully. "If it was in the attic, it wouldn't have been mine. I don't think I've ever been in the attic of that house in my whole life. And when we moved in here, we brought all our things with us."

Janet stared at her. "You were *never* in the attic? But you lived in that house so many years—"

Anna's eyes met hers. "But I never went to the attic. I started to, once, but Amos stopped me. He told me there was nothing up there, and that it was dangerous. He told me the floor's weak, and if I went up there, I'd fall through and break my neck."

"And so you never went?" Janet asked, amazed. "If Mark had ever told me something like that, you can bet it would be the first place I'd go." Of course, she thought, Mark never would have told me something like that.

Anna set her darning aside and wheeled herself over to the stove where a pot of coffee was simmering. Picking it up with one hand, she used the other to maneuver herself back to the table, where she poured each of them a cup of the steaming brew. Only when she'd set the pot on a trivet did she speak. "Well, Mark wasn't Amos, and I wasn't you. When Amos told me to leave the attic alone, I did just that."

"But what about the children? Didn't they ever go up there?"

"If they did, I don't know about it," Anna replied. "And I suspect that if their father told them not to, they didn't. Both Laura and Mark had great respect for their father."

"But still, they were children—"

"Children can be controlled," Anna replied, her voice oddly flat.

Suddenly Michael's words flashed through Janet's mind, but when she spoke, she managed to keep her voice light.

"What did he do, beat them?"

Anna stiffened in her chair. "Did Mark tell you his father beat him?" she asked.

Janet shrank back defensively. "No—no, of course not."

"Amos may have used the strop now and then," Anna went on, ignoring Janet's words as if she'd never uttered them. "But I'm not sure I call that a beating." Her voice took on a faraway note that made Janet wonder if the old woman was aware she was still speaking out loud. "A child needs to know respect for his elders, and he needs controls. Yes, controls. . . ." Her voice faded away, but a moment later she seemed to come back into reality. "Amos always controlled the children," she finished.

"But a razor strop—"

"My father used one on me," Anna replied. "It didn't hurt me."

No, Janet thought to herself. It didn't hurt you at all. All it did was make you think that whatever a man told you to do, you had to do. All it did was make you into a nice obedient wife, the kind of wife I could never have been, and the kind that Mark, thank God, never wanted. No wonder he ran away.

But even as she allowed the thoughts to come into her mind, she rejected them. They struck her as somehow disloyal, not only to Anna and Amos, but to Mark as well. Mark, after all, had been her husband, and she had loved him, and who was she to begin questioning the manner in which he had been raised, particularly when the people who had raised him were showing her nothing but kindness. Once again, she retreated to safer waters.

"But what about the things we found in the attic? What shall I do with them?"

Anna's eyes suddenly became expressionless. "I'm sure I don't know," she said. "I don't know what there is."

"There's a lot of silver and china. And there's a—" She stopped short, for Anna's eyes were suddenly angry.

"Don't tell me," Anna commanded. "There are some things I don't want to know about. If there were things in that attic, then Amos knew they were there, and knew what they were. They would have come from *his* family—that house was built by his ancestors over a century ago."

Janet's mind churned.

Abby Randolph's diary, written just a hundred years ago.

But Abby had died. All her children had died except Nathaniel, and then, after that terrible winter, Abby and Nathaniel, too, had died.

"*. . . that house was built by his ancestors. . . .*"

And then she remembered. According to the old legend and the diary, Abby Randolph had been pregnant that winter.

The child must have survived.

It must have been a girl, and it must have survived.

Janet felt a sickness in her stomach as she realized what had gone on in her house so many years ago. She gazed at Anna, who had once more picked up her darning and was now placidly stitching her husband's sock.

How much did Anna know? Had Anna known she was living in Abby Randolph's house, that her husband was a descendant of the only survivor of that long-ago tragedy?

Janet decided she didn't, and knew that she would never tell her. Indeed, Janet wished that she herself had never found the diary. Suddenly, the ghosts of Abby and Nathaniel were very real to her.

CHAPTER 17

Michael followed his grandfather into the barn, then up the ladder to the loft, where the bales of hay—what was left of last winter's supply—were neatly stacked under the sloping roof. He stood back while Amos cut the wire from three bales, and when Amos handed him a pitchfork, he seemed reluctant to take it.

"It won't hurt you," Amos admonished him. "Not unless you get careless and stick the tines through your foot."

Michael took the fork gingerly, then made a desultory stab at one of the bales. A few pieces of hay came loose, but the fork stuck in the bale itself.

"I'll break 'em up, and you pitch it over the edge," Amos offered. He peeled off his shirt, and a moment later set to work, his powerful torso moving rhythmically as he quickly began breaking the neat bales down. Hesitantly, Michael began using his own fork to throw the hay down into the bin below the loft. As he worked, his head began to ache.

He tried to ignore the now-familiar pain, tried to concentrate on what he was doing, but it grew worse, radiating out from his temples and growing into a throbbing that seemed to fill his head. Then the light in the barn began playing tricks, fading away so that the loft seemed to disappear into a black void, only to come back with a brilliance that washed the color out of everything.

In his mind, filtered by the pain, he heard Nathaniel whispering to him, telling him to beware, warning him of danger.

And then he saw his father.

It was like last night, and though Michael worked on, doggedly forking the hay over the edge of the loft, he suddenly was no longer aware of himself. It was as if his mind had left his body and was now in the far corner, watching as some other being went on performing his tasks. But then, as he watched, something changed, and suddenly he was watching his father.

And his grandfather was there too, breaking up the bales for his father just as he had been for Michael himself.

And then the two men weren't working anymore, but were facing each other, and Michael could see the anger in both their faces. His father was staring at Amos, and there was something in his eyes that Michael recognized. And then he knew. His father's eyes had the same emptiness he'd seen in Nathaniel's eyes. And then he heard his father speak.

"You killed her, didn't you? You were there when she was born, and you took her away and killed her."

"No, Mark—"

"I saw it, Pa. I saw what you did. Nathaniel showed me, Pa. This afternoon, Nathaniel showed me."

Amos's eyes widened. "Nathaniel? There is no Nathaniel, damn you."

"There is, Pa," Michael heard his father say. "Nathaniel lives, and he showed me what you did. He wants vengeance, Pa. He wants it, and he's going to get it."

And then, as Michael looked helplessly on, his grandfather began moving forward, moving toward his father.

Michael knew what was about to happen.

He wanted to cry out, wanted to warn his father, just as he had wanted to warn him in the dream last night.

In the distance, as if from very far away, he could hear a dog barking. It was Shadow, and though Michael knew the big dog was nowhere around, he also knew that the shepherd was trying to help him.

Suddenly his voice came to him, and a scream erupted from his throat to fill the vastness of the barn and echo off the walls in a keening wail. The pain in his head washed away, only to be replaced by another pain, a searing that shot up through his body like a living thing, twisting him around so that suddenly he was facing his grandfather, his eyes wide, his face contorted into a grimace of agony.

Then, as he felt himself begin to slip into the darkness that was gathering around him, once again he heard Shadow. The barking grew louder. It sounded furious—as if Shadow was about to attack. . . .

At first he was only aware of a murmuring sound, and was sure that Nathaniel was talking to him again, but slowly the voices became more distinct, and he recognized his mother's voice, and his grandmother's. And there was a third voice, not quite so familiar, but one that he recognized. And then he knew—it was Eric's mother. He opened his eyes to see Ione Simpson smiling at him.

"Well, look who's back," Ione said. "Feeling better?"

Michael tried to remember what had happened, but what he could remember made no sense. He'd seen his father, but that was impossible. And he'd had a headache, and Nathaniel had been talking to him, warning him about something. Slowly, he became aware of a throbbing pain in his right foot, and he struggled to sit up. Ione placed a gently restraining hand on his shoulder.

"Not yet," she told him. "Just lie there, and keep your foot up. Okay?"

Michael let himself sink back onto the cushion that was under his head, and fought against the pain that seemed to be growing every second. He looked around, recognizing his grandmother's parlor. His mother was there, and so were his grandparents, and they looked worried.

"What happened?" he asked at last.

"A little accident," Ione told him. "It seems you aren't quite an expert with a pitchfork yet."

Michael frowned, and another fragment of memory came back to him: his grandfather, moving toward his father. But it hadn't been his father. It had been himself. "I—I didn't—" he began, but his mother interrupted him.

"Of course you didn't, sweetheart," she assured him. "It was just an accident. The pitchfork slipped, and went through your foot."

Now Michael raised his head just enough to gaze at his right foot, which was propped up high on a second cushion, swathed in bandages.

"It isn't nearly as bad as it looks," Ione Simpson assured him. "It looks like the fork went right between the bones, and it doesn't seem like anything's very badly hurt."

Michael stared at the foot for a long moment, then gazed curiously around the room. Something was wrong—if he was hurt, where was the doctor? He frowned worriedly. "Is Dr. Potter here?"

Ione's smile faded away, and her eyes left Michael. Then his mother was bending over him. "Dr. Potter couldn't come," she said. "But it's all right, honey. Mrs. Simpson's a nurse, and she knows what to do."

But Michael's frown only deepened. His mind was continuing to clear and as it did, another memory came back to him, a memory from the previous night. "Dr. Potter," he whispered. "Why couldn't he come? Did—did something happen to him?"

A silence fell over the room, finally broken by the gruff voice of Amos Hall. "He might as well know," he said.

"Amos—" Janet began, but the old man shook his head.

"Dr. Potter died last night, Michael," he said. Michael's eyes widened, and the color drained from his face. "Do you know what a stroke is?" Mutely, Michael shook his head. "It's a blood vessel bursting inside the head. That's what happened to Dr. Potter last night. They found him this morning."

In his mind's eye, Michael had a sudden vision of Dr. Potter, slumped in a chair in front of a fire, his face scarlet, his eyes filled with pain and fear. He shook his head. "I'm sorry," he whispered. "I didn't mean to do it. I didn't mean to . . ." His voice trailed off, and his eyes met his grandfather's. There was a look in his grandfather's eyes that terrified him, and after only a second, he tore his eyes away and listened to his mother's voice.

"It's all right, sweetheart," she was saying. "No one thinks you meant to hurt yourself—it was just an accident. And you'll be all right. The foot will heal right up in no time at all."

Michael started to say something, but then, once again, he saw the strange look in his grandfather's eyes, and he changed his mind.

"Can you tell us what happened, honey?" Janet asked. "Do you remember any of it?"

Michael ignored her question. "Can we go home, Mom? Please?"

Janet's encouraging smile gave way to a worried frown. "Now?"

Michael nodded.

"But Michael, you need to rest for a while."

"I don't want to rest," Michael said. "I want to go home."

Suddenly Amos's voice cut in. "Your mother has some things to do, and you need to rest. And you need to be looked after. You'll stay here."

Now a look of real fear came into Michael's eyes. "Can't I go with you?" he begged his mother. "I can stay in the truck, and my foot doesn't hurt much. Really, it doesn't."

"You need to rest, at least for a little while," Janet said.

"Of course he does," Anna declared, rolling her chair close to the couch. "He should just lie here and take it easy, and you should do your errands."

"But I don't *want* to stay here," Michael argued. "I want to go home."

"Hush, child," Anna told him. "Your mother has a lot to do, and she can't do it and take care of you, too. And Mrs. Simpson can't stay here all day either." Suddenly she smiled. "But just because I can't get out of this chair doesn't mean I don't know how to look after someone. In fact, I was thinking of making some cookies."

Michael turned his attention back to his mother. "I don't want any cookies," he said, his voice taking on a sullen tone. "I want to go home."

Janet wavered. She wanted to give in to Michael, wanted to take him home and give him all the attention she thought he needed. And yet, there was something that was holding her back, and she immediately knew what it was. It was that tone of voice he'd just slipped into, the tone of a spoiled child, which Michael had never been. She made up her mind.

"I want you to stay here," she told him. "I won't be gone very long, and you'll be fine. Just stay here, and keep your foot up on the cushion. That way it won't throb so much. I'll be back as soon as I can, and then we'll get you home. Okay?"

Michael hesitated, but finally nodded.

A few minutes later, he was alone with his grandparents.

Janet left the drugstore, then turned the battered green truck away from the square and drove the two blocks to Laura and Buck Shields's house. She parked the car in the driveway and was starting toward the front door when she heard Laura's thin voice calling to her from the upstairs window.

"It's unlocked. Let yourself in and come upstairs." A wan smile drifted across her face, then disappeared. "I'm afraid I'm still not quite up to coming down."

Janet found Laura dressed, but propped on the bed, resting against several pillows.

"I should be *in* bed, but I just couldn't stand it anymore," Laura told her. "So I got dressed this morning, and I'm spending the day *on* bed. At least I don't feel quite so useless this way." She patted the mattress. "Come and sit down and tell me what's happening. I feel like I've been cooped up here forever."

Janet sighed, and lowered herself gratefully onto the bed. "I suppose you've already heard about Dr. Potter."

Laura's gentle eyes hardened. "The only thing I want to hear about him is that he's dead," she half whispered. "I hate him, Janet—I hate him so much . . ."

Janet reached out to touch Laura's hand. "He—Laura, he *is* dead."

The other woman paled, and a tear suddenly welled in her eye. "Oh, God, Janet. I didn't mean—"

"Of course you didn't." She shrugged helplessly. "It was a stroke, I guess. They found him this morning."

Laura fell silent for a moment, then slowly shook her head. "I should be sorry, shouldn't I, Janet? But you know something? I'm not. I just feel sort of—sort of relieved, I guess. After what he did—"

"No," Janet interrupted her. "Laura, stop torturing yourself. Please?"

But Laura only shook her head again. "I can't help it. I believe what I believe, and I believe they killed my baby." Then, seeing Janet's discomfiture, she decided to change the subject. She made herself smile. "Where's Michael?"

"And that's the rest of the news," Janet replied. Briefly, she told Laura what had happened.

"Is he all right?" Laura asked when Janet was done.

Janet nodded. "But it just seems so stupid. And Michael's always been so good with things like that."

"It *is* stupid," Laura agreed. "But I'll bet it won't happen again—one thing about farms: you usually only make a mistake once. After that, you know better. And how are you doing? Is the house all in order?"

"Hardly, but I guess some progress is being made. And last night Michael and I cleaned out the attic."

"The attic? I thought it was empty."

Janet frowned. "You mean Anna was right? You and Mark never went up there?"

"Mark did, once," Laura told her. "Dad gave him a beating he never forgot. Or anyway, one I never forgot. I guess it was one time I learned by someone else's mistake."

"Amos beat Mark?"

Laura gave her a puzzled look. "Of course he did. He'd told Mark never to go up there, and Mark disobeyed him."

"So he *beat* him?" Janet pressed. "Not just spanked him?"

Laura chuckled hollowly. "I wouldn't call a razor strop an ordinary spanking, but it's amazing how effective it was."

"It's no wonder Mark got out as soon as he could," Janet observed, making no attempt to hide her disapproval.

"That wasn't it at all," Laura said quickly. "That had something to do with the night mother had her last baby. By then, Dad hadn't given Mark a beating in—well, it had been a while. What did you find in the attic?"

Janet made an instinctive decision: what Anna Hall wouldn't talk about, her daughter might. "Among other things, I found Abby Randolph's diary."

Laura stared at her. "You're kidding, of course."

Janet shook her head. Then as casually as she could, she said, "Anna told me that the house has been in your family since the day it was built."

Laura nodded. "The old family homestead, and all that sort of thing. But there was never any mention of Abby having lived there. In fact, if I remember right, we were always sort of led to believe that her house had burned down. If it ever existed at all. Personally, I was never sure there ever was an Abby

Randolph. And I certainly don't believe she did all the things she's supposed to have done."

"Well, apparently she did exist, and if I read her diary correctly, it seems that she did exactly what the old stories claim she did."

Laura's face paled. "I—I can't believe that."

"It's in the diary," Janet said gently. "Would you like to see it?"

Quickly, Laura shook her head. "And I don't want to talk about it, either. The whole idea of it makes me sick."

Janet wished she'd never brought the subject up. "Well, none of that matters now anyway," she said quickly. "Whatever happened, it's ancient history. But there was a lot of other stuff—china and silver—and I thought we ought to split it between us. I've talked to Anna about it, and she insists it wasn't hers. In fact, she said if it was in the house, it must be mine, since the house is mine. But that just doesn't seem fair."

Laura looked at her curiously. "But if it wasn't hers, then whose was it?" When Janet made no reply, she suddenly understood. "Oh, God," she groaned. "You're not thinking—" Then, seeing that that was exactly what Janet was thinking, she shook her head. "I could never use it. I couldn't look at it, or touch it, let alone eat off it! And anyway, I've got loads of china and silver of my own, which I never use. It came from Mother's mother, and it's all stowed up in the attic. Limoges china, and the most garish silver you've ever seen."

"Limoges?" Janet repeated. "But that's what was in my attic. Maybe it's from the same set."

"I don't see how—"

But Janet was on her feet. "Can I go up and look? Please?"

"Well, if you want to—" Laura told her where the china and silver were stored, and a few minutes later, Janet was rummaging through the Shieldses' attic. She found the trunk Laura had described, opened it, and felt a pang of disappointment. The china and silver were there, all right, but these things bore no resemblance at all to the things she'd found in her own attic. Slowly, she closed the trunk, and was about to go downstairs when something in the far corner of the attic caught her eye.

It was a crib, and though it was not new, neither was it an antique. Indeed, it seemed barely used. And it was not the crib that Laura had set up in her bedroom in preparation for the baby who had died—that crib was still downstairs, a lonely reminder of Laura's loss. Curious, Janet moved toward the crib. Only when she was near it did she see the rest of the nursery equipment.

A tiny rocking chair, painted pink, and hardly used.

A bassinet, used, but, like the crib, in nearly new condition.

Behind the crib, there was a small chest of drawers, just the right size for a three- or four-year-old. Hesitantly, Janet opened one of the drawers. Inside, clean and neatly folded, she found several stacks of clothing, all of it in infant sizes. Tiny dresses, playsuits, blouses, and pajamas, much of it in pinks and whites.

And then, in the bottom drawer, she found an album. Bound in white leather, it was thin and, like the rest of the things in that far corner, barely used. Frowning slightly, she opened it. On the first page, beneath a blank space neatly outlined in green ink, there was a neatly lettered caption:

REBECCA—HER FIRST PICTURE

Janet stared at the odd page for a moment, then quickly flipped through the book. Where the pictures had once been, now there was nothing. Someone had gone through the album, taking out the photographs, leaving nothing but the eerily hollow captions.

She stared at the album for several seconds, wondering what could have happened to the pictures. Should she take it downstairs and ask Laura about it? Then, before she could make up her mind, she heard Buck's voice, his furious tones carrying clearly into the attic.

"She's up there? By herself? For God's sake, Laura, what are you thinking of?"

Startled, Janet closed the album and hurriedly slipped it back in the dresser drawer. Then she moved quickly toward the attic door, opened it a crack, and listened. Now she could hear nothing except indistinct mutterings, muffled by the closed door to the master bedroom. Janet reached up and pulled the light cord, plunging the attic into darkness, then started down the steep stairs to the second floor. Only when she reached the landing, though, could she hear Buck's voice once again.

"But what if she does see it? What if she wants to know where it came from, and why it's there?"

"She won't," Laura's terrified voice replied. "It's way back in the corner, and there's so much other stuff, she won't even notice it. And even if she does, I'll just say we're storing it for someone. Ione—I'll say we're storing it for Ione Simpson. She has a little girl."

"I told you to get rid of it." There was a silence; then, again: "Didn't I tell you to get rid of it?"

"Y-yes."

"Then why didn't you?"

"I—I couldn't."

"You will," Buck said, his voice holding an implacability Janet had never realized was in him before. "As soon as you're strong enough, you'll bring all that stuff down from the attic, take it out back, and burn it."

"Buck, don't make me—"

"It has to be done," Buck said. "Not today. Not until you're well again. But you have to get rid of that stuff. Do you understand?"

Then, as Janet shrank back against the wall, the door to the bedroom opened, and Buck emerged, his face set with determination. Without seeing Janet, he turned the other way and disappeared down the front stairs. A moment later she heard the front door slam.

For a long time, Janet stood where she was, wondering what to do. At last, forcing herself into a composure she didn't feel, she returned to the bedroom, where Laura, still on the bed, was blotting her face with a Kleenex.

"Was Buck here?" Janet asked. "I thought I heard his voice."

Laura nodded. "He just came by to see how I was doing. Wasn't that sweet of him?"

"Yes," Janet agreed. Then: "The china's all different from what I found, and so's the silver. But I found some stuff in the corner. Some nursery furniture." She watched as Laura swallowed hard, then seemed to search for words.

"It—it's Ione Simpson's," she said at last. "It's been there for a couple of years now. She didn't have any room to store it."

Janet hesitated only a moment, then nodded. Laura had lied, just as she'd told Buck she would.

Michael woke up, and for a moment couldn't remember where he was. Then the room came into focus, and he recognized his grandmother's parlor. Drifting in from the kitchen, he could smell the aroma of fresh-baked cookies. Tentatively, he sat up and lowered his bandaged foot to the floor. The throbbing had eased, and when he tried to stand up, he found that the pain wasn't bad at all as long as he kept his weight on his heel. Slowly, he began hobbling toward the door that would take him into the hall and then back toward the kitchen. But when he came to the dining room, he heard his grandfather's voice, and stopped. His grandfather was talking about him.

"There's something about him, Anna. Something in his eyes. I'm sure of it."

There was silence for a moment, and then his grandmother spoke. "Don't, Amos. Don't start. Not on Michael."

"But what about the headaches? He's having 'em, you know. Just like Mark did. And this morning—"

"What about this morning?" Anna demanded, when Amos showed no sign of going on.

"It was in his eyes," Amos finished. "The same look I saw in Mark's eyes. It's Nathaniel. There's the mark of Nathaniel on that child. They told me when I was a boy—"

Suddenly his grandmother's voice grew loud and angry. "They told you a bunch of lies and stories. They ruined your life and my life and Laura's life. The only one who got away was Mark, and now all those old stories have killed him, too!"

"What happened to Mark was an accident."

"If that's what you believe, then believe it. But I don't believe it. I believe you might as well have killed him with your own hands."

Now his grandfather sounded as angry as his grandmother. "Don't say that, Anna. I've always done what I had to do, and nothing more."

"And look at me," Michael heard his grandmother say. Her voice was trembling now, as if she were starting to cry. "Just look at me. Five babies, and all I have left is Laura. And look at her—she's going to wind up just the way I am, and it's going to be on your head. So help me, if you start trying to see your unholy family curse in Michael, I'll see to it that Janet takes him and goes right back to New York. They're stories, Amos! None of it is anything but stories."

"Abby Randolph was no story. And neither was Nathaniel. It won't end, unless I end it."

"Leave it alone, Amos," his grandmother said after another long silence. "There's nothing wrong with Michael."

"We'll see," his grandfather replied. "When Janet's baby comes, we'll see."

Slowly, Michael backed away from the kitchen door, then turned and made his way back to the parlor. With his heart pounding, he lay down on the sofa again and carefully propped his foot back up on the cushion. Then he closed his eyes and tried to make his breathing come evenly, but he couldn't control the terror in his soul: *He knows,* Michael thought. *Grandpa knows about Nathaniel, and he knows about me.*

CHAPTER 18

Janet sat in the small living room, staring apprehensively at the last box remaining to be opened, knowing that its contents were going to be the most difficult for her. Everything else had long since been put away—as spring had given way to stifling summer, she and Michael had spent the long still evenings sorting through the remnants of their lives in New York, putting some things away, consigning others to the trash barrel. Finally there had been nothing left, except this single box which Janet had been assiduously avoiding. It was Mark's box, the remnants of his life, all the things that had been retrieved from his desks—both at home and at the university. Janet had been putting off opening it, working around it, moving it constantly farther into the corner of the room, but now it sat there, conspicuously alone, and there were no more excuses for ignoring it. Unless she put it in the tiny attic, consigned it to that easily forgettable storage room where it might lie undisturbed through several generations.

Like Abby's diary.

She turned the idea over in her mind as she sat enjoying the peace of the midsummer evening. The day's heat had finally broken, and a gentle breeze drifted over the plains. The soft chirping of crickets seemed to fill up the vast emptiness of the landscape, lulling Janet into a sense of peace she hadn't felt in the months since Mark had died. But tonight, with Michael asleep upstairs —apparently peacefully asleep—she began to wonder if she really needed to open that box at all. Perhaps she shouldn't. Perhaps she should simply put it away, as someone had long ago put Abby's diary away, and forget about it.

But Abby's diary had not remained forgotten, nor had Abby herself.

And, Janet was sure, it would be the same with Mark. To her, the plain cardboard container had become a Pandora's box. Despite all logic, she had the distinct feeling that when she opened it, serpents were going to spew forth, devouring what was left of her faith in her husband. And yet, no matter how long she argued with herself, she knew that in the end she would open it. She sighed, and began.

On top, she found all the things she remembered from his desk in the apartment—even the too-short stubs of pencils and the bent paperclips had been packed. She went through things quickly, only glancing at the stacks of canceled checks, the financial records of their life together, the scribbled notes Mark had often made to himself during the course of an evening, only to tuck them away in the desk and forget them.

Only when she came to the contents of his desk at the university did she slow down, pausing to read the files—the notes on his students, the notes on the various studies he always had in mind but never seemed to get around to. And then, at the bottom of the box, she found a large sealed envelope with her name written across it in Mark's distinctive scrawl.

With trembling hands, she ripped the envelope open and let its contents slide onto her lap. There wasn't much there: a copy of Mark's will—the same will that had been on file with their lawyer—and another envelope, again with its flap sealed and her name written on it.

She stared at this envelope a long time, still toying with the idea of putting it away unread, but in the end, she opened it, too. Inside, she found a note in Mark's choppy hand, and yet a third envelope, which had been opened and resealed with tape, this one postmarked Prairie Bend, but with no return address.

She read Mark's note first:

Dearest Janet,

I can't really imagine circumstances under which you would be reading this, but still, I think I'd better write it down. While I'm in Chicago next week, I'm going back to Prairie Bend. There's something that's been bothering me—it goes back many years, and since it's probably nothing, I won't go into it now. There's a lot I've never told you, but I've had my reasons. Anyway, if anything should happen to me, I want you to know that I love you very much, and would never do anything to hurt you. Also, there's something I'd like you to do. I have a sister—Laura—and I'd like you to take care of her. She might not even know she needs help, but I think she does. If you read this, then you'll be reading her letter, too, and perhaps you'll understand. Do whatever you can. I know this note doesn't shed much light on anything, but until I know more, I won't say more.

All my love forever,
Mark

Janet read the note again, then once more. With each reading the tension inside her increased until she felt as if she'd been tied in knots.

"Damn you," she whispered at last. "Damn you for telling me just enough to make me wonder about everything, but not enough for me to *know* anything."

Finally, she picked up the letter from Laura, and feeling as if she were somehow invading her sister-in-law's privacy, she reluctantly pulled it out of its envelope and unfolded it. It was written in a shaky scrawl, and the signature at the bottom was totally illegible. And yet, in spite of the agitation reflected in the penmanship, Janet recognized it as coming from someone closely related to Mark.

Dear Mark,
I know I haven't written to you for ages, and I know you probably won't answer this, but I have to ask you a question. If I don't, I think I'll go crazy. I'm going to have another baby, and after what happened last time, I'm so frightened I don't know what to do. I think they killed my baby. They said it was born dead, but for some reason, I know it wasn't. Mark, I know *it wasn't born dead!*

I keep thinking about that night—the night you ran away while I was in the storm cellar. I keep thinking I remember something about that night, but I can't quite remember what. Do I sound crazy? Maybe I do. Anyway, I need to know about that night, Mark. I need to know what happened. I keep thinking the same thing is happening to me that happened to Mother. Did they kill her baby? For some reason, I think they did, but I was in the storm cellar the whole night, so how could I remember? Anyway, did you run away because you saw what happened that night? Please, Mark, if you did, tell me. I don't care what you saw, or think you saw—I just need to know. *I need to know I'm not going crazy.*

As she had with Mark's letter, Janet reread the note from Laura.

There was nothing really new in the note—it was filled with the same illogical speculations Laura had made after her miscarriage, the speculations Janet had attributed to Laura's grief over losing the baby.

Except that when Laura had written this note, she had not yet lost her baby.

But she had lost another one, a little girl, a little girl named Rebecca—Becky? But that didn't make sense either. Becky had lived, at least for a while—there had been pictures of her, neatly mounted in an album and captioned, only to be torn out later, after the child had died. Laura must have torn them out herself, unable to handle the memories of her lost daughter.

And what was there in the note that had brought Mark back to Prairie Bend after all his years away? He could have answered Laura's questions with a letter, however long or short. But he hadn't—instead, he'd come back to Prairie Bend himself, intent on looking for something.

Something, Janet was sure, that was related to the night he'd run away.

Had he found it?

Was that what the letters meant? That if Janet read the letters, it would mean he'd found what he was looking for, and it had cost him his life?

The idea was barely beginning to take hold in her mind when, upstairs, Michael began to scream.

Janet opened the door to Michael's room, and the first thing she heard was Shadow's soft growl. He was next to Michael's bed, his teeth bared, his hackles bristling, and his yellow eyes gleaming in the darkness. But then, as she spoke to him and he recognized her, his fur settled down and his snarl gave way to a soft whimper. A moment later Janet gathered her son into her arms, rocking him gently until his sobbing eased. "What is it, honey? Is it the pain? Do you want one of the pills?"

Michael shook his head, his eyes wide with fear.

"It isn't your foot?" Janet asked. The foot had been slow to heal, and even after eight weeks Michael still had a slight limp. Sometimes, when he was tired, it still ached.

But again Michael shook his head.

"Then what is it, sweetheart? Can't you tell me?"

"Grandpa," Michael sobbed. "I had a dream about Grandpa, and I saw what happened. Just like before, when I saw Grandpa beating Daddy."

Janet had a sinking feeling. She'd hoped the dreams in which Michael saw his father and his grandfather were over and that Michael had forgotten them. "You had another dream?" she asked.

"Only it wasn't really a dream," Michael insisted. "It was like I was there, and I saw it. And this time, I saw what happened when I hurt my foot. I saw Grandpa try to kill me."

"Oh, Michael," Janet breathed. "Grandpa wouldn't hurt you. He wouldn't hurt you for the world. He loves you."

"No, he doesn't," Michael replied, snuggling closer to his mother and twining his arms around her. "I saw what happened! I didn't stab my own foot —it was Grandpa! He was going to stab me. He was trying to kill me!"

Janet gasped. "Stab you? What are you talking about, Michael?"

"W-with the pitchfork. He was going to stab me with the pitchfork, just like he did to Daddy."

A chill ran through Janet, and her arms tightened around the terrified boy. "No, honey. That's wrong. Daddy fell. He fell from the loft, and landed on the fork. It was an accident. Grandpa wasn't even there."

"He was!" Michael wriggled free from her arms and sat up. Even in the dim light, his eyes were flashing angrily. "He was there! I saw him!"

Suddenly Shadow leaped up onto the bed, and Michael slipped his arms around the big dog's neck. "We saw it, didn't we, Shadow? We saw it!"

With a sinking feeling, Janet realized there was going to be no arguing with Michael. "All right," she said softly. "I won't try to tell you what you saw and what you didn't see." Michael seemed to relax a little, and Janet reached out to take his hand. Shadow growled softly, then subsided. "Why don't we put Shadow outside tonight," she suggested. "Then you can sleep with me."

"But Shadow likes to sleep with me—"

"I'll bet he'd like to spend a night outside," Janet countered. "Wouldn't you, Shadow?" The dog's tail moved slightly. "See? He's wagging his tail."

Michael looked at the dog, then reached out to scratch his ears. "Is that okay?" he asked, and as if he understood his master, this time the dog truly wagged his tail. Janet stood up.

"Okay, I'll put him out, and you go crawl into my bed. I'll be there in a minute. Come on, Shadow."

The dog sat up, but didn't move from the bed. Instead, his head swung around, and his eyes fixed expectantly on Michael.

"Go on, boy," Michael said softly. "Go with Mom."

Shadow jumped off the bed and followed Janet out of the little bedroom and down the stairs. Then, when she held the kitchen door open for him, he dashed out into the night. She watched him lope off in the direction of Ben Findley's place, but after a few seconds the blackness of his coat blended into the darkness, and he was gone. Silently, Janet hoped the dog would be as invisible to the cranky old man as he was to her.

She toured the downstairs, turning off lights and checking doors and windows. Just before she put out the last light, she picked up Mark's letter and reread it, then reread Laura's note as well. At last she put both of them back into the envelope she'd found them in, and put the envelope into the bottom drawer of the desk, far in the back. Thoughtfully, she turned out the lights, went upstairs, undressed, and slipped into bed next to her son.

"Are you still awake?" she whispered.

Michael stirred, but made no reply.

"Sleep then," she said, her voice barely audible. "In the morning you'll have forgotten all about it."

"No, I won't," Michael replied, his voice echoing hollowly in the darkness. "I won't forget about it at all. Not ever." He fell silent for a moment, then stirred and turned over.

"Honey? Is something wrong?"

"Unh-unh," Michael replied. "I just have a headache, that's all."

"Do you want me to get you some aspirin?"

"Unh-unh. It's almost gone."

"You mean you've had it all evening?"

In the darkness, Michael shook his head. "I woke up with it," he said. "I had it in the dream, and then I still had it when I woke up. But it's almost gone now."

Janet lay awake for a long time, thinking about Michael. He'd grown quiet over the last few weeks, and even though he'd made up with Ryan, he still wasn't as close to his cousin—or any of the other children of the town—as she wished he were. And his feelings about his grandfather seemed to be getting almost obsessive.

And then, just before she drifted into sleep, she remembered Michael's words the day Ione had bought the Raggedy Ann.

"I bet they killed her. . . . I bet they buried her in Potter's Field."

No, Janet told herself. It's not possible. He's only imagining things. None of it is possible. . . .

It was just after dawn when Amos Hall glanced out the kitchen window, frowning. "There's that damned dog again," he said softly. Anna's eyes followed his gaze, and in the distance she could see Shadow, his tail tucked between his legs, skulking outside the barn.

"If he's after those hens, I'll have his hide," she said, rolling herself toward the door. "You, Shadow, get out of here! Go home!"

The dog tensed, and his large head swung around so that he faced the house.

"That's right," Anna called. "I'm talking to you. Get on out of here!" Then, as Shadow disappeared around the corner of the barn, she turned back to Amos. "What's he doing over here this early? He never leaves Michael. Did you hear Janet's truck come in?"

"I didn't hear it, 'cause it didn't come in," Amos replied. He got up and went into the dining room, then the living room. A minute later he was back. "And Michael's bike's not around either. So he's not here, unless he hiked along the river. I'll go out and have a look behind the barn."

He left the house and strode across the yard toward the barn, then around the corner. There was nothing behind the barn, neither Shadow nor Michael. Puzzled, Amos came to a halt and surveyed the fields. The ripening grain, nearly three feet high, waved in the breeze, and Amos studied it for a few minutes, trying to find a spot where the boy and the dog could be hiding. And then, as the seconds went by, he began to have an odd sense of eyes watching him.

He turned around, half expecting to see Michael grinning at him, but there was nothing.

Nothing, except—still—the uneasy feeling of being watched. Finally, he looked up.

In the loft door, only his head visible, was Shadow. He was panting, and his mouth was half open, and he seemed to be staring down at Amos.

"What the— You, Shadow! Get down from there!"

Shadow's hackles rose, and a low growl rumbled from his throat. He stayed where he was.

For a long moment the man and the dog stared at each other, and then Amos noticed that the door to the tack room was ajar. And yet he was sure he'd closed it last night, and he hadn't used it today.

Michael *had* to be around, and he must be inside the barn. Amos went inside the tack room, pulling the door closed behind him. "Michael? You in here, son?"

There was no answer, only a soft scratching sound overhead as Shadow moved across the loft floor.

"Come on, Michael," Amos called out a little louder. "I know you're in here. If you make me come and find you, you're going to regret it. And I want that dog of yours out of the barn right now!"

Still there was no answer, and Amos went on through the tack room and into the barn itself. Something scurried in the silence, and once again he heard Shadow prowling around the loft. Slowly, Amos walked down the center of the barn, inspecting the stalls one by one.

All of them were empty.

At last, when he was at the front of the barn, he turned to gaze upward to the loft.

Shadow gazed back at him.

"I know you're up there, Michael," Amos said. "Someone had to let that dog in here, and dogs don't climb ladders."

Still the silence in the barn was undisturbed.

Amos moved toward the foot of the ladder that led to the loft, and started up it. A second later, Shadow appeared at the open trapdoor at the top of the ladder, a soft snarl escaping his lips as he bared his fangs.

Amos stopped and stared upward, his heart beating a little faster. "Get that dog away, Michael," he commanded. After a few seconds, Shadow backed away from the trapdoor.

Quickly, Amos clambered to the top of the ladder and glanced around the loft.

Shadow had disappeared.

"All right, Michael," Amos said, the softness of his voice concealing his anger. "The joke's over. Wherever you're hiding, show yourself."

Nothing happened.

Amos moved toward the small pile of hay bales. They stood beneath the slanting roof, and Amos had to bend down to peer into the narrow space behind him.

Glaring back at him, his eyes glowing, was Shadow.

Startled, Amos stood up, and his head struck one of the beams that supported the barn roof. He staggered back, and Shadow, as if sensing his advantage, growled and moved forward.

"Get back, damn you," Amos muttered. He glanced around the loft, searching for a weapon, and spotted a pitchfork lying near the edge of the loft.

Moving slowly, his eyes never leaving the dog, he began edging toward the fork.

Shadow advanced, his hackles raised now, and his growl grew into an angry snarl.

Suddenly Amos made his move and had the pitchfork in his right hand. The dog tensed and came to a halt, as if sensing that the situation had changed.

Amos felt his heartbeat begin settling back to normal, and tightened his grip on the pitchfork. He began jabbing it at the dog, and slowly Shadow began to retreat, his growl subsiding into a sullen whimper.

And then Shadow's sinewy rump hit the stacked bales of hay, and he could move no further. His hackles rose once more, and his tail, still tucked between his legs, began to twitch. His yellow eyes, glinting in the shadows of the loft, seemed to narrow into evil slits, and fastened on the fork as if it were a snake.

"Not so brave now, are you?" Amos whispered. "Goddamn cur—lots of courage a minute ago, but look at you now."

Suddenly, Shadow leaped, twisting in midair to clamp his jaws onto the handle of the pitchfork, the force of his weight wrenching the tool out of Amos's grip. Before Amos could react, the dog darted toward the open door to the loft, and a moment later the fork dropped harmlessly to the ground below.

And then, as Amos watched, Shadow turned back, and began advancing on him once more, stalking him as if he were a rabbit, watching him, closing the gap between them, waiting for the right moment to strike.

Once again, Amos began backing away, and once more his eyes searched for a weapon.

There was none.

And suddenly Amos felt the edge of the loft. He came to a halt, glaring at the dog with a mixture of fear and anger.

"Down, damn you," he whispered. "Down!"

Shadow ignored him and came even closer, crouching on his haunches, his eyes glowing malevolently, the snarl in his throat settling into a steady evil hum.

And finally, once more, he leaped. His mouth wide open, he hurled his body forward.

Instinctively, Amos's hands and arms came up to ward off the attack, but he knew it was useless. The animal's jaws were about to close on his throat, its teeth about to sink into his flesh, tearing him apart.

Shadow's weight crashed against him, and Amos lost his balance, tumbling backward off the edge of the loft.

He could almost feel the tines of the waiting pitchfork, feel them plunging into his back, impaling him as they'd impaled Mark.

The split second it took before he struck the bin seemed like an eternity, and he half wished that Shadow's jaws would close on his throat, ripping his life out before the tines of the fork slashed through his body. At least with the dog, death would be quick, and the pain short lived.

And then, just before the fall ended, he blacked out.

The telephone was ringing as Janet returned from feeding her small flock of chickens. She hurried to answer it, but Michael got to it first. A moment later, he called out from the living room.

"Mom? It's Grandma, and she wants to talk to you." Then, as Janet took the receiver, he added, "She sounds real funny."

"Anna? I was going to call you in a few—"

And then she fell silent, lowering herself onto the chair next to the desk. "I see," she said at last. "But he's going to be all right? You're sure?" She listened once again, then hung up the phone and turned to face Michael. "Grandpa's had an accident," she said, reaching for her purse. "We have to go over there right away." Suddenly her eyes darted around the small living room, and she frowned. "Where's Shadow?"

As if in answer to her question, there was a soft woofing at the front door, and Michael went to let the big dog in. He nuzzled eagerly at Michael for a minute, but then, as if he felt Janet's eyes studying him, went to her and laid his head against her side. She hesitated, but finally gave him a tentative scratch behind the ears. As he watched, Michael felt suddenly worried.

"What happened to Grandpa?" he asked, and finally his mother looked at him, removing her hand from Shadow at the same time.

"I'm not sure," she said softly. "Apparently he fell from the hayloft. He's all right, but he says Shadow attacked him."

Instantly Michael was kneeling next to the dog, his arms around the beast's neck. "He did not! Shadow wouldn't hurt anyone. Besides, he was here when I got up, weren't you, Shadow?"

The dog whined happily and licked Michael's face.

"But we've only been up an hour," Janet pointed out. "Your grandfather's been up since dawn. Shadow could have been over there."

"But why would he go to Grandpa's? He doesn't even like Grandpa!"

Janet sighed, and got to her feet. "Well, we don't really know what happened, do we? So why don't we go over there and find out?"

Suddenly Michael stiffened. "No!"

"Michael!"

"I don't want to go over there. Grandpa's going to try to blame everything on Shadow, and it's not fair."

Suddenly Janet's own thoughts from the night before came back to her. *Don't argue with him.* "All right," she agreed. "You can stay here. But I want you to stay in the house, and rest. You still limp, even if it's just a little."

"Can't I even go out to the backyard and play with Shadow? I could just throw sticks for him."

Janet was already at the front door. "Okay, but that's as far as you go. The yard. Understood?"

"Uh-huh."

"I'll be back as soon as I can."

And then she was gone, and Michael and Shadow were alone in the house.

"Did you get him, Shadow?" Michael said softly when the sound of the old truck had faded away. "Did you really get him?" The dog whimpered, and pressed closer. "Good boy," Michael whispered. "Next time, maybe you can make him die."

The scene at the Halls' was eerily familiar: there was Anna, her wheelchair pushed close to the sofa in the parlor, and there was Ione Simpson, doing her best to fill the gap left by Dr. Potter's death, bending over the supine figure on the sofa. But this time, it was Amos Hall, not Michael, on the sofa. Janet paused at the doorway for a moment, but Anna motioned her into the room.

"He's all right," she assured the younger woman. "Nothing's broken, and Ione doesn't think there're any internal injuries. Mostly, he got the wind knocked out of him, and his dignity's taken a beating." Suddenly she frowned. "Where's Michael?"

"I left him at home," Janet replied hastily. "I didn't know what was happening here, and I was afraid he'd just add to the confusion."

"It's his dog, I want," Amos suddenly growled. He struggled a moment, then sat up, fury in his eyes. "That mutt attacked me, and I want it destroyed."

"Now, Amos," Anna began, but her husband cut her off.

"You saw him, Anna. You saw him sneaking around the barn. And then he went for me."

"Oh, Amos, I'm so sorry," Janet said. "What happened? Why did he attack you?"

"How the hell do I know why?" Amos snorted. Briefly, he told them what had happened. When he was done, Janet sighed.

"We'll just have to get rid of the dog then, I suppose."

"Get rid of him?" Ione asked. "What do you mean?"

Amos glared at her. "She means have it destroyed. Don't you understand English anymore?" Ione's lips tightened but she said nothing.

Janet leaned forward. "Amos, I didn't mean that—"

"Well, you should have. The dog's dangerous. I told you that when it first came around, but you didn't believe me. Well, do you believe me now?"

"I—"

But this time it was Ione Simpson who didn't let Amos finish. "Are you sure the dog attacked you, Amos?"

Amos's angry eyes shifted back to the nurse again. "What the hell do you mean, am I sure?"

"We've had a lot of dog bites over the years," Ione replied, keeping her voice calm in the face of Amos's wrath. "Most of them were just nips, but a few of them were good hard bites. And a few years back, a dog about the size of a collie did attack someone around here."

"And?" Amos asked.

Ione shrugged. "At least those people had a break in their skin for their trouble. And remember Joe Cotter? Both his arms were torn up, and he was lucky he survived."

For a long moment, Amos was silent, glowering malevolently at Ione. When he finally spoke, his voice was dangerously low. "Are you accusing me of lying?"

Ione shook her head tiredly, knowing arguing with Amos Hall was useless. "I'm only suggesting you might think it was a lot worse than it was. I mean, where are the bites?"

"Goddamn it, it didn't bite me," Amos roared. "It backed me up to the edge of the loft, then jumped at me and pushed me off."

"Amos, calm down," Anna cut in. "No one's accusing you of anything, and I'm sure you think Shadow attacked you. But couldn't you be wrong? Just once in your life, couldn't you be wrong about something?"

"No," Amos snapped. "I know what happened, and I want that dog destroyed. He's dangerous. Sooner or later he'll attack someone else." His attention turned back to Janet. "How would you feel if he attacked Michael?"

Janet stared at the old man, aghast. "Michael?" she replied. "Why on earth would he attack Michael? He adores him. It's almost as if the two of them can communicate with each other."

Amos's eyes darkened. "Well, if something happens to Michael, it won't be my fault."

Suddenly Janet found herself angry with the old man. "Amos, stop it," she said. "Nothing's going to happen to Michael, and if it does, it won't be because of Shadow. Right now, that dog is Michael's closest friend, and unless you can come up with something more than talk to back up your claims that he attacked you, I'm not getting rid of him. Ione's right—if he'd attacked you, it seems to me you'd at least have some scratches. I think you simply stumbled off that loft yourself, and you don't want to admit it. And frankly, you should be ashamed of yourself for trying to put the blame on Shadow." She rose to her feet and left the front room, followed immediately by Anna, who stopped her just as she was leaving the house.

"Janet? Wait a minute."

Her anger already spent, Janet turned back to face her mother-in-law. "Oh, Anna, I'm sorry—I just don't know what got into me."

"No," Anna said softly, shaking her head. "Don't apologize. It wasn't your fault—none of it. I'm sure you were right about what happened. But Amos has always been that way—he can't stand to be contradicted, or criticized, or made to feel he's wrong. He'll get over it. Just give him a little time."

Janet nodded. "Of course." She smiled sadly at Anna. "Is that what happened with Mark? Did he suggest that Amos was wrong about something?"

Anna hesitated a moment, then nodded. "I suppose you could say that." Her eyes met Janet's, and Janet could almost feel the sadness in them. "Don't you do it, too," she pleaded. "Don't turn away from him—from us. I know he's not always easy, but he loves you, and he loves Michael. I know he does."

Janet reached out and touched the older woman's cheek. "I know," she said softly. "And it will be all right. I won't hold anything against him, and neither will Michael."

Anna stayed by the door until Janet was gone, then slowly wheeled herself back to the living room, where Ione Simpson was giving Amos a shot. Anna sat silently in her chair, her eyes fixed on her husband.

But in her mind, she had gone back twenty years, back to the house where Janet lived now, the house Mark had fled from.

She has to know, Anna thought. *Sometime, Janet has to know what happened that night, and why Mark left. And I will have to tell her.* But even as she entertained the thought, Anna was not at all sure she could ever tell the truth about that night and what had gone before. Even after all these years, it was still too painful to think about.

She came back to the present, and focused once more on her husband. Silently, she wondered what had really happened in the barn that morning, wondered if Shadow had, indeed, attacked Amos. Or had it been another accident, like Mark's. Like Michael's.

With a shudder, Anna recalled her husband's words on the day Michael's foot had been hurt. The trouble would go on, she realized. The trouble that had started twenty years ago, then erupted again when Mark finally came home.

And suddenly she knew, with dreadful certainty, that the trouble wouldn't end until Amos was dead. Amos, or Michael. Her husband, or her grandson.

Slowly, Anna turned and wheeled herself out of the room.

"Get it, Shadow! Go get it, boy!" The stick had arced through the air, landing with a thud in the dust near the entrance to the cyclone cellar. Shadow took a few steps away from Michael, then turned back to look uncertainly at his master. "That's right, Shadow," Michael told him. "Fetch. Fetch the stick." The big dog hesitated, then as if finally understanding what was expected of him, trotted off toward the little dugout. But before he got to the stick, he veered off to the right, and a moment later began snuffling around the edges of the closed door. At last he looked back at Michael and barked loudly.

"Aw, come on, Shadow, we're supposed to be playing fetch," Michael complained. He began trudging once more toward the piece of wood which had so far entirely failed to capture the dog's attention. When he had the stick in hand, Michael called to Shadow again. "Come on, boy. Look what I've got!" But Shadow ignored him, his nose still pressed against the crack between the doors of the storm cellar. Frowning slightly, Michael dropped the stick and started toward the dog, and as he drew close to the big animal, he began to feel a slow throb begin in his temples. "What is it?" he asked.

As if in answer, Shadow whined eagerly, and pawed at the door.

"Is something in there?" Michael struggled with the door for a moment and finally succeeded in getting it halfway open. Shadow immediately disappeared into the gloom of the little room, but Michael hesitated, searching the darkness for some hint of what had attracted the dog.

And then he heard the voice.

"Michael."

"N-Nathaniel? Are—are you in here?"

"Go inside," the voice instructed him. "Go inside, and close the door."

As if in a trance, Michael obeyed the voice, moving carefully down the steep steps, lowering the door closed behind him. Slowly, his eyes began adjusting to the darkness. Enough light seeped through the cracks in the weathered doors to let him see Shadow crouching attentively in the corner, his ears up, his tail twitching with eagerness.

"Nathaniel? Are you in here?"

"I am in you, Michael. I am in you, and you are in me. Do you understand?"

In the semidarkness of the subterranean room, Michael slid his arms around Shadow's neck, pulling the dog close. "N-no."

"We are part of each other," Nathaniel's voice said. "I am part of your father, and I am part of you."

"My father?" Michael breathed. "Is—is that why Grandpa killed him?"

"He found out. He found out, so he killed your father."

Michael's eyes darted around, searching for the familiar face of Nathaniel, but there was nothing in the room, nothing but the coolness and gloom. "What did Dad find out?" he whispered.

"The children. He found out about the children. I told him, and showed him, and he believed. But he was afraid."

"He wasn't!" Michael protested. "My dad wasn't afraid of anything!"

"He was afraid to act, Michael," the strange voice replied. "He was afraid to punish them, even after he saw what they did."

"Y-you mean he wouldn't fight?" Michael's voice quavered as he asked the question, for slowly he was beginning to understand what was going to be asked of him.

"He wouldn't make them die, Michael." Nathaniel's voice took on a strangely compelling quality, and even though Michael was sure he ought to resist the voice, he knew he wouldn't. "Will you, Michael? When the time comes, will you be with me and help me make them die?"

"I—I don't—"

"You do know, Michael," Nathaniel's voice insisted. "You know what you must do. You told us so."

"Told you? Told you what?"

There was a long silence, and then, from inside his head, Michael heard his own words—the words he'd spoken to Shadow that very morning—repeated to him in the voice of Nathaniel: "Next time, maybe you can make him die."

Deep down inside, far down in the depths of his subconscious, Michael understood what was expected of him.

He was to avenge his father's death.

He was to kill his grandfather.

His head pounding with the throbbing pain, Michael tried to drive the voice of Nathaniel out of his mind. His arms dropped away from Shadow, and he hurled himself toward the cellar door, scrambling up the steep steps, bursting out into the morning sunlight. But even then, Nathaniel's face lingered inside him.

"You will, Michael. When the time comes, you will help me. You will make them die, Michael. You will . . ."

CHAPTER 19

Ryan Shields was working on his bicycle, adjusting the seat and the handlebars, when he heard the back door slam. He looked up, then watched curiously as his mother brought a bundle of clothes down the back steps and made her way across the yard to the graveled area where the incinerator stood. "Whatcha doing?"

"Cleaning out the attic," Laura told him. "It's gotten too full, and your father wants me to burn some things."

"Want me to help?" Ryan asked, eagerly abandoning the bike in favor of the prospect of a bonfire. But Laura shook her head.

"I can do it." Carefully, she set the bundle on the gravel, stared at it a moment, then returned to the house. A few minutes later she appeared once again, struggling to maneuver a crib through the back door. Immediately, Ryan recognized the crib.

"You're going to burn that?" he asked. "But that's—"

"I know what it is," Laura said, and there was something in her voice that made Ryan fall silent. "I know what all of this stuff is, and I don't want to talk about it, Ryan." She glared at him for a second. Then: "Don't you have anything to do? Do you have to hang around here all the time? Why don't you go out and see Michael?"

Abashed, Ryan scuffed at the ground for a moment. "Well?" Laura demanded with a severity that startled her son. "You haven't seen Michael for a long time. Did you two have a fight?"

"Not exactly—"

"Then go," Laura told him.

"But Dad told me not to go anywhere," Ryan protested. "He told me to stay around here in case you needed anything."

"Well, I don't need anything," Laura declared. "And I'm getting tired of having you underfoot all the time." Then, as she saw her son's chin begin to quiver, she suddenly relented. "Oh, honey, I'm sorry. It's just that I'm upset right now, and I have to do something I really don't want to do. It'll be easier if I'm by myself. Do you understand?"

Even though he didn't understand at all, Ryan nodded his head. "But if you don't want to burn that stuff, how come you're going to?"

"Because your father says I have to. I've put it off as long as I can, and I have to do it by myself. All right?"

Reluctantly, Ryan got to his feet. "Okay. Maybe I'll go out and see what Eric's doing. Maybe we can go fishing."

"Why don't you go see Michael? Are you mad at him?" she asked again.

Ryan hesitated, and dug at the ground with the toe of his sneaker. "He's always got his dog with him," he finally said.

"Shadow? Don't you like him?"

"He doesn't like me. He only likes Michael, and whenever anyone else is around, he starts growling. He scares me."

"He's just being protective—he wouldn't hurt you. Now run on along."

When Ryan was gone, she finished bringing Becky's things down from the attic.

She went over them once more—the clothes Becky had never worn, the crib Becky had never used, the mobiles Laura had never been able to hang over Becky's bassinet, and the toys she had never been able to see Becky touch for the first time. Finally there was nothing left except the album, the album which should have eventually filled with pictures of Becky's first years.

The captions were all there: "Her first meal," "Sunning in the backyard," "First step—wobbly, but she did it!"

She turned the pages slowly, as if studying for the last time the pictures that weren't there—had never been there.

She'd nearly lost herself over Becky. She could remember some of it so well, and yet so much of it was a blank.

She could recall the days of waking up and listening for the cries of the baby, only to remember that there would be no cries, for there was no baby. Other days—the worst days—she'd known from the moment she awoke that Becky had died, and those days had been desolate ones.

The best days had been the days—sometimes two or three of them in a row—when she truly believed that Becky was still there in the house, sleeping, perhaps, and would soon wake up and call for her. It was during one of those times that she'd ordered the Raggedy Ann doll, a gift for Becky to make up for her own neglect.

No one had known she'd done it until the doll arrived, and when Buck had asked her about it, she'd blurted out the truth without thinking. "It's for Becky—I've left her alone so much."

That's when they'd sent her away for a while—not very long, really, only a few weeks. And when she'd come back, she'd been all right. Except that every now and then, she still crept up to the attic to go through Becky's things, to pretend, if only for a few minutes, that Becky was all right, that Becky had survived the birth, that Ryan—despite all the love she felt for him—was not her only child.

But she knew Buck was right, she knew she had to get rid of the last of Becky's things and put the child out of her mind, finally and forever. If she didn't, she would destroy herself.

She placed the empty album on top of the heap, then doused the whole thing with kerosene. Finally she stood back and tossed a match onto the pyre. A moment later all that was left of her memories of her daughter began to go up in flames.

For a long time Laura watched the blaze, standing perfectly still, her attention focused totally on the conflagration. When the touch on her shoulder came, she jerked spasmodically, then whirled around to see Janet standing behind her.

"I'm sorry," Janet said. "Are you all right? I spoke to you, but you didn't answer me."

"I—I—" Laura floundered, then fell silent and turned back to gaze once more at the fire which was fast diminishing to nothing more than a bed of glowing coals. "I was just burning some trash," she whispered at last, her eyes filling with the tears she had been doing her best to control.

"Some trash," Janet repeated softly. "It's the stuff from the attic, isn't it? Ione Simpson's stuff?"

Laura hesitated, then nodded mutely.

"Ione didn't want it back?"

Again the hesitation, longer this time, but finally Laura shook her head. "No . . . no, she didn't."

When she spoke once more, Janet was careful not to look at Laura. "I wish you'd called me—I could have used those things for my baby."

At last Laura faced Janet, and when Janet looked into her eyes, she saw a depth of pain there such as she'd never seen before. "Your baby?" Laura asked, her voice as hollow as her eyes. "Did you say your baby?"

Slowly, Janet nodded, and suddenly a bitter smile warped Laura's pretty features. "You really think you're going to have it? You really think they'll let you have it? Go away, Janet. Go away now, while you still can. If you want your baby, go away now, before it's born. They'll kill it, Janet." Laura's voice began rising to that hysterical pitch Janet had heard once before, right after Laura had lost her baby. She reached out to place a calming hand on Laura's arm, but her sister-in-law shrank away from her.

"Who, Laura?" Janet asked. "Who will kill my baby?"

"Father," Laura whispered; then, again, "Father. He'll do it, Janet—he always does it." For a long time she stared into Janet's eyes, as if trying to see whether the other woman believed her, then finally broke her gaze, and glanced once more at the smoldering coals. "That's all that's left of her now. She's gone, Janet. Now, she's really gone."

"Who?" Janet asked. "Please, Laura, who's gone?"

"My little girl," Laura suddenly wailed. "My little girl, my Becky."

And as Laura collapsed sobbing into her arms, Janet once again remembered Michael's words. *"I bet they killed her. I bet they buried her in Potter's Field."*

"Come on, Laura," Janet said softly. "I'm taking you home with me. I'm taking you home, so we can talk."

"Is Father all right?" Laura suddenly asked. The two of them were sitting in Janet's living room, and Laura was sipping at the cup of tea Janet had fixed for her. It had taken nearly an hour for her to calm down, but now she seemed better.

"He'll be all right," Janet told her. "He claims Shadow attacked him, but nobody else agrees with him."

"I wanted to go out there, you know," Laura said as if she hadn't heard Janet's words. "When Mother called, I offered to go out and help her take care of him, but she wouldn't let me."

"I'm sure she was only thinking of you."

"No!" Once again Laura's voice rose. "They don't think of me," she said bitterly. "At least not Father. He—he thinks I'm crazy, you know."

"I'm sure he doesn't," Janet protested.

"But he does," Laura replied. "He thinks all women are weak, but especially me. And I suppose he's right. After Becky was born I fell apart."

Janet frowned, remembering the letter Laura had sent to Mark.

"Tell me what happened." But Laura shook her head. "I can't talk about it. If I do, you'll think I'm crazy, too."

"I won't," Janet promised. "Laura, I need to know what's happened here, too. I need to know what happened to you, and to Mark. I don't care what you say, I promise you I won't think you're crazy."

Laura grinned crookedly. "That's what the doctors said, too. But when I told them what happened, they didn't believe me. For a while, I thought they did, but it was only an act. Pretty soon they started trying to convince me I was imagining things. So finally I agreed with them, and they let me go."

"Let you go?"

"I—I was in a hospital for a while. A mental hospital. I finally got out by telling them what they wanted to hear. Do you know how hard it is to do that, when you know all they want to hear is what makes sense, but the truth doesn't make sense? In order to prove you're sane, you have to lie. And that's crazy, isn't it?"

Janet ignored the question. "But why were you there? Because of Becky?"

Laura nodded. "I wouldn't admit she was dead. Even now, sometimes I think she's still alive. I wake up in the middle of the night, and I can almost hear her crying. Then I remember where she is, and I remember what happened. But I didn't used to. Sometimes I'd forget for days at a time. So they sent me away."

"Where is she, Laura?"

"Out there," Laura said. Her eyes drifted toward the window, but when Janet followed her gaze, she saw nothing but the fields: her own fields, the ripening crops beginning to tinge the prairie with a golden hue, and, further away, the overgrown expanse that was called Potter's Field. "Becky's buried out there?" Janet breathed. "But why? Why would she be buried out there?"

Laura shook her head. "I don't know," she whispered. "All I know is that's where they bury them. That's where they see Abby, you know. But it's not Abby, Janet. It's not Abby Randolph looking for her children. It's Father, or Dr. Potter, burying my children."

Janet shuddered, for Laura's words were too much like Michael's own. For a moment, she had an urge to flee, to take Michael and run away. But she knew she wouldn't—couldn't—until she learned the truth.

Michael, unaware of how long it had been since he'd come out of the storm cellar, stared at the river. It was much lower than it had been in the spring, and its water was getting clearer every day. As Michael watched, he thought he saw a small school of fish swimming against the current. He started walking upstream, toward the village, with Shadow next to him, though the dog stopped every few seconds to sniff at a bush, a small hole in the ground, or a rock. Then, after they'd gone some fifty yards, Shadow suddenly stiffened, and a low growl emerged from his throat. Michael stopped and stared curiously at the dog.

"What is it, boy?"

The dog stood perfectly still, one foreleg slightly raised, his eyes fixed on a point somewhere in the distance. Michael studied the woods, then shrugged and started forward again.

Again, Shadow growled, and Michael turned back to face him. "Come on, Shadow. There's nothing there," he said, his voice implying a certainty he didn't feel.

For a long moment, the dog remained frozen on point, but then slowly began to relax. His growling faded, and the fur on his neck settled back. Finally he went to Michael, sat down in front of him, and licked his hand. Michael patted him on the head. "See? I told you there was nothing there." But a second later, when he started forward once more, Shadow blocked his way. Michael paused, then started to step around the dog.

Shadow countered his move, then nudged at Michael, pushing him slightly backward.

"Stop that," Michael said, and once more tried to move around the dog. This time, a low growl rumbled up from Shadow's throat as once more he blocked Michael's way.

"What's wrong with you?" Michael complained. "Why can't we go this way?"

And then, from a few yards ahead and off to the right, he heard a twig break. Shadow whirled and once more went onto point, his growl turning into a snarl.

Michael peered into the shadows of the forest, but could see nothing. "Who's there?" he called. Then, when there was no reply, he called out again, "Is someone there?"

Another twig snapped, closer this time. Shadow's hackles rose, and his tail dropped slightly, curving close to the ground. Then his snarl escalated into a howl, and he leaped forward, charging into the woods. A moment later he was gone, though his baying filled the woods with an eerie din.

Michael hesitated only a moment, then spun around and ran back down the path, his feet pounding on the ground, the sound of Shadow's fury diminishing in the distance.

At last, out of breath, Michael came to a stop and sank down on the riverbank. From far away, he could still hear Shadow barking. Suddenly, the bark turned into an anguished yelp.

Then there was silence.

Ryan Shields and Eric Simpson saw Michael and came to a sudden halt. They were on their way to their favorite fishing hole, but now, as they watched Michael, they began to wonder if maybe they shouldn't change their minds.

They glanced at each other uneasily; then, though neither of them spoke, each of them began scanning the area, looking for the big dog that was always with Michael. Today, Shadow was nowhere to be seen.

"You wanta go somewhere else?" Ryan finally asked Eric, and Eric shrugged.

"I don't know. Maybe he's gone."

"Maybe he's hiding in the woods," Ryan countered.

"You scared of him?"

Ryan hesitated, but finally nodded. "He's always growling, and acting like he's gonna bite."

"But Michael says he never bit anyone."

"So what?" Ryan replied, his voice scornful. "Michael doesn't even know where he came from."

Eric frowned. "Are you mad at Michael?"

"I don't know. He's just sort of—well, he's sort of weird."

Eric nodded his agreement. "But my mom says I ought to be nice to him. Why don't we ask him if he wants to go fishing with us?"

Ryan was about to shake his head when he remembered his own mother's words earlier that day, so he shrugged, then called out to his cousin. Michael looked up, then waved.

"Whatcha doin'?" Eric asked as he flopped down on the riverbank next to Michael.

"Waiting for Shadow," Michael replied, but there was something in his voice that made both the other boys suspicious.

Ryan eyed his cousin. "Did he run away?" he finally asked.

"N-no," Michael stammered. Then he told them what had happened, and finished by asking, "You wanta help me look for him?"

The three boys started slowly back up the path that followed the riverbank, but a few minutes later, Eric suddenly stopped. Michael looked at him curiously. "It was further than this," he said.

"But this is where old man Findley's land starts," Eric replied. "What if he sees us out here?"

Michael's eyes narrowed. "I thought you said you weren't afraid of old man Findley."

Then, before Eric could reply, they heard the sound of an animal whimpering.

"Shadow?" Michael called. "Shadow, is that you?"

From up ahead and off to the right in the forest, came an answering bark. Michael began running toward the sound. A second later the other two boys followed him.

Michael found the dog first. Shadow was lying at the base of a tree, his back curled protectively against a root, licking at his left forepaw. Michael knelt down and reached out to touch the injured leg. The dog stiffened for a moment, then seemed to relax under the boy's gentle fingers. But seconds later, when Eric and Ryan came into sight, his hackles rose, and he struggled to his feet, supporting himself on three legs.

"It's all right, boy," Michael whispered. "Lie down. It's all right."

The beginnings of a growl died in the dog's throat, and then he eased himself back down to the ground. Warily, Ryan and Eric approached.

"What's wrong with him?" Ryan asked.

"It's his leg," Michael explained. "Something's wrong with his leg."

"Is it cut?"

"I don't know. I don't think so—there isn't any blood."

Eric dropped down next to Michael, and reached out to touch the injured leg, but quickly pulled his hand back when Shadow bared his fangs.

"No, Shadow," Michael said to the dog. "It's all right. Eric won't hurt you." Then, keeping his hands on Shadow's head, he nodded to Eric. "Go ahead—he won't bite you."

Eric still looked uncertain. "How do you know?"

"I know, that's all," Michael told him.

Eric took the dog's leg in his hand, and though a low rumble came from Shadow, and his eyes fixed balefully on Eric's, he didn't move. Gingerly, the boy explored the injured leg, and though Shadow yelped twice, he made no move either to pull the leg away or to snap at Eric. Finally Eric released the leg and looked at Michael. "It's swollen, but there isn't any cut or anything. It's like maybe somebody hit him with a stick or something."

"Is it broken?" Michael asked, his voice anxious.

Eric shrugged. "I don't know."

"I bet it was old man Findley," Ryan said. "I bet he was coming after you with his gun, and Shadow went for him."

The three boys fell silent, staring at each other, and suddenly Michael felt a chill go up his spine as if someone were watching him from behind. His hands fell away from Shadow, and he scrambled to his feet just as Ben Findley stepped out from behind a tree ten yards away.

The old man glared at them for a moment, then his eyes came to rest on Michael. When he spoke, his voice was hard and angry. "You're damned lucky I didn't shoot him," he said. Only then did Michael see the shotgun that he held loosely in one hand.

At the sound of the old man's words, Shadow bared his fangs once more, snarled, and struggled to his feet.

"What'd you do to him?" Michael demanded. Findley grinned, exposing crooked teeth.

"Hit him," he said. "Hit him with the barrel of this here gun, just when he thought he was gonna get me. Now you three get the hell off my land, hear? Get off right now, and don't come back."

As he gazed at the old man, the familiar pain began in Michael's temples, and a thought drifted fleetingly through his mind. *I could make him die . . . right now, I could make him die. . . .* And then, barely discernible in the far reaches of his mind, he heard Nathaniel's voice: *"Not yet. Not now. . . ."*

"I—I didn't know this was your land," Michael stammered as his headache passed. "There wasn't any sign or anything."

Findley fixed him with a hard look, but then nodded. "That's why I didn't shoot the dog," he said. "If it'd been one of theirs," he went on, nodding toward Eric and Ryan, "I woulda shot it. They know where my land starts and where it stops. And now you know, too. So take the dog and get off. And don't come back."

Slowly the three boys began backing away. For a moment, Shadow held his ground, his yellow eyes flashing even in the filtered light of the woods, but then he, too, began backing off, his gait an awkward hobble as he held his left foreleg off the ground. As the three boys watched, Ben Findley moved deeper into the woods, disappearing almost as if he'd never been there.

"C-come on," Ryan whispered, breaking the sudden silence that hung over the forest. "Let's get out of here before he comes back."

As one, the three boys wheeled around and ran back the way they'd come, not stopping until they were well away from Ben Findley's land.

Limping clumsily and favoring his injured leg, Shadow struggled to keep up.

When they finally emerged from the woods at the foot of the Halls' small farm, Michael stopped to stare at the weed-choked acreage of Potter's Field. Eventually, though, his gaze shifted to Ben Findley's ancient barn.

"That's what he really wants us to stay away from," he whispered, his eyes narrowing angrily. "It's not the woods he cares about, it's the barn."

Ryan and Eric stared at him curiously. "How come? What's so special about the barn?" Ryan asked.

Michael turned to the other two boys, an odd smile coming over his face. "You really want to know?"

The boys hesitated, then nodded.

"Maybe I'll show you sometime," Michael said softly. "Maybe when Shadow's leg gets better, I'll show you."

CHAPTER 20

As the summer wore on, the heat of the prairie filled Janet with a languor she was unused to. At first she attributed it only to the weather, but when she finally talked to a doctor in North Platte about it, she was told that she had to expect her body to concentrate most of its energy on the baby growing inside her and that the best thing she could do was listen to the messages her body was sending her, and take life as easy as possible. And for a while, she was able to relax.

The farm needed little attention, and Michael was more than able to feed their few chickens, tend the cow, and keep the barn in order. Janet concentrated on turning the third bedroom into a nursery, and discovered that even that was no trouble. Just as they had for the farm itself, now people dropped by with things they "thought the baby might be able to use."

For a while, Janet kept a watchful eye on Michael, but as July passed into August, and he complained less and less about his headaches, she began to feel that perhaps the worst was over. Even Laura seemed to have been calmed by the summer weather.

Laura and Janet had grown closer. As Laura's strength returned to her, she began spending more and more time at the farm, helping Janet with her first experiments at canning, teaching her the little tricks that made running the farm easier. And she had an endless curiosity about Janet's life in New York.

At first, Janet assumed that Laura's primary interest was in her brother, that she wanted to know what Mark had been like in all the years of their estrangement. But as time went on, it became clearer that for Laura, talking to Janet was the closest she would ever come to the life she had always dreamed about, and when Janet described the rhythms of the city, told her about the galleries and museums, the shows and the parties, it was almost as if Laura was experiencing them herself.

It was on a day in late August, when the prairie was shimmering with heat and they were sitting on the front porch whiling away the afternoon by talking about all the things they should be doing—and would do, once the heat broke—that Janet finally asked Laura why she had stayed in Prairie Bend.

Laura smiled, a soft smile that reflected both sadness and longing. "By the time I knew what I wanted, it was too late," she said. "I was already married, and Ryan was born, and I just let myself drift along. For a while, I thought about taking Ryan and just leaving, but I always seemed to get pregnant just when I had my mind made up. When you're pregnant, you may feel like running away from home, but it just isn't practical, is it?"

Janet let one hand fall to the swelling in her torso, then brushed a damp strand of hair from her brow. "Not practical doesn't begin to express it. It's funny—when I was pregnant with Michael, I had so much energy I used to frighten Mark. He was always telling me to slow down—take it easier. He was sure I was going to lose the baby. But this time, it's all different. I don't even feel like getting up from this chair."

"You're not as young as you were then," Laura pointed out.

"But look at you," Janet argued. "You weren't taking it easy in May, and you're not that much younger than I am." Then, as Laura's smile faded away, Janet started to apologize for her careless words, but Laura stopped her.

"It's all right, Janet," she said. "And you're right, I wasn't taking it easy. But it wouldn't have made any difference. They would have killed my baby anyway. That's one of the reasons I didn't take it easy—sometimes I can pretend that what happened to the baby was my fault. Isn't that silly? It's easier for me if I can pretend that the baby would have lived if I'd just done something differently. But it isn't true. With Becky, I was so terribly careful, and then—well, I won't go into that anymore." Suddenly she stood up and went to the end of the porch. Though Janet couldn't see her face, she knew that Laura was gazing at Potter's Field.

"I keep thinking I ought to go out there," Janet said when the silence at last became unbearable. "Sometimes I wake up in the middle of the night, and think I ought to go out there and look around that field."

Laura turned around to face her once more, and when she spoke her voice was low, and slightly trembling. "Do you?" she asked. "Or are you just saying that? Do you really believe what I've told you about what's happened to my babies, or are you just like the doctors, only pretending to believe me?"

Janet had been hoping this confrontation would never come, hoping that her failure to argue with Laura would be enough. But now the question had been asked, and she had to answer it.

"I don't know," she said. "It seems totally illogical. I just can't imagine Amos and Dr. Potter doing such a thing. Amos seems so—well, so steady—and so did Dr. Potter."

"Then you don't believe me," Laura pressed.

Janet sighed heavily, and before she replied, she looked around for Michael. But neither he nor Shadow were anywhere in sight. "Michael believes you," she said, her voice low.

"Michael?" Laura replied, her voice sounding dazed. "What do you mean, Michael believes me? Have you talked to him about it?"

Janet shook her head. "I didn't have to. He talked about it himself." Briefly, she told Laura what had happened at the dry goods store the day after they had moved into the little house.

"And then when Ione Simpson said there weren't any little girls named Becky around here, Michael said he bet Becky had been killed, and buried in Potter's Field."

Laura's face paled, but Janet pressed on. "He seems to think his grandfather killed your baby. Not only that, but he thinks Amos killed Mark, and wants to kill him as well."

"Dear God," Laura whispered. "But how does he know?"

"It sounds crazy," Janet replied, then smiled in spite of herself. "There's that word again. Anyway, he claims he saw Amos kill Mark in a dream, and he claims he saw something happen to your baby the night it was born."

"But he wasn't there—"

"No, he was out here that night—out at the Simpsons'. Eric's mare was foaling, and Michael was watching. And then on the way home, something happened. He said he fell off his bicycle, but when he got back to the Halls', he was incredibly upset. He wasn't hurt, except for a few scratches, but he seemed terrified by something. And then there were the headaches," she added, though her mind was already on something else. It was only a fleeting memory, an image of Michael, bent over Anna's chair, while Anna kissed him goodnight.

Except Anna hadn't been kissing him. She'd been whispering something to him, her voice so low that no one but Michael had been able to hear her.

"Laura," Janet asked, the memory of that brief whisper refusing to disappear, "what about Anna? Does she know what you think happened to your babies?"

Laura's face set in bitterness. "She knows. But in the end, she always believes whatever Father tells her. Out here, that's the way it is. No one believes me, Janet."

"Except Mark. Mark believed you, didn't he?"

Laura's pallor increased, but she said nothing.

"It's all right," Janet told her. "I read the letter you wrote him. He left it for me, along with a note." She fell silent, wondering how much to tell Laura. "The note was strange, Laura," she said carefully. "It was as if he knew he might die if he came back here."

"And he did, didn't he?" Laura replied, her voice lifeless. "It's my fault, isn't it? I should never have written to him at all. But I was so frightened. I put that letter off for so long, but then, after I got pregnant again, I just had to write to him. I *had* to, Janet. I never wanted him to come out here—I just wanted him to tell me what happened the night he ran away. But I guess he thought I was crazy, didn't he?"

Janet nodded. "That's what I thought, when I read the notes. But now I'm not so sure. What if he believed you? What if he came out here because he believed you?"

"But—"

Janet ignored the interruption. "Your mother, Laura. Let's go talk to your mother. She must know something."

Anna's gaze wandered from Laura to Janet, then returned to her daughter. "I've never spoken about that night to anyone," she said finally. "Why should I tell you about it now?"

Laura's eyes brimmed with tears. "Because I *have* to know," she pleaded. "Can't you understand, Mother? I've been terrified most of my life. And my babies. What about my babies, Mother? What really happened to them?"

Anna's eyes narrowed. "Your babies were born dead, just like mine."

"Were they, Anna?" Janet asked. "Laura doesn't think so, and I don't believe Mark thought so, either."

"How do you know that?" Anna's voice rose, and her hands gripped the arms of her chair. For a moment, she seemed about to lift herself up, but then she slumped back. "Did Mark say something?" she asked. "Did he ever talk about the night he left?"

"No," Janet replied. "But he left me a note. And a letter he'd gotten from Laura."

"You wrote to him?" Anna demanded of her daughter. "After he abandoned us, you wrote to him?"

Laura hesitated, then nodded her head. "He was my brother. I loved him.

And I needed to know why he went away. But now he's dead, Mother, and so you have to tell us. You *have* to."

"I don't have to," Anna replied, her voice low. "I've never talked about that night because I don't know what happened that night." Her voice broke, and her eyes filled with tears. "It's been the same for me as it has for you, Laura. Don't you understand? I—I thought they killed my baby, too."

"Dear God," Janet whispered. "But why? Why would anybody want to kill a baby?"

"I didn't say they did. I said I thought they did. But I could never prove it. They told me the baby was born dead, and I could never prove it wasn't. But I felt that baby. I felt that baby alive inside me, and deep inside, I've never been able to convince myself that Amos didn't kill it. And I've never forgiven him for it, even though I don't know if he did it." Suddenly a twisted smile distorted her face. "Maybe that's what crippled me," she whispered. "Maybe this is my punishment for my evil thoughts about my husband." Her voice turned wistful. "I want to walk, you know. Maybe if I knew myself what happened that night, I might be able to walk again."

There was silence in the room for several long seconds, a silence that was finally broken by Laura. "Maybe Michael knows what happened that night," she said at last. Anna stared at her with disbelieving eyes. "He—he knows what happened to my baby, Mother," she went on. "He told Janet he saw them kill it—"

Anna swung around, her eyes locking on Janet. "That's impossible," she said. "He wasn't there that night. He couldn't have seen anything."

"I know," Janet agreed, her voice reflecting her own disbelief. "But he says he saw it." She hesitated, then went on. "He says Nathaniel showed him what happened."

"Nathaniel?" Anna repeated. "But there is no Nathaniel—"

"Michael says there is," Janet replied.

"Do you believe him?"

Janet shrugged helplessly. "I don't know what to believe anymore—"

"I want to talk to him," Anna said suddenly. "Alone. I want to talk to him alone. And I want you to tell me everything else Michael has said."

Michael stared down into the depths of the swimming hole, and saw the collection of boulders that choked the bottom. Here and there, the larger ones rose nearly to the surface, and not more than five feet from the place where he had dropped into the water only three months ago, a broad flat plane of rock had replaced the water entirely. He looked up, and met his cousin's gaze.

"I said you were lucky," Ryan told him as if he'd read the thoughts in Michael's mind.

But Michael shook his head. "I knew I wasn't going to get hurt," he said.

"Bullshit," Ryan replied. He gave Eric a disgusted look. "You shoulda seen it—it was all muddy, and you couldn't see anything. And he did a backflip off the tire."

Eric turned suspicious eyes on Michael, but when he spoke, it was to Ryan. "Maybe he came down here earlier and found out where the rocks were."

"I did not," Michael protested. "I'd never even been here before. But I knew I wasn't going to get hurt."

"How did you know?" Eric demanded.

Michael knew he couldn't explain it. How could he tell them what it had been like, when he couldn't really figure it out himself? Still, Ryan and Eric were staring at him, and he had to say something.

"It—it was like somebody was there, whispering into my ear, telling me where to dive. I wasn't even scared. I just sort of knew that nothing could happen to me."

Ryan stared at him with scorn in his eyes. "If nothing can happen to you, how come you managed to stick a pitchfork through your foot?"

"I didn't do that. Grandpa did that."

"Aw, come off it, Michael. Grandpa didn't do it. You're so full of shit!"

"I am not!" Michael flared.

"You are too," Ryan shot back. "Like remember that day old man Findley caught us in the woods, and you said what he was really worried about was the barn?"

"Y-yes—" Michael admitted.

"Well, you said you'd show us what he was so worried about sometime, but you never did. You're just as scared of him as everybody else is."

"I am not!"

"Are too!"

Michael's eyes narrowed. His head began to ache, and in the depths of his mind, he heard Nathaniel's voice, warning him. But it was too late. If he backed down now, Ryan and Eric would never let him forget it. Besides, it would be an adventure, and a forbidden adventure at that.

He ignored Nathaniel's warnings. "All right then, let's go over there."

Shadow suddenly stirred from his position at Michael's feet, and a low growl rumbled up from deep in his throat. Michael reached out and scratched the dog's ears, and the growl faded away.

"When?" Eric challenged.

Michael shrugged with feigned nonchalance. "Tonight?"

Ryan and Eric exchanged a glance, each of them waiting for the other to call Michael's bluff. "Okay," Eric said at last. "But I bet you don't show up. I bet you chicken out, and then claim your mother stayed up late and you couldn't sneak out."

"Mom goes to bed early," Michael argued. "And even if she doesn't, I'll still get out."

"But what if she sees us?" Ryan asked.

"She can't," Michael replied. "Her bedroom's on the other side of the house. She can see Eric's house, but she can't see old man Findley's at all."

"What if she sees Eric?"

But Eric shook his head. "She won't. There isn't any moon tonight."

Ryan, though, was still uncertain, and his brows knit into a worried frown. "If my dad catches me, he'll beat the shit out of me."

Eric shrugged. "Then stay at my house tonight. My room's downstairs, and I can sneak out any time I want to. I never get caught."

A little later the three of them started home, but as they ambled through the woods and across the fields, none of them said much. Each boy was thinking of the night's adventure, Eric and Ryan with anticipation, but Michael with a strong sense of unease. Maybe, he decided as he and Shadow turned up the driveway to his house, it would have been better to have let Eric and Ryan think he was chicken. But it was too late now.

Shadow barked happily and dashed ahead. Michael looked up and saw his grandmother seated in her wheelchair just in front of the porch. As he watched, the big dog bounded up to her and reared up to put his paws on the old woman's lap, his tongue licking at her face.

"Get down," Michael yelled, breaking into a run. "Shadow, get down!"

"It's all right," Anna assured him. "He's a good dog, aren't you, Shadow?" She patted him on the head, then began to ease his weight off her lap. The dog quickly settled down at her feet, though he kept his head high enough so she could scratch his ears. Anna smiled at Michael. "I thought it was time you and I had a good talk."

Michael glanced around uncertainly. "Where's Mom?" he asked. "And Grandpa?"

"Your grandfather's at home, and your mother and Aunt Laura had some errands to run. But I wanted to talk to you, so here I am."

"T-talk to me?" Michael asked. "About what?"

"All kinds of things," Anna replied. "For one thing, why don't we talk about why your grandfather killed your father?"

Michael stared at his grandmother. Her eyes were on him, and though he expected them to be angry, instead he saw only a soft warmth. And she was smiling.

"D-did Mom tell you that?"

Anna hesitated, then nodded. "She told me that's what you think. She told me you saw him do it."

Michael swallowed, then nodded. "Mom says it was only a dream, though."

"I know," Anna said. "And I didn't argue with her. But what if it wasn't a dream? What if you really did see it?"

"You mean you believe me?"

"I don't believe you're a liar, Michael. As far as I know, you've only lied once, and I believe you had your reasons for that lie." She paused a moment, then went on. "It was the night Aunt Laura's baby was born," she said. "You saw them bury her baby out in the field, didn't you? Out in Potter's Field?"

Michael froze, a wave of fear washing over him.

"Is that what happened, Michael?" Anna pressed.

"I—I'm not supposed to tell. I'm not supposed to tell anybody. H-he told me—" Michael broke off, already sure he'd said too much.

"But you didn't tell me," Anna reassured him. "I told you, didn't I? I told you what happened."

Uncertainly, Michael nodded.

"And what about that day in the barn, Michael, when your grandfather stabbed your foot? Are you allowed to tell me about that?"

"Mom said that was an accident—" Michael began, but Anna held up a quieting hand.

"I'm sure your mother thinks it was an accident. But I want you to tell me what really happened. Can you do that?"

Slowly, Michael told his grandmother what had happened in the loft. When he was done, Anna sat silently for a long time. Then she reached out and took Michael's hand. "Michael, do you know what it was your father thought your grandfather had done? What Nathaniel had shown him?"

"N-no."

"Well, don't you think we ought to find out?"

Michael frowned. "But Mom says I only imagined it all. Mom says I only dreamed the things I saw."

"But what if you didn't, Michael? What if you really saw it all?"

"You mean you believe me? You don't think I'm crazy?"

Anna put her arms around the boy and drew him close. "Of course you're not crazy," she told him. "And you mustn't be afraid of what you know. It's what you don't know that's frightening, Michael. That's the way it always is," she said, almost to herself. "The things that you don't know about are the most frightening." She let her arms fall away from the boy, and straightened herself in her chair. "Now, let's you and I go and find out just what's in Potter's Field, all right?"

Michael's eyes widened apprehensively. "But Mr. Findley—"

"Ben Findley won't stop us," Anna replied. "I've known Ben Findley most of my life, and he won't do anything. Not to me. Not when he knows I'm sitting right there, watching him. Now, help me with this chair."

With Michael behind her and Shadow at her side, Anna Hall moved across the yard. Then she started out through the pasture toward the barbed wire fence that surrounded Potter's Field, her chair fighting her every inch of the way.

"Leave me here," Anna said. She gazed at Ben Findley's ramshackle house, partly hidden from her view by his barn. A few feet away lay the barbed wire, and beyond it the tangle of brush and weeds that choked the abandoned field. "You and Shadow go out into the field, and see what you can find." When there was no reply, she twisted around in her chair.

Michael's expressionless eyes seemed fixed on a point in the distance. Anna followed his gaze, but all she saw was the barn. "Michael? Michael, is something wrong?"

Michael came out of his daze, and his eyes shifted to his grandmother. "But what if old man Findley—"

"He won't come out," Anna told him. "He might try to scare children, but he won't try to scare me. Now, go on."

As Anna watched, Michael made his way carefully through the fence, the big dog following close behind him. Once, Michael glanced up toward the barn, but then he concentrated on the ground in the field. He moved slowly, knowing he was looking for something, but unsure what it might be.

For ten minutes, the boy and the dog ranged back and forth across the field, finding nothing. Then, suddenly, Shadow stiffened and went on point.

And at the same time, a headache began to form in Michael's temples.

There was a stone on the ground, a stone that didn't quite seem to belong in the field. Though it was weathered, it seemed to have been purposely shaped, flattened and rounded as if it was meant to mark something. As Michael stared at the stone, Shadow moved slowly forward, his nose twitching, soft eager sounds emerging from his throat.

"Here." Though it was only one word, the voice inside his head was unmistakable. The word resounded in his head, echoing, then gradually faded away. As it died, the headache cleared.

Michael knelt on the ground and carefully moved the stone aside. He began digging in the soft moist earth beneath the stone.

Six inches down, his fingers touched something, and after a little more digging, he was able to unearth the object.

It was a piece of bone, thin and dish shaped, and even though Michael had never before seen such a thing, he knew at once what it was.

A fragment of a skull.

In twenty minutes, Michael and Shadow found five more of the flat, round stones, and beneath each of the stones, there were pieces of bone.

At last, Michael returned to his grandmother and told her what he'd found.

"What are we going to do?" he asked as they began making their way back toward the house.

For a long time, Anna was silent, but when they were finally back on the front porch, she gazed into Michael's eyes. "Michael, do you know how you see the things you've seen?"

Michael nodded.

"Can you tell me?"

Michael gazed fearfully at his grandmother. "I—I'm not supposed to tell. If I tell, I'll die."

Anna reached out and touched Michael's cheek. "No," she said softly. "You won't die, Michael. Whatever happens, I won't let you die."

Michael paled slightly. "You're not going to tell Grandpa, are you?"

Anna drew the boy close. "I'm not going to tell anybody, and neither are you. Until we decide what to do, this is our secret. But you mustn't be frightened. Do you understand that?"

Michael nodded silently, then pushed his grandmother's chair through the front door. When his mother and his aunt arrived a few minutes later, neither he nor his grandmother said a word about what had transpired between them.

It was their secret, and, Michael decided, he liked having a secret with someone else. Since his father had died, there had been no one to share secrets with.

No one except Nathaniel.

Ben Findley let the curtain drop back over his window as the woman and the boy disappeared into the house next door. For a long time, he thought about what he ought to do, wondered if, indeed, he ought to do anything at all. In the end, though, he went to the telephone, picked it up, and dialed. When it was finally answered, he explained exactly what he'd seen. "I don't want them there," he finished. "I don't want your family snooping in my field."

"All right, Ben," Amos Hall replied. "I'll take care of it."

CHAPTER 21

Michael lay in bed, wishing he'd never promised Ryan and Eric that he'd take them into old man Findley's barn. This afternoon, when they'd been at the swimming hole, it had seemed like it might be a great adventure. But now he wasn't so sure—ever since he'd been in Potter's Field and his head had started hurting, he'd begun to remember Nathaniel's warnings once again. Now, in spite of his grandmother's words, he was frightened, but he'd told Eric and Ryan he'd meet them, and if he didn't, they'd think he was chicken.

At last, when he was sure his mother was asleep, he slowly began getting dressed. Only when he had double-knotted his tennis shoes and checked his pocket for his house key three times did he finally open the door to his room and whisper to Shadow, "Go on." The dog obediently slipped through the narrow opening and padded silently down the stairs. Closing the door, Michael went to the window and peered out into the darkness. As Eric had said, there was no moon, but the night was clear, and the soft glow of starlight softened the blackness. Michael opened the dormer window, then climbed gingerly out onto the steeply sloping roof. A shingle cracked under his weight, and Michael froze for a moment, listening for any slight movements from within the house. When he heard nothing, he began making his way carefully toward the eave.

He crouched at the edge, his eyes fixed on the rain gutter. The pipe seemed as if it was about to collapse under its own weight, and finally he decided not to risk it. Surely his mother would awaken if the gutter pulled loose, and the jump looked pretty easy. He lowered himself to a sitting position and let his legs dangle over the edge. A moment later he launched himself off the roof, letting his knees buckle as he hit the ground so that he rolled into the kind of somersault he'd seen his father use when he was skydiving. He lay still for a moment—something else his father had always done—and then stood up to brush the dust off his jeans. Then he went to the front door, unlocked it, and let Shadow out.

Ryan and Eric were waiting for him next to the storm cellar.

"How we gonna do it?" Ryan whispered. "Old man Findley hasn't gone to bed yet. There's a light on in the downstairs window."

"Maybe we better not try it," Michael suggested.

"You chickening out?" Eric asked.

"N-no. But what if he catches us?"

"If we do it right, he won't," Eric said. "We can cut down to the river, then come back through Potter's Field. That way the barn'll be between him and us. Come on."

They moved out of the shelter of the storm cellar's slanting roof and began zigzagging down the length of the pasture, hunched low, pausing every few seconds to watch and listen.

Except for the soft chirping of insects and the lowing of cattle floating over the prairie, the night was silent. They came to a stop at the fence separating the pasture from the wheat field beyond, and Michael peered intently into the darkness. The night seemed to thicken over Potter's Field, just to the west. Shadow, crouching at his master's feet, whined softly.

"What is it?" Ryan asked, his voice barely audible.

Michael said nothing. His head was beginning to hurt, and in the darkness he was almost sure he could see a slight movement. And as if from a great distance, a voice—Nathaniel's voice—was whispering to him. The words were indistinct, but Michael knew it was a warning.

"Something's out there," he said at last. "In Potter's Field. I can feel it."

"Come on," Eric said. He climbed the fence and began making his way down the wheat field toward the woods next to the river. Ryan followed him, and, a moment later, so did Michael. But even as he came to the strip of cottonwoods and stepped into the near-total darkness beneath the trees, Michael's headache grew worse, and the voice in his head became more urgent.

Their progress slowed. They moved with all the care their imaginations demanded, and every time a twig snapped under their feet, they came to a halt, waiting for an answering movement that would tell them they were not alone in the woods. After what seemed an eternity, they emerged from the forest, and found themselves at the south end of Potter's Field. They gazed out at it. In the gloom of the night, its growth of tumbleweeds seemed to have turned threatening.

"Maybe Michael's right," Ryan whispered. "Maybe we ought to go home."

"You scared?" Eric asked.

Ryan nodded.

"Well, I'm not," Eric declared. "Come on." He started to worm his way through the barbed wire fence that surrounded the field, but suddenly Michael's hand closed around his arm.

"There's something out there."

Eric hesitated. "Bullshit." Then: "What?"

"I—I don't know. But I know there's something in the field. I can—I can sort of feel it."

The three boys, their eyes squinting against the darkness, peered into the field, but saw nothing more than the blackness of the night and the strange forms of the tumbleweeds etched vaguely against the horizon.

Suddenly Shadow tensed, and a low growl rolled up from the depths of his throat.

"Oh, Jeez," Ryan whispered. "Let's go home."

And then, in the distance, a light appeared, and Shadow's growl turned into a vicious snarl.

"It's Abby," Ryan breathed. "It's gotta be Abby, lookin' for her kids."

"M-maybe it's not," Eric said, but his voice had suddenly lost its conviction. "Maybe it's old man Findley—maybe he saw us."

Only Michael remained silent, his eyes concentrating on the light, his ears hearing only the words that were being whispered within his head.

"If he finds you, you will die."

The light moved, bobbing slowly through the field, stopping every few feet. With every movement, it seemed to come closer, almost as if whatever was in the field knew the three boys were there, and was searching for them.

Shadow, too, seemed to be concentrating on the light. Every muscle in his body was hard with tension under Michael's hands, and the end of his tail twitched spasmodically. A menacing sound, barely audible, welled up from deep within him, and his ears lay flat against the back of his head.

And then, as if he'd responded to the hunter's instinct buried deep in his genes, he shot off into the night, disappearing almost instantly, as his black fur blended into the darkness.

The dog's sudden movement triggered Ryan and Eric, and suddenly they were running, oblivious now to the sounds of their feet pounding through the underbrush as they dashed back into the cover of the forest.

Only Michael, his head throbbing, stayed where he was, peering into the darkness, searching the field for someone—or something—he knew was there, but couldn't quite find. And then, following the voice that seemed to come from within, he carefully crept through the fence and began making his way across Potter's Field toward the barn beyond.

Amos Hall had been making his way carefully through the field. He knew where each of the markers lay, which were the stones that marked the children's graves. He paused at each of them, though only for a second at the ones that still lay undisturbed.

The stones that had been turned over that afternoon took more of his time, for when he came to those, he knelt in the earth, carefully sifted the soft soil through his fingers, smoothing it as well as he could, then replacing the stone markers with an odd sense of reverence.

He'd been in this field only four times since the day when he was a young man and his father had brought him out here, shown him the stones, and told him the story of Abby Randolph.

"And our children still die," his father had told him. "It's as if there's a curse on us, almost as if Abby and Nathaniel want us to remember how they felt, want us to feel the pain they must have felt that winter." Amos had started to protest his father's words, but his father had stopped him. "It'll happen to you, too, Amos. You'll have children, and some of them will be all right. But there will be others who will be born dead. Bring them here, Amos. Bring them here and bury them with Abby's children."

Amos hadn't believed it at first, not until the first time it had happened. He and Anna had been young then, and as Anna's belly swelled with the growing child they had made plans for it, begun to love it, cherishing it even before it was born.

And then, finally, one night it had come.

And it had been dead.

Amos remembered that birth still, remembered being in the little downstairs room with Anna, helping her as her labor began. And then the child had emerged from the womb, and he had known immediately that it was dead.

Anna had denied it.

It couldn't have been dead, she'd said. It couldn't have been dead, because she'd felt it moving inside her, right up until the very end. If it had been alive then, how could it have died?

Amos hadn't been able to tell her. He'd tried, done his best to make her understand the tragedy that had befallen their family so many years ago, but in the end, he'd failed. Stories and old wives' tales, Anna had insisted.

Despite what Anna had thought, Amos had brought the child out to this field and buried it with Abby's children. And when he'd returned, Anna had changed. A hurt had entered her soul, a hurt that had never healed. Slowly, over the years, she'd come to think he had killed her child.

When it had happened again, her bitterness had only increased. And once more he had come to Potter's Field, burying what he had come to think of as Nathaniel's child near its brother.

Then there had been Mark. And Laura. Healthy children, who had lived though both had seemed frail at birth.

With Anna's last child, it had been different. Amos still could not bring himself to remember that night. On that night, he had not come to the field. That night, Charles Potter had done it for him, and Amos had never even asked where that child lay.

He didn't want to know, for it was after that night that Mark had left, and Anna had retreated to her wheelchair, and Laura's mind had begun to weaken.

Laura.

He hadn't even tried to explain the truth to Laura. Instead, he'd merely been there, as he'd been there for Anna, to help her with her labor, and take away the tiny bodies when she inevitably gave birth to one of Nathaniel's children. For Laura, he'd been here twice.

If other people ever came to Potter's Field, Amos Hall had never known about it.

Except for Mark.

Mark had come to the field twice. Once, the night Anna's last child had been born. That night, he'd said nothing. Instead, he'd simply disappeared. But then, last spring, he'd come home, and once more he'd come to Potter's Field. And after that night in Potter's Field, he'd sought Amos out, confronted him with wild ravings about dead children who still lived, shouting about Nathaniel and punishment.

Amos had tried to explain the truth of what had happened so many years ago. But Mark hadn't wanted to hear. Instead, he'd only stared at Amos with hate-filled eyes. "I was there, Pa," he'd said. "I was there the night my brother was born. You thought you'd killed him, didn't you? And you gave him to Doc to bury. But he wasn't dead, Pa. I could hear him, crying out, calling to me. I followed him that night, Pa. While Doc carried him into the field, I followed him, and I watched what happened. Doc buried him, Pa. The baby wasn't dead, but Doc buried him anyway. And he's still not dead, Pa. He's alive. Nathaniel's alive."

Mark had been shouting, shouting and screaming, and then, Mark had died. And Amos, in his own mind, was still not sure if it had been an accident, or if he had meant to kill Mark. All that had mattered was that suddenly there was silence in the barn. Silence and peace. There had been too many years of pain, too many years of misunderstandings. Now, all that mattered to Amos was that Potter's Field lay undisturbed, that Nathaniel's children have their peace.

But today, Anna had come, and Michael, and Michael had prowled the field, turning over the stone markers, disturbing the soil that covered Nathaniel's children.

Tonight, carefully, reverently, Amos was repairing the damage.

He worked slowly, moving from grave to grave, checking each stone.

Twice, he thought he heard sounds in the night, sounds that didn't fit. Twigs snapped, and he knew well that the creatures of the night moved silently, never betraying their presence with more than a rustling of leaves that could be mistaken for the wind. Tonight, there was no wind.

He paused each time he heard a sound, and listened, but all he heard was silence, and after a few moments he returned to his work.

Then, as he was replacing the sixth stone, he felt something. It was a presence, and it was near him. And suddenly the night was filled with sound—the sound of running feet, human feet, fleeing into the woods by the river. And yet, despite the sounds, Amos still had the feeling that he was being watched. Nervously, he cast the beam of light in a circle around him, and finally saw them. Two yellow eyes gleaming in the darkness, and beneath them the bared fangs of Shadow, his lean body slung close to the ground in readiness for the attack.

His rifle. Amos had to find his rifle. He groped around in the dark, but it wasn't there. Finally, in desperation, he used the flashlight. The gun lay on the ground a few feet away, just out of reach. As Amos moved toward it, Shadow launched himself into the air.

Neither the man nor the dog uttered a sound, and for Amos the dog's silence was the most frightening thing about the attack. Shadow's first lunge knocked him off his feet, and he tumbled to the ground, expecting the dog's fangs to sink into his flesh immediately. It didn't happen.

Instead the dog placed himself between Amos and the gun, his cold yellow eyes fixed on the man, his teeth bared. For several seconds, Amos lay still on the ground, waiting for the dog to renew his attack.

Then, when Shadow made no move toward him, he pulled himself up onto all fours. Shadow watched him, but still made no move.

But when Amos started forward, moving slowly and carefully, Shadow tensed, and his tail began to twitch.

Amos backed off, and Shadow's tail stopped moving, but he inched forward, closing the distance between himself and Amos to what it had been before.

Every time Amos tried to move toward the gun, it happened again. The bared fangs, the dangerously twitching tail, the tensing of the body.

Slowly, Amos began backing away, and just as slowly Shadow closed on him, never crowding him, but never letting the distance between them increase.

Then Shadow began playing Amos, moving him slowly across the field, circling him slowly, guiding him toward the fence that separated the field from the woods. At first Amos rejected what was happening, but each time he tried to define the direction of his own retreat, Shadow countered him.

And still there was no sound, either from the man or from the dog.

Minutes later, Amos felt the sting of barbed wire as the lowest strand of the fence gouged into his leg. He stopped, sank into a crouching position for a moment, then finally stood up. Shadow, too, came to a halt, as if sensing that for the moment the man could go no further.

After a few seconds had passed, Amos took a step to the left. For the first time, Shadow growled, then countered the move. Amos tried going to the right. Again, the growl, and the counter.

"Goddamn you," Amos muttered. Carefully, he made his way through the fence. The moment he was free of it, Shadow slipped easily beneath the bottom wire and began relentlessly driving the old man through the woods toward the river beyond.

CHAPTER 22

Michael made his way slowly across Potter's Field, carefully avoiding the worst of the undergrowth but nevertheless having to stop every few yards to free himself from the weeds and vines that seemed to grasp at his ankle with every step. For a while he kept a careful watch on the light that still bobbed in the darkness fifty yards away, but even as he watched it, he knew it posed no threat: Shadow was out there, and Michael was certain that the dog was stalking whatever was in the field. Soon he shifted the focus of his attention to the barn.

His headache began to ease as he drew close to the looming structure, and by the time he had come close enough to touch it, his mind was clear, and the pain was gone.

And all his memories of Nathaniel had returned. He could remember everything he had talked about with Nathaniel, every word Nathaniel had told him.

And he knew he had disobeyed Nathaniel.

He moved slowly around the corner of the barn to the side door. When he had achieved his goal, he stopped for a few moments and gazed out into Potter's Field, but the light was gone now, and the darkness of the night was once more complete. All he could see was the silhouette of the forest against the night sky, and even that was little more than a vague line across the horizon. Above, he could see the stars; beneath, there was nothing but blackness.

Creeping as quietly as he could, he slipped through the darkness to the front of the barn.

Mr. Findley's lights were still on, and once, through the curtains, Michael saw the form of the old man himself, pacing restlessly across his kitchen floor. But no dogs barked, and the silence of the night remained undisturbed. Michael returned to the side door, removed its bar, and slipped inside the barn.

The barn was filled with a musky odor that made Michael want to sneeze, but he resisted it. And even though he could see nothing, he moved through the blackness with the same confidence he would have felt if it had been broad daylight. Somewhere in the darkness, Nathaniel was waiting for him.

And then came the words, whispered in that odd toneless voice that seemed to originate deep inside his own head.

"Outside, Michael. I want to go outside."

Michael froze in the darkness, knowing that Nathaniel was close to him, very close.

"Wh-where are you?"

"I am here, right next to you. Now we will go outside."

As if an alien force was moving him, Michael started back toward the door. A moment later, with Nathaniel beside him, he was outside again in the fresh night air.

"It smells good." For the first time that night, the voice came through Michael's ears, and he turned to face Nathaniel. Suddenly the night seemed brighter, and he looked curiously at Nathaniel's clothes.

They looked old-fashioned, and they didn't seem to fit very well.

"Where'd you get those clothes?" he asked. "Are they from a store?"

Nathaniel looked puzzled. "Someone made them for me," he said as he carefully placed the door bar back in its brackets. Then, before Michael could ask him another question, Nathaniel started off into Potter's Field.

"They are here," Nathaniel said softly, pointing to one of the stones that marked the children's graves. "Can you feel them, Michael? Can you feel the children around you?"

And strangely, Michael realized that he could feel something. It was almost as if he and Nathaniel were not alone in the field; all around him he could feel strange presences, and on the edge of his consciousness he thought there were voices, voices he couldn't quite hear. They weren't like Nathaniel's voice, clear and strong even when Nathaniel wasn't speaking out loud. These voices were soft, indistinct, but there was something about them that made

Michael feel sad. They were lonely and abandoned, and Michael wanted to help them.

"Who are they?" he finally asked.

"My mother's children," Nathaniel whispered softly. "Abby's children."

"But why are they here?"

"My father kills them," Nathaniel replied. "My father comes for them, one by one, and brings them out here. But tonight we will kill my father."

"Kill him," Michael repeated, his voice suddenly as toneless as Nathaniel's.

"If we don't, he will kill us," Nathaniel whispered. "And he is here, tonight. He was looking for you, Michael. He knew you were coming tonight, and he was looking for you. The light in the field, Michael. It was my father." He stopped talking and crouched down for a moment. When he straightened up, there was a rifle in his hands. "He was going to kill you with this," he said.

Michael stared at the gun, and knew immediately where he'd seen it before. Still. . . . "He won't—" he protested, but even as he uttered the words, he knew they weren't true.

Nathaniel had been staring off toward the river, but now his head swung around, and his blue eyes fixed on Michael, holding him in their grip.

"He killed your brothers and sisters, Michael."

Michael felt fear begin to grow in him. "I—I don't have any brothers or sisters," he whispered.

"Here," Nathaniel breathed. "Here around you are your brothers and sisters. And there will be more."

There will be more.

His mother. His mother was pregnant; very soon she was going to have a baby—a brother or sister for him. So Nathaniel was right. In the darkness, he nodded. Nathaniel's powerful eyes released him from their hold, and he turned away once again.

They moved quickly now, and Michael had no trouble avoiding the tangle of vegetation that overran the field. Though he was seeing with his own eyes, it was as if Nathaniel was showing him the way. They climbed over the fence. Silently, confidently, Nathaniel stepped into the trees, with Michael close behind him. And even here, though nothing in the quality of the starlight had changed, Michael found he could see clearly.

Then, from close by the river, he heard a low growl and knew without being told that it was Shadow. Ahead of him, Nathaniel came to a stop. He turned around to face Michael once again, his hypnotic gaze drawing Michael's spirit close.

"Will you help me?" he asked.

Almost unwillingly, Michael nodded.

"He's nearby, Michael. Ahead, by the river. Come."

They moved slowly now, slipping from tree to tree. Every second Shadow's menacing snarl grew louder. And then, through the trees ahead, Michael saw his grandfather.

Amos felt his heart pounding, and tried to think how long he had been here, trapped against the river, held at bay by the dog who never made a move to attack him, never came close enough for Amos to strike out at him with the flashlight, yet never dropped his vigilance, but instead paced back and forth, his head low and his tail drooping, his eyes flashing in the starlight, a steady snarl raging in his throat.

In the darkness behind the dog, Amos sensed a movement. "Who's there?" he called out. "Is someone there?" Then, sure that he knew who it was lurking in the woods, he forced his voice into a tone of command. "I know you're there, Michael. Come out and call off your dog."

In the woods, Michael stiffened as he heard his name, but suddenly he heard Nathaniel's voice, heard it as he had heard it so many times before, emanating from within his own head.

"Say nothing. Say nothing, and do nothing."

But he knows I'm here, Michael thought. He called my name, and he knows I'm here.

"Wish him dead."

Nathaniel moved forward through the darkness, and Michael stayed where he was, watching and listening, watching with the strange clarity of Nathaniel's vision, and listening to the soft sounds of Nathaniel's instructions.

"Wish him dead."

The seconds crept by—each of them, to Michael, an eternity.

An unnatural silence seemed to fall over the night. Shadow, his growl dying on his lips, suddenly lay down on the ground, his ears up, his eyes still fixed on Amos.

Amos, too, sensed the change in the atmosphere, and suddenly felt his skin begin to crawl. Whatever was out there, he was suddenly certain, it was not Michael, and it was coming for him.

With shaking fingers, he pressed the switch on the flashlight and began playing its beam over the forest.

And then Amos saw him.

Standing perfectly still, his face a pale mask in the white light of the torch, his blue eyes wide and steady—the same blue eyes of all the Halls—the figure of the oddly dressed boy seemed to Amos to have about it the calmness of death.

"W-who are you?" he asked, forcing the words from his throat. Suddenly he was having difficulty breathing, and his heart was pounding with a fury that frightened him almost as much as the visage that glared at him with malevolent eyes from a few yards away.

The words suddenly filled the night.

"I am Nathaniel."

Amos staggered. "No," he gasped. "No. Nathaniel's dead. Nathaniel's been dead for a hundred years. Who are you? Tell me who you are!"

Again, the same words: "I am Nathaniel."

Amos staggered, and the flashlight dropped from his trembling hands.

Michael, still rooted to the spot where Nathaniel had left him, watched as his grandfather sank to his knees, and listened as Nathaniel whispered to him once again:

Wish him dead.

Then, as Amos clutched at his chest, his terrified eyes still fixed on the spot where the apparition stood, Michael began to feel Nathaniel's power within him.

Die. Die. Die.

The word echoed in his mind, his lips silently formed it, the thought transfused his soul, and as he watched, his grandfather sank slowly to the ground.

You killed my father. Die. Die. Die.

And then, as the night sounds slowly began again, Michael knew it was over. Shadow rose to his feet and padded over to sniff at Amos's body. He whined a little; then, wagging his tail, he trotted toward Michael, sat at his feet, and licked his hand.

In the darkness, Nathaniel smiled at him.

"Go home now, Michael," he heard Nathaniel say. "Go home, and wait."

Michael hesitated uncertainly. "But what about Grandpa?"

"They will come and find him," Nathaniel said quietly. "It will not be very long. Go home and wait, Michael. I will tell you what to do."

With Shadow beside him, Michael turned and started back through the forest. Suddenly he turned back. "Nathaniel?"

But all Michael saw was the blackness of the night.

Nathaniel was gone.

Michael slipped his key in the lock of the front door, twisted it, then gently pushed the door open, silently praying that the hinges wouldn't squeak. As soon as Shadow scuttled through the narrow opening, Michael followed, and closed the door as carefully as he had opened it. Then he made his way up the stairs, testing each tread before putting his weight on it. After what seemed to him to be forever, he made it to the second-floor landing, and paused to listen. From behind the closed door to her room, he could hear the even sound of his mother's breathing. A moment later, he was safe in his own room. He undressed, then slipped into bed, where he lay wide awake listening to the night and waiting.

Suddenly he heard Nathaniel's voice whispering inside his head, and at the same moment, the quiet of the night was shattered by the sound of a gunshot. Obeying Nathaniel's instructions, Michael leapt out of bed, and ran to his mother's room. He pounded on the door, then burst inside.

"Mom! Mom, wake up!"

Janet's eyes flew open, and she sat up, reaching instinctively for the lamp next to her bed. As light flooded the room, she heard a sound, then another.

Two shots.

"There was another one," Michael told her, climbing onto her bed. "It woke me up, Mom. Someone's down by the river, and they're shooting at something."

Janet swung her legs off the bed, struggling to drive away the last vestiges of heavy sleep. A moment later she was at the window, peering out. All she could see was darkness, suddenly pierced by a light from the Simpsons' house, a few hundred yards away. A moment later, the phone started ringing.

"Go answer it, honey," Janet told Michael as she struggled to find the sleeves of her bathrobe and pull it on over her ungainly bulk. As Michael jumped off the bed and dashed out of the room, Janet followed him as quickly as she could. Another shot rang out as she took the receiver from Michael.

"It's Mrs. Simpson," Michael told her.

"Ione?" Janet asked. "Ione, what on earth is going on?"

"Then it's not coming from your house?" Ione asked.

"Our house? Ione, Michael and I were both sound asleep. And I don't even own a gun. Michael says it sounds like it's coming from down by the river."

"That's what Leif thinks, too."

"Maybe it's hunters," Janet suggested.

"In the middle of the night? Don't be silly."

"Then what could it be?"

Ione hesitated a moment, then: "Janet, did you say Michael was asleep?"

Janet frowned, and her eyes went automatically to Michael. "Yes."

"Didn't Michael go out tonight?"

"Go out? What are you talking about?"

"Boys," Ione said in a weary voice. "It seems Eric and Ryan decided to have themselves a little midnight adventure. But I caught them at it. They said Michael was with them. Was he?"

Janet was silent for a moment, then: "Just a minute." She covered the receiver with her hand. "Michael, did you go out with Ryan and Eric tonight?"

Michael opened his mouth to deny it, but then changed his mind. "Yes," he admitted. "We—we were just messing around."

Janet spoke once more into the phone. "He was with them," she told Ione. "But what's that got to do with the shooting?"

"I don't know," Ione replied. "But the boys said they saw someone in Potter's Field. They—well, they thought it was Abby. But I've never heard of a ghost carrying a gun before." Then, before Janet could make a reply: "Hold on, Janet." There was a murmuring, then Ione came back on the line. "We're coming over there, Janet. Leif thinks it might be Ben Findley shooting, and he wants to find out. There've been stories of Ben shooting at kids before, but so far, no one's ever heard the shots." Ione's voice hardened. "I don't care what old Ben does, but if he was trying to shoot at the kids, he's in big trouble. And while we're at it, we might as well find out from all three of the boys exactly what they were up to. Okay?"

Janet sighed. "Okay. I'll put on some coffee." She hung up the phone, and turned to confront Michael. "You are in trouble, young man," she told him. "You know better than to go out by yourself at night, and if you were trespassing on Mr. Findley's property, you should know that he would have been perfectly within his rights to shoot you." Then her worry overcame her anger. "My God, Michael, you could have been killed! Why did you do it?"

Suddenly Nathaniel's warning voice sounded in his head. *"Not yet!"*

"I—I don't know," Michael stammered.

Janet glared at him. "Well, you'd better figure it out," she told him. "And whatever you have to say had better match pretty well with whatever Ryan and Eric have to say. Understand?"

Michael nodded; then, as Janet started toward the kitchen, he sank down to the floor and slipped his arms around Shadow. "I'm scared," he whispered to the big dog. "What'll they do when they find Grandpa?"

Shadow nuzzled at his master, and his tail thumped against the wall as he wagged it. Then, once more, Nathaniel's voice came to him. *"It will be all right. In a little while, it will be all right."*

When the knock came at the front door, Janet hurried to answer it, opening the door wide in the expectation that the Simpsons and Ryan Shields would be on her porch.

Instead, it was Ben Findley.

His hooded eyes were glowering, and his threatening demeanor was made no less frightening by the shotgun in his left hand.

"Where's that brat of yours, Mrs. Hall?" he demanded.

Janet ignored the question. "Was that you shooting just now?"

"That wasn't no shotgun," Findley growled. "That was a rifle. Is your kid here?"

"Of course he's here," Janet finally replied. Then her eyes narrowed. "I just talked to Ione Simpson," she told him coldly. "Her husband thinks the shooting might have been you."

Findley hesitated a moment, then nodded his head. "Can't say as I blame him for that," he said.

Janet was about to demand that the old man leave her property when a car turned into the driveway and the porch was suddenly flooded with the glare of headlights. A moment later, the Simpson family and Ryan Shields piled out of the car. But when they saw who was on the porch, their words of greeting died on their lips. It was Leif Simpson who finally broke the silence.

"What're you doing over here, Findley?"

"Checkin' up," the old man replied, his voice sullen. "I came over to make sure her kid was here where he belongs."

Leif's eyes narrowed. "What made you think he might not be?"

Findley's rheumy eyes shifted toward Janet, then went back to meet Leif's steady gaze. "Why don't you and I have a little talk, and let the ladies go inside?" he asked.

Leif nodded his agreement, and Janet held the door open while Ione, carrying Peggy, followed the two boys into the little house. Janet hesitated a moment, then closed the door, leaving the two men on the porch.

A few minutes later, Leif joined them in the kitchen. "You'd better call Buck," he told Janet. "It seems Amos Hall was out here tonight, and Findley thinks it must have been him shooting. But he hasn't seen Amos's light for a while, and he and I are going to go down toward the river and have a look around."

"Amos?" Janet repeated. "Why would Amos be out there? Where was he?" And then she remembered Ione's words. "Potter's Field?"

"That's what Ben Findley says."

"But—but why?"

"Don't know," Leif replied. "But he also said it might be a good idea if you got hold of a doctor."

Janet made the calls, then joined Ione and the children at the table. "All right," she said softly. "It's time for you three to tell us what you were up to tonight."

One by one, the three boys recounted the story of the evening.

Each of them told about sneaking out, and each of them told about making their way down the Halls' pasture, across the field, and into the woods.

Each of them told about seeing the light in Potter's Field.

Ryan and Eric talked about losing their nerve, and running pell mell back the way they had come, and bursting back into the Simpsons' house, too frightened to worry about the noise they were making.

At last Janet turned to Michael. "What about you, Michael?" she asked. "Did you come home when you saw the light in the field?"

Michael shook his head. "I—I went into Mr. Findley's barn," he said softly.

Janet frowned. "Weren't you frightened, too?"

Again Michael shook his head.

"But why not?"

Michael hesitated, and then he heard Nathaniel's voice:

"Tell them. Tell them now."

"Because of Nathaniel," he breathed. "Nathaniel and I killed Grandpa."

Janet stared at her son, his words battering at her mind. But Michael's face was placid, and his eyes were calm.

"Nathaniel said we had to," he went on. "Grandpa was going to kill us, Mom. He killed Daddy, and he was going to kill me, too."

A wave of dizziness swept over Janet, and suddenly the lights in the room seemed to go out.

CHAPTER 23

Janet opened her eyes and stared without comprehension at the unfamiliar face that loomed over her. But then, as she came totally awake, she remembered what had happened. She struggled to sit up, but the stranger put a restraining hand on her shoulder.

"Don't," he said. "Just lie there, and try to take it easy. You very nearly lost your baby a little while ago. You didn't, but you're not out of danger yet. I'm Dr. Marsden," he added.

A small groan escaped Janet's lips, and she sank heavily back onto her pillows. "Amos," she whispered. "Did they find Amos?"

Marsden nodded. "He's downstairs." But then, as Janet sighed with relief, he went on: "They found him by the river, Mrs. Hall. I'm not sure exactly what happened, but your son couldn't have had anything to do with it."

Janet gazed at the doctor for a moment, then looked away, her eyes fixing on a point somewhere near the ceiling. "You mean he's dead?" she asked, her voice hollow.

"It looks like a heart attack. His gun was right next to him, and one of his hands was still on the stock. He must have been shooting at something, but whatever it was, it doesn't look like he hit it. Anyway, the men didn't find anything out there except Mr. Hall. In the morning, they'll look again."

"But Michael said—"

"I know what the boy said," Marsden interrupted. "Mrs. Simpson told me. But you heard the shots yourself, didn't you? Wasn't your son here at the time?"

"But you said they found him down by the river. That's where Michael said—"

"That's where the shots came from, Mrs. Hall. Now, I want you to rest. If I have to, I'll give you something—"

"No! I don't want anything, Dr.—" She struggled to remember his name, but couldn't. "I'll be all right. But I want to see Michael. Can I? Please?"

Marsden hesitated, then finally nodded. He left the room, and a minute later Michael appeared in the doorway. "Mom? Are you okay?"

Janet beckoned him over to the bed. "I'll be all right," she assured him. She reached out and took Michael's hand. "Honey, what you said just before I fainted. About killing Grandpa?"

"Uh-huh," Michael mumbled.

"What did you mean by that?"

"I already told you," Michael replied. "It was me and Nathaniel. Nathaniel told me I should wish him dead, so I did. And he died."

Janet fought the wave of dizziness that threatened to overwhelm her. "But that's not possible," she told him, her voice unsteady. "You can't wish someone to death. You were here when Grandpa died. You were with *me.*"

Michael shook his head. "I was with Nathaniel," he said. "I had to talk to him tonight. Grandpa wanted to hurt us. He wanted to kill us, just like he killed Daddy, and Aunt Laura's babies."

"No, Michael," Janet wailed. "Grandpa didn't do any of that."

Michael's face set stubbornly. "Yes he did," he replied. "I saw him. Nathaniel showed me. And besides, the night Aunt Laura had her baby, I saw them. I saw them kill the baby, and then I saw them out in the field. They were burying Aunt Laura's baby. I was with Nathaniel that night, and we both saw it."

"But Michael, Grandpa was home that night, remember? When you came home, Grandpa was there."

"I don't care," Michael said. "I know what I saw, and I'm not lying."

Suddenly Janet wanted to shake Michael, as if somehow she might physically shake his impossible ideas out of his head. Where had they come from? What did they mean? Then her weakness overcame her, and she collapsed back onto the pillows. "Tomorrow," was all she could say. "We'll talk about it tomorrow. . . ."

Michael got off the bed and started toward the door, but then turned back. "Mom?"

Janet opened her eyes. Michael was studying her with an intensity so great she had to look away.

"Everything's going to be all right now," he said softly. "I don't think I'm going to have my headaches anymore. I think they only came when Nathaniel was showing me things." He paused for a moment, then went on. "We had to make him die, Mom. He was going to kill the baby. Even if he didn't kill me, he would've killed the baby."

Janet's head turned, and she stared at Michael. "Stop it," she whispered. "Just stop saying those things." Her voice rose to the edge of hysteria. "They're not true, Michael. *They're not true!*"

Michael returned her gaze, his face suddenly angry. Then he left her alone, closing the door behind him.

Anna Hall was dozing in her chair, her ever-present mending on her lap, her head lolling on her breast.

In the hall, the clock began to strike, and Anna came half awake, certain that Amos had finally come home.

"Amos? Is that you?"

There was no answer, but even as silence settled once more over the house, Anna had a strange sense that she was no longer alone.

She tried to clear the fogginess from her mind, and opened her sleepy eyes to peer around.

Then, at the window, she saw it.

A face, a face she recognized.

It was Mark's face, but younger than he'd been the last time she saw him, almost as young as he'd been when he ran away so many years ago.

And yet it wasn't Mark's face. It was a face like Mark's, but different.

Then she heard the voice.

"He's dead, Mama. He's dead."

The words struck Anna almost like a blow. For a moment she wasn't certain she'd heard them at all. There was a flat atonality about them that made her wonder if the face at the window had spoken the words, or if she'd only imagined them.

Then the voice came again. *"He's dead, Mama. You must not be frightened anymore."*

Then the face disappeared from the window, and once more Anna felt the solitude of the house.

She sat for a long time, listening to the soft ticking of the clock, amplified by the night, trying to decide what had really happened to her. Had it been real, or had it only been a dream?

Then, as the hours wore on, a sense of peace slowly settled over her, a sense of peace she hadn't felt in years, not since before the night so many years ago when she had given birth to her last child. Suddenly she smiled. That was who the face had reminded her of. The face at the window had looked like her last son, just as she'd always imagined he would look—if only he had lived.

And with the sense of peace came something else.

It was Amos of whom the boy had spoken. As the night wore on, and Anna waited, she became increasingly sure that Amos was not coming home that night, that he would never come home again.

At last, as the clock was striking two, she heard a car pull up the drive. She rolled herself over to the window and stared out into the night, squinting against the darkness as she tried to make out the face of her visitor.

And then, as the figure of a man emerged from the pickup truck in front of the house, Anna gasped.

It was Ben Findley.

Trembling, Anna slowly backed away from the window. Her eyes searched the room as if looking for a place to hide. But there was no place to hide, and in the end she let the chair drift to a stop in the center of the room. A moment later she heard the front door open, and then Ben Findley stood framed in the doorway, his gaunt figure looking like a ghost from the past.

"Hello, Anna," he said at last.

The seconds ticked by, and Anna felt the color draining from her face, felt her whole body, even the legs that had been lifeless so long, trembling.

"You," she breathed at last.

Ben Findley nodded. His eyes left Anna for a moment and drifted slowly over the room. He nodded almost imperceptibly, then turned back to Anna. "Amos is dead, Anna. Leif Simpson and I found him down by the river."

"The river?" Anna asked blankly, her mind reeling not only at the confirmation of her strange sense that her husband was dead, but at the presence of Ben Findley in her house. "What was he doing down at the river?"

Findley shrugged. "I called him today. I saw you and the boy this afternoon, and I told Amos I didn't want anyone poking around that field."

Anna's eyes narrowed. "What happened, Ben. Did you kill him?"

Findley shook his head; then, without asking Anna's permission, he came into the room and lowered himself onto the sofa. Slowly he told Anna what he and Leif Simpson had found. When he was done, Anna fell into a reflective silence for a few moments. Then her head came up, and her eyes roved to the window and the blackness of the night. "Perhaps it was the children," she said in a voice that was only partially audible. "Perhaps the children finally got their revenge." Suddenly she looked at Ben Findley. "Ben, do you believe in ghosts?"

Findley looked puzzled for a moment, then shook his head. "No, I don't. Why?"

Anna shook her head, as if trying to clear her mind. "I don't know. I just thought I saw one tonight, that's all." She paused, then went on. "I knew Amos was dead, Ben. I wasn't waiting for him to come home. I was waiting for someone to come and tell me what I already knew."

Findley's body tensed, and his hooded eyes darkened. "How?" he asked. "How did you know?"

Anna shrugged. "I told you—a ghost."

"Nathaniel . . ." Findley said softly.

Anna's head came up angrily. "Nathaniel!" she echoed, her voice suddenly regaining its strength. "Don't be a fool, Ben. There is no Nathaniel. There was never a Nathaniel. All my life, since I married Amos Hall, I've heard of nothing except Nathaniel. He doesn't exist, Ben. He was never anything but a fantasy of Amos's."

"No, Anna—"

"Yes! He killed my children, Ben. He killed my children, and somehow, in his twisted mind, he managed to blame it on his holy Nathaniel. But it was a lie, Ben! Amos was insane, and a murderer. I could never prove it, but I knew. I always knew."

"How?" Ben Findley suddenly demanded. He rose to his feet, towering over Anna, his blue eyes blazing. "How did you know, Anna?"

Anna cowered in her chair, her burst of strength suddenly deserting her. "I knew," she whispered. "That's all. I just knew."

"And is that why you stayed with him?" Findley asked. "Is that why you stayed with him all those years, Anna? Because you knew he'd killed your children? It doesn't make sense. If you truly knew, you'd have left him, left him and gone away. If you truly thought he'd killed your children, you never would have stayed with him."

Anna shook her head helplessly as her eyes flooded with tears. "No," she protested. "You don't understand. I—I couldn't walk, Ben. I couldn't walk, and I couldn't prove what he'd done." Suddenly she looked up at him imploringly. "Don't you understand, Ben? Don't you understand at all?"

Findley ignored her question. "And what about our child, Anna?" he asked softly. "Did Amos kill our child, too?"

Anna recoiled from his words. "No . . ." she whimpered. "No, don't talk about that. Please . . ."

"Tell me, Anna," Findley pressed, his voice relentless. "Tell me what you think you know about our son."

"Dead," Anna whispered. "He was born dead. That's what Amos always told me. But I never believed him, Ben. I never believed him. Amos killed our baby that night, just like the other two. He killed him, and they buried him in Potter's Field."

"No, Anna," Findley told her. The anger drained out of his voice, and Anna responded to his sudden gentleness, gazing at him with frightened eyes. "He didn't die, Anna. He wasn't born dead, and he didn't die. Potter brought him to me that night. He brought him to me, and I've had him ever since." He paused, then, "I named him Nathaniel, Anna. That's who you saw tonight. You saw Nathaniel, and he's our son."

A terrible silence fell over the house as Anna tried to comprehend Ben Findley's words. The room seemed to turn around her, and her mind reeled as twenty years of her life shattered into meaningless pieces.

And then, gathering her strength, Anna Hall grasped the arms of her wheelchair. "No," she breathed. "No. None of it's true!" Her voice pitched to a scream, as slowly, supporting herself on trembling arms, she began to rise from the chair. "Why are you lying to me?" she wailed. "Why? Why?" She took a halting step toward him, and suddenly her fists came up. "Lies," she screamed. "It's all lies! I know the truth, Ben. I know it!" She began pummeling at his chest, her legs wobbling, but still somehow supporting her.

Ben Findley's arms went around Anna, and he held her tight. "No, Anna, I've told you the truth. It's all over now. Amos is dead, and he can't hurt you anymore. It's all over. Amos is dead, and our son is alive, and it's over."

But Anna shook herself loose. "It's not over," she hissed. "I wasn't wrong, Ben. I wasn't! You're lying to me, but I'll find the truth! So help me, I'll find the truth!" Then she turned, and with an effort of sheer willpower, she walked slowly across the room and disappeared into the tiny room that had been her private retreat for the last twenty years.

A moment later, when Ben Findley tried to follow her, he found the door locked. When he called to her, Anna Hall refused to answer him.

The next morning, Anna began to hear the rumors. People called—nearly everyone in town—to express their sympathies, and Anna listened to them, and made all the proper responses. But some of them didn't stop with condolences about Amos's death. Some of them made oblique references to Michael:

"Such a terrible thing for a boy his age—"

"Of course, losing his father must have been a terrible trauma for him, but to blame his grandfather—"

"Of course, he couldn't have seen a ghost, but he must have seen *something*—"

"Of course, I can't believe it's true. Why would a little boy want to do a thing like that—"

Anna listened to it all, and slowly pieced it all together. Finally she turned to Laura, who had arrived during the night, after Ben Findley had left. She hadn't seen Laura last night, but she'd told her through her closed door that she was all right and that she needed to be alone for a while. Laura had accepted it, as Laura always accepted everything. Only this morning, when Anna had slowly and shakily walked out of the tiny room, had Laura tried to confront her.

Anna smiled grimly at the memory.

Laura had stared at her, speechless, then finally opened her mouth to protest. "Mother—you can't—"

Anna had silenced her. "Obviously I can," she'd said. "Since I am."

"But—but—how?"

"I don't know," Anna admitted. "Something happened to me last night. I'm not sure what it was, and I won't talk about it. But after I found out your father had died, something inside me changed." She'd smiled sadly at Laura. "Maybe I've stopped punishing myself. Or maybe I could have done it long ago," she said. "Maybe my chair was nothing more than my own way of running away from things. I've been thinking about it all night, Laura, and that's the only thing that makes sense. Charles told me that years ago, you know. From the very beginning, he told me there was nothing wrong with my legs, that I'd just decided I didn't want to walk." A tear welled in her eye, then ran slowly down her cheek. "And it worked, you know," she whispered. "Your father used to beat me, years ago—"

"Mother!"

"He did, Laura. But then he stopped. When I couldn't walk anymore, he stopped."

Then, with a strength she hadn't felt for years, Anna had begun taking charge of her own life, a task she'd ceded to Amos on the day she'd married him.

"I want to go to Janet's," she said now.

"But mother, Janet's in bed. The doctor's ordered her to stay in bed for at least a week."

"Then she'll need help," Anna replied. "I can at least take care of the cooking. I won't have my grandson rummaging around eating God only knows what."

"Mother, no one expects you to do anything right now. Ione Simpson's looking after her, and Michael can spend the nights with us, if it's too much trouble for the Simpsons."

Anna's face set. "Laura, I know you're trying to do what's best for me, and I appreciate it. But I'm not senile, and if I have to sit here listening to idle gossip about my grandson—"

Suddenly Laura's expression turned wary. "Gossip? What gossip?"

"It seems," Anna replied, "there are some people in town who think Michael might have had something to do with Amos's death."

Laura paled. "I know what they're talking about, but it isn't true, mother. It isn't possible—"

"I'll decide for myself what's possible and what isn't," Anna snapped. "Now, will you take me over there, or do I have to learn to drive again the same day I have to learn to walk?"

"Mother, you really should stay home—what will people think? And Father—think of Father."

Anna made no reply. Instead, she simply began making her slow way to the front door, then out onto the porch. She was starting down the steps when Laura finally decided that she was not bluffing. "All right, Mother," she said, and followed the older woman out to her car.

Ione Simpson looked up in shocked surprise, then got quickly to her feet as Anna Hall, leaning heavily on Laura's arm, walked slowly into Janet Hall's small living room. "Anna! What are you—" She paused, floundering, then recovered herself. "I'm—I'm so sorry about Amos."

Anna nodded an acknowledgment, and quickly scanned the room. "Is Michael upstairs?"

Ione hesitated, then shook her head. "He's in the kitchen, I think."

Wordlessly, Anna turned toward the kitchen. Laura moved quickly to help her, but Anna brushed her aside. "I want to talk to him alone." Slowly, but with remarkable steadiness, Anna walked out of the living room.

She found Michael at the kitchen table, staring sightlessly at a bowl of cold cereal. As if coming out of a trance, his eyes suddenly focused, and he looked at her. "Aren't you going to give your grandmother a kiss?" she asked.

With obvious reluctance, Michael got up from the table and approached her. "I—I'm sorry, Grandma," he whispered. Anna put her arms around him.

"It's all right, Michael. I know it's hard, but he was an old man, and whatever happened, it wasn't your fault." Then she held him at arm's length and looked directly into his eyes. "It wasn't your fault, was it?"

Michael trembled slightly, then nodded his head.

"I see," Anna breathed. She let her hands drop from Michael's shoulders and moved to the table, where she carefully lowered herself into a chair. "Sit down, Michael," she said softly. "Sit down and tell me what happened. Can you do that? Can you tell me all of it?"

Slowly, Michael recounted his story of the night before, and when he was done, Anna slumped tiredly in her chair. "You wished him dead," she whispered. "You and Nathaniel wished him dead."

She reached out then, reached out to comfort the sobbing boy who sat across from her, his head buried in his arms. At her touch, he looked up.

"I'm sorry, Grandma. I'm sorry!"

"Michael," Anna said almost fearfully. "There's something you haven't told me."

Slowly, Michael's sobbing subsided, and at last he looked up at his grandmother, his eyes red, his cheeks splotched with tears.

"Who is Nathaniel?" Anna asked. "You haven't told me who Nathaniel is." She hesitated, then asked the question she'd been dreading. "He's—he's a ghost, isn't he?"

Michael's eyes widened, and for a long moment he stared at his grandmother in silence. At last, he shook his head.

"No, Grandma," he said softly. "He's real."

CHAPTER 24

Ben Findley stared at the tray of food that still sat where he'd left it on the table in the little room beneath the barn.

It was untouched.

He hadn't really expected anything different, not since he'd come down here late last night to find the room empty. That, too, had not been unexpected, but still he'd gone over the barn carefully, inspecting everything. Everything had been as it should have been. The door to the tack room, as always, was barred from the outside. The planks that formed the siding of the barn were as solid as ever, despite their appearance from the outside. Upstairs in the loft, the door was still nailed shut.

Yet despite the fact that the security of the barn did not appear to have been breached, Nathaniel was gone. He was gone, and he had not come back.

Findley picked up the tray and, balancing it expertly on one hand, used the other to steady himself as he climbed the ladder out of the tiny cell. He left the barn, not bothering to lock it, and quickly crossed the yard.

Inside his house, he put the tray on the sink and stared idly at his little kitchen. A puddle of coffee had spread across the kitchen counter, and he automatically moved to wipe it up before the stain could penetrate the butcher-block top.

He and Nathaniel had made that top together, and he wasn't about to let it be ruined.

Impulsively, he decided to inspect the entire house, and he began moving slowly through its few rooms, examining everything, making sure everything was in the perfect condition he had always maintained.

The interior of the little house was in remarkable contrast to its ramshackle exterior. The hardwood floors gleamed under his feet, their mellow oaken planks polished to a soft glow. The walls were lined with leatherbound books, stored in cases he had built himself, all the joints carefully dovetailed so that as the years went by they would remain as true as they had been the day he and Nathaniel had put them together.

The furniture was sparse. Two chairs—one his, the other Nathaniel's, for the times, much more frequent than Charles Potter had ever suspected, when Findley had felt safe enough to have Nathaniel inside the house.

At times, Ben Findley had wondered if he'd begun taking a perverse pleasure in keeping the interior of the house in such perfect contrast to its exterior, but deep inside he knew he had not. It was just that he liked things to be right, and over the years he had come to want them to be as nice as possible for Nathaniel.

At first, of course, it had not been for Nathaniel at all.

It had been for Anna.

For a long time after that night when Nathaniel was born, Ben Findley had hoped that Anna Hall would finally leave Amos and come to live with him. Him, and Nathaniel.

He had fantasized in those years, picturing the light that would come into Anna's eyes when he told her that their son was alive. That fantasy had kept him going those first years, after Jenny had left him.

Even twenty years later, he could clearly remember that night. It was the night Nathaniel had been born, and Charles Potter had brought the baby to him, meeting him in the field, while a storm howled around them.

"Amos thinks he's dead," Potter had told him that night. "I made him think so, or he might have killed him. He knows the child's yours." He'd handed the blanket-wrapped infant to Ben. "Amos thinks I'm burying him. I'll stay here for a while, in case he's watching."

Ben had peeled a corner of the blanket back, and gazed down into the face of the son that Anna Hall had borne him, the son that his own wife had never been able to conceive. "What about Anna?" he'd asked, but Potter had shaken his head.

"I don't know. It was hard, and she thinks the baby's dead." Then he'd met Ben's eyes. "He's yours, Ben. Yours and Jenny's."

Except that Jenny hadn't wanted the child, wouldn't even look at it.

"Anna's?" she'd demanded. "You expect me to raise a child you had by Anna Hall? Never! Never, Ben!"

That night, she, like Mark Hall, had gone away.

Unlike Mark, she had never come back.

And so Ben had begun to raise the child himself, hoping, at first, that Anna Hall would one day recover from the child's birth and walk again.

He'd hidden the child, knowing that he had no reasonable explanation for its being there, and slowly, over the years, his life had changed.

For a long time, he'd whiled away the time by preparing the house for Anna, but when he'd finally come to accept that Anna was never coming, he hadn't stopped working on the interior of the house.

By then, he was doing it for Nathaniel.

Nathaniel became the sole focus of his life. Ben Findley became consumed with the need to provide whatever was necessary for the little boy who was growing up in his house.

What was needed for Nathaniel was isolation, for isolation meant safety. So Ben constructed his shield, and made himself into the town recluse, the rundown appearance of his farm discouraging most visitors, his surly façade—a façade that had finally become his true personality—repelling those few who braved the tangle of overgrowth of the yard to knock on the peeled and weathered boards of the front door.

It had worked. Years ago, people had stopped trying to be friendly toward him, and he had ended up being as trapped as Nathaniel within the limits that he had set for them.

The limits had been simple: No one must know, or even suspect, that Ben Findley was not living alone.

At first it had only been temporary. When Anna came, they would bring Nathaniel out in the open, and live as the family they were.

But Anna hadn't come.

Instead, she'd retreated to her wheelchair, and soon moved away from the little house where the two of them had loved. She had wiped Ben Findley from her life.

Ben had resented that, and he knew that there had been times when he'd taken Anna's rejection of him out on little Nathaniel. Sometimes, for no reason at all, he'd found himself punishing the child, beating him.

But as the years wore on, he'd come to care totally for the boy. And so he'd raised him, isolating himself along with Nathaniel. He'd done what he could to make Nathaniel's life comfortable, and if it wasn't enough, Ben was sorry.

He knew the boy was peculiar, but he also knew there was nothing he could do about it. Nathaniel's oddness, he was sure, was only a result of his isolation.

And he'd taught the boy, taught him everything he knew. What he did without in the way of human companionship, he tried to make up for with books. Ben clothed Nathaniel, making the boy's garments himself; buying clothes in Prairie Bend was out of the question, and doing it through the mails was equally risky. Catalogs would begin coming, catalogs of children's clothes and toys, and the woman at the post office would begin to wonder why Ben Findley was getting such things. And if she wondered, she'd talk, and then she'd want to know. So he took no risks.

Still, Ben knew it hadn't worked. Nathaniel was different from other children, ill-equipped to deal with the world. There had been times when Nathaniel had seemed to drift off into a private world of his own, and Ben had been unable to reach him. It was as if he'd been listening to voices only he could hear. But it didn't happen often, and he always came out of it. And there had been the other times, the times when the children—what his cousin Amos had always called "Nathaniel's children"—had been born. Those nights, Ben had sometimes heard Nathaniel in the barn, moaning softly, almost as if he were in pain. Sometimes he'd tried to comfort the boy, but he'd never been able. Nathaniel had never even seemed aware of his presence.

By the mornings after those terrible nights, though, Nathaniel had always seemed to be all right, and Charles Potter—still the only other person who knew of Nathaniel's secret existence—had maintained that the odd spells meant nothing.

And then, last spring, Mark Hall had come home.

Ever since then, Nathaniel had been different.

He'd become odder, and seemed to disappear deeper into his private world every day.

He'd stopped speaking to Ben, preferring to spend his time alone in his room beneath the barn, lying on his cot, his eyes wide open but blank, staring at something Ben could never see.

His voice, never expressive, had taken on an atonality that sometimes frightened Ben, and when he looked at Ben now, it always seemed to be with anger.

And when he'd spoken, he'd said strange things.

"I know what happened," he told Ben once. "I can see it now, and I know what happened."

That was all he'd said, but in his words, and in his eyes, Ben had sensed danger.

Then, last night, Nathaniel had disappeared from the barn.

And Amos Hall had died.

* * *

It wasn't until dusk that Findley went back to the barn. He carried Nathaniel's dinner with him, not because he expected Nathaniel to be there to eat it, but because he had taken Nathaniel's dinner to the barn every night for so many years that when he'd fixed his own meal that evening, he'd automatically cooked for them both. He opened the barn door, slipped inside, and pulled the door closed behind him.

And then he felt it.

Nathaniel was there.

Nathaniel's presence was in the atmosphere of the barn, just as his absence had been palpable the night before.

Findley paused, then spoke softly into the gloom of the building. "Nathaniel?"

There was no answer. Ben started toward the tack room, but had taken only a few paces when suddenly he felt something behind him. He turned slowly, and stared at the glistening tines of a pitchfork hovering a few inches from his chest. Beyond the cold, glittering metal, his hands grasping the fork's handle, Nathaniel's eyes blazed at him, penetrating the deep shadows of the barn. The tray clattered to the floor. "Nathaniel—"

The finely honed points of the fork inched closer to his chest. "Where are they?" Nathaniel demanded.

Ben frowned. "What? Where are what, Nathaniel?"

"The children. The children in the field. Where are they?"

"Nathaniel—"

A single tine of the fork touched the skin of Ben Findley's throat, pierced it. A drop of blood began to form, then slowly ran down the inside of Ben's shirt.

"Tell me where they are. I have to find them."

"I don't know what you're talking about, Nathaniel," Ben said softly. "Now put down the fork, and tell me what you mean."

But it was too late. The look was in Nathaniel's eyes, the look Ben Findley had seen before, and he could almost imagine he heard the voices himself, the voices Nathaniel was listening to.

He's going to kill me, Findley thought. He killed Amos, and he killed Charles, and now he's going to kill me. Then another thought came to him: Why shouldn't he kill us? One way or another, all of us killed him.

He felt the tines of the fork pressing against his throat again, and began backing away. Behind him, he suddenly felt the wall of the barn, and there was nowhere else to go. He stopped, his eyes fixing on Nathaniel's.

"I'm sorry," he whispered, even as he knew it was too late. "I'm sorry I took your life away from you."

Nathaniel nodded, then hurled his weight against the pitchfork.

Ben opened his mouth to scream, but no sound came out, as two of the tines plunged through his flesh, then on into the soft pine planks of the barn wall.

A stream of blood welled up from his torn throat, then overflowed and began pouring down the front of his shirt.

A few seconds later, his eyes rolled backward and his body went slack.

Nathaniel stared for a moment at the man who had raised him, and killed him, then went out into the gathering night.

CHAPTER 25

Janet awoke with a start, her heart pounding. The dream had come again, the nightmare in which she stood helplessly by and watched as flames consumed the house she'd grown up in. Only this time, the dream was different. This time, as she cowered in the night, transfixed by the smoke and flames, it wasn't her brother who was calling to her.

This time, the voice she heard was Michael's, and the face she saw at the upstairs window was Mark's.

And in the background, barely audible, was another voice, a voice she recognized as that of her unborn child.

This time it wasn't her parents and her brother who were dying. This time it was her children and her husband.

She shook off the remnants of the dream and lay in the gloom, listening to the throbbing pulse of her heart, staring at the ceiling where strange shadows were cast by the soft glow of her nightlight. Inside her, she could feel the baby stirring—that was good, for as long as the baby moved it still lived, and for a while during the past twenty-four hours, she was sure she had lost it. Then, as her pulse slowly returned to normal, she shifted her attention, listening to the sounds of the house. Voices drifted up from downstairs. Though she couldn't make out the words, the murmuring itself was comforting to Janet.

She knew who was downstairs: her mother-in-law, her son, and Ione Simpson.

Earlier in the day, when she'd first mentioned that Ione had volunteered to stay with them and look after them, she had expected Anna to object. But she'd been wrong. Anna, without Amos and without her chair, had literally changed overnight.

"She has a level head," Anna had said of Ione. "And I don't feel like talking tonight. With Laura, I'd have to talk. But with Ione, I can just sit and think. I need to think, Janet," she'd added in a tone that had almost frightened the younger woman. "I need to think about a lot of things." And then, sounding more like her usual self, she'd glanced pointedly at Janet's belly. "Aren't you supposed to be staying in bed?"

Janet nodded. "But I feel so useless up there. And the baby's all right. The doctor said—"

Anna's eyes flashed with sudden anger. "Doctors are fools! Never believe what they say. Never! I believed Charles Potter once."

The force of Anna's words struck Janet almost physically. She sank back against the cushions of the sofa. "Anna, what are you saying? He was your doctor for years—"

"Amos's. He was Amos's doctor, Janet. To me, he was—" Suddenly she fell silent, but Janet had the distinct feeling there was something the older woman wanted to talk about.

"He was what, Anna?"

Anna's eyes suddenly shifted away from Janet, and she appeared to be trying to come to a decision. Finally, her empty eyes met Janet's. "I don't know what he was," she said at last. "I don't know what's the truth, anymore, and I don't know who lied to me all my life. I don't know anything anymore, Janet. For twenty years, I sat in a wheelchair, but at least I thought I knew why I was there. I thought it was Amos's fault. I thought he'd done something to me when my last baby was born, thought somehow he or Charles Potter had hurt me when they killed my baby."

"Anna," Janet pleaded, "don't say that."

"Wait," Anna said quietly. "I'm not saying what I believe, Janet. I'm only telling you what I thought." Suddenly she seemed to straighten up. She took a deep breath. Then she said: "Ben Findley was the father of my last child."

Janet stared at her mother-in-law, unable to make any reply at all.

"It's true. Ben was different then. Not like he is now. In some ways he was very like Amos—like all that family—except there was nothing of Amos's cruelty about him. Amos *was* cruel. He beat the children, and he beat me. And he was absolutely convinced that some awful curse had been placed on his family. It all went back to Abby Randolph, and Nathaniel, and the child that survived."

"But you said—"

"I know what I said." Anna sighed, then went on talking. "I think Amos killed two of my children. I don't know anymore. Not after last night. But what's important is that I *believed* he did. That's one of the reasons I fell in love with Ben Findley. I blamed Amos for so much, and in Ben I found the parts of Amos I was attracted to, without the parts I hated. Can you understand that?" She paused, but Janet made no reply. "Anyway, I fell in love with him, and I got pregnant by him. And Amos knew." Slowly, her voice trembling with the pain she felt at reliving the story, Anna told Janet what had happened twenty years ago, when her last child had been born. "He had sworn he'd kill it," she finished. "He'd said he'd kill it, but then, when it came, he told me it was stillborn. He told me, and Charles Potter told me. But I didn't believe them. I believed they killed it, just as I believed Amos had killed my other children. I believed they killed it. And later on, I believed they killed Laura's children."

"But if that's what you believed—"

"Why did I stay? Because Amos was my punishment, and I deserved to be punished for my . . ." Her voice faltered. "For my sins. I stayed out of my own guilt, Janet. I hated Amos, but I stayed."

Janet felt sick. Sick and betrayed. "And you didn't warn me, either," she said, her voice suddenly bitter. Her eyes turned angry. "What about Michael? Did he beat Michael, too? And would you have stood by when my baby came, even though you thought Amos might kill it?"

Anna shook her head helplessly. "I don't know," she whispered. "I just don't know. But it's over now, Janet. Nathaniel—" She fell suddenly silent.

"Nathaniel!" Janet demanded. "What about Nathaniel? That's only a ghost story."

"Is it?" Anna broke in. Then her body seemed to droop. "Maybe it is, at that. But Michael doesn't think so. Nor do I. Nathaniel is real, at least in some ways. For me, he's real, and he's bringing me an odd kind of peace." She fell silent, then smiled softly. "I'm going to have another grandchild, Janet. I'm going to see Mark's second son, and Amos isn't going to kill him. It will be almost like having my own son back."

Janet had gone upstairs then, trying to puzzle out the meaning of all that Anna had told her. She had fallen asleep for a while, then awakened. Now, as she listened to the calming drone of voices from below, Anna's words seemed to fade from her mind. Perhaps, as Anna had said, everything would be all right now.

And then came the scream.

* * *

Anna jerked out of the half sleep she'd fallen into, and stared at the contorted face of her grandson. Shadow, his tail twitching nervously, was licking at Michael's face, but the boy didn't seem to notice. "What is it?" Anna asked, her eyes leaving the screaming boy and fixing on Ione Simpson. "My Lord, what's wrong with him?"

Ione had been sitting on the floor studying the chessboard between herself and Michael, but was now crouched beside the boy, cradling him in her arms. "It's all right," she told Anna. "It's going to be all right."

Michael's screams subsided, and as he calmed down, so did Shadow. Finally, his weight still resting against Ione's breast, his eyes opened and he looked up into his grandmother's face.

"He killed him," he whispered. "It happened just now. He killed him."

"Who?" Ione asked. "Who killed someone, Michael?"

"Nathaniel," Michael whispered. "I saw it. Just now. I saw him in the barn, and he was hiding. And then Mr. Findley came in. And—and Nathaniel killed him."

Instinctively, Ione glanced toward the window, but the rapidly gathering darkness revealed nothing of what lay beyond the glass. Whatever Michael was talking about, he hadn't seen it with his eyes.

"All right," Ione said, automatically reverting to the soothing voice she'd cultivated during her years of nursing. "Tell us what happened. Tell me what you saw, and how you saw it. Can you do that?"

Michael gazed up at her for a moment, then his eyes shifted back to his grandmother.

"It's all right," she assured him. "Whatever you tell us, we'll believe you. Just tell us what happened."

Michael swallowed. "I was looking at the board," he said. "I was trying to decide whether or not to move my bishop, and then all of a sudden I got a headache. And I heard Nathaniel's voice."

Ione frowned and started to say something, but Anna silenced her with a gesture.

"Only he wasn't talking to me," Michael went on. "He was talking to Mr. Findley. He was asking about the children. He wanted to know where the children were, and Mr. Findley wouldn't tell him. So Nathaniel killed him."

"How?" Anna asked. "How did Nathaniel kill him?"

Michael's voice shook. "The way Grandpa killed Dad," he said softly. "With a pitchfork."

Suddenly, from the doorway, they heard a low moan, and both Ione and Anna turned to see Janet, her face pale, leaning heavily against the doorframe. "I can't stand it," Janet whispered. "I just can't stand it."

"Ione, help her," Anna said, but the words were unnecessary: Ione was already on her feet, offering Janet a supporting arm. But Janet brushed her aside, her eyes fixed on Michael.

"It isn't possible, Michael," she said. "You couldn't have seen anything like that." Hysteria began to edge her voice. "You were sitting right here. You couldn't have seen anything. You couldn't!"

Michael stared at his mother, his eyes wide and frightened. "I did, Mama," he said. "I know what I saw."

"No!" Janet screamed. "You're imagining things, Michael! Can't you understand?" Her eyes, wide with distress and confusion, flicked from Michael to Anna, then to Ione. "Can't any of you understand? He's imagining things! He's imagining things, and he needs help!" She broke down, her sobs coming in great heaving gulps, and now she let herself collapse into Ione's arms. "Oh, God, help him. Please help him!"

"It's all right, Janet," Ione soothed. "Everything's going to be all right. But you have to go back up to bed. You have to rest." Without waiting for her to reply, Ione began guiding her back up the stairs.

Suddenly alone with his grandmother, Michael looked fretfully at the old woman. His hands played over Shadow's thick coat, as if he were seeking comfort from the dog. "Why doesn't she believe me?" he asked. "Why doesn't she believe I saw what I did?"

"Maybe she does," Anna told him. "Maybe she does, but just doesn't want to admit it to herself. Sometimes it's easier to pretend things aren't happening, even when you know they are. Can you understand that?"

Michael hesitated, then nodded. "I—I think so."

"All right. Now, would you do something for me?"

"Wh-what?"

"I want you to call Aunt Laura and ask her to come out here. And have her bring Buck and Ryan, too."

Michael's brow knitted into a worried frown. "Why?"

"To help Mrs. Simpson take care of your mother. You and I and your Uncle Buck are going to go over and have a look at Ben Findley's barn."

The enormous barn door stood slightly ajar, and an ominous silence seemed to hang over the unkempt farm like a funeral pall. The little group stopped in the center of the barnyard, Michael on one side of Anna, Buck Shields on the other, supporting her with his arm. Shadow, his tail between his legs, whined softly.

"He's gone," Michael whispered. "Nathaniel's gone."

"There's no such person as Nathaniel," Buck Shields said, his voice angry. Anna silenced him with a glance, then switched on the flashlight she held in one hand, playing its beam over the walls of the barn. Nothing showed, nothing moved.

"Stay here with your grandmother," Buck said. "I'll go have a look inside."

"No!" Anna's voice crackled in the darkness. "We'll all go inside. Whatever's there, Michael's already seen it. And whatever's there, I want to see it."

They started toward the barn, and suddenly Shadow stiffened, then a growl rumbled up from the depths of his throat.

"Someone's there," Michael whispered. "Someone's inside the barn."

As if in response, Shadow whimpered, then leaped forward into the darkness, disappearing into the building. There was a scuffling sound, and Shadow began barking. Then his barking subsided into a steady snarl, and Buck Shields moved forward, taking the light from Anna Hall's hands.

He slipped through the door, then paused. Shadow's snarling was louder, coming from the far end of the barn. Buck made his way slowly along the inside of the door, then felt on the wall for a light switch.

The blackness of the barn's interior was suddenly washed away with a brilliant white light from three overhead fixtures. Buck blinked, and shaded his eyes with one hand.

Sixty feet away, at the far end of the barn, he could see Ben Findley, his eyes still open, his clothes covered with blood, held upright only by the pitchfork that impaled his throat, pinning him to the wall. Buck stared at the dead man for a few seconds, trying to control the churning in his stomach that threatened to overwhelm him. Then his eye was caught by a flicker of movement.

Slowly, Buck started down the center aisle of the barn, approaching Ben Findley as if he were some grotesque religious icon hovering above an altar.

Like a supplicant at Ben Findley's feet, Shadow was crouched low to the ground, his tail sweeping the floor in slow movements, his eyes fixed on the dead man's face.

Nathaniel lay in Potter's Field, his eyes fixed on the barn. Light glimmered through the cracks in the barn's siding, and it almost looked as if the building were on fire.

He knew he should get up and move. Soon, he was sure, people would come looking for him, and when they found him—

Not yet. They couldn't find him yet.

Even though the three of them were dead now—the one who had wanted to kill him when he was born, and the two who had kept him a prisoner all his life—there was still something he had to do.

He had to go home. His eyes turned away from the barn, and focused on the little house where he'd been born.

With his mind, he reached out to it, exploring it.

There were people in it tonight. His sister—Laura—was there, and Michael's mother was there. And someone else, a stranger. So he couldn't go there tonight. Tonight, he must hide, and stay hidden until it was safe. Softly, inaudibly, he sent out an urgent signal.

In the barn, Shadow suddenly rose from his position at Ben Findley's feet and trotted out into the night.

CHAPTER 26

There was no funeral for Amos Hall, none for Ben Findley. Anna had forbidden it.

"I won't do it," she'd said. "I won't pretend to shed tears for Amos, and as for Ben Findley—well, he lived alone for twenty years, and he can be buried alone, too."

She'd told no one of her conversation with Ben Findley the night Amos had died, and now she knew she never would. There was no point, she'd decided. There was no one left who knew the whole truth of what had happened all those years ago. And she'd decided it no longer really mattered. Finally, it was over. They were all dead, and even though they could no longer give her the answers to her questions, neither could they hurt her any more than they already had.

They'd talked to her about Ben Findley, of course, when they came down from Mulford to investigate his death.

She hadn't told them about Nathaniel. That, too, was something she'd decided never to speak of again. So when they'd asked her if she had any idea who might have killed Ben Findley, she'd only shrugged. "A drifter, I suppose.

Ben didn't have any friends, but he didn't have any enemies, either. So it must have been a drifter."

No one else in Prairie Bend had been able to offer a better idea, nor had anyone given credence to Michael's insistence that Nathaniel had killed the recluse.

The investigators went over Ben Findley's farm, but paid scant attention to the little room below the barn, dismissing the cell as nothing more than the storm cellar it appeared to be. In the end, they went back to Mulford, sure they would never find Ben Findley's killer, and equally sure that no one in Prairie Bend would care.

For Janet, the days following the deaths were increasingly difficult. She found herself watching Michael closely, guarding herself against the moment when he would suddenly be attacked by one of his headaches, then insist that Nathaniel had shown him something both hideous and impossible. Even as the days went by, and nothing happened, she did not calm down. Instead, she only grew more nervous, sure that whatever was happening to Michael had not yet ended.

Part of her certainty that things were not over involved Shadow.

Since the night Ben Findley had been found dead in his barn, the huge black dog had not been seen. Nor had Michael seemed upset by his disappearance.

"He's helping Nathaniel," Michael had said. "He'll come back. Nathaniel will bring him back."

And so Janet was waiting.

It was on the fifth day, near dusk, that Shadow returned.

Janet and Michael were in the kitchen. Michael was at the sink, doing the last of the supper dishes, while Janet sat at the kitchen table laboriously attempting to master the basic manipulations of the knitting needles that Anna had given her that afternoon. "Learn now," Anna had told her. "In the winter, it will help pass the time." And so she was trying, but it was not going well. In fact, Michael could already do it better than she could.

"I just don't get it," she said at last, dropping the work on the table. "I can't keep the same number of stitches in a row, and they just keep getting tighter and tighter." Then, when Michael made no reply, she looked up to see him staring out the window. His right hand was raised as he rubbed at his temples. "Michael?" When he still said nothing, Janet rose to her feet. "What is it, honey? Is something wrong?"

Then her eyes followed his, and in the distance, in Potter's Field, she saw the familiar black mass that was Shadow.

"He's looking for the babies," Michael said in a far-away voice. "He's looking for the babies that Grandpa killed."

Holding her emotions tightly in check, Janet slipped her arms around her son. "No, Michael. There's nothing out there. . . ."

"There is," Michael repeated, his voice growing stronger. "Shadow's out there looking for them, helping Nathaniel find them."

"No!" Janet exclaimed.

Michael pivoted to face her, glaring at her with furious eyes. "Yes! They're out there, and Nathaniel has to find them, and I have to help him."

He began struggling in her arms, trying to wriggle free, but Janet hung on. "No!" she screamed. "There's nothing out there, and there is no Nathaniel, and you have to stop pretending there is! You have to stop it, Michael! Do you hear me? *Just stop it!*"

Michael was still in her arms, but suddenly his eyes, blazing with fury, gazed into hers.

"You don't know," he whispered. "You don't know, because you don't know Nathaniel."

For several long minutes the two of them stood frozen in a contest of wills. Then, at last, Janet knew what she had to do.

"All right," she said, letting go of Michael. "Let's go find out. Right now, let's go find out what the truth is."

Taking Michael by the hand she left the house and strode across the yard to the toolshed. Seconds later, Michael's arm still firmly gripped in her right hand, a shovel in her left, she started toward Potter's Field. "We'll dig them up," she told Michael as they climbed through the barbed wire. "If there are any bodies in this field, we'll dig them up right now, and look at them."

Shadow's head came up, and he watched them as they approached. Then, as he recognized them, he bounded over, his tail wagging, a happy bark ringing out over the prairie. Michael threw himself on the dog, scratching him and petting him, but Janet stood still and silent. Finally, when Michael had begun to calm down, she spoke.

"Where are they?" she asked. "Where are they buried?"

Shadow's ears suddenly dropped flat against his head, and his joyful barking faded into a wary growl.

"It's all right," Michael soothed. "It's all right, boy. We're gonna help you." Then, slowly, Michael began moving through the field with Shadow at his side.

"Here," Michael said.

Janet moved the stone at Michael's feet aside, and plunged the shovel into the earth. She worked silently, not heeding the stress she was putting on her body, caring more about proving to Michael that there was nothing in the field than about any danger to her unborn child.

And then, a moment later, the bone fragments appeared.

Janet stared at them, then reached down to pick one of them up. She studied it a moment, then handed it to Michael. "Look at it," she said. "It's old and crumbling, and it could be anything. It might be human, and it might not. But whatever it is, it's far too old for your grandfather to have buried it here."

Michael's temples were pounding now, and he glowered at his mother with barely contained fury. "There's more," he whispered. "All over the field, there's more."

"Where?" Janet demanded. "Show me where. You keep telling me Aunt Laura's babies are buried out here, Michael. But where are they? If they're here, show them to me."

Trembling, Michael glared at her, then silently hurried away. He moved across the field, then finally stopped. "Here," he said once more. "If you want to see it, it's right here."

Wordlessly, Janet began digging once more.

Nathaniel watched for a few moments, then turned away and moved slowly through the barn, looking at it all for the last time. The little room beneath the trapdoor where he'd spent so many years; the tack room, from which he'd watched the burials on those strange nights when the children had been born and then died.

His children, the children he could reach through the powers of his mind. There hadn't been many of them, but he still thought of them as his.

There had been his brother. On the night Nathaniel was born, he had called out to his brother, and his brother had answered him. But then he'd gone to sleep, and when he woke up, his brother was gone. For a long time after that, Nathaniel had called out to his brother, called to him for help, but his brother had never come to him.

There had been two others since then, two others that he had felt, but in the end, they had brought them to the field, and buried them.

And then, a few months ago, his brother had come back. Nathaniel remembered it so well—he'd awakened one morning and sensed that he was no longer alone, that at last his brother had returned to help him avenge all the wrongs that had been done. For a long time, he and his brother had talked, and his brother had promised to come for him, to take him outside, to help him destroy their enemies.

But then his brother had died. He'd tried to warn Mark, but he couldn't. Mark was older than he and had ignored his warnings. And the old man had killed him.

And then, a few days later, Michael had come. He'd called out to Michael, too, and Michael had answered him.

And with Michael's help, he had destroyed his enemies.

And now, Michael and his mother were in the field, and would find the children, and know the truth.

Now, at last, Nathaniel could go home.

He left the barn and in the gathering darkness crossed the yard. He ignored the house—the house that had been part of his prison through all the years of his life, but that had, in these last days, been his secret refuge. Instead, he concentrated his mind on his goal: the house where he'd been born.

He moved quickly, slipping easily through the barbed wire, and in a few seconds, he was there. . . .

Janet's shovel struck something, something that stopped the blade's penetration of the earth, but was too soft to be a rock. As Michael stood by, with Shadow quivering at his side, Janet lowered herself to her knees, and began digging with her hands.

A moment later she felt the soft folds of a blanket.

Her heart began to beat faster as she worked, and then she pulled the object she had uncovered free from the earth that had hidden it.

She stared at it for a long time, afraid to open it, afraid it might actually be what she thought it was.

But she had come too far to turn back now. With a shaking hand, she folded back one corner of the blanket.

She could only stand to look at it for a second. Already, the flesh had begun to rot away, and the skin was entirely gone from the skull. Her stomach lurched, and involuntarily, Janet dropped the tiny corpse back into its grave. Her face pale, her whole body trembling now, Janet turned to gaze at her son.

"How did you know?" she breathed. "How did you know?"

"Nathaniel," Michael said, his voice steady. "Nathaniel told me."

"Where is he?"

Michael fell silent for a moment, then his eyes filled with tears.

"He's gone home," he said. "He's gone home to die."

Michael stopped, his eyes fixed on the window of his room. Janet, too, stopped. Following Michael's gaze, she looked up. The house was dark except for a single, oddly flickering light that glowed from Michael's window. Shadow bounded ahead to scratch eagerly at the back door.

"What is it, Michael?" Janet asked.

"Nathaniel. He's here. He's in my room."

"No," Janet whispered. "There's no one here, Michael. There's no

Nathaniel." But even as she said the words, Janet knew she no longer believed them. Whatever Nathaniel was, whether he was someone real, or a ghost, or no more than a creature of Michael's imagination, he was real. He was as real to her now as he was to Michael, and to Anna.

Slowly, Janet moved toward the back door of the house. Michael followed her, his face suddenly gone blank, as if he was listening to some being that Janet couldn't see.

She pulled the door open, and reached for the light switch. Nothing happened. Shadow slipped inside, immediately disappearing through the kitchen and up the stairs.

Janet could sense the presence in the house now, and her instinct was to flee, to abandon the house to whatever had invaded it, to take Michael and run out into the darkening night.

Instead, she went into the living room and picked up the poker that hung from the mantelpiece. Then she turned, and as if in a trance, moved toward the foot of the stairs, and started up.

Michael followed. Once again, his head was pounding, and once again, his nostrils seemed filled with smoke. And once again, Nathaniel's voice was whispering in his head.

"This is my house, and I have come home."

Michael moved on, his vision starting to cloud.

"This is my house, and I will never leave it. Never again."

They reached the landing. The presence of Nathaniel was almost palpable. Shadow, too, was there, his great body stretched on the floor in front of Michael's door, a strangled whimpering coming from his throat.

"This was my mother's house, and this is my house. I will not leave my house again."

Michael stopped, staring at the closed door, listening to Nathaniel's voice, knowing what Nathaniel was going to ask him to do.

Janet, too, stopped, but then she moved forward again, and put her hand on the knob of the door to Michael's room.

She turned it, then gently pushed the door, letting it swing open.

In the center of the room, his empty blue eyes fixed on her, his ashen face expressionless, Nathaniel stood, illuminated by the soft light of an oil lamp.

"This is my house," he said. "I was born here, and I will die here."

Janet recognized them all in the strange face she beheld. It was an ageless face, and it bore no emotion, and all of them were there.

Mark was there, and Amos.

Ben Findley was there.

And Michael was there.

For endless seconds, Janet searched that face, her mind reeling. Even now, as she saw him, she still was uncertain if he was real or only an apparition.

"Who are you?" she breathed at last.

"I am Nathaniel."

"What do you want?"

"I want what is mine," Nathaniel replied, his toneless voice echoing in the small room. "I want what was taken from me. I want—"

"No!" Janet suddenly screamed. All the torment that had built inside her over the last months, all the tensions, all the fears, overwhelmed her now, focusing on the strange being in Michael's room. "No," she screamed once again. "Nothing. You'll get nothing here."

She raised the poker, swinging it at Nathaniel with all the force she could muster. Nathaniel staggered backward under the blow, and then Janet dropped the poker, hurling herself forward.

"Help me, Michael!" The words thundered in Michael's head as he watched his mother throw herself on Nathaniel. Then, again, Nathaniel's words came: *"Help me!"*

Everything Michael saw was fogged now, fogged by the smoke that was choking him, and by the sound of Nathaniel's words ringing in his head.

"Help me, Michael. Please help me . . ."

His mind began to focus, and Nathaniel's wish began to take shape within him.

And then, as Michael silently commanded him, Shadow suddenly rose to his feet and launched himself into the room. To Michael, it was as if he was seeing it in slow motion: the dog seeming to arc slowly through the air, his lips curling back to expose his gleaming fangs, his ears laid flat against his head, droplets of saliva scattering from his jowls.

"Help me!" Nathaniel's words filled the room now, battering Michael's ears as well as his mind.

Then Shadow reached his target, his body twisting in midair and knocking over the little table that held the oil lamp as his jaws closed firmly on a human throat.

A scream filled the room as the oil lamp burst, and flames suddenly shot in every direction. The bedcovers caught first, and then the curtains.

Suddenly the room was filled with real smoke, and Michael understood with certain clarity that this was the smoke he'd been smelling all along, that Nathaniel, while showing him the past, had been showing him the future as well. And now he could hear his mother's terrified screams drowning out Nathaniel's bellows of pain and anguish.

His fogged mind cleared, and he watched for a moment, frozen to the spot, as his mother began flailing at the quickly spreading fire.

On the floor, his throat bleeding, Nathaniel lay calmly beneath the still attacking dog.

"No," Michael screamed. He hurled himself into the room. "No, Mom. Stop it—it's too late! Out! We've got to get out!"

Without waiting for her to reply, Michael grabbed her arm and began dragging her from the burning room.

For Janet, none of it was real anymore. Not Nathaniel, not Michael, not even the fire. She was caught in her nightmare again, but this time, she had to save them. Her family was going to die, and she had to save them.

She fought against the hands that restrained her, tried her best to stay in the burning room, tried to combat the growing flames.

Then, out of the smoke, a great weight hurled itself against her, and she fell to the floor. She recovered herself and got to her knees, then once again regained her feet.

But the weight was pressing at her now, pushing her toward the door, while the insistent hands still pulled.

And then she was out of the burning room and on the stairs. Her mind began to clear, and she recognized Michael in front of her, pulling her along. Behind her was Shadow, barking furiously, prodding at her, his large body preventing her from going back up the narrow stairs.

Then they were out of the house, huddled together in the yard, watching as the flames consumed the tinder-dry wood. Once, as she looked up, Janet thought she saw a face at Michael's window, but a second later it disappeared as the house crashed in on itself.

Then people began to gather around her; first the Simpsons, then the Shieldses, and then others, until soon most of Prairie Bend was there.

No one tried to save the house, no one tried to save anything that was in it: as the house burned, Janet's labor began.

EPILOGUE

"We'll take her to our house," Leif Simpson said.

Janet lay on the ground, her head cradled in Laura Shields's lap. Her face, glistening with a film of perspiration, was a mask of pain made grotesque by the orange light of the fire. The first violent contraction of her premature labor had wrenched a scream from her lips, and only Buck Shields's strong arms had kept her from collapsing. But now she drew on what few reserves of strength she still had. "No," she whispered. "Anna's . . . I want to go to Anna's."

"But there's no time, Janet," Ione protested.

"There is," Janet gasped. "I'll make time. But I want to have my baby at Anna's. Please . . . please." Another contraction seized her, and she moaned.

"I'll take her," Buck Shields said. "We'll put her in the back of the Chevy. It won't take more than an extra minute or two." He glanced at Ione Simpson. "Can you meet us there?" As soon as Ione had nodded, Buck leaned over and picked Janet up in his strong arms. "It's going to be all right," he told her. "We're taking you home." Janet sighed, and let her eyes close, blotting out the sight of the smoldering farmhouse, giving in to the pain that was wracking her body.

As Buck carried her to the car, she numbly tried to remember what had happened that night, how the fire had started.

But all she could remember was being at the kitchen table, then going upstairs to bed. A few minutes later, the house had burned.

She had no memory of going out to Potter's Field that night, no memory of what she had found there.

She had no memory of seeing Nathaniel that night.

For in dying, Nathaniel had taken her memories of him with him.

Ten minutes later, Ione Simpson arrived at Anna Hall's house, a determinedly cheerful expression masking the dread she was feeling. Janet's baby, she knew, was at least a month early, possibly more. And from the look in her eyes, Ione had known that Janet was in shock even before she went into labor. Nonetheless, she did her best to ease the fear that was plain in Michael's eyes as he sat in Anna's parlor, staring up at her. "Isn't this going to be exciting?" she asked. "Just like Magic foaling last spring, except this time you're going to have a baby brother or sister." Then, when Michael failed to react to her words, her tone changed. "Where's your mother?"

"Upstairs," Michael replied in a dazed voice.

"All right. Now, I want you to do something for me. I want you to find all the clean towels you can, and bring them into your mother's room. Okay?"

Michael seemed to come out of his trance, and nodded.

A few minutes later, his arms filled with folded towels, he appeared in the doorway of his mother's room. He stared at Janet, who was propped up against the pillows, her face drawn, lines of pain etched around her eyes. "Are you okay?" he asked, his voice filled with anxiety. "Does it hurt?"

Janet said nothing, but Laura Shields took the towels from Michael and eased him out of the room. "She's going to be fine, Michael. She and the baby are both going to be fine."

Michael gazed at the faces around his mother, but in none of them could he see anything to give him a hint about what was going to happen to his mother. His grandmother was sitting beside his mother, gently wiping her face with a damp cloth, while his uncle hovered in one corner. At last, understanding that right now no one had time for him, Michael went back downstairs to wait.

It was just after midnight, and Michael was in the parlor doing his best to shut out the sound of his mother's labor as it echoed through the house. Outside, the wind had begun to rise. He was alone—had been alone for hours as everyone in the house gathered upstairs to help with the delivery. Michael had wanted to be there, too, but his wishes had been denied. It would be easier for everyone, particularly his mother, if he stayed downstairs.

He was lying on the sofa now, staring out the window into the darkness, listening as the wind rose, howling around the house. Then, slowly, in the back of his mind, he felt something reaching out to him. It was a voice, and though the words were unclear, he understood the meaning.

Someone, somewhere, needed his help.

There was something oddly familiar about the sensation. It seemed like something that had happened before, but that he had forgotten about.

Then, as the wordless pleas for help became more insistent, the sounds of the wind and of his mother's agony began to grow dim. Unconsciously, Michael folded his arms over his chest, then drew his knees up, curling himself into a tight ball.

There was something surrounding him. Something damp and warm, and very comforting. And then, slowly, he began to feel pressure on his head, and the damp warmness around him began to move, producing an undulating rhythm that seemed to rock him gently.

The pressure on his head increased, turning into pain, and suddenly Michael moaned, a soft cry muffled by the damp folds that bound his limbs. The pain sharpened, and he felt as if his head was being crushed. Then the moist strictures of his bonds suddenly tightened around him, squeezing him, moving him. . . .

"It's coming," Ione said. "I can see the top of its head now. Bear down, Janet. It's almost over—just bear down hard."

Janet, sweat running off her body to soak into the already damp sheets, groaned softly, and tried to comply with Ione's instructions. But it was hard—so hard.

Suddenly Michael's bonds closed tightly around him. He felt as if he were being crushed, and he tried to fight against the restraints, but he had no strength. He screamed now, a long, high-pitched howl of agony.

Shadow, who had been asleep on the floor, suddenly awoke and rose to his feet. He moved to the couch, paused a moment, whimpering, to lick at Michael's face, but if Michael was aware of the big dog's presence, he gave no sign. Then, with Michael's next scream, Shadow turned and trotted upstairs to lie by the door to Janet's room, his ears laid back against his head, his tail twitching nervously, an odd sound halfway between a whine and a snarl drifting up from his throat.

In the parlor, the terrible pressure on Michael's head suddenly stopped. He tried to move his body, but couldn't. And then there was something else.

Something seemed to be twisting itself around his neck, making it hard for him to breathe.

He began struggling, fighting against the new restraint, but he couldn't get loose, couldn't throw it off. He could feel himself choking, feel himself beginning to gag.

Then, in the distance, he heard a voice.

"Here it comes," the voice whispered. "Here comes the pretty baby." Then: "Once more, Janet. Just once more."

Suddenly the pressure on Michael's body increased, squeezing, squeezing him ever harder, and he could feel himself being moved forward.

But with each forward motion, the pressure on his throat increased. There was no air now, and he could feel something strange happening in his brain. His sensations were growing dim, and his pain was easing.

There was a blackness around him, a gathering darkness that threatened to swallow him up. For a moment, he fought the blackness, tried to fight his way into the light. In the end, though, the darkness won, and he gave in to it.

"The umbilical cord," Ione Simpson gasped. The baby had stopped moving, only its head having emerged from the womb, and she knew instantly what had happened. "The cord's wrapped around his neck. It's strangling him. Hard, Janet. Bear down hard. Now!"

With a final effort that was more sheer will than strength, Janet forced the last of her energy into her torso. Her body heaved on the bed, and she cried out in exhaustion and agony. But slowly, the baby moved.

"Now," Ione whispered. "Now . . ."

With sure fingers and strong hands, she grasped the baby's body and drew it forth from the womb. Working as quickly as she could, she cut the umbilical cord away from the child's neck, then gave it a gentle thump on the back.

Nothing happened.

She tried again, a little harder, then felt for a pulse.

There was nothing.

Her eyes left the baby for a moment and scanned the room. Anna still sat by the head of the bed, her face pale and impassive. Laura Shields, her eyes fixed on the motionless infant, was crying, shaking her head in apparent disbelief. In the far corner, Buck Shields stood, his lower lip caught between his teeth, his entire body quivering with tension.

"Like Laura's," he said softly. "It's like Laura's."

Then, though she knew it was too late, and that there was nothing that could be done, Ione tried once more to bring the baby back to life.

Michael opened his eyes in the dimly lit room. Upstairs, he knew, his brother had been born, and he'd helped in the birth. Already, he understood that the odd voice he'd heard in his head a little while ago had been his brother's voice, and that his brother had needed his help. And he'd given his help, taking on the pain of the birth as he would take on whatever other pain his brother ever felt.

His brother, he knew, was his responsibility. It would be up to him to take care of the tiny child, comfort him when he was unhappy, tend to him when he was sick.

And protect him from evil.

Michael got up from the sofa and started slowly up the stairs. As he approached the landing, Shadow got to his feet, then moved slowly toward Michael, his tail low. He whimpered softly, then licked at Michael's hand.

Michael opened the door to the room in which his mother lay, and stepped inside.

His gaze roved through the strangely silent room, drifting from one face to the next. Finally his eyes fell on the tiny bundle that was cradled in Ione Simpson's arms.

"Let me see him," Michael whispered. "Let me see my brother."

Ione hesitated, then slowly shook her head. "I'm sorry, Michael . . ." she whispered.

"Let me see my brother," Michael repeated.

Now it was Anna Hall who spoke. She rose to her feet and moved slowly across the room until she stood in front of Michael. "He's dead, Michael," she said quietly. "Your little brother was born dead."

Michael's eyes widened, and he backed away from his grandmother. "No," he said. "He wasn't dead. I know he wasn't dead." His voice began to rise. "I could feel him. I could feel him, and he was alive!"

Turning away from the people in the room, the people he knew had killed his infant brother, Michael fled from the house, out into the night and the shrieking wind. He ran aimlessly, scrambling through fences, stumbling in the fields. At last, exhausted, he collapsed to the ground, where he lay sobbing and panting. Shadow crouched beside him, licking at his face.

He didn't know how much time passed by, but when he looked up, the night had grown even darker. The wind had ceased. All was silent.

In the distance, there was a soft reddish glow, and slowly Michael came to realize that he was seeing the dying embers of the house that had burned that night.

And then he saw another light, the yellow flame of a lantern, looming in the darkness. He watched it for several long minutes, and when it didn't move, he began creeping forward, huddling low to the ground, Shadow beside him.

And then, in the darkness, he could see.

There was someone there, working in the dim light of the lantern, and Michael knew what they were doing.

They were burying his brother, burying the brother he knew they had killed, but who was not dead.

As he watched, Michael knew what he must do.

In his own mind, his brother was Nathaniel, and his brother still lived.

Now, it was for Michael to avenge Nathaniel.

THE GOD PROJECT

For Sarita,
and the memory of Leon

CHAPTER 1

Sally Montgomery leaned down and kissed her daughter, then tucked the pink crocheted blanket that her mother had made in honor of Julie's birth—and which Sally hated—around the baby's shoulders. Julie, six months old, squirmed sleepily, half-opened her eyes, and gurgled.

"Are you my little angel?" Sally murmured, touching the baby's tiny nose. Again Julie gurgled, and Sally wiped a speck of saliva from her chin, kissed her once more, then left the bedroom. She had never quite gotten around to converting it into a nursery.

It wasn't that she hadn't intended to. Indeed, the room had been planned as a nursery ever since Jason had been born eight years earlier. She and Steve had made elaborate plans, even gone as far as picking out wallpaper and ordering curtains. But Sally Montgomery simply wasn't the decorating type. Besides, though she had never admitted it to anyone but Steve, the idea of redoing an entire room just for the enjoyment of an infant had always struck her as silly. All it meant was that you had to keep redoing it as the baby grew up.

In the gloom of the night-light, Sally glanced around the room and decided she had been right. The curtains, though they were blue, were still bright and clean, and the walls, still the same white they had been when she and Steve had bought the house nine years ago, were covered with an array of prints and pictures that any self-respecting baby should enjoy—Mickey Mouse on one wall and Donald Duck opposite him, with a batch of Pooh characters filling up the empty spaces. Even the mobile that turned slowly above Julie's crib had been chosen as much for the quality of its construction as for its design, though Sally had, almost reluctantly, come to appreciate the abstract forms which the saleslady had assured her would "do wonders for Baby's imagination." When they were grown, and had children of their own, she would pull the pictures and the mobile out of the attic and split them between Jason and Julie, who by then would have come to a new appreciation of them.

Chuckling at what she knew was an overdeveloped sense of practicality, Sally quietly closed the door to the baby's room and went downstairs. As she passed the door to the master bedroom she paused, listening to Steve's snoring, and was tempted to forget the report she was working on and crawl into bed with him. But again, the practical side of her came to the fore, and she pulled that door, too, closed and went downstairs.

She glanced at the papers covering the desk. Better to get the report done tonight, and have the papers cleared off before Steve came down in the morning and demanded to know why "his" desk was cluttered with "her" things. Years ago she had given up trying to convince him that the desk was "theirs." Steve had certain territorial ideas. The kitchen, for instance, was hers, even though he was a better cook than she was. The bathrooms were hers, too, while the family room, which by all rights should definitely have been theirs, was his. On the other hand, their bedroom, which they both loved, was hers, while the garage, which neither of them particularly wanted, was his.

The yard, being apart from the house, had somehow managed to wind up being "theirs," which meant that whoever complained about it had to do something about it. All in all, Sally decided as she wandered into "her" kitchen and began making a pot of tea, the division of the house and yard had worked out very well, like everything else in their marriage. She stared at the pan of water on the stove and idly wondered if it was true that as long as she watched it, it wouldn't boil. Then, for her own amusement, she picked up a pencil and began jotting figures on the scratch pad beside the telephone. Figuring the resistance of the metal in the electrical coils, the power of the current, and the volume of water, she came to the conclusion that the water should start boiling in eight minutes, give or take fifteen seconds, whether she watched it or not.

And that, she thought as the water began bubbling right on time, is the pleasure of having a mathematical mind. She poured the water over the tea bags and carried the pot and a cup back to the desk.

Much of the clutter was made up of computer printouts, and it was Sally's job to analyze the program of which the printouts were the results. Somewhere in the program there was a bug, and the college admissions office, which had dreamed up the program in the first place, had asked Sally to find it. The program, designed to review the records of hopeful high school seniors, had disqualified every applicant for the fall semester. When Sally had suggested that perhaps the program was perfect and the applicants simply weren't qualified, the dean of admissions had been less than amused. Soberly, he had handed Sally the program and the output, and asked her to find the problem by Monday morning.

And find it she would, for Sally Montgomery, as well as being beautiful, was brainy. Too brainy for her own good, her mother had always told her. Now, as she began analyzing the program in comparison to the printout it had produced, she could almost hear her mother's voice telling her she shouldn't be down here working in the middle of the night; she should be upstairs "loving her husband."

"You'll lose him," Phyllis Paine had told Sally over and over again. "A woman's place is in the home, loving her husband and her children. It's not normal for a woman your age to work."

"Then why did I go to college?" Sally had countered back in the days before she had given up arguing with her mother.

"Well, it wasn't to major in mathematics! I'd always hoped you'd do something with your music. Music is good for a woman, particularly the piano. In my day, all women played the piano."

It had gone on for years. Sally had finally stopped trying to explain to her mother that times had changed. She and Steve had agreed from the start that her career was every bit as important as his own. Her mother simply couldn't understand, and never missed an opportunity to let Sally know that in her opinion—the only one that counted, of course—a woman's place was in the home. "Maybe it's all right for women to work down in New York, but in Eastbury, Massachusetts, it just doesn't look right!"

And maybe, Sally reflected as she spotted the error in the program and began rewriting the flawed area, she's right. Maybe we should have gone out to Phoenix last year, and gotten out of this stuffy little town. I could have found a job out there, probably a better one than I have here. But they hadn't gone. They had agreed that since Sally was happy at the college, and Steve saw a glowing future for both of them in Eastbury's burgeoning electronics industry, they should stay right where they were, and where they'd always been.

Until the last few years, Eastbury had been one of those towns in which the older people talked about how good things used to be, and the younger people wondered how they could get out. But then, five years ago, the great change had begun. A change in the tax structure had encouraged fledgling businesses to come to Eastbury. And it had worked. Buildings which had once housed shoe factories and textile mills, then lain empty and crumbling for decades, were bustling once again. People were working—no longer at slave wages on killing shifts, but with flexible hours and premium salaries, creating the electronic miracles that were changing the face of the country.

Eastbury itself, of course, had not changed much. It was still a small town, its plain façade cheered only by a new civic center which was a clumsy attempt at using new money to create old buildings. What had resulted was a city hall that looked like a bank posing as a colonial mansion, and an elaborately landscaped "town square" entirely fenced in with wrought iron fancywork. Still, Eastbury was a safe place, small enough so the Montgomerys knew almost everyone in town, yet large enough to support the college that employed Sally.

The tea was cold, and Sally glanced at the clock, only slightly surprised to see that she'd been working for more than an hour. But the program was done, and Sally was sure that tomorrow morning it would produce the desired printouts. Eastbury College would have a freshman class next year after all.

She meticulously straightened up the desk, readying it for the onslaught of telephone calls that greeted Steve every morning. Using his talents as a salesman in tandem with the contacts he had made growing up in Eastbury, Steve had turned the town into what he liked to refer to as his "private gold mine." Mornings he often worked at home, and afternoons he spent either in his office or at the athletic club he had helped found, not out of any great interest in sports, but because he knew the executives of the new companies liked to work in what they called casual surroundings. Steve believed in giving people what they wanted. In turn, they usually gave him what he wanted, which was invariably a small piece of whatever action was about to take place. When asked what he did, Steve usually defined himself as an entrepreneur. In truth, he was a salesman who specialized in putting people together to the benefit of all concerned. Over the years, it had paid handsomely, not only for the Montgomerys, but for the whole town. It had been Steve who had convinced Inter-Technics to donate a main-frame computer to Eastbury that would tie all the town's small computers together, though Sally had never been convinced that it was one of his better ideas.

But now Steve was beginning to get bored. During the last few months he had begun to talk about the two of them going into business for themselves. Sally would become an independent consultant, and Steve would sell her services.

And mother will call him a pimp, Sally thought. She closed the roll-top desk and went into the kitchen. She was about to pour the untouched tea down the drain when she changed her mind and began reheating it. She wasn't tired, and her work was done, and the children were asleep, and there were no distractions. Tonight would be a good time for her to think over Steve's idea.

In many ways, it was appealing. The two of them would be working together—an idea she liked—but it also meant they would be together almost all the time. She wasn't sure she liked that.

Was there such a thing as too much togetherness? She had a good marriage, and didn't want to disturb it. Deep inside, she had a feeling that one of the reasons their marriage was so good was that both of them had interests beyond the marriage. Working together would end that. Suddenly their entire lives would be bound up in their marriage. That could be bad.

Sally poured herself a cup of the tea, still thinking about the possibilities. And then, in her head, she heard Steve's voice, and saw his blue eyes smiling at her. "You'll never know till you try, will you?" he was asking. Alone in the kitchen, Sally laughed softly and made up her mind. No, she said to herself, I won't. And if it doesn't work, we can always do something else. She finished the tea, put the cup in the sink, and went upstairs.

She was about to go into the bedroom when she paused, listening.

The house was silent, as it always was at that time of night. She listened for a moment, then went on into the bedroom and began undressing. The near-total darkness was broken only by the faint glow of a streetlight half a block away.

She slipped into bed next to Steve, and his arms came out to hold her. She snuggled in, resting her head on his shoulder, her fingers twining in the mat of blond hair that covered his chest.

She pressed herself closer to Steve and felt his arm tighten around her. She closed her eyes, ready to drift off to sleep, content in the knowledge that everything was as close to perfect as she could ever have wanted it, despite what her mother might think. It was, after all, her life, and not her mother's.

And then she was wide-awake again, her eyes open, her body suddenly rigid.

Had she heard something?

Maybe she should wake Steve.

No. Why wake Steve when she was already awake?

She slipped out of his arms and put on a robe. In the hall she stood still, listening carefully, trying to remember if she had locked the doors earlier.

She had.

She could remember it clearly. Right after Steve had gone up to bed, she had gone around the house, throwing the bolts, a habit she had developed during Steve's time on the road, when she had been alone with Jason for so many nights. The habit had never been broken.

The silence gathered around her, and she could hear her heart beating in the darkness.

What was it?

If there was nothing, what was she afraid of?

She told herself she was being silly, and turned back to the bedroom.

Still, the feeling would not go away.

I'll look in on the children, she decided.

She moved down the hall to Jason's room and opened the door. He was in his bed, the covers twisted around his feet, one arm thrown over the teddy bear he still occasionally slept with. Sally gently freed the covers and tucked her son in. Jason moved in his sleep and turned over. In the dim glow from the window, he looked like a miniature version of his father, his blond hair tangled, his little jaw square, with the same dimple in his chin that Sally had always thought made Steve look sexy. How many hearts are you going to break when you grow up? Sally wondered. She leaned over, and kissed Jason gently.

"Aw, Mom," the little boy said.

Sally pretended to scowl at her son. "You were supposed to be asleep."

"I was playin' possum," Jason replied. "Is something wrong?"

"Can't a mother say good night anymore?" Sally asked.

"You're always kissin' me," Jason complained.

Sally leaned down and kissed him again. "Be glad someone does. Not every kid is so lucky." She straightened up and started out of the room. "And don't kick the covers off. You'll catch pneumonia." She left Jason's room, knowing he'd kick the covers off again in five minutes, and that he wouldn't catch pneumonia. If Julie grew up as healthily as Jason had, she would be twice blessed. As she approached Julie's room, she began trying to calculate the odds of raising two children without having to cope with any sicknesses. The odds, she decided, were too narrow to be worth thinking about.

She let herself into the room, and suddenly her sense of apprehension flooded back to her.

She crossed to the crib and looked down at Julie. The baby was as different from her brother as she was from Steve. Julie had Sally's own almost-black hair, dark eyes, and even in her infancy the same delicate bone structure. She's like a doll, Sally thought. A tiny little doll. In the dim light the baby's skin was pale, nearly white, and Sally thought she looked cold, though the pink blanket was still tucked around her shoulders as Sally had left it earlier.

Sally frowned.

Julie was an active baby, never lying still for very long.

Apparently she hadn't moved for more than an hour.

Sally reached down, and touched Julie's face.

It was as cold as it looked.

As she picked up her tiny daughter, Sally Montgomery felt her life falling apart around her.

It wasn't true.

It couldn't be true.

There was nothing wrong with Julie.

She was cold. That's all, just cold. All she had to do was cuddle the baby, and warm her, and everything would be all right again.

Sally Montgomery began screaming—a high, thin, piercing wail that shattered the night.

Steve Montgomery stood in the doorway staring at his wife. "Sally? Sally, what's wrong?" He moved forward tentatively, watching her as she stood near the window, rocking back and forth, muttering in a strangled voice to the tiny form in her arms. Then he was beside her, trying to take the baby out of her arms. Sally's hold on the child tightened, and her eyes, wide and beseeching, found his.

"Call the hospital," she whispered, her voice desperate. "Call now. She's sick. Oh, Steve, she's sick!"

Steve touched Julie's icy flesh and his mind reeled. No! No, she can't be. She just can't be. He turned away and started out of the room, only to be stopped by Jason, who was standing just inside the door, his eyes wide and curious.

"What's wrong?" the little boy asked, looking up at his father. Then he looked past Steve, toward his mother. "Did something happen to Julie?"

"She's—she's sick," Steve said, desperately wanting to believe it. "She's sick, and we have to call the doctor. Come on."

Pulling Jason with him, Steve went into the next room and picked up the phone on the bedside table, dialing frantically. While he waited for someone to answer, he reached out and pulled his son to him, but Jason wriggled out of his father's arms.

"Is she dead?" he asked. "Is Julie dead?"

Steve nodded mutely, and then the operator at Eastbury Community Hospital came on the line. While he was ordering an ambulance for his daughter, he kept his eyes on his son, but after a moment Jason, his face impassive, turned and left the room.

CHAPTER 2

Eastbury Community Hospital, despite its name, was truly neither a hospital, nor a community service. It was, in actuality, a privately owned clinic. It had started, thirty years earlier, as the office of Dr. Arthur Wiseman. As his practice grew, Wiseman had begun to take on partners. Ten years before, with five other doctors, he had formed Eastbury Community Hospital, Inc., and built the clinic. Now there were seven doctors, all of them specialists, but none of them so specialized they could not function as general practitioners. In addition to the clinic, there was a tiny emergency room, an operating room, a ward, and a few private rooms. For Eastbury, the system worked well: each of the patients at Eastbury Community felt that he had several doctors, and each of the doctors always had six consultants on call. It was the hope of everyone that someday in the not-too-distant future, Eastbury Community would grow into a true hospital, though for the moment it was still a miniature.

In the operating room, Dr. Mark Malone—who, at the age of forty-two, was still not reconciled to the fact that he would forever be known as Young Dr. Malone—smiled down at the unconscious ten-year-old child on the table. A routine, if emergency, appendectomy. He winked at the nurse who had assisted him, then expertly snipped a sample of tissue from the excised organ, and gave it to an aide.

"The usual tests," he said. He glanced at the anesthetist, who nodded to him to indicate that everything was all right, then left the operating room and began washing up. He was staring disconsolately at the clock and wondering why so many appendixes chose to go bad in the wee hours of the morning, when he heard his name on the page.

"Dr. Malone, please. Dr. Malone."

Wiping his hands, he picked up the phone. "Malone."

"You're wanted in the emergency room, Dr. Malone," the voice of the operator informed him.

"Oh, Christ." Malone wracked his brain, trying to remember who was supposed to be on call that night.

The operator answered his unasked question. "It's—it's one of your patients, Doctor."

Malone's frown deepened, but he only grunted into the phone and hung up. He slipped off his surgical gown, put on a white jacket, then started for the emergency room, already sure of what had happened.

The duty man would have handled the emergency. The call to him meant that one of his patients had died, and, since he was in the clinic, someone had decided he should break the news to the parents. He braced himself, preparing for the worst part of his job.

He found the nurse, shaken and pale, just outside the emergency room. "What's happened?" he asked.

"It's a baby," the nurse replied, her voice quaking. She nodded toward the door. "She's in there with her mother. It's Julie Montgomery, and Sally won't let go of her. She just keeps insisting that she has to make the baby warm." Her voice faltered, then she went on. "I—I called Dr. Wiseman."

Malone nodded. Though Julie Montgomery was his patient, the child's mother was Art Wiseman's. "Is he coming?"

"He should be here any minute," the nurse promised. Even as she spoke, the distinguished gray-haired figure of Arthur Wiseman strode purposefully through the door from the parking lot.

The older doctor sized the situation up at once.

Sally Montgomery was sitting on a chair, with Julie cradled in her arms. She looked up at Wiseman, and her eyes were wide and empty.

Shock, Wiseman thought. She's in shock. He moved toward her and tried to take Julie from her arms. Sally drew back and turned away slightly.

"She's cold," Sally said, her voice no more than a whisper. "She's cold, and I have to make her warm."

"I know, Sally," Wiseman said softly. "But why don't you let us do it? Isn't that why you brought her here?"

Sally stared at him for a moment, then nodded her head. "Yes . . . I—I guess so. She's not sick, Dr. Wiseman. I know she's not sick. She's—she's just cold. So cold . . ." Her voice trailed off, and she surrendered the tiny body to the doctor. Then she covered her face with her hands and began to cry. Wiseman gave Julie to Mark Malone.

"See what you can do," he said softly.

Leaving Sally Montgomery under Wiseman's care, Malone took Julie Montgomery's body into a treatment cubicle. For the child, he knew already, there was no hope of resuscitation. But even knowing it was already far too late, he began trying to revive her. A few minutes later, holding Julie as if his will alone could bring her back to life, he felt a presence in the room and glanced up. It was Wiseman.

"Is she gone?" he asked.

Malone nodded. "There's nothing I can do," he said. "She's been dead at least an hour."

Wiseman sighed. "Any idea what happened?"

"I can't be sure yet, but it looks like SIDS."

Wiseman's eyes closed, and he ran his hand through his hair, brushing it back from his forehead. Damn, he swore to himself. Why does it happen? Why? Then he heard Malone's voice again.

"Is Steve here?"

"He was calling someone. His mother-in-law, I think. I ordered Valium for Sally."

"Good. Do you want me to talk to Steve?"

Wiseman, his eyes fixed on Julie Montgomery's tiny body, didn't answer for a moment. When he did, his voice was hollow. "I'll do it," he said. "I know Steve almost as well as I know Sally." He paused, then spoke again. "Will you do an autopsy?"

"Of course," Malone replied, "but I don't think we'll find anything. Julie Montgomery was one of the healthiest babies I've ever seen. And I saw her two days ago. Nothing wrong. Nothing at all. Shit!"

Malone looked down into the tiny face cradled in his arms. Julie Montgomery, to look at her, seemed to be asleep. Except for the deadly pallor and the coldness of her flesh. No injuries, no signs of sickness.

Only death.

"I'll take her downstairs," Malone said. He turned away, and Wiseman watched him until he disappeared around a corner. Only then did he return to the waiting room, where Steve Montgomery was now sitting by his wife, holding her hand. He looked up at the doctor, his eyes questioning. Wiseman shook his head.

"There was nothing that could be done," he said, touching Steve on the shoulder. "Nothing at all."

"But what happened?" Steve asked. "She was fine. There wasn't anything wrong with her. Nothing!"

"We don't know yet," Wiseman replied. "We'll do an autopsy, but I don't think we'll find anything."

"Not find anything?" Sally asked. The emptiness was gone from her eyes now, but her face was filled with a pain that Wiseman found almost more worrisome than the shock had been. She'll get over it, he told himself. It'll be hard, but she'll get over it.

"Why don't you two go home?" he suggested. "There's no reason to stay here. And we'll talk in the morning. All right?"

Sally got to her feet and leaned against Steve. "What happened?" she asked. "Babies don't just die, do they?"

Wiseman watched her, trying to judge her condition. Had it been anyone but Sally Montgomery, he would have waited until morning, but he'd known Sally for years, and he knew she was strong. The Valium had calmed her down and would keep her calm.

"Sometimes they do," he said softly. "It's called sudden infant death syndrome. That's what Mark Malone thinks happened to Julie."

"Oh, God," Steve Montgomery said. He saw Julie's face, her dancing eyes and smiling mouth, her tiny hands reaching for him, grasping his finger with all her own, laughing and gurgling.

And then nothing.

Tears began running down his face. He did nothing to wipe them away.

As the spring dawn crept over Eastbury, Steve Montgomery stood up and went to the window. He and Sally were in the living room, where they'd been all the long night, neither of them wanting to go to bed, neither of them willing to face whatever thoughts might come in the darkness. But now the darkness was gone, and Steve wandered around the room, turning off the lamps.

"Don't," Sally whispered. "Please don't."

Understanding her, Steve turned the lights back on, then went back to sit beside her once more, holding her close against him, neither of them speaking, but drawing strength from each other's presence. After a while there was a sound from upstairs, and then footsteps coming down the stairs. A moment later Sally's mother was in the room. She paused, then came to the sofa and drew Sally into her arms.

"My poor baby," she said softly, her voice soothing. "Oh, my poor baby. What happened? Sally, what happened?"

Her mother's voice seemed to trigger something in Sally, and her tears, the tears that should have been drained from her hours earlier, began to flow once more. She leaned against her mother, her body heaving with her sobs. Over her daughter's head, Phyllis Paine's eyes met her son-in-law's.

"What happened, Steve?" she asked. "What happened to my granddaughter?"

I have to control myself, Steve thought. For Sally, I have to be strong. I have to tell people what happened, and I have to make arrangements, and I have to take care of my wife and my son. Then another thought came to him: I'll never be able to do it. I'll come apart, and my insides will fall out. Oh, God, why did you have to take Julie? Why not me? She was only a baby! Just a little baby.

He wanted to cry too, wanted to bury his head in his wife's bosom, and let go of his pain, and yet he knew he couldn't. Not now, perhaps not ever. He met his mother-in-law's steady gaze.

"Nothing happened to her," he said, forcing himself to keep his voice steady. "She just died. It's called sudden infant death syndrome."

Phyllis's eyes hardened. "A lot of nonsense," she said. "All it means is that the doctors don't know what happened. But something happened to that child. I want to know what."

Her words penetrated Sally's grief. She pulled herself from her mother's embrace and faced her. "What do you mean?" she asked, her voice strident. "What are you saying?"

Phyllis stood up, searching for the right words. She knew where the blame lay, knew very well, but she wouldn't say it. Not yet. Later, when Sally had recovered from the shock, they would have a talk. For now, she would take care of her daughter . . . as her daughter should have taken care of Julie.

"I'm not saying anything," she maintained. "All I'm saying is that doctors like to cover for themselves. Babies don't just die, Sally. There's always a reason. But if the doctors are too lazy to find the reason, or don't know enough, they call it crib death. But there *is* always a reason," she repeated. Her eyes moved from Sally to Steve, then back to Sally. When she spoke again, her voice was gentler. "I'm going to stay here for a few days—I'll take care of Jason and the house. Don't either of you worry about anything."

"Thanks, Phyl," Steve said quietly. "Thanks."

"Isn't that what mothers are for?" Phyllis asked. "To take care of their children?" Her eyes settled once more on Sally, then she turned and went back up the stairs. A moment later they heard her talking to Jason, and Jason's own voice, piping loud as he pummeled his grandmother with questions. Sally was silent for a long time, then she spoke to Steve without looking at him.

"She thinks I did something to Julie," she said dully. "Or didn't do something. She thinks it was my fault."

Inwardly, Steve groaned at the hopelessness in his wife's voice, and reached out to hold her. "No, honey, she doesn't think that at all. It's just—it's just Phyllis. You know how she is."

Sally nodded. I know how she is, she thought. But does she know how I am? Does she know me? Her train of thought was broken as Jason came pounding down the stairs. He stood in the middle of the floor, his pajamas falling down, his hands on his hips.

"What happened to Julie?" he asked.

Steve bit his lip. How could he explain it? How could he explain death to an eight-year-old, when he didn't even understand it himself? "Julie died," he said. "We don't know why. She . . . she just died."

Jason was silent, his eyes thoughtful. And then he nodded, and frowned slightly. "Do I have to go to school today?" he asked.

Too tired, too shocked, too drained to recognize the innocence of her son's words, Sally only heard their naive callousness. "Of course you have to go to school today," she screamed. "Do you think I can take care of you? Do you think I can do everything? Do you think . . ." Her voice failed her, and she collapsed, sobbing, back onto the sofa as her mother hurried down the stairs. Jason, his face pale with bafflement and hurt, stared at his mother, then at his father.

"It's all right," Phyllis told him, scooping him into her arms. "Of course you don't have to go to school today. You go upstairs and get dressed, then I'll fix your breakfast. Okay?" She kissed the boy on the cheek and put him back on the floor.

"Okay, Grandma," Jason said softly. Then, with another curious glance at his parents, he ran up the stairs.

When he was gone, Steve put his arms around his wife. "Go to bed, sweetheart," he begged. "You're worn out, and Phyllis can handle everything. We'll take care of you, and everything will be all right. Please?"

Too exhausted to protest, Sally let herself be led upstairs, let Steve undress her and put her to bed, let him tuck her in. But when he had kissed her and left her alone, she didn't sleep.

Instead, she remembered her mother's words. "Isn't that what mothers are for? To take care of their children?" It was an accusation, and Sally knew it. And she knew, deep in her heart, that she had no answer for the accusation. Perhaps she had done something—or not done something—that had caused Julie to die.

Hadn't she considered aborting Julie? Hadn't she and Steve talked about it for a long time, trying to decide whether they really wanted another child? Hadn't they, finally, talked until it was too late?

But they had loved Julie once she was born. Loved her as much as Jason, maybe even more.

Or had they?

Maybe they had only pretended to love her because they knew it was their duty: You have to love your children.

Maybe she hadn't loved Julie enough.

Maybe, deep inside, she still hadn't wanted Julie.

As she drifted slowly into a restless sleep, Sally could still hear her mother's voice, see her mother's eyes, accusing her.

And her daughter was dead, and she had no way of proving that it hadn't been her fault.

She couldn't prove it to her mother; she couldn't prove it to herself.

As she slept, a germ of guilt entered Sally Montgomery's soul, a guilt as deadly for her soul as a cancer might be for her body.

In one night, Sally Montgomery's life had changed.

CHAPTER 3

Randy Corliss poked aimlessly at the bowl of soggy cereal. He had already made up his mind not to eat it.

Five more minutes, and his mother would be gone.

Then he could throw the cereal into the garbage, swipe a Twinkie, and be on his way. He stared intently at the minute hand on the clock, not quite sure if he could actually see it moving. He wished his mother would buy a clock like the ones at school, where you could really see the hands jump forward every minute, but he knew she wouldn't. Maybe if he asked his father next weekend . . .

He mulled the idea over in his nine-year-old mind, only half-listening as his mother gave her usual speech about coming right home after school, not answering the door unless he knew who was outside, and reporting his arrival to Mrs.-Willis-next-door. At last she leaned over, kissed him on the cheek, and disappeared into the garage adjoining the kitchen. Only when he heard her start the car, and knew she was really gone, did Randy get up and dump the loathsome cereal.

At five minutes after eight, Randy Corliss went out into the bright spring morning and began the long walk that would take him first to Jason

Montgomery's house, and then to school. All around him children his own age were drifting from their homes onto the sidewalks, forming groups of twos and threes, whispering and giggling among themselves. All of them, it seemed, had plenty of friends.

All of them except Randy Corliss.

Randy didn't understand exactly why he had so few friends. In fact, a long time ago, when he was six, he'd had lots of friends. But in the last three years, most of them had drifted away.

It wasn't as if he was the only one whose parents were divorced. Lots of the kids lived with only their mothers, and some of them even lived with just their fathers. Those were the kids Randy envied—the ones who lived with their fathers. He decided to talk about that with his father this weekend too. Maybe this time he could convince him. He'd been trying for almost a year now—ever since the time last summer when he'd run away.

Last summer hadn't been much fun at all. Nobody would play with him, and he'd spent the first month of the summer watching the other kids, waiting for them to ask him to play ball, or go for a hike, or go swimming, or do any of the other things they were doing.

But they hadn't, and when he finally broke down and asked Billy Semple what was wrong, Billy, who had been his last friend, only looked at him for a long time, then stared at the cast on his leg, shrugged, and said nothing.

Randy had known what that was all about. He and Billy had been out playing in the Semples' backyard one day, and Randy had decided it might be fun to jump off the roof. First they had tried the garage roof, and it had been easy. Randy had jumped first, landing in the Semples' compost heap, and Billy had followed.

Then Randy had suggested they try the house roof, and Billy had looked fearfully up at the steep pitch. But in the end, not wanting to appear cowardly, Billy had gone along with it. The two of them had gotten a ladder and climbed to the eaves, where they had perched for a couple of minutes, staring down. Randy had been the first to jump.

He had hit the ground, and for a second had felt a flash of pain in his ankles. But then he had rolled, and by the time he had gotten to his feet, the pain was gone. He'd grinned up at Billy.

"Come on!" he'd yelled. "It's easy." When Billy still hesitated, Randy had begun taunting him, and finally, just as Billy made up his mind, Mrs. Semple had come out to the backyard to see what was going on. She'd appeared just in time to see her son hurtle down from the roof and break his right leg. Furious, she'd ordered Randy out of the yard, and later that afternoon she'd called Randy's mother to tell her that Randy was no longer welcome in her home.

Enough, she'd said, was enough. She'd hoped that it wouldn't come to this, but after today she had to join the rest of the mothers in the neighborhood, and forbid her son to play with Randy Corliss anymore.

The fact that it had been an accident had made no difference. Randy was a daredevil, a bad influence.

And so the summer had dragged on. Randy, getting lonelier every day, had begun going off by himself, roaming in the woods, prowling around the town, wishing he knew what had gone wrong.

Then he had met Jason Montgomery, and even though Jason was a year younger than he was, he'd liked Jason right away. Jason, he'd decided, wasn't like the rest of the kids. The rest of them were all cowards, but not Jason. They'd become best friends the day after they met, and all this year Randy had stopped by Jason's house every day on his way to school.

Today he arrived at the Montgomerys' house, and went around to the back, as he always did.

"Jason! Jaaaason!" he called. The back door opened, and he recognized Jason's grandmother. "Isn't Jason here?" he asked.

"He's not going to school today," Jason's grandmother told him. She was starting to close the door, when Jason suddenly appeared, scooting out from behind his grandmother and slipping through the door.

"Hi," Jason said.

Randy stared at his friend curiously. "You sick?" he asked.

"Naw," Jason replied. Then he looked directly at Randy. "My little sister died last night, so I don't have to go to school today."

Randy absorbed the information and wondered what he was supposed to say. He'd only seen Jason's baby sister once, and to him she hadn't seemed like anything special. All she'd done was cry, and Jason had told him she peed all the time. "What happened to her?" he asked at last.

Jason hesitated, then frowned. "I dunno. Dad says she just died. Anyway, I get to stay home from school."

"That's neat," Randy said. Then he frowned at Jason. "Did you do something to her?"

"Why would I do that?" Jason countered.

Randy shifted uncomfortably. "I don't know. I just—I just wondered. Billy Semple's mother thought—" He broke off, unsure how to say what he was thinking. Billy Semple's mother had thought he was trying to hurt Billy, even though she never said it out loud.

"Did you push Billy off the roof?" Jason asked.

"No."

"And I didn't do anything to Julie," Jason said. "At least, I don't think I did."

Then, before Jason could say anything else, his grandmother opened the back door and told him to come back into the house. Randy watched as his friend disappeared inside, then started once more on his way to school.

He didn't really want to go today. Without Jason there, it wouldn't be any fun at all. It would be like it had been last summer, before he had met Jason, while he was waiting for his friends to come back.

Waiting, though, is much easier for an adult than for a nine-year-old, and while he was waiting, Randy had begun entertaining himself by getting into mischief. He'd started swiping things from the dime store. Nothing big, just a few little things.

Then one day Mr. Higgins, who owned the dime store, had caught him.

Randy would never forget that day. He'd almost been out of the store when he'd felt a hand on his arm and turned to see Mr. Higgins glowering down at him, demanding that he empty his pockets.

The yo-yo didn't have a price tag on it, but Randy didn't even try to pretend he hadn't stolen it. His face pale, his eyes brimming with tears, he'd stammered out an apology and promised never to do it again.

But Mr. Higgins hadn't let the matter go. He'd called the Eastbury police and explained that while he didn't want to press charges, he thought it would be a good idea if someone put the fear of God into Randy Corliss. "A good scare," Randy had heard him say into the phone. "That'll straighten him out." Randy had been taken to the police station, and shown a cell, and told that he might have to spend the night there. Then they'd fingerprinted him and taken his picture, and warned him that if he ever tried to steal anything again, he'd be sent to prison.

When they let him go, Randy was shaking. That night, he began to think about running away.

Nobody liked him, and his mother never seemed to have any time for him. The only person who cared about him, he decided, was his father. He'd called his father, and begged him to come and get him, but Jim Corliss had told him that he couldn't, not yet. Then his father had asked to speak to his mother, and Randy had listened to his mother arguing with his father, telling him that she'd never let Randy go, and that his father better not try to take him. Finally, when the fight was over, he'd talked to his father again.

"I'll see what I can do," Jim had promised. "But there are laws, Randy, and if I just came and got you, I'd be breaking them. Can you understand that?"

Randy tried, but he couldn't. The only thing he could understand was that he hated Eastbury, and he hated his mother, and he hated his friends-who-weren't-his-friends-anymore, and he wanted to go live with his father. Then he got the idea. Maybe his father couldn't come and get him, but what if he went to his father?

Two days later he had made up his mind. When he was sure his mother was asleep, he dressed and sneaked out of the house. He knew where his father lived—it was only five miles away, if you didn't stay on the roads. And he knew the woods; he'd been wandering in them all his life. He figured it would take him an hour or two to get to his father's.

What he hadn't figured was how different the woods would look at night. For a while he walked rapidly along, lighting his way with the flashlight he'd taken from the kitchen drawer, enjoying the adventure. But when the path forked, he began to get confused.

In the daylight, it would have been easy. Everything would have been familiar—the trees, the rocks, the stream that wound its way through the woods toward Langston, where his father lived. But in the darkness, with shadows dancing everywhere, he wasn't sure which way to go. Finally, he made up his mind and told himself everything was fine, even though he didn't believe it.

A little while later he came to another fork in the path. This time he had no idea at all which way was the right way. He stood still for a long time, listening to the sounds of the night—birds murmuring in their sleep, the rustlings of racoons foraging in the underbrush—and finally decided that maybe going through the woods hadn't been a good idea after all. He turned back and started toward home.

Another fork in the path.

Now Randy was getting worried. He didn't remember this fork at all. Had he really passed it before?

The sounds around him were suddenly becoming ominous. Was there something in the darkness, just beyond the beam of the flashlight, watching him?

He spun around, sweeping the woods with the light, and flashes of light came back to him.

There *were* eyes in the night—glowing yellow eyes—and now Randy was frightened. He began running down the path, no longer thinking about where he was going or which path he was on. All he wanted was to get out of the woods.

And then, ahead of him, he saw a light moving in the darkness. Then another, and another. He hurled himself toward the lights, but they disappeared.

They came back, flashing across the trees, then disappearing again.

He stopped short, knowing at last what it was. He was at the edge of the forest, near a road. But which one? He had no idea.

He stayed where he was for a while, wondering what to do next. He really wanted to go home, but he wasn't sure which way home was. He tried to remember what roads went by the woods, but couldn't. Finally, as the night grew colder, he decided he had to do something. He stepped out of the forest and started walking along the road, the flashlight clutched in his right hand.

A car pulled up beside him. An Eastbury police car.

"Goin' somewhere, son?" the policeman asked him.

"H-home," Randy stammered.

"Eastbury?" the cop asked.

"Uh-huh."

"Well, you're goin' the wrong way." The policeman leaned over and opened the door. "Hop in."

Terrified, visions of jail cells dancing in his head, Randy did as he was told. "Are you arresting me?" he asked, his voice even smaller than he felt.

The policeman glanced over at him, a tiny smile playing around the corners of his mouth. "You a big-time crook?"

"Me?" Randy's eyes opened wide. He shook his head. "I—I was going to visit my father."

"Thought you said you were going home."

Randy squirmed in the seat. "Well—my dad's house is home. Isn't it?"

"Not if you live with your mother. You running away?"

Randy stared glumly out the window, sure that he was going to jail. "I—I guess so."

"Things that bad?"

Randy looked up at the cop, who was smiling at him. Could it be possible the cop wasn't mad at him? He nodded shyly.

The cop scowled at him then, but Randy was suddenly no longer scared, and when the man spoke, his worries vanished completely. "I'm Sergeant Bronski," the policeman told him. "Want to have a coke and talk things over?"

"Where?" Randy countered.

"There's a little place I know." Bronski turned the patrol car around and started back toward Eastbury. "You want me to call your mother?"

"No!"

"How about your dad?"

"Could you call him?"

"Sure." Bronski pulled into an all-night diner, and took Randy inside. He ordered a Coke for Randy and a cup of coffee for himself. Slowly, the story came out, ending with the fight the Corlisses had had on the phone. When Randy was through talking, the policeman looked him squarely in the eye.

"I think we better call your mother, Randy," he said.

"Why?"

"Because that's who you live with. If we call your father, he'll have to call your mother, and she might think he planned all this. Then she might not let you see him at all. Understand?"

"I—I guess so," Randy said uncertainly. The call had been made, and then Sergeant Bronski had taken him home and turned him over to his mother.

His mother had been furious with him, telling him she had enough to worry about just trying to raise him, without having to worry about him running away too. Finally she had sent him back to bed, and Randy had lain awake all night, wondering what to do next.

Ever since that night, he had been wondering what to do. He had begged his father to take him away, and his father, never really saying no but never quite saying yes, had told him to wait, that things would get better.

But months had gone by and not much had changed.

He'd finally met Jason, but his mother still had no time for him. And every time he approached his father, his father told him to wait, told him that he was "working on it." Now spring was here, and soon it would be summer. Would it be another summer to spend by himself, wandering in the woods and prowling around town, looking for something to do? It probably would. If something had happened to Jason's sister, Jason probably wouldn't be allowed to play with him anymore. Once again, he would be all alone.

A horn honked, pulling Randy out of his reverie, and he realized he was alone on the block. He looked at the watch his father had given him for his ninth birthday. It was nearly eight thirty. If he didn't hurry, he was going to be late for school. Then he heard a voice calling to him.

"Randy! Randy Corliss!"

A blue car, a car he didn't recognize, was standing by the curb. A woman was smiling at him from the driver's seat. He approached the car hesitantly, clutching his lunch box.

"Hi, Randy," the woman said.

"Who are you?" Randy stood back from the car, remembering his mother's warnings about never talking to strangers.

"My name's Miss Bowen. Louise Bowen. I came to get you."

"Get me?" Randy asked. "Why?"

"For your father," the woman said. Randy's heart beat faster. His father? His father had sent this woman? Was it really going to happen, finally? "He wanted me to pick you up at home," he heard the woman say, "but I was late. I'm sorry."

"That's all right," Randy said. He moved closer to the car. "Are you taking me to Daddy's house?"

The woman reached across and pushed the passenger door open. "In a little while," she promised. "Get in."

Randy knew he shouldn't get in the car, knew he should turn around and run to the nearest house, looking for help. It was things like this—strangers offering to give you a ride—that his mother had talked to him about ever since he was a little boy.

But this was different. This was a friend of his father's. She had to be, because she seemed to know all about his plans to go live with his father, and his father's plans to take him away from his mother. Besides, it was always men his mother warned him about, never women. He looked at the woman once more. Her brown eyes were twinkling at him, and her smile made him feel like she was sharing an adventure with him. He made up his mind and got into the car, pulling the door closed behind him. The car moved away from the curb.

"Where are we going?" Randy asked.

Louise Bowen glanced over at the boy sitting expectantly on the seat beside her. He was every bit as attractive as the pictures she had been shown, his eyes almost green, with dark, wavy hair framing his pugnacious, snub-nosed face. His body was sturdy, and though she was a stranger to him, he didn't seem to be the least bit frightened of her. Instinctively, Louise liked Randy Corliss.

"We're going to your new school."

Randy frowned. New school? If he was going to a new school, why wasn't his father taking him? The woman seemed to hear him, even though he hadn't spoken out loud.

"You'll see your father very soon. But for a few days, until he gets everything worked out with your mother, you'll be staying at the school. You'll like it there," she promised. "It's a special school, just for little boys like you, and you'll have lots of new friends. Doesn't that sound exciting?"

Randy nodded uncertainly, no longer sure he should have gotten in the car. Still, when he thought about it, it made sense. His father had told him there would be lots of problems when the time came for him to move away from his mother's. And his father had told him he would be going to a new school. And today was the day.

Randy settled down in the seat and glanced out the window. They were heading out of Eastbury on the road toward Langston. That was where his father lived, so everything was all right.

Except that it didn't quite *feel* all right. Deep inside, Randy had a strange sense of something being very wrong.

CHAPTER 4

It had not been one of Lucy Corliss's better days. She had spent the morning making the rounds of new listings coming onto the market. Houses that she privately thought weren't worth the land they were built on were being priced at well over a hundred thousand dollars. Between the prices and the mortgage rates, she didn't see how anyone was going to be able to afford to buy. That meant her commissions were going to be off. While pretending to be interested in the houses, she had privately begun reviewing her financial position, and making plans for cuts in her budget. For the moment, the situation wasn't perilous—she had three closings coming up over the next couple of months, and those commissions, if she was careful, would see her through a year. Then what?

Over lunch, she discussed the matter with Bob Owen, who was not only her employer, but her friend. She'd known Bob since childhood, and he'd seen her through a lot.

When her marriage had begun to sour, Bob had been there, listening to her complaints with a sympathetic ear, finally telling her that at some point she was going to have to stop complaining and take some action. When the crunch had at last come, she'd gone to Bob for advice.

The problem, at the time, had been twofold. She was pregnant, and her husband had walked out on her. In fact, she'd admitted to Bob, Jim Corliss had walked out on her *because* she was pregnant, accusing her of trying to tie him down with a baby.

"Did you?" Bob had asked. It had taken Lucy a long time to come up with an answer. At last she had admitted that perhaps, subconsciously, she had. Perhaps she had thought that the responsibilities of fatherhood would calm Jim down, make him see that there was more to life than fast cars and dreams of quick money.

Bob—practical Bob—had advised her to file for a divorce and prepare to go to work. It had even been his idea for her to learn real estate while she was pregnant, so that after the baby was born she would have a way to earn a living. For nine years she had worked out of Bob's office, and she was good at her job. At first she had hired a sitter to come in and look after Randy, but last year she had decided that Randy was old enough to stay by himself for the two hours between the end of the school day and the end of her work day. Margaret Willis, who lived next door, had agreed to keep an eye on Randy. So far it had worked out. Except that today she had a vague sense of unease.

"What's the matter with my girl?" Bob asked, pushing the menu aside and making up his mind to settle for a salad. He looked enviously at Lucy, who ate enormous lunches and dinners and never gained an ounce.

"Your girl—and I don't think your wife would like to hear you call me that, even though she knows it isn't true—is feeling worried today," Lucy replied. She put the menu aside.

"Anything in particular, or everything in general?"

"Well, the market isn't doing a lot for my mood. I can't see who's going to buy the overpriced dogs we saw this morning."

"Someone will," Bob said complacently. "People have to buy houses. We'll just have to think up new ways to finance them."

"But the houses aren't worth it," Lucy complained.

Now Bob frowned, his bushy eyebrows plunging toward the bridge of his nose. "With an attitude like that, you're certainly not going to be selling any of them."

Lucy smiled wanly and brushed a strand of her pale blond hair out of her eyes. "I'm not sure I want to. Lately, every time I sell someone a house, I feel like I'm making him an indentured servant for the next thirty years."

"Then maybe you'd better do something else."

"Forget it. Besides, it's not really the market that's bothering me—it's Randy."

"Randy? Is something wrong with him?"

"Nothing new. It's just that he seems so unhappy. He doesn't seem to have many friends anymore, and he hates school and home and me and everything else. Sometimes I think maybe I should let Jim take him, for a while at least. Except I don't trust him."

"You don't even know him anymore," Bob pointed out. There were times, every now and then, when Lucy suspected that Bob was trying to get her back together with Jim. Lately, he seemed to be pushing her to see her ex-husband more often than she had to. So far, she had resisted him. "Hasn't it occurred to you that he might have changed?" Bob asked now. "It's been almost ten years. People grow up."

"Even Jim Corliss?" Lucy scoffed. "Do you know how many jobs he's had since he left me? Seven! Seven jobs in nine years, Bob. You call that mature?"

"But only one in the last four years, Lucy. And he's good with Randy."

"Who he never wanted in the first place," Lucy shot back, her voice bitter. "To Jim, Randy's nothing more than a part-time hobby he can deal with over a weekend now and then. But all the time? Come on, Bob, you know damned well Jim would send him back in a week. And what would that do to Randy? He's miserable enough already—having his father reject him could destroy him. I won't do it." She wondered if she should tell Bob that Jim had mentioned the possibility of going to court over Randy, and decided against it. Bob —reasonable Bob—would only suggest that it might not be best for anyone to have a court fight over Randy, and that perhaps she should consider at least sharing the boy with Jim. And that, she knew, was something she wasn't prepared to do.

"I'm sorry," she said as their food arrived. "I don't know why I always wind up crying on your shoulder. Let's talk about something else, okay? Like when you and Elaine can come over for some of my famous burnt steaks? The weather's getting nice, and I feel in the mood for a barbecue. How about this weekend?"

And so the afternoon passed, and Lucy kept her mind off her problems. Or, more exactly, she *tried* to keep her mind off her problems. But by five o'clock, when she left the office, Randy was once more looming at the forefront of her mind.

As she pulled into the driveway of the small house she had bought five years before, her feeling of unease increased. Usually, Randy was there, standing at the living-room window, watching for her.

She went inside and called out to him. There was no answer. Quickly, she went through the house, but nowhere was there any sign of Randy. His room was as it had been this morning, and his school clothes, which he usually left in a heap on the floor, were nowhere to be seen. Satisfied that Randy was not in the house, Lucy went next door to talk to Margaret Willis.

"But why didn't you call me?" Lucy asked when the elderly widow told her that Randy had not been seen at all that afternoon.

Mrs. Willis's hands fluttered nervously. "Why, I simply assumed he'd gone to play with friends," she said, then flushed a deep red as she realized her error. Even on the days when Randy didn't come home immediately after school, he was always home long before his mother was expected. But today, the afternoon had slipped away, and she hadn't seen Randy.

Margaret Willis's ample chin began to quiver. "Oh, dear, I've made a terrible mistake, haven't I? But surely you don't think anything's happened to him? Why, it's not even five thirty yet. Why don't you let me fix you a nice cup of tea?" She tried to draw Lucy into her house, but Lucy pulled away.

"No, no, thank you, Mrs. Willis. I'd better try to find out what's happened to him." Lucy tried to keep her voice calm, but her eyes revealed the fear that was beginning to grip her. Margaret Willis reached out and touched her arm.

"Now, what could have happened to him?" she asked gently. "It's not as if this was Boston, dear. Why, nothing ever happens in Eastbury, you know that. I'll tell you what—I'll make some tea and bring it over to your house."

Tea, Lucy thought. Why is it that half the people in the world think that a nice cup of tea will fix everything? But she was too upset to argue. "All right," she agreed. "I'll leave the front door open."

She hurried down the steps of Mrs. Willis's front porch and cut across the lawn that separated the large Willis house from her own. Inside, the silence pushed her unreasonably close to the edge of panic. She went to the kitchen and made herself sit down at the table that was still littered with breakfast dishes. Consciously, she forced the panic back, telling herself that Margaret Willis was undoubtedly right, that Randy was fine, and would show up any minute. Her fears were silly; she was overreacting to a commonplace situation. Small boys often took off without telling anyone where they were going.

Her intuition told her otherwise. She went to the phone and began searching through her address book, looking for the names of people whose children had once been Randy's friends. She was on her third phone call when Margaret Willis appeared at the back door, carrying a steaming teapot. Lucy stretched the phone cord and reached the knob, feeling irritated that the woman hadn't used the front door. But in Eastbury, neighbors, except for herself, always used back doors. As Mrs. Willis came into the kitchen, she looked inquiringly at Lucy, who only shrugged, then began speaking as Emily Harris came back on the line.

"Geordie says Randy wasn't at school today, Lucy."

"Wasn't there at all?" Lucy asked, her voice hollow.

"That's what Geordie says," Mrs. Harris told her. "And he should know—he's in Randy's class."

"I—I see," Lucy said. There was a silence as each of the women wondered what to say next. It was Emily Harris who finally spoke.

"Lucy, have you talked to Sally Montgomery?"

Lucy groaned to herself. Sally Montgomery should have been the first call she made. If Randy was anywhere, he'd be with Jason. "Oh, God, Emily, I feel like such a fool," she said.

"It's tragic," she heard Emily Harris saying. "I mean, what do you say when something like that happens?"

Lucy felt her stomach tighten. "What are you talking about?" she asked. "What happened?"

Again there was a silence, and when Emily eventually spoke, her voice had dropped to the conspiratorial level that signaled the sort of bad news she loved best. "You mean you haven't heard? Their little girl died last night. They *say* it was crib death . . ." She let the words hang, clearly indicating that she was sure there was more to the story than that. Then her voice brightened, and Lucy suddenly realized why she had never really liked Emily Harris. "But I'm sure nothing's wrong," Emily said. "Jason wasn't at school today, of course, and Randy probably decided to play hookey with him. Geordie's done it more than once," she lied. "All boys do it, especially in spring. I'll bet he'll be home in time for dinner."

"I suppose so," Lucy said without conviction. She decided she had had quite enough of Emily Harris. "Thanks, Emily. Sorry to bother you."

"No bother at all," Emily Harris replied. "Let me know when you find him, all right? Otherwise I'll worry."

Sure you will, Lucy thought angrily. And you'll be on the phone all night, spreading the latest news too. She hung up, then sipped the tea that Margaret Willis had placed in front of her, and told the older woman what she had just heard.

"Oh, dear," Margaret murmured. "Well, I suppose you'd better call Mrs. Montgomery, hadn't you?"

"I don't know," Lucy replied unhappily. "Oh, I know I should, but what good would it do? Randy couldn't possibly be there, not today. And what would I say to her? Do I tell her I'm sorry her daughter died, but has she happened to see my son? Margaret, I can't! I just can't!"

"Then I will," Margaret said, reaching for the phone book. But before she had found the Montgomerys' number, Lucy suddenly hit the table with her fist.

"His father!" she exclaimed. "Damn it, that's what happened. Jim took Randy!" Once more she picked up the phone, and began dialing furiously, her eyes, filled with worry only a moment ago, now glittering with anger. "That bastard," she rasped through clenched teeth as she listened to her ex-husband's telephone ring on with that strange, impossible tone that seems to occur only when no one is going to answer. Finally, she pressed the button to disconnect the call and dialed the emergency number that was taped to the phone. "I want to report a kidnaping," she said, her voice level.

Ten minutes later she sank back in her chair and tiredly closed her eyes. She could feel Margaret Willis's burning curiosity permeating the kitchen. Even though she knew it would be all over the neighborhood by this evening, she had to talk.

"They said they can't do anything," she began, her voice reflecting the frustration she was feeling. "They said they can't even list him as missing yet, and they said if his father took him, it's a civil matter, and I should talk to a lawyer instead of the police."

"But what do they expect you to do?"

"Wait. They told me to wait, and try to get hold of Jim. Then, if Randy isn't back by morning, and I can't get hold of Jim, I should call them back." She shook her head helplessly. "How can I do that, Margaret? How can I just sit here and wait?"

"We'll do it together," Margaret Willis said firmly, standing up and beginning to clear the breakfast dishes off the table. "We'll clean up the kitchen and fix supper, and then we'll start cleaning the house."

"But it's clean—" Lucy started to protest, but the elderly woman waved a gentle finger at her.

"Then it will be cleaner. No such thing as too clean, Lucy, and I've always found that cleaning house makes the time pass faster. So we'll clean all night if we have to." Then she smiled affectionately. "But I bet we won't have to," she added. "I'll bet the little rascal will show up in an hour or two, tired, hungry, and dirty. Then we'll feed him and send him to bed. How's that sound?"

To Lucy it sounded horrible, but she knew she would give in to Margaret Willis. It was either that or sit alone, watching the clock tick off the endless minutes while improbable fantasies transformed themselves into frightening realities in the far reaches of her imagination. She would, she knew, go mad with worry if she had to wait alone. Better to fill the time and the emptiness with Margaret's relentless cheerfulness than to try to cope with the hysteria that was building inside her. Morosely, she began cleaning her house.

It was nearly midnight, and the house was spotless, when Jim Corliss finally answered his phone.

"Jim? It's Lucy. I want him back, do you hear? I want you to bring him back right now, or I'm going to call my lawyer."

Jim Corliss knew by the hysteria in her voice that something was wrong. She never called him, except to demand support payments or argue with him about Randy. Suddenly, he became worried. Did she think Randy was with him? But he wasn't scheduled to see his son for another week. "Are you talking about Randy?" he asked cautiously.

"Of course I'm talking about Randy," Lucy exploded. "Who do you think I'm talking about? How dare you!"

"How dare I what? Isn't Randy there?"

There was a silence, then Lucy spoke again, her voice suddenly breaking. "You don't have him? You didn't pick him up this morning?"

"Oh, my God," Jim said, his heart pounding as he realized the implications of what his ex-wife was saying. "Lucy, what's happened? Tell me what's happened."

"He's gone, Jim."

"What do you mean, gone? Gone where?"

"I—I don't know," Lucy stammered, her rage dissipating, only to be replaced by the fear she had felt earlier. She explained what had happened that afternoon. "I—I thought you must have picked him up," she finished. "I know how he's been after you to take him away from me. I thought you'd done it."

"I wouldn't, Lucy. I wouldn't do that to you."

"Wouldn't you?" Lucy asked, her voice brittle with suspicion. "I wonder . . ."

"I'm coming over," Jim said suddenly. "I'll be there in twenty minutes."

"No," Lucy protested. "Please, Jim—"

"He's my son too," Jim said firmly. He hung up the phone. Within minutes he was on his way to Eastbury.

There was an awkwardness when Jim and Lucy Corliss faced each other across the threshold of Lucy's house, the kind of uncomfortable silence that comes over two people who have once been close but are no longer sure what to say to each other. For years Lucy had done her best to avoid Jim when he came to pick up Randy, restricting her conversations to a few stilted sentences conveying nothing more than what she deemed to be vital information. Now, as Lucy examined her ex-husband's face, she had an impression of age, but then, noting that Jim's face was as unlined as ever, and his hair the same thick, wavy thatch that it had always been, she decided that it wasn't age that had come to Jim, but something else. The word that came to mind was maturity, but she tried to reject it. If Jim had, indeed, matured over the years, she would have to see more evidence of it than a look in his eyes.

"May I come in?"

Lucy stepped back nervously, stumbled, then quickly recovered herself. "I'm sorry," she said. "Of course." She held the door open as Jim came in and Mrs. Willis, hands fluttering, mumbled a series of greetings, apologies, sympathies, and good-byes. Then she was gone, and a nervous silence settled over the Corlisses.

Jim glanced around the little living room, then offered a tentative smile. "Did I ever tell you I like this room? It's nice—looks just like you. Pretty, warm, and tidy."

Lucy returned Jim's smile stiffly and settled herself into a chair that would, by its placement in the room, separate her from him. The thought that Jim was still very attractive came into her mind, but she put it determinedly aside and began telling him what had happened, ending up with her fear that Randy had been kidnaped.

"But he ran away last summer," Jim pointed out when she had finished.

"This is different," Lucy insisted. "Last summer he ran away in the middle of the night, after that problem with the Semple boy. But nothing's happened recently—there's no reason for him to have run away this morning. And I'd have known—I'd have sensed something at breakfast. But he was just like he always is." She paused, then met Jim's eyes. "He's been kidnaped, Jim. Don't ask me how I know, but I know Randy didn't just run away. Someone took him." Her eyes narrowed. "And I'm still not entirely convinced it wasn't you."

"Oh, God . . ." Jim groaned.

"It's just the kind of thing you'd do, Jim. And I swear, if you've taken him and hidden him somewhere—"

"I haven't," Jim said vehemently. "Lucy, I wouldn't do something like that. I—well, I just wouldn't. Look. Let's call the police again. It seems to me that he's been gone long enough so they should at least be willing to take a report."

"They told me they couldn't do anything for twenty-four hours."

"Twenty-four hours!" Jim exploded. "My God, he's not an adult—he's only nine years old! He could be lost—or hurt." Jim stood up and stormed into the kitchen. A moment later Lucy heard him talking to someone, then shouting. His voice dropped again, and she could no longer make out what he was saying. At last he rejoined her.

"They're sending someone out," he said. But as Lucy looked at him hopefully, he had to tell her what the police had told him. "They'll take a report, but they said the odds are that he's a runaway." He fell silent, and Lucy prodded him.

"Which means what?"

Jim avoided her eyes. "I'm not sure. It could mean anything. Kids are—well, they're running away from home younger every year. They said if he was a little older, we'd probably only see him again if he wants to see us."

Lucy frowned. "What does that mean?"

"Just that with the young ones—the real young ones, like Randy—sometimes they don't know what to do, and after a night or two, they turn themselves in."

"And if he doesn't?" Lucy asked quietly.

"I—I'm not sure. They said something about a search, but they said searches usually don't do much good either. If something's happened to Randy, it's more likely that someone will . . . well, that someone will find him by accident."

"You mean if he's dead." Lucy's voice was flat, and her eyes cold, and Jim found himself unable to make any reply other than a nod of his head.

"But he's not dead," Lucy said softly. "I know he's not dead."

Jim swallowed. There was one more possibility the police had mentioned. "They said he might have gone to Boston . . ." he began, but then let his words trail off. Better to let the police try to explain to Lucy what could happen to a small boy in Boston.

CHAPTER 5

At the same time Jim and Lucy Corliss were trying to deal with the loss of their son, Steve and Sally Montgomery were trying to deal with the loss of their daughter.

All afternoon, and into the evening, ever since they had returned from the hospital and their talk with Dr. Malone, Sally had been strangely silent. Several times Steve tried to talk to her, but she seemed not to hear him.

Steve had spent several hours with Jason, trying to explain to him what had happened to Julie, and Jason had listened quietly, his head cocked curiously, his brows furrowed into a thoughtful frown. He seemed, to Steve, to accept the death of his sister as simply one more fact in his young life.

It was, indeed, not so much the fact of Julie's death that worried Jason, but the reason for her death. Over and over, he'd kept coming back to the same question.

"But if there wasn't anything wrong with her, why did she die?"

His eyes, larger and darker than his mother's, looked up at Steve, pleading for an answer Steve couldn't give. Still, he had to try once more.

"We don't know why Julie died," he repeated for at least the sixth time. "All we know is that it happens sometimes."

"But why did it happen to Julie? Was she a bad girl?"

"No, she was a very good girl."

Jason's brows knit as he puzzled over the dilemma. "But if she was a good girl, why did God kill her?"

"I don't know, son," Steve replied through the sudden constriction in his throat. "I just don't know."

"Is God going to kill me too?"

Steve pulled his son to him and hugged him close. "No, of course not. It didn't have anything to do with us, and it isn't going to happen to you."

"How do you know?" Jason challenged, wriggling loose from his father's embrace. Steve wearily stood up and began tucking Jason in.

"I just know," he said. "Now I want you to go to sleep, okay?"

"Okay," Jason agreed. Then his eyes wandered over to the far corner of his room where a black-and-white guinea pig named Fred lived in a small cage. "Can Fred come sleep by me tonight?" he asked.

Steve smiled. "Sure." He brought the cage over and set it down next to Jason's bed. Inside the cage, Fred began patrolling the perimeter, examining his environment from the new perspective. Then, satisfied, he curled up and buried his nose in his own fur. "Now that's what I want you to do," Steve said. "Bury your nose and go to sleep." He bent down and kissed Jason's cheek, snapped out the light, and left the room.

A moment later, as he came downstairs, his mother-in-law drew him into the den, and the two of them talked for a long time. At last Phyllis shook her head slowly.

"I just don't understand it," she said. "It seems so strange that a perfect child like Julie could just—what? Stop living? Terrible. Terrible! There must have been a reason, Steve. There must have been."

But Steve Montgomery knew there was no reason, at least no reason that the doctors understood. That, he was coming to realize, was the most difficult part of the sudden infant death syndrome: there was nothing to blame, no germ or virus, no abnormal condition—nothing. Simply the fact of unreasonable death and the lingering feeling of failure. Already it was beginning to gnaw at him, but there was nothing he could do about it. He would simply have to live with it and try to put it out of his mind. Even if it meant putting Julie out of his mind too.

"Life is for the living."

The words had sounded reasonable when Malone had spoken them, and Steve knew they were true. Then why did he feel dead inside? Why did he feel as though he might as well bury himself tomorrow along with his daughter? He couldn't feel that way, couldn't *let* himself feel that way. For Sally, and for

Jason, he would have to go on, have to function. And yet, would he be able to do any better for them than he had for his daughter?

He shut the thought out of his mind. From now on, he decided, there would have to be places in his mind that were closed off, sealed forever away from his conscious existence. It was either that or go crazy.

Now he sat with Sally, tiredness weakening every fiber in his body, his mind numb, his grief pervading him. Sally was looking at him, and he saw something in her eyes that chilled his soul.

Her eyes, the sparkling brown eyes that had first attracted him to her, had changed. The sparkle had been replaced by a strange intensity that seemed to glow from deep within her.

"She didn't just die," Sally said softly. Steve started to speak to her, but was suddenly unsure whether she was talking to him or to herself. "Babies don't do that. They don't just die." Now her eyes met his. "We must have done something, Steve. We must have."

Steve flinched slightly. Hadn't the same thoughts gone through his own mind? But he couldn't give in to them, and he couldn't let Sally give in to them either. "That's not true, Sally. We loved Julie. We did everything we could—"

"Did we?" Sally asked, her voice suddenly bitter. "I wonder. I wonder, Steve! Let's face it. We didn't want Julie—neither of us did! One child was all we were going to have, remember? Just one! And we had Jason. A little sooner than we'd planned, but we agreed that he was the only child we wanted. But it didn't happen that way, did it? Something went wrong, and we had Julie, even though we didn't want her. And she died!"

Steve stared at his wife, his face pale and his hands shaking. "What are you saying, Sally?" he asked, his voice so quiet it was almost inaudible. "Are you saying we killed Julie?"

Tears suddenly overflowing, Sally buried her face in her hands. "I don't know, Steve," she sobbed. "I don't know what I'm saying, or what I'm thinking, or anything. I only know that babies don't just die—"

"But they *do*," Steve interrupted. "Dr. Malone said—"

"I don't care what Dr. Malone said!" Sally burst out. "Babies don't just die!"

She ran from the room. Steve listened to her heavy step as she went upstairs.

A little later he followed her and found her already in bed. He undressed silently, slipped into bed beside her, and turned out the light. He could hear her crying and reached out to take her in his arms.

For the first time in all the years of their marriage, Sally drew away from him.

* * *

Jason lay in his bed, listening to the silence of the house and wondering when things would get back to the way they used to be.

He didn't like the way his mother had been crying all the time. Up until last night, in fact, he'd never seen her cry at all.

It had frightened him at first, seeing her standing in Julie's room, holding Julie just like she always did, except for the tears running down her face. Usually, when she held Julie, she laughed.

His first thought when he saw her was that she had found out about what he'd done to Julie and was going to be mad at him. But that hadn't been it at all—she was crying because Julie was dead.

Julie hadn't been dead when he'd gone in earlier to look at her.

She'd only been sleeping.

He knew she was sleeping, because he could hear her snuffling softly, like his mother did when she had a cold. So he'd wiped her nose with a corner of the sheet.

That couldn't have hurt her.

But it did wake her up and she'd started crying.

And that was when he'd put the blanket over her face, so no one would hear her crying.

But he hadn't left it there long enough for her to smother. It couldn't have been that long; as soon as she'd stopped crying, he'd taken the blanket off her face and tucked it back around her just the way it had been when he went in to look at her.

But had she still been breathing?

He tried to remember.

He was sure she had. He could almost hear her now, in the silence of the house, even though she was dead.

He listened hard and was sure he heard, very faintly, the sounds of tiny breaths.

And then he remembered: Fred was sleeping next to his bed.

He slid out of bed and knelt next to the guinea pig's cage. The sounds Fred were making were just like the sounds Julie had made after she stopped crying.

Very quiet, but there.

He opened the cage, and Fred, hearing the slight rattle, woke up, opened his eyes and stared at Jason through the gloom. Jason reached in, gently picked up the guinea pig, and took it into bed with him. Soon Fred fell asleep again, this time curled up in the crook of Jason's arm.

Jason listened to the guinea pig breathe, sure that he had heard the same sounds in Julie's room last night just before he had left it. So he hadn't done anything to Julie, not really.

Still, tomorrow or the next day he'd talk to Randy about it. It was, he realized, sort of like what had happened to Randy after Billy Semple jumped off the roof. Even though Randy hadn't really done anything to Billy, he'd still gotten blamed for Billy's broken leg.

As he fell into a fitful sleep, Jason wondered if the same thing would happen to him, and he'd get blamed for Julie's dying.

Maybe the next time Randy came over they'd do the same thing to Fred that he'd done to Julie and see if Fred died.

At least then he'd know for sure. . . .

CHAPTER 6

Randy Corliss scrunched under the covers, trying to avoid opening his eyes to the morning light. He was cold, and all night long his sleep had been broken by nightmares. But now the sun was warming his room, and he wanted to drift back to sleep, wanted to forget the loneliness that had overcome him the previous afternoon when he realized his father was not coming for him, at least not that day.

"But it's going to be all right, Randy," Miss Bowen had explained. "Your father is very busy, and for the moment he wants us to take care of you."

"Why?" Randy had asked. Since he'd seen the fence around the Academy, he'd wondered why his father had had him brought here. It didn't, to Randy's eyes, look quite like a school. For one thing, you couldn't even see it from the road. There was just a long driveway and then a gate without a sign. And there weren't any of the kind of school buildings he was used to, only a huge house that looked almost like a castle, with the windows of the second floor covered with bars. He'd seen a couple of boys who looked like they were about the same age he was, but hadn't been able to talk to them. Instead, he'd been taken into an office, where Miss Bowen had told him why he was there.

"It's a special school, for special boys," she assured him. "Boys like you, who've had problems in regular school."

"I haven't had any problems," Randy said.

"I mean problems making friends." Miss Bowen smiled at him, and a little of Randy's apprehension dissipated. "Lots of boys your age have that kind of trouble, you know. Boys who are special, like you."

"I'm special?"

"All the boys here are special. Most of them come from families just like yours."

"You mean where their parents are divorced?"

"Exactly. And most of the boys here didn't want to live with their mothers anymore and didn't like the schools they were going to. So their fathers sent them here, just like your father sent you."

"But where is he?" Randy's face darkened belligerently, and as he watched her, he could see that she wasn't going to answer him. That was the trouble with grown-ups, even his father. When they didn't want to answer your questions, they never even explained why not. They just said you weren't old enough to know. Or sometimes they just pretended they hadn't heard the question, which was what Randy thought Miss Bowen was about to do.

"Wouldn't you like to meet the other boys?" she asked, confirming his suspicions.

"I want to talk to my father," Randy replied, his voice turning stubborn. He was sitting uncomfortably on a high-backed wooden chair, but he folded his arms, and his eyes sparked angrily. "Why can't I call him? I know his number at work."

"But he's out of town. That's why he sent me to pick you up. He *couldn't* come for you. But he'll be back in a few days."

"How many days?" Randy demanded. He was beginning to squirm in his chair now, and his face was flushing. The woman opened her desk drawer and took out a small bottle filled with white tablets. "What's that?" Randy demanded.

"It's some medicine. I want you to take one of these."

"I'm not sick, and I don't ever take pills."

"It's just to calm you down. I know all this is very strange, and I know you're frightened. This pill will help."

"What'll it do to me?" Randy stared at the pill suspiciously. "Will it make me go to sleep?"

"Of course not. But you won't be frightened anymore, or worried."

"I won't take it, and you can't make me." Randy's mouth clamped shut, and his body stiffened. His eyes began darting around the room as he searched for a way out. There was none. The woman was between him and the door, and there were no windows in the office.

"Then you're going to sit there until you change your mind," she told him. "You can make up your own mind. Take the pill, and come with me to meet the other boys, or sit there all day. It's up to you." She set the pill in the center of the blotter on her desk and picked up a file folder. Five minutes passed.

"It won't make me go to sleep?" he asked, coming to the desk and picking up the pill, studying it as if it were an insect.

"It won't make you go to sleep." She got up to go to the water cooler, keeping her eyes on Randy in case he tried to bolt out the door. He didn't.

She handed him a cup of water, still watching closely to be sure he really swallowed the pill. Ten minutes later, when he began to relax, she took him outside and introduced him to his schoolmates.

There were five of them, and they eyed Randy with all the suspicion of preadolescence, silently daring him to pick a fight. He watched them, trying to decide which of them to challenge, but none of them stepped forward, nor did any of them back away. Only when Miss Bowen left them alone with the newcomer did any of them speak.

"Did she give you the pill?" one of them finally asked. His name was Peter Williams, and when he spoke, his voice was neither friendly nor belligerent.

"Uh-huh," Randy replied. "What is it?"

"I think it's Valium," another of the boys said. "My mom used to take it when she was nervous."

"Do you have to take it every day?"

"Nah. Only the first day. Then they don't make you take anything. How come you're here?"

Randy thought about it before he answered, and when he finally spoke, he avoided the others' eyes. "My dad sent me. Mostly to get me away from my mom, I guess."

There was a silence as the other boys exchanged glances and shrugs. "Yeah," Peter said at last. "That's why we're all here, except Billy." He gestured toward the skinny brown-haired boy who stood slightly behind him. Billy stared at his shoes, as Peter explained importantly. "*His* mom sent him here to get him away from his dad. But who cares? It's better than being at home."

That had been yesterday, and this morning Randy was still not convinced that Peter was right. He felt terribly alone, and when he went to look out the window, and saw nothing except forest beyond the fence that surrounded the Academy, a slight chill rippled over him. But then there was a tap at the door, and Adam Rogers stuck his head in.

"You better get dressed. If we aren't down for breakfast in five minutes, we won't get any." Adam came into the room and perched himself on the bed while Randy pulled his clothes on. "You from around here?"

"Eastbury." Randy sized Adam up as he tied his shoelaces. He looked younger than Randy, and was smaller, but his body was wiry and he looked like he was fast. "Where you from?"

"Georgia. That's down south."

"I know where it is. I'm not stupid."

"Nobody said you were," Adam said by way of apology, "but lots of people don't know where anyplace is. Come on." He hopped off the bed and led Randy out of the bedroom and down the stairs into a large dining room. There were two tables in the room, around one of which the other four boys were seated. At another, smaller table sat Louise Bowen. "She thinks she's a den mother or something," Adam whispered as the two of them slid into the two vacant chairs at the big table with the other boys. "But she never talks to us in the morning. Just watches us."

"Why?"

"Search me. But that's one of the neat things about this place—they watch you all the time, but they practically never tell you what to do."

"Yeah," Peter Williams agreed, grinning happily. "Not like at home. My mom was always telling me I was going to hurt myself, or get in trouble, or kill someone, or something. And then I ran away one day, and the cops picked me up, and ever since then she was always on my case."

The other boys began chiming in. As Randy listened, he began to think maybe he'd been wrong to be so suspicious yesterday. All the stories sounded familiar. Most of the boys had been lonely before they came to the Academy, and some of them bragged about how much trouble they'd caused in the schools they'd gone to before.

"But what do you do here?" Randy asked.

"Go to class and play," Peter replied. "It's neat, because we don't have as many classes as regular school. But we play lots of games. They teach us boxing and wrestling and some other stuff, but a lot of the time they just let us do what we want."

"Anything?" Randy asked.

Peter looked at the other boys questioningly, and when they nodded, so did he. "I guess so. At least, they never told any of us *not* to do anything." He paused, as if turning something over in his mind, then went on, his voice more thoughtful. "But they always watch us. It's funny. There's always someone around, like they want to know what we're doing, but they never tell us much about what to do. Except in class. That's just like regular school."

"How come there's only six of us?" Randy suddenly asked. It seemed to him that the house was big enough for a much larger group than they made up, and he'd always thought private schools had hundreds of students.

Adam Rogers glanced toward Louise Bowen, then leaned close to Randy and whispered. "There used to be more," he said. "When I got here, there were ten of us."

"What happened to the others?" Randy asked.

Peter frowned at Adam. "They left."

"You mean their dads came for them, or they went to another school?"

Across from Randy, a red-headed boy with a sprinkle of freckles across his nose shook his head. "No. They—"

"Shut up, Eric," Peter broke in. "We're not supposed to talk about that."

"Talk about what?" Randy demanded.

"Nothing," Peter told him.

Randy turned his attention back to Eric. "Talk about what, Eric?" he asked again, his eyes locking onto the other boy's. Eric started to open his mouth, then closed it and looked away. "Tell me," Randy insisted.

Eric glanced uneasily toward Louise Bowen. She appeared not to be listening to them. Still, when he spoke, his voice dropped to a whisper, and Randy had to strain to hear him.

"Sometimes kids just—well, they just disappear. We think they die."

"Die?" Randy breathed.

"We don't know," Peter said. "We don't know what happens to them."

"Yes, we do," Eric whispered miserably. "Nobody's been here more than a few months, and everyone who's gone died. That's what happens. You come here, and you die."

"Shut up, Eric," Peter said once again. "We don't know what happened to David and Kevin. Maybe their fathers came for them."

"I hope so," Adam Rogers said, and when Randy looked at him, he saw that Adam's face was pale. "I've been here almost six months. Longer than any of you. I—I hope . . ."

His voice trailed off. The six boys finished their breakfast in silence.

Lucy Corliss sat at her kitchen table and tried to decide what to do. All night she had lain awake, hoping to hear the front door opening signaling Randy's return, or the sound of the telephone notifying her that the police had found him. That was the one thing Sergeant Bronski had promised her last night—that he would put together a search party and comb the woods in which Randy had gotten lost a year ago. He hadn't promised anything; indeed, he had reluctantly told Lucy that the odds of finding Randy in the darkness were almost nil.

But all night long her house had been filled with an eerie silence. Finally, as the eastern sky had begun brightening into dawn, she had made one more call to the police, only to be told that no trace of Randy had yet been found;

then she drifted into a fitful sleep, from which she had awakened an hour later. Since then she had been sitting in the kitchen, waiting, resisting the constant impulse to call the police yet again, knowing that if there was anything to report, they would call her.

When the phone suddenly came to life just before nine, its jangling sound nearly made Lucy drop her coffee cup. She grabbed for the receiver, her heart pounding.

"Hello? Hello?"

"It's Jim, Lucy." There was a hopelessness in his voice that told her instantly that the search party had found nothing, but she had to confirm it. "You didn't find him, did you?"

"No."

"Oh, God, Jim, what am I going to do? I just feel so helpless, and—and—" Her voice broke off as she fought to control the tears that threatened to engulf her.

"Take it easy, Lucy," she heard Jim say. "It's not over yet." There was a short silence, then he added, "Are you going to work?"

"Work?" Lucy echoed. She felt a tentacle of panic at the edge of her consciousness, and her voice pitched higher. "How can I go to work? My God, it's my *son* that's missing. I've got to *do* something about it." The panic was beginning to grow, and Lucy lit a cigarette, drawing deeply. As she exhaled the stream of smoke, a little of her tension eased.

"I didn't mean it that way," she heard Jim saying. "I just meant that there's nothing you can do right now. It won't do you or Randy any good for you to sit around the house going out of your mind."

"You're a fine one to say that," Lucy shot back. "How would you know what's going to do me or Randy any good? You can't just come waltzing back into my life after nine years and start telling me what's good for me and what's not. Was it good for me to have you walk out and leave me to bring our son up by myself?"

If he was stung by her words, he showed no sign. "Tell you what," he said. "You do what you think is best, and I'll keep at it with the police. It's all we can do. Okay?"

Lucy took another puff on her cigarette and nodded, even though there was no one to see her. "Okay. But call me if you find anything. Anything at all!"

"Sure." There was a long silence, and then Jim's voice came over the line once again. "Lucy? Are you going to be all right? Do you want me to come over?"

"No. I mean, yes, I'm all right, and no, I don't want you to come over."

"Gotcha," Jim said, and the word almost made Lucy smile. It was a word he had used throughout their marriage on those rare occasions when he understood exactly why she was angry with him and was trying to apologize for having gone too far with whatever excess he was currently involved in. Now, as the word echoed in her mind, she could almost feel the warmth she knew must be in his eyes. "If you need anything," he went on, "you know where to find me."

The line went dead. Lucy held the receiver in her hand for a moment before hanging it up. As she poured herself another cup of coffee, she suddenly made up her mind.

Jim was right—she couldn't hang around the house all day. She quickly drained the coffee cup, then began dressing for work.

For Sally Montgomery, there was a chill to the morning that even the spring sun couldn't penetrate. She stared at herself in the mirror for a long time, studying the strange, haggard image that confronted her—slender arms wrapped protectively around a body she barely recognized as her own, hair limply framing a face etched with lines of exhaustion that even careful makeup hadn't been able to erase—and wondered how she was going to get through this day.

The sounds of morning drifted up the stairs, unfamiliar, for it should have been herself rattling around the kitchen, murmuring to Steve, urging Jason to hurry up. Instead it was her mother's voice she heard, and even the sounds of the coffeepot being put back on the stove and the frying pan clunking softly as it was placed in the sink bore the unmistakably purposeful tenor of her mother's efficiency. She moved to the closet and tried to decide what to wear.

She owned nothing black, never had. Navy blue? Her hands, shaking slightly, plucked a suit from a hanger. Something caught, and instead of stopping to disentangle the unseen snarl, Sally simply yanked at it. The rasping sound of a seam giving way raked across her nerves, and she knew she was going to cry.

I won't, she told herself. Not now. Not over a torn seam. Later. Later, I'll cry. She glanced at the tear in the lining of her suit jacket and felt that she'd won a small victory.

She went to her dresser next, and as she was about to open the second drawer where all her blouses lay neatly folded in tissue paper, her eyes fell on a picture of Julie. The tiny face, screwed into an expression somewhere between laughter and fury, seemed to mock her and reproach her at the same time. Now the tears did come. Sally backed away from the picture, sank to her bed, and buried her face in her hands.

That was how Steve found her a few moments later. He paused at the door, watching his wife, his heart aching not only for her, but for his own inability to comfort her, then crossed the room to sit beside her. With gentle hands he lifted her face and kissed her. "Honey? Is there anything . . ." He left the sentence unfinished, knowing there was no real way to complete it.

". . . anything wrong?" Sally finished for him. "Anything you can do for me? I don't know. Oh, Steve, I—I just looked at her picture, and it all came apart. It was like she was staring at me. Like she wanted to know what happened, wanted to know if it was a joke, or if I was mad at her, or—oh, God, I don't know."

Steve held her for a moment, sharing the pain of the moment but knowing there was nothing he could do to ease it. Then Sally pulled away from him and stood up.

"I'll be all right," she said, more to herself than to her husband. "I'll get dressed, and I'll come downstairs, and I'll eat breakfast. I'll take each moment as it comes, and I'll get through." She took a deep breath, then went once more to her dresser. This time she kept her eyes carefully averted from the picture of Julie as she opened the drawer and took out a soft silk blouse. Then, taking her pantyhose with her, she disappeared into the bathroom.

Steve stayed on in the bedroom for a while, his eyes fixed on the picture of his daughter, then suddenly he turned the picture face down on the dresser top. A moment later he was gone, back to the kitchen where his son was waiting for him.

CHAPTER 7

The car moved slowly through the streets of Eastbury, and Sally found herself looking out at the town and its people with a strange detachment she had only felt a few times before. The last time had been when her father had died, and she had been driven through these same streets toward the same cemetery. On that day, as their car passed through the center of town, where the charm of old New England had still been carefully preserved, the people of Eastbury had nodded respectfully toward Sally and her mother. They had understood the death of Jeremiah Paine and been able to express their sympathy toward his family.

But today, Eastbury looked different. People seemed to turn away from the car. What Sally had always perceived as Yankee reserve, today seemed like icy aloofness. Even the town had changed, Sally realized. It had begun to take on a look of coldness, as if along with the new technology had come a new indifference. Where once the town and its inhabitants had seemed to fit each other comfortably, now the people Sally saw moving indifferently through Eastbury's picturesque streets were mostly newcomers who looked as if they had been cut from a mold, then assigned to live in Eastbury. Cookie-cutter people, Sally thought, who could have lived anywhere, and nothing in their lives would change. The new breed, she reflected sadly. It seemed to her that there was some vital force lacking in them, and as the car moved into the parking lot next to the First Presbyterian Church and its adjoining cemetery, she wondered if she, too, had become infected by the malaise that seemed to have chilled the town.

A few minutes later, as she stood in the cemetery where her father was buried, and where, she supposed, she herself would someday lie, Sally Montgomery still felt the chill, though she knew the day was unseasonably warm. There were few people gathered around the grave. Apparently most of Sally's friends were feeling the same way she was feeling: numb and unable to cope. Funerals were to pay final respects to old people and to comfort the living for the loss of someone who had been part of their lives for years. What did you say when an infant died?

Suddenly all the soft murmurings sounded hollow.

"Perhaps it was a blessing . . ." for someone who had been sick for years.

"At least it happened quickly . . ." for someone who had never been sick a day in her life.

"I know how you'll miss her . . ." for a mother or a sister or an aunt.

"I don't know what I'll do without her . . ." to share the burden of loss.

But for a six-month-old baby? Nothing. Nothing to be said, nothing to be offered. And so they stayed away, and Sally understood.

She watched the tiny coffin being lowered into the ground, listened as the minister uttered the final words consigning Julie Montgomery to the care of the Lord, moved woodenly toward the grave to deposit the first clod of the earth that would soon hide her daughter from the sight of the living, then started toward the car, intent only on getting home, getting away from the ceremony that, far from easing her pain, was only intensifying it.

From a few yards away, Arthur Wiseman watched Sally's forlorn figure and wondered once again why he had come to Julie Montgomery's funeral. He rarely attended funerals at all, and particularly avoided the funerals of his patients. To him, a funeral was little more than a painful reminder of his own failure.

But this one was different. Julie Montgomery had not been his patient, not since the day he'd delivered her. No, this time his patient was still alive. But he had delivered Sally herself, as well as her two children, and she had been on his roster for as long as she had needed the services of an obstetrician-gynecologist. Over the years he had come to regard her with an almost paternal affection. One of his special girls, as he thought of them.

So he had come today, even though he hated funerals, and now, as the service drew to a close, he was beginning to wish he'd stayed away after all. He was going to have to speak to Sally, and he knew the words of condolence would not come easy to him. In the familiar surroundings of his office, the right words always came easily. But here, faced with a patient whose problem was beyond his medical expertise, he was at a loss. And yet, something had to be said. He started toward Sally.

She had nearly reached the car when she felt a hand on her arm. She turned and found herself looking into the troubled eyes of Arthur Wiseman.

"Sally—" he began.

"It was good of you to come, Dr. Wiseman," Sally said, her voice barely audible.

"I know how difficult this must be for you . . ." Wiseman said. Then his voice faltered, and he fell silent.

Sally stared at him for a moment, waiting for him to continue. "Do you?" she asked at last. Suddenly, with no forewarning at all, she found her entire being flooded with anger. Why couldn't he find the right words to comfort her? He was a doctor, wasn't he? *Her* doctor? Wasn't it his *job* to know what to say at a time like this? She glared at him, her face a mask of pain and anger. "Do you know how difficult it is for me?" she demanded. "Do you know what it feels like to lose your baby and not even know why?"

Stung, Arthur Wiseman glanced around the cemetery as if he were looking for a means of escape. "No, of course I can't feel what you're feeling," he muttered at last as Sally's gaze remained fixed upon him. "But I hope I can understand it." He could see that she was no longer listening to him as she searched the cemetery for—what? Her husband, probably. Wiseman kept talking, hoping Steve would appear. "I do know how hard it is, Sally. Even for doctors who see death all the time, it's still hard. Especially in cases like Julie's—"

"Julie?" Sally repeated. At mention of her daughter's name, her attention shifted back to the doctor. "What about Julie?"

Wiseman paused, looking deeply into Sally's eyes. There was something in them—a sort of flickering glow—that told him Sally was on the edge of losing control. He searched his mind for something to say, anything that might ease her pain. "But we're learning, Sally. Every year we're learning a little more. I know it's no help to you, but someday we'll know what causes SIDS—"

"It wasn't SIDS," Sally interrupted. "Something happened to Julie." Her voice rose and took on a shrillness that Wiseman immediately recognized as the beginnings of hysteria. "I don't know what it was," Sally plunged on, "but I'm going to find out. It wasn't SIDS—it was something else. Julie was fine. She was just fine!"

Wiseman listened helplessly as Sally's hysteria soared, certain that he'd been wrong to come to the funeral, wrong to speak to Sally Montgomery right now. Here, today, he could see the true depths of her grief. When the time came for her to begin dealing with the reality of her loss, would he be able to help her? He was glad when Steve Montgomery, accompanied by Sally's mother and Jason, appeared beside her.

"Sally?" Steve asked. Sally's gaze shifted over to him, and Steve, too, saw the strange light in her eyes. "Are you all right?"

"I want to go home," Sally whispered, the last of her energy drained by her outburst. "I want to go home, and get away from here. Please? Take me home." She moved once more toward the nearby car, Steve by her side, Jason trailing along behind them. Only Phyllis Paine stayed behind to speak to Wiseman, and there was an anger in her voice that he had rarely heard in the long years of their friendship.

"Arthur, what did you say to her?" she demanded. "What did you say to my daughter?"

"Nothing, Phyllis," Wiseman replied tiredly. "Only that maybe someday we'll have some idea of what causes SIDS."

"At the funeral?" Phyllis asked, her voice reflecting her outrage. "You came to the funeral to talk about what killed Julie?"

Wiseman groaned inwardly, but was careful to maintain a calm façade. "That's hardly what I was doing, Phyllis, and when you think about it, I know you'll realize I would never do something like that. But it's important that Sally understand what happened, and I wanted to let her know that if there's anything I can do, either as her doctor or her friend, I'll do it."

As Wiseman spoke, Steven Montgomery came back to escort his mother-in-law to the waiting car. "There *is* something you can do, Dr. Wiseman," he said. "Just try to let us forget about it. It's over, and nothing can be done. We have to try to forget."

He led Phyllis to the car, helped her in, then turned back to face the doctor once again. "You understand, don't you?" he asked with a bleakness in his voice that Wiseman had rarely heard before. "There's nothing we can do now. Nothing at all." Then Steve, too, got into the car, and Wiseman watched as the Montgomerys drove away. When they were gone, the agony of Sally's eyes and Steve's words remained.

As he left the cemetery, Wiseman pondered the true depth of the tragedy that had befallen the Montgomerys.

For Julie, the tragedy was over.

For her parents, it had just begun.

Jason Montgomery jammed the shovel into the ground, jumped on it, then pulled on the handle until the clod of earth came loose. He repeated the process again and again, then stopped to inspect his work.

There was a square, four feet on a side, from which he'd stripped the topsoil. He'd been working for almost an hour—ever since he'd gotten home from his sister's funeral. So far, no one had come out to tell him to stop.

Maybe today, no one would.

If it happened that way—and Jason thought the chances were pretty good—then he would have his fort done by suppertime. It would be four feet deep and covered over with some planks he'd found behind the garage last week. His father had said they were going to be used for a chicken coop, but Jason had decided that since they had no chickens, he might as well use them for the roof of his fort. Besides, all he had to do was lay them on the ground side by side. They wouldn't even have to be nailed. The work was all in the digging. He wished Randy Corliss were there to help him, but he hadn't even been allowed to call Randy today, so now he had to build the fort all by himself.

He picked up the shovel once more and plunged it deep into the softer earth that lay beneath the surface. He felt the shovel hit something and pushed harder. It gave a little, then a lot. Putting the shovel aside, he knelt down in the dirt and began digging at the loose soil with his bare hands.

A moment later he hit the broken bottle.

It had been whole when the shovel struck it, but now its sharp edges slashed at him, cutting deep into the index finger on his left hand. Reflexively, Jason jerked his hand out of the dirt and stuck the finger in his mouth. He sucked hard, tasting the sweet saltiness of the blood, then spat onto the ground.

He inspected his finger carefully. Blood was oozing thickly from the cut, running down his hand, then dripping slowly onto the pile of loose dirt. He squeezed the finger, remembering someone once telling him that you had to make a cut bleed a lot to keep it from getting infected.

When the bleeding slowed a minute later, he inspected the cut. It was about a half-inch long and looked deep. He decided he'd better go wash his hand.

He slipped through the kitchen and dining room, avoiding the living room where he knew his parents were sitting. Even though he didn't really miss his little sister, he knew they were very upset, and he didn't want to bother them. He could take care of the cut himself, or, if he decided he couldn't, he could get his grandmother to help him.

He went upstairs to the bathroom and began washing his hands. The dirt and already-clotting blood swirled down the drain. Once more Jason squeezed at the finger.

This time it didn't bleed.

Puzzled, Jason held his hand up to the light and inspected it.

He couldn't find the cut.

He stared at his finger, and in a moment found the faintest tracing of a scar where the injury had been.

His brow furrowed into a curious scowl as he tried to figure out what had happened.

It had bled a lot.

Now there was nothing.

Did cuts heal that fast? In the past when he'd skinned his knee or something, the Band-Aid always had to stay on for a couple of days.

Of course, who knew what happened *under* the Band-Aid? His mother had never let him look.

Maybe all cuts healed this fast.

Or maybe the cut hadn't been as bad as he'd thought.

He tried to remember how much it had hurt and couldn't remember it having hurt much at all. Not like when he skinned his knees or his elbows, when it stung for a couple of seconds. With the cut, he'd hardly felt anything. In fact, if it hadn't been for the blood, he probably wouldn't even have noticed it.

He turned off the water, dried his hands, then went back downstairs and outside. He looked at the ground where all the blood had dripped. There didn't seem to be much left. And then, from next door, he heard a voice calling him, and looked up to see Joey Connors waving to him.

"Hey, Jason," Joey was saying, "you wanna come over and see my puppies?"

"Puppies?" Jason repeated, his eyes widening with eagerness, the cut finger forgotten. "You got puppies?"

Joey nodded. "Daisy had 'em day before yesterday, but my mom wouldn't let me call you."

"How come?" Jason asked as he climbed over the fence and dropped into the Connors' yard.

" 'Cause of your sister. Did you go to the funeral?"

"Uh-huh."

"What was it like?"

Jason stopped a minute, thinking. "Like a funeral, I guess," he said. Then, "Can I have one of the puppies?"

To an adult, Jason Montgomery's reaction to the death of his sister might have seemed callous. To him, her death was as unreal as she had been, and in his life, not much had changed. In fact, for Jason, the most notable event of the day was probably the finger that healed in ten minutes flat.

In her daughter's guest room, Phyllis Paine packed the last of her belongings into her suitcase and snapped it shut. Her eyes scanned the room absently. She was sure she had left nothing out. In her own mind she was already at home, taking up the myriad details of which life, for her, was composed. Phyllis was not a cold woman. When Julie died, Phyllis had experienced one of those private moments of unutterable grief, and then, taking herself in hand, had risen to the occasion. For two days she had run her daughter's home as she ran her own—efficiently, quietly, and with a sense of purpose. She had done her best to give Sally room in which to mourn. Now Sally had to begin putting her life back together again. All Phyllis's instincts told her to stay on, and "do" for Sally. She knew the pain Sally was feeling; she had felt it herself so long ago when her own first child had been stillborn. But no one had "done" for her. She had been forced to deal with her feelings, cope with the turns life can take, and persevere. And so she had buried her little boy, as Sally had just buried her little girl, and then gone on with life.

She picked up her suitcase and carried it downstairs. Sally and Steve were in the living room, sitting on a sofa, a distance between them that seemed greater than the few inches that separated them.

"Steve, would you call a taxi for me, please?"

Sally's head swung slowly around, and her eyes, clouded by tears that still threatened to overflow at any moment, seemed puzzled. "A taxi?" she repeated vacantly. "Where are you going?"

"Home, dear," Phyllis said gently. She forced herself to remain impassive to the barely perceptible shudder that passed over her daughter. Her gaze shifted to her son-in-law and she nodded slightly; Steve left her alone with Sally. Only then did she move to the sofa and sit by her daughter, taking Sally's hand in her own.

There was a long silence between the two women, and for a moment Phyllis wasn't sure how to bridge it. Finally she squeezed Sally's hand reassuringly.

"I was wrong yesterday, dear," she said, "and I want to apologize."

Sally's eyes, full of fright and dazed, met her mother's. "Wrong? About what?"

"About Julie," Phyllis said. "About how she died. I don't know why I said what I did before—about babies not just dying. It was stupid of me."

Sally's expression cleared slightly. "I don't know what you mean."

"I mean I was wrong to insinuate that something must have happened to Julie. I know now that nothing did. She simply died, and we have to accept that."

"Like you accepted what happened to my brother?" Though her voice was level, there was a coldness in her tone that shocked Phyllis even more than the words.

"How did you know about that?"

"Daddy told me. A long time ago."

"He had no right—" Phyllis began.

"He had every right, Mother," Sally replied. "He was trying to explain to me why—well, why you're the way you are."

"I see," Phyllis replied, sinking back into the depths of the sofa. It was the first time her son had been mentioned in Phyllis's presence since the day he had been born. "And did it explain anything?" she heard herself asking.

"No, not really," Sally replied, her voice distant, as if she were thinking of something else.

"Then let me try," Phyllis said, choosing her words carefully, afraid that even talking of that time nearly thirty years in the past might destroy the careful structure she had built for herself. "I blamed myself for the fact that your brother was born dead, even though the doctors told me it wasn't my fault. Just as you might be blaming yourself for what happened to Julie. In the months afterward, I wanted to die myself. I almost did. I—well, I almost killed myself. But then something changed my mind. Don't ask what—I don't even remember. But I suddenly realized that no matter how I felt about the son I never knew, I had responsibilities. To your father, and, a few years later, to you. And so I took each day as it came, and I got through. And I'm still getting through, Sally, just as you must. One day at a time. Don't think about what Julie might have been. Don't even think about what she was. Just take each day as it comes, and do what you must do. Life is for the living, Sally, and no matter how you're feeling now, you're still alive."

There was a silence as Sally tried to absorb her mother's words. They sounded so cold, so uncaring. And in her mind, Sally kept seeing her daughter, asleep in her crib, but not asleep.

Dying.

Dying from what?

For how long?

She swallowed, trying by the gesture to drive the image from her mind, but knowing it was useless. And then she saw Steve standing a few feet away, watching her. How long had he been there? Had he been listening?

"She's right, you know," he said. He *had* been listening. For some reason Sally felt betrayed. "We have to put our lives together again, darling, and we have to do it by ourselves."

"But I need—"

"You need Jason, and you need me," Steve went on, his voice firm. "You need to pick up the threads of your life. And you can't do that as long as Phyllis is here. Don't you see that?"

Sally shifted on the couch, drawing herself away from her mother. "You want me to forget about Julie, don't you?" she said. "You want me to do what Mother did and pretend she didn't exist at all. Well, I can't do that. I won't do that. She was my daughter, Steve. She was my little girl, and something killed her. I have to find out what! I have to, and I will!"

"Sally—" Steve started toward his wife, but the sudden jangling of the telephone stopped him. His eyes, beseeching, stayed on Sally for a moment. "Oh, Jesus," he muttered. He disappeared into the kitchen to answer the phone while Sally and her mother sat in tense silence in the living room. And then Steve was back.

"Sally, someone wants to talk to you."

"Not now," Sally said, her voice dull.

"I think you'd better take it. I think it's important."

Sally started to protest once more, but the expression in her husband's eyes changed her mind. Stiffly, her body aching with exhaustion, she got to her feet and went to the kitchen.

"Hello?"

"Mrs. Montgomery? My name is Lois Petropoulous. You don't know me, but—"

"My husband said you have something to say to me," Sally broke in. "This isn't a good time for me—"

"I know. I'm terribly sorry about your daughter. I know what you're going through. The same thing happened to me six months ago."

"I beg your pardon?"

"There's a group of us, Mrs. Montgomery. Six couples. We meet once a week, trying to deal with the deaths of our children."

Sally frowned. What was the woman talking about? A group for the parents of dead children? "I'm sorry," she said, "but I don't—"

"Don't hang up, Mrs. Montgomery, please? It's the SIDS Foundation. They set up these groups so we can try to help each other understand what happened. We meet on Tuesdays, and I hope you and your husband might come tonight."

Sally fought to hold her temper. They weren't going to leave her alone. None of them. Not her husband, not her mother. And now the strangers were going to start on her, meddling in her life, trying to tell her what was good for her. Well, she would have none of it. She'd deal with her problems in her own way. "Thank you for calling," she said politely, "but Julie did not die of SIDS, so there would be no point in my coming to your meeting, would there?" Without waiting for a reply, she hung up the phone and returned to the living room. Through the window she could see a cab pulling up in front of the house. Her mother was standing up, looking at her expectantly. Sally composed herself, intent on hiding the resentment she was feeling for both Phyllis and Steve.

"Shall I walk you to the cab?"

Phyllis ignored the question. "Who was on the phone? Was it something to do with Julie?"

"No, Mother. It was nothing." She began guiding her mother toward the door. "I'm sorry for what I said. I'm just terribly tired right now. But you're right—life *is* for the living. I'll be all right." She gave her mother a quick hug, and kissed her on the cheek. "Really I will."

The two of them paused at the front door, but there was nothing left to say. And then Phyllis was gone, and Sally returned to her husband.

"We're going to that meeting," Steve said as soon as Sally had returned to the living room.

Sally looked at him, her eyes clear. "But why? It's a meeting for SIDS parents, and that's not us."

"It *is* us, Sally," Steve said quietly. "I'm going to that meeting, and you're going with me, and that's that. Do you understand?"

The hardness of his voice hit Sally like a blow. She searched his face, trying to see what had changed. He had never spoken to her that way before, never as long as she had known him. And yet his voice had left no room for doubt—he had given her an order and expected to be obeyed. Her eyes narrowed, and when she spoke, there was a hardness in her own voice that was foreign to her. "Then we'll go," she said. "But I still see no purpose to it."

A few minutes later she went into the room where Julie had lived to begin the process of clearing out all the things she would never need again. She stripped the bedding from Julie's crib, then folded up the crib itself. She went through the chest of drawers, pausing over each tiny dress or blouse—so many of them had never been worn, and now never would be. Finally, she took down the mobile that had been drifting over Julie's crib since the very beginning, stared at it sadly for a moment, then reluctantly dropped it into the wastebasket.

Everything was changed.

Her family was changed.

Her husband was changed.

She herself was changed.

From now on everything was going to be different.

Oh, she would do her best to be like her mother. She would accept her responsibilities. She would live for the living.

And yet, deep inside, a part of her was convinced that there was a reason for Julie's death, and even as she put away Julie's things, she knew that sooner or later she would have to discover that reason. And so, when she eventually left that room for the last time, she knew that she would never be like her mother at all.

In two days Sally Montgomery had changed in ways that the people close to her had not even begun to understand.

CHAPTER 8

Eastbury Elementary School, its whitewashed exterior turning gray and its grounds unkempt, sat defensively huddled in the midst of a small grove of maples as if it was trying to hide. As Lucy Corliss approached it, she found herself feeling oddly sorry for the bedraggled building—it was almost as if the school itself was aware of the fact that it was on the edge of ruin, and was hoping that if no one noticed it was there, someone would forget to tear it down. As Lucy passed through the front door, she could sense that the depressing appearance of the school's façade had permeated throughout. There was a feeling of gloom that the dim lights in the corridor did nothing to dispel. It was nearly four o'clock on Tuesday afternoon, and the silence of the place made her wonder if anyone was still there. She walked purposefully toward Randy's classroom, her heels clicking hollowly on the wood floor.

Harriet Grady, nearing sixty but carrying the strain of her thirty-five years of teaching as gracefully as anyone could, was preparing to leave for the day when Lucy appeared in her classroom. She recognized Lucy immediately and rose to her feet. "Mrs. Corliss," she said warmly. "Please come in. Is there any news about Randy?"

Lucy glanced around the room. It, too, needed a coat of paint, and there were several cracked panes in the large casement windows that broke the west wall. She walked to one of the windows and stared out, not seeing anything really, but trying to decide where to begin. Now that she was here, she was no longer sure why she had come. "Do you think Randy ran away?" she asked at last. A moment later she felt the teacher's hand touching her arm.

"I don't know," Harriet replied. "It's so hard to know the children these days. They all seem—what? Older than their years, I suppose. So many of the children just don't seem like children anymore. It's almost as if there are things in their minds they don't want you to know."

Lucy nodded. "Randy's been that way since he was a baby. I always have the feeling I don't quite know him. I suppose it's because I don't get to spend as much time with him as I should."

"Children need their parents," Harriet commented, and Lucy sensed a trace of condemnation in her tone.

"Unfortunately, marriages don't always work out."

"Or people don't work them out," the teacher countered.

Lucy's eyes narrowed angrily. "Miss Grady, I didn't come here to talk about my marriage. I came here to talk about my son."

The two women's eyes met and Harriet Grady's expression softened. "I'm sorry," she said. "I suppose I'm getting to be a crotchety old lady. I can't get used to the fact that most of my children have only one parent. It seems such a pity, and I always wonder if it isn't one of the reasons so many of the children have problems."

"Like Randy?" Lucy asked.

"Randy, and a lot of others." Harriet Grady appraised Lucy Corliss carefully and decided there was no point in mincing words. "But of course you know that Randy's been more of a problem than most."

"How?"

Harriet moved back to her desk, sat down, and pulled a file folder from the top drawer. She began glancing through it.

"Discipline problems. Except it's not quite that easy."

"I'm not sure I understand," Lucy said. She reached out to take the file, but Harriet Grady held on to it.

"I'm sorry," she apologized. "I'm afraid I'm not supposed to let you see these."

Lucy stared at the teacher, trying to grasp what she was saying. "Not let me see them? My God, Miss Grady, my son is missing! And if there's information about him in that file that I need to know about, you have no right to keep it from me. I'm his mother, Miss Grady, I have a right to know everything about my son."

"Well, I really just don't know," Harriet Grady fretted. "You have to understand, Mrs. Corliss—files on students contain all kinds of information, much of it quite objective, but some of it purely subjective. And we just don't like anyone to see the subjective portions. Anyone at all."

"Except the teachers," Lucy interjected, her voice grating with anger.

"Except the teachers," Harriet agreed. She leaned back in her chair and brushed a strand of hair from her eyes. "Mrs. Corliss," she went on, "I know how you must feel and I wish I could tell you something to make you feel better. But what can I say? Randy has tried to run away before."

"He was going to see his father," Lucy protested. "And he was only gone a few hours."

"But he still ran," the teacher insisted. "There's something about Randy—something odd. He doesn't always seem to have good judgment."

"Good judgment?" Lucy echoed. "He's only nine years old. What on earth are you talking about?"

Harriet Grady sighed and fingered the file for a moment. "I wish I could tell you. It's something I can't quite put my finger on. It's as if Randy thinks he can do anything any time he wants. He doesn't seem to be afraid of anything, and it gets him into trouble."

Lucy frowned. "What kind of trouble?"

"Nothing serious," Harriet assured her. "At least not yet. But we're always afraid that someday he's going to hurt himself."

"Hurt himself? How?"

Harriet Grady searched her mind, trying to think of a way to illustrate what she was trying to say. Finally, she gave up, and reluctantly handed Lucy the file. "Look at the top page," she said. "And I suppose, if you insist, you might as well look at the rest of the file too. It's all more or less the same."

Lucy took the file, opened it, and quickly read the first page. Her skin began to crawl, but she forced herself to finish reading the report, then glanced through the other pages. As Miss Grady had said, it was all the same. Her hands trembling, she returned the folder to the teacher.

"Tell me what happened," she whispered. "Tell me about that day."

Harriet Grady cleared her throat, then began. "It was last September. One of the children brought a black widow spider into class. It was in a jar, but I kept it on my desk, and let the children come up to look at it. I warned them that it was poisonous, and they were all very careful. Most of them wouldn't even pick up the jar. Randy not only picked it up; he opened it and put his hand inside."

"Good Lord," Lucy whispered. "What happened?"

"He started poking at it, and the spider tried to get away from him. But it finally attacked. I tried to take the jar away from him, but he wouldn't let me. He didn't seem frightened—he seemed fascinated."

"Even when the spider bit him?"

"Fortunately, it didn't. I finally knocked the jar out of his hands, and smashed the spider. Then I took him to the nurse and had her look at the hand. There were no bites."

"It didn't bite him at all?"

"Apparently not. And even when the nurse explained to him what a black widow bite can do, he didn't seem worried. He just said he'd played with them before, and nothing had happened."

Nausea rose to Lucy's throat as she began to realize what might have happened to Randy. "Why didn't you tell me?" she asked. "Why didn't someone—"

Harriet Grady's mouth twisted into a frosty smile. "Do what, Mrs. Corliss? Send a note home with Randy saying 'Dear Mrs. Corliss, today Randy didn't get bitten by a spider?' You'd have thought I was crazy."

Lucy closed her eyes and nodded. "I probably would." She thought for a moment, trying to decide what significance the teacher's information might have for her. But there was nothing. Nothing but a history of dangerous stunts and pranks, any of which might have seriously injured or even killed Randy, but none of which, so far, had apparently harmed him. When she opened her eyes, Harriet Grady was looking at her with an expression that told Lucy the teacher was sharing her thoughts.

"I suppose it's possible that Randy could have gone off on some kind of an adventure and it went wrong," the teacher offered. Then she stood up and began leading Lucy to the door. "I wish I could tell you more, Mrs. Corliss, but I never knew what Randy was going to do next. Now I don't know what to think." She squeezed Lucy's arm reassuringly. "He *will* be found, Mrs. Corliss. And knowing Randy, whatever's happened, he'll come out all right. He always has so far."

But when Lucy left her classroom, Harriet Grady went back to her desk and scanned Randy Corliss's file once again. To her, Randy was a hopeless case. If there ever was a boy who was going to get himself in trouble, it was Randy. She closed the file, put it back in the desk, and locked the drawer.

Lucy was almost out of the building when she noticed the small sign identifying the nurse's office. She hesitated, then tapped on the frosted glass panel.

"Come in," a voice called out. Lucy opened the door and stepped inside. A woman only slightly older than herself, dressed in a white uniform, was sitting at a desk reading a paperback novel. She glanced up and grinned.

"If you're an irate taxpayer, I'm technically off duty. I just hang around most afternoons in case one of the kids hurts himself on the playground. Everyone says I'm dedicated."

Lucy laughed in spite of herself. The nurse had an open expression that was in sharp contrast to the stern visage of Randy's teacher.

"I'm not an irate taxpayer," Lucy told her. "I'm a worried mother."

Immediately the grin faded from the nurse's face, and she stood up.

"Are you Mrs. Corliss?" she asked. "We're all so worried about Randy. Is there anything I can do?"

"I don't know," Lucy admitted. "I was on my way out, and I happened to see the sign. And Miss Grady was just telling me about something that happened last fall—"

"The black widow," the nurse interrupted. "Your boy was very lucky there."

"That's what Miss Grady said. She—she thinks Randy ran away. Everybody does."

"Everybody except you, right?" The nurse gestured toward a chair. "Sit down. I'm Annie Oliphant, and I've heard all the possible jokes having to do with orphans and elephants." Once more her expression turned serious. "I'm afraid there's not much I can do for you. Randy was one boy I hardly ever saw." She went to a filing cabinet, pulled out a thin folder, and glanced quickly through it.

"May I see that?" Lucy asked, her tone deliberately sarcastic. "Or is it confidential?"

Annie Oliphant handed her the file. "Nothing in there that's a deep, dark secret. And I'll bet there's nothing in any of Randy's other files that's going to shake national security either. I think secrets just make everyone around here feel important."

Lucy flipped through the pages of Randy's medical file. The information was sparse and mostly meaningless to her. "I don't suppose any of this could relate to Randy's disappearance, could it?" she asked.

"I don't see how," the nurse agreed. "The only thing interesting about that file is that it describes a disgustingly healthy kid. If they were all like Randy, I wouldn't have a job. Look at this." She took the file out of Lucy's hands and started from the beginning. "No major illnesses. No minor illnesses. No injuries, major or minor. Tonsils intact and healthy. Appendix in place. Even his *teeth,* for heaven's sake! The lower ones are at least crooked, but not enough to bother with braces, and there isn't a cavity in his head. What did you do, raise him in a box?"

Again, Lucy couldn't help laughing. "Hardly. I guess we've just been lucky. Up till now." She paused, and when she spoke again, her voice was lower. "Do you know Randy very well?"

The nurse shook her head. "All I ever did was look him over once a year. He wasn't one for getting sick in the cafeteria or banging himself up. I'm afraid the only kids I really know are the sickly ones, and as you can see, Randy can hardly be called sickly."

Lucy flipped through the file once more. "Could I have a copy of this?" she asked.

"Sure." Lucy followed her down the hall, and watched from the doorway as the nurse began duplicating the file.

"I can't imagine what good this will be," Annie said uncertainly as she gave the copies to Lucy.

"I can't either," Lucy replied, her voice suddenly quavering. "I suppose it just makes me feel as though I've *done* something. You don't know what it's like, having your child missing. I feel so helpless. I don't even know where to begin. I thought maybe someone here might know something, or have noticed something—anything." Lucy could hear her desperation in her trembling voice and was afraid for a moment that she was going to cry. She fell silent, fighting the tears.

"I'm so sorry, Mrs. Corliss." The nurse's voice was gentle as she guided Lucy toward the main doors of the school. "It just seems to be the times we live in. Things happen to children when they're younger now. First the teenagers started running away, and now it seems like the preteens are starting to do it. And they're drinking and using drugs too. I wish I knew why."

Lucy's tearfulness gave way to anger. "Randy doesn't drink, and he doesn't use drugs! And he didn't run away!" Her voice rose dangerously. "Something happened to him, and I'm going to find out what!"

She ran through the doors and down the steps, then hurried toward her car. She could feel the nurse's eyes on her as she started the engine, but she didn't glance back as she jammed the car into gear, pressed the accelerator, and sped away.

"Anything?"

"Nothing."

Jim and Lucy Corliss stood facing each other. After a long moment Lucy stepped back to let him come into her house. He glanced around the dimness of the living room, then went to the window and opened the drapes. Evening sunlight seemed to wash some of the strain from his ex-wife's face.

"You can't live in darkness, Lucy. That won't help you or Randy."

Lucy sighed heavily, and sank into a chair. "I know. The truth is, I didn't even realize they were closed. I guess I never opened them at all this morning."

"You've got to—"

"Don't lecture me, Jim. I don't think I can stand it. Isn't there any trace of him at all?"

Jim shook his head. "Nothing. They're doing everything they can, Lucy, believe me. I was with them all day. We searched the woods he got lost in last year, and talked to practically everyone on his route to school. No one saw him; no one knows anything. They'll keep searching tomorrow, but after that—" He shrugged despondently.

"You mean they'll stop looking?" Lucy demanded. "But he's only a little boy, Jim. They *can't* stop looking for him, can they?"

Jim moved to the sideboard and helped himself to a drink, and Lucy, even in the midst of her anguish, found herself gauging its strength. Surprisingly, it appeared to her to be fairly weak. "Fix me one?" she asked.

"Sure." He poured a second highball and crossed to her, handed her the drink, then retreated to a chair a few feet away. "You have to understand, Lucy. It isn't that they don't want to look for him. They *are* looking, and they say they'll keep on. But they simply can't keep doing it full-time. Eventually, unless there're signs of violence, or a ransom note, they're going to have to assume he ran away."

"But he didn't," Lucy insisted. "I know he didn't. And please, Jim, don't ask me how I know. I just do."

"I wasn't going to ask you that," Jim said gently. "I was going to ask you if you've had dinner."

Lucy looked at him sharply. Did he expect her to cook for him now? He seemed to read her mind.

"I'd like to take you out, Lucy." He saw her body stiffen and her eyes become guarded. "Don't," he said. "I know what you're thinking. You're wondering what I'm after. Well, I'm not after anything, Lucy. It's just that—well, we've lost our son, and for some reason right now I'm finding it very difficult to relate to anyone but you. And I'm worried about you."

"About me?" Lucy asked, her skepticism clear in her voice.

"I know. I know, I know, I know! I was a thoughtless inconsiderate selfish bastard, and I deserved to be thrown out. In fact, I probably should have been drawn and quartered, then strung up for the vultures to feed on. Perhaps even keelhauled"—her lips were beginning to twitch just slightly—"or marooned on a desert island . . ."

"I'd draw the line at the keelhauling," Lucy burst out. "You never could hold your breath for more than a few seconds." She fell silent, examining him carefully, looking for a clue as to what was going on in his mind. She wanted to believe him, to believe that he wanted nothing more from her than company for dinner and the companionship that, right now, only she could give him.

She made up her mind.

"Do you remember the Speckled Hen?" she asked. It was a little place, a few miles out of Eastbury. When they were first married, it had been their favorite place, but she hadn't been there for nearly ten years.

"Is it still there?" Jim asked.

"It was last week," Lucy said. "I had a listing out there, and I almost went in for lunch."

"Why didn't you?"

This time there was something in his eyes that made Lucy keep her own counsel. "I just changed my mind," she said. She finished her drink and stood up. "Let's go. I don't promise to be great company, but you're right. I need to eat, and I need to be with someone this evening."

"Even me?"

"Even you. Maybe, tonight, only you."

As they drove to the restaurant, Lucy tried to analyze what it was about Jim that had changed. Several times she caught herself watching him out of the corner of her eye. The profile was still perfect, though his jaw seemed even stronger than it had been twelve years ago.

No, the changes weren't in his physical being; they were somewhere else.

His manner had changed. He seemed, to Lucy, to be more aware of things beyond himself. Also, there was a stability to him, and a hint of humor that was unfamiliar to her. Oh, he'd always been funny, but it had always been at the expense of someone else, usually her.

"What changed you?" she suddenly heard herself asking. If the question surprised him, he gave no sign.

"Life," he said. "I guess I got tired of landing on my ass. It was either change my ways or pad my butt, and I decided wearing a pillow wouldn't work. Maybe your throwing me out was the best thing that ever happened to me. For the first time, I didn't have anyone to fall on, so I decided to stop falling."

There was a long silence then, and Lucy didn't speak again until they were in the parking lot of the restaurant.

"Jim?"

He turned to face her, and once more it was as if he'd read her mind.

"Don't worry," he said. "For a while, at least, I can take care of both of us. If you want to fall apart, you go ahead. You may not think I'm good for much, but right now I'm all you've got. And you can depend on me, Lucy. Okay?"

Her tears brimmed over, and she sat still, letting them flow. Jim sat quietly beside her, holding her hand in his own.

The Speckled Hen was very much as they remembered it, and for the next few hours they talked of things other than their son.

They talked of times past, when things had been good, and times past, when things had been bad.

Mostly, they were silent. No one watching them would have known they'd been divorced for nearly ten years. To an outsider they would have appeared very much married, with much on their minds, but little need to talk.

By the time he took her home, Jim and Lucy Corliss were becoming friends again.

CHAPTER 9

The night was warm and humid, a precursor of the summer that was soon to come, and Steve Montgomery left his window rolled down as he searched for the right house. "It should be in this block," he said, slowing the car and peering through the darkness for the numbers which seemed to him to be deliberately hidden from anyone who might be looking for them.

"I still don't see why you insisted on coming." Sally's voice was cold. She sat stiffly upright on the seat next to him, her arms folded across her breast, the fingers of her right hand kneading the flesh of her left arm. Steve brought the car to a halt, switched off the ignition, and turned to face his wife.

"It can't hurt, and it might help," he said. He reached out to touch his wife, but she drew away from him. He sighed, and when he spoke again, he was careful to keep his growing impatience out of his voice. "Look, honey, how can it possibly hurt? You don't have to say a word if you don't want to. But all these people have been through the same thing we've been through. If anyone can help us come to grips with this thing, they can."

He searched Sally's face, hoping for a sign that perhaps she was willing to face the reality of what had happened to Julie. But her face remained unchanged, her eyes brooding, her expression one of puzzled detachment.

Steve knew what was happening. She was sifting through her mind, trying to find a clue that would unlock the mystery of Julie's death for her. It had begun that afternoon, when instead of beginning to put her life back together, as Steve was trying to do with himself, she had sat straight up on the sofa, a medical book in her lap, reading intently page after page of material that Steve was nearly certain she didn't understand. But he understood very well what she was doing.

She was looking for what he had already come to think of as The Real Reason for Julie's death.

It had begun the night before. As Steve lay trying to fall asleep, and thinking about the funeral to be faced the next morning, Sally had left their bed and begun wandering through the house as though she were looking for something. Steve heard her footsteps in the hall, heard the soft click of a door opening and closing, and knew that she had gone to Jason's room to reassure herself that her son was still alive. Twice he had gone downstairs to talk to her, only to find her hunched up on the sofa, a book open on her lap, reading.

And refusing to talk to him, except to doggedly repeat the litany: Babies don't just die. But tonight, he hoped, Sally might begin to accept that theirs had. He got out of the car and went around to open the door for Sally.

Holding her arm, he guided her up the steps of the large frame house, then pressed the bell. A moment later the door was opened, and a friendly-looking woman about the same age as Sally smiled at them.

"You must be the Montgomerys," she said. "I'm so glad you could come. I'm Lois Petropoulous." She guided them into the living room and introduced them to the twelve people who were gathered there. There was a disparity to the group that Steve found startling at first. There was a black couple, and an Oriental man with his Caucasian wife. Two of the women had no husbands, and one couple stood out only for the apparent poverty of their lives. The woman's face, like her husband's, was gaunt, and there was a hopelessness in her eyes that was reflected in the shabbiness of her dress. Steve scanned the group, searching for a common bond among them, but there was none. Apparently all that had brought them together was the fact that each of them had lost a child to sudden infant death syndrome.

Two places had been held for them on a large sofa. Steve lowered himself gratefully into its soft comfort. Sally, next to him, remained rigidly erect, her hands clasped together in her lap.

"We don't really have a leader in the group," Lois Petropoulous explained. "In fact, we don't really have a regular meeting place either. The group keeps changing, and we keep moving from house to house, as people come and go."

"How long do people stay in the group?" Steve asked.

"As long as they need to, or as long as they feel needed," the gaunt-looking woman, whose name was Irene, said. "Kevin and I have been part of it for over a year now."

Another woman—Steve thought her name was Muriel—suddenly grinned. "We think Irene and Kevin stick around because we're cheap entertainment." Steve felt himself flushing and was surprised to hear several people, including Irene and Kevin, chuckling.

"Don't be surprised at anything you might hear," Lois said, smiling kindly. "We all have to deal with SIDS in our own way, and sometimes humor is the only way. But we also shed a lot of tears, and sometimes we get pretty loud. You have no idea how much anger builds up after you lose a child the way we all have. One of the reasons we're here is to vent that anger. In this group there are no rules. Say what you feel, or what you think, and be assured that someone else here has felt and thought exactly the same thing. What's most important is to realize that you're not alone. Everyone here has gone through what you're going through." She glanced around the room. "Well," she said, her voice suddenly nervous, "I suppose we've already begun, but I'm going to make my big announcement anyway, even though I'd planned to start the meeting with it. I'm pregnant."

All the eyes in the room suddenly fastened on Lois, and she squirmed self-consciously. "And the first person who says 'after what happened?' gets the award for bad taste for tonight."

"After what happened?" five voices immediately asked. When the laughter died, Muriel Flannery spoke out of the silence.

"But aren't you scared, Lois? I mean, really?"

"Of course I'm scared," Lois replied. "I'm terrified. And you can believe I don't expect to get much sleep the first couple of years. I'll be watching this baby like a hawk, even with the alarm."

"I'm not sure I could do that to a baby," another voice said. "I mean, wire it up like that. It seems so—so cruel. Almost like a lab experiment, or something."

"But without it, I'd be afraid to let the baby sleep."

Steve Montgomery stared from one face to another. What were they talking about? An alarm for children? He'd never heard of such a thing. Seeing his expression, Kevin tried to explain. "We're talking about an infant monitor. You attach it to the baby when its sleeping, and it goes off if the baby stops breathing. Except that no one knows if it really works for SIDS. There's something else, called apnea, where the baby just seems to forget to breathe."

"But I thought that's what SIDS was," Steve said.

"I wish it were," another of the men put in. "But it seems there's more to

SIDS than that. With SIDS, there's a constriction of the throat, so even if the baby tries to breathe, it can't. And for that, the alarm doesn't seem to do any good at all."

The conversation went on, moving from subject to subject. Steve found himself listening intently. These people, he began to realize, were just like himself—ordinary people who had become the victims of something they had always assumed could only happen to someone else. Each of them was dealing with it in a different way. There was grief and puzzlement in the room and a lot of anger. But for all of them, there was understanding.

Beside her husband, Sally Montgomery listened to the voices droning on and wondered why Steve had insisted they come to this meeting. There was nothing here for her, and she had a distinct feeling that she was wasting her time. She should be at home, looking after Jason, and studying her books, searching for the answer that kept eluding her as to what had happened to her daughter.

Suddenly, she heard a voice addressing her. It was Alex Petropoulous, and his intelligent eyes were fixed on her, his expression quizzical.

"You don't seem to be paying much attention, Mrs. Montgomery," he said. "Is there something on your mind?"

She made herself relax and sink back onto the couch, her hands smoothing the soft linen of her dress. "I'm afraid I've got a lot on my mind," she explained. "You see, my baby didn't die of SIDS. It was something else."

Across the room, a woman who had been quiet all evening suddenly spoke.

"I'm Jan Ransom, Mrs. Montgomery," she said. "Would you mind telling us what happened to your baby?"

"I—I don't know yet," Sally admitted. "But I'll find out."

"Of course you will," Jan agreed. "Just like I did. I spent nearly a year trying to find out what happened to my daughter, and I finally did."

Sally looked at the woman sharply. "What was it?" she asked.

"SIDS," Jan said, shrugging her shoulders. "You know, one of the hardest things to accept is the simple fact that with SIDS no one can tell you what happened. For me, the idea that the doctors—the people who are always supposed to know what happened and why it happened—didn't have the slightest idea why my baby died was absolutely unacceptable. So I started reading and studying and talking to everyone I could think of. And no one knew. Of course, what I was really doing was burying my head in the sand. Deep down, I was afraid that if there was no reasonable explanation for my baby's dying, I must have made it happen myself."

"No one would want to kill her own baby," Muriel Flannery said softly.

"No?" Jan Ransom replied bitterly. "People kill their own babies every day. And I never wanted a baby in the first place."

For the first time, Sally Montgomery began listening.

"I had my life all planned," Jan went on. "I was going to finish my master's —I'm in communications—then go to New York and get a job in advertising. When I was in my thirties, I'd get married, and my husband would be as career-minded as I am. No children. They only get in the way, and besides, what kind of world is this to bring up children in? Energy shortages, overpopulation, all the usual things. And then one day I turned up pregnant."

"Why didn't you have an abortion?" someone asked.

Jan Ransom smiled bitterly. "Did I forget to tell you? I was raised a Catholic. I thought I'd gotten over that, but it turned out I hadn't. Oh, I went for the birth control—that didn't bother me at all. But when it came right down to having an abortion, I just couldn't do it. And then, when the baby came, I couldn't put it up for adoption either. Maybe I should have."

"It wouldn't have made any difference," Lois Petropoulous told her. "SIDS doesn't have anything to do with who's raising the baby."

"Doesn't it?" Jan shot back. "Who says? And how do they know? If they don't know what SIDS is, how can they say it doesn't have anything to do with the parents? Maybe," she added, her voice trembling, "the baby senses that its mother doesn't want it and just decides to die."

Sally felt her fingers digging into her thighs as she listened to Jan Ransom. Right here, in front of all these people, the woman was voicing all the dark suspicions with which Sally had tormented herself in the small hours of the night. Now she could feel Jan Ransom's eyes on her. When she looked up, the young woman was smiling at her gently.

"I don't think I killed my baby anymore, Mrs. Montgomery," she said softly. "And I'm sure you didn't kill yours either. I don't know exactly why you're so sure that SIDS didn't kill your baby, but I do know that if the doctors say that's what happened, it's best to believe them. You can't spend the rest of your life searching for answers that don't exist. You have to go on with your life and accept what happened."

"I'm not sure I can do that," Sally said, suddenly standing up. "But I know that I have nothing in common with you people. Steve?" Without waiting for a reply, Sally started toward the door. Steve, his face flushing with embarrassment, tried to apologize for his wife.

"It's all right," Lois Petropoulous told him. "This isn't the first time this has happened, and it won't be the last. When she needs us, we'll still be here. If not us, then there will be others. Take care of her, Steve. She needs you very badly right now."

She stood by the door and watched Steve and Sally Montgomery disappear into the night. As she returned to the living room, she wondered if Sally Montgomery would come back and get the help she needed, or if she would insist on bearing her problems alone until the day came, as it inevitably would, when those problems would close in on her, and destroy her.

* * *

Jason Montgomery sat on the floor of his room, watching as his guinea pig happily darted from corner to corner, enjoying its respite from the confines of its cage. From downstairs Jason could hear the sound of the television droning on as the sitter dozed in front of it. He'd gone down a few minutes ago, but when he'd found her asleep, he'd decided not to wake her up. She wasn't like some of the sitters he'd had, who were always baking cookies or willing to play games. She was too old, he'd decided long ago, and all she wanted was to be left alone. And if she wasn't, sometimes she got crabby. So Jason had stood at the door for a minute, watching her, then gone back upstairs to play with Fred.

His parents, he knew, had gone to some meeting, but he wasn't sure what it was about. Something to do with his sister and getting used to the fact that she was dead. But Jason didn't understand why his parents had to go to a meeting. Hadn't there already been a funeral? He'd thought that's what the funeral was for, but now he guessed he'd been wrong.

He decided it was one more thing he'd talk to Randy Corliss about the next time he saw him.

Except that this afternoon Joey Connors had told him that Randy had run away, and most of the kids thought that even if he came back, he'd probably be sent to Juvenile Hall, where he'd be punished.

Fred moved across the floor, his tiny nose snuffling at the carpet, then crept into Jason's lap to be petted. Jason began scratching the rodent behind the ears and talking quietly to it.

"Is that what'll happen to me?" he asked. "But I didn't really do anything to Julie. All I did was put the blanket on her face for a minute." He stared down at the guinea pig, wondering for the hundredth time if he could really have hurt Julie by putting the blanket over her head. He was almost sure he hadn't.

Almost.

But what if he had? How would he ever know?

He picked up the guinea pig, pulled his extra blanket off his bed, then knelt down on the floor once again.

"Now, you pretend like you're Julie," he said. He put Fred on the floor, and rolled him over on his back. The guinea pig struggled for a moment, then, as Jason began tickling its stomach, lay still.

"There," Jason said. "Doesn't that feel good?" Then he stopped tickling his pet and waited. The tiny animal lay still, waiting for the petting to resume.

Carefully, Jason wrapped the blanket around the guinea pig and held it firm. He began counting.

Fred wriggled and squirmed in the woolen folds, and Jason could feel him trying to bite, but it was no use.

By the time Jason had counted to one hundred, there was no more movement within the blanket.

He tried to remember—had Julie stopped struggling? He thought she hadn't, and he was almost sure he'd held the blanket over her face for much longer than he'd kept Fred wrapped in it.

Almost sure.

Carefully, he lifted the blanket, sure that Fred, suddenly freed, would scurry under the bed.

The guinea pig lay still. Even when Jason prodded it with his finger, it didn't move.

Maybe, he decided, he *had* done something to Julie. But if he had, he hadn't meant to. No more than he'd meant to kill Fred.

He picked the guinea pig's body up and cradled it in his hands for a minute, wondering what to do.

Maybe, he decided, guinea pigs were like babies.

Maybe they just died sometimes.

He put Fred back in his cage, then went to bed, and by the time his parents came home, he was fast asleep.

It was Sally who found the guinea pig.

While Steve drove the baby-sitter home, she slipped into Jason's room to make sure he was all right. She bent over him, listened to him breathe for a moment, then gently kissed him on the forehead. She was about to leave his room, when she realized something was wrong.

The scuffling noises that Fred made whenever his sleep was disturbed were missing. Sally switched on the lamp next to Jason's bed and went to the cage in the corner. Fred, looking strangely unnatural, was sprawled on the bottom of the cage. She knelt, opened the cage, and picked him up. As she realized he was dead, an involuntary sound escaped her lips.

"What's wrong?" she heard Jason asking from behind her. She turned to see her son sitting up in bed, sleepily rubbing his eyes. "Is something wrong with Fred?"

"He's dead," Sally breathed, fighting off the terrible emotions that were welling up inside her. It's only a guinea pig, she told herself. It's not Jason, it's not Julie, it's only a damned guinea pig.

But still, it was too familiar. Bursting into tears, she dropped the dead animal and fled from the room. Behind her, she heard Jason's voice.

"What happened to him, Mommy? Did the same thing happen to Fred that happened to Julie?"

CHAPTER 10

Sally Montgomery sat in her living room, a small pool of light flooding the book she was trying to read.

The words on the pages made no sense to her. They kept drifting away, slipping off the pages, and over and over again she realized that she had read a paragraph but had no memory of it.

When Steve had come back from taking the sitter home, and Sally had told him about the guinea pig, all he had done was tell her to forget about it, then gone upstairs, brought the dead rodent down, and taken it outside to bury it in the backyard. By morning, he assured her, both she and Jason would have forgotten about it.

But would she?

She kept hearing Jason's words echoing in her head.

"Did the same thing happen to Fred that happened to Julie?"

What had happened to Julie?

Involuntarily, images of her son began to flit through her mind.

Jason, standing at the door of the nursery, staring at her as she held Julie's body.

Jason at the funeral, watching as his sister's coffin was lowered into the ground, his eyes dry, his expression one of—what?

It had been, she admitted to herself now, an expression of disinterest.

As the long night wore on, she had twice gone upstairs to check on Jason. Each time she had found him sleeping peacefully, his breathing deep and strong, one arm thrown across his chest, the other dangling over the side of the bed. If either the loss of his sister or the loss of his pet was bothering him, it wasn't keeping him awake. Twice she had stood at the foot of his bed for long minutes, trying to drive horrible thoughts from the edges of her mind. And both times she had at last forced herself to leave his room without waking him just to prove to herself that he was all right.

Or to ask him questions she wasn't at all sure she wanted to voice.

Now, as she tried once more to concentrate on the book of childhood diseases that lay in her lap, she found herself once more thinking of Jan Ransom's words.

"Never wanted a baby in the first place . . ."

"Maybe the baby senses that the mother doesn't want it . . ."

Finally, heedless of the time, she picked up the phone book and flipped through it.

There it was:

RANSOM, JANELLE 504 ALDER ESTBY 555-3624

The phone rang seven times before a sleepy voice answered.

"Miss Ransom? This—this is Sally Montgomery. I was at the meeting tonight?"

Instantly the sleepiness was gone from the voice at the other end of the line. "Sally! Of course. You know, I had the strangest feeling you might call tonight. I—well, I had the feeling I hit a nerve."

Sally wasn't sure what to say, and as she was trying to decide how to proceed, she suddenly felt as if she was being watched. Turning, she saw Steve standing in the doorway. She swallowed hard, and when she spoke into the phone, her voice sounded unnaturally high.

"I—I thought perhaps we could have lunch next week."

"Of course," Jan Ransom replied immediately. "Any particular day?"

"Whatever's good for you."

"Then let's not wait for next week," Jan suggested. "Let's say Friday at noon. Do you know the Speckled Hen?"

They made the date, and Sally slowly put the phone back on its cradle, still not sure why she wanted to talk further to Jan Ransom. All she knew was that she did.

Steve came into the room and sat down beside her. "Can I ask whom you were talking to?"

"I wish you wouldn't," Sally said uncertainly.

Steve hesitated, then, seeing clearly the strain and exhaustion in Sally's whole being, decided not to press the issue. He stood up and switched off the light. "Come on, honey. Let's go to bed."

Sally let herself be led upstairs and helped into bed, and she didn't resist when Steve drew her close. But when he spoke again, her body went rigid.

"Maybe we should have another baby," she heard him saying. "Maybe we should start one right away."

Silently, Sally moved away from him, and as the hours of the night wore on, she felt the gulf between herself and her husband slowly widening.

CHAPTER 11

Lucy Corliss glanced at the clock. It was nearly eleven, and another day, the third since Randy had disappeared, was nearly over. "Here's to tomorrow," she said bitterly, raising her empty cup. "Want some more coffee?"

Jim shook his head and watched as Lucy moved to the stove. They'd been sitting at the kitchen table all evening, Jim doing his best to keep Lucy calm. It had begun six hours ago, when he'd shown up at her door, his face pale. "What is it?" she'd asked. "Did you hear something?"

Jim had shaken his head. "Not really. Could I come in?"

Puzzled, Lucy had let him into the house and taken him to the kitchen. To Jim, it had seemed a sign of acceptance; when he was growing up, his mother had entertained her friends only in the kitchen—the living room was for the minister.

"I just came from the police station," he told her after she'd poured him the first of the endless pots of coffee the two of them had consumed during the evening. "I talked to Sergeant Bronski."

"And?" Lucy prompted when Jim seemed reluctant to go on.

"And he started talking about statistics."

"What sort of statistics?"

"About cases like ours," Jim replied, his eyes meeting hers. "Cases like Randy."

"I see," Lucy said softly. Her mind wandered back over the day she had just spent talking to people, knocking on every door along Randy's route to school, pleading with people, begging them to try to remember anything they'd seen that day, anything that might give her a hint as to what had happened to her son. Always the answer had been the same.

People were sorry, but they had seen nothing, heard nothing, noticed nothing. And all of them, both before and after the search of the forest, had been interviewed by the police.

"Lucy," she heard Jim saying, "they told me we have to prepare ourselves for the fact that when Randy is found—if he's found . . ." His voice trailed off, and he felt tears brimming in his eyes. He looked away from Lucy.

". . . he'll be dead?" Lucy asked, her voice devoid of emotion. "I know that, Jim. Anyway, I've been told that. I don't believe it. I just have a feeling—"

"Lucy," Jim groaned. "Lucy, I know what you think, I know how you feel. But you have to be ready. Bronski told me that if there were anything—a note, or a phone call, or even some sign of a struggle somewhere, it would be one thing. But with nothing, no clues, all they can think is that Randy either ran away, or—or whoever took him wasn't interested in ransom."

"You mean some pervert picking him up for sex?" Lucy asked, her voice uncannily level. "Raping him, and then killing him?"

"Something like that—" Jim faltered.

"That didn't happen," Lucy stated. "If that had happened, I'd know it. Deep in my heart, I'd know it. He's not dead, Jim, and he didn't run away."

"Then where is he? Why haven't we heard *something?*"

But Lucy had only shaken her head. "Jim, I've talked to everyone I can think of, asked questions, looked for God-knows-what, and all I can think of is that in a book, or in a movie, it's always different. The mother goes out looking for her child and she finds him. But it's not that easy. I haven't found anything. Not one damned thing. All I've got after three days is this."

She had picked up the file that the school nurse had given her and tossed it across the table to her ex-husband, who flipped through it, then put it aside. It still lay on the table, where it had lain all through the evening as they ate dinner, talked, sipped at their coffee, tried to figure out what to do next, talked of other things, and always, inexorably, returned to the subject of their son.

Now, as Lucy refilled her cup and came back to the table again, Jim picked up the report once more. He looked through it.

The only thing about it that made it unique was the picture it painted of a remarkably healthy little boy.

Too healthy?

Jim began studying the file again, searching it for all the things that should have been there.

The absences from school.

The upset stomachs after lunch.

The skinned knees from inevitable falls.

The sore throats and colds that no child escapes.

None of it was there.

Jim went over the report yet again, searching for anything he might have missed. Finally, he closed the folder and faced his wife. "Lucy, did you notice anything odd about Randy's file?"

She looked at him pensively. "Odd? How do you mean?"

"According to this, Randy's never been sick a day in his life, never had a cavity in his mouth, never even so much as skinned his knee."

"So?"

Jim frowned. "Well, I don't know about you, but I've never heard of such a thing before." He reopened the report and began quoting it to Lucy. All of it was clear—all except for a small notation at the bottom of the first page:

CHILD #0263

"What's this mean? Do they assign each of the kids a number now?"

Lucy shook her head. "It's a survey code. I wondered about it, too, so I called the school nurse this morning. CHILD stands for Children's Health Institute for Latent Diseases, and oh-two-six-three was the number assigned to Randy."

"Assigned to him for what?" Jim asked.

"Some sort of survey. Miss Oliphant said they've been tracking Randy for a long time."

"Tracking him? You mean watching him?"

"Not exactly. Every few months the school forwards Randy's health records to the Institute, that's all."

"How many of the kids are they tracking?"

Lucy frowned. "What do you mean?"

"Are they tracking all the kids at the school? All the ones in Randy's class?"

"I don't know," Lucy said. She picked up the file and looked at the notation once again, trying to remember just what Annie Oliphant had told her about the survey. Had she even asked how many of Randy's schoolmates were involved? She couldn't remember. She went to the phone and began dialing.

"Lucy, it's after midnight," Jim reminded her.

"But it might be important." Lucy waved him silent and turned her attention to the phone. "Miss Oliphant? It's Lucy Corliss. I hate to bother you so late, but I keep wondering about this survey Randy was involved in. Was his whole class being studied?"

She listened for a moment, asked a few more questions, then thanked the nurse again, and hung up.

"Well?" Jim asked.

"It's strange," Lucy said. "She told me she doesn't know anything about the survey. There are several children from Eastbury involved, and Randy's the oldest. Every month she sends copies of the children's records to Boston, to the CHILD headquarters. They supply the envelopes and the postage, but they've never told her what the survey is about or what the results are."

"But who authorized the survey?" Jim asked. "I mean, don't you have to give your permission for Randy's records to be sent out?"

"I don't know," Lucy replied. "I suppose I might have signed some kind of consent form somewhere along the line. You know how it is—kids bring home so many forms, and they never give them to you until breakfast the day they're due."

"Actually," Jim commented, his voice not unkind, "I don't know about such things. I guess there's a lot I don't know much about."

His eyes had taken on a look of such loneliness that Lucy went to him and slipped her arms around him. "Well, don't start worrying about all that now," she told him. "I can guarantee you that if you *had* been around, you wouldn't have read all the forms either."

Jim grinned at her. "You mean you'd have forgiven me for being irresponsible?" Lucy drew away from him, and Jim wished he'd left the mild taunt unsaid. "I'm sorry," he apologized, but Lucy was already studying Randy's medical file again.

"Miss Oliphant said something else. She said that all the subjects of the survey have one thing in common: All their files read like Randy's. It seems they're all in perfect health and always have been."

Now Jim stared at her.

"All of them?" he said.

Lucy nodded.

"But—but how can that be?"

"What do you mean?"

"How long has the survey been going on?"

"At least since they started school."

"And all the kids they're surveying have perfect health?"

"That's what Annie Oliphant said." What was he getting at?

"Lucy, doesn't it strike you as odd that this survey has been going on for some time—we don't really know how long—and all its subjects have perfect health? I mean, it seems to me that it would be reasonable if when Randy was, say, ten years old, someone came along and suggested that *because* he'd been in perfect health all his life, they'd like to start tracking him to see what's going to happen. But apparently this outfit in Boston had some reason to think there was going to be something special about Randy and the others and started tracking them early."

"What are you saying, Jim?" Lucy asked, sure she already knew what was coming.

"I'm saying that it seems to me we might have some kind of clue about Randy after all. I think tomorrow one of us better get in touch with CHILD, and find out just what this survey is about, and how Randy fits in. Apparently there *is* something special about Randy. We'd better find out what it is."

As she went to bed later that night, Lucy wondered what could possibly come of talking to the Children's Health Institute for Latent Diseases. Was Jim just sending her off on another wild-goose chase?

Still, it would be something to do, and anything, right now, was better than nothing.

With nothing to do, she would go crazy, and she couldn't allow herself to do that.

Not until she knew what had happened to her son.

CHAPTER 12

After only three days at the Academy, Randy Corliss had grown accustomed to the routine. For the first time, he felt as though he belonged somewhere. The sense of being alone in the world, of being somehow set apart from the other kids his age, was gone. At the Academy he was like all the other boys.

School at the Academy wasn't like school in Eastbury. Here, all the classes were compressed into the morning, except for physical education, and the things they studied seemed to Randy much more interesting than the things they had been taught at home. Also, at the Academy everyone seemed to care whether or not you learned. It wasn't like the public schools at all. As long as Randy could remember, if he got bored with something and stopped paying attention, no one seemed to care. All his teachers had just gone along at their own pace, never noticing that their students had lost interest.

But here, everything seemed to go faster. Here, they expected you to learn, so you learned. And they spent most of their time on subjects Randy liked. A lot of history, which Randy liked because most of history seemed to be, one way or another, about war, and Randy found war fascinating. There was, to his young mind, something wonderful about men marching into battle. And the way Miss Bowen taught it, war was almost like a game. You obeyed the rules, and did exactly as you were told, and you won. Time after time, in lesson after lesson, Randy learned that battles were lost only because the troops had not done as they'd been told. To him, it all made perfect sense, because as he thought about it, he realized that in all his nine years, the only times he'd really gotten into trouble were the times he'd disobeyed someone.

At the Academy it was the same way. As long as you followed the routine, everything went fine. When you were supposed to do something, you did it. If you failed, you did it again until you got it right. But the main thing was to do as you were told. Otherwise things happened.

The quick hand of retribution had fallen on Randy only once, on the night after he'd arrived at the Academy. It had been dinnertime, and Peter had come to his room to take him down to the dining room. Randy had been reading, and the end of the chapter was only two pages away. He had told Peter he'd be down in a minute and finished the chapter.

By the time he got to the dining room, his place at the table was gone—even his chair—and none of the other boys even looked at him. Miss Bowen got up from the staff table. Dinner was at six o'clock, she said, not five after six; he'd missed it. He was about to protest that the other boys hadn't even started to eat yet, but as he faced her, something in the woman's eyes told him that anything he might say would be useless. He was sent to his room and spent the rest of the evening by himself. No one came to his room, no one even spoke to him, though he left his door open all night. From then on Randy was careful to do exactly as he was told.

Not that it was difficult. Mornings seemed to be the time when discipline was strictest, and in the afternoons, after gym class, they were turned loose, free to do as they pleased. In the afternoons no one ever told them what to do or how to do it. Indeed, though Randy always felt as though someone was watching him, he'd never been able to see the watchers. It was, he'd finally decided, like some kind of test, but he didn't know what the rules were or what was expected of him. Nor did he know what would happen to him if he failed.

For the first few days, of course, Randy had wondered exactly why he was there and why his father hadn't come to see him or at least called him. Then, as he got used to the Academy, he began to stop worrying about it.

Now it was Thursday afternoon, and Randy and Peter had just finished gym. The afternoon stretched before them, and they were wandering in the woods that lay close by the main building of the Academy.

"You wanna play King of the Mountain?" Peter suddenly asked.

Randy looked around. As far as he could tell, the ground the Academy sat on was perfectly flat, except for a shallow pond they used for swimming. "What are we gonna use for a mountain?"

"Come on," Peter replied. He started through the woods, and in a few minutes they came to a path. A few hundred yards farther, there was a clearing in the woods. In the center of the clearing stood a massive granite outcropping, towering thirty feet above the ground.

"What is it?" Randy breathed.

"It's a rock, dummy," Peter said scornfully. "How do I know what it is?"

"Can you climb it?"

"Sure. I've climbed it lots of times. Me and another guy used to play on it all the time."

"Who?"

"Jeff Grey."

Randy had never heard the name before. "Who's he?"

"He used to be here before you came."

"Where is he now?"

"How should I know?" Peter replied, but something in his voice told Randy that he knew more than he was telling. Suddenly Eric's words, half forgotten, came back to him.

"Sometimes kids . . . just disappear. We think they die."

Was that what had happened to Jeff Grey? He was about to ask, but Peter was already starting the game. "You wanna play or not?" Peter called. "First one to the top tries to keep the other one from getting up!" Peter charged up the heap of rubble, then began scrambling up the rock, his hands and feet moving instinctively from ledge to ledge. Randy watched for a moment, then began climbing a few feet away from Peter.

For the first ten feet the climb was easy. The rock rose out of the ground at an angle, and over the centuries its surface had been cracked and split by the freezing New England winters. Randy concentrated on moving upward as fast as he could, paying little attention to Peter.

And then, as the rock grew steeper, he felt a hand close on his shoulder, tugging at him. He turned, and there was Peter, right next to him, bracing himself against a ledge, grinning.

"Good-bye!" Peter sang out. He shoved hard, and Randy felt himself lose his balance as his left foot slipped out of place. He grasped at a branch of laurel that was growing out of the rock, then felt it break off in his hand. Suddenly, he was skidding downward, his arms and legs jarring against the stone, but never finding support. He hit the ground and lay on his back, wondering if he'd hurt himself. But it hadn't been a bad fall, and he could feel no pain. Then, from above him, he heard the humiliating sound of Peter's laughter.

As Peter once more began working his way upward, Randy got to his feet and began looking for another place to climb. He circled the crag carefully, knowing there was now no chance of beating his friend to the top. Now he would have to fight his way onto the summit.

He found a spot where the first part of the climb would be the most difficult, but where there seemed to be a fairly wide ledge, high up, on which he could brace himself while he tried to wrestle Peter down.

He began climbing slowly, trying to memorize each step he made so that in the event he fell again he might be able to catch himself before he tumbled all the way down. He ignored the taunts that floated down to him as Peter proclaimed himself king of the mountain.

Then he was on the ledge, and the flat top of the outcropping was level with his chest. Peter stood above him, grinning maliciously.

"That's as far as you get. Come any farther, and I'll push you off."

Randy put his arms on the summit, but before he could scramble onto it, Peter had pushed him back. "Give up?" Peter demanded.

"Why should I?" Randy shot back. "You cheated."

"I didn't either," Peter told him. "All I said was you had to get to the top. I didn't say you couldn't push the other guy back down."

Once more Randy tried to scramble over the ledge, and once more Peter stopped him, this time stepping on Randy's fingers to make him let go of his handhold. Randy jerked his hand free, then sucked on his injured knuckles for a moment while he tried to decide what to do next. He glanced backward over his shoulder, and there, beyond the trees, he could see the forbidding mass of the Academy. He could almost feel eyes watching him and began to wonder if he was going to get in trouble when he got back.

Then he looked down.

Far below him, the rubble around the base of the crag looked threatening, and Randy realized that if he fell from here, the first part of the fall would be the easy part. If he didn't stop himself in the first ten feet, there would be no way to keep himself from plunging the last twenty. And if that happened . . .

He turned his attention to Peter once more.

"Give up?" Peter asked again.

"No!" Randy shouted. He made a move with his right hand, but pulled it away just as Peter's foot came out to crush his fingers.

He grabbed Peter by the ankle, using both hands even though he knew it was risky.

Peter, surprised, stared at him for a moment, then tried to jerk his leg free.

Randy held on.

Peter tried to kick him with his free foot, but Randy twisted his leg, and Peter lost his balance, and had to use his other foot to keep from falling.

He bent down and picked up a rock.

"Let go of my leg."

"No."

"Let go, or I'll bash your head in!"

"No!"

Randy looked up and suddenly realized Peter wasn't kidding. The rock, large and heavy, was swinging downward.

Instinctively, Randy yanked at Peter's leg, bracing himself carefully on the lower ledge. As he watched, Peter's eyes widened, and the rock fell from his hand.

And then Peter teetered a moment, his balance gone, and began swaying forward. Both boys realized what was happening at the same moment.

"Catch me!" Peter screamed.

It was too late. Randy reached for his friend's leg, but his fingers only brushed against the denim of Peter's jeans. As Randy watched helplessly, Peter plunged headfirst into the pile of rubble below.

Louise Bowen knelt next to Peter's limp body and checked for a pulse. Satisfied, she carefully opened one of the little boy's eyes and examined the dilation of the pupil. Next to her, Randy Corliss hovered nervously, tears streaming down his terrified face.

"Is he dead?"

"Of course not," Louise assured him. "He's unconscious, but he's alive."

"I didn't mean to do it," Randy wailed. "Really, Miss Bowen, it wasn't my fault. We were playing King of the—"

"I *know* what happened."

The impatience in her voice made Randy subside into silence, and as he watched her examine Peter, he wondered what would happen to him now.

When Billy Semple had jumped off the roof and broken his leg, everyone had been furious with him, even though it hadn't been his fault. But what about this? He *had* deliberately tripped Peter, even if it was because Peter was going to hit him with a rock. What if Peter died? Would they take him to jail?

As Randy watched, Louise Bowen carefully turned Peter over, and it was suddenly obvious what had happened.

Peter must have landed on his head, pitching over onto his back. His hair was matted with blood, and the back of his skull was caved in. Fragments of bone were embedded in the bloody scalp.

By rights, Louise Bowen knew, Peter Williams should be dead.

Then, while Randy Corliss vomited into the bushes, Louise Bowen picked Peter up, and began making her way toward the huge gothic building that housed the Academy.

His stomach still churning with horror at what had happened to Peter, and his mind whirling with thoughts about what might still happen to him, Randy followed a few minutes later.

Randy listened to the muffled chimes of the clock in the downstairs hall as it struck midnight. As its last note faded away, he listened for other sounds, but there were none. And yet the silence didn't feel right to him. It wasn't the kind of peaceful silence he was used to, but another kind; it made him feel like something was wrong.

And, of course, something was: Peter Williams.

At dinner Peter Williams's place had been removed from the table. If the other boys had noticed—and Randy was sure they must have—none of them said anything. Instead, they quietly ate their dinners, then excused themselves, and disappeared upstairs.

Randy had waited until they were gone, then shyly approached Miss Bowen.

"Is Peter going to be all right?" he'd asked.

Miss Bowen had met his gaze, hesitated, then reached out to touch him on the cheek.

"He's gone," she'd told him. "He's gone, but you mustn't worry about it. We know what happened, and nobody blames you. It was an accident, and nobody is responsible for accidents. Do you understand?"

Randy had nodded his head uncertainly, then he, too, had retreated to the upper reaches of the building. But instead of joining the other boys, he had stayed in his room, trying to figure out what Miss Bowen had meant.

And now, at midnight, he was still trying to figure it out.

"He's gone." That was what Miss Bowen had said. She hadn't said Peter was dead, just that he was gone.

But that didn't make any sense. Where had he gone and when? Randy had been in the building ever since the accident, and no ambulance had come for Peter. No cars had even left the Academy. So where had Peter gone?

The silence and darkness suddenly closed in on Randy, and he got out of bed, put on his robe, and went to the door. He opened it and peered out into the hall. A few yards away, at the head of the main stairs, there was a desk where someone always sat, as if guarding the house.

Tonight there was no one at the desk.

Puzzled, Randy left his room and moved down the hall until he was standing at the top of the stairs. He paused and listened.

All he could hear was the soft ticking of the clock.

He descended the stairs slowly, stopping every few steps, sure that at any moment Miss Bowen would appear in the foyer and send him back to bed. But then he was in the foyer himself and still there was no sound.

From where he stood, he could see that the living and dining rooms were both empty, so he turned and started toward the back of the house, where the offices were. He went past Miss Bowen's office, then past several other closed doors. And then, as he was about to turn back, he heard the sound of muffled voices coming from behind the next door.

He crept closer, and listened. Then, hesitantly, he reached out and turned the doorknob. He waited, sure that someone would call out to him, but no one did.

Finally, he pushed the door open a crack and pressed his eye close so he could see into the room.

It was all white, with a table in the center that was surrounded with what looked to Randy like medical equipment. In fact, the room looked just like the operating rooms of hospitals that he'd seen on television. And around the table, five people were gathered.

They were wearing white gowns and face masks, but Randy was able to recognize Miss Bowen from her eyes and the wisps of curly hair that stuck out from under her cap. He was sure that the man at the end of the table was Mr. Hamlin, who he knew was the director of the Academy.

And then someone moved, and Randy saw who was on the operating table.

It was Peter Williams. His head was locked into a metal frame. His hair had been shaved off and the back of his skull cut away.

Randy froze, his eyes wide, his heart pounding.

So Peter wasn't gone after all, and he wasn't dead. He was still here.

But what were they doing to him? Were Mr. Hamlin and Miss Bowen doctors?

They must be, or they wouldn't be operating on Peter.

And then he heard Miss Bowen speak.

"What are you doing? You'll kill him!"

"I won't kill him," Randy heard Mr. Hamlin reply. "If he was going to die, he already would have."

Randy stood transfixed for a few more minutes, listening to the doctors as they worked, understanding only a few of their words, but knowing with a terrifying clarity that something was very wrong. At last, when he could stand it no longer without screaming, he pulled the door quietly shut, and crept back up to his room.

George Hamlin, who was, indeed, a doctor as well as the director of the Academy, glanced around at the other members of his surgical team and wished their masks were transparent. He would have liked particularly to be able to read Louise Bowen's expression right now. Of all his staff, he knew that only Bowen was likely to object to what he had done. The others, whatever roles they performed for the subjects at the Academy, were all doctors who shared not only his medical skills, but his devotion to research. But Bowen was different. She had never, as long as she had been part of Hamlin's team, been able to develop the proper scientific objectivity. Indeed, had it not been for the importance of keeping the project a secret for the time being, he would have fired her long ago. For the moment, though, he would simply have to tolerate her. "All right," he said softly. "I think that's about it."

The operation had taken nearly three hours. During that time an anesthetist had stood by, ready to move in should Peter Williams have shown signs of regaining consciousness. But Peter had not; throughout his ordeal, he had remained in the coma that had come over him at the time of his fall.

George Hamlin had begun working on Peter at ten o'clock, narrating his findings and his procedures as he went.

"The scalp is healing; all bleeding has stopped. Clear signs of osteoregeneration."

He had carefully picked pieces of bone from Peter's head, dropping them into a jar of saline solution that stood at his elbow. He worked quickly and expertly, and in moments the wound was cleaned.

Beneath the hole in Peter's skull a badly damaged brain had lain exposed.

"Jesus," someone whispered. "It's a mess."

But Hamlin had ignored the interruption and begun cutting at the cortical material, removing the damaged tissue. That, too, had gone into a bottle of saline solution.

"The damage doesn't seem to have gone too deep," Harry Garner, Hamlin's senior assistant had commented. "Are there any signs of regeneration?"

"Not yet." Hamlin's manner, as always, had been curt. He was making up his mind what to do next, and it was at that moment, as he had stared down into the gaping hole filled with living matter, that the part of him that was devoted to pure research took over.

The scalpel flashed downward, slicing deep into the cerebral cortex, cutting inward and downward through the occipital lobe until the cerebellum was exposed. Behind him he heard a gasp and wasn't surprised when Louise Bowen's voice penetrated his concentration with the words that had so terrified Randy Corliss.

"What are you doing? You'll kill him."

"I won't kill him," Hamlin had replied coldly. "If he was going to die, he already would have."

And now, an hour later, the operation completed, Peter Williams lay in a coma, his face placid, his breathing slow and steady, his vital signs strong.

But inside his head, part of his brain was gone. Hamlin had cut a core through the occipital lobe and the cerebellum, penetrating deep into the medulla oblongata.

The wound was still open.

"Do you want us to close for you?" Garner asked.

"I don't want it closed at all. Put him in the lab and watch him twenty-four hours a day."

"He'll never survive twenty-four hours," someone said quietly.

"We won't know that until tomorrow, will we?" Hamlin replied. "I want this subject watched. If there's any sign of regeneration in the brain—and I think you all know I mean unusual regeneration—I want to know about it immediately."

"And if he wakes up?" Louise Bowen asked.

Hamlin faced her. His expression was impassive, but his eyes glinted coldly in the bright lights of the operating room. "If he wakes up," he said, "I trust you'll ask him how he feels. In fact," he added, "it would be interesting to find out if he still feels anything at all." And then George Hamlin was gone, leaving his associates to do whatever was necessary to facilitate the survival of Peter Williams.

For Hamlin himself, Peter Williams as a person had never existed.

He was simply one more subject, Number 0168. And the subject was apparently a failure. Perhaps he would have better results with the new one, Number 0263. What was his name?

Hamlin thought for a moment, and then it came to him.

Corliss. That was it: Randy Corliss.

Starting tomorrow, he must begin watching the new subject more carefully.

CHAPTER 13

Sally Montgomery paused just inside the entrance to the Speckled Hen, and wondered if she shouldn't turn around and walk back out again. She glanced at herself in the enormous mirror that dominated the foyer of the restaurant and felt reassured. Nothing in her reflection betrayed her nervousness. To an observer she would look to be exactly what she was—a young professional woman. She was wearing a red suit with navy blue accents, deliberately chosen to draw attention to itself and away from the strain in her face, which she had tried to hide behind a layer of carefully applied makeup.

"I'm Mrs. Montgomery," she told the smiling hostess. "I'm meeting Mrs. Ransom."

"Of course," the hostess replied. "If you'll follow me?" With Sally trailing behind her, the woman threaded her way through the crowded restaurant to a small table tucked away in an alcove near the kitchen. Jan Ransom was sipping a spritzer and said nothing until the hostess had left the table.

"I asked for this table because it's far from prying ears. No sense whispering our secrets to the world, is there?"

Sally let herself relax a little and glanced around, relieved to see that there wasn't a familiar face anywhere in the room. A waiter appeared, and she ordered a glass of wine, then turned her attention to Janelle Ransom.

"I suppose you must have thought I was crazy, calling you in the middle of the night," she began. Jan Ransom made a deprecating gesture.

"Don't be silly. All of us are like that at first. For a while I thought I was going crazy. I was calling people I hardly know and trying to explain what had happened to my little girl. I suppose I was really trying to explain it to myself." She fell silent as the waiter reappeared with Sally's drink. When he was gone again, she held up her glass. "To us," she proposed. "Lord knows, people who've been through what we've been through need to stick together." The two women sipped on their drinks for a moment and scanned the menu.

"Can I ask you something?" Jan asked after the waiter had taken their orders. "Why did you choose me to call? Did I say something the other night?"

Sally nodded. "I don't quite know how to start . . ." She faltered. Jan smiled at her encouragingly.

"Start any way you want, and don't worry about my feelings. One thing you learn after you lose a baby to SIDS is that there are times when you have to say everything you're feeling, no matter how awful it sounds, and hear everything people are saying, no matter how much it hurts."

Sally took a deep breath. "You said the other night that you hadn't wanted your baby—"

"Until she was born," Jan broke in. "Once she was born, I fell in love with her." A faraway look came into Jan's eyes and she smiled. "You should have seen her, Sally. She was the most beautiful baby you ever saw, even right after she was born. None of that wizened-monkey look. She was tiny, but I swear she came into the world laughing and never stopped. Until that day . . ." She trailed off and the smile disappeared from her face. When she spoke again, there was a hard edge of bitterness to her voice. "I still wonder, you know. I still wonder if it was something I did, or didn't do."

"I know," Sally whispered. "That's what's terrifying me too. I—well, I hadn't planned on having Julie either. Even my son was a couple of years ahead of schedule. Funny, isn't it? Some women want children desperately and can't have them. And then there are women like us, who do our best not to get pregnant, but nothing works."

"Forget the pill?" Jan asked.

Sally shook her head. "I'm allergic. I was using an IUD."

"So much more romantic, right? You know it's there, and nobody has to stop to install equipment. No worrying about whether you remembered to take the pill. Just a little tiny device and all the peace of mind in the world. And then you're pregnant."

"You had a coil too?"

"Uh-huh. It seemed like the best way. You know why? Religion. You want a laugh? I had it all figured out that with the IUD, I'd only be committing one sin, and I thought I could get away with that. The pill was going to be a sin a day, and even though I don't go to church, I knew I'd have a little twinge of guilt every time I took it. So I went into Dr. Wiseman's office one day, got my coil and my guilt, and went home and forgot about it."

Sally frowned. "Dr. Wiseman?" she repeated. "Arthur Wiseman?"

"Do you know him?"

"He's my doctor."

Jan Ransom chuckled hollowly. "Now what do you suppose the odds are on that? Two women, the same doctor, the same device, the same failure, and then SIDS."

Sally Montgomery did not share Jan's amusement. What, she wondered, *were* the odds? She began calculating in her head, but there were too many variables.

". . . and you have to go on living," she heard Jan saying.

"You sound like my mother."

"And like my own. Sally, it's hard to accept what's happened. No one knows that better than I do. But there's nothing else you can do. Nothing's going to bring Julie back and nothing's going to make you feel better. All you can do is try to let the wounds start to heal."

"But I can't do that," Sally said quietly. "I can't just go on as if nothing happened. Something did happen and I have to know what it was." She held up a hand as Jan started to say something. "And don't tell me it was SIDS. I won't accept that. It just doesn't make any sense."

"But that's just it, Sally. Don't you see? SIDS *doesn't* make sense—that's the awful part of it."

Sally sat silently, her eyes meeting Jan Ransom's. "Do you think I'm going crazy?" she asked at last.

Jan chewed on her lower lip a moment, then shook her head. "No. No more than I went crazy the first few months. Do what you have to do, Sally. In time it will all work out." Then she smiled ruefully. "You know something? I was hoping I might be able to help you today—help you cut some corners. But I can't, can I? All I can do is let you know that I understand what you're going through. You have to go through it yourself." She raised her glass.

"Good luck."

The clinic seemed oddly quiet as Sally walked down the green-walled corridor toward Arthur Wiseman's office, and the sound of her heels clicking on the tile floor echoed with an eerie hollowness. But it's not the clinic that seems empty, she decided as she turned the last corner. It's me. I don't know exactly what I'm doing here, so it seems strange. Strange and scary. Then she stepped into Dr. Wiseman's outer office. His nurse looked up at her, smiling uncertainly.

"Mrs. Montgomery? Did you have an appointment today?" She reached for her book.

"No," Sally reassured her. "I was just hoping maybe I could talk to the doctor for a couple of minutes. Would it be possible?"

The nurse turned her attention to the appointment book, then nodded. "I think we can just shoehorn you in." She grinned and winked conspiratorially. "In fact, it's an easy fit—I had a cancellation an hour ago, and the doctor was counting on an hour to himself. We just won't give it to him." She stood up, then, after tapping briefly on the closed door to the inner office, went in. A moment later she reappeared. "Go right in, Mrs. Montgomery."

Arthur Wiseman was waiting for her, his hand outstretched, his expression cordial. "Sally! What a pleasant surprise." The smile melted from his face to be replaced by a look of concern. "Nothing's wrong, is it?"

"I don't know," Sally said pensively, settling herself into the chair next to his desk. "I just wanted to ask you about a couple of things. I've been talking to some people, including Janelle Ransom."

Wiseman's brows rose a little. "Jan? How did you meet her?"

"The SIDS Foundation. Steve and I went to one of the meetings they sponsor."

"I see. And Jan was there?"

Sally nodded. "We had lunch today, and I discovered something that worries me. We were both using IUDs when we got pregnant."

"And?" Wiseman asked.

"And, well, I suppose it just seemed like too much of a coincidence that we were both using IUDs and both got pregnant and both lost our daughters to SIDS."

Wiseman sighed heavily and leaned back. Here it comes, he thought. When there is no easy explanation for a death, the family turns on the doctor. "Just what is it you think might have happened?"

"I don't know," Sally admitted. "It just occurred to me that perhaps the IUD might have . . . well . . ."

"Injured the fetus?" Wiseman asked. He leaned forward, folding his arms on the desk. "Sally, that's patently impossible. In order for you to have conceived, the IUD would have to have been flushed out of your system. And that, statistically, happens in two out of ten cases. I told you that right from the start, if you remember. Except for the pill, which you can't use, there's no foolproof method of birth control. And with an IUD, you never know when your body rejects it. It happened to you years ago, and you had Jason. Then, for eight years there was no problem. Maybe it was the new device we tried and our mistake was in trying a third kind a couple of years ago. But I'm not sure it would have mattered. You don't feel it when it's in, and you don't feel it when it's gone. But it absolutely couldn't have affected the fetus, that I can assure you. The similarities between your case and Jan Ransom's are simply coincidence. And not much of a coincidence, except for the fact that you both lost your babies to SIDS."

"Don't you think that's enough to make me wonder?" Sally asked.

"Of course it is," Wiseman said, relaxing back into his chair. "And of course you should have come to see me. But I'm not sure what I can do for you."

Sally's eyes moved to the CRT on Wiseman's desk. It was, she knew, a remote terminal of the computer that served most of the needs of the town. "Perhaps you could show me Julie's records," she suggested.

Wiseman hesitated, instinctively searching his mind for a valid excuse to deny Sally's request. There was none. "All right," he agreed at last. "But since she was Mark Malone's patient, I think he should be here too." He picked up the phone, spoke briefly, and then hung up.

"Do you really think we'll find anything in Julie's records?" he asked as they waited.

"I don't know," Sally said truthfully. "In fact, I'm not even sure I'll be able to understand them."

"Well, I can understand them," Wiseman assured her. A moment later the office door opened, and the pediatrician appeared. He greeted Sally, then looked questioningly toward Wiseman, who explained what Sally had proposed.

"Sounds like a good idea," Malone said, after quickly reviewing what he remembered of Julie's records. There was nothing, as far as he knew, that could upset Sally. He switched the computer terminal on and swiftly tapped in some instructions. Then he smiled encouragingly at Sally. "Come around here."

Sally went around the desk to stand close to Malone as the CRT screen began to fill up with the medical record of her daughter. Other than the birth data, there wasn't much: the results of the monthly examinations that Julie had been given, the last just two days before she died, all of which, Wiseman explained, reflected a picture of a remarkably healthy baby. Then there was the final report of her death, with a copy of the death certificate.

"I don't even know what I might be looking for," Sally said as she scanned the screen.

"You'd be looking for something wrong," Wiseman told her. "But according to this Julie wasn't damaged in any way, either before or after the birth." He looked to Mark Malone for confirmation, and the younger doctor nodded his agreement.

Sally pressed one of the cursor keys on the console, and the record began scrolling upward until the screen was filled with a series of letters and numbers that looked, to Sally's untrained eyes, like gibberish. "What's all this?" she asked.

Malone shrugged indifferently. "Test results. Analyses of blood samples, tissue samples, urine samples. All of it very routine and very normal."

"I see," Sally muttered. Then she frowned. As the data continued to roll up the screen, a number, set off by itself, suddenly appeared in the lower right-hand corner. Sally took her finger off the cursor key. "What's that?"

Wiseman stared at the number, frowned slightly, then looked up at Malone. "Do you know what this is?"

"It's just a code number," Malone replied. "It refers to a survey being done by a group in Boston, the Children's Health Institute for Latent Diseases."

"And they were surveying Julie?" Sally asked. "What for?"

Malone shrugged. "I don't really know. In fact, I doubt they're sure themselves."

"I don't understand." Sally moved back to her chair, and faced the two doctors. "This group—"

"It's called CHILD," Malone said.

"CHILD is studying children, but they don't know why?"

"It's what they call a random survey," Malone began. He started to explain it to Sally, but she held up a hand to stop him. She knew very well how such a survey operated. She had, indeed, designed several of them herself.

Basically, it involved the use of a table of random numbers to select a small fraction of a population that would accurately reflect the population as a whole. Sally herself had helped the Health Department design a survey of the population of Eastbury a few years back, to determine the incidence of swine flu in the town. It had boiled down to a matter of choices: either survey the entire town, or use a computer to assign everyone in town a number, then employ a table of random digits, itself devised by the computer, to choose a cross-section that would accurately reflect the whole.

To a layman, Sally knew, it sounded like hocus-pocus, but she also knew it was a statistically correct and absolutely accurate method of surveying a population for practically anything. And the beauty of it was that as the size of the population to be studied grew, the proportion of the population that actually would have to be surveyed grew smaller.

In Eastbury, for instance, only a few hundred people had needed to be surveyed in order to project the exact incidence of swine flu within the town.

"I know how studies like that work," Sally said. "But what's the study about?"

"As far as I know, it's just a general survey," Malone replied. "Apparently their computer constantly scans the records in our little computer—and a lot of others too—and randomly chose Julie for the survey. I think they were planning to track her right through her first twenty-one years."

"And you let them do that?" Sally asked. She was all too familiar with computers and their ability to pry into people's lives. "You let them simply invade your records? I thought medical records were supposed to be confidential."

"But they are," Wiseman told her as Malone glanced at him helplessly. "I'm sure the Institute assured us when we agreed to the survey that even they wouldn't know the names of the subjects. Otherwise we wouldn't have gone along with it." He glanced down at Julie Montgomery's records once more and smiled at Sally. "All they know about Julie is that child number nine-six-eight-two was a victim of SIDS, plus her medical data. They don't know her name, and they don't care about it. Studies like this go on all the time, Sally. You must know that. And you also must know that the computers make their selections, then are programed to forget the names of the subjects as soon as they've been assigned numbers."

"And you believe this?" Sally asked, her voice suddenly growing bitter. "How do you think they keep track of their subjects? If no one knows who belongs to what number, how are they going to keep up with their subjects? People move, you know. And someone has to put the data into a computer somewhere, along with the numbers, so that your Institute's computer can get it out again. My God, Julie's number—which you yourself just said is supposed to be confidential, is right there on her records for anybody to see!" Wiseman started to interrupt her, but Sally plunged on, her anger growing as she talked. "You're doctors, both of you, and I won't question your knowledge of medicine. But I'm a computer expert. I've been trained to use them, and I know what they can do. Do you? Do you know how easy it is for computers to talk to each other, to go through each other's files? Anybody in this country can find out anything about anybody else if he knows how to use a computer and can get the access codes. And if you're good enough with computers, you can program them to give you the codes that are supposed to hide the secrets." Sally was on her feet now, pacing the room. "Why wasn't I told about this survey?" she demanded. "I'm Julie's mother. If someone was watching my child, I had a right to know about it."

"Sally . . ." Malone began, but she ignored him.

"Maybe there *was* something wrong with Julie. Maybe they knew something was wrong with her!"

Now Wiseman, too, stood up. "Sally," he said firmly, "I want you to sit down and listen to me." Her eyes glazed with indignation, Sally stared at him and he thought she was going to bolt from his office. Then, as he and Malone watched, she forced her anger back and sank once more into the chair next to the desk.

"I'm sorry," she said. "It's just that I can't get over the feeling that something happened to Julie—something terrible."

Wiseman returned to his place behind the desk, but kept his eyes on Sally, searching her face carefully. He could see the signs of stress behind her makeup—the dark circles lurking beneath her eyes, the high color of her cheeks, the strain in the set of her mouth.

"Sally," he began, his baritone voice filling the room with its soothing tones. "I want you to understand something. There was nothing wrong with Julie. Nothing at all." He could see her body stiffen and knew she was resisting his words. He turned to Malone for assistance.

"It's true, Mrs. Montgomery," the pediatrician agreed. "There was nothing wrong with her, and there was nothing in her records—*anywhere*—that could lead anyone else to think anything was wrong with her."

Now Wiseman picked up the thread. "As for CHILD, they're a highly respected institution. They've contributed a great deal of knowledge to the field of medicine, particularly with regard to children. To think that there was anything"—he searched for the right word, and finally found it—"anything *menacing* about the fact that Julie was a subject of one of their surveys is simply beyond reason." Dr. Wiseman's voice dropped, and even through her anger Sally began to feel that he was patronizing her. "Now, what I'm going to do is this," he went on. "I'm going to give you their address, and I want you to go to them and find out for yourself just what the survey was all about, how Julie was selected for it, and what's being done with the data they're collecting. All right?"

Sally smiled at Wiseman, but the smile was cold. "Dr. Wiseman, did you really think I wouldn't do all that on my own?" She rose to her feet, picked up her bag, and went to the door. Then she turned back to face the two doctors. "Something happened to my daughter. I know you both think I'm a hysterical woman, and perhaps you're right. But I'm going to find out what happened to Julie. Believe me, I'm going to find out."

When she was gone, Arthur Wiseman switched off the CRT, then turned to Malone.

"I'm sorry," he said. "I wish none of this had had to happen, but with cases like this, you just can't avoid it."

Malone smiled at the older man. "It's all right, Arthur. Part of the job."

Wiseman nodded and returned to his desk. He picked up a medical journal, a clear signal for Malone to leave the office. But when he was alone, Arthur Wiseman's thoughts stayed on Sally Montgomery. Her adjustment to the loss of her daughter was not proceeding within the parameters that he considered normal. Sally, he was sure, was beginning to exhibit obsessive behavior, and if it continued, something would have to be done.

He turned the matter over in his mind, examining it from every angle. Finally, sighing heavily, he picked up the telephone and began to dial.

Sally moved swiftly down the corridor toward the entrance of the clinic, her emotions roiling. Wiseman's manner—his insufferable calm in the face of her tragedy and his patronizing attitude—infuriated her. It seemed to her that there was an arrogance about the man that she had never seen before.

Never seen, or chosen to ignore?

She emerged from the clinic and paused, letting the spring air flow over her, breathing deeply, as if the warm breeze could clear away the feeling of oppression that had come over her in Wiseman's office. She could still hear his voice, resonating in her mind, as he rambled on about "accepting reality," "going on with life," and all the other platitudes that, she suddenly realized, had been flowing from his lips for the last ten years.

From now on, she decided, she would be on her guard when she talked to Dr. Wiseman.

CHAPTER 14

Sally Montgomery glanced at the clock on the dashboard. It was a few minutes past three, and Eastbury Elementary was only a block out of her way. She made a left turn on Maple Street and pulled up in front of the school. Maybe she'd treat Jason to an ice cream cone on the way home. She waited in the car, still trying to calm the anger she was feeling from her talk with the two doctors.

And yet, as she thought about it, she realized that her anger really shouldn't be directed toward them. It was that group in Boston—CHILD—that was doing the snooping. And snooping, Sally was sure, was exactly what it was. That was the trouble with computer technology: It had turned the country into a nation of gossips. Everywhere you turned there was information stored away on tapes and disks and dots, much of it useless, most of it forgotten as soon as it was collected, but all of it stored away somewhere. And why? Sally, over the years, had come to the conclusion that all the data collecting had nothing to do with research. It was just plain old nosiness, and she had always half-resented it.

Only half, because Sally was also well aware that she was part of that snoop-culture, and while she had often questioned the uses to which computers were put, she had always been fascinated by the technology. But today, she realized, the chickens had come home to roost. That incredible ability to invade an individual's privacy had been turned on her own child.

In her head she began to speculate on how CHILD might have been planning to track Julie for twenty-one years. Just through hospital records? But what if Julie had grown up to be as healthy as Jason? There would have been no hospital records.

And then it came to her.

School records.

Sally got out of her car just as the school bell rang and children began to erupt from the building. She spotted Jason in the crowd, waved to him, and waited as he ran over to her.

"I thought I'd pick you up and take you out for an ice cream cone," she said. Jason grinned happily and scrambled into the car. Sally started back around to the driver's side, then changed her mind. "Wait here a minute," she told her son. "I have to talk to someone." Without waiting for Jason to reply, she walked purposefully into the school.

"Miss Oliphant?"

The nurse glanced up, trying to place the face. Not a member of the school staff, therefore a parent. She put on her best welcoming smile and stood up. "Guilty."

"I'm Sally Montgomery. Jason Montgomery's mother?"

"That explains why I didn't place you," Annie Oliphant replied. "I know the mothers only of the sick ones." Then the smile faded from her lips as she remembered what had happened to Jason's sister. "Oh, Mrs. Montgomery, I'm sorry. What a stupid thing for me to say. I can't tell you how sorry all of us were to hear about your baby."

"You know about Julie?" Sally asked, relieved that at least she wouldn't have to try to explain Julie's death to the nurse.

"Everyone in town knows. I wish there was something I could do. In fact, I wondered if I ought to talk to Jason about it, but then decided that I'd only be meddling. I've been keeping an eye on him though. He seems to be handling it very well. But, of course, he's a remarkable little boy anyway, isn't he?"

Sally nodded distractedly, wondering how to broach the subject she wanted to discuss with the nurse. "He's out in the car waiting for me," she said at last. "And since I was here, I thought I'd ask you a question."

"Anything," Annie said, sinking back down into her chair. "Anything at all."

"Well, it might be a dumb question," Sally went on. "It has to do with an organization in Boston, one that studies children—"

"You mean CHILD?" Annie interrupted, her brows arching in surprise.

"You *do* know of them?"

"Of course. They're surveying some of our students."

"Surveying them? How?" But even as Sally spoke, she answered her own question. "Through a computer, right?"

"You got it. Every few months they request an update. It's some kind of project that involves tracking certain children through a certain age—"

"Twenty-one," Sally interrupted.

"Oh, you know about the project. When I talked to Mrs. Corliss the other day, the whole thing seemed to come as a complete surprise to her. I'd always assumed the parents of the children knew all about the study, but Mrs. Corliss hadn't even known it existed." Then her expression clouded. "It's such a shame about Randy running away, isn't it?"

Sally's mind whirled as she tried to sort out what Annie Oliphant had just told her. She lowered herself onto the chair next to the nurse's desk and reached out to touch the other woman's arm.

"Miss Oliphant—"

"Call me Annie."

"Thank you. Annie, I just found out about this study today." She told the nurse what had happened that afternoon and how she had come to ask the question that had started the conversation. "But what you just said sounded as though I should have known about the survey all along."

Annie Oliphant frowned. "But I thought you *did* know," she said. "Jason's part of the survey too. Jason, and Randy Corliss, and two younger boys."

"I see," Sally breathed. Suddenly she felt numb. What was going on? And what had Annie just said about Randy Corliss?

"He seems to have run away," the nurse answered when Sally repeated her question out loud. "Except that his mother thinks he was kidnaped." She shook her head sympathetically. "I suppose she just can't accept the idea that her own child might have run away from her, and she's trying to find some other reason for the fact that he's gone. Some reason that takes the final responsibility off herself."

"I suppose so," Sally murmured as she rose from the chair. Her mind was still spinning, but at least she knew where to go next. "Thank you for talking to me, Annie. You've been very helpful." Then her gaze fell on the file folder that still contained Jason's health records. "Could I have a copy of that?"

Annie hesitated. She had already broken the rules by giving Lucy Corliss a copy of Randy's file, and she wasn't at all sure she wanted to repeat the offense. Still, the circumstances of the two mothers seemed to her to have certain parallels. She made up her mind and disappeared from the room for a few minutes. Finally she returned and handed Sally the Xerox copies of the file. "I don't see how I've helped you, but if I have, I'm glad," she said. She walked with Sally to the front door and watched as Sally hurried down the steps and went to her car. Then she returned to her office and stared at the file cabinet for a moment. She began straightening up her office, but as she worked, her mind kept going back to CHILD and the survey. How much information did they have? And what were they using it for? She didn't, she realized, have the faintest idea. All she really knew was that slowly, all over the country, banks of information were being built up about everybody. But what did it mean?

For one thing, no one would be able to disappear. No matter who you were, or where you went, anyone who really wanted to could find you. All they'd have to do would be to ask the computers.

Annie wasn't sure that was a good idea.

Sometimes people need to hide, and they should be able to.

For the first time, it occurred to Annie Oliphant that the whole idea of using computers to watch people was very frightening.

If there was a computer watching nine-year-old boys grow up, was there also, somewhere, a computer watching her?

While Jason Montgomery played in the tiny backyard, Sally and Lucy sat in Lucy's kitchen, sipping coffee and talking. The first moments had been difficult, as each of the women tried to apologize for not having offered her sympathy earlier, yet each of them understood the pain of the other.

For the last half-hour they had been discussing the survey their children were involved in.

"But what are they doing?" Sally asked yet again. "What are they looking for?"

Lucy shrugged helplessly. "I wish I could tell you, Sally. Maybe next week I'll be able to. I've got an appointment on Monday, and I won't leave until I know what that study is all about."

"Do you really think it has anything to do with Randy's disappearance?"

Lucy sighed. "I don't know anything anymore. But it's the only really odd thing I can come up with. Extra-healthy boys. They're studying extra-healthy boys; but how could they know which ones are going to be extra-healthy when they're babies? It doesn't make any sense."

"Maybe it does," Sally said thoughtfully. "Maybe they started out with a huge population and began narrowing it down as some of the subjects began showing the traits they were looking for. Maybe by the time the children get to be Randy's and Jason's ages, they've been able to focus on the population they're interested in."

"And maybe the moon is made out of green cheese," Lucy snapped. "Think about it, Sally. Annie Oliphant told you there are only four boys at the school involved in the survey and all of them are younger than Randy. According to your idea, there should be a lot of children being surveyed, at least in kindergarten and the first couple of grades. But there are only four. So there was something special about those four, and the Children's Health Institute for Latent Diseases knew about it."

"And what about Julie?" Sally asked, her voice quivering. "Was there something special about her too?"

Lucy reached across the table and squeezed Sally's hand. "Oh, Sally, I'm sorry. It's just that I'm trying to figure out what might be going on. And—and maybe there was something about Julie that nobody knows about."

"And maybe there wasn't," Sally replied. She stood up and began gathering her things together. "Maybe we're both a little bit crazy, Lucy. Maybe I'd better go home and do what everyone wants me to do—forget about Julie and go on with my life."

"And what about Jason?" Lucy countered. "Julie's dead, and Randy's missing, and Jason's part of that study too! What about him?"

Sally's eyes suddenly blazed. "What about him? What about *all* the other children in the survey? Apparently nothing's wrong with the others, at least not the ones here in Eastbury." And then, as she saw the hurt in Lucy's eyes, it was Sally's turn to apologize for her hasty words. "Lucy, forgive me. I didn't think—I just let loose. Of course I'm worried about Jason. Ever since Julie died, I've been worried sick about Jason. I'm edgy all the time, and I can't work, and half the time I think I'm losing my mind. But I don't know what to do next."

"Then don't do anything," Lucy said. "Don't do anything at all. Wait until Monday. I'll go to Boston, and I'll talk to the people at the Institute. Then we can decide what to do next. Okay?"

Silently, Sally nodded her head. A few minutes later, as she and Jason were on their way home, Sally found herself glancing over at her son.

Was there something about him that made him special?

Deep in her heart, she hoped not. All she really wanted for her little boy right then was for him to be just like all the other little boys.

Certainly, he *looked* just like other boys.

But was he?

* * *

For Steve and Sally Montgomery, the evening was like a play, with each of them trying, as best as possible, to pretend nothing was wrong between them, or within their home.

And yet the house itself seemed not to have recovered from the loss of its youngest occupant, and there was an emptiness to the rooms of which both Steve and Sally were acutely aware.

Steve tried to fill the void with three martinis, but even as he drank them, he knew it was useless. Instead of feeling the euphoria that ordinarily enveloped him with the second drink, he was becoming increasingly depressed. As he fixed the third drink, his back to his wife, he heard himself speaking.

"Aren't you making dinner tonight?" There was a cutting edge to his voice and, as the words floated in the atmosphere, he wished he could retrieve them. He turned to face Sally, an apology on his lips, but the damage had already been done.

"If you're in such a hurry, you might start fixing it yourself."

Jason, sprawled on the floor in front of the television, looked up at his parents, sensing the tension in the room. "Why don't we go out?" he suggested.

"Because money doesn't grow on trees," Steve snapped. As his son's chin began to tremble, he set his drink down, then knelt down to tousle Jason's hair. "I'm sorry, sport. I guess your mom and I are just feeling edgy."

Jason squirmed uncomfortably. "It's okay," he mumbled. A moment later he slipped out of the room and Sally heard him going upstairs. When the sound of his footsteps had disappeared, she turned to Steve.

"They're studying him too, you know," she said. "It wasn't just Julie. They're watching Jason too."

"Oh, Jesus," Steve groaned. He'd listened to Sally's recital of the day's events earlier. As far as he could see, none of it meant anything. It was all nothing more than coincidence. Why wouldn't she drop it? "For Christ's sake, honey, can't you leave it alone?" he demanded, but remorse at his own words immediately flooded over him.

It had been that way ever since the funeral. It was as if, with her burial, Julie had thrown him off balance, had somehow disturbed the symmetry of his life, drained away the joy he used to feel. Now he felt as though a stranger was living in his body, an angry, mournful stranger who had no way of dealing with the equally strange people around him. The only solution, he knew, was to forget about Julie, to forget that she had ever existed, and somehow to go back to the time before she had been conceived, when there had been only Sally and Jason and himself. If he could do that—if *they* could do that—then things would be all right again. They would be a family again.

But every day, every hour, something happened, or something was said, that reminded him of his little girl, and the scabs were ripped from his wounds and he began to hurt all over again.

And then he would lash out.

Lash out at Sally, lash out at Jason, lash out at anything or anyone that was available. The worst of it was that even though he understood what was happening to him, he could do nothing to stop it, nor could he bring himself to try to explain it to Sally.

He no longer knew what to do about Sally. He had thought that time would take care of her wounds, as he hoped time would take care of his own. But then, late this afternoon, he had had that call from Dr. Wiseman.

Wiseman was worried about Sally. His conversation had been filled with words and phrases of which Steve had only a vague understanding.

"Obsessive behavior."

"Paranoid tendencies."

"Neurotic compulsion."

All of it, Steve knew, boiled down to the fact that while he was trying to forget what had happened, his wife was refusing to face it. Instead, she was grasping at straws, looking for plots where there were no plots. And if it continued, according to Wiseman, Sally could wind up with serious mental problems.

Dinner, when it finally was on the table, was an unhappy affair, with Steve at one end of the table, Sally at the other, and Jason caught in the middle, understanding only that something had gone wrong—something connected with his sister's death—and his parents didn't seem to love each other anymore. He ate as fast as he could, then excused himself and went up to his room. When he was gone, Steve carefully folded his napkin and set it next to his plate.

"I think we have to talk," he said.

Sally, her lips still drawn into a tight line that reflected the anger she had been feeling since before dinner, glared at him. "Are you going to apologize for the way you spoke to Jason and me?"

"Yes, I am," Steve replied. He fell silent, trying to decide how to proceed. Finally, as the silence grew uncomfortable, he made himself begin. "Look, Sally, I know both of us are under terrible strain, and I know we both have to handle this in our own way. But I'm worried about you. Dr. Wiseman called today—"

"Did he?" Sally cut in. There was a coldness to her voice that Steve had never heard before. "Somehow, that doesn't surprise me," she said. "Did he tell you he thinks I'm a hysteric? He does, you know."

"Sally." Steve made his voice as soothing as he could. "He didn't say anything of the sort. He's worried about you, and so am I. We can't go on this way. We're tearing ourselves apart. Look at us. Barely speaking to each other, and when we do, it's not very pleasant. And what about Jason? We're hurting him too."

The words stung Sally, for she knew they were true. Yet she couldn't keep from thinking about Julie and what might have happened to her. She had to find out, had to know that whatever had happened to Julie had not been her own fault. If she couldn't do that, how could she go on living, go on being a mother to Jason? How could she ever know a moment's peace if the thought was ever-present in the back of her mind that she might have done something that killed her own baby. And yet, Jason was still there, and Steve, too, and she loved them both very deeply. For tonight, at least, she would put her problems out of her mind and take care of her family.

"You're right," she said out loud. "Steve, I'm sorry." She leaned back in her chair and toyed with her fork. "That sounds hollow, doesn't it? Our world is falling apart, and all I can do is say 'I'm sorry.' But what good does it do?" Without waiting for an answer, she stood up and started toward the stairs. "I'll go try to make up with Jason. Can you take care of the dishes?"

"Sure." As his wife disappeared from the dining room, Steve began clearing the table. At least, he decided, it was a beginning.

As she passed the door to the little room that had been Julie's, Sally steeled herself against the urge to open it, to look inside, knowing that the wish was futile, that it would not all turn out to have been a nightmare, that Julie would not be miraculously returned to her crib, breathing softly and steadily, gurgling in her sleep. She forced herself to walk steadfastly onward until she came to Jason's room. The door was slightly ajar.

There was no sound from within, and for a moment Sally felt an unreasonable sense of panic. Again she steeled herself, and she pushed the door open.

Jason was sitting at his little worktable, his chemistry set spread out in front of him, his face a study in concentration as he carefully poured a liquid from a plastic bottle into a test tube.

"Hi!" Sally said. "May I come in?"

Startled, Jason jerked his head upward, and the plastic bottle slipped from his hand. He grabbed at it, catching it just before the contents spilled into his lap. Some of the liquid splashed onto his hand, and he screamed in sudden pain.

Sally's eyes widened in fear as she watched her son rise up from his chair and stare at his hand. Already, it was beginning to turn an angry red. Then Sally came to her senses and rushed forward to pick the terrified boy up and carry him to the bathroom.

"What was it?" she asked as she turned the water on full force and held Jason's hand under the faucet.

"Acid," Jason stammered. "Muriatic acid. I was di—"

"Never mind what you were doing with it," Sally told him. "Let's get it off."

Through the rushing water she could see the blistering skin on Jason's hand. On his fingers the acid had already burned into the flesh.

"I've told you never to play with anything dangerous," she said. "Where'd you get muriatic acid?"

"At the pool store," Jason said placidly. The cool water had flushed the pain out of his hand, and he stared at it now with more curiosity than fear. "I was diluting it down. Why'd you have to come in like that?"

"I came in to see what you were doing, and it's a good thing I did." Sally shut off the water and examined the hand. Now, without the water running over the burn, it didn't look so bad. There were blisters, but apparently the skin wasn't broken after all. Still, burns were easily infected. "Come on, let's take this hand down to your father."

Steve, though, was on his way up the stairs. "What's going on? Did one of you scream?"

"It's your son," Sally said, falling back into that odd form of defense whereby the misbehaving child is ascribed solely to the other parent. "He was playing with acid, and it spilled on his hand."

"It was Mom's fault," Jason chimed in. "If she hadn't startled me . . ."

"Never mind that," Sally cut him off. "Steve, take a look at it. I flushed it with cold water, but it's blistered horribly. At first I thought it had gone right through his skin. Maybe we should take him to the hospital—"

But Steve was already examining the injured hand.

There were no blisters.

All he could see was a slight redness to Jason's skin, and even that seemed to be clearing up as he watched. The redness, he decided, was nothing more than a reaction to the cold water. He grinned at Jason encouragingly. "Does it hurt?"

Jason shook his head.

"Not at all?"

Again, Jason shook his head. "It stung a little, but as soon as Mom ran the water on it, it stopped."

Steve shifted his attention to Sally, who was staring at her son's hand. "You really want to take him to the hospital for this? Sally, there's nothing wrong with his hand."

But it was blistered, Sally thought. I *know* it was. Just two minutes ago it had looked horrible.

Or had it? Had she overreacted to the whole thing? Had her eyes and her emotions played tricks on her?

She felt Steve's eyes on her, and when she faced him she could read his thoughts as clearly as if he was speaking to her.

Are you crazy? he seemed to be asking. Is that what's happened? Have you gone crazy?

As she turned away and went up to her bedroom Sally realized that even if Steve had asked the question out loud, she would have had no answer.

Lucy Corliss pulled up to the building in which her ex-husband lived and let the engine idle for a moment before switching it off and getting out of the car.

She walked up the front steps of the building and pressed the buzzer next to Jim's name.

The apartment was on the second floor, in a corner of the building, and Jim was anxiously waiting for her at the door.

"Has something happened? Have you heard something?"

"Not really," Lucy said uncertainly as she stepped into the living room. She stopped just inside the room and stared. "For heaven's sake," she muttered. The room was small, but one side of it was dominated by a fireplace around which were a love seat and two wing chairs covered in the rust-brown material she had nearly selected for her own almost identical furniture. Between the chairs and the couch was a glass and brass coffee table, on which rested a sculpture that Lucy had never seen before, a bronze figure, obviously oriental, one leg raised, and the arms arched into the air.

"It's a Thai dancer," Jim told her. "I couldn't really afford it, but I decided I could live without two years worth of nights on the town, and I bought it."

"It's beautiful," Lucy breathed, moving closer to the statue and lowering herself onto one of the wing chairs.

"And you never thought I'd spend money on something like that?" Jim asked, his voice lilting with a half-taunting humor. "I'm afraid I gave up on Mediterranean furniture and decor by *Playboy* about the same time I moved out of Adultery Acres." He sat down on the sofa opposite her, and his expression turned serious. "Something *did* happen, didn't it?" he asked.

Lucy nodded, then told him about the visit she had had with Sally Montgomery that afternoon.

"And is that why you came over here?" Jim asked when she was done. "To see if I could figure out what's going on?"

"Not really," Lucy replied. "I'm putting all that on hold till Monday. There just isn't anything I can do right now. It seems like both of us have done everything we can, and—" Her voice broke, and she let herself sink into the softness of the chair. "I guess I'm just wearing out, Jim. And I almost didn't come over here. But I was lonely, and I was driving around, and suddenly the only person I could think of to talk to was you." She glanced at Jim sharply, hoping he wouldn't misunderstand her. "I mean, right now you and I have a lot in common, despite our differences."

"Maybe there aren't so many differences anymore," Jim suggested. Then, before Lucy could answer, he stood up. "Can I fix us some drinks?"

"Do you have any gin?"

"Tanqueray."

"With some tonic." As Jim disappeared into the kitchen, Lucy stood up and wandered around the room. In a bookcase against the wall opposite the fireplace she found several books she had read over the past few years and a series of framed pictures.

Mostly, they were of Randy.

Several of them were of herself, and all but one had been taken before the divorce. One of them, though, was recent.

"I see you found my gallery," Jim observed as he came back into the room.

"Where did you get this?" Lucy asked, picking up the picture. It had been taken two years earlier.

Jim blushed slightly. "I'm afraid I got sneaky. Randy told me you'd had a portrait made for his grandmother, and I called every studio in town till I found it." He paused for a moment. "I'm sorry about your mother. I always liked her, even though she never thought much of me."

Lucy smiled at him. "I think if she knew you now, she might change her mind."

The two of them stood still for a moment, and Lucy had a feeling Jim was going to kiss her. And then, as if he sensed her sudden unease, he moved away from her. "You doing anything for dinner?"

"I hadn't really thought about it," Lucy admitted. All day she'd been dreading the evening alone in the empty house. Then, after Sally had gone, she'd finally gotten into the car and driven aimlessly for nearly two hours, trying to decide where to go, until a little while ago, when she'd found herself a few blocks from Jim's apartment. "You want to go out somewhere?"

"Not really," Jim replied, his easy grin spreading over his face. "I still have to pay for the Thai dancer, and there's Randy's education to think of. So I've learned to cook. Feeling brave? I make a mean Stroganoff."

"Fine," Lucy decided. The idea of spending a quiet evening with Jim was suddenly very appealing. Then she said, "Jim? When you mentioned Randy's education just now, were you . . . Do you really think we're going to find him?"

Jim hesitated for a moment, forcing himself to maintain a cheerful façade. "Who knows? I know what Sergeant Bronski thinks, and I know what the statistics are, and I don't have any more of an idea than you do as to what to do next. So, I suppose, we should accept the fact that he's gone. But deep down inside I don't believe he ran away either. I believe in you, Lucy, and if you think someone took him, then someone took him. If you think he's alive, then he's alive. And if you think we'll find him, then we'll find him. So I guess I better not spend his college money yet, had I?"

Lucy felt her eyes tearing, and made no move to wipe the dampness away. Instead, she reached out and tentatively touched Jim's hand.

"Thank you," she whispered.

Their eyes met, and then suddenly Jim winked. "And on Monday, you get down to CHILD and find out what they did with our son. Okay?"

Silently, Lucy nodded.

CHAPTER 15

The glass-and-steel monolith that housed the offices of CHILD rose up out of the heart of the city like a great impersonal tombstone. The faceless people within it would continue their endless sojourn, year after year, until one day they would finally leave their offices and begin their "golden years," unaware they had spent most of their lives within a spiritual graveyard. As Lucy Corliss approached its expressionless façade on that unusually muggy spring morning, she felt as though she already knew what would happen inside.

Nothing.

The people at CHILD, she was sure, would be reflections of the building in which they worked—efficient, featureless, bland, and, in the end, impenetrable. Still, she had to try.

The elevator rose swiftly and silently to the thirty-second floor, and when its doors slid open, Lucy was confronted with a wide corridor stretching away in both directions. At the end of the hall was a pair of imposing double doors. Behind those doors lay the CHILD offices. Steeling herself, Lucy opened the doors and slipped into a mahogany-paneled reception room containing a small sitting area—empty—and a desk behind which sat a cool blonde who appeared to be cut from the same die as morning talk-show hostesses. Lucy approached the desk, but the receptionist, talking softly on the telephone, held up her hand as if forbidding Lucy to get too close. A moment later she hung up the phone and turned on her smile.

"May I help you?"

"I'd like to see Mr. Randolph. Paul Randolph?"

The receptionist, who neither wore a name badge nor had a nameplate propped helpfully on her desk, looked doubtful.

"I'm afraid Mr. Randolph is very busy."

"I have an appointment," Lucy said firmly.

The receptionist frowned. "With Mr. Randolph?"

"That's right," Lucy replied, her original sense of intimidation turning rapidly to irritation. "My name is Lucy Corliss. If you'll just tell me where his office is—" But the receptionist was already on the phone, talking softly to someone hidden in the depths of the offices. Then she was back to Lucy, smiling brightly.

"If you'll just take a seat, Mrs. Corliss? It'll just be a minute, and I'll be happy to get you some coffee while you wait."

But Lucy didn't want coffee. She simply wanted to sit for a minute and savor her tiny victory over the cool blonde. The blonde, however, saw fit to ignore her.

A moment later a much older woman strode into the reception room and offered Lucy her hand.

"I'm Eva Phillips, Paul Randolph's secretary. We're so sorry to keep you waiting, but you know how things can be."

She ushered Lucy through the offices, chattering amiably all the way, and finally showed her into a large corner office dominated by an enormous desk. Behind the desk sat a man who was obviously Paul Randolph.

He was in his indeterminate forties, his face smooth and handsome in a bland sort of way. His sandy hair was thinning, and, to his credit, he made no attempt to hide that fact. He rose to greet Lucy, and as he came around the end of his desk, he moved with a lithe grace that Lucy had always associated with old money, private schools, and summers on the Cape. When he spoke, his voice was perfectly modulated, his accent pure Brahmin.

"Mrs. Corliss, how nice to meet you. Won't you sit down?" He indicated a sofa that sat at right angles to his desk, and without thinking about it, Lucy seated herself where Randolph intended her to sit. He himself took a chair that was substantially firmer than the sofa, and Lucy, not quite understanding the psychological ploy, suddenly felt that she was somehow at a disadvantage. From his slightly higher position, Paul Randolph smiled cordially down at her. "Would you like coffee?"

"No, thank you," Lucy replied. With a quick gesture, Randolph dismissed Eva Phillips, who silently closed the door as she left the room.

"Now, what can I do for you?" Randolph asked. "May I assume you've become interested in our work?"

My God, Lucy thought, he thinks I want to donate money. "Yes, I have," she said. "You see, I just found out a few days ago that your people have been studying my son."

The smile on Randolph's face stayed firmly in place, but something in his eyes changed, and Lucy immediately realized that the man was suddenly on guard. When he spoke, however, his voice was as mellow as before.

"I see. Of course, we study thousands of children here. And I must say," he added with a touch of a chuckle, "this is the first time one of the children's parents has come to see me."

"Mr. Randolph, my son has been kidnaped."

Finally, the smile faded from the man's lips. "I beg your pardon, Mrs. Corliss?"

"I said my son has been kidnaped. At least that's what I think happened to him. The police . . ." She faltered for a moment, then, in a rush, poured out the whole story of the last few days. When she was done, Randolph sat silently, his eyes clouded with concern, his hands clasped together.

"But what brought you here, Mrs. Corliss? Surely you don't think that we could have had anything to do with your son's disappearance?"

Lucy hesitated. Put so bluntly, in surroundings as eminently respectable as those of CHILD, it sounded unthinkable. And yet, that was exactly what she thought.

"I don't know," Lucy hedged, sure that if she told him the truth he would show her the door. "I don't know what to think. But when I found the notation in Randy's medical files and learned that he'd been part of a project I knew nothing about, well, naturally I began to wonder."

Randolph's head bobbed understandingly. His smile returned. "So you want to know what we're doing, is that it?"

"Exactly."

Randolph rose and began to pace the room. "Well, I'll do my best, but I have to tell you that I'm not even sure I understand it all myself. I'm afraid I'm an administrator, not a scientist."

"Then you'll use language I can understand."

"I'll try. To begin with, the work we're doing here is what you might call passive work, as opposed to active work. We conduct surveys and put together statistics, primarily concerning genetics."

"I'm not sure I do understand."

Randolph lowered himself into the chair behind his desk and leaned back, folding his hands across his stomach. "All right, let's go back to the beginning. Are you aware that almost all babies, at birth or even before, go through a process of genetic screening?"

"Sort of." Lucy was beginning to feel that she was going to get lost right at the start. But Randolph smiled at her encouragingly.

"It's really not terribly complicated. Samples of the baby's tissue are taken, and the chromosomes are analyzed. We can often discover genetic weaknesses that, if left uncorrected, can lead to various problems, the most obvious, but not the least of which, is Down's syndrome."

Lucy held up a protesting hand. "I'm sorry, but you're losing me," she said.

Randolph tried again. "All right. The chromosomes, or genes, act as a pattern for the cells. They dictate what chemicals the cells will produce, and, therefore, determine the cell's shape, function, and purpose. Over the years, we've discovered that certain genetic deficiencies cause chemical imbalances that, in turn, cause certain mental or physical problems later on in life."

"And what, exactly, does CHILD do?"

"It's very simple, really. All we do is track certain children, from the time of birth through adulthood. We keep track of their genetic records and then simply observe them. For instance, let's suppose that there are two children who, at the age of, say, ten or eleven, begin to develop symptoms of mental illness. Say, also, that there are no environmental similarities between the children. But say, even further, that when we go through our records, we discover that both children share a specific genetic abnormality. Bingo! It would appear that the particular disorder displayed by the two children may have its roots in genetics."

Lucy shook her head. "It sounds too simple."

"Yes," Randolph agreed. "But even granted the over-simplification, that's basically what we do. In the long run, of course, the idea is to determine which genetic deficiencies are benign and which ones are going to cause problems to the child later. It's up to other researchers to try to figure out ways of correcting or compensating for the deficiencies and abnormalities."

"And that's all you do?" Lucy asked.

"That's all we do," Randolph assured her.

"Then why wasn't I told you were studying Randy?"

"Perhaps you were and don't remember it," Randolph suggested.

"Where my son is concerned, I wouldn't have forgotten," Lucy shot back. "I would have wanted to know exactly what the study was about, what would be required from Randy, and how he had been chosen."

"But that's just the point, Mrs. Corliss." Randolph's voice was gentle and soothing. "The study was no more than a survey, it required nothing from

Randy, and he was chosen at random. It was purely a matter of chance that Randy was selected for our study."

"Then you won't mind showing me the results of the study, will you?"

"Results? But, Mrs. Corliss, there aren't any results yet. The survey will go on until the children are all grown up."

"But what about the ones who don't grow up?" Lucy asked. "What about the ones who die in infancy, or get sick, or are victims of accidents? Surely you must have *some* results? If you don't, I should think you'd have given the whole thing up by now."

For the first time, Randolph seemed at a loss for words. Lucy decided to press her advantage. "Mr. Randolph, the nurse at Randy's school says that of all the children in the school, Randy and the three others you're studying have the best health records. Randy's never been sick a day in his life, never hurt himself badly, never shown any signs of being slow, or abnormal, or anything else. Now, doesn't it seem reasonable that if I discover someone has been studying him, I might also wonder just *why* they were studying him? And if Randy is remarkable—and he is—doesn't it seem reasonable that I might begin to think the people who are studying him might want a closer look?"

The color had drained from Randolph's face, and his smile had settled into a tight line of anger. "Mrs. Corliss, are you suggesting that CHILD kidnaped your son?"

"I don't know, Mr. Randolph," Lucy replied coldly. "But I know it would do a great deal toward setting my mind at rest if you would show me the study Randy was involved in, together with any results that have come from that study. I don't pretend that I'll understand it, but I'll be able to find someone who will. And although I can't be sure of it right now, I suspect that what you've been doing without my consent, and without Randy's consent, amounts to invasion of privacy."

Randolph sank back into his chair. His right hand brushed distractedly at his hair. "Mrs. Corliss, I'm not sure what I can do for you," he said at last. "But of course, I'll do my best. It will take a little time to find out exactly which of our surveys Randy was involved in and put together a report for you. Believe me, we'll do it. Nothing like this has ever happened before, and CHILD has been functioning for nearly twenty years. But I can tell you right now that we had nothing to do with the disappearance of your son."

"How long will it take?" Lucy asked.

"A couple of days."

Lucy stood up. "Then I'll expect to hear from you, Mr. Randolph. Day after tomorrow?"

"I'll call you, Mrs. Corliss. If you'll just leave your address with my secretary . . ."

Lucy smiled icily. "I'll do that, Mr. Randolph, but I can't imagine it's necessary. I'm sure that somewhere in your files you already have my address."

She picked up her purse, and without offering Randolph her hand, left his office.

When she was gone, Paul Randolph sat down heavily at his desk. Sweat had broken out on his brow.

What he had always feared was starting to happen.

Randy Corliss was spending the afternoon playing a game he still didn't quite understand. It was sort of like hide-and-seek, and sort of like tag, but there was something else involved, and Randy wasn't quite sure he liked it.

The game had started simply enough.

One of the boys was 'it,' and he had to count to a hundred while the other boys scattered and hid. Then the boy who was 'it' began hunting for his friends. When he spotted one of them, he yelled the boy's name, and began chasing him, trying to tag him. If he succeeded, that boy became 'it.'

The catch was that once the boy who was 'it' had named his prey, the other boys could come out of hiding to help the prey.

Suddenly, whoever was 'it' was transformed from hunter to victim.

Randy had made his first mistake right at the start. When the counting had begun, he had run off by himself while the rest of the pack stuck together. He had found a hiding place deep in the woods, near the creek. He waited, sure that he wouldn't be found, listening for a name to be called out, at which point it would be safe to emerge.

The minutes had passed interminably, and Randy tried to figure out what was going on. Finally, he rose from his hiding place only to find that Adam Rogers, who was 'it,' was standing only a few yards away.

"Randy!" Adam screamed and the chase was on.

And that was when Randy realized his mistake. The other boys, all together, were too far away to help him. Within a few seconds Adam had slammed him to the ground, crowing at having won a victory in the first round.

And now Randy was 'it.'

He counted through to a hundred as fast as he could, then looked up.

No one was in sight.

He moved away from the base point next to the main house and started across the lawn, his eyes searching the woods for a sign of his friends.

Nothing.

He moved into the woods, searching carefully, knowing that he would have to find one of the boys alone if he was going to have a chance at winning.

He caught a glimpse of Adam and started to shout his name, but then saw one of the other boys, Jerry Preston, peeking out from behind a tree only a few feet away. Pretending not to see either of them, Randy moved deeper into the woods.

He stopped every few seconds, listening, sure that all the other boys were following him, yet unable to hear them.

Then, ahead of him, he saw Eric Carter, his red hair giving him away, crouched in a clump of laurel near the fence. He moved closer, trying to pretend he hadn't seen Eric.

He looked around, searching the woods behind him for the others. There was silence.

When he judged he was close enough, he suddenly let out a scream.

"ERIC CARTER!"

He hurtled himself forward as Eric exploded out of the laurel and began to run parallel to the fence. For a second Eric seemed to be outdistancing him, but then Randy began to gain. He had almost caught up with his prey, when three boys suddenly burst out of the forest, one of them slightly ahead of him, one next to him, and the other just behind him.

Once again, Randy had fallen into a trap.

He turned to face Adam, who was the closest to him, but Adam suddenly paused, and Randy felt a blow from behind. He stumbled, then fell to the ground as Billy Mayhew and Jerry piled onto him. In the distance, Eric Carter had stopped running and was now watching the fracas, his face wreathed in a smile.

Randy fought as hard as he could, his arms and legs flailing, but it did no good.

"Throw him into the fence," Jerry suggested. "That'll finish him off."

Suddenly the boys were off him, but Adam was holding him firmly by the shoulders as Billy and Jerry each grabbed one of his legs.

"On three," Adam yelled. The boys began swinging Randy, with Adam counting off the cadence.

On three they let go and hurled Randy into the fence.

There was a shower of sparks, and the air was suddenly filled with the odor of burning flesh.

Randy fell to the ground.

The game was over, and the boys gathered around Randy, staring at him curiously. Adam Rogers glanced at Billy Mayhew.

"Do you suppose we'll get in trouble?"

Billy shrugged. "We didn't last time. Why should we this time?"

Then, chattering among themselves, the boys started back through the woods toward the Academy, leaving Randy lying on the ground next to the electrified fence.

* * *

Sally Montgomery had spent much of the weekend in her office at Eastbury College. What she was doing, she knew, was probably illegal. It was definitely unethical, but she had wasted no time at all worrying about that. Instead, she had devoted all her time to discovering the access codes that would allow her to tap into the Eastbury Community Hospital records that were stored in the county's computer. It was, like most programing, a matter of trial and error. For anyone without Sally's background, it would have been nearly impossible; for Sally, it was simply a matter of knowing how the codes were constructed, then having the computer begin trying all the possibilities within the framework. The code, when she finally found it, turned out to be ridiculously obvious:

M-E-D-R-E-A-C-H. *MED*ical *R*ecords, *EA*stbury *C*ommunity *H*ospital? Probably. Indeed, when she finally found the code, it had occurred to her that in an age of acronyms, she ought to have been able to figure it out without the aid of the computer.

Now, on Monday morning, she was tapping into the records, attempting to find out whether or not the children that CHILD was surveying had truly been selected through random sampling.

She began by instructing the computer to search the records and put together certain populations.

Children who were being surveyed by the Children's Health Institute for Latent Diseases.

Children who had been victims of SIDS.

Children whose records reflected no health problems.

She went back twenty years. Without the computer it would have taken months simply to compile the data.

Now, after only two hours of work, Sally had begun to see a pattern emerge.

The computer had constructed the populations Sally had asked for and begun comparing them.

Until ten years ago there had been no discernible differences between the children who were being studied by CHILD and the entire population of juvenile patients for the entire county.

The same percentage of each population had come down, at one time or another, with such diseases as mumps, measles, and chicken pox.

The same proportion of each group had displayed a similar incidence of emotional problems.

The same proportion of each group had fallen victim to SIDS.

On and on, it had been the same. As far as Sally could see, the CHILD surveys had involved a genuinely random sampling of all the children born at Eastbury Community Hospital.

And then, ten years ago, things began to change.

The incidence of sudden infant death syndrome seemed to have increased among children in Eastbury, particularly among those born at Eastbury Community Hospital.

In itself, Sally knew that such a fact could be statistically meaningless.

What *was* meaningful was that among the entire population of children in Eastbury, SIDS had increased by four percent.

Among the population being surveyed by CHILD, SIDS had increased by nearly ten percent.

Furthermore, the composition of the group of children struck down by SIDS had changed. For the first ten years, the syndrome had appeared with equal frequency in boys and girls. But ten years ago, the statistics began to skew, and baby girls became more frequent victims of the syndrome than baby boys. And among the population of children being surveyed by CHILD, an even higher ratio of girls to boys had died from SIDS.

Sally printed out the lists of populations, and the strange correlations between the two. Then she turned her attention to the other group she was looking at, the population of children whose medical records were remarkable for the excellent health they reflected. Here, Sally ran into a problem. Over the years, too many children had simply moved away from Eastbury, and their records had come to an abrupt end, to be continued in other areas of the country. Areas to which Sally had no easy access.

Still, she thought there was a pattern. It appeared, even from the sketchy records, that over the last ten years, the proportion of remarkably healthy little boys on the CHILD lists had risen.

Again, Sally Montgomery printed out the statistics.

Toward noon Sally asked the computer to complete one more task.

Given all the data in the records, she requested the computer to come to a determination as to whether or not the subjects of the CHILD surveys had, over the last ten years, been chosen on a truly random basis.

The minutes crept by as the computer began digesting all the material stored away in its data banks. At last the screen on Sally's console came to life.

The computer's answer brought tears to Sally's eyes. Through the blur, she read the computer's final summation one more time.

"Insufficient data to make determination."

Sally switched off her terminal, gathered up all the printouts her morning's work had produced, and left her office.

All her work, according to the computer, meant nothing. And yet she was sure that the computer was wrong. Then, as she thought about it, she came to the slow realization that the computer had not said the CHILD surveys weren't random. It had simply refused to take a stand on the question.

That was the problem with computers. They were too objective. Indeed, they were totally objective.

But CHILD, Sally was convinced, was *not* totally objective. The survey, she was sure, was a cover for something else.

A conspiracy.

But would she be able to prove it?

She didn't know.

All she knew was that the more she learned, the more frightened she became.

CHAPTER 16

Steve Montgomery paused on the front porch of his mother-in-law's house, wondering if he'd been right in his decision to share his problems with Phyllis Paine. When the idea of talking to her about Sally had first occurred to him, he'd immediately rejected it. But then, this morning, he'd changed his mind. After all, who knew Sally as well as her own mother?

He pressed the button next to the front door and listened to the soft melody of the chimes. When there was no answer, he pressed the bell again. Then, just as he was about to turn away, the door opened, and Phyllis, her eyes rimmed in red, and her face suddenly showing her years, gazed out at him.

"Steve." Her eyes darted around as she looked for Sally, then her brows furrowed in puzzlement. "Isn't Sally with you?"

"No." Offering no further explanation, Steve asked if he could come in, and Phyllis suddenly stepped back.

"Of course. I'm sorry, Steve. I—well, I'm afraid I haven't been having a very good day."

Steve paused. "Maybe I should come back another time."

"No, no." She closed the door, and led Steve into the parlor. "I was just getting rid of some things." Sighing tiredly, she seated herself on the edge of the sofa. "Some dresses I was making for Julie," she went on. "They were in the sewing room, all cut, and I've been waking up every night, feeling guilty about not having finished them." Her lips twisted into a desolate smile. "You know me—once I start something, I have to finish it. Anyway, I've been waking up in the middle of the night and going to the sewing room to finish the dresses, and it isn't until I start working on them that I remember . . . what happened. So just now I threw them away. I took them out to the garbage can and threw them away."

Her eyes, reflecting an uncertainty that Steve had never seen before, searched his face. "It seemed like a terrible thing to do," she whispered. "And yet, I couldn't think of anything else. It was a symbol, I suppose. A way of forcing myself to face up to what's happened." Suddenly she straightened up and folded her hands in her lap. "But that's not why you're here, is it?" The uncertainty in her eyes disappeared, to be replaced by the penetrating sharpness Steve was used to. "It's Sally, isn't it?"

Steve shifted uncomfortably, then nodded his head.

"Things aren't going well, are they? I mean, even considering the circumstances?"

"No," Steve said quietly. "And I'm beginning to wonder what to do."

Phyllis's brows rose. "About Sally?"

"Dr. Wiseman called me on Friday. He's worried about her—he seems to think she's avoiding facing up to the fact that Julie's death can't be explained by trying to prove that something else happened. Something more reasonable."

"I see," Phyllis said. "And what do you think?"

"I don't know what to think. I barely saw her over the weekend. When she wasn't at her office, she was holed up in the den, and she wouldn't tell me what she was working on. But I'm sure it had something to do with"—he faltered, then plunged on—"with Julie. And she's been talking to Lucy Corliss."

"Lucy Corliss? Why does that name—oh! The mother of that little boy who's missing. What's his name?"

"Randy. He was a friend of Jason's. But that's not what she was talking to Mrs. Corliss about, at least not directly. It seems that Jason and Randy as well as Julie were being studied by some group in Boston."

Phyllis's brows arched skeptically. "What's unusual about that? These days it seems as if someone's studying all of us all the time." Then her expression changed. "Oh, God, she hasn't come up with some sort of conspiracy theory, has she?"

"Well, I wouldn't want to go—"

"*Has* she?"

"I'm afraid so," Steve replied, his shoulders sagging.

Phyllis shook her head sadly. "Have you talked to Arthur about it?" she asked.

"No. I wanted to talk to you first. I guess I was afraid Dr. Wiseman might see what Sally's doing as some sort of—what? Neurotic behavior?" He groaned. "Oh, Christ, Phyllis, I can hardly believe we're having this conversation."

"And yet we are," Phyllis replied firmly. "And since we are, the question is, what are we to do about it? Do you want me to talk to Arthur?"

"Would you?"

Now it was Phyllis's turn to sigh. "I suppose so. I have to talk to him anyway. I'm afraid I was quite rude to him at the funeral, and I had no right to be. I owe him an apology. I'll drop by the clinic this afternoon."

"I'd appreciate it," Steve told her. "I know how you hate getting—"

Phyllis waved his words away. "Don't be silly. You know I try not to interfere, but I'm still Sally's mother, and I still worry, even though I try not to show it." Her expression changed slightly, and her eyes fell appraisingly upon Steve. "What about you? Are you all right? You look terrible."

"I'm holding myself together."

"See that you continue to," Phyllis said. She rose to escort her son-in-law to the door. "You're a man, Steve, and Sally's going to have to count on you." Her voice dropped, as if she were about to impart a secret. "I've never thought Sally was as stable as she appears to be, you know. It's always seemed to me there were tensions in Sally, and under the wrong circumstances—" She suddenly fell silent, and as he left her house, Steve knew she thought she'd said too much.

"Want some more coffee?" Sally asked.

Lucy Corliss shook her head. "What I really want is a drink, but I'll be damned if I'll have one this early in the day." The clock read three twenty, and she had been sitting at Sally's kitchen table for nearly two hours. She fingered the stack of computer printouts, then leaned back and folded her arms across her chest. "So all this might mean something, or it might not," she said. Sally had already explained the meaning of the computer's evaluation of its own work.

"It does," Sally insisted. "I'm sure it does. It's just that the damned computer can't prove it."

"So we're nowhere," Lucy said. "It looks like something is going on, but we can't prove it. And you can bet I'll get nothing out of Randolph. God, how I hate those smooth bastards."

"But he said he'd have *something* for you?"

"Oh, sure. But you can bet that whatever it is, it won't be the truth. If there was no secret about what they're doing, why wouldn't they have let us know they were studying our children? And they didn't," Lucy added bitterly. "I'm one of those people who keeps everything. I even have laundry receipts from Randy's diaper service. They're getting yellow, but I have them. Anyway, I went over everything—everything! There's nothing about a survey, no forms, no requests for permission, nothing! And you know what, Sally? The more I think about it, the angrier I get. Even if it has nothing to do with Randy's disappearing, the whole idea just gets to me. I mean, if they've been watching Randy and Jason, and even Julie, what about us? Are we all being watched? Don't any of us have any privacy anymore? It's scary!"

"It's the new age," Sally said quietly. "I don't think there's anything any of us can do but get used to it. But what about all these?" she asked, gesturing toward the printouts. "We've *got* to do something about this."

Suddenly Lucy had an idea. "Could I have them?" she asked.

Sally frowned. "What for?"

"I want to show them to someone," Lucy replied. Sally started to ask another question, but Lucy held up her hand. "Just trust me," she said. "I might wind up looking like a fool, but there's no reason why you should too."

The back door slammed open, and Jason appeared. "Hi, Mom," he called. "I'm—" Then he saw Lucy, and his words died on his lips. "Hi, Mrs. Corliss," he went on. Suddenly he looked hopeful. "Is Randy back?"

Lucy had to fight to control the tears that came into her eyes at Jason's words, but she made herself smile. "Not yet," she told him, "but I'm sure it won't be long now. Do you miss him?"

Jason nodded solemnly. "He's my best friend. I hope nothing happened to him."

Lucy stood up abruptly, picked up the printouts, and started toward the door. "I'll take good care of these, Sally," she promised. Then, before either Sally or Jason could say anything more, she was gone. Sally, still seated at the kitchen table, held her arms out to her son.

"Come here," she said softly, and Jason, though unsure what his mother wanted, let himself be hugged. "I love you," Sally whispered. "I love you so much."

Jason, wriggling in her arms, suddenly looked up and grinned. "Enough to let me make fudge?" he asked.

For some reason, the devilish look on her son's face broke the tension Sally had been living under for over a week, and she began laughing.

"Sure," she said, releasing Jason and standing up. "In fact, making fudge seems like the best idea I've heard all day!"

* * *

Jason watched as Sally mixed together the milk, sugar, and chocolate, added a dash of salt, and put the pan on the stove.

"Want me to check the thermometer?" he asked.

"You can if you want," Sally said with a shrug. "But it's never been off yet, has it?"

"No," Jason agreed, "but my chemistry book says you should always check your equipment before you start an experiment."

"When you're as old as I am, making fudge isn't an experiment anymore."

Jason filled a pan with water, put the long candy thermometer into it, and set it on a vacant burner. Then he turned the heat on, and while he waited for the water to boil, fished a bottle of pop out of the refrigerator. Sally glared at him.

"Drink that, and you won't get to scrape out the pan," she warned.

Jason glanced at the stove where the fudge was just barely beginning to heat, then at the bottle in his hand, which was all ready to be drunk. "Aw, Mom," he muttered.

"Make up your mind."

Reluctantly, Jason put the pop back in the refrigerator. "Dad would have let me drink it," he complained as he went back to check on his pan of water. It was beginning to simmer, and he climbed up on the kitchen stool to watch the thermometer.

It read 200 degrees, but even as he watched it, he could see the mercury climbing. He shifted his attention to the fudge. It, too, was beginning to boil.

"The thermometer'll be ready in a minute."

Sally was buttering a pan. She glanced up, smiling at the intensity with which Jason watched the thermometer.

"When it gets to two-twelve, let it sit a minute. If it doesn't go up any farther, it's reading right. Then you can move it over to the candy pan. But *don't* stir the candy!"

"I know," Jason said, his voice filled with scorn. "If you stir it, it crystallizes. Anybody knows that."

"You didn't till I taught you," Sally teased. She began chopping up some walnuts, but kept an eye on Jason when, a few moments later, he moved the thermometer from the boiling water into the candy. "Now, don't let the candy go above two-thirty-four."

Jason, his eyes glued to the steadily creeping mercury, ignored her.

He watched as the temperature reached 230 degrees, then 232. He was about to get down from the stool, ready to pick up the pan as soon as it rose two more degrees, when suddenly the temperature seemed to spurt.

As the red column in the thermometer started past 234, he picked up the pan and groped with his left foot for the step that should have been there.

It wasn't.

Startled, he tried to set the pan back on the stove, but it was too late. His balance was gone, and he tumbled to the floor, the pan of boiling fudge still clutched in his right hand. His scream of fright made Sally look up just in time to see the searing liquid gush over Jason's arm and spread out on the floor.

Sally forced back the scream that boiled up from her own throat. She dropped her knife as she scooped Jason up from the floor and instinctively moved him toward the sink. Then she began running cold water while she held his arm under the tap.

As the brown mess washed away, she saw the blistering skin underneath.

Jason, strangely still, stared at his arm.

"Why doesn't it hurt?" he asked. Then, again, "Why doesn't it hurt?"

Pausing only to snatch her car keys from the table and wrap his arm in a towel, Sally rushed Jason out the back door. A moment later she was on her way to the hospital.

Last time, she had been too late, and her daughter had died.

This time she would not be too late.

Jason was her only child now; she would allow nothing to happen to him.

As Jason sat silently beside her, his arm swathed in a kitchen towel, she sped through the streets of Eastbury.

Arthur Wiseman was walking Phyllis Paine out to her car. They had talked for nearly an hour, but reached no conclusions. All that had been decided was that for the next few weeks they would keep a careful eye on Sally. And then, as they passed the emergency room, they heard her voice.

"But I *saw* it, Dr. Malone," she was saying, her voice strident, and her face flushed with anger. "I tell you, I *saw* the blisters. Don't tell me he's all right! He's *not* all right. He's burned! Don't you understand?"

"Who?" Phyllis demanded. Sally whirled around, staring at her mother in surprise. "Who's burned?" Phyllis repeated.

"Mother, what are you doing here?"

"Never mind that," Phyllis replied. "Has something happened to Jason?"

Sally's eyes brimmed with tears and she nodded. "We were making fudge. He—he slipped, and the fudge poured out all over his arm." Suddenly she was sobbing, and Phyllis gathered her into her arms. "Oh, Mother, it was horrible. And it was my fault. I should have been doing it myself."

"Hush, child," Phyllis crooned. Her eyes shifted to Mark Malone, who stood to one side, slowly shaking his head. "How bad is it, Doctor?"

Malone shrugged. "Not that bad at all, Mrs. Paine. In fact, it really doesn't look like anything."

Phyllis Paine's expression hardened, and a scowl formed on her brow.

"Now see here, young man. If that pan of fudge was boiling, the boy must have been hurt. Where is he?"

Malone nodded toward a small treatment room. Phyllis helped Sally into a chair, then strode toward the door. Inside the little room she found Jason, stripped to the waist, sitting on a table.

"Hi, Grandma," he said, grinning at her. "Wanna see my arm?"

He offered his right arm for her inspection. Phyllis bent over it, examining it carefully. "Well, it doesn't look like much, does it?"

Jason shook his head. "And it hardly hurt at all," he announced proudly. "But it was real hot, Grandma. The thermometer read two hundred and thirty-four. That's what they call the soft-ball stage. It means that if you drop the fudge in cold water—"

"I know what it means," Phyllis said severely. "And I also know what heat like that does to little boys like you. You stay right where you are, young man." She let go of his arm and returned to the waiting area. Sally, blotting at her eyes with a Kleenex, looked up at her anxiously. "It certainly doesn't look like much," Phyllis said.

Sally's face crumpled. "But it was blistered," she whispered, almost to herself. "I saw it, and it was blistered."

Over Sally's head, Phyllis's eyes met Malone's. "It seems to me there must be some confusion," she said. "Apparently it was my grandson who was watching the thermometer, and he must have misread it. It was probably only *one* hundred and thirty-four."

Slowly, Sally's head came up, and she stared at her mother. "But it wasn't, Mother," she said. "It was boiling, and it burned Jason's arm very badly." She stood up and went to the treatment room. A moment later she returned, holding Jason by the hand. "I'm sorry you don't believe me," she said. She turned to Malone. "Is there any reason for us to stay?"

"Mrs. Montgomery, it *couldn't* have been as bad as you think. You must have been upset—"

"Of course I was upset," Sally shot back. "Anyone would have been. But I saw what I saw. Now please answer my question. Does Jason need to stay here or be bandaged?"

"No—"

"Thank you," Sally said, her voice icy. She turned, about to speak to her mother, then paused. There was something about the way her mother and Dr. Wiseman were looking at her that made her feel strange, as if she had just been tested, and found wanting. But then, as they became aware she was watching, their expressions changed. Wiseman extended his hand to Phyllis.

"Now, if there's anything else you need, just call me. How about dinner on Wednesday?"

"Fine, Arthur," Phyllis replied. She turned to Sally. "Well, shall we go? I'll follow you home and help you clean up the mess."

"Never mind, Mother." Sally's voice was cold, but Phyllis ignored it.

"No arguments! That's what mothers are for." But as she guided Sally and Jason out into the parking lot, she glanced back at Arthur Wiseman.

He looked as worried as she felt.

Sergeant Carl Bronski stared at the pile of computer printouts, and shrugged helplessly. "I'm sorry, Mrs. Corliss, but I'm afraid I'm just not following you."

Once again Lucy tried to explain what the columns of numbers meant, and once again Bronski listened attentively. When she was done, though, he shook his head sadly.

"But even you admit it doesn't really mean anything."

"It means that CHILD is up to something," Lucy replied. "I don't know what, and I don't know why, but something's going on."

Bronski nodded tiredly. It had been going on for two hours, and though he understood full well how Lucy Corliss was feeling, he didn't see what he could do about it. "But if you won't even tell me where these came from, and if you can't really explain what they mean, what do you expect me to do?"

"I expect you to find out what CHILD was doing with my son," Lucy said. "I expect you to do what you're supposed to do, and investigate this."

"But, Mrs. Corliss, there isn't anything to investigate. A few pages of numbers that don't really mean anything. It's just not something I can use to justify an investigation of an outfit the size of CHILD."

There was a long silence. Lucy sank back in her chair. "All right," she said, her voice suddenly calm. "How about this? How about if I talk to the person I got this information from, and they agree to talk to you, to explain what all this means? Will you at least listen to h—them?"

Her, Bronski thought. Will I listen to *her*. But who is she? Another hysterical mother? But if that's all she is, where'd she get this stuff? Finally, he said, "Okay. You talk to her, and if she wants to talk to me, I'll listen."

Seeming satisfied, Lucy Corliss gathered her things together and left the Eastbury police department. But long after she was gone, Carl Bronski sat at his desk, thinking.

He remembered Randy Corliss very well, and though he had never admitted it to anybody, he had had his private doubts that the boy would run away.

Yes, he decided, if Lucy Corliss's friend wanted to talk to him, he would listen.

CHAPTER 17

Randy Corliss lay in bed in a small room at the rear of the main floor of the Academy. His breathing was steady, and all the instruments wired to his small body displayed normal readings. His hands, covered with bandages, rested at his sides. A white-clad figure hovered over him, observing him closely, comparing the readings on the instruments to the evidence displayed by Randy's physical being.

Randy's eyes fluttered slightly, then opened.

He looked up and frowned uncertainly. Above him, the ceiling was unfamiliar. It was the wrong color, and the cracks in the plaster weren't in the right places.

He tried to remember what had happened. He'd been playing a game with his friends, and they'd done something to him, something that had frightened him.

He'd been running, and then they'd caught him, and—and what?

The fence. They'd thrown him against the fence, and he'd felt a burning sensation, and—and—

But there wasn't any more. After that, it was all a blank.

Suddenly, a face loomed above him, and he recognized Dr. Hamlin, who seemed to be smiling at him.

"How are we doing?" he heard Hamlin ask.

"What happened?" Randy countered. He hated it when people acted like however you felt was how they felt too.

"You had a little accident," Dr. Hamlin explained. "Someone left the electricity on in the fence, and you stumbled into it. But you're going to be fine. Just fine." He reached out to touch Randy, but Randy suddenly had a vision of Dr. Hamlin holding a scalpel, and cutting into Peter Williams's brain. He shrank away from the doctor's hands.

"What's going to happen to me?"

"Happen to you? What could happen to you?"

"I—I don't know," Randy faltered. Then, for the first time, he became aware that his hands were bandaged. "Is something wrong with my hands?"

Again, Hamlin smiled. "Well, why don't we just take those bandages off and have a look," he suggested. He seated himself on a chair next to the bed and began unwrapping the gauze from Randy's hands.

The skin, clear and healthy-looking, showed no signs of the severe burns that had been apparent when Randy had been brought in that afternoon.

For the first few minutes, as he had examined the unconscious child, Hamlin had been tempted to order full-scale exploratory surgery, to determine the effects the 240 volts of electricity had had on Randy's body. But then, as he had watched, Randy's vital signs had begun to improve, and he had decided to wait.

Perhaps, finally, he was on the verge of success.

And so he had spent the last several hours observing Randy and watching the monitors attached to the child. Slowly, but miraculously, Randy's pulse and respiration had returned to normal.

His brainwaves, monitored by the electroencephalograph, had evened out, until they once again reflected a normal pattern.

And now, even Randy's skin had healed.

Randy Corliss, who should have been dead, was in perfect physical condition.

"Can I go back to my room?" he heard Randy ask.

"Well, now, I don't really see why not," Hamlin agreed. "But you're a very lucky little boy. Did you know that?"

"If I was lucky, I wouldn't have had the accident, would I?" Randy asked, his voice filled with a suspicion that Hamlin couldn't quite understand. Wasn't the boy even glad he was all right? He decided that he would never understand the mentality of children. "Maybe not," he agreed. "But you have to admit that you were lucky it happened here, where we have lots of doctors. If you'd been somewhere else, you might have died."

Randy looked up at him, his eyes dark and serious. He appeared to Hamlin as if he was seeing something far away, something in his memory. "But I'm going to die anyway, aren't I?"

Hamlin scowled. "What makes you say that?"

Randy twisted at the bed covers, and his eyes roamed the room as if he didn't want to look at Hamlin. "Some of the boys talk. Some of them say that lots of boys die here. But they say we're not supposed to talk about it. Is that true?"

Hamlin sat silently, cursing to himself. That was the trouble with little boys. If you told them not to talk about something, invariably that was the one thing they talked about. And the problem, of course, was that what the boys were saying was true. So far, every one of the boys who had been brought here had died. But could he tell that to the little boy in the bed? Absolutely not. Instead, he reached out to pat Randy reassuringly on the hand.

"A few of our boys have died. But that happens in every school, doesn't it? But I'll bet you won't. I'll bet you'll be the first of my perfect children. And now's the time to find out."

As Randy nervously waited, Hamlin left the room, then returned with a piece of equipment that looked to Randy like nothing more than a box with a dial on it, some cord, and two shiny metal handles.

"What's that?" he asked suspiciously while Hamlin plugged the box into an oversize socket in the wall.

"It's a rheostat," Hamlin explained, carefully keeping the anxiety he was feeling from betraying itself in his voice. "I just want to do one more test, to see if you're really all right. Then you can go back to your room."

"What kind of test?"

Hamlin hesitated. "A sensitivity test," he finally explained. "All you have to do is hold on to these handles, and tell me when you feel something."

Randy scowled at the box. "What kind of something?"

"Anything. Anything at all. Warmth, or cold, or some kind of sensation. Just anything. All right?"

Randy wondered what would happen to him if he refused. Would they strap him down and clamp his head in a vise, like they'd done to Peter? He didn't know, and he decided the best thing he could do was to go along with whatever Dr. Hamlin wanted. He took one of the electrodes in each of his hands.

George Hamlin turned on the power and slowly began turning the rheostat up, his eyes flickering from the dial on the transformer to the instruments monitoring Randy, to Randy himself.

For the first few seconds, as he steadily increased the force of the electrical current that was passing through Randy's body, there was no reaction at all.

Then, as the current reached 200 volts, Randy's eyes widened slightly. "It tickles," he said.

Tickles.

The word thundered in Hamlin's mind. A few hours ago, only a little more voltage than this had knocked the boy unconscious and done severe damage to his heart, his nervous system, and his brain.

And now, all it did was tickle him.

Not only had Randy's regeneration been quick and complete, but he seemed to have built a resistance against the source of the trauma itself.

Impulsively, George Hamlin twisted the rheostat to full power.

Randy Corliss only giggled.

It had worked. At last, it had worked. Hamlin shut off the power and assured himself once more that all Randy's vital signs were still normal. Then he disconnected the monitoring equipment and squeezed Randy's shoulder.

"You can go back to your room," he said. "It's all over, and there's nothing wrong with you. Nothing at all." Without another word, he left the room.

When Hamlin was gone, Randy lay still for a while, wondering what the doctor had meant. Then he got out of bed, gathered up his clothes, and went to the door. He started down the hall that would take him back to the main section of the Academy, but then he paused outside a closed door. He looked up and down the hall, and, seeing no one, tried the door. It was unlocked, and Randy slipped inside.

In the room, lying in bed, his face expressionless and his body perfectly still, was Peter Williams. Slowly, Randy moved close to Peter's bed.

He could hear Peter breathing, but the sound was shallow and rasping, as if something were stuck in Peter's throat.

So Peter wasn't dead. Peter was still alive, even after everything that had happened to him.

Was that what Dr. Hamlin had meant by being a perfect child? That no matter what happened to you, you wouldn't die?

As he left the infirmary and started walking toward his own room in the dormitory, Randy began to wonder if he wanted to be a perfect child.

He decided he didn't—not if it meant ending up like Peter Williams.

George Hamlin peeled off his horn-rimmed glasses and used two fingers to massage the bridge of his nose. The gesture was more habitual than anything else; his energy level, as always, was high. He was prepared to work through the night.

First, there had been the apparent breakthrough with Randy Corliss.

Then there had been the call from Boston.

Paul Randolph's call had disturbed him more than he had let on. It was nothing, he was sure, no more than an upset mother clutching at any straw that might lead her to her son. Even so, it had disturbed him that the mother had turned out to be Lucy Corliss. Why today? Why should the security of the project be threatened today, and by the mother of the one subject who offered a promise of success?

But he had put his concerns aside. All it meant, really, was that he would simply have to work faster. He picked up his laboratory analyses once more and began studying them.

The problem, he knew, had always had to do with the restrictive endonuclease-ligase compound—the combination of enzymes that altered the genetic structure of the egg just prior to conception. The process was basically a simple one, once he had developed the tools to accomplish it. It was a matter of cutting out a section of the deoxyribonucleic acid—DNA—then repairing it in an altered form. But it had taken Hamlin years to develop the compounds, all of which had to be tested by trial and error.

They had been years of lonely, unrecognized work that, so far, had led only to a series of total, if unspectacular, failures.

Failures that had not been, and never would be, noticed by the scientific community, but failures, nevertheless.

George Hamlin did not like failures.

He turned back to the first page of the report and began reading it through once more. He flipped through page after page of charts, graphic correlations of causes and effects, chemical analyses of the enzymes they had used, medical histories of every subject since the project had begun.

The key, he was now certain, lay in Randy Corliss. He turned to the page describing the genetic analysis of the boy.

It was the introns that interested him.

The answer, he had always been sure, was locked in the introns that lay like genetic garbage along the double helix of DNA. Ever since he had begun studying them, George Hamlin had disagreed with the prevailing theory that the introns were nothing more than gibberish to be edited out of the genetic codes as the process of converting DNA into RNA, and finally into the messenger RNA that would direct cell development, was carried out.

No, Hamlin had long ago decided that introns were something else, and he had finally come to the conclusion that they were a sort of evolutionary experimentation lab, in which nature put together new combinations of the genetic alphabet, then segregated them off, so they wouldn't be activated except by genetic chance. Thus, only if the experiment proved successful, and the organism lived, would the activated intron, now an exon, be passed on to succeeding generations.

What Hamlin had decided to do was find a way to activate the introns artificially, determine their functions, and then learn to control them and use them.

And slowly, over the years, he had succeeded.

That was when he had begun experimenting on human beings.

That was when the secrecy had begun, and that was when the failures had begun.

And now, locked somewhere within the small, sturdy body of Randy Corliss, the final answer seemed to be emerging.

It was too soon to tell, but it was only a matter of a few months now.

All that had to happen was for Randy Corliss to survive.

The years of secrecy would be over, and George Hamlin would take his place in the ranks of preeminent genetic engineers.

He wished, as he had many times over the years, that he could carry out his experiments entirely in his lab. But that was impossible.

Extrauterine conception was no problem—combining a sperm with an egg outside the womb had been accomplished years ago.

The problem was that there were so many subjects, so many embryos to be brought to maturity, and not nearly enough women who would agree to bear those "test-tube babies," particularly knowing full well that those babies would be far more the children of George Hamlin than the children of themselves and their husbands.

And so he had made the decision.

The DNA in the ovum would be altered *in utero* rather than *in vitro*.

If the experiments failed, the parents would never know exactly what had happened.

If they succeeded, the parents would raise, albeit unknowingly, a group of wonderfully healthy, if not quite human, children.

And success seemed imminent. If Randy Corliss lived.

The four of them sat stiffly in Lucy Corliss's small living room: Lucy and Jim on the love seat, Sally Montgomery and Carl Bronski on the wing chairs.

It had not been easy for Sally to get there. After hearing what had happened that afternoon, both from Sally and her mother, Steve had suggested that Sally was overwrought. Sally, though she thought the word was ridiculous, had let it pass. Then, rather than argue with him, she had quietly agreed that a good night's rest would be the best thing for her. A few minutes later, Lucy had called and asked if she would be willing to explain the computer data to Sergeant Bronski. She had agreed, and that was when the fight had started. And now, along with Steve, she had her mother to contend with. Phyllis had sat impassively at first, trying to ignore the argument. At last she had, in her infuriatingly rational voice, sided with Steve.

Sally, she declared, should not get involved with the problems of strangers. Certainly, she went on, Sally had enough to cope with right now, without taking on the problems of Lucy Corliss.

Finally, Sally had had enough. Barely retaining her civility, she told her husband and her mother where she was going and stormed out of the house.

Now, after explaining to Sergeant Bronski and Jim Corliss what she thought the computer printouts meant, she was beginning to wonder if she'd done the right thing.

All in all, she realized, there wasn't really much of a parallel between Randy Corliss's disappearance, and Julie's death.

The only real link, indeed, seemed to be that both children had been under study by CHILD. And then, as a silence fell over them, Sally suddenly remembered a thought that had crossed her mind while she was working with the computer that morning. A notion that had been tugging at her mind since her lunch with Jan Ransom.

"Lucy," she said, "I know this may sound like a strange question, but—well, did you want Randy? Before he was born, I mean. Did you get pregnant on purpose?"

Before Lucy could answer, Jim Corliss shook his head. "I was the one who didn't want a baby," he said. "In fact, it was Randy who put an end to our marriage. I guess Lucy thought he'd bring us closer together, but that's not the way it happened." His gaze shifted away from Sally, and he began talking directly to Lucy. "I know you meant well, but I . . . when you told me you were pregnant, I felt like a prison door was slamming on me. So I bolted."

"But I wasn't trying to get pregnant!" Lucy protested. "Randy wasn't my idea. Just the opposite—I'd had a coil put in because I was pretty sure I knew what would happen if I got pregnant. Unfortunately, I was one of those women who doesn't hold an IUD, but by the time I found that out, it was too late."

Sally sat stunned, trying to sort it all out. Was she being hysterical, or was the whole situation becoming more ominous? There were four of them now, four children, all of them unplanned, all of their mothers "protected" by IUDs when the pregnancies occurred, all of them under study by the Children's Institute for Latent Diseases. Now two of them were dead and one was missing. Only Jason was left.

"It's horrible," she said, not realizing she was speaking out loud.

"What?" Carl Bronski asked her. "What's horrible?"

Abashed, Sally glanced from one face to another. All of them were looking at her curiously, but all the faces were friendly. "I was just thinking," she began. "Thinking about you, and me, and Jan Ransom, and all the coincidences." She went through them one by one, half-expecting someone—Bronski probably—to tell her she was overreacting, to explain to her that she was seeing a conspiracy where none existed, to suggest that she get some counseling.

No one did.

When she was finished, there was a long silence that was finally broken by Sally herself.

"Lucy," she asked, her voice oddly constricted. "Who was your obstetrician?"

Lucy frowned thoughtfully. "Somebody over at the Community Hospital. After Randy was born, I never saw him again. I'm afraid I'm just not much of a one for doctors. But his name was Weisfield, or something like that."

"Was it Wiseman?" Sally asked, knowing the answer.

Lucy brightened. "That's it! Arthur Wiseman. I hated him, but at the time he was all I could—" She broke off, seeing the twisted expression on Sally's face. "What is it? What did I say?"

"Wiseman is my doctor too," Sally explained. "And Jan Ransom's." Her voice suddenly turned bitter. "He and his bedside manner and his fatherly advice. What the hell was he *doing* to all of us?"

"We don't know that he was doing anything," Carl Bronski said quietly. But privately he decided that it was time for him to devote a great deal more attention to finding out exactly what *had* happened to Randy Corliss.

The house was dark when Sally returned, except for one light glowing upstairs in the master bedroom. Her mother, apparently, had finally gone home. Sally slipped her key into the lock, let herself into the house, then checked the lower floor to be sure all the windows were closed. As she started upstairs she wondered how she was going to tell Steve that far from withdrawing from Lucy Corliss's problems, she was now going to become even more deeply involved. She knew what his response would be, and she didn't want to hear it. Yet, she wouldn't—couldn't—begin lying to him about what she was doing.

Somehow she would have to make him understand. She knew now that something was happening at Eastbury Community Hospital. Something had happened to her there, and it had happened to Jan Ransom, and it had happened to Lucy Corliss. How many others had it happened to? How many other babies had died, and how many children were missing? She had to know, and Steve had to understand that.

They owed it, if not to themselves or to Julie, to all the women and children to whom, so far, nothing had yet been done.

She reached the top of the stairs and started toward the bedroom, but then changed her mind. She would look in on Jason first, just to reassure herself that everything was all right.

He lay in bed, sound asleep, his right arm dangling over the side of the bed. When she bent down to kiss him, he stirred, and turned over to look up at her.

"Mom? Is that you?" The words were mumbled sleepily, and Jason's eyes, half opened, seemed to be searching for her.

"It's me, honey," she whispered, kneeling by the bed and slipping her arms around him. "How are you? Is everything all right?"

"I'm fine," Jason replied. "Me and Dad spent the whole night playing games with Grandma, and I won." There was a note of accusation in his voice, and Sally half-wished she had been home to enjoy the games. And yet, she knew, if she *had* stayed home, she would have felt guilty all evening.

She reached down and touched the hand gently.

"Doesn't it hurt at all?" she asked.

"Uh-uh," Jason said. Then he added, "I guess Grandma was right. I guess the fudge wasn't as hot as I thought."

Sally frowned in the darkness and felt her heart beat a little faster. Even Jason no longer believed that anything serious had happened to him.

And yet her eyes hadn't deceived her. Or had they? How could she ever know? Maybe—just maybe—she *had* been too upset to realize how little damage had truly been done.

Once more she kissed him good night, then tucked him in. She pulled his door closed behind her and went down the hall and into the room she shared with Steve.

He was already asleep, a book open on his chest. For a few minutes Sally stood still, trying to decide whether to wake him. In the end she decided not to. Instead, she undressed, switched off the light, and slid into bed beside him.

For a long time, though, she didn't sleep. There were too many visions dancing in her head.

Julie, lying dead in her crib. From what?

Jason, his hand ravaged by the acid one minute, but only slightly red a few minutes later.

Again Jason, his hand covered with boiling chocolate, blistered and red, then, a few minutes later, nothing.

And I hadn't meant to have him either, she thought bitterly to herself.

It had been a little over eight years ago, but still she remembered how frightened she'd been when she'd gone to Dr. Wiseman to have that first IUD inserted.

She had been almost as frightened that day as she was today.

CHAPTER 18

Steve Montgomery stared glumly at the report on his desk. After four readings, would a fifth bring it into focus? Probably not. Besides, he already knew what was in the report. It was one more merger proposal, one more report on a small company that was eagerly waiting to be swallowed up by a larger one with all the executives of the former taking a profit on the sale, then going to work for the latter at twice the salaries they had been earning before. Steve's job was to find the right conglomerate to make the merger. Under ordinary circumstances he would have relished the challenge.

Today his concentration was shot. Nothing would come from wading through the charts and profit projections one more time. He put the report aside and swiveled his chair around, but even the view of the soft spring morning beyond the windows did nothing to change the bleakness of his mood.

Until nine days ago, his life had been nearly perfect. A wife he loved, children he adored, work he enjoyed. And now, in a little over a week, his daughter was gone, his wife had changed, and his son . . .

What about his son?

An image of Jason came into his mind, and for a moment a hint of a smile played around his lips. But then the smile faded. For just the briefest of moments, he saw the small, still body of the guinea pig that had been his son's pet.

Steve shook himself, banishing from his consciousness the half-formed thought that had flashed through his mind.

The thought, he told himself, had nothing to do with Jason. Rather, it had come from Sally, and her growing obsession that something had been wrong with Julie. That obsession was spreading like a disease to include Jason as well.

It was time, he decided, to have a long talk with Sally's doctor.

Arthur Wiseman grinned at Steve and gestured toward the empty seat in front of his desk. "Is this your first visit to a gynecologist? If it is, let me assure you that you have nothing at all to fear. The examination is painless, and . . ." He let the joke trail off as he saw the dark expression in Steve's eyes. "Sit down, Steve," he concluded softly.

The two men watched each other in silence for a moment, Steve wondering if he'd made a mistake in coming to Wiseman, while Wiseman waited patiently for Steve to begin talking. When it became obvious to him that Steve wasn't going to begin, he broke the silence.

"I take it this has something to do with Sally?" he asked, his voice professionally neutral.

Steve nodded. Once more a silence fell over the small office.

Wiseman tried again. "Has something else happened?"

"I'm not really sure," Steve admitted uncomfortably. "I can't really put my finger on anything. It's just that she's—well, she's changed. She's so edgy, and she overreacts to everything. Like yesterday, when Jason had a little accident in the kitchen."

"I know," Wiseman interrupted. "I was here when she brought Jason in. Sally seemed to think it was a lot worse than it was."

"Exactly! And she's like that with everything. She's found out about a survey that included both Julie and Randy Corliss, and now she and Randy's mother have cooked up some kind of plot."

Wiseman groaned, remembering his own talk with Sally. "You think she's getting paranoid?" he asked.

The question startled Steve. He hesitated, his brows furrowing deeply. But before he could answer, Wiseman smiled genially.

"It's only a catchword," he said. "Loaded with all kinds of prejudices and connotations. But it does rather get to the heart of the matter, doesn't it?"

"I suppose so," Steve replied, his voice almost inaudible. Then, inhaling deeply, he made himself meet the doctor's eyes. "Do *you* think she's paranoid?"

Wiseman shrugged. "I'm not a psychiatrist, and I don't like to make psychiatric judgments. But," he went on, as relief flooded over Steve Montgomery's face, "that doesn't mean she's not having some severe problems. How could it be otherwise, considering what's happened? The loss of a baby is the worst thing that can happen to a mother, Steve. Most mothers would prefer to die themselves than lose their child. He paused for a moment, drumming his fingers on his desk top. "Would you like me to find someone for Sally to talk to?"

"You mean a psychiatrist?"

"Or some other kind of therapist. I'm not at all sure Sally needs a psychiatrist. If her problems were coming from something physical, that would be one thing. But I think we both know the source of her trouble, and it seems to me that a good psychologist should be able to help."

Steve shook his head slowly. "I don't know," he said at last. "I'm just not sure she'd go. She doesn't think anything's wrong with her."

Wiseman stood up, pointedly glancing at his calendar, and Steve, almost by reflex, echoed the movement.

"No, she'll never do it," Steve said. "I know her, and I just don't think she can be convinced."

"Sometimes," Wiseman replied, "we almost have to force people to do what's best for them."

Before the implications of his words had fully registered on Steve Montgomery, Wiseman showed the young man out of his office, then returned to his desk. He began jotting notes on a pad of paper, then made a list of five psychologists. At the bottom of the sheet he made one final note, reminding himself to check on the status of his malpractice insurance. He tore the sheet off the pad and slid it into the top drawer of his desk just as his nurse opened the door to announce his first patient of the day.

Wiseman rose, smiling warmly, and moved around his desk to greet the young woman who shyly followed the nurse. He took the file the nurse proffered, and waved the woman, Erica Jordan, into the chair so recently occupied by Steve Montgomery. Only when Erica Jordan was settled in the chair and the nurse was gone did Wiseman return to his own seat. He opened the file, glanced over its contents, then smiled at the woman.

"Well, it seems that an IUD is the indicated method," he said.

Erica Jordan paled slightly. "Then I *am* allergic to the pill?"

"Well, I wouldn't go that far," Wiseman replied. "It isn't really a matter of allergies. It's just that the pill has certain side effects, and you seem to be prone to some of them. Migraine headaches for instance. And then there's the cancer in your family."

"I didn't think cancer was hereditary," Erica Jordan protested.

"It isn't, as far as we know. But still, we hesitate to prescribe the pill where there's a history of cancer. Not that there's any direct connection, but it's better to be safe than sorry."

"Damn," Erica said softly. "Why do I have to be allergic to everything? And what if I turn out to be allergic to the IUD too?"

Wiseman shrugged. "It could happen," he admitted. "Maybe you'd better think about a diaphragm again."

Erica screwed up her face and shook her head. "Nope. I know myself too well for that. Let's go with the coil and hope for the best."

Wiseman picked up the phone and spoke to the nurse, then turned his attention back to Erica Jordan. "If you'll go on into the examining room, Charlene will help you get ready. And I have something that just might help with any possible allergic reaction. It's a salve, and it goes in with the device itself. It's supposed to lessen any irritation and help your body accept the presence of the coil."

"For how long?"

"Quite a while," Wiseman replied. "According to the literature it's effective for up to a month. And of course, I'll want to see you again in a month's time, just to be sure." He smiled encouragement as he guided her to the door. "I'll be with you in a minute."

Half an hour later, with the procedure completed and Erica Jordan on her way back to work, Wiseman slowly and carefully began amending Erica Jordan's medical records to reflect the insertion of an intrauterine contraceptive device into her womb. He was also careful to note that, "in view of the patient's susceptibility to allergic reaction," the application of bicalcioglythemine (BCG) had been both indicated and implemented.

When the record had been updated to his satisfaction, he keyed the proper codes into the computer terminal on his desk and added the new information to the permanent files that were stored in the Shefton County computer.

Paul Randolph sped through the countryside, acutely aware of the budding trees and the warmth of the air. He was, he knew, spending altogether too much time in Boston, cooped up in either his office or his apartment, seldom escaping the city. He shouldn't have left the city today—his desk was piled high with work, and he had been forced to juggle appointments with three possible donors to CHILD. Still, it seemed to him that today he had had no choice. Today, he had a problem.

The long narrow drive ended at the gates of the Academy. Except that Paul Randolph still thought of it as The Oaks. He rolled down the window and punched a code number into the lock-box that was discreetly concealed in a clump of laurel, and watched the gates swing slowly open. He put the car in gear, drove through, then watched in the rearview mirror as the gates closed behind him. Only when he heard the distinctive clunk of the lock did he continue along the winding driveway to the house.

He parked in front of the main entrance, got out, and had already started up the steps when he changed his mind. Turning, he retreated from the house, stepping back to examine it, to *feel* it, much, he imagined, as a prospective buyer might. For himself, he decided, the inspection would end right there. The house, even though it appeared quiet and peaceful, no longer felt right to him. In the months since the project had been relocated to the estate the house seemed to have changed. The warmth it had held during his childhood here was gone, and now it was as if the house itself didn't approve of what was being done within its walls.

And neither, Paul Randolph told himself as he started once more toward the door, do I.

With the authority of familiarity he strode through the entry hall and went directly to the clinic. He recognized Louise Bowen, but when she started to speak to him, he ignored her greeting. "Where's Hamlin?" he demanded.

Her welcoming smile fading from her lips, Louise gestured toward a closed door. "I think he's—" She fell silent as Randolph opened the door, marched through, and closed it behind himself.

Inside the office George Hamlin looked up from his work. He frowned, set his pencil aside, then turned cool eyes on his visitor.

"It really wasn't necessary for you to come out here, Paul," he said. "Your call yesterday was quite sufficient."

Paul Randolph made no immediate reply. Instead, he went to stand at a window, where he stared unseeingly out at the expanse of lawn and woods. When he spoke, he still faced the window, his back to Hamlin. "I've been thinking all night, and what I have to say today is too important to talk about on the telephone."

He waited for Hamlin to speak. Seconds passed by, marked only by the soft ticking of an antique clock on Hamlin's desk. Finally Randolph turned, wondering if, by some incomprehensible chance, Hamlin had actually left the room.

Hamlin hadn't. He was now leaning back in his chair, his feet propped up on his desk, his arms folded across his chest, his features placid. As Randolph turned to face him, he smiled. "It's a good trick, Paul," he said easily. "But I've used it too often myself. If you want to talk to me, face me."

The eyes of the two men locked in a silent struggle for control of the situation. It was Randolph who finally looked away, doing his best to cover his defeat by sinking into a chair and lighting a cigarette. Hamlin watched him wordlessly.

"I've come to a decision, George," Randolph said at last as he slipped his lighter back into his pocket. "I've decided to close the project down."

Hamlin's eyes widened in disbelief, and his feet came off the desk to be planted firmly on the floor. "You can't do that," he said softly. "We're too close to success, and we've got too much time, money, and research invested here."

"And we've also done some things that you and I know are both unethical and illegal," Randolph shot back. "It's no longer a question of money and research. It's now only a question of time, and I'm afraid we've run out of that. We're going to close the project down while we still can."

"What are you talking about?"

"Lucy Corliss," Randolph replied, his voice oozing with deliberate sarcasm. "Have you forgotten already?"

"Of course not," Hamlin replied, carefully ignoring Randolph's baiting. "Randy Corliss's mother. You told me about her yesterday."

"But apparently it bears repeating. It seems she's looking for her son, George, who I assume is still here. She found out that he was being surveyed by CHILD, and she wants to know what the study was all about."

"So you stall her."

"Exactly. I stall her. In fact, I already have. I told her it would take some time to comb the records, and that I'd get back to her."

Hamlin nodded. "Then what's the problem? You have a hundred projects you can give her."

"The problem, George," Randolph replied coldly, "is that you have consistently maintained that there was no way anyone could find out about our surveys, particularly this one. And yet, Lucy Corliss found out that her son was being 'watched,' as she put it. If she found out that we were watching her child, then others will too."

"That doesn't hold, Paul."

"Doesn't it?" Randolph began pacing the room. "I'm afraid I don't have as much faith in what you tell me as I used to, George. Do you remember when we began the project? It would only take a couple of years, you said. That was twelve years ago. It could all be done with lab animals, you said. But that was ten years ago, and you haven't used an animal since. I still don't know how I let you convince me on that point, George—it's going to ruin us all. You also assured me there was no possibility that the integrity of the project could be compromised. But Lucy Corliss has become suspicious. In short, this project is not what it was originally presented to be, it has gone on far too long, and has become a liability to the Institute. I have no other choice than to close it down."

Hamlin leaned forward, resting his clasped hands on the polished surface of the desk. "I'm not closing this project down, Paul," he said in carefully measured tones. As Randolph started to protest, Hamlin cut him off. "I listened to you, and now you can listen to me. All that's happened is that a woman has stumbled across our studies. Statistically, that doesn't surprise me. There's nothing in the world that can be kept a total secret, nothing at all. But what has she found out? Has she actually found out about *this* project? I doubt it."

"So do I," Randolph agreed. "And it's my job to see that she doesn't. It isn't just *this* project, George. CHILD has many other projects going, all of them valuable, and none of them dangerous. But this project could bring down the entire Institute."

Hamlin's eyes narrowed angrily. "It could also make the Institute the most important research center in the world."

Randolph shook his head ruefully. "You just don't understand, do you, George? That's been the problem between you and me since the very beginning. You have no idea of what could be involved here. Sometimes I don't think you even understand exactly what you're doing." He paused, wondering how far he should go. Still, the showdown between them had been coming for years, and now there seemed no point in avoiding it any longer. "I've read your reports, George. All of them. All the euphemisms. 'Nonviable subjects.' 'Failed experiments.' 'Defective organisms.' " Suddenly Randolph's voice dropped, as if he were no longer talking to Hamlin, but to himself. "Do you know how long it was before I let myself admit to what you were doing? Years. For years I read those reports and told myself you were talking about rats or rabbits. Maybe even monkeys. I wouldn't let myself know the truth." He tried to smile, but produced nothing more than a twisted grimace. "I think I'd have made a good Nazi, George, and I think you would have too."

His jaw clenched with fury, Hamlin glowered at Randolph. "I'm a scientist, Paul," he rasped. "There's no room in my world for sentimentality."

"Is that what you call it? Sentimentality?" He shook his head in disbelief. "My God, George, how many children have you killed over the last ten years?"

Hamlin rose, his fury no longer containable, his eyes glowing with unconcealed hatred for the man to whom he had always been forced to answer. "None," he shouted. "God damn it, you fool, it's you who doesn't understand. You've never understood, and you probably never will. These aren't children here, and the women who produced them aren't mothers. They're exactly what I call them in my reports. *Laboratory animals.* Granted, they look human, and they act human, but genetically, I can't *tell* you what they are. It will be up to the courts and the legislatures to decide what they are, but only after I've made them functional. But as long as they keep dying, they're nothing more than failed experiments. But they won't keep dying. God damn it, they won't!

I'm on the verge of success, Randolph. I won't be stopped now." Suddenly his rage disappeared, and his eyes took on the look of a hunted animal. "Don't try to stop it, Paul. If you do, I'll bring the Institute down myself. Stay with me, and you can share the glory. Abandon me, and believe me, I'll take you down right along with the project."

And so, at last, it was out in the open. As he watched Hamlin, Randolph realized that he had known it for years: At some point this moment would come. And he had even, deep inside of himself, known what the outcome would be. Hamlin was right. The project was far too extensive and far too close to completion to be abandoned now, unless Hamlin himself agreed to it. And barring the possibility of immediate exposure, and the inevitable end of the project that would follow, nothing would make George Hamlin agree to suspend the project.

So now it was Hamlin who was in control, and as Randolph began trying to adjust himself to his new circumstances, he suddenly remembered the name Hamlin had suggested for the experiments so many years ago.

The God Project.

Now, as it neared completion, Randolph realized that Hamlin himself was playing God.

CHAPTER 19

Randy Corliss glared at the instruction book, his face screwed into an expression that combined concentration with disgust. "It's wrong," he said, his eyes moving from the picture to the Lego construction that he and Eric Carter had been working on since lunchtime. The pieces—blue, red, and yellow—were strewn across the floor of Randy's room. "I don't see how they expect us to figure out what's underneath the battle deck."

Eric rocked back, balancing himself on the balls of his feet, and stared at the model. "So what if it's wrong? It doesn't have to be just like the picture. We can make it any way we want to."

"But it should be right," Randy insisted. He pointed to a bright blue plastic gun mount. "That should be farther back, and there's supposed to be something else in front of it. Only I can't figure out what it's supposed to be."

"Lemme see." Eric picked up the book, stared at it for a moment, then made a face. "I can't even figure out what step we're on."

"Fourteen. Right here, after the bridge and the flight deck go on." While Eric studied the diagram, Randy wandered over to the open window and gazed out at the lawn below. The day had warmed up, and there was a dank humidity to the air that made it hard to breathe. Unconsciously, Randy's right hand moved to the bars over the window. "Did you ever feel like running away?" he suddenly asked.

"I did last year," Eric replied.

"I mean from here. Do you ever want to run away from here?"

"Why should I?"

"I don't know. Just to see if you could, I guess."

"Naa." Eric went back to the diagram, comparing it carefully to the half-finished model on the floor. "I got it!" he exclaimed. "Look!"

Randy glanced once more out the window, then returned to the model. Eric was busy pulling the super-structure apart. When he was finished, he began counting the tiles from the bow of the ship to the stern, then grinned at Randy. "See? We didn't put in enough tiles on the deck. That's why there's no room for the lifeboat."

And then, as Randy began examining the model, an odd, choking noise came from Eric. Randy looked up, then frowned.

Something was wrong with Eric. His eyes were opened so wide, they seemed to bulge from his face. His mouth hung slack, and a strange gurgling noise bubbled from his throat.

"What's wrong?"

But Eric made no answer. Instead, as Randy watched, his arms began to flail, and the color drained slowly from his face. In a moment, his flesh had taken on a bluish hue, and he had toppled over onto his side. His legs jerked spasmodically, and then he was still.

"Eric?" Randy's voice suddenly grew into a scream of fear. "Eric!"

Leaving his friend lying on the floor, Randy ran from his room, his terror translating into a scream that echoed through the entire building.

Louise Bowen was sitting moodily in her tiny office, trying to decide what to do. She knew she shouldn't have lingered outside Dr. Hamlin's door, knew she shouldn't have listened to his conversation with Paul Randolph. In fact, she hadn't heard the entire conversation, but when Dr. Hamlin had suddenly raised his voice and begun shouting about the children, she couldn't help but overhear him.

So now, after three years at the Academy, she knew that all her suspicions were true. To Hamlin, the children simply weren't human. And in a way, Louise suspected he might be right. These children were different from other children. Yet they still had names, they still had personalities, they still thought, and felt, and reacted just like all the other children she had ever known.

And deep in her heart, Louise reacted to them as she always had to children. She cared about them, loved them. Every time one of them died, she felt as if she'd lost a baby of her own.

It was time, she reluctantly decided, for her to leave the Academy.

The decision made, Louise pulled a pad from her desk and began composing her letter of resignation. She wrote out the first draft quickly, and was about to begin rewriting it when Randy Corliss's scream rang through the house. Reflexively, she dropped her pen and dashed out of her office into the foyer just as Randy Corliss, his face pale and his eyes wide with fear, charged down the stairs. He looked wildly around; then, seeing Louise, he hurled himself into her arms.

Louise dropped to her knees, holding the boy close. "What is it, Randy?" she asked. "What's happened?"

"It—it's Eric. He's—I think he's dead!" Randy's words dissolved into a choking sob as his body heaved with emotion. And even while part of Louise's mind accepted his words and began to make all the decisions concomitant to yet another death at the Academy, a voice sounded deep within her.

He's human, it said. This little boy is human.

Slowly, she disentangled herself from Randy, and, holding him by the hand, began leading him back upstairs.

"Where is he?"

"In—in my room. He's on the floor, and he's all blue, and—" Randy broke off, his sobs overcoming him once again. Louise said nothing more until they were in Randy's room and she had checked Eric Carter's body for any signs of life. As she had expected, there were none. She pulled the spread from Randy's bed, covered Eric's body, then led Randy out of the room.

Keeping the terrified little boy with her, she moved to the desk at the head of the stairs, picked up the telephone, spoke into it for a moment, then started down to the first floor.

Randy hesitated at the top of the stairs. "Aren't we going to do anything?"

"There's nothing we can do, darling," Louise said quietly. Taking Randy by the hand once more, she led him down the stairs and into her office. She closed the door, then took Randy to a sofa, sat down, and drew him into her lap. Randy, despite his size, made no move to resist. His arms slipped around her neck, and he rested his head against her breast. For a long time, neither of them said anything, and when Randy finally broke the silence, his voice was shaking.

"What happened to Eric?"

Louise wondered how to answer the boy. She knew that she should make up a story. Eric has been sick for a very long time, she would say, and his death wasn't unexpected; what happened to him certainly wasn't going to happen to Randy.

And she knew that she couldn't.

She'd done it so many times before, talked to so many frightened little boys who had lost their friends, told so many lies to so many children.

With Randy she wouldn't lie.

"We don't know what happened to Eric," she said at last.

Randy was silent for a moment, digesting what he'd just been told. Then he asked, "Is that what's going to happen to me? Am I gonna die too?"

It happens to all of you here, Louise thought. But how could she tell Randy that? She couldn't. She felt Randy tense in her arms and knew her silence must be terrifying to him, but still she couldn't bring herself to lie to him. Not to him, not to any of them, not ever again. And yet, did she have the right to frighten Randy so? She tried to think of something she could say that would ease his terror. "I—I don't think it hurt Eric very much. I think it happened very quickly. I suppose it must have been sort of like fainting. Have you ever fainted?"

"No."

"I have. Just once, but I remember it very well. I was fine one minute, and then all of a sudden I started sweating, and things started going black. And then I woke up, and it was all over. It didn't hurt. It just felt sort of—funny."

"But you woke up," Randy said. "Eric won't."

"No," Louise whispered. "He won't."

And it *does* hurt, Randy added to himself. Miss Bowen hadn't been there and didn't know. But he'd seen Eric's eyes and the expression on his face. He'd heard the awful sounds Eric had made and watched him turn blue. He'd seen Eric's arms waving helplessly in the air and watched him wiggle on the floor.

Deep in his heart, Randy was sure that dying hurt a lot.

He didn't want to die, and he didn't want to hurt. But he didn't know what to do about it. All he knew was that he'd just found out what happened to all the boys who disappeared. They died. And they died because they were at the Academy.

Here. It happened here.

So, if he could get away . . .

But where could he go? He couldn't go to his father. His father had sent him here, so his father must have—

The thought was too horrible, and he made himself stop thinking it.

His mother.

Somehow, he would have to get away from here and find his mother.

He snuggled closer to Louise Bowen, but in his mind he was nowhere near her. In his mind, he was with his mother.

If he was with his mother, he wouldn't die. . . .

* * *

Sitting at his desk in the Eastbury police station, Carl Bronski loosened his necktie, opened the collar of his shirt, and cursed the anachronistic regulation that forbade the wearing of summer uniforms before June twenty-first. But even as he felt the freedom of releasing his neck from the too-tight collar, he realized that it was neither the heat of the day nor the weight of his uniform that was keeping him from concentrating on the file that lay open and unread on his desk.

Rather, it was the conversation he'd had last night with the Corlisses and Sally Montgomery. It had been on his mind all morning, and now, in mid-afternoon, it kept picking at him, niggling at him, demanding his attention when he should be thinking about other things. At last he stood up, retrieved the Corliss file from the cabinet, and took it to the chief's office.

Orville Cantrell, whose florid face and close-cropped white hair had never quite seemed to fit with the warmth of his personality, waved Bronski into a chair, and brought his telephone conversation to a close. Dropping the receiver back on the hook, he rolled his eyes toward the ceiling. "Wanna go out and bust Harrison's peacock again? Old Mrs. Wharton still swears she hears a baby crying in his barn." When Bronski failed to respond, Cantrell held out his hand for the report his sergeant obviously wanted him to see. He glanced at it, dropped it on his desk, and shrugged. "Runaway. I've already seen it."

"Except I'm not so sure it's a runaway."

"Aw, come on, Carl, they're taking off younger every year. And this one's got a previous."

"Still, I don't believe it."

"I've got a couple of minutes—explain."

As carefully as he could, Bronski tried to explain what Lucy Corliss and Sally Montgomery had discovered, leaving nothing out, including Sally's suspicions about Dr. Wiseman. But even as he unfolded the tale, he suspected that Cantrell was only half-listening, and when he was finished, the chief confirmed it.

"You find out anything about that burglary down at the A&P?"

"I thought we were talking about Randy Corliss."

"Carl, *you* were talking about Randy Corliss. *I* was thinking about the A&P. Charlie Hyer's giving me a lot of trouble about that—thinks we should have solved it by now."

"And Lucy Corliss thinks we should have found her son by now," Carl Bronski said doggedly. "Now I ask you, Orv, which is more important—a couple of thousand dollars, or a nine-year-old boy?"

"To Charlie? The couple thousand."

Carl groaned. "Come on."

Cantrell leaned back and folded his hands behind his head. "Carl, I'm gonna tell you something. When I was your age, which I grant you was quite a ways back, I thought I could spend all my time trying to solve the cases I thought were important. But you know what? I found out that every case is important to the people involved. I know it sounds lousy, but to Charlie Hyer, his couple of thousand are just as important as Lucy Corliss's little boy."

"I'm afraid I don't agree."

"Which is why you're a sergeant and I'm the chief." Cantrell glanced at the clock. "Now, you've got half an hour of duty left, and I want you to spend it on that A&P file. As far as we're concerned, Randy Corliss is a runaway—"

"Didn't you even listen to me?"

"I heard you, and it sounds to me like you got suckered in by a couple of hysterical women who don't want to face reality. What have they got? A bunch of crap out of a computer that probably doesn't even mean anything to the people who put it in! Know what I read? I read that ninety-some percent of everything that goes into computers is never even looked at again. It's just stowed away and forgotten. Hell, as far as I can tell, nobody even knows *what's* in the damn computers anymore. So I don't want you wasting your time trying to figure out what those numbers you were talking about mean." As Bronski started to protest, Cantrell held up a restraining hand. "Carl, I'm sorry about Randy Corliss running away, and I'm sorry that other woman's baby died. Hell, I'm sorry about a lot. But when you talk about Arthur Wiseman maybe 'doing' something to his patients, I've got to think something's wrong. Are you starting to get the picture?"

Bronski stood up. "I get it. No more duty time on Randy Corliss, right?"

"Very right."

Bronski started out of the chief's office. He had the door half-open when Cantrell spoke again, this time in the soft tones his men referred to as his "off-duty" voice.

" 'Course, I can't really be held responsible for what you do on your own time, can I? And you might want to keep in mind that even when you're not here, the lights are on, the telex works, and nobody really gives a damn about what facilities are used for what case during what hours."

Bronski turned back. "Did you say something?"

The off-duty voice disappeared as fast as it had come. "I didn't say a damn thing, Sergeant. Now get back to work."

Bronski pulled Cantrell's door shut as he left the office and started back toward his own desk. In the far corner, the telex suddenly began chattering, and Bronski changed course to go over and watch as the tape spewed out of the machine.

There was the usual lot of APBs, mixed with some idle chatter among operators who had become equally idle acquaintances over the years. One item caught Bronski's eye. It was from Atlanta, Georgia, a request for any information about a boy who was assumed to be a runaway. His name was

Adam Rogers, and he was nine years old. The message was being sent to Eastbury because the boy's father had once lived there, and the mother thought the child might be looking for him. The name of the father and his last known address followed the body of the communiqué.

Carl Bronski frowned, then reread the message. The thing that struck him as odd was that the last name of the father was not Rogers. It was Kramer, Phillip J. Kramer.

Bronski was suddenly uneasy. "Anybody on this?" he asked the desk sergeant.

The sergeant didn't even look up. "Since it just came in, it doesn't seem likely, does it?"

"Then I'll take it myself." He tore the strip of paper out of the machine and took it back to his desk. After rereading the message one more time, he picked up the Eastbury phone book and flipped to the K's.

No Phillip Kramer was listed.

Turning to the city directory, he looked up the address. The current occupants were Mr. and Mrs. Roland P. Strassman.

Bronski picked up the phone, dialed their number, and a moment later was talking to Mrs. Roland P., whose name turned out to be Mary.

She and her husband had bought the house from Phillip Kramer eight years ago.

No, Mr. Kramer had not been married. Yes, she was sure. In all the papers she and Rolly had signed, Mr. Kramer had always been referred to as "a single man," which had struck her as funny, even though Rolly had told her it was the proper way to talk about someone in legal papers. So she was sure Mr. Kramer hadn't been married.

Bronski thanked her for the information, then sat at his desk, thinking.

His mind kept coming back to the telex.

First the chief had mentioned it, and if Bronski knew Cantrell as well as he thought he did, there was a reason. And then this message, which seemed totally irrelevant, yet made him uneasy.

Nine-year-old boy. Father's name different from son's.

Unwanted child?

Possibly born in Eastbury?

Bronski looked at the clock once more, then at the closed door of Orville Cantrell's office. Making up his mind, he buttoned his collar and slipped into his coat. As he started out of the building, the desk sergeant grinned at him. "Hot case, or cold beer?"

Bronski returned the grin, though he didn't feel amused. "Maybe a little of both. But if the chief asks, tell him I'm working on the A&P thing, okay?"

"Sure."

As he headed toward Lucy Corliss's house, Bronski made a special point of driving down Brockton Street, past Charlie Hyer's A&P. And just as he passed it, he noted with a certain amount of pleasure, it turned four o'clock.

He was off duty.

CHAPTER 20

Jason Montgomery wriggled uncomfortably in his chair and began counting the raisins in his cereal. Usually it was no more than a game. First he'd try to guess the number, then see if he was right. But this morning it was more: He was concentrating on his cereal in a vain attempt to shut out the sound of his parents' voices.

It seemed to Jason as if the fighting was getting worse. Last week, when he had first become aware that his mother and father were mad at each other, they'd at least waited until he'd gone to bed before they started arguing.

This morning they didn't even seem to know he was there. It was as if he were invisible. He looked up at his parents, who were sitting at either end of the dining-room table. Neither of them seemed aware of him. They were staring at each other, his mother's face stony and his father's red with anger.

"All I want you to do is go see Wiseman this afternoon," he heard his father say. "Is that going to be so horrible? For God's sake, he's been your doctor for years. How can it hurt to go see him?"

"I already saw him," Sally replied. "And I don't trust him anymore."

"But you do trust a woman you hardly know who's not exactly in good shape herself?"

Sally's eyes narrowed as she glared down the length of the table. "And just what is that supposed to mean?"

Steve sighed. Even though it was only 7:30, he already felt exhausted. "It just means that maybe Lucy Corliss could use some counseling herself."

"How would you know?" Sally flared, the pitch of her voice rising dangerously. "You've never even talked to Lucy! How could you know what her mental condition is? Sometimes you talk like a damned fool!"

Putting down his spoon, Jason slid off his chair and left the dining room. But as he went upstairs to get his schoolbooks, his parents' voices drifted after him, fighting about things he didn't understand.

Was something wrong with Randy's mother?

And why did his father want his mother to talk to Dr. Wiseman. Was something wrong with *her?*

He gathered up his books, stuffed them into his green bookbag, then went back downstairs. He looked through the living room into the dining room, and though he couldn't see his father, he could see the tears on his mother's cheeks.

Should he go in and kiss her good-bye? But if he did, and she didn't stop crying, he'd probably start crying himself.

He hated to cry.

Silently, speaking to neither his father nor his mother, Jason slipped out the front door into the warmth of the spring morning. The sounds of his parents' fight faded away as he started along the sidewalk toward school.

Half a block ahead, he saw Joey Connors. Even though he and Joey had never been best friends, Jason decided to catch up with him. He broke into a trot, and in a few seconds was right behind the other boy.

"Hi," he said, falling into step with Joey.

Joey looked at him, made a face, and said nothing.

"What's wrong with you?"

"Nothing. What do *you* want?"

Jason shrugged. "Nothing." What was wrong with Joey? Was he mad too? The two boys walked along in silence for a few minutes, then Joey spoke again.

"Why don't you walk by yourself?"

"Why should I?" Jason demanded. He hadn't done anything to Joey. Besides, what was he supposed to do, just stand there while Joey walked ahead of him? What if someone was watching? He'd look stupid.

"My mom doesn't want me to hang around with you," Joey replied, facing Jason for the first time.

Now Jason stopped, and Joey did too.

"Why not? What did I ever do to you?"

Joey stared at the sidewalk. "My mom says there's something wrong with your mom, and I shouldn't hang around with you."

Anger welled up in Jason. "You take that back."

"Why should I? Ever since your sister died, your mom's been acting funny, and besides, my mom says something must have happened to your sister."

"What's that supposed to mean?" But even as he asked the question, Jason wondered if Joey's mother knew what he'd done to Julie that night. "She just died."

"Bull!" Joey grinned maliciously. "I bet you did something to her. I bet you and Randy Corliss did something to her, and that's why he ran away."

Suddenly all the tension and confusion that had been churning in Jason fused together. His right hand clenched into a fist, and almost before he realized what he was doing, he swung at Joey.

Joey, too surprised to duck, stood gaping while Jason's fist crashed into his stomach, knocking the wind out of him. He gasped, then hurled himself on Jason. Jason buckled under Joey's weight, falling to the ground with the other boy on top of him. He struggled under Joey, ignoring the fists that were punching at his sides, but when Joey began beating him in the face, he screamed, and heaved himself over, rolling Joey under him. He sat astride Joey, returning the pounding he had just taken, while Joey thrashed on the ground, kicking out and flailing at Jason with his fists.

Suddenly Jason heard sounds, and looked up to see two other children running toward them. Joey used the distraction to wriggle free, but he was bleeding from the mouth, and his left eye was already swelling. He was crying, partly from pain and partly from anger, and as Jason lay on the ground, Joey began kicking at him. Jason grabbed at Joey's foot, caught it, and jerked the other boy off balance.

Again, they became a tangle of churning arms and legs, but suddenly Joey, realizing he was getting the worst of it despite his larger size, sank his teeth into Jason's arm.

Jason screamed at the sudden pain, jerked free, and stood up. "You chickenshit!" he yelled. "You bit me!" Then he leaped onto Joey and held a threatening fist over the bigger boy's face. "Give up," he said. "Give up or I'll bust your nose."

Joey stared up at him, his eyes wide as he watched the fist. His arms were pinned to his sides by Jason's legs, and he realized that if he tried to move, Jason's fist would crash down into his face.

"I give," he said. Jason hesitated, then climbed off Joey. He waited while Joey got to his feet, then took a step toward the other boy.

Joey hesitated, tears streaming down his face. "I'm gonna tell," he yelled. "I'm gonna tell my mother, and you're gonna be in trouble." Then he turned and began running back down the street toward his house.

Jason watched him go, then faced the other children who were watching him uneasily. Jason sensed that they, too, had heard things about him.

"Whatcha gonna do?" someone asked.

Jason glared at his questioner. "Well, I'm not gonna run home to Momma like some people," he said. Turning his back on the others, he started down the street. No one tried to follow him.

He walked another block, then stopped, wondering if maybe he should go home after all. His clothes were torn and covered with grass stains, and his face was bloody.

But what if his parents were still fighting? Wouldn't they get mad at him too?

He stood indecisively for a minute, then made up his mind.

He wouldn't go home, but he wouldn't go to school either.

Instead, he'd play hookey for the day, and go off by himself.

At least if he was by himself, no one would be mad at him. . . .

"You've decided I'm crazy, haven't you?" Sally's voice reflected the fear that lay like a caged beast within her. As she spoke, she could feel the beast begin to stir, begin to wake into panic. "The two of you have decided I'm crazy."

"Sally, it's not that at all. We just think you've had too many problems bearing down on you, and you need someone to talk to. It won't even *be* Wiseman. He said himself that he's not qualified, but he thinks he can find someone who can help you."

"Someone who can help me to do what? Help me find out what happened to Julie, or help me try to pretend that nothing happened to her at all?"

Before Steve could answer, there was a loud knock at the back door. Steve threw down his napkin, disappeared into the kitchen, and was back a moment later, followed by a furious Kay Connors clutching her son by her hand. When Sally saw Joey's bruised and swollen face, and the bloodstains on his clothes, she gasped.

"Joey, what hap—"

"Your son happened," Kay interrupted, her eyes blazing with indignation. "Look at him. One eye's black, his cheek is cut, he's bruised all over his body, and his knee is bleeding."

Sally dabbed at her own eyes with her napkin. What was Kay talking about? What did Jason have to do with all this? "But Jason's here," she said. "He hasn't left for school yet." She glanced around, sure that Jason would be standing in the door to the living room.

He wasn't.

Her gaze shifted uncertainly to Steve. "Isn't he here? He must be. He didn't say good-bye."

"He must be upstairs." Steve crossed the living room and went into the foyer to stand at the foot of the stairs. "Jason? Jason!"

Upstairs, the house was silent.

"If he's there, he's in the bathroom cleaning himself up," Kay Connors said angrily.

"Kay, I don't know what you're talking about," Sally protested.

"I'm talking about Jason. He picked a fight with Joey, and then proceeded to do this to him."

Steve came back into the dining room, looking puzzled. "He's not here. I checked his room, and his books are gone. He must have left without saying good-bye."

Sally sat quietly for a moment, digesting what her husband had said. It made a sad kind of sense, really. Why would Jason say good-bye that morning? Neither of them had really spoken to him. They'd been too involved in their own struggle.

And what must he have thought of that? She tried to remember him sitting at the table, listening to them. Had she even seen him?

Not really.

Vaguely, she remembered him leaving the table, but that was all. What must he have been feeling, watching her cry, watching his father's angry face, hearing the bitter words that had flowed so freely. Of course he hadn't said good-bye. He must have wanted nothing more than to be out of the house, away from the anger. Sally tried to speak, but her throat constricted, and as her tears began to flow once more she clutched the damp napkin to her mouth and hurried from the room. Steve watched her go, then turned to face Kay Connors.

"What happened, Kay?"

Kay's fury had been dissipated by Sally's tears. She drew Joey closer. "I don't know, really," she admitted. "Joey left for school, and about ten minutes later he was back. He said Jason picked a fight with him."

"But you're a lot bigger than Jason," Steve said to Joey.

"He hit me first," Joey replied sullenly.

"But why did he hit you?"

Joey's gaze shifted guiltily away from Steve. "I don't know."

"Come on, Joey. There must have been a reason. I can't believe Jason just walked up to you and hit you."

"Well, that's what he did. I was just walking along, and Jason came up behind me and yelled at me. When I turned around, he slugged me."

"Had they had a fight before?" Steve asked Kay.

"I don't see how they could have," Kay said. "I—well, I've tried to keep Joey away from Jason. First there was that Corliss boy—"

"Randy?"

"Randy, yes. He's always been troublesome. And then the last week or so —well, I know Sally's been . . . upset, and it just seemed to me that Joey should stay away."

"I see," Steve said softly. He could see in Kay's eyes the discomfort she was feeling, and wondered just what she'd said to Joey, and what Joey might have said to Jason. But the long hesitation before she'd said the word *upset* told him all he needed to know. "I'll talk to Jason about this, Kay, and try to find out what happened. And if what Joey says turns out to be true, I can assure you that Jason will be punished."

"He's already been punished," Joey said. "I bet he's got two black eyes, and I bit him."

Kay Connors stared down at her son. "You *what?*"

"I bit him," Joey said. "He was on top of me, hitting me in the face, so I grabbed his arm and bit it. It was bleeding."

"Oh, God, Joey," Kay groaned. "Why didn't you tell me that before?"

"You didn't ask."

Feeling suddenly foolish, Kay wondered what to say. But when she looked at Steve Montgomery, there was a trace of a smile playing around his lips. "Maybe I overreacted a bit," she said.

"And maybe the fight wasn't quite as one-sided as we thought."

Kay nodded. "And maybe someday I'll learn to understand little boys." She took Joey by the hand. "As for you, young man, the next time you get into a fight, don't come crying to me unless the boy was twice your age and four times your size. Now let's get you cleaned up and off to school."

"Aw, Mom, do I have to?"

"Yes, you do. You're going to be late, but that's going to have to be your problem too. The next time you think about fighting, maybe you'll think twice."

Their voices were suddenly cut off as Kay pulled the back door closed behind her. Steve sank back into his chair and poured himself another cup of coffee. But instead of drinking it, he left it sitting on the table while he went upstairs to Sally.

He found her lying on the bed, staring up at the ceiling. She made no move when he came into the room, nor did she speak to him. He crossed to the bed, sat gingerly on its edge, and took her hand.

"Sally?"

Her eyes, large and pleading, suddenly met his, and what he saw frightened him. There was terror there, and confusion, but most of all, sadness.

"What's happening to us?" she asked in a whisper. "Oh, God, Steve, I'm so frightened. Everything's closing in, and I have the most awful feeling."

Steve gathered her up and cradled her against himself. "It's all right, honey," he crooned. "You'll see, everything's going to be all right. We'll go see

Dr. Wiseman together and see what he has to say. You're just worn out. Don't you see? There's nothing wrong except that you're worn out from worrying. You can't do this to yourself, Sally. You have to let go of it."

Sally was too exhausted, and too frightened, to argue further, but even as she agreed to see Arthur Wiseman that afternoon, she made up her mind that no matter what happened, she would remain calm and rational.

After all, she reminded herself, I'm *not* irrational, I'm *not* paranoid. I am *not* insane.

She would give Wiseman no reason to suspect otherwise.

Mark Malone was sipping on his coffee and leafing through a copy of the AMA journal when the intercom on his desk suddenly came to life.

"Dr. Malone, this is Suzy. In the emergency room?"

"Yes."

"We've got a patient coming in, and since it's one of yours, I thought you might want to handle it."

"Who?"

"Tony Phelps."

Tony Phelps was two years old and one of Malone's favorite patients, since all he ever had to do for the boy was agree with his mother's assessment that he was certainly "the world's most perfect child." And even privately, Malone wasn't sure the assessment wasn't too far off the mark.

"Tony? What's happened to him?"

"I'm not sure," Suzy replied. "Mrs. Phelps wasn't really too coherent. You know how she is about Tony—it was all she could do to tell me who she was. She was crying, and all she said was 'my baby . . . my baby . . .' I sent an ambulance. They should be back in about ten minutes."

"Okay." Malone shoved the magazine to one side, and switched on his CRT. When the screen began to glow, he quickly entered his access codes, then tapped out the instructions that would retrieve Tony Phelps's medical records from the computer's memory banks. Except for the usual vaccinations and inoculations, Tony's chart was unremarkable except in its brevity. Malone unconsciously nodded an acknowledgment to the machine, and was about to turn it off again when he noticed the small notation on the chart that identified Tony Phelps as another of the children being studied by CHILD. Malone's brows arched slightly.

Then he heard the faint wailing of a siren in the distance. He shut off the console and started toward the emergency room.

Three minutes later, two paramedics burst into the emergency room. One of them carried a screaming child; the other followed, supporting a trembling Arla Phelps. Her face was pale and tear-streaked, but she seemed calmer than she had been when she'd called a few minutes earlier. She glanced around the room, recognized Malone, and hurried over to him.

"Dr. Malone, he drank some Lysol. I don't know how it happened. I was only out of the kitchen a minute, and when I came back—"

But Mark Malone was already gone, following the medics into a treatment room, snapping out orders to the nurse. Arla Phelps, left suddenly alone, sank onto a sagging plastic-covered sofa, and shakily lit a cigarette.

In the treatment room one of the medics restrained Tony Phelps, who had by now stopped screaming but was doing his best to struggle out of the strong hands that held him. Malone began the unpleasant task of forcing a Levin tube through the child's nose, down his throat, and into his stomach. A moment later, the lavage began.

"Will he be all right?" the nurse asked.

"I don't know," Malone replied, his voice grim. "It depends on how much he drank, how strong it was, and how long ago it happened."

Tony began vomiting, and the nurse tried futilely to catch the orangish mess in a bowl. Malone ignored the fact that most of it wound up on his coat.

"Well, at least he has orange juice in the morning," the nurse said by way of an apology.

"Let's get some more water down there."

They repeated the lavage process until Tony was throwing up nothing more than the clear water they were pumping into him. "Okay," Malone said at last. "Clean him up, and keep an eye on him, while I go talk to his mother." Without waiting for a reply, he strode out to the lobby area, where Arla Phelps was working on her fourth cigarette.

"Is he going to be all right?"

"He's still alive," Malone told her. "Tell me exactly what happened. I need to know exactly what he drank, and how much."

"It was Lysol," Arla told him. "I'm not sure how much, but I think it must have been a lot."

"What do you mean by a lot?"

"Half a bottle," the unhappy woman whispered.

Malone's eyes widened in surprise. "Half a bottle?" It was unbelievable. The first swallow should have been enough to make even a two-year-old choke and start screaming. "That doesn't make any sense."

"I was only out of the kitchen a few minutes. Doctor, he's never done anything like that before—never! But when I came back in, he was sitting on the floor, holding the bottle in his hands, drinking it just like it was pop."

Malone thought furiously. If he was to avert a disaster, he had to act quickly and make no mistakes. "Just a minute," he said. He went back to the treatment room, intent on having the contents of Tony Phelps's stomach analyzed.

But when he got there, the emergency seemed to have passed. Tony Phelps, sitting up on the examining table, was giggling happily while the nurse teased him. Malone stood at the door and stared.

"Suzy?" he said at last.

The nurse turned and grinned at him. "Still the world's most perfect child."

"So I see," Malone said. "Do me a favor, will you? Have the lab check out the contents of his stomach to see if there's anything there besides orange juice. I have a feeling our young Mr. Phelps may be playing a bad joke on all of us."

As the nurse hurried out of the room, bearing the bowl and its contents, Mark Malone picked up the gurgling child and held him high in the air. "Is that what you're doing, Tony? Playing a game on us?"

"Where's Mommy?" the little boy asked.

"Right out here." Malone carried Tony out to the lobby and turned him over to Arla, who looked up at him anxiously as she took her son.

"Is he all right?"

"Apparently. But I'd just as soon you stayed around for a while. I'm having the lab check out just what it was that he swallowed."

Twenty minutes later, a laboratory technician appeared, his face a mask. He signaled to Malone, then went into the treatment room. Malone followed.

"I don't know what's with that kid," the technician said softly. "He must have swallowed at least twelve ounces of straight Lysol. You ask me, he should be dead."

So the crisis wasn't over after all.

For Mark Malone, it promised to be a long day, and a difficult one.

CHAPTER 21

For the first time in five years, Sally Montgomery wished she had a cigarette. The problem, she knew, was her hands. If she only had something to do with them, perhaps she wouldn't feel so nervous.

She was lying to herself, and she knew it.

It was Dr. Wiseman who was making her nervous, with his calm eyes and placid expression, his understanding smile and his low-pitched voice.

She had been listening to him for half an hour while Steve waited outside. All he really wanted, he kept insisting, was for her to talk to someone—a stranger, someone who had never met her before and knew nothing about her. A stranger who would listen to her objectively and then try to help her sort things out. Perhaps, Wiseman even admitted, this stranger might actually agree with her that something was "going on," and his fears for her would prove groundless.

Or perhaps, Sally thought, your friend will be one more voice hammering at me to stop worrying, face reality, and go on with my life. Isn't that what you all say? That I should bury my head in the sand? Pretend nothing's happening? She felt indignation rising up from the pit of her stomach, flooding through her like a riptide, threatening to tear away the veneer of false serenity in which she had wrapped herself.

"Would you like something?" she heard Wiseman saying.

"No—no, nothing at all," Sally said a little too quickly. She forced a smile. "I'm afraid I was just regressing a bit, wishing I had a cigarette." She bit her lower lip, regretting her words even as she spoke them. "It happens every now and then, but I always resist."

"Just as you're resisting me now?" Wiseman said, lounging back in his chair and smiling genially.

Exactly, Sally thought. Aloud she said, "I didn't know I was resisting you. I didn't think I needed to. Do I?"

"I don't see why." He leaned forward, folding his hands and resting them on his desk. "We've known each other for a long time, Sally. If you can't trust me, and you can't trust Steve, whom can you trust? You seem to have decided that for some reason we've turned against you."

Sally frowned in studied puzzlement. "I do? I'm sorry if I've given you that impression. I've listened to every word you've said."

"And dismissed them," Wiseman replied. "Sally, I'm your doctor. I've known you for ten years, but I'm sitting here talking to a stranger. Don't you *want* me to help you?"

Sally felt her guard slip just a little. Did he really want to help her? "Of course I want you to help me. But I want you to help me with my problem, and you only want to help me with what you *think* is my problem. I'm not crazy, Dr. Wiseman—"

"No one has said you are."

Sally's resolve crumbled around her, and all the feelings she had been struggling to control boiled to the surface. "*Everyone* has said so." The words burst out of Sally, and there was nothing she could do to stop them. "I keep hearing it from everyone—you, Steve, my mother, even the neighbors are starting to look at me strangely. 'Oh, dear, here comes poor Sally—you know, ever since her baby died, she's been a little odd.' By next week, they'll be crossing the street to get away from me. But I'm not crazy, Dr. Wiseman. I'm not crazy, and neither is Lucy Corliss. Do you remember her, Dr. Wiseman? You probably don't, but you did the same thing to her that you did to me, and to Jan Ransom, and to God-only-knows how many other women. We didn't want children, so you gave us IUDs. But we had children anyway—for a while. But mine died, and Jan's died, and Lucy's is gone. Is that your kind of birth control? After the fact?"

She started sobbing in fury and frustration. She was dimly aware of Wiseman getting up and moving from behind his desk to lay a gentle hand on her shoulder.

"Sally," she heard him say, "I tried to explain it to you at the time. IUDs don't always work. Sometimes your body rejects them. There's nothing I can do about that."

Sally shook his hand away and rose to face him. "Isn't there? I wonder, Dr. Wiseman. I wonder if there's nothing you could have done, or if there's something you *did* do. And I'll find out! You can't stop me, Dr. Wiseman. Not you, not Steve, not my mother, none of you!" The last vestiges of her control, the control she had nurtured all day, slipped away from her. She stumbled toward the door, grasping at the knob. It stuck, and for a frightening moment she wondered if she had been locked in. But then it turned in her hand and she pulled it open, lurching into the waiting room. Steve, on his feet, reached out to her, but she brushed him aside. As quickly as it had deserted her, her self-control returned. She glared at her husband. "Leave me alone," she said coldly. "Just leave me alone." And then she was gone.

Sudden silence hung in the air for a moment, and then Steve heard Arthur Wiseman's voice. "You'd better come in, Steve. I think we need to talk."

Numbly, Steve allowed himself to be led into the inner office. Wiseman guided him to the chair that Sally had just vacated, then closed the door. He waited while Steve settled into the chair, speaking only after the young man seemed to have recovered from his wife's outburst.

"You heard?"

"Only Sally, and only at the end. My God, what happened in here?"

"I'm not exactly sure," Wiseman said thoughtfully. "I talked to her, and for the first few minutes I thought she was listening to me. And then I had the strangest feeling she'd just sort of clicked off, shutting me out. It was as if she was only willing to listen to what she wanted to hear." He paused, then went on. "And then at the end, when I asked if she wanted our help—well, you heard her. She lost control."

"Oh, God," Steve groaned. "What am I going to do?"

Wiseman's fingers drummed on the desk top. "I'm not positive, Steve, but it seems to me that Sally's on the edge of a major collapse. I hate to suggest it, but I think it might be wise if she had a good rest. Not for a long time, but for a week or two at least. Get her out of Eastbury, away from everything that might remind her of Julie."

"I suppose I could get away for a while," Steve mused.

"That's not what I meant," Wiseman said quietly. "I think Sally needs to be by herself in an environment that's structured for people with her kind of problem."

Steve reluctantly met Wiseman's steady gaze. "You mean a mental hospital."

"I think it might be best."

Steve shook his head. "She won't agree to go."

Wiseman's fingers stopped drumming, and he picked up a pencil. "It isn't always necessary that—well, that the patient agree."

Steve swallowed hard, trying to dissolve the lump that had formed in his throat. "I—I'm not sure I could do that."

"If it's best for Sally, I'm not sure either of us has a choice," Wiseman countered.

Steve took a deep breath and shifted his weight forward in the chair. Surely, there was a better way. "Do we have to decide now?" he asked at last.

"This minute? No. But it shouldn't be put off too long. Unless Sally gets some help, I don't know how far she might go with this thing. And I can't tell you what effect it might have on your son either."

It was the mention of Jason, coupled with the memory of the morning, that made up Steve's mind.

"All right," he said, his shoulders sagging with defeat. "Let's go find her."

Sally paused in the corridor and took a deep breath. She had her control back, and no matter what happened, she must not lose it again.

Not in front of Wiseman, and not in front of Steve.

But who was left for her to talk to?

Her world, the world that only two weeks ago had seemed limitless, had suddenly narrowed to three people: Lucy and Jim Corliss, and Carl Bronski.

Three people she barely knew.

But three people who believed in her.

She moved through the corridor quickly, intent only on getting out of the clinic, getting to her friends. She was almost through the lobby when she suddenly heard her name.

"Mrs. Montgomery?" the voice said again. It was a familiar voice, but still Sally had to curb her impulse to run. She turned to face the speaker.

It was Dr. Malone, and his brows were furrowed with worry. He was watching her intently. "Is something wrong?" he asked, his voice solicitous.

Sally glanced at a window and caught a vague reflection of herself. Her hair looked messy and her face drawn. She made herself smile. "I'm fine, Dr. Malone. I was just on my way home."

But Malone shook his head. "You're not fine, Mrs. Montgomery. Something's upsetting you. Won't you tell me what it is?"

"I—" Sally's eyes flickered nervously over the lobby. "I really have a great deal to do—"

"Does it have something to do with what happened on Monday?" Malone pressed.

Monday. Monday. Sally's memory churned, trying to sort things out. What was he talking about? And then she remembered. Jason's arm. "What about it?" she asked coldly.

Malone moved closer to her and Sally took a step backward. He stopped, sensing that she was on the verge of running. "You still think the burns were worse than they looked, don't you?"

"Yes," Sally admitted. "But nobody else does. Something's going on, Dr. Malone, and I'm going to find out what it is. No one's going to stop me. No one's going to convince me that I'm crazy. So please, just let me go."

Malone stood silently for a moment, wishing he knew Sally Montgomery better. Was she buckling under the strain of losing her baby, or had she really stumbled onto something? He decided he'd better find out.

"I don't think you're crazy," he said at last. "I think things on Monday happened exactly the way you told it. Burns and all," he added, seeing the suspicion in Sally's eyes.

"Thank you," Sally breathed, moving toward the door. "I really have to—"

"I think we ought to talk, Mrs. Montgomery," Malone said quietly. He watched Sally carefully, sure that if he said the wrong thing, she would bolt. "Could we talk in my office? I promise we won't be disturbed. By *anyone.*" Sally still hesitated. "There's a door from my office directly into the parking lot. Your car is right next to it. That's how I knew you were here." He moved toward her, and again she backed away. "In fact, why don't we go through the parking lot? Then if you still don't want to come into my office, you can just leave."

Sally was silent for a moment, then nodded her head in agreement. The two of them left the lobby and began walking along the side of the building.

"Something happened today, Mrs. Mont—is it all right if I call you Sally?"

She nodded, but said nothing.

"The same kind of thing happened again today, Sally. A woman brought in her son, and from what she said, the little boy should have been dead. Not just burned—dead. But nothing was wrong with him."

Sally stopped and turned to face Malone. She looked deep into his eyes. Was he telling the truth, or was it some kind of trap? Maybe he was just trying to delay her, trying to keep her here until—what? And yet, there was nothing in his eyes to suggest that he was lying to her. "Was the boy being surveyed by CHILD?"

Malone hesitated for a moment, then nodded.

They were near Sally's car now, and she began fishing in her purse for her keys. "Then if I were you, I'd keep a very careful eye on that boy," she said. "And I'd bet money that his mother hadn't planned to have him, and that Dr. Wiseman was his mother's doctor."

Malone knew it was all true. He reached out and touched Sally's arm. This time she didn't draw away.

"Come in for a minute. Please?" He went to the outside door of his office, unlocked it, and went in. Through the window Sally watched him cross to the other door, turn the bolt, then rattle it to prove to her that it was locked. At last, conquering her fear, she went inside.

Mark Malone talked steadily for ten minutes, and when he was done, Sally sighed heavily. "And there's no mistake? The Lysol should have killed him?"

Malone nodded. "If not, he should have been in so much pain that he would have been unconscious. He wasn't. He was mad as hops about the way he was being treated, but as soon as the lavage was finished, he was fine. And there was no mistake about how much of the stuff he'd drunk. He'd gone through it like root beer, and for the amount of damage it did, it might as well have *been* root beer."

The intercom on Malone's desk suddenly crackled, and the voice of Arthur Wiseman filled the room. "Mark, it's Arthur. Have you happened to see Sally Montgomery anywhere around the hospital?"

Malone glanced quickly at Sally, who shook her head vehemently. "No."

"Damn. Okay. If you see her, talk to her, and keep talking to her until I get to you."

"Why? Is something wrong?"

There was a short silence, then he said, "She's been having some problems, Mark. Her husband and I have decided she needs some help, but she doesn't agree. I'm afraid we're going to have to take the decision out of her hands."

Sally was on her feet and at the door to the parking lot by the time the intercom fell silent.

"Sally?" She paused and turned back to face him. "If I'm going to help you, I have to know where you'll be." She stared at him, and he knew that even now she didn't quite trust him. "Just a name," he said softly. "Don't argue, and don't waste time thinking. Just give me a name and get out of here."

"Lucy Corliss," Sally said.

"I'll be there tonight," Mark promised. "We have a lot to talk about." But by the time he'd finished speaking, Sally was gone. He moved to the window and watched as her car skidded out of the parking lot and disappeared down Prospect Street. Only then did he unlock his office door and hurry down the corridor toward Arthur Wiseman's office.

Louise Bowen paused for a moment on the lawn of the Academy to watch the three boys playing some kind of game with a ball. Although she didn't quite understand the point of the game, she could see that it was rough. The idea seemed to be to retain possession of the ball, but with the odds two against one, the game had the appearance of a constantly shifting wrestling match in which there could be no winner until all but one of the boys dropped in exhaustion.

Only Randy Corliss was not playing, and it was Randy in whom Louise was primarily interested.

She knew that what had happened yesterday afternoon was preying heavily on Randy's mind. He had been quieter than usual at breakfast. Then at lunch, while the rest of the boys wrangled about how to spend the afternoon, he had remained completely silent, his expression blank, as if he were somewhere far away, in a world of his own. And then, after lunch, he had disappeared. Now Louise was looking for him, determined to do what she could to assuage his fears.

Randy was in the woods. After lunch he had ignored his friends' pleas for him to join in their game and gone off by himself.

But it wasn't that he wanted to be alone.

He was looking for a way out.

For an hour he had worked his way along the fence, searching for a tree that had a limb extending beyond the strand of barbed wire that topped the barrier.

There was none.

All along the perimeter of the property the trees had been cleared away. Here and there a remaining tree that might once have had long lower branches showed the scars of some long-ago chain saw. But nowhere was there a place where the fence could be scaled without touching it. And then, when he had only fifty yards to go to the gate, he found it.

It was a stream flowing through a culvert that carried it under the fence. The pipe was small, but Randy was almost sure that if he hunched his shoulders together, he could get through. He scrambled down the bank of the stream and tried to peer through the culvert. At the far end, he thought he could see traces of light.

Should he try it now?

He glanced around, wondering if anybody was watching him.

He wasn't sure. At first, he had always felt the eyes on him, and it had bothered him. But after those first few days, he had grown used to the watching. That odd sixth sense had become dulled, and now that he needed to know if he was truly alone, he had no way of telling.

But one thing he was sure of. If he tried to run now and got caught, he wouldn't have another chance. Reluctantly, he turned away from the stream and started back toward the main building. If he was going to try to escape, he would have to do it at night, and he would have to do it from the house. But the windows were barred, and there was always someone awake, watching.

He moved through the woods slowly, trying to figure out what he could do. As he stepped from the forest onto the edge of the lawn, he saw an answer.

On the slope of the roof there seemed to be some kind of trap door. Randy stopped and stared at it for a long time. Was it really a trap door? But what was it for? What if it wasn't a trap door at all? What if it was just a skylight, and wouldn't open.

He frowned, trying to puzzle it out. And then, in his innocence, he decided that it *had* to be a trap door, and it *had* to open. Otherwise there was no way out.

But once he was on the roof, what would he do?

A tree. All he had to do was find a tree that reached to the eaves of the three-story building, and he could climb down it. He was about to begin searching for the right tree when he heard his name being called. He recognized Louise Bowen coming toward him.

"Randy, I've been looking all over for you."

"I was just off in the woods, messing around."

She smiled at him and tousled his hair. "I was worried about you."

Randy's first impulse was to pull away from her, but he thought better of it. If he was really going to try to run away, he couldn't let anyone know he might even be thinking about it. Otherwise they would watch him. He slipped his arms around Louise and hugged her. "I was just thinking about what we talked about last night," he said. His heart began pounding, and he prayed she wouldn't see through the lie he was about to tell her. "And I decided God must have wanted Eric to die, and what happened to him isn't going to happen to me."

Louise patted him on the back. "Well, that seems very sensible," she told him. "What made you decide that?"

Randy looked up at her, trying to hide the fear he was feeling. "I don't know. But I'm not scared anymore."

"Well, that's good," Louise said. But when she looked into his eyes, she saw something that told her he was lying. There was a look in his eyes and something about his smile that rang false.

He's going to do something, she thought. He's going to try to run away.

"Do you think I could build a treehouse here?" Randy suddenly asked.

"A treehouse?" Louise echoed. What was he talking about? One minute he was talking about dying, and the next minute he was talking about treehouses.

"You know," Randy said. "A treehouse. All you need is the right tree and some boards and nails."

Louise frowned, certain that somehow there was a connection. "Where do you think you might put it?"

"I don't know," the little boy conceded. "Over there, maybe?"

He pointed toward a grove of maples near the house, and as her gaze followed his gesture, her eyes wandered to the roof of the house. Clearly visible to her, and obviously to Randy too, was the trap door that allowed access to the roof. Suddenly she understood.

"Why, I don't know," she said. "Why don't we go have a look?"

Pleased that she had fallen so easily into his plans, Randy skipped off toward the trees, with Louise Bowen slowly and thoughtfully following after him.

Half an hour later, amid much planning of an elaborate treehouse, both Randy and Louise knew which tree Randy would use when he tried to escape.

As they returned to the house, Louise Bowen tried to decide what to do. She knew she should report her conversation with Randy, as well as her suspicions, to Dr. Hamlin. And yet she couldn't. She knew perfectly well that to Hamlin, Randy was no more than an animal, and she suspected that he wouldn't hesitate to lock the boy up like an animal. So, for the moment, she would say nothing. Instead, she would simply watch Randy very carefully. Then, when she knew exactly what he was planning, she would decide what to do about it.

As for Randy, he was positive that the woman suspected nothing. Tonight he would run away, and he was childishly sure that he wouldn't be caught.

CHAPTER 22

The long twilight of the spring evening was just beginning to fade as Sally steered her car toward Lucy Corliss's house. She had been driving aimlessly all afternoon, intent only on staying away from Eastbury until dark, stopping only once to try to eat supper. Supper, it turned out, had been a salad that had sat untouched before her while she sipped cup after cup of bitter coffee.

Twice she had considered calling Steve; twice she had discarded the idea. What could she say to him? That she was sitting by herself in a diner in another town, wondering if it was safe to come home? It would only confirm what he already believed.

She had considered other alternatives. Her mother? But her mother would only call Steve. What about friends? An image of Kay Connors came into her mind. No, there was only one place to go—the place that she had named while talking to Dr. Malone a few hours before.

And so she pulled up in front of Lucy Corliss's house, set the handbrake, and got out of her car. She started toward the house, then paused, frowning.

There was a strange car in Lucy's driveway, a car with medical plates.

Dr. Malone?

Or Arthur Wiseman?

Perhaps she shouldn't go in. Perhaps they were both there, waiting for her.

She forced the idea out of her mind. Paranoid. It was a paranoid thought, and she wouldn't entertain it. With a confidence she didn't feel, she climbed the three steps up to Lucy's front door and rang the bell. The door opened immediately, and Lucy drew her inside.

"Sally—where have you been? We've been so worried. I was watching for you, and then it looked like you weren't going to come in—my God, you look awful!"

Sally instinctively brushed at her hair, and when she spoke she heard her voice quaver. "It was the car in the driveway. I didn't know whose it was."

"It's Mark Malone's. He got here an hour ago."

Sally started to breathe a sigh of relief, then caught it back. "He came alone?"

"All alone," Lucy reassured her. She led Sally toward the living room. "He told us what happened at the hospital today."

As they walked into the living room, Jim Corliss rose to offer his chair to Sally, but she ignored the gesture, choosing instead to settle on the love seat next to Lucy. "All of it?"

"All of what I saw, and all of what you told me," Mark Malone said. "And after you left, I went into Wiseman's office." A look of alarm came over Sally, and Mark quickly reassured her. "I only wanted to find out what they were doing and give you a little time. I'm afraid they were talking to your mother, explaining that if you showed up at her house, she should try to keep you there and call them."

"Oh, God, what am I going to do?"

"You're going to forget all about it for a while." It was Carl Bronski, and the firmness in his voice puzzled Sally. Forget it? How could she? Bronski continued speaking, almost as if she'd voiced her questions. "They can't just come and get you, Sally. They'd have to get a court order, and that involves a hearing. All that takes time, plus a lot more evidence than they've got right now. Also, don't forget that there are four people sitting right here who don't think you're crazy at all, including a doctor and a cop. So even if they're serious about trying to commit you, it isn't going to happen tomorrow, or the next day either. And by then, if we're lucky, we'll know just exactly what the hell is going on."

"Then something *is* going on? I'm not crazy?"

"If you are, we all are," Jim Corliss said. "It seems there's been another coincidence. Carl called Lucy last night about a little boy who's disappeared from Atlanta. He's the same age as Randy and was born here. His parents weren't married."

Sally's eyes met Jim's, and when she spoke, the calmness of her voice told all of them that she had put her personal fears aside. "Was he being surveyed by CHILD?"

"That's what we don't know," Carl said. "I was hoping you could find out for me. Most of those statistics you pulled out of the computer didn't have any names attached to them. They were just numbers."

"Well, it's easy enough to find out," Sally told them. "All I have to do is go down to my office—" Her heart sank as she pictured the keys to her office dangling from the key rack in the kitchen closet. "We can't go to my office. I don't have my keys."

"Can't a security officer let you in?" Bronski asked.

Sally shook her head. "They can, but they won't. If you don't have your keys, they aren't allowed to open any doors for you."

Mark Malone paced the room, weighing the risks of what he was about to suggest against the idea's possible advantages. He made up his mind. "What about the hospital? Why can't Sally and I go down to the hospital and use the terminal in my office?"

"But they'll be looking for me there, won't they?"

"They won't see you," Malone assured her. "We won't even have to go through the lobby. Then we'll see if you and your computer expertise can figure out exactly what's going on."

They rose, ready to leave, when the phone suddenly began ringing. Lucy hesitated, then went to answer it. A moment later she reappeared. "It's for you," she said to her ex-husband, frowning slightly. "It's a woman." Ignoring her faintly accusatory tone, Jim hurried into the kitchen. Moments later, he, too, reappeared.

"That was a friend of mine in Boston," he said, his eyes on Lucy. "Her name's Joan Winslow, and she works for an ad agency. And I haven't dated her for two years. Anyway," he went on as Lucy's eyes narrowed suspiciously, "I asked her to see if she could find out who funds CHILD."

"Who *funds* them?" Lucy sounded exasperated. "What on earth difference could that make?"

"A lot," Jim told her. "You don't really think all these foundations are as independent as they claim to be, do you? Almost all of them, somehow, are funded by people with one sort of an ax to grind or another."

"And CHILD?" Carl Bronski asked.

Jim looked at him bleakly. "A lot of minor grants from a lot of places. But two big ones. Continuing support from an outfit called PharMax—"

"Which is one of the biggest drug companies in the country," Mark Malone interrupted. "It seems like they'd have a natural interest in a group like CHILD."

"It's the other grant that intrigues me," Jim Corliss said quietly. "It makes all the other funds, including the ones from PharMax, look like peanuts."

"Who is it?" Lucy demanded.

Jim's eyes locked on hers, his puzzlement clear in the frown that knotted his forehead. "The Defense Department," he said slowly. "Now, why would the Defense Department be interested in a group like CHILD?"

Jason Montgomery came home just as the full darkness of night was falling over Eastbury. He walked the last few yards very slowly, knowing very well that he was in a lot of trouble. His father, he was sure, would give him a spanking, and his mother—well, she would just look at him, and he would know from her eyes that he'd disappointed her. That would be even worse than the spanking. Jason had found out years ago that spankings only stung for a split second, no matter how hard his father slapped his bottom. He paused, staring at the house.

How much, he wondered, did they know? Had Joey really told on him? Maybe he hadn't. He could explain his torn clothes by saying that he'd—he'd what? He searched in his mind for a reasonable explanation. Maybe he'd climbed a fence and slipped? That was it. He and somebody else had climbed the fence around the schoolyard, and he'd slipped.

But what if they'd found out he skipped school?

He didn't even want to think about that.

Wondering if the fun of ditching school had been worth whatever was waiting for him inside the house, he slid through the front door. "Mom? I'm home!"

From the kitchen, he heard his father's voice.

"Jason? Is that you?" His father came through the dining room, his face red with anger. "Where have you been?"

"I—I—" Jason stammered. Then, in the face of his father's wrath, words failed him. He stared up at his father, his eyes brimming with tears.

Looking down at his son, Steve felt his anger drain away, to be replaced by relief.

His afternoon had not been easy. He'd left the clinic to find the car—and Sally—gone. He'd started walking home and decided to stop by the school to pick up his son.

But even though he'd waited until the school grounds were deserted, Jason hadn't appeared. Finally he'd gone in, found Jason's room, and talked to his teacher.

Jason hadn't been at school that day.

For the rest of the afternoon Steve had spent his time worrying alternately about his wife and his son, neither of whom came home. He'd called everyone he could think of, including Lucy Corliss, but no one had seen either of them. Several times he'd started to take his car and go looking for them, but he'd always changed his mind, afraid that one or the other might call him, needing help, and he wouldn't be there. So he'd waited, nervously pacing the house, willing the phone to ring, glancing out the window every few minutes in hopes of seeing one of the people he loved best.

And at last his son had come home.

"Where've you been?" he asked again, his voice gentle now. "Why didn't you go to school?"

Jason, sensing that his father was no longer angry at him, sniffled a couple of times.

" 'Cause of the fight," he said.

"The fight with Joey?"

The little boy shook his head.

"Then why didn't you come home?"

" 'Cause of the fight you and Mom were having," Jason explained. Then, as if sensing something wrong, he glanced uneasily around. "Isn't Mom here?"

"Not right now," Steve replied. What could he say to Jason? That his mother had run away, and no one knew where she was? Then, for the first time, he noticed Jason's torn clothes. "That must have been some fight you had with Joey," he commented. "Want to tell me about it?"

Slowly Jason began to unfold the story. "And my eye was swollen," he finished, "and my arm was bleeding, and my clothes were torn, so I didn't go to school. But he started it, Dad."

Steve nodded absently, not really hearing Jason's last words. Instead, he was trying to match Jason's list of wounds with what he saw.

His eye was swollen?

His arm was bleeding?

And the torn leg on his pants. Where had that come from?

"What happened to your jeans?"

Jason scowled. "He pushed me down on the sidewalk, and I skinned my knee."

"Show me."

Obediently, Jason rolled up his pant leg. The skin on his knee was clear and smooth. And yet, when Steve examined the jeans, he could see what looked like blood on the inside.

"And what about your arm? Where did he bite you?"

"Right here." Jason touched a spot just above his wrist. It showed no signs of damage either. Nor was there any blemish on Jason's face.

What the hell was going on? Both boys gave the same account of the fight, and Joey Connors had been a mess this morning. "Come on, son," he said quietly. He led Jason into the kitchen, opened a Coke for the boy, then picked up the phone.

"Kay?" he asked when the connection was made. "This is Steve Montgomery. I was just wondering how Joey's doing."

There was a slight pause, then a sigh. "All right, I guess. He's sore, and his bruises won't go away for a couple of days, but there's no real damage." She paused, then added, "Has Jason come home yet? Or Sally?"

"Jason's here," Steve said.

"Is he okay?"

"I'm not sure," Steve said slowly. "But apparently the fight went just about the way Joey said, except that Jason insists Joey started it."

"Which he did," Kay Connors admitted. "What do you mean, you're not sure if Jason's okay? Is he hurt?"

"No, no—nothing like that." He laughed, but the sound was hollow. "In fact, it seems to me he should be hurt worse than he is. I'm afraid that Joey got by far the worst of it."

"I see," Kay replied, her voice noticeably cooler. In fact, she did not see at all, but privately decided that in the future, Joey would be instructed to have nothing whatever to do with Jason Montgomery. Indeed, from now on, the entire Connors family would avoid the Montgomerys. A moment later she found an excuse to end the conversation and cut the connection.

Steve sat silently, wondering what to do. There was no damage where there should have been damage. Even Jason said he'd been hurt in the fight. But what had happened to the wounds?

And then he remembered the fudge and the muriatic acid. Both times it had been Sally who claimed to have seen the damage, and both times he'd thought she was overreacting. But what about now? This time Joey, and Jason himself, had seen the damage. Were they lying? But there was no reason for them to. He reached for the phone again, glancing at the numbers that were scrawled all over the cover of the directory. A moment later he was talking to Eastbury Community Hospital.

"This is Steve Montgomery. Is Dr. Malone in?"

"No, he isn't, Mr. Montgomery."

"Can he be reached somewhere else?"

"One moment." He was put on hold for what seemed an interminable length of time, but at last the operator came back on the line. Dr. Malone was not at home, nor had he informed his service where he was. Could another doctor help?

"Dr. Wiseman," Steve said. "Can you put me in touch with Dr. Wiseman?"

"Of course, Mr. Montgomery." He was put back on hold, and then, seconds later, a new connection was made.

Arthur Wiseman listened quietly while Steve tried to explain what had happened. When he was finished, there was a short silence. Then Wiseman spoke, his voice low and calm.

"Bring the boy down to the hospital, Steve. It doesn't sound like there's anything to worry about, but it won't hurt to have a look at him." He paused, then he added, "Heard anything from Sally yet?"

"No."

Wiseman's voice turned grim. "We can talk about that too."

Randy Corliss waited until the Academy was silent, then waited some more. The minutes crept by. After what seemed like hours, he slipped out of bed and began dressing. Finally he opened his door a crack and peeped out into the hall. At the far end there was a dim light and a desk. At the moment, no one was sitting at the desk.

Randy edged out into the hall and began moving as quietly as he could toward the narrow set of stairs that led from the rear of the second floor up into the attic. He had almost reached the stairs when he heard footsteps behind him. Someone was coming up from the main floor. He dashed the last few feet, scuttled up to the top of the stairs, and waited. He heard a scraping sound and decided that whoever had come up was now sitting at the desk. Gingerly, he tried the door to the attic.

It was unlocked.

He slipped inside, eased the door closed behind himself, and felt around for a light switch. But even as his hands found one, he changed his mind. What if someone were outside and saw lights in the attic? He'd never even make it out of the house.

He'd have to do it in the dark.

He started across the floor, but his footsteps seemed to echo loudly. He stopped again and took off his sneakers, tied the shoelaces together, then hung the shoes themselves around his neck. Once more he began creeping across the attic floor, testing each step before he put his weight on his foot. He moved slowly, his eyes straining to penetrate the near-total blackness, but after what seemed an eternity he found himself under what he believed to be a skylight.

He stared upward.

It *was* a skylight, but in the dimness he could just make out a folding ladder and a latch. From the ladder, a cord dangled just out of his reach. He stretched upward, and his fingers barely brushed its frayed end.

Should he try to find something to stand on? But how? He could grope around in the dark all night and never find anything.

He decided to risk a jump. He flexed his legs a couple of times, judging the distance carefully, then lofted himself off the floor.

His right hand grasped the rope, and as he dropped back to the attic floor with a soft thump, the ladder creaked and moved down six inches. The thump and the creak made Randy freeze, listening.

* * *

On the floor below, Louise Bowen looked up from the report she was working on. Was it her imagination, or had she heard a faint sound? Frowning, she rose from her chair and began making her way down the hall, checking on each of the boys.

Hearing nothing, Randy slowly pulled the ladder down. Its ancient springs groaned in low protest, but to Randy the sound was like blaring trumpets. At last, the ladder touched the floor and he scurried up it. It took him a moment to figure out how the latch worked, but then with a scatter of flaking rust, it came free. He pushed the skylight upward and crept out onto the roof.

The pitch looked much steeper than it had from below, and the slate of the roof felt slippery under Randy's bare feet. Quickly, he put his sneakers back on, laced them tightly, then stood up and tested the footing. The rubber soles seemed to grip the slate firmly, but he wasn't too sure of his balance. Finally, he spread himself out, until he was almost lying flat against the incline, and began crabbing sideways across the roof.

There was only one more room to check, and Louise Bowen hesitated before opening its door. What if Randy was not inside?

But he had to be. Surely, if he were planning to run tonight, he would wait until much later.

Or would he?

She turned the knob of his door and pushed it open.

"Randy?"

There was no answer. She switched the light on. Randy's bed was empty.

Slowly, reluctantly, Louise started toward the main stairs. She would have to report that Randy Corliss was gone.

Randy could see the treetop looming twenty feet in front of him. All he had to do was ease himself down to the eave, then climb onto the large branch he had spotted this afternoon. But going down the steep angle of the roof was not as easy as scooting across it. He had to place each foot carefully, bracing himself with both hands as he shifted his weight from one foot to another.

And then it happened. His right foot hit a patch of moss and he slipped. He began sliding down the roof, his hands scrabbling for a grip on the worn slate. He felt himself begin to go over the edge and made a desperate grab at the gutter that rimmed the eave. It screeched at the sudden strain, and pulled away from its supports, but it held. Randy swung in the air for a moment, searching wildly for his branch.

It was only a foot away, and with the strength born of fear, Randy worked his way over and swung onto it. Pausing only a moment to catch his breath, he began scrambling down the tree. In a few seconds he was on the ground, sprinting across the lawn toward the woods. Only when he reached them did he stop to look back.

All over the house lights were coming on.

He turned and plunged into the forest, relying on his memory to guide him to the stream and the culvert that would take him under the fence. A faint glow from the moon lighted his way, and he was able to keep moving at a dead run, dodging this way and that, moving steadily away from the house. His breath was getting short, and he was beginning to think he'd taken a wrong turn, when suddenly he heard the sound of running water. And then he was at the top of the bank, the stream just below him.

From behind, he heard the barking of dogs.

He slid down the bank and waded into the water, ignoring its chill. He started upstream and came to the end of the culvert. Without considering the possible consequences, hearing only the baying of the dogs as they searched for his scent, he dove into the narrow pipe.

It was tight, and his shoulders rubbed against both sides as he crept through the rushing water. But then, as his hands and feet began to grow numb from the cold, he saw a faint glow ahead.

He was almost out.

Urging his small body onward, he squirmed the last few feet.

With his goal only inches away, he discovered his mistake.

Firmly imbedded in the end of the culvert was a wire-mesh grate, its heavy screening blocking the passage of anything but the rushing stream.

Hopelessness flooded over Randy for a moment, then receded. Determinedly, he began backing out of the culvert. It seemed to take forever, but at last he was free of the confining pipe, standing in the water, his body charged with a combination of fear and exhilaration.

The dogs were coming closer now. Randy scrambled back up the bank, his mind whirling, searching for a solution.

The fence.

He would have to climb the fence.

He could see one of the dogs now, a huge shadow charging toward him out of the dimness. Turning, he hurled himself toward the fence, but he was too late.

The doberman was on him, snarling, its jaws clamping onto Randy's left ankle. The dog planted its feet firmly in the ground and began shaking its head. Randy tripped, collapsed, then tried to kick out at the dog. His right foot connected with the animal's head, and it let go for a moment. Randy scrambled to his feet, the fence a foot behind him. The dog hesitated, snarled, then leaped toward him. Randy twisted aside, grabbed the dog in mid-leap, and shoved hard.

With a high-pitched scream, the dog died as the voltage of the fence surged through it. Randy, his hand still clutching the animal's skin, stared at it for a moment.

Dimly, he was aware of an odd sensation in his arm. It was an inner tingling and a slight burning sensation. The last time he had touched the fence, he had been knocked out. Suddenly he remembered the test Dr. Hamlin had given him, and now he knew what it had meant. The electricity hadn't killed him the first time, and now it couldn't hurt him at all.

Very close by, he heard the other dogs. Letting go of the dead animal at his feet, Randy reached out and grasped the fence.

Again, there was the strange tickle, and the sensation of warmth, but nothing more.

So everything he had been told while he was growing up was wrong.

Electricity didn't hurt you at all. In fact, it felt kind of good.

A moment later he dropped to the ground on the other side.

CHAPTER 23

Darkness shrouded the parking lot of Eastbury Community Hospital, but still Mark Malone drove around to the back entrance and switched his lights off before he pulled in and parked his car next to his office.

"No sense alerting everyone that we're here," he commented. Sally nodded her agreement as she got out of the car and waited for Malone to unlock his office door. Only when they were inside, with both doors securely bolted and the lights turned on, did Sally speak.

"I feel as though I'm doing something illegal."

"You're not," Malone assured her. "Although you were when you broke the codes to the medical records the first time. But this time, it's perfectly legal. If anyone ever asks any questions, I hired you as a computer operator to compile some statistics for me. Okay?"

"Okay." Sally set her purse on Malone's desk and switched on the computer terminal. Moments later she began tapping in the proper codes. "First things first," she murmured. Her fingers flew over the keyboard, finally coming to rest on the key marked ENTER. Sighing slightly, she leaned back in her chair and smiled wanly at Malone. "It'll take a couple of minutes."

Malone shrugged. "How'd you know what to tell it?"

"It's all one computer," Sally explained. "Even though I spend most of my time with the college records, the instructions are pretty much the same for anything. Right now it's putting together a list of the names and birth dates of every child ever born in this area that CHILD is studying or has ever studied."

Even as she spoke, the screen was filled with a list of names. Sally pressed the cursor key that would allow her to scroll down the cathode ray tube until the entire list had been exposed.

"My God," she breathed. She glanced up at the information line at the top of the screen. The list stopped at line 153, and there were five names on each line. She glanced at the printer that sat a few feet away. Three lights, one red, one amber, and one white, glowed softly, indicating that the machine was ready for use.

Seeing her intent, Malone moved to the printer and rolled a sheet of paper into its platen. "Okay."

Once again Sally's fingers flew over the keyboard, and a second later the printer began chattering. "It'll take three pages," she said. Malone nodded silently, wishing he'd bought the automatic paper feeder he'd seen last year.

While the printer worked, Sally studied the screen. "I wonder if they're all part of the same study? But they can't be," she went on. "CHILD does all kinds of surveys, doesn't it?"

"As far as I know."

Once again, Sally's fingers moved over the keyboard. "I'm having the computer analyze the code numbers CHILD uses and see if it can find any relationships," she said.

The printer suddenly stopped for the last time, and Malone pulled the final sheet from the platen. "The name Carl Bronski gave us is here," he said. "Adam Rogers." He stapled the three pages together. "What shall we do with these?"

"Keep them," Sally replied. "They may be all we get." But then the screen suddenly came alive again, this time filled with four blocks of numbers.

Malone frowned at the screen. "What's that mean?"

"Apparently CHILD is doing four studies, and they've assigned the code numbers by multiples of certain other numbers." She pointed to the block of numbers in the upper left-hand quadrant of the screen. "Those are all multiples of 13. The others are multiples of 17, 19, and 21."

"I'm not sure I get it," Malone said.

Sally's voice became grim. "It means that Dr. Wiseman is lying. According to him, CHILD uses random numbers to decide whom to survey. But these numbers aren't random—they only appear to be when they're all mixed together. What CHILD is really doing is studying selected children and keeping them grouped together by means of the code numbers. Let's try something else."

For the third time, her hands manipulated the keyboard, and once more the screen began to fill with numbers, but this time there were names attached to them. As Sally stared at the names, her eyes brimmed with tears.

"I told it to find Julie's case number, then list all the names and numbers of the rest of that group," she explained.

All the names were on the list.

Randy Corliss.

Adam Rogers.

Julie Montgomery.

Eden Ransom.

Jason Montgomery.

In all, there were forty-six names. Sally Montgomery and Mark Malone stared at the list for several seconds, each deep in his own thoughts.

"We'd better print it out," Malone said at last.

Sally nodded silently, and her fingers once more began moving over the keyboard, but slowly this time, as if by committing the list to paper she would somehow seal whatever fates awaited the children whose names appeared on it.

Fifty feet away, Arthur Wiseman sat in his office listening quietly while Steve Montgomery once again described Jason's misadventures.

"And that's it?" he asked when Steve had finished his recital.

"That's it."

Wiseman turned to Jason.

"And what about you, son? Did it happen the way your father told it?"

"I—I guess so," Jason faltered. "I mean, the fight happened, and I was bleeding."

"Well, why don't we just have a look at you and see what we can find, all right?"

Jason frowned. He hated it when Dr. Malone poked and prodded at him, and stuck the ice cream stick in his mouth and made him say *aaahhh.* It wasn't as if he was ever sick, or anything was wrong with him. "I'm okay," he said.

"And who said you weren't?" Wiseman countered with mock severity. "All I want to do is take a peek. I haven't seen you since the day you were born, and it seems to me it's only fair if you let me admire my work."

"Were you the doctor who delivered me?" Jason asked. He'd always thought it was Dr. Malone.

"Sure was. Popped you a good one on the bottom, then handed you over to

Dr. Malone. You were a scrappy little critter, as I recall. Nearly tore the roof off this place with the screaming and yelling."

Still talking, Wiseman led Jason into the examining room and boosted him up onto the table.

"What are those?" the little boy asked, staring curiously at the stirrups that rose from one end of the table.

"Just something I use now and then. Why don't you take off your shirt?"

Obediently, Jason stripped to the waist, then waited to see what would happen. A moment later he felt the cold chill of the stethoscope as the doctor listened to his heartbeat and his breathing. Then he looked from side to side while Dr. Wiseman carefully watched his eyes.

"Which one got the fist?"

"This one," Jason replied, holding his hand up to his right eye.

Wiseman compared the boy's eyes carefully, and saw no evidence of a bruise. "Couldn't have been much of a punch."

"I guess it wasn't," Jason admitted. "It only hurt for a second."

"And what about the other day, when you spilled the fudge on your arm. Did that hurt?"

"Not much," Jason said, scratching his head while he tried to remember. "I guess it did at first, but not very long. Like the day I cut my finger."

"Your finger?" Wiseman asked.

Jason nodded. "I was making a fort and I cut myself."

"Badly?"

"Nah. It bled for a minute, and I was going to put a Band-Aid on it, but then it healed up."

Now it was Wiseman who scratched his head. "Healed up? Before you put a Band-Aid on it?"

"Sure."

Wiseman thought for a moment, then spoke again. "How would you like to have your blood tested?" he asked.

"What for?"

"Just to find out something," Wiseman replied.

"Okay."

A moment later, while Jason watched, Wiseman plunged a needle into the boy's arm and drew out five cc's of blood. With a single practiced motion, he drew out the needle, placed an alcohol-soaked wad of cotton on the point where the needle had pierced Jason's skin, then folded the boy's arm so that the cotton was held in place. "Just hold your arm like that for a few minutes," he said. Taking the blood sample with him, he returned to his office and picked up the phone. He issued a series of orders, then, putting the receiver back on the hook, he turned to Steve Montgomery.

"Is something wrong?" Steve asked anxiously.

"I don't know," Wiseman replied. "At the moment it doesn't look like it, but I want some tests run on his blood. Also, it appears that Jason may have an unusual ability, which I'm testing right now." He glanced at his watch. Two minutes had elapsed since he had withdrawn the needle from Jason's arm. "Just sit tight a minute."

He returned to the examining room and smiled at the boy. "All right," he said. "Let's have a look and see if you're bleeding."

Jason unfolded his arm, and Wiseman removed the cotton wad from the small wound.

Except that there was no wound there.

He examined the skin very closely, but nowhere could he find so much as a mark indicating that the skin had recently been punctured.

Chewing his lip thoughtfully, Wiseman led Jason back to the office, then sent him on out to the waiting room. "I want to talk to your father for a few minutes. Okay?"

Jason, glad that the examination was over, grinned happily. "Okay." Then something occurred to him. "I always get a sucker from Dr. Malone."

"Well, I'm afraid I don't have any," Wiseman told him. "But maybe, if you're a good boy, I can go down to Dr. Malone's office in a few minutes and find one. How's that?"

"Okay."

Jason disappeared into the waiting room, and Wiseman closed the door behind him.

"Well?" Steve asked.

"Well," Wiseman said softly, "I just don't know. It appears to me that Jason heals at an abnormally fast rate."

"What does that mean?"

Wiseman shrugged helplessly. "I can't tell you. It would seem to me that it means Jason has some kind of abnormality in his body, and it's manifesting itself in an accelerated regeneration of tissue. But I can't be sure what else it might be doing."

Steve frowned. "I don't follow you."

Wiseman wondered what to say, and finally decided to say as little as possible. His fingers began their habitual drumming on the desk top.

"I think perhaps it might be wise to keep Jason here for a day or two," he began. "Jason seems to have some kind of abnormality, and until we find out just what it is and just what its effects are, I'd like to keep him under observation."

"You mean here?" Steve asked. If nothing was wrong with Jason, why should he stay in the hospital?

"Here," Wiseman agreed. Then, after a slight hesitation, he added, "Or perhaps in a diagnostic clinic." He began carefully explaining to Steve exactly what he had in mind.

As he listened to the older man, Steve began to feel as if he had lost control over his life and the lives of his family. First Julie, then Sally, now Jason. What had happened? What *was* happening? He could understand none of it, and as Wiseman continued talking, it all began to sound more and more unreal. By the time Wiseman had finished, Steve's resistance to the idea of putting an apparently healthy child in the hospital had begun to erode. Perhaps, he had begun to think, Jason *should* be put under observation. At least for a while . . .

Randy Corliss stood uncertainly outside the fence. The howling of the dogs grew louder. He wondered how many of them there were.

He'd never heard them before, or seen them. Had they been there all the time? But where? Maybe they'd been kept locked up in the basement. But what did it mean that they were loose now? Did they already know he had escaped, or were they loose every night, guarding the grounds. And then he saw them—three of them—moving steadily along his trail to the point where he'd gone into the water. They paused there; their baying stopped suddenly while they sniffed curiously around, first at the ground, then at the air. And then they turned and began moving toward him. Randy stood still, fascinated by the huge beasts, his fear eased by the high fence that separated him from them.

As he watched they discovered the fourth dog, lying dead near the fence, and suddenly their snuffling and sniffing gave way to whining. They poked at the corpse, pawing at it almost as if they were uncertain of what it was. And then, as one, they caught Randy's scent. Their dead companion suddenly forgotten, they turned toward the fence, fangs bared, and began snarling. The ugly sound grew until the night was once again filled with their terrifying voices.

Randy fled into the woods.

For the first few minutes he simply ran, but then, as the baying of the dogs faded slightly, he paused. He had to think.

If they knew he was gone, they would turn the dogs loose in the forest. Not only that, but they would find the dead dog and know exactly where to let the live ones hunt. And as soon as they caught his scent, he wouldn't have a chance.

And then an image of the dogs at the edge of the stream came to his mind. His trail had ended there, and they hadn't known what to do.

He must get back to the stream.

It was off to the right somewhere.

Or was it?

He'd been so frightened, he hadn't paid much attention to where he was going. He thought he'd run in a straight line, at least as straight as he could while still threading his way through the trees, but had he really?

He stood still. The blackness seemed to close in around him, shutting out everything—even the howling dogs—and he felt the first ragged edges of panic reaching out for him. It was like when he was learning to swim, and he'd gotten into deep water for the first time. His mother had been there with him, only a couple of feet away, but still he had begun thrashing at the water, terrified that he was going to die.

And then he'd heard his mother's voice calmly telling him not to panic, to let himself float. And now, as that strange sense of terror began flooding over him, he repeated his mother's words.

"Don't panic," he said out loud. Then, again, "Don't panic."

And it worked. The terror eased. The rushing sound in his head that had momentarily blocked out the sounds of the night disappeared, and once more he could hear the dogs. He turned, so the sound seemed to be coming from behind him. And then, slowly and deliberately, he turned to the right and began walking through the woods. He moved slowly, pausing every few minutes to listen.

Finally, he heard it. Ahead of him was the soft, gurgling sound of running water. He began to run.

He came to the brook and waded in, turning left to begin making his way upstream. The bottom was covered with water-smoothed rocks, and even the rubber soles of his sneakers failed to find a firm purchase on them. Randy found himself slipping and sliding, falling into the water, only to pick himself up and keep going.

He waded on and on, with no idea of the direction in which the stream was leading him or what his goal might be. All he knew was that he had to get away from the Academy, or he would die. And in order to get away, he must stay in the water, where the dogs couldn't follow him.

Suddenly the noise of the water increased. Randy searched the darkness ahead. Vaguely he could see that he was approaching a fork; the brook he had been wading in was only an offshoot of a larger stream. What if it was too deep, or the current was too fast? And yet he knew he had no choice. Doggedly, he made his way into the larger stream, and began battling against the current. The water was over his knees now.

He came to a small waterfall, and his path was suddenly blocked. He stopped, staring at the four-foot cascade, and wondered what to do.

To the left there seemed to be a path.

Should he leave the stream?

But what if the dogs came this way and found his scent on the path?

He stayed in the water and began groping for a handhold that would allow him to pull himself up directly through the torrent. At last his right hand found the slippery surface of a branch that had lodged in the rocks. He clung to it while his feet battled the current to find a toehold. And then, for just a moment, his right foot caught and he hauled himself over the ledge to lie gasping and choking in the stream. He looked up. Just ahead of him a large rock rose out of the water. He heaved himself back to his feet and struggled toward it, not sure he had the strength to get to it, but unwilling to sink back into the cold water.

And then he was there. He sank down onto the rock, his breath coming in a series of heaving gasps. He was soaked through, and cold, and his teeth were chattering.

But, for the moment, he was safe.

He had no way of knowing how long he sat on the rock, but it seemed like hours. And then, finally, his teeth stopped chattering, and his breath came easily and evenly. He listened, straining to hear the baying of the dogs, but if it was there, the rushing water made it indistinguishable from any other sound.

At last he got to his feet and continued wading. The stream leveled out, and the rocky bottom was replaced by sand. The wading became easier, and Randy was no longer even tempted to leave the stream.

Ahead a light flashed.

Randy stopped and stood stock-still, staring into the darkness.

Was someone out there with a light, looking for him?

Once again the light flashed. Suddenly, Randy knew what it was.

Ahead of him there was a road, and the flashes of light were cars. He redoubled his efforts and forged ahead, splashing through the water, his mind filled with the memories of the previous summer, when he had been alone in the dark, then seen lights, and finally come to a road. Maybe it would happen like that again, and someone would find him and take him home.

He came to the bridge that carried the road over the stream. He was about to scramble up the bank to wave at the first car that came along, when he suddenly stopped.

What if Dr. Hamlin was out there in a car looking for him? Or Miss Bowen? Or any of them?

He couldn't just climb out.

But he couldn't just keep wading up the stream either. He listened carefully. Here, where the stream slid quietly over a smooth bottom, the night was silent. No matter how hard he tried, he could hear no dogs barking, no sounds of animals crashing through the forest toward him.

Maybe, if he was very careful, it was safe to leave the stream.

He tried to figure out which way the Academy might be. Behind him, he thought, and to the left.

Reluctantly, Randy left the water and made his way up the right bank, then, staying well back from the road, he began moving through the woods, making sure every few steps that the road was still in sight.

To pass the time he began counting his steps.

He had counted to six hundred and thirty-four, when he suddenly became aware of a light flashing in the distance.

Not the headlight of a car, for it wasn't moving.

No, it was the light of a sign. He began running, and in a few moments he was able to read it.

The sign was for a diner, and its flashing message pulsated through the darkness:

OPEN ALL NIGHT

At last, Randy was safe.

CHAPTER 24

George Hamlin glanced up at the clock on the wall of his office. It was nearly ten, he was tired, and a long night of work stretched ahead of him. It was work he hated to have to do. Nevertheless, it had to be done. Now he faced his staff, and wondered if he looked as bad as they did. The five of them sat nervously in a semicircle around his desk, their faces drawn, their eyes furtive. Louise Bowen, upon whom Hamlin placed full responsibility for what was about to happen, sat with her head down, her fingers twisting at the fringe of a woolen shawl that was draped over her shoulders.

She looks old, Hamlin thought irrelevantly. She looks old and tired. Then he took a deep breath and began speaking.

"You all know what's happened. This evening's unfortunate events leave me no choice. The God Project is going to be suspended."

A low murmuring rippled through the room, and the laboratory technician raised a tentative hand. "Isn't there anything we can do?"

"I wish there were," Hamlin replied. "But Randy Corliss is gone, and we have no way of recovering him. The dogs—the dogs lost his scent when he went into the stream. He's gone, and that's that. We have to assume that he's alive, and that he's going to get home, and that he's going to talk about where he's been."

"But what about the burn-out?" someone asked.

Hamlin responded to the question with a twisted smile. "I suppose a miracle could be happening, and Randy could be lying dead out there somewhere right now. But I don't think we can count on that, can we? We have to assume the worst—that Randy Corliss is alive. And so we are going to close the Academy. Tonight."

Louise Bowen's head came up, and she stared at Hamlin with a dazed look. "Tonight?" she repeated. "But—but what about the—"

Hamlin's eyes fastened on her, their icy blue matching the coldness of his voice. "All the subjects will be destroyed. Please bring them to the lab."

"But—" Louise started to protest.

"Now." The two of them stared at each other for a moment, and then Louise rose and made her way out of the suddenly silent room. When she was gone, Hamlin turned his attention to the others. The four of them had been with the project since the beginning, and no matter what happened, he knew he could count on their loyalty. But what about Louise Bowen? Could he count on hers? Probably not. It was one more thing he would, in the end, have to deal with himself. He sighed and began issuing orders. "We'll pack all the records and as much of the equipment as we can. Paul Randolph is sending three trucks from Boston." A note of sarcasm crept into his voice as he watched his staff exchange doubtful glances. "They'll have to be enough, since they're all we have." He paused for a few seconds, then began speaking again, his voice as bitter as his words. "I told Randolph this was a stupid idea. We should have moved to the desert somewhere or out of the country. Using this place was asking for trouble." His voice rose dangerously. "Ten years of work—ten *years!* And after six months out here it's gone. Gone! It makes me—" Hearing the tone of his own voice, he bit back his words. "Never mind," he said, forcing himself to hold his emotions in check. "Let's get started. It's going to be a long night."

Louise Bowen climbed the stairs slowly. She had made a mistake, and now the price for that mistake was going to have to be paid.

It didn't seem right: the mistake had been so small, and the price was so high.

All she had done, really, was hesitate. She had found Randy's room empty and started for the stairs, intent on telling Hamlin that Randy was gone. But then she had hesitated.

Instead of going downstairs, she had gone up to the attic, certain that she would find Randy there. The attic had been empty, but the ladder, normally folded up against the roof, was down, and the skylight was propped open. She had climbed the ladder and looked out over the roof just in time to see Randy slip, catch himself, and start down the tree.

At that point Louise had hesitated no more. She had hurried downstairs to report what had happened, but it was already too late. Randy was gone, and now the others would have to follow.

Louise opened the door to Adam Rogers's room. Adam, his unruly hair falling over his forehead, was propped up in his bed. He looked at Louise apprehensively. "Did they find Randy?"

"No," Louise admitted. Now came the hardest part. "But since everyone is up, we've decided to have a little party. We're all going down to the dining room, and then we have a surprise for each of you."

Adam's face broke into an eager grin, and he scrambled off the bed. "Shall I get dressed?"

"No," Louise said quietly. "You'll be fine just the way you are."

Then, as Adam scampered down the stairs, Louise continued along the hall, stopping at each room to repeat what she had told Adam to Jerry Preston and Billy Mayhew. And both of them, their eyes glowing with anticipation, had followed Adam down the stairs. Her heart breaking, Louise, too, made her way to the dining room, forced herself to smile at the three boys, then went on through the kitchen and into the lab. George Hamlin turned to look at her.

"Are they ready?"

Louise nodded and tried to swallow the lump that had formed in her throat. "I—I told them we were going to have a party," she said, her voice shaking. "Can I make them some cocoa?"

Hamlin scowled in barely contained fury. *"Cocoa?* You want to make *cocoa* for them?"

Louise's expression hardened with determination. "They don't have to know what's going to happen," she said. "Can't they at least *think* it's a party? It will only take a minute."

Hamlin glanced at the clock, then back at Louise. Then, realizing it would take as long to argue with her as it would to let her have her way, he shrugged indifferently. "All right," he said. "You have fifteen minutes."

As Louise set about making the cocoa, she used the time to compose herself. Whatever happened, she must not let the children see how upset she was. It would be easier for them if they suspected nothing. Forcing a smile, she carried a tray with the pot and four cups into the dining room.

"Here we are," she said as brightly as she could. The three little boys grinned happily.

"What's the surprise?" Jerry Preston asked.

Louise hesitated only a split second. "It's from Dr. Hamlin. He'll tell you all about it."

She poured the cocoa and passed the cups around. And then, four minutes later, George Hamlin appeared at the door as if on cue.

"Jerry?"

Pleased to be the first selected, Jerry Preston grinned at his friends and got up to follow Hamlin out of the dining room.

Once more Hamlin came back, and then Louise Bowen was alone with Adam.

"How come I'm always last?" the little boy complained.

"Are you?" Louise said, not really listening.

"It must be because I'm youngest," Adam said thoughtfully. "When I'm older, will I get to do things first?"

Louise's eyes brimmed with tears as she looked at the solemn face of the little boy. "I don't know," she whispered.

Adam cocked his head and frowned. "Is something wrong?"

Louise bit her lip and brushed at her eyes, but before she was forced to find a reply to his question, Hamlin appeared once more at the door. "All right, Adam," he said. Then his gaze swung over to Louise. "And you come, too, please, Louise."

Hamlin led them through the kitchen and laboratory to a small room at the rear of the house. Adam stared at the odd machine that stood in the middle of the floor. "Is that the surprise?"

"No," Hamlin explained. "It's for a new test we want to give you. Can you get into it by yourself, or do you need some help?"

"I can do it," Adam replied. The machine looked to him like a huge fat metal cigar with a glass door at one end. "What's it do?"

"It's to test your breathing," Hamlin said. "It only takes a minute, and then you can go back to your friends." He helped Adam climb into the machine. "All set?"

The little boy nodded uncertainly, and Hamlin closed and sealed the heavy glass door. Then he turned to face Louise. "Open the valve," he said.

Louise's eyes widened. "No," she whispered. "No, I can't do it—"

Hamlin's voice hardened. "When the project is a success we will all share the glory. Until then we will all share the responsibility. Turn the valve."

Almost against her will, Louise's hand moved to the valve that would open the decompression lines. "I can't—"

But Hamlin was inexorable. "You can, and you will!"

Watching Adam Rogers through the glass door, Louise turned the valve. There was a quick *whoosh* as air rushed out of the chamber, and a fleeting look of surprise came into Adam's eyes. Then it was over.

Five minutes later Adam Rogers's body joined the others in the crematory that had long ago been installed in this room, and the fires were started.

Lucy Corliss picked up the telephone on the third ring, expecting to hear either Sally Montgomery or Mark Malone at the other end. Instead, when it was a voice she didn't recognize, her heart skipped a beat.

"Is this Mrs. Corliss?" the voice asked again.

"Yes."

"The mother of Randy Corliss?"

Lucy felt her legs begin to shake and quickly sat down on one of the kitchen chairs. Was this it? Was she finally hearing from the people who had taken Randy?

"Yes," she said into the phone. Then louder. "Yes, it is." She covered the mouthpiece. "Jim? Jim!" As her former husband hurried into the room, she strained to hear what the man on the phone was saying.

"This is Max Birnbaum. I got a diner out on the Langston road."

"Yes?" Lucy asked once more. What was the man talking about?

"Anyway, Mrs. Corliss, about ten minutes ago, a kid comes wandering in, all soaking wet, and asks me to call you."

"Randy?" Lucy breathed. "Randy's there?"

"Right here, ma'am."

There was a pause, and then Lucy heard Randy's voice, shaking slightly, but unmistakably Randy's. "Mom?"

"Randy? Oh, Randy, what's happened? Where are you?"

"I ran away, Mom. I got scared, so I ran away. I was afraid I was going to die."

"Die?" Lucy echoed. He ran away from home because he was afraid he was going to die? Where had he ever gotten such an idea? "Oh, Randy, I've been so worried—so frightened."

"Will you come and get me?"

"Yes! Oh, Randy, yes! Where are you? I'll come right now. Right now!"

"I'm at Mr. Birnbaum's diner. It's—I don't know. Mr. Birnbaum can tell you how to get here."

Lucy signaled frantically, but Jim already had a pen and paper ready. She scribbled down the directions, spoke to Randy once more, then hung up.

"He's all right," she cried, the strain of the last week draining from her eyes. "Oh, Jim, he's all right!" She hurled herself into his arms, hugging him tightly. "He's back, Jim. Our son's back." And then, seeing Carl Bronski standing in the doorway, his face sober, she drew away from Jim. "Carl? Is something wrong?"

"I don't know," the policeman said. "I hope not. But it could be a trick."

Her happiness deserting her as fast as it had come, Lucy sank back onto her chair. "A trick?"

"What did he say?"

Lucy repeated Randy's words as closely as she could remember them. When she was done, Bronski nodded. "So he ran away after all," he said softly.

"But he wants to come home now," Lucy replied. "It's not a trick—I know it isn't." She turned to Jim, and her voice suddenly grew shy. "Come with me, Jim. Let's go get him together." She looked from Jim to Bronski, then back at Jim again. "It's over. Oh, God, it's over. I'll get my coat, and my purse, and then—" She ran out of the room, and the two men heard her rummaging in the closet for her coat.

"It isn't over at all," Bronski said softly. Jim Corliss looked puzzled. "It still might all be a trick," Bronski went on. Then, while Jim watched, Bronski picked up the telephone book, flipped through the pages, and finally dialed a number. He spoke briefly, then weighed his options. Finally, he decided to gamble on his instincts. "Okay," he told Jim. "I don't think the call was a fake, so I'll let you two go get Randy by yourselves. I can wait until you get him home to hear his story. But keep something in mind, Jim." His voice dropped so Lucy would not overhear his words. "He said he ran away because he was afraid he was going to die. But he didn't say he ran away from *home.* He—well, he might just as easily have run away from whoever took him."

"*If* anyone took him," Jim countered.

"There's still Adam Rogers, and God knows how many others."

Jim sighed, knowing Bronski was right. "Okay. But don't tell that to Lucy right now, will you? Let her have a few minutes. It's been so rough—"

"I won't," Bronski promised. "Tell you what—I'll stay here and man the phone in case Sally or Malone calls. And see if you can keep Randy from talking until you get him back here, all right? I'd like to hear what he has to say first hand."

As they drove through the night toward Langston and the diner where Randy was waiting, Lucy slowly became aware that Jim was not sharing her happiness. At last she could bear it no longer.

"What's wrong?" she asked. "What did Carl say to you while I was getting my coat?"

"Nothing."

Lucy looked at him carefully. Even in the dim light, she could see the worry in his face.

"Don't lie to me, Jim. Not now. Please?"

Jim forced a smile and patted her hand as it rested on his thigh. "There's nothing, sweetheart. Really."

But Lucy was not convinced. They drove on in silence, and twenty minutes later, in the distance, they saw a flashing neon sign.

"That must be it," Jim said softly.

Lucy leaned anxiously forward in the seat, her excitement growing as they pulled into the parking lot next to the diner. She was out of the car even before Jim had finished parking it, running toward the front door. Then she was inside, and there was Randy, sitting with a heavy set, middle-aged man who wore a greasy chef's hat. Recognizing his mother, Randy leaped off his chair.

"Mom! Oh, Mom, I was so scared!" He was in her arms, burying his face in her breast, the tears he had been holding back all night finally flowing.

"It's all right, sweetheart," Lucy whispered. "I'm here now, and it's all right." She patted him gently and held him, rocking him slowly back and forth until his sobbing subsided. Then, as Jim came through the front door, she whispered to him again. "I have a surprise for you."

He looked up at her through his tears. "A surprise? What?"

"Turn around."

Randy turned around. Lucy expected him to tear himself loose from her arms and run to his father. Instead, she felt him stiffen.

"Dad?" he said uncertainly.

"It's me, son," Jim replied. He held his arms out to Randy, but Randy only shrank closer to his mother.

"Don't make me go back there," he said. "Please don't make me go back there."

As she listened to Randy's words, Lucy felt a chill. So that was why Jim had not shared in her happiness. All along, while he was pretending to help her, pretending to be worried about Randy, it had been a lie. All along, he had been the one. She'd been right. Right from the start, she'd been correct to suspect him. Fury rose in her, and she stood up to face Jim Corliss, but before she could speak, he came over and put his hands on her shoulders.

"Don't say it," he begged. "I know what you're going to say, and I know you'll regret it later. It's not over, Lucy. I don't know any more about it than you, but I know it's not over. That's what Bronski told me in the kitchen. He said we don't know *where* Randy ran away from."

"Randy said he ran away from home because he was afraid he was going to die."

"No, I didn't, Mom," Randy said. His parents looked down at him. "I ran away from the Academy. The one Daddy sent me to."

Jim looked steadily into Lucy's eyes. "I swear I don't know what he's talking about, Lucy."

As they drove home Lucy wondered whether to believe him or not. She wanted to. God, how she wanted to. But could she?

The printer was spewing out the last of the computations Sally had ordered when the knock came at the door opening into the corridor. Mark Malone glanced at Sally, whose eyes filled with sudden fear.

"Who is it?" he called.

"Dr. Malone, is that you?" a woman's uncertain voice answered.

Malone moved toward the door and opened it. "It's me."

The nurse smiled in relief. "Thank God. I saw the light under your door and was afraid someone might have broken in." She glanced into the office, recognizing Sally. "Why, hello, Mrs. Montgomery. Are you looking for Jason?"

"Jason?" Sally asked in surprise.

If the nurse noticed Sally's blankness, she gave no sign. "He's in Dr. Wiseman's office with your husband."

"I—what—?"

But before she could say anything else, Mark Malone held up a warning hand. "Thank you," he said to the nurse. "Mrs. Montgomery and I were just discussing the problem." Then, without waiting for the nurse to reply, he closed the door. He turned to Sally, whose expression of surprise had turned to one of worry.

"Jason and Steve are *here?* But why?"

"I don't know," Malone said. "But I don't think we'd better wait around to find out. Someone's sure to tell Wiseman you're here." He began stuffing his briefcase with the printouts. "Shut that thing off, and let's get out of here."

Sally switched the terminal off, stood up, and began gathering her things together. Malone had already opened the door to the parking lot, waiting for her. And then, as she started across the room, Sally stopped. "I can't go."

Malone stared at her. "Sally, we've got to."

But Sally was shaking her head. "I can't go. Jason's here, and I have to find out why."

"Sally—"

"Mark, you have all the data. Take it and go." She looked up at him imploringly. "Mark, he's my son. If something's wrong, I've got to be with him. Don't you see?"

Malone's mind raced, and he came to a quick decision. "I'll go with you," he said. He closed the outside door and moved toward Sally, who took a step back.

"No. Take those printouts and go back to Lucy's. I'll get there as soon as I can."

"If Wiseman gets his hands on you, you might not get back at all," Malone said, his voice tight. He patted the briefcase. "And right now we need you to lead us through all this. Come on."

Taking her by the arm, he led her out of his office and through the corridors to Arthur Wiseman's waiting room. There, sitting on a chair leafing through a magazine, was Jason. He looked up and grinned.

"Hi, Mom. Hi, Dr. Malone."

Sally dropped to her knees and hugged the boy. "Honey, what are you doing here? Are you all right?"

"I'm okay," Jason said, wriggling free of the embrace.

"Then what are you doing here?"

Jason did his best to explain what had happened. "So Dr. Wiseman told Dad to bring me down, and he took some of my blood, and I think he wants me to go somewhere else."

"Somewhere else?" Sally breathed.

Jason looked guilty. "I put my ear against the door and listened," he admitted. "He wants me to go somewhere for ob—" He frowned, then remembered the word. "Observation."

Sally looked up at Malone. "I don't understand—"

"Don't you? I think maybe I do." He reached down and swung Jason up off the chair. "How'd you like to go for a ride with your mother and me, sport?"

"Where?"

"Over to visit some friends." He started out of the waiting room, speaking to Sally over his shoulder. "Come on."

With an uncertain glance at the closed door leading to Dr. Wiseman's inner office, Sally followed.

CHAPTER 25

Then it's settled," Arthur Wiseman said. He stood up, stretched, and came around to lean on the edge of his desk. "CHILD has the best children's diagnostic clinic in the country. If they can't find out what's going on with Jason, nobody can. Now, it seems to me that we might as well keep the boy here tonight and send him to Boston in the morning."

But Steve was still not quite sure. "Can't he stay home tonight? It seems to me—"

"And it seems to *me*," Wiseman interrupted emphatically, "that you have quite enough to worry about tonight."

"But there's nothing really wrong with him."

"So it would appear," Wiseman agreed. "But appearances can be deceiving." His voice dropped slightly. "Don't forget Julie."

At mention of his daughter's name, the last of Steve's resistance crumbled. He rose to his feet and went to the door, opening it. "Jason?"

The waiting room was empty. "Jason?" he repeated, more loudly this time. Then Wiseman was beside him.

"He probably got bored and went to the emergency room," the older man suggested.

But when they got to the emergency room, it, too, was empty, with only the duty nurse sitting placidly at her desk.

"Did Jason Montgomery come through here?" Wiseman asked.

The nurse shook her head. "I haven't seen him. Maybe he's in Dr. Malone's office."

"Malone? Is he here?"

Now the nurse's smile faded into an uncertain frown. "Of course. Didn't you see him? He and Mrs. Montgomery—"

"Mrs. Montgomery!" Wiseman flared. Blood rushed into his face as sudden fury raged through him. "I gave orders that if anybody—*anybody*—saw Mrs. Montgomery, I was to be notified immediately."

The nurse trembled under his wrath. "I—I'm sorry, Dr. Wiseman," she stammered. "I didn't know. No one told me when I came on shift, and—" But she was talking to an empty room. Wiseman, followed by Steve Montgomery, was striding down the hall toward Malone's office.

It, too, was empty.

The two men stood silently for a moment, and it was Steve Montgomery who at last spoke, his voice quiet, defeated. "I don't get it."

"Neither do I," Wiseman replied tightly. "But it seems that Sally must have convinced Malone that there's something to her fantasies."

And suddenly Steve knew exactly where his wife had gone. "Lucy Corliss," he said. "They're with Lucy Corliss." He started through Malone's office. "Come on."

"Wait a minute," Wiseman said. Steve turned to face him. "What are you going to do?"

"I'm going to get my wife and son!"

"And if Sally doesn't want to go with you?"

"She has to—I'm her husband!"

"Think, Steve. She doesn't trust you, and she doesn't trust me. Apparently, she only trusts this Corliss woman, and maybe Mark Malone. Nor does she have to do anything she doesn't want to. You can't barge in there and drag her out, even if you think it's for her own good."

Steve's shoulders slumped; suddenly he felt exhausted—exhausted and frustrated. "But I have to do something," he said at last. "I can't just let her take Jason, let things go. I can't . . ."

"For now," Wiseman said softly, "there isn't anything else you can do. Wait until morning, Steve." He led the unhappy man back to his own office, where he opened his drug cabinet, shook four tablets out of a bottle and into an envelope, and handed it to Steve. "Go home and try to get some sleep. If you need to, take these. And stop worrying—Mark Malone is a good man. He won't let anything happen to either Sally or Jason. Then, tomorrow, if she hasn't come home, we'll take whatever action is necessary to protect her."

Steve Montgomery, his mind whirling with conflicting doubts and emotions, made his way out into the night.

"But *why* did you go with that woman?" Lucy asked for the third time. Once again, Randy repeated his answer.

"She said Daddy sent her. They said Daddy was on a trip, and when he got back, he'd come and visit me."

"But I haven't been anywhere, son," Jim Corliss told the little boy. "Ever since the day you disappeared, I've been right here, trying to help your mother find you."

Randy's expression reflected his uncertainty. He turned to his mother.

"It's true, darling," she assured him. "He hasn't been on a trip at all."

"And I'm not going to die?" Randy asked, his voice quavering.

Lucy gathered him into her arms. "Of course you're not going to die," she whispered. "You're a very healthy little boy, and there's no reason on earth for you to die." And yet, as she recalled the strange story he'd related, she wondered.

Nothing about the Academy sounded right. It didn't sound like a school to her, at least not a school she'd ever heard of.

Had he told the truth?

Once or twice, as Randy had talked, she'd caught a glimpse of Carl Bronski's face, and she'd seen doubt. She'd seen it in his eyes, in the set of his mouth, in the nearly imperceptible shakings of his head. Bronski, she knew, didn't quite believe what he was hearing.

And then, with the arrival of Sally, Jason, and Malone, her doubts were shunted aside while she explained to Sally what had happened. Finally she turned to Malone. "Could you look at him? We got his clothes off him and bathed him, and he seems to be all right, but after what he told us . . ."

"No problem," Malone replied. He turned to the two boys, who were happily whispering together. "Randy? How'd you like to have me take a look at you?"

"I'm okay," Randy said, but before Randy could protest further, Lucy stepped in.

"You're going with Dr. Malone, and then you're going to bed. It's past midnight."

"And Jason's going with you," Sally added.

Suddenly, with the prospect of his friend sleeping over, Randy grinned. "Okay. Can Jason watch the examination?"

"Sure," Malone agreed. "But it's not going to be very interesting. I'm just going to make sure you're breathing. Come on." He led the boys off to Randy's room, and a sudden silence fell over the group in the living room. It was Sally who finally broke it.

"Lucy, I'm so happy for you—it's like a miracle. But where was he?"

"Better wait for Malone," Bronski said. "No point in going through it all twice. What did you find?"

"A lot," Sally replied. "It's all in Mark's bag, at least as much as we could get. And there's no question that something's going on. Dr. Wiseman lied to me, and CHILD lied to you, Lucy. Those children weren't picked randomly."

"You're sure?" Bronski asked.

"I'm sure," Sally said quietly. "I don't know yet how they were picked for that study or what it's all about, but it's all there. Wait until you see." She opened Malone's briefcase and began pulling the printouts from its depths.

"My Lord," Lucy whispered as the pile grew. "So much."

"And most of it probably doesn't mean a thing. A lot of this is nothing more than copies of medical records."

"What for?"

"For us to search through. Somewhere there's a common factor that makes all these children special. We're going to have to find it."

"What's all this?" Carl Bronski asked. He was holding several sheets of paper that were stapled together. Sally glanced at them.

"The correlations. On the third page there's a list of names of all the children involved in Group Twenty-one."

Jim Corliss, who was also thumbing through the stacks of documents, looked at Sally curiously. "Group Twenty-one?"

"It's a name Mark and I have been using." Quickly, she explained the system CHILD had used for keeping track of its subjects. "And all of our children are in that group," she finished. "Jason and Randy, and Julie, and Jan Ransom's baby."

Bronski pulled the list of names loose from the rest of the papers. "I'll be back in an hour," he said. Before anyone could protest, he was gone.

A few minutes later Mark Malone rejoined the others.

"Randy's fine," he told them. "Not that I expected anything else. Now tell us what happened to him."

Between them Jim and Lucy did their best to retell Randy's story. "I know it doesn't sound plausible," Lucy finished. "I mean, no one can climb over an electrified fence."

"And no one can spill boiling fudge on himself without getting burned, or drink Lysol without even getting sick," Sally added. "But we *know* those things happened too."

Lucy felt a chill go through her. The happiness she had been clinging to ever since she had heard Randy's voice on the telephone began to slip away. "You mean it could all be true?" she asked, turning to Malone.

"I don't know," Malone replied carefully. "But that's why we're here, isn't it? To see if there's any proof in these records." Sighing heavily, he sat down and picked up the medical charts. "Let's start going through them," he said in a weary tone. "And don't ask what we're looking for, because I don't know. Similarities. Just start reading them and try to spot similarities." He passed them out to Jim and Lucy and Sally.

The room fell silent as the four of them began reading.

The desk sergeant at the Eastbury police station looked up in surprise when Carl Bronski walked in.

"What the hell are you doing here?"

"Got a message to put on the telex."

The sergeant, who was a terrible typist, tossed a few obscenities at Bronski. Only when he was done did Bronski tell him that he planned to do the work himself. The desk sergeant brightened. "In that case, help yourself."

Bronski seated himself at the console, and began typing. He worked steadily for twenty minutes, then transmitted his message. He stood up and stretched.

"What's it all about?" the desk sergeant inquired with an obvious lack of interest.

"Don't know yet," Bronski said. "But if you get an answer to any of those, you call me right away. Okay?" He scribbled Lucy Corliss's number on the desk calendar.

"Those?" the sergeant asked. "I thought you said it was *a* message. Singular."

"It was," Bronski replied. "But I sent it to every police department in the country."

The sergeant stared at him. "Holy shit, Bronski. Do you have any idea what the chief's going to say when he sees the bill?"

Bronski grinned. "Probably just about what you said. But by then, I have a feeling he won't really give a damn. Keep an eye on that machine, will you?" He started out the front door, but the sergeant stopped him.

"Mind telling me what it's all about?"

Bronski paused, scratching his head thoughtfully. "I'm not sure," he said at last, "but I'll tell you one thing. If we get back the replies I think we will, you're going to be part of a bigger case than you ever even dreamed of." Then, leaving the mystified sergeant wondering what had gotten into him, Bronski started back to Lucy Corliss's house. On the way, he bought a lot of coffee in little white plastic containers.

It was going to be a long night, and for some reason coffee in cups never kept him awake. If it was cold, it was even better. He made a mental note to take the lids off all the containers as soon as he got back to Lucy's.

"I don't believe you," Jason whispered in the darkness. He was lying on an air mattress that had been inflated and put on the floor next to Randy's bed, with Randy's bedspread wrapped around him as a makeshift blanket. For an hour he had listened while his friend had bragged about his adventures. But the last thing had been too much.

"Well, it's true," Randy insisted. "I threw the dog against the fence, and he died, and then I climbed the fence, and it didn't hurt at all."

"I bet someone turned it off," Jason argued. "If they didn't, you'd be as dead as the dog."

"Bull!" Randy said as loudly as he dared. If his mother heard them, she'd come in and tell them to go to sleep, and he'd hardly begun telling Jason about all the things that had happened to him. "Besides, one day three of the other guys threw me into the fence. That time I got knocked out, but I still didn't really get hurt. I guess I sort of got used to it."

"Maybe there wasn't much electricity in it," Jason suggested.

"Boy, are you stupid. They either have it all on, or they have it all off. There isn't any partway."

"So you say electricity doesn't hurt you?" There was a note of challenge in Jason's voice.

"That's what I've been telling you, isn't it?"

"Prove it."

"How?"

"Just prove it."

Randy turned on the light by his bed and sat up. He looked around the room, his eyes coming to rest on the radio that sat on one of his bookshelves. "All right, I will." He got out of bed, unplugged the radio, then rummaged in a drawer until he found the Swiss Army knife his father had given him the previous Christmas. Bringing the knife and the radio, he squatted down on the floor next to the air mattress.

"Whatcha gonna do?" Jason asked.

"Watch." Randy opened the knife, and cut the cord off the radio. Then, holding the knife in one hand and the cut end of the cord in the other, he carefully stripped away six inches of insulation. When the wires were bare, he put down the knife and took one of the exposed wires in each hand.

"Plug it in," he said.

Jason stared at him, his eyes wide with a mixture of awe and fear. "No," he whispered. "You'll get hurt."

"I won't either," Randy replied. "Go on—plug it in."

Jason picked up the plug and looked around. There, under Randy's bed table, was a double socket, with only the lamp plugged into it. "Are you going to do it or not?" he heard Randy ask.

Jason tried to make up his mind. Was he being chicken? What if something happened to Randy, as he was sure it would? He remembered Julie, and he remembered his guinea pig. With both of them he'd done something he shouldn't have, and they were both dead.

"I can't," he said finally. "I'll hurt you."

"Then I'll do it myself," Randy announced. He jerked the cord out of Jason's hand and jammed the plug into the empty socket. His eyes fixed on Jason, he took one of the bare wires in his left hand.

"Now watch," he whispered. Slowly, while Jason's eyes followed his movements, he reached out with his right hand for the second bare wire. He smiled as he saw Jason holding his breath.

He grabbed the wire and Jason gasped.

"See?" Randy said, grinning broadly. "Look at that."

"So what?" Jason said, trying to sound as if he wasn't impressed. "Maybe there isn't any current."

"Wanna bet?"

"What do you mean?"

"You try it."

The two boys faced each other, Randy confidently holding the bare ends of the radio cord, his expression clearly telling Jason what he thought of him. Then, as if to confirm it, Randy spoke. "Are you chicken?"

"No."

"Then try it."

Jason's voice suddenly grew belligerent. "Okay, I will. Lemme have the cord."

Silently Randy handed the cord over to Jason. Jason took it gingerly with his right hand, staring fearfully at the gleaming strands of wire. Tentatively, he touched them with his left forefinger.

Nothing.

Encouraged, he closed his left hand around the naked end of one side of the cord, then moved his right hand toward the other bare wire.

As he touched it, a spark jumped, and there was a soft crackling sound.

Reflexively, Jason's hand came away from the wire.

"Chicken," Randy sneered.

Jason barely heard him. He was staring curiously at the cord. It had hurt, but not nearly as much as he had been expecting.

"Try it again," Randy urged.

Once more, Randy touched the bare wire, and this time he was able to overcome his reflexes and feel the electricity surge through him.

It didn't hurt. Not really. At first there was a sort of burning sensation, but that subsided to be replaced by something else.

Something not really unpleasant.

Suddenly confident, he closed his right hand tightly over the live wire.

There was still no pain. As the current flowed through him, there was only a faint tickling sensation. He looked at Randy, and slowly a smile came over his face.

"Hey," he said softly. "That's kind of neat, isn't it?" Then he saw the look of disappointment on Randy's face, and suddenly realized that Randy had been hoping it wouldn't work for him, that he'd get a shock. "Are you mad?" he asked.

Randy stared at him for a moment. "I don't know," he said at last. Then he licked his lips. "Why do you suppose it doesn't hurt us?"

"Lots of things don't hurt me," Jason suddenly blurted. "That's why I had to go to the hospital tonight."

Randy cocked his head. "What kind of things?"

Jason's eyes fell on the knife, and he suddenly remembered the day of his sister's funeral, when he'd been playing outside. "I'll show you," he whispered. He picked up the knife and stared at the blade for a second. Then, closing his eyes tightly, he slashed the blade across his hand.

This time it was Randy who gasped.

Jason opened his eyes and stared at his hand. Blood was welling up from a deep cut on his palm.

"It's going to get all over the floor," Randy said.

"No, it won't," Jason told him. "See? It's not bleeding anymore. Got a Kleenex or something?"

Randy rummaged in a drawer and found a rumpled handkerchief. While he watched, Jason sopped up the blood on his hand. The wound had, indeed, stopped bleeding.

"It's pretty bad," Randy whispered.

"Just wait."

As the two boys watched, the gash in Jason's hand began to heal. Three minutes later, even the skin had mended, and there was not even so much as a trace of a scar to mark where the wound had been.

Now it was Randy who stared at Jason with wonder. "Did it hurt?"

Jason shrugged with studied indifference, pleased that he'd outdone his friend. "Just for a second."

"I'm gonna try it," Randy said, picking up the knife. Without giving himself time to change his mind or even think about it, Randy plunged the knife deep into the palm of his hand. He flinched slightly, then stared at the knife. Blood welled up around it.

"Pull it out," Jason whispered.

Jerking hard, Randy wrenched the blade loose, then began mopping at the wound with the already-bloody handkerchief. When the bleeding stopped, the two boys watched.

As with Jason, Randy's wound disappeared within a few minutes.

"Wow," Randy breathed. Then he grinned at Jason. "Know what?" he asked.

"What?"

"We can do anything we want to now, Jason. We can do anything we want to, because nothing can hurt us."

CHAPTER 26

As the first light of dawn glowed dimly through the east windows of his office, Paul Randolph massaged his temples in a vain effort to ease the tensions that had built up through the long night. The two other men in his office were gazing at him, and he had the feeling he was being judged. Overcoming his exhaustion with an effort of sheer will, he attempted to regain control of the meeting.

"Very well, then. The situation as I see it is this: We have the records of the project—the physical records—locked in the vault, ready to go to Washington this afternoon. The computer banks have been emptied of all data pertaining to the project, and the house has been vacated. What about the staff?"

George Hamlin flicked an imaginary speck from his left pantleg. "I can personally guarantee the security of the project as far as my people are concerned. They've all been with me for years, and each of them has a compelling interest in seeing it through."

"And the boy?" the third man in the room asked. He was a middle-aged man whose hard-muscled body denied the appearance of aging that his close-cropped gray hair suggested. When he had first entered the room an hour earlier, Hamlin had known who he was even before Paul Randolph introduced them. The man's military bearing had given him away.

"Well?" Lieutenant General Scott Carmody prodded.

"Ah. That *is* the problem, isn't it?" Hamlin replied. A wintry smile molded his lips into an expression that Randolph had long ago come to associate with Hamlin's less humane ideas. This morning was no exception. "It seems to me that that is the very area in which we need your help. What I believe some of your people sometimes call 'wet activities'?"

"Let's call a spade a spade," the general dryly translated. "You mean you want us to kill him."

Paul Randolph rose from his chair. "Now just wait a minute, George. There are some things that I cannot allow this Institute to be a party to."

When he replied, Hamlin's voice clearly conveyed the contempt he felt for Randolph. "Are there? It seems to me that this is rather an inappropriate time for you to begin setting moral standards for yourself. Or for any of the rest of us, for that matter." Randolph tried to interrupt, but Hamlin pressed on. "Besides, I see no moral dilemma in having some of the general's personnel pacify Randy Corliss."

"You mean kill him," Randolph corrected.

"As you will. Kill him. Remove him. Whatever. The point is that as far as we know, he's alive, and if he's alive, he's undoubtedly talking. That makes him, and anyone he's talked to, a threat to all of us."

"But to kill him?"

"In all likelihood he's going to die anyway, Paul. All the others have."

The general frowned. "All of them? I thought you were on the verge of success."

"I am," Hamlin told him. "Indeed, at the point that one of the subjects survives to maturity, I *will* have succeeded, and we're not that far away. In fact, I think Randy Corliss just might be our first success, but unfortunately, circumstances don't allow us to continue working with him. He's become a threat."

"George, he's only a little boy—" Randolph broke in.

"*God* makes little boys, Paul. *I* made Randy Corliss." He leaned forward, gazing intently at Randolph. "You've never really grasped the nature of the project, have you, Paul?"

"You know that isn't true, George."

"Isn't it? You keep referring to my subjects as little boys. But Randy Corliss and the others are not boys at all. They are a new species, which I created through genetic engineering. Someday they will serve a specific function for our country"—he nodded toward General Carmody—"but we must never make the mistake of regarding them as human beings. Granted, they bear a great resemblance to our species, but genetically they are different. So I am not talking about murder, Paul. I am simply talking about plugging what could become a disastrous security leak." He turned his attention fully on the general now. "As far as the world knows, what we are doing is not yet possible. That gives us an advantage. It means that our country will soon be able to match biological form to technological function. We will be able to create the people we need. Except that they won't be people. They will be living robots, designed with specific purposes in mind. It seems to me that we have no choice but to do whatever is necessary to protect the integrity of the project."

General Carmody nodded and turned to Randolph. "The Department has a very large investment in this project, Paul. I—*we* expect you to do everything you can to protect that investment. Is that clear?"

"Very." Paul Randolph sighed. "Do whatever you think is best." In his heart, Randolph knew that he had just agreed to the murder of a nine-year-old boy.

"I don't get it," Mark Malone said. "None of this makes any sense at all." He stood up, stretched, then poured himself yet one more cup of steaming hot coffee. Taking a careful sip, he glared malevolently as Carl Bronski gulped down half a cup of his remaining supply of cold brew. "Did you know that cold coffee causes cancer?" he taunted.

Carl ignored the bait. "What doesn't make sense? It seems to me it's all coming together."

"It is," Malone agreed. "And that's what I don't get. According to Sally, CHILD chose all these kids for their survey practically on the day they were born. They assigned the numbers, and the numbers show they assigned the children to the groups right away. And with three of the groups, there's nothing special. But look at Group Twenty-one."

Jim Corliss repeated what all of them had known for hours. "All the girls are dead. Every one of them, and all before the age of eleven months, and all of SIDS."

"But nobody knows anything about SIDS," Malone said doggedly. "It was only a year or so ago that the University of Maryland correlated hormone T-3 with the syndrome, and they still aren't sure whether the high level of T-3 is a cause or effect. So how did CHILD know those girls were going to die?"

"Maybe they didn't," Lucy offered. "Maybe it's coincidence."

"It's no coincidence," Sally told her. "It can't be. The odds are astronomical. And it's not just the girls," she reminded them. "It's some of the boys too. Particularly in the first few years. And then the boys stopped dying, but the girls didn't."

"And everywhere you look," Lucy replied, "it seems to come back to Dr. Wiseman. He was the obstetrician for all forty-six children in Group Twenty-one."

"About four a year," Sally mused. "I wonder how many babies he actually delivers each year?"

"It was twenty-seven last year," Malone replied. His voice suddenly turned grim. "Twenty-seven new little patients for me, and now this."

A silence fell over the group as, once more, they tried to figure out what it could all mean. Then, as Sally started to speak, the intrusive sound of the telephone interrupted her. Jim Corliss picked it up, spoke for a moment, then handed it to Bronski.

"Bill? Is that you?" Bronski asked.

"Yeah," the desk sergeant said. "Where the hell did you get that list of names?"

"Never mind. Have we gotten any replies?"

"From all over the place," the sergeant replied. "And it's weird. How many names were on that list?"

"Twelve."

"Twelve, huh? Well, eight of 'em are listed as runaways. From towns all over the country."

"Runaways?" Carl echoed. Lucy Corliss unconsciously moved closer to her ex-husband.

"That's right. All those cases are still open, and none of them have turned up in the morgues."

"Give me the names and the dates they disappeared." As the desk sergeant droned out the list, Bronski scribbled names and numbers on a piece of paper. "Got it," he said, handing the paper to Malone, who immediately started annotating the correlation sheets. "Thanks a lot, Bill, and if any—"

"Carl, there's more," the sergeant interrupted. The timbre of his voice had changed. Bronski felt his body tense.

"What is it?"

"The rest of them are dead."

"Dead?" Bronski repeated. "With police reports on them? You mean homicides?"

"Apparently not. I told you it was weird. It seems like your other four boys were found dead in public areas."

Bronski suddenly knew what was coming. "Tell me about them," he said softly.

"I got reports from all over the place—Washington State, Kansas, Texas, and Florida. The bodies were found in parks, playgrounds, vacant lots, that sort of thing."

"And?"

"And nothing. No marks on them, no signs of foul play or violence. Nothing. The coroners ruled the same in all the cases."

" 'Unknown natural causes?' "

There was a short silence, then he said, "What's going on, Carl? If you know something about all this, you better let the rest of us in on it."

"Just give me the names and dates, Bill," Bronski said, ignoring the other man's question. It would take far too long to begin explaining it now.

Once again, the desk sergeant began reciting names, places, and numbers.

At last Bronski hung up the phone and faced the others. "More pieces," he said. "It seems Randy isn't the only runaway in Group Twenty-one, and we've got some more deaths."

Sally stared bleakly at the list of names the computer had generated. Of the original forty-six, all the girls—twenty-two—were dead. Of the twenty-four boys, the nine oldest, including Randy Corliss, were listed as runaways, and four were dead. The name of the oldest boy on the list who had neither died nor run away was Jason Montgomery. As for the other eleven boys, ranging in age from six months to seven years, nothing was known.

"But that doesn't mean they're okay," Bronski said softly. "I sent out only the names of the oldest ones, the ones who could have disappeared and been considered runaways. If a kid under seven turns up missing, we usually assume foul play."

"Maybe now you'll raise the age limit," Lucy said. Then, seeing the hurt in Bronski's eyes, she quickly apologized: "Carl, I shouldn't have said that. You've been wonderful. I had no right to—well, I'm sorry."

"It's all right, Lucy. And I'm not really blameless, am I? Maybe if I'd believed you right away—"

"Never mind," Jim Corliss broke in. "None of us needs to say any of those things to each other. What we need is a plan. What do we do next?"

Instinctively, they all turned to Bronski.

"It's daylight," he said. "I think we'd better get Randy up and see if he can show us where he was."

"You mean go back there?" Lucy cried. "No! You can't make him do that."

Jim took her hand and held it tightly. "Lucy, it'll be all right. Carl and I will be with him. And we won't do anything."

"We have to know where he was, Lucy," Bronski added.

Lucy opened her mouth as if to protest further, then shut it again, nodding her head. "All right," she murmured.

She went to the bedroom where the two boys were still sleeping, and, being careful not to disturb Jason, woke Randy. He looked at her sleepily, but let himself be led to the living room. Bronski explained to the little boy what he wanted him to do. "Do you think you can?" he asked.

Randy looked uncertain. "I don't know," he finally admitted. "I was scared, and it was dark, and I don't know how far—" He broke off, as if sensing that perhaps no one really believed the story he had told last night.

"I can find it," he said. "I know I can." He disappeared into his room and dressed, then returned to the living room. Five minutes later, together with his father and Sergeant Bronski, he was on his way back to the Academy.

Sally Montgomery, Lucy Corliss, and Mark Malone silently went back to the stack of reports.

Two hours later Mark Malone began to recognize the answer that was buried deep within the records.

"Damn," he said softly. "God damn it to hell."

CHAPTER 27

The car moved slowly ahead, and Randy Corliss, sitting between his father and Sergeant Bronski, fidgeted nervously. It seemed to him that they were wasting time. The bridge, he was sure, was still way ahead. He twisted in his seat and peered out the back window. He could still see the diner.

"It's farther up the road," he said. "I couldn't see the diner at all, so it has to be way up ahead."

"Things seem farther at night," Bronski told him. "Besides, you weren't on the road—you were in the woods, so you wouldn't have been able to see as far."

"I just don't think it was this close."

They came to a bend in the road, and a hundred yards farther was a bridge.

"Is that it?" Jim Corliss asked his son.

As Bronski pulled off the road a few feet from the bridge, Randy looked at it uncertainly. "I guess so," he said at last. The three of them got out of the car, and Randy scrambled down the bank to stand beside the stream. Now he was sure. "This is it," he called up to his father.

"Okay. There's a path up here," Jim replied. Randy climbed back up.

"We have to go downstream," he announced.

"How far?" Bronski asked.

"I don't know," Randy replied. He started down the path, with his father and the policeman following. Every few minutes he glanced down at the stream. This morning, in the bright sunlight, everything looked different. Last night the stream had been swift and deep, and he could remember its roaring in his ears. But now its sound was a murmur, and he could see that it was only a couple of feet deep.

Maybe it was the wrong stream, and the bridge had been the wrong bridge. What if he was lost and couldn't find the Academy? Would they think he'd lied about everything?

As he kept walking, he became increasingly nervous. The two men with him exchanged a glance.

"It seems like an awfully long way," Bronski finally commented.

Randy said nothing. Had it really been this far? He tried to remember how far he'd waded, but there were no landmarks, nothing he recognized.

And then he heard the waterfall. He broke into a run, and the two men had to jog to keep up with him.

"This is it," Randy yelled. "This is the waterfall. See?" He pointed excitedly at the cascading stream and the large rock looming above it. "That's the rock I sat on after I climbed the waterfall." He began recounting the struggle he'd had fighting the current, too afraid of the dogs to leave the stream. "Come on," he finished. "There should be a fork just a little way farther." He dashed ahead, and disappeared around a bend in the trail.

"What do you think?" Jim asked.

Bronski shrugged. "I don't know. He found the bridge, and he found the waterfall." Then they heard Randy's voice floating back to them.

"I found it! I found the fork! We're almost there."

Jim and Carl caught up with Randy at the point where the stream split into two smaller channels. "Which fork do we take?" Jim asked.

"This one," Randy said, no longer uncertain. "Come on!"

The path disappeared, and the three of them began pushing their way through a tangle of laurel, keeping as close to the brook as they could.

"It'd be easier to wade," Randy suggested.

"How much farther is it?"

"I don't know. Not much. I could still hear the dogs barking when I got to the fork."

And then they were there. The brook suddenly disappeared into a metal culvert, the end of which was covered by a heavy wire-mesh grating. A few yards beyond the opening of the culvert they could see a high fence. Randy stared silently at the fence for a moment, then turned to look up at his father. "We're here," he said. "That's the fence around the Academy."

Bronski moved forward. The fence stretched off in either direction, and beyond it he could see nothing but more woods. "Where's the house?" he asked.

"You can't see it from here," Randy told him. "It's off that way." He started walking along the fence, but the sound of Sergeant Bronski's voice stopped him.

"Randy? Didn't you say there was a dead dog right about here?"

Randy nodded. "I threw it against the fence, and it got electrocuted."

"Where is it?"

Randy stared through the fence, trying to remember exactly where he'd climbed it.

He couldn't.

He looked for the body of the dog.

It wasn't there.

Tentatively, he reached out and touched the fence.

There was no current.

"But it was here," he said. "I know it was here." He looked up at the two men, sudden tears brimming in his eyes. "I'm not lying," he said. "The gate's off that way, and from there you can see the house." Determinedly, he began walking along the fence, with the two men once again trailing after him.

They came to the gate, and Randy stood still, staring through the bars. In the distance he could see the massive brick house, its barred windows clearly visible in the bright morning sunlight. Flanking him on either side were his father and Sergeant Bronski. Bronski's eyes swept the house and lawn and came to rest on the rusted chain that was wrapped around the gates, holding them securely together.

"Doesn't look like there's anyone here."

"But there's *got* to be," Randy wailed. And yet, as he looked at the house, he knew the policeman was right. There was just something about it, a stillness, that made him sure that everyone had gone. "We could climb the fence and go in," he suggested.

"No, we can't," Carl Bronski said. "All we can do is try to get a search warrant. Come on."

Randy started to protest. "But—"

"No buts," Jim Corliss told his son. "Sergeant Bronski's right."

"But this is where I was!" Randy insisted. "This is where I ran away from last night!"

Bronski knelt down so his eyes were level with Randy's. "And we're going to find out all about it, Randy. But we're going to do it legally. Do you understand? Otherwise the people who kidnaped you will get off scot-free. So we're going to find out who owns this place, and we're going to get a search warrant. Then we can go in, and you can show us all of it. All right?"

Randy scowled. "I don't see why we can't just go in. If there's nobody here—"

"Because that's the way it is," Jim said, the severity of his voice leaving no more room for argument.

They turned away from the gate and started along the driveway that eventually led them back to the main road, where a second chain blocked the drive against intruding traffic. Next to one of the support posts for the chain stood a mailbox with a number painted on its side. Bronski jotted down the number.

Half an hour later, they were back at Bronski's car. It was nearly nine A.M., and they had been gone from Lucy's for nearly two hours.

Steve Montgomery, with Arthur Wiseman sitting next to him, pulled up in front of Lucy Corliss's house. He switched the ignition off and set the emergency brake. "There's Sally's car," he said as he opened the door.

"And Mark Malone's," Wiseman added. "Has he been here all night too?"

Having no answer for the question, and sensing that no answer was required, Steve got out of the car and, with Wiseman following, mounted the steps to Lucy's small front porch. He rang the bell, waited a moment, then rang it again. After a moment, the door opened a crack, and a woman's face looked out suspiciously.

"Mrs. Corliss?" Steve asked.

Lucy frowned, her eyes darting between the two men. The older one looked familiar. And then she recognized him. But before she could speak, the younger one was talking again.

"I'm Steve Montgomery. Sally's husband."

The door shut in his face.

On the other side of the closed door, Lucy hesitated, then hurried into the living room where Sally and Mark were still poring over the computer printouts. "Sally, it's your husband," she said in an urgent whisper. "And he's got Wiseman with him."

Sally's tired eyes took on the look of a hunted animal, and instinctively she turned to Mark Malone for help. Malone was already rising to his feet.

"We might as well let them in," he said. Then, as Sally shrank into the chair on which he had been sitting, he tried to reassure her. "It'll be all right. I'm here, and Lucy's here, and Jim and Carl should be back any minute." He moved past Lucy, stepped into the hall, and opened the door.

The two men on the porch looked at him. It was Steve who finally spoke. "Is Sally here?"

"Yes, she is." Malone stepped back to let the two men enter, and Steve moved directly to the living room.

"Sally—" He fell silent, staring at his wife. Her face was pale and her hair, oily and disheveled, hung limply over her shoulders. "My God," Steve whispered. "Sally, what's happened to you?"

"She's exhausted," Malone said. "We're all exhausted. You would be, too, if you'd been up all night."

But Steve Montgomery wasn't listening to him. He had gone to his wife and knelt by her chair, slipping his arms around her to draw her close.

"Sally . . . oh, Sally, it's going to be all right, baby," he whispered. "We've found a place for you. You'll like it there. You can rest, and relax, and stop worrying about everything. Dr. Wiseman found it for us, and he thinks it'll only take a few weeks—"

Sally shook herself free, the exhaustion in her eyes suddenly replaced with fury. When she spoke, her voice was low and trembling, but still the force of her words shook her husband.

"Dr. Wiseman found a place? Oh, God, I'll *bet* he did. A nice little place, is it? Pretty? Good service? And lots of nice doctors who will spend all their time making me well again? But I'm not sick, Steve."

"Sally—" Steve moved toward her, but she backed away.

"Don't touch me," she whispered. It was all catching up with her now, all the anger, all the hurt, all the boiling emotions she'd been holding in check for so long. "Don't put your arms around me and tell me you love me and that you'll make me well again." Her voice began to rise as her self-control slipped away. "Don't tell me that, Steve. It's a lie. *It's all lies.* Everything that man has told you is a lie!" She wheeled around to face Wiseman, her expression a mask of fury. "What have you done to us?" she shrieked. "What have you done to us and to our children?" She hurled herself on Wiseman, her fists pounding against his chest. "How many of us were there? Five? Ten? A hundred? How many dead babies? How many little boys gone? How many? And why? God damn you! *Why?"*

The last of her energy drained, she collapsed to the floor, her screams giving way to sobs. Lucy Corliss crouched beside her, stroking her gently, but her eyes, as they fastened on Wiseman, reflected a cold fury that seemed to cut through to the old doctor's soul.

"I don't understand—" he began.

"Don't tell us that." Lucy cut him off. "Sally isn't crazy. None of us is. We're tired because we've been up all night trying to figure out what you've been doing. But we're not crazy."

"I?" Wiseman asked, his voice hollow. "What *I've* been doing?"

Before anyone could say anything else, Jason came into the room, rubbing sleep from his eyes. At the sight of his father and Dr. Wiseman, he hesitated a moment, his eyes confused, then made up his mind. "I don't *want* to go to that hospital," he cried. "There's nothing wrong with me, and I don't want to go!" He ran to his mother.

Though she was still huddled on the floor, Sally gathered him into her protective arms. She peered up at Lucy with frightened eyes. "Don't let them take us away, Lucy. Please don't let them take us away."

As he watched his wife and son on the floor Steve felt himself begin to come apart. He sank into a chair, his face pale, his hands working helplessly. There before him were the two people he loved best in the world, and they were terrified of him. His eyes searched the room, looking for help, and finally came to rest on Mark Malone.

"I—I—" His voice faltered, then fell silent.

Arthur Wiseman's eyes, too, turned to Malone. "What's going on, Mark?"

Malone coldly eyed the older doctor. "You don't know?"

Wiseman lowered himself uncertainly into a chair. "All I know is that for ten days I've watched one of my favorite patients change from a normal, level-headed, charming woman, into—" He gestured toward Sally, was silent for a moment, then continued. "And now she accuses me of things I can't even imagine. Dead babies? Missing boys? What is she talking about?"

Malone walked to the coffee table and picked up a sheaf of papers. "Maybe you'd better take a look at these." He offered them to Wiseman, who made no move to take them.

"What are they?"

"Records. Correlations. Data that Sally took out of the computer last night."

Wiseman frowned. "The hospital computer? She had no right—"

"I authorized it," Malone told him. "I'm a doctor, remember? Not that I give a damn right now who had the right to do what. The only thing that matters is what's here and what it means."

When Wiseman still hesitated, Malone's voice grew cold. "We're not crazy, Arthur. And it's not just us. It's Jim Corliss and Carl Bronski too. And unless you have an explanation for what's here, I don't mind telling you that I'll see to it you're barred from practice, stripped of your license, and put in prison for the rest of your life. I don't know if I can prove it, Arthur, but all this looks to me like the closest thing I've ever seen to mass murder. I don't know how you did it, and I don't know why, but I know it's all here."

His hands trembling, Wiseman reached out to take the sheaf of papers from Malone. When he spoke, his voice shook. "I don't know what you're talking about, Mark. Believe me, I don't."

"Then you'd better read those," Malone replied. "If you have any questions, I'll try to help you out. Sally's taken me through them so many times, I think I know the correlations by heart. And frankly, I don't think she's in any condition to start over with you."

Steeling himself, Wiseman began reading the sheets of correlations.

Across the street and a quarter of a block down, two men sat in a gray van. While one of them stared through a pair of binoculars and read off license plate numbers, the other took notes. When he had dictated the letters and numbers of all five cars that were parked in Lucy's driveway and on the street in front of her house, Ernie Morantz put the glasses away. "I don't like it."

"What's not to like?" Victor Kaplan asked in reply. "It's just another job."

"Taking out a nine-year-old kid isn't what I call just another job," Morantz said. His face settled into what Kaplan had long ago come to think of as "the mule face," as in "as stubborn as a . . ."

"Orders are orders," he reminded his partner.

"And I've never disobeyed one yet," Morantz snapped. "But terrorists and traitors are one thing. Even picking up illegal aliens. But what's this kid done? They don't think he's going to leave a bomb at Logan Airport, do they? Or is that the new thing? Foreign governments subverting the schoolboys of America? Come off it."

"It doesn't matter," Kaplan insisted. "We've got our orders."

"But nobody told us we'd be walking into a mob scene. And here come some more." The two men fell silent as they watched a sixth car pull up in front of Lucy Corliss's house. Two men and a boy got out, and Morantz, who was once more using his field glasses, spoke quietly. "That's the kid. Shit, he can't be more than four-and-a-half feet tall, and he looks just like any other kid. Wonder who the two other guys are?"

Kaplan took the glasses and watched until all three had disappeared into the house. "One's a cop," he said softly. "The one who was on the right. The other's probably the kid's dad."

"Yeah," Morantz grunted. He started the engine, slipped the van into gear, and cruised slowly past the house.

"Where are we going?" Kaplan asked.

"Coffee. And you're going to call Carmody and tell him this job isn't going to be all that easy. It's one thing to bust in on a woman, all by herself, and grab her kid. I'm not saying I like it, mind you, but at least it's possible. This is different, and I want to know what Carmody wants. You see a Ho-Jo on the way in?"

A few minutes later they slid into an orange Naugahyde booth, ordered, then Morantz adjourned to the men's room while Kaplan made the phone call. When he returned to the table, Morantz found himself still alone, so he passed the time fiddling with a puzzle that had apparently been left by the management for just such an occasion. At the next table a little boy, no more than six years old, had solved the puzzle and was gleefully explaining it to his sister. Morantz strained to hear what the boy was saying, but by the time Kaplan returned, he still had gotten nowhere. "Well?"

The look on Kaplan's face told most of the story. "It's getting worse. Carmody's running a check on all the cars to find out who's in the house. Then he'll make a decision about beefing up the team. We're to call him back in fifteen minutes, and he'll let us know what's happening."

"Shit," Morantz said softly. He picked up the puzzle, which involved some pegs and a triangular board. "Try this," he said, shoving it across to Kaplan. Kaplan stared at the gadget for a minute, studied the directions, then tentatively began jumping the pegs over each other, removing each one he jumped. When he was done, there were three pegs left, and no legitimate way of getting to them.

"So?" he said.

"So the kid in the next booth just solved it. And I bet that kid we're supposed to grab could do it too."

Kaplan frowned. "I don't get it, Ernie. What's this puzzle got to do with anything?"

Ernie Morantz stretched, then slouched deep into the booth. "I don't know," he said. "But it just seems to me that there's something wrong. Kids these days are brighter than adults. They can do things and understand things that don't make any sense to us at all. So what's this Corliss kid done that's so horrible? Hell, I bet Carmody himself doesn't know. But I ask you, does it make any sense that you and I, who were trained to believe in apple pie, motherhood, and the U.S. of A. are now being asked to grab a little American kid and take him out and drown him? I understand commies, and I understand traitors, and I hate them. But I don't hate kids. I don't understand them, but I don't hate them. In fact, I love them. And I'll tell you, Vic—it rubs me the wrong way to be told to go out and kill a little kid."

"So what does all that mean?" Kaplan asked.

There was a long silence. Ernie Morantz shrugged his shoulders. "I don't know, Vic. I just don't know. I guess it means I'll wait and see what Carmody wants. But I can tell you, if he wants us to go into that house like a SWAT team after the S.L.A., he's got the wrong man. I'm not sure I could do it."

"But you're not sure you couldn't either."

Morantz drained his coffee, then slid out of the booth. As he tossed some change on the table, he shook his head sadly. "No, I guess I'm not. Come on, let's go call Carmody and get the bad news."

The news, when they got it three minutes later, was as bad as either of them had expected.

CHAPTER 28

Arthur Wiseman, his complexion drained of all color and his hands trembling, silently squared the stack of documents and placed them neatly in the center of Lucy Corliss's coffee table. Finally his eyes began wandering over the room, pausing for a moment on each of the faces that were watching him, pausing almost as if he were seeking refuge, then, seeing none, moving on. At last his eyes came to rest on Sally Montgomery.

"There is no question about these statistics? No possibility of a mistake?"

"None worth talking about," Sally said, composed now.

"I suppose not," Wiseman said almost to himself. "I can remember too much of it all—"

"Then you *did* know," Sally flared.

Wiseman stared at her with eyes that had suddenly aged. "No," he said softly. "I should have, but I didn't. You have to understand—all this happened over so many years. What I remember are incidents. The babies—the ones that died. We don't forget them, you know. We learn to deal with the things that happen to children, we even learn to accept their deaths. But we don't forget." His eyes moved away from Sally, moved to the coffee table where, on the top of the stack, the list of children in Group Twenty-one lay. Once again he scanned the names. "They're my children. All of them."

Sally bit her lip. "Julie wasn't your child. She was my child. Mine and Steve's."

"I didn't mean it that way—"

"What are they doing?" Sally demanded. "What is CHILD doing?"

"Sally, I've known you all your life, and you've known me. Can you really believe that I would know about some sort of conspiracy and remain silent?"

But Sally was implacable. "Then why does it all come back to you?"

Wiseman shook his head helplessly. "I don't know. I haven't the slightest idea." He picked up the medical records and began going through them. Suddenly, he looked up. "What about the chromosome analyses?"

Malone frowned. "What about them?"

Wiseman handed him the medical records of the children in Group Twenty-one, his expression uncertain. "I order a chromosome analysis on a child only if there's reason to suspect a problem. And even then, I have to rely on the specialists to identify a defect in a particular chromosome and analyze it."

"So?"

"So, the records of all those children in Group Twenty-one indicate that a complete chromosome analysis was done, but there were no indications of any abnormalities."

Malone's eyes fixed on the older man. "Then who ordered the analyses? And why?"

"I'm sure I don't know—"

"Don't you?" Malone challenged, his voice icy. He turned to the others. "It's the obstetrician who orders tests like these. They're usually done prenatally, when there's a suspected problem with the fetus. But with all these children, there were no apparent problems, none whatsoever. Until they were born, and began dying." He turned back to Wiseman. "So my question, Arthur, is, who ordered these tests, and what were they looking for?" Without waiting for the old doctor to answer, Malone plunged on. "I think the first part of the answer is clear: You were the obstetrician for all of these children. But what were you looking for? Is there something genetically abnormal about these children that *isn't* reflected in the chromosome analyses?"

Wiseman seemed to sink deeper into his chair, and the records he was holding fluttered to the floor. "My God," he breathed. "What you're suggesting is monstrous."

"What's happened is monstrous," Malone countered, his voice suddenly level. "I'm sure you never expected anyone to find it. Not you, or anyone at CHILD. But Sally found it, Arthur. And if she could find it, others can too. So it's going to come out. We're going to find out what you did to these children's genes."

"No!" Wiseman protested. "I did *nothing* to these children. Whatever's wrong with them, it had to start with their parents. It had to!" But before he could go on, the front door suddenly flew open and Randy Corliss burst into the room, followed by his father and Carl Bronski.

"I found it," Randy crowed. "I found the house!"

Lucy's eyes went immediately to Jim, who nodded. "We stopped at City Hall," he said. "The place is owned by Paul Randolph."

Wiseman frowned. "Paul Randolph is executive director of CHILD."

"Right," Bronski said. He looked curiously at Wiseman and Steve Montgomery, guessing immediately who they were. "What are you two doing here?"

Malone explained to them what had happened. "We still don't know how it was done," he finished. "For that matter, we don't even know exactly *what* was done to these children's genes. But you can bet that somehow they've been altered."

"Can we find out what they did?" Sally asked.

Malone shrugged. "It depends on you. If the information's in the computer, you're the only one of us that can fish it out."

Sally started to speak, but Bronski took over. "Then that'll be your job, Sally. I want you to go to the hospital with Mark and start working with that computer." His eyes shifted over to Wiseman. "And I want you to go with them, is that clear?"

Wiseman, his face haggard, made a gesture with a trembling hand. "Of course," he mumbled. "Anything . . ."

"The house," Bronski went on. "I can get a search warrant for it by telephone. We think it's empty, but I want to go in. And I'd like to take Randy with me."

"No!"

"Lucy, there's no other way," Jim said.

"There must be, or you wouldn't have come back here," Lucy snapped. "You'd have just gone ahead and done whatever you thought you had to do."

Now Carl Bronski spoke again. "Lucy, that isn't it at all. We came back here because Jim wouldn't agree to taking Randy in unless you agreed too."

"Which I don't," Lucy said.

Jim Corliss sat on the sofa and drew Lucy down next to him. "Honey, you've got to—" Seeing the stony look in her eyes, he broke off and started over. "Of course, you don't *have* to let Randy go. But without Randy, there's not much point in Carl even going in there. As far as we could tell from outside, the place is empty. Carl's excuse for getting a search warrant is that he needs to verify Randy's story of what's inside that house, and that means Randy has to show him."

Lucy, too exhausted to think it all through, turned to Sally for advice.

"If it was Jason, I'd feel the same way you feel," Sally told her. "But still, if CHILD was using that house for something—"

Lucy took a deep breath and stood up. "You're right," she said. "Of course you're right. We have to know what was going on out there." As Carl Bronski picked up the phone, dialed, then began speaking quietly to the judge at the other end, Lucy turned back to Jim. "You'll be careful?"

"Lucy, you have to believe that I'd never let anything happen to Randy."

"Something's already happened to him," Lucy whispered. She reached out and touched his arm. "But it's not just Randy," she said, her voice suddenly shy. "You be careful, too. I—well, I feel as though I just found you again, and I don't think I could stand to lose you now. I'm going to need help from now on, Jim."

"And you're going to have it," Jim promised.

The small group began to break up. Mark Malone packed the computer printouts into his briefcase, then led an ashen-faced and silent Arthur Wiseman out of the house.

Sally and Steve Montgomery left to take Jason to his grandmother's, where he would stay while his parents went to the hospital to work with Mark Malone.

Carl Bronski, with Jim and Randy Corliss, prepared to return to Paul Randolph's estate.

And then, as they were about to depart, Lucy suddenly stood up. "I'm going with you," she told Jim. "I can't stay here by myself—I'll go crazy."

Jim started to protest, but Lucy touched his arm. "I have to go, Jim," she said softly. "I have to be with Randy, and with you."

Their eyes met, and a gentle smile came over Jim's face. "Wherever I go, you go?" he asked.

Lucy hesitated only a moment, then nodded. "From now on."

The Montgomerys drove slowly through the streets of Eastbury, Steve at the wheel, Sally sitting silently next to him, Jason in the back. Jason, too, was uncharacteristically silent, but his parents were too deeply involved in their own thoughts to notice.

It was Steve who finally broke the silence. "I'm sorry, honey."

Her reverie disturbed, Sally glanced over at him. "Did you say something?"

"I was trying to apologize," Steve said. "I thought—well, you know what I thought. But the whole thing seemed so crazy—" He fell silent, regretting his choice of words.

"It *is* crazy." The calmness in her voice surprised Sally as much as it did

Steve; by rights she should be screaming, or sobbing, or pounding her fists on something. Anything but this eerie sense of calm that had come over her. But she knew the calmness was only a temporary reaction, a protective device she had wrapped herself in, a screen to ward off for a little while the despair she knew was bound to overtake her when she came to grips with reality.

For reality was contained in the term that had flashed into her mind when Mark Malone had said the words "genetically altered."

Reality was that Jason was not what she had always thought he was. He was something else, something she was unfamiliar with.

A mutant.

Not an eight-year-old boy, not the innocent and perfect product of the mating between herself and her husband.

A mutant.

Something different, something unfamiliar, something unknown.

What was he?

Suddenly all the words she had heard over the past few years held new and sinister meaning for her.

Recombinant DNA.

She barely knew what DNA was.

Genetic engineering.

She knew about that. That was the new science, the science that was going to offer glorious solutions to age-old problems.

But what else was it going to do? Was it going to create a glorious new world, or was it going to create a world full of altered beings, *mutants,* designed for—for what?

She didn't know. And perhaps she never would. Perhaps whatever had been done to Jason had been done for no specific reason at all. Perhaps he was nothing more than an experiment.

The thought chilled her, and she turned around, gazing at her son, trying to fathom how he might have been changed. She reached back to caress Jason's cheek, but he drew back from her touch, his eyes large and worried.

"Why do I have to stay at Grandma's?" he wanted to know.

"It's only for a little while, sweetheart," Sally managed to tell him through the constriction that had formed in her throat. "Just a few hours."

"Why couldn't I stay with Mrs. Corliss, so I could be there when Randy gets back?"

Randy.

Jason and Randy.

Sally tried to remember how long they had been friends, and how long it had been since Jason had had other friends.

Thoughts flickered through her mind, disconnected thoughts that suddenly fit together.

Mutants.

Was that why Jason and Randy had become friends? Did they know about themselves and each other? Had they recognized each other long ago, sensing that the two of them, different from others, were not different from each other?

Sally sank back into her seat without having answered Jason's question.

He didn't look any different. He looked as he'd always looked: a miniature version of his father, with the same deep blue eyes and unruly blond hair, the same energy and enthusiasm for everything, the same stubbornness.

But he was not his father's child, nor was he his mother's child.

Dear God, what had they done to her child? What had they done to *her?* She reached out and took Steve's hand in her own.

"Steve?"

He glanced over at her, and squeezed her hand.

"Take care of us, Steve," she said. "Take care of all of us."

"I will, darling," he promised. But even as he made the promise, Steve Montgomery wondered whether he could keep it. There were so many questions in his mind, and so few answers.

He still wasn't altogether sure that there was any kind of conspiracy. Wiseman, he was sure, was right. Whatever had gone wrong with the children in Group Twenty-one had started with their parents.

It wasn't a conspiracy. It was simply a genetic weakness passed on to the next generation.

It was, actually, his fault.

His fault, and Sally's.

CHILD, in all likelihood, was doing nothing more than watching the children, trying to isolate the defect and find a means to correct it.

So there was really nothing for him to "take care of." All he had to do was learn to live with the fact that he'd failed his children.

Or, anyway, he'd failed Julie.

But had he failed Jason? After all, Jason had never been sick a day in his life. Maybe with Jason, he hadn't failed at all. Maybe Jason, through some strange combination of his genes—and Sally's—was truly the perfect child they had always thought he was.

Maybe everything was going to be all right after all.

By the time they reached Phyllis Paine's house, he was feeling much better about everything.

Jason was fine. Jason was his son, and Jason was alive, and Jason was perfect. And in a few hours, working with Dr. Malone and the computer, Sally would find out that nothing was wrong, and they, like the Corlisses, could get back to the reality of being a family.

Steve relaxed, sure the end of the nightmare was near.

* * *

One by one, Arthur Wiseman retrieved the medical histories of the women who had given birth to the children in Group Twenty-one, sure that somewhere in those records his vindication would be found. The pattern emerged very quickly, both to him and to Mark Malone.

It wasn't just Sally Montgomery, and Lucy Corliss, and Jan Ransom.

It was all of them.

Forty-six women, none of whom had wanted children.

Forty-six women, all of whom he had considered to be poor risks for the pill.

Forty-six women, for whom an intrauterine device had been the indicated method of birth control.

Not an unusual number over the space of more than ten years. Indeed, Arthur Wiseman had inserted far more than forty-six IUDs over those years.

But for these forty-six, there was something else. All of them, at one time or another, had complained of one symptom or another—often a history of allergic reactions—which had suggested that their bodies might reject the intrusion of such an object.

And so he had applied, in the uterus of each of these women, and perhaps a hundred others, bicalcioglythemine.

"But what is it?" Mark Malone asked.

"BCG? It's a salve that helps reduce the likelihood of the uterus rejecting the IUD."

"I've never even heard of it," Malone said. "Who makes it?"

"PharMax."

Malone groaned, and Wiseman looked at him curiously. "What's wrong? I've been using it for ten years."

"Which is just about how long we've had this problem, even though we didn't know about it."

"I don't see what the connection could be—"

"PharMax is the source of CHILD's funds. In fact, PharMax set CHILD up in the first place. And why haven't I ever heard of this—what do you call it?"

"BCG. And there's a simple reason why you've never heard of it—you're not an OB-GYN."

"But I keep up with the literature, and I talk to the reps. And Bob Pender's never mentioned anything about BCG to me."

Wiseman's temper began to slip. "Why the hell would he?" he demanded. "You'd have no use for the stuff. And I can tell you, it's nothing more than an antiseptic and a relaxant."

"Maybe," Malone replied quietly. "But I think we'd better have it analyzed, just to see what's in it."

Wiseman glared at the younger man. "Just what are you suggesting?"

"I'm suggesting we find out what you've been treating these women with. My God, Arthur, we've got forty-six children here, more than half of whom are dead. And if you look at the dates on those charts, every one of them would have been exposed to this BCG stuff exactly at the time of conception. Now, if DNA is going to be tampered with, when is it done?"

"In the embryo—"

"Even before that, Arthur. In the egg. In the nucleus of the egg."

The anger he had been feeling—the anger of affronted pride—suddenly drained out of Wiseman, to be replaced by fear.

Fear, and a memory.

How many women had he treated with BCG? Not only treated, but followed up on, reapplying the salve month after month. But had it done its job, the job it was intended for? No, it hadn't. For even in women he had treated with BCG, the devices had still sometimes been rejected, though the salve itself remained. Remained, to do what?

There had been a drug—how many years ago? Nearly thirty. The drug had been called thalidomide, and it had been a tranquilizer.

And doctors all over the world, unaware or uncaring of the fact that it had never been exhaustively tested, had prescribed it for pregnant women. The results had been a nightmare of congenitally deformed infants.

And there had been DES, where the consequence of the drug's use was not immediately apparent, but rather lay like an invisible time bomb deep within the children—the daughters—waiting to explode into a devastating cancer.

Now BCG. What was it going to do? What had it already done?

"I'll take it to the lab," he said quietly. "But I can't believe—" His voice dropped. "I'll take it to the lab."

Leaving Malone in his office, Arthur Wiseman went into his examining room and opened his medicine cabinet. He scanned the shelves quickly, then again, more carefully this time.

Where he was sure the jar of BCG had been, there was now only an empty space on his shelf.

He picked up the phone and reached his nurse. "Has anyone been in my treatment room this morning?"

"Why, yes, Dr. Wiseman. Bob Pender dropped by, and I let him take an inventory of the PharMax products you use."

Wiseman felt a sudden pain in his chest as his heart began to pound. "I see," he said. "Thank you."

Sensing the strain in his voice, the nurse spoke again. "Wasn't that all right? Bob's been inventorying your drugs for years."

"It's all right, Charlene," Wiseman assured her. "I'm sure it's quite all right." He hung up the phone and slowly made his way back to his office. Mark Malone looked up at him, then, seeing the expression on his face, rose.

"What is it, Arthur?"

"Bob Pender was here," Wiseman said softly. "And the BCG is gone."

"Then we'll order more," Malone said. He picked up the phone and asked the hospital operator to connect him with the PharMax sales desk.

"BCG?" the man at the other end repeated. "I'm not sure I've ever heard of that."

Malone started to explain what it was he wanted, then changed his mind and handed the phone to Wiseman.

"Bicalcioglythemine," Wiseman snapped. "I want a twelve-ounce jar, and I want to pick it up today."

There was a pause. Wiseman could hear pages being turned. Finally the voice at the other end spoke again. "Are you sure you have the right company? This is PharMax."

"PharMax is who I want. I've been getting BCG from you people for ten years."

"And this is Eastbury Community Hospital?"

"That's right."

"One moment."

This time Wiseman was put on hold. Nearly two minutes later the voice came back on the line.

"I'm sorry, sir, but this company does not make a product called bicalcioglythemine, and I've just checked your records on our computer. I see nothing indicating that you've ever ordered such a thing before, nor have we ever shipped it or billed you for it. I'm afraid you must have the wrong company."

"I see," Wiseman whispered. When he faced Malone again, his whole body was trembling.

"I don't think we need to have it analyzed, Mark," he said softly. "I suppose, if I did enough research, I could tell you which enzymes must have been in it. There must have been some kind of restriction endonuclease and a ligase. Maybe even some free nucleotides to zip into the DNA. And, of course, the calcium base. But I don't think I could tell you how they put it together or made the whole process work. As far as I knew, what that compound must have done isn't possible even now, let alone ten years ago. But they must have done it. Recombinant DNA, accomplished within the uterus."

The phone rang on Wiseman's desk and he spoke with the nurse once more. When he hung up the phone, his eyes avoided Mark Malone's. "Sally and Steve are here," he said. "Will you talk to them? I don't think I can face them right now. I think I have to . . . well, I have to think this thing through. I have to decide what it all means."

Mark Malone rose and started toward the door. Then he turned back and faced Wiseman. "Arthur," he said, his voice low and deadly, "are you sure you didn't make this compound yourself?"

What little color still remained in the old man's face drained away. "Mark, what are you saying?"

"Only that when the time comes, I doubt that anyone will believe you got that stuff from PharMax. Frankly, I don't believe it myself." Malone turned away, and a moment later Arthur Wiseman was left alone in his office.

CHAPTER 29

Jim Corliss cast doleful eyes on the chain blocking the driveway to the Randolph estate. "Maybe we'd better just leave the car here and walk."

"Nope. I want it near the house." Bronski opened the trunk of his car and took out a large set of chain cutters. "These should do the trick." A moment later the chain, its end link neatly severed, lay on the asphalt, leaving the drive clear. They proceeded on to the gate, where Bronski cut the second chain, then dismantled the electric opening device so the gates swung freely. "After this, the house should be a cinch," he remarked. He put the chain cutters back into the trunk, slid behind the wheel, and gunned the engine.

They drove around to the back of the house, parking the car where it couldn't be seen from the gates. Then, with Lucy and Randy trailing them, the two men approached the house. They knocked loudly at the back door, waited, then knocked again. When there was still no response, they went around to the front and repeated the procedure.

"There's no one here," Lucy said at last. "They've all gone."

"We still have to try," Bronski replied. "Let's go in." He stepped back from the house and gazed up at the barred windows of the second floor. "Seems as though it would be the lower windows they'd keep bars on."

"It was to keep us in," Randy said. "And they always had someone in the hall too. Except that Miss Bowen didn't always stay there."

"Well, at least that makes it easy for us," Bronski murmured. He led the others around to the side of the house, where French doors opened onto a terrace overlooking the lawn. Using the butt of his gun, he shattered a pane of one of the doors, then reached through and twisted the dead bolt. He winked at Randy. "Just like in the movies." He opened the door and led the way in.

"It's the dining room," Randy explained. "And through there is the kitchen. The other doors lead to a big hall, and in the back everyone had offices." He started eagerly across the room, but Bronski stopped him.

"I'll go first."

"Aw . . . there's no one here."

"I'll still go first," Bronski insisted, even though he agreed with Randy. He led the way through the dining room and stopped in the foyer, staring up the broad staircase. "What's up there?"

"The bedrooms," Randy explained. "Mine was almost at the end of the hall. Wanna see it?"

"Okay."

They moved up the stairs, Bronski still in the lead. At the top, situated so that it had a full view of the wide corridor that ran the length of the hall, was a desk, emptied of its contents. They started down the hall.

"This was Eric's room," Randy said, pausing at a closed door.

Bronski glanced at Lucy. "Eric who?" he asked.

"Carter. I think he was from California."

So there it was. Eric Carter had been reported as a runaway from San Jose. Unless . . .

"Randy, did you look at all that stuff we were reading last night?"

Randy shook his head.

"You're sure?"

Randy shrugged. "It was only a bunch of numbers and stuff like that. Why would I want to read that?"

"Okay. You said this *was* Eric's room. Isn't it anymore?"

"Eric died," Randy said. Lucy gasped, and Randy looked anxiously up at her. "That's why I ran away. After Eric died, I got real scared. So I ran away."

"Of course you did," Jim Corliss said. "Why don't you show us how you got out of the house?"

Randy led them to the end of the hall, then up the narrow stairs to the attic, where the ladder, still extended, led up to the open skylight. "Then I went across the roof, and climbed down a tree," Randy explained. "It was easy."

Bronski nodded. Everything was exactly as Randy had said it would be. "Let's go back downstairs."

Now it was Randy who led the way, explaining to his parents and the sergeant what each of the rooms had been used for. At last they were in the clinic area, and Randy showed them the room where Peter Williams had lain unconscious for several days.

"And what's back there?" Bronski asked, pointing to the only door they had not yet opened. Randy stared at it, his lips pursed, and his brows knit together in puzzlement.

"I don't know," he finally admitted. "I was never back there."

"Then let's have a look." Bronski, followed by the three Corlisses, started toward the door that would lead them into the laboratory.

Morantz and Kaplan moved through the trees, being careful to stay well back in their shadows. The boy, they had been told, was the primary assignment. And so, when the house in Eastbury had suddenly disgorged its occupants an hour before, it was the two men, the woman, and the boy whom they followed. It had been an easy tail, for they had known within minutes exactly where they were going. They had hung back, well out of sight, until their quarry reached its destination. Now they were closing in.

"There's the car," Morantz said. Even though there were no prying ears, he still used his habitual working voice, just above a whisper, which he knew only Kaplan could hear.

"We'll go in from behind the garage," Kaplan replied in the same lowered tone. His grip tightened on the canvas bag he was carrying. "Even if they look out, we shouldn't be visible for more than a second or two."

They worked their way a little farther south, putting the large garage between themselves and the house. Only when they were certain they couldn't be seen did they leave the shelter of the woods and dash across the narrow expanse of lawn to crouch beside the brick wall of the outbuilding. Once there, Kaplan opened the bag and removed its contents.

It was a small device—no larger than a cigar box—and all that was visible on its exterior were several tiny, but very powerful, magnets. Kaplan opened the box, carefully rechecking the receiver, the capacitor, and the firing cap. Satisfied, he made the final attachments that would allow the cap to accomplish its purpose, imbedded it in the mass of gelignite that took up the bulk of the space in the box, and reclosed it.

"See anything?"

Morantz, his binoculars pressed to his eyes, shook his head. "If they're in there, they're still up front. Looks like right now is as good a time as any."

Kaplan crouched and, keeping his head low, darted out of the lee of the garage and moved swiftly across the concrete apron upon which Carl Bronski's car, closed and carefully locked, was parked. He stopped next to the right rear wheel, knelt down, and reached under the car with his left hand. A moment later he had found the spot he was looking for, and heard a distinct *thunk* as the magnets on the exterior of the box clamped themselves firmly to the gas tank of the car.

A few seconds later, both Kaplan and Morantz had faded back into the woods.

For now, all they had to do was get back to their van, and wait.

Lucy Corliss stared at the mess and instinctively touched her son. "But what is this place?" she asked, although she knew the answer even as she spoke.

Even in its disheveled state, it was still obvious that the room was some kind of a laboratory. There was a long counter that took up most of one wall, with various pieces of equipment that neither Jim nor Carl Bronski recognized. On the wall opposite the counter, five filing cabinets stood, most of their drawers open, all of them empty.

"Seems like they took the records and left the hardware," Bronski commented.

"Which fits in with a government operation," Jim Corliss pointed out. "Generate a mass of paper, never lose track of a single piece of it, but let the equipment rust. But what was it all about? If all they were doing was medical research, why the secrecy?"

"Come on, Jim. Let's not kid ourselves," Bronski said. "This wasn't just research. Children were being kidnaped and brought out here, where apparently they died." He glanced toward Randy, who was already disappearing into yet another room. When he spoke again, his voice was grim. "And I'll bet that even after they died, they stayed on the premises. Let's see what's in there." The trio moved toward the door of the lab.

They found Randy standing in the small room behind the laboratory, staring at a large piece of equipment, his face puzzled.

"Is that an iron lung?" he asked.

Carl Bronski shook his head. "Not quite," he said, his voice shaking slightly.

"What is it, then?" Lucy asked.

"It looks like a decompression chamber." He hesitated, his eyes once again flickering toward Randy. Lucy, reading Bronski's expression, gently nudged her son.

"Wait for us in the other room, sweetheart," she said. Then, when he was gone, she turned her attention back to the sergeant. "What's it for?" she asked.

Bronski swallowed hard. "It's the kind of thing they use in dog pounds," he said at last.

Lucy, still not quite comprehending, turned to Jim.

"They use it for the puppies," he explained. "For the puppies nobody wants."

Lucy paled. "Dear God," she whispered. "You mean they used that thing to—?"

"That's the way it looks," Bronski said, his voice suddenly hard. "But they still had bodies to dispose of. And it looks to me like that's why they had that thing."

Lucy, her face ashen, stared at the firebox. "Isn't it just a furnace?"

"It's not like any furnace I ever saw," Bronski replied. "The only place I've ever seen anything like that is in a crematorium." As the Corlisses numbly looked on, he approached the crematory and touched the door.

It was still warm, but not too warm to prevent him from opening it.

The chamber inside was empty.

"They cleaned it up pretty well, but not quite well enough."

In the corners of the chamber there were a few flecks of grayish matter. Producing a plastic bag from his coat pocket, Bronski scooped up a sample of the stuff, sealed the bag, and replaced it in his pocket.

"Come on," he said. "Let's get out of here. We've seen enough, and it'll take a team of techs to go over this place properly. But offhand, I'd say it ought to be pretty easy to find out who was here. There'll be prints all over the place, and God only knows what else." He chuckled, but there was not even a trace of humor in the sound. "When you clear out as fast as they did, you don't stop to clean up after yourselves. You take what you can and run. And that's what these people did. I'll bet they didn't even waste time looking for Randy. Just packed up everything and took off."

A few minutes later they were back in Bronski's car and heading down the driveway. They stopped to reclose the main gate, but ignored the chain that still lay on the ground where they had left it.

"What now?" Jim asked as they turned back onto the main road.

"As soon as we get into radio range, I'll call headquarters and have a team sent out here. Then I think I ought to have a little talk with Paul Randolph. That's right," he added, seeing in the rearview mirror the look of dismay on Lucy's face. "Just me, and maybe someone else from the department. You're out of it now, Lucy. You, and Jim, and the Montgomerys too. From here on in, it's all got to be official." Then, still watching Lucy's face, he caught a glimpse of something moving in the distance. He slowed the car slightly. Behind them, a van was pulling out of a side road.

"Something wrong?" Jim asked.

Bronski said nothing, his eyes glued to the slow-moving van. Only when it turned in the opposite direction did he relax.

"Nothing," he said. "For a second there, I just thought maybe we were being followed."

And yet, even as he continued driving, he felt uneasy. There was something about the van . . .

As they rounded a bend in the road, and Carl Bronski's car disappeared from their view, Morantz spoke softly to Kaplan.

"About ten more seconds," he said. "Give them that, but no more."

Bronski's brain was working furiously now, trying to remember where he'd seen that van before.

Not long ago.

This morning?

But where? And why was the memory so vague?

And then he knew. Lucy Corliss's block, part way down the street. He'd barely noticed it.

But was it the same van?

If it was, then they were being followed. Except the van had gone the other way. Instead of following them, it was going to—

But if it *had* followed them, whoever was in it knew where they'd been.

And no longer cared.

"Holy Christ!" he yelled. His foot slammed onto the brake and the car spun into a four-wheel skid. "Get out! Get the hell out of the car!"

As the car skewed off the road, he yanked at the door handle. Maybe, just maybe, there was still time.

With a sudden roar, the gelignite attached to the gas tank exploded, ripping the tank loose from the car, splitting its welded seams and igniting its contents.

What a moment before had been an automobile lurching toward a ditch was now a massive fireball rolling into that ditch, through it, then coming to rest a few yards from the edge of the forest.

Carl Bronski died instantly, crushed by the weight of the car, his body a mangled mass resting grotesquely in the bottom of the ditch.

For Jim Corliss, it was worse. As the car rolled, the roof gave way, pressing him down into the front seat, his legs jammed immobile beneath the twisted dashboard.

Flaming gasoline gushed from the ruptured tank, inundating the car, and soon the choking, acrid smell of burning rubber filled the air. Gasping, Jim tried to twist in the seat to help his wife and son, but it did no good. His one free arm groped through the smoke, finding nothing. And then the flames began to eat at him.

"Randy!" he screamed. And then again, "Randy! Lucy!" He took a deep breath, and superheated air flooded into his lungs, searing their delicate tissue, and ending his last slim hope of survival.

In the back seat, Lucy had instinctively grabbed for her son when the car began to skid, and now, as it lay overturned and burning, her mind suddenly went blank with panic. She was going to die, and Randy was going to die, and it was all going to be for nothing. She clutched Randy closer and began screaming.

Randy himself thrashed wildly in his mother's arms, trying to wriggle free. "Mom!" he yelled. "Mom, let go of me!"

But Lucy, too terrified to understand, knew only that she somehow had to protect her son from the roaring flames. Her mind, filled with a fog of terror, tried to sort things out, tried to make decisions.

Jim. She needed Jim. "Help us," she cried, her voice already beginning to weaken. "Oh, Jim, help us!" And then, through the fear and the heat and the smoke, she became aware that Randy was no longer in her arms. She reached out and finally grasped him. He was wriggling toward the gap between the two front seats of the car. As her hand closed on his ankle, he looked back at her. His eyes were wide and angry, and Lucy suddenly thought she must be hallucinating.

While the flesh on her hand, the hand that held her son's ankle, was seared and blistered, Randy's flesh seemed uninjured. It glowed red in the strange light of the fire, but it seemed to her that it had not yet been harmed. And then she heard Randy talking to her.

"Let me go," he hissed. "I'm not going to die, Mother. I *won't* die." And then, kicking violently, he escaped Lucy's weakened grasp and slipped away from her.

Lucy, a vision of her son's angry face etched in her mind, slipped into unconsciousness.

Randy scrambled through to the front seat. The smoke burned his eyes, and for a moment he lost his orientation. Then he tried to force his way past a blockage and heard a soft moaning sound.

It was his father.

But suddenly all he knew was that he had to get out, that it was getting too hot to breathe. Then he felt a hint of cooler air and realized that the door on the driver's side was open. He wriggled toward it, his clothes burning now, and caught his foot in the steering wheel. Kicking wildly, he jerked himself free and burst out of the flaming wreckage.

He fell to the ground, then almost instinctively rolled through the pool of burning gasoline that surrounded the car. Getting to his feet, he staggered toward the woods.

Away from the flames, Randy collapsed to the ground, his breath coming in faint gasps, his heart pounding. The last thing he saw before his eyes closed was his father's face, barely visible through the shattered glass of the windshield, unrecognizable in the agony of death.

Then blackness closed in around Randy, and he felt nothing more.

But even as he passed into unconsciousness, George Hamlin's genetic miracle had already been triggered. Randy's clothes were gone, burned completely away, and here and there the smooth skin of his body showed faint signs of blistering. But even now the blisters were beginning to dry up and peel away to reveal healthy skin beneath. The injured tissues of Randy's body were regenerating themselves.

Morantz and Kaplan heard the sound of the explosion just as they turned into the driveway of the Randolph estate. Kaplan nodded with satisfaction. "So much for that part of it. How much time do you think we have?"

"As much as we need," Morantz replied. "No one's going to come around here—all the excitement's going to be back there."

"What you might call a diversion."

Morantz threw his partner a dirty look. "We just killed four American citizens, two of whom were a woman and a child. I don't call that a diversion. I call it . . . shit, I don't know what to call it." He was silent for a moment, then he said, "I think when this is over, I'm getting out."

"I've heard you say that before," Kaplan countered. "In fact, I hear you say it in the middle of practically every job." The car drew to a halt in front of the gates, and Kaplan got out of the van to open them, then hopped back in when Morantz had driven through. "You want me to do the next one?"

"Not particularly."

They took the van around to the back of the house, parking it in the exact place where Bronski's car had been only a few minutes before. "Okay," Morantz said as he set the brake and switched off the engine. "Let's get it set up, then get out of here. It's getting along toward noon."

Working swiftly and efficiently, the two men unloaded their supplies and took them into the house. They surveyed the interior with professional detachment, ignoring everything except the layout of the building. When they had decided on the exact layout of the explosives, Morantz shook his head.

"I don't know how they're going to cover this one up," he said. "I can give them rubble, but I can't hide the fact that it was a professional job. What they want done here can't be made to look like an accident."

"Maybe no one's ever going to see it," Kaplan suggested.

"Don't hold your breath. The explosion alone is going to bring everyone running from miles around. And it won't take long to find out what caused it either. Any fire department worth its salt'll figure this one out in about five minutes."

For thirty minutes the two of them worked. Finally, Morantz made the last connection. He straightened up after hiding the timer under the counter in the laboratory and stretched.

"About five hours?" he asked.

Kaplan frowned. "Why so long? What if somebody comes in here this afternoon?"

"They won't," Morantz promised. "But we might as well let them get that mess with the car cleaned up before they have to start on this one." He glanced at his watch, then set the timing device. "Come on. Let's get out of here."

Without looking back, the two men left the house, climbed into the van, then drove back to the road. Morantz parked the car just beyond the gates, got out of the van, closed the gates, and wrapped them with a chain he produced from the back of the van. Then he returned to the van once more, this time to fetch a large painted metal sign. He took it back to the closed gates, and wired it securely into position. Standing back, he read the sign:

DANGER

THIS PROPERTY UNDER QUARANTINE BY ORDER OF THE UNITED STATES GOVERNMENT

Beneath the warning there was a carefully written paragraph regarding the penalties involved for ignoring or removing the sign and a telephone number which could be called if further information was required.

Satisfied, Morantz got back into the van and started the engine. "Dumb, isn't it?" he remarked as he drove on and eventually turned into the main road. "We could string up barbed wire and every kid in the area would crawl through it just to find out why it was there. But that sign could sit there for years and no one would ignore it."

And then, ahead, they saw three police cars, a fire truck, and two ambulances gathered around the smoldering wreckage of Carl Bronski's car. As they passed it, threading their way through the fleet of emergency vehicles, Kaplan carefully examined what was left of the demolished automobile.

"Nobody could have survived that," he said, his voice betraying a note of satisfaction. "Nobody in the world."

CHAPTER 30

Arthur Wiseman moved slowly around his office, touching things, examining things, remembering.

His medical diploma, neatly framed, but yellowing with age even under the protective glass, hung discreetly behind his desk, a silent reassurance to his patients that he was qualified to do his job.

Around the diploma, in frames of their own, were all the certificates he had gathered over forty years of practice. An array to be proud of, documenting a life devoted to service. Commendations from the town, the county, even the state. Citations from the medical association. The gavel that had been his the year he had served as its president. All of it suddenly confronted him with an overwhelming sense of guilt.

How many had there been?

How many children over the years whom he had unknowingly sentenced to death? How many men and women whose lives he had unwittingly shaken, if not destroyed?

He knew the statistics. It wasn't simply the children who were the victims. It was the families too. The families like the Montgomerys, for whom the loss of an infant seemed to strike a mortal blow to the basic structure of their lives, leaving them floundering helplessly, unable to cope with their own feelings, or those of their mates, or their surviving children.

Until today he had been able to blame that destruction on sudden infant death syndrome. An unknown killer creeping out of the shadows to claim a victim, then slipping away into the nether regions, its identity cloaked in mystery.

Except that for him the cloak had slipped. Arthur Wiseman had seen the face of the enemy.

It was his own face.

Too busy, he thought.

Always, he had been too busy. Too busy caring for his patients, too busy improving his clinic, too busy raising funds so that Eastbury could have a hospital to be proud of.

Too busy to analyze every medication he used.

Too busy to question each new product that came on the market touted by its manufacturers as the latest "medical miracle."

Too busy to question the motives of the manufacturers, too busy to question the results of their own testing programs, too busy, even, to demand the documentation behind the products.

Instead, he had simply accepted the products and used them to treat the symptoms for which they had been created, grateful that the pharmaceutical companies kept developing new products to help his patients.

Except that this time the product had not helped.

This time the product had done something else, and the children were dying.

But not all of them. No, not all of them. Some of them lived.

Lived as what?

What were they, these altered beings that seemed so normal? Were they really the healthy little boys they seemed to be? Or were they something else, created for some specific purpose?

What could the purpose be?

Arthur Wiseman thought about it, and the puzzle was not too difficult for him to figure out.

Children who healed at an unnaturally rapid rate. On the way back to the hospital Malone had mentioned the Defense Department.

Perfect little soldiers, that's what they were.

Children who could grow up to fight battles, and not be killed.

War, suddenly, could be waged at no cost. Send in the killers who can't be killed.

Who would argue that war was wrong if only the other side died?

Arthur Wiseman, alone in his office, looked into the future and saw the new man, bred for a single purpose. To kill. But there would be others.

He could envision entire classes of people, each of them bred to serve a specific need, to perform a specific function which regular people could not, or would not, perform.

Regular people.

And that, Wiseman knew, was the attitude that soon would prevail. Society, barely learning to function without racial segregation, would turn to genetic segregation. Each person would be assigned to his station in life according to his genetic structure, with the "regular people" at the top. But for how long?

Not long. A few generations, perhaps, before the mutants, human in all respects except for a tiny genetic change that gave them special abilities, rebelled. And then what?

Arthur Wiseman neither wanted to know, nor wanted to be a part of, whatever the future might hold. And yet he was already a part of it.

Nothing more than a pawn, perhaps, but it was enough. Never again would he be able to face a patient, let alone try to administer to a patient's needs.

For Arthur Wiseman, his career, and his life, had just come to an end.

He went into his examining room, unlocked his drug cabinet, and removed a bottle. Then, taking the bottle and a hypodermic syringe, he returned to his office.

For a few minutes he worked with the computer, deleting all references to BCG from his records. His reputation, at least, would remain intact.

Moments later, he was dead.

Randy Corliss opened his eyes. For a moment he wasn't sure where he was, but then, seeing the branches above his head, he began to remember.

He'd been in the back of Sergeant Bronski's car, with his mother. And then something had happened. Sergeant Bronski had started yelling, and the car had skidded, and then—and then—

He sat bolt upright and looked around. Through the trees he could see the smoldering wreckage. All around it there were people.

People, and ambulances, and a fire truck, and—

He got to his feet and stared down at his body. His skin was all reddish, and he wasn't wearing any clothes. And his head felt cold.

Curiously, he touched his head.

Where there should have been hair, he felt only bare skin.

Fire.

There had been a fire. But where were his parents?

He began stumbling out of the woods. "Mommy? Mommy, where are you? Daddy?" Suddenly, he stopped, as the memory of what had happened flooded back to him. Now he was screaming and running toward the blackened car. "Mommy! Daddy!"

The crowd gathered around the wreck turned to stare at the strange apparition that had appeared out of the woods.

"Where the hell did *he* come from?" one of the medics muttered. Grabbing a blanket, he moved toward the naked child, then tried to wrap the blanket around him. Randy struggled against him.

"Mommy!" he screamed again. "Where's my mommy?"

"Easy, son, take it easy," the medic told him. "Where'd you come from?"

But Randy was beyond hearing. Thrashing in the confines of the blanket, he could only keep shouting for his parents, tears streaming down his face. Finally, exhausted, he fell to the ground, where he lay sobbing helplessly.

"Get him into the truck," a second medic said. "He must have been in the car with them. Let's get him to a hospital. Fast."

They carried Randy to one of the ambulances. A moment later, its siren wailing, the vehicle began racing toward Eastbury Community Hospital. The medic carefully unwrapped the blanket and stared at Randy's skin.

"I don't get it," he said to his partner. "Look at him. His clothes are gone, and his hair is gone. He must have been right in the middle of that fire. He should be dead, just like the others."

And yet, as they examined Randy, neither of the medics could find anything more than what appeared to be a few first-degree burns on what was otherwise baby-smooth skin.

Mark Malone stared somberly across his desk, trying to read Sally Montgomery's eyes.

She had sat silently next to her husband while Malone recited what had happened in Wiseman's office. Twice she had been about to interrupt him, but both times Steve had gently squeezed her hand. Now she was sitting still, her eyes thoughtful. Slowly, she rose from the sofa. "I'm going to see him," she said, her voice coldly furious. "I want to hear it all from him."

"I'm not sure he'll see you," Malone said softly. "When I left him, he said he was all through as a doctor—"

"All through as a *doctor?*" Sally exploded. "He's a *killer,* Mark. He killed Julie. Whether he knew what he was doing or not—and if you ask me, he knew exactly what he was doing—he killed her. And God knows how many others. That's why he wanted to commit me—I was finding out too much." She started toward the office door just as the phone rang.

Malone picked up the receiver and listened for a moment. When he hung up, his hands were trembling. "It's too late, Sally," he said softly. "That was Arthur's nurse. She just found him in his office. He's dead."

"Dead?" Sally repeated. "He's dead?"

"There was a hypodermic on his desk. Apparently he killed himself."

Her fury suddenly deserting her, Sally sank back onto the sofa. "Oh, God," she mumbled. "What next?"

As if in direct response to her question, the phone rang once more. This time, as he listened, Malone closed his eyes and nodded, almost as if he'd been expecting more bad news. When he hung up, he seemed unable to speak.

"What is it?" Steve asked. "Mark, has something else happened?"

Malone nodded. "There—there was an accident. Anyway, they think it was an accident."

Sally lifted her head and her eyes widened. "Where—who—?"

"Carl Bronski," Malone whispered. "He's dead. And Lucy and Jim Corliss too."

"No!" Sally screamed. She was on her feet again. Her eyes wild, she staggered toward Malone. "No! It's a lie—they can't be dead. They can't be." Suddenly her legs buckled beneath her, and she fell, sobbing, to the floor.

Malone rose from his desk and came around to help Steve move her back onto the sofa. "I'll give her a sedative," he said. He went to his drug locker, and a moment later Sally's eyes closed, and her breathing evened out. Only then did the doctor speak again.

"Randy's alive," he said. "They're bringing him here now."

"But what happened?" Steve asked.

"I told you—they don't know. The car went off the road and exploded. If they know why, they didn't tell me."

Steve's mind was reeling. He looked from his sedated wife to the doctor, then back to Sally. "What—oh, Christ, Mark, what the hell's happening?"

"I don't know, Steve," Mark Malone said quietly. "All I know is that right now we have to deal with one thing at a time. Let's get Sally into a bed, and then I'd better get to the emergency room. I want to be there when they bring Randy Corliss in."

Paul Randolph nervously paced his office, wishing he still smoked. But smoking was no longer part of the proper image for anyone even remotely connected with medicine, so no matter how badly he wanted a cigarette, he would not light one. He glanced at the other two men in his office and wondered how they could sit so calmly, as if nothing were happening.

They had been waiting all morning now, and still they had heard nothing from Carmody's team, nothing past that first phone call, when they'd found out who had gathered at Lucy Corliss's house.

Damn the woman. Damn her and her friend Mrs. Montgomery both. And that fool, Dr. Malone. How on earth had they gotten *him* involved in their snooping? And what had they found? Damn them all!

"It isn't really so bad, you know," George Hamlin said softly, breaking the silence that had hung over the room for the last half hour. "We deliberately formulated a base that would be used only on women who didn't want children in the first place. It's not as if our failures were children somebody wanted. Just the opposite is true. These women specifically did not want children! Frankly, I can't see how we've damaged them."

"Apparently, they don't see it that way," Paul Randolph replied, his voice oozing as much sarcasm as he was able to muster. "Apparently, they're under the impression that we've murdered and kidnaped their children. And, damn it, we have done just that, haven't we?"

Lieutenant General Scott Carmody shifted his weight uncomfortably. He wasn't used to waiting, and sitting for any length of time made him stiff. "There's always a price," he said. "The army needs these boys, Randolph, and the sooner this project comes together, the better off this country will be."

"No matter what the cost?"

Carmody's voice grew hard. "We've lost men in every program we've ever started. Sacrifice is part of the price of progress, and we all know it."

Randolph groaned. "Please," he said. "Spare me the old saw about eggs and omelettes. We're talking about children here."

"That has yet to be determined," Hamlin interrupted. He rose, and, stretching, ambled over to the window where, with his arms clasped behind his back, he gazed out at Logan Airport. With the same pleasure he had taken from the sight since he was a boy, he watched a plane hurtle down the runway, then soar into the sky. "I wonder if *my* boys enjoy that?" he mused more to himself than to the others.

"Pardon?" Randolph asked, but before Hamlin could repeat his question, the phone on Randolph's desk jangled to life. Randolph picked it up, then handed it to Carmody, who listened for a few moments, issued some instructions, then hung up. He turned to face the others, the tension of the long night and morning suddenly gone.

"I think we've got it contained," he said. "Lucy and James Corliss are dead, along with Bronski. And Wiseman is dead too."

"Wiseman?" Randolph asked. "What happened?"

"Killed himself."

"What about Randy Corliss?" Hamlin demanded. "Is he dead?"

"No," Carmody replied. "He's not dead. He survived the explosion, and the fire, and got out of the wreckage. He's at Eastbury Community Hospital."

Randolph turned white. "Then how can you say it's contained? If that boy talks—"

But George Hamlin had already grasped the point. "It doesn't matter anymore. What's he going to talk about? We've washed the computers, and by tonight the Academy will be gone too. There's no evidence of anything anymore."

"Except that Randy Corliss knows the names of everyone on the project."

Carmody shrugged. "Not one of whom will ever be traceable. If you were to go searching for them right now, Randolph, you would have trouble proving that anyone connected with the God Project ever lived. Up to, and including, Dr. Hamlin here. Computers not only allow us to keep track of people, Randolph. They also allow us to bury them."

Randolph sank into his chair. "Then it's over?"

"No," Hamlin replied. "There are still the Montgomerys to contend with. And that, Paul, is going to be your job."

As he listened to George Hamlin outline what he had in mind, Paul Randolph once again wished he had a cigarette.

An hour later, though, as he drove to Eastbury and thought over Hamlin's plan, it began to make sense to him.

Perhaps it was going to work out after all.

And if it didn't?

Paul Randolph didn't even want to think about that possibility.

CHAPTER 31

Sally Montgomery opened her eyes, and the first thing she saw was the ceiling. Acoustical plaster, the kind she had always hated. And the color—that awful shade of pale green that was supposed to be restful but was faintly nauseating. So she was in a hospital bed. She had a moment of panic and struggled to sit up. Then she heard Steve's voice.

"It's all right, honey," he was saying. "There's nothing wrong. You just—well, you sort of came apart a couple of hours ago, so Mark gave you something to put you to sleep for a while."

Sally sank back onto the pillow and gazed silently at her husband for a few moments. Was it a trick? Was it really Mark who had given her the shot, or Wiseman?

Wiseman.

Wiseman was dead. Wiseman, and . . . and the Corlisses, and Carl Bronski. Tears welled up in her eyes and brimmed over. Steve reached out and gently brushed them away.

"They're all dead, aren't they?" she asked, her voice hollow.

"All except Randy," Steve replied.

"What happened?"

"Not now," Steve protested. "Why don't you go back to sleep?"

"No. I want to know what happened, Steve. I *have* to know."

"It was an accident. Apparently Bronski lost control of the car—a blowout, maybe. Anyway, it skidded off the road, turned over, and the gas tank ruptured."

"Oh, God," Sally groaned. "It must have been horrible." Her eyes met Steve's. "They . . . burned?"

Steve nodded. "Jim and Lucy did. Carl was thrown out of the car. It rolled on him."

"And Randy?"

"He got out. Somehow, he got out. His clothes burned completely off him, and all his hair . . ."

Sally closed her eyes, as if by the action she could erase the image that had come into her mind. "But how could he have survived? The burns—"

"He did survive. And he's all right, Sally. It's like what happened with Jason."

The door opened and Mark Malone appeared. He closed the door behind him, then stepped to the foot of Sally's bed, glanced at her chart, and forced a smile. "I wish I could say you looked better than you do."

"Steve just told me about . . . about . . ." Her voice faded away as her tears once again began to flow. She groped around her bedside table and found a Kleenex. Wiping away the tears, she pushed herself a little higher up in the bed, then forced herself to meet Malone's eyes. "What does it mean, Mark? What's going on?"

"I wish I could tell you," Malone replied. He hesitated, then spoke again. "You have a visitor. But you don't have to see him."

"A visitor? Who?"

"Paul Randolph."

Sally's eyes widened. "From CHILD? He's here? But—but how? Why?"

"He telephoned about an hour ago. He wanted to know if we'd done something to our computer programs."

Sally felt her heart skip a beat. "The programs?"

Malone nodded. "That's what he said. His story was that their computer tried to do a routine scan of the updates of our records and couldn't."

Steve frowned. "What does that mean?"

"It means all the codes are gone," Malone said. "It means that all our evidence has disappeared."

"But it doesn't matter," Sally said. "We've got the printouts—" Malone's shaking head stopped the flow of her words.

"They're gone, Sally. Before Arthur killed himself he destroyed everything. He altered records in the computer and burned all your printouts. It's all gone, Sally. Everything."

As the full meaning of his words sank in, Sally felt suddenly tired. Tired, and beaten. It was over. The information was gone, all of it. But where? And even as she asked herself the question, she knew the answer. "They did it themselves, didn't they?" she asked. "The people at CHILD dumped the whole thing out of the computer."

"Undoubtedly," Malone agreed. "Although Randolph denies it. That's why he came out here. I told him what's been happening out here, and he wants to hear the whole story from you. He says he also wants to tell you what they know about Group Twenty-one. Except they call it the GT-active group."

"What does that mean?" Steve asked.

"It refers to something called introns," Malone said. "I think Randolph can explain it better than I can, but if you don't want to talk to him," he added, turning his attention back to Sally, "you don't have to."

Sally's eyes grew cold. "I want to," she said. "I want to know what they've been doing to the children, and I want to know why."

Malone hesitated, then turned to Steve as if for confirmation. Steve nodded.

"If Sally wants to see him, bring him in. But don't leave us alone with him."

"I won't," Malone promised grimly. "I want to hear this as much as you do." He left the room, and a moment later returned, followed by Paul Randolph, who immediately moved to the side of the bed and took Sally's hand in his own.

"Mrs. Montgomery," he said, "I can't tell you how sorry I am about what's happened. I'm Paul—"

"I know who you are," Sally said, withdrawing her hand from his grasp and slipping it under the sheet. "What I don't understand is why you want to talk to me."

"I need help," Randolph said. "May I sit down?"

Sally nodded.

"I need to know exactly what you found out about what you've been calling Group Twenty-one. I gather you found evidence that their flaw may have been caused by some external stimulus."

"You know that better than I, Mr. Randolph."

"All I know, Mrs. Montgomery," Randolph said earnestly, "is that a number of years ago our Institute came upon a genetic irregularity which we've recently named the GT-active factor. It's very complicated, but basically what it means is that in certain children there is a normally functionless genetic combination called an intron that for some reason has become functional. It has to do with the enzyme bases that mark the beginning and end of the intron sequences in DNA. For some reason, the guanine-thymine sequence, which normally marks the beginning of an intron, has failed in these children. We've only recently identified which intron it is that has become active."

Sally's eyes narrowed with suspicion. "But you've been tracking these children for years," she pointed out.

"Because of a hormone present in their bodies in higher quantities than is normal," Randolph explained. "Hormones, as you may know, are produced under the direction of DNA, just as are all the other compounds in the body. We suspected a genetic irregularity because of the hormone, but it was only recently that we were able to trace it to the GT-active factor. Our next step will be to determine the source of the factor itself, which, until now, we've assumed was hereditary—a combination of the genetic structures of the parents that produces the GT-active factor. But apparently you've discovered evidence to the contrary."

"Yes," Sally said, "I have." Slowly, she began to repeat the story that had begun the night her daughter had died. She talked steadily for nearly an hour, while Paul Randolph sat listening to her, taking occasional notes, but never interrupting her. When she finished, she sank, exhausted, into the pillows, then stared bitterly at Randolph. "But you knew all about it," she said. "It was all there, and it all pointed directly to CHILD. You killed our children, and you kidnaped them, Mr. Randolph."

Paul Randolph avoided her gaze, rose, and drifted distractedly toward the window. When he finally began speaking, his back was still to the room. "You're partly right, of course. We *did* kidnap some children, Mrs. Montgomery. In fact, the next child we intended to take is your son, Jason."

As Sally gasped, Steve rose to his feet, his hands clenched into white-knuckled fists. But then Randolph turned around, his face slack and his eyes bleak. "I'm sorry to have to tell you this," he said softly, "but your son is dying."

Sally flinched. "No!" she cried. "Jason's not dying. He's fine! He's never been sick a day in—"

"None of them are, Mrs. Montgomery," Randolph said quietly. Though his voice was soft, there was a tone to it that demanded the attention of everyone in the room. "That's what makes the whole thing so incredibly difficult. These children, the children with the GT-active factor, seem healthy. They *are* healthy, incredibly so. The hormone appears to be triggered by trauma. That is, any damage to the tissue of these children from any source whatsoever—germs, viruses, injuries—triggers production of the hormone. And the hormone, in turn, spurs tissue regeneration. These children have a regenerative ability that is nothing short of miraculous. Damaged tissue which should normally take days or weeks to repair itself regenerates in a matter of minutes, sometimes even seconds."

Sally's eyes met Steve's as they each remembered the incidents with Jason —the acid, the boiling fudge, the fight with Joey Connors. The unexplainable was suddenly explained.

Reluctantly, she turned her attention back to Randolph. "But you said Jason was—was dying."

"And he is, Mrs. Montgomery. That's the other side of the coin. Although the hormone makes the children appear abnormally healthy, in the end it kills them. It's as if at some point the hormone has drawn on every bit of energy these children possess, and they die. From what we know, they simply seem to burn out. With the little girls it happens very quickly. So far none of them have survived past the age of one year. With the boys the process is slower. Some of them have lived to be nine. None has lived to see his tenth birthday. And that's why we kidnaped some of them."

"Did it occur to you that kidnaping is a federal crime, Mr. Randolph?" Steve asked, his voice crackling with indignation.

"Of course it did," Randolph snapped. "But in the end, it was the only possible course of action."

Steve stared at the distinguished-looking man with a mixture of revulsion and curiosity. "In the end?"

"When we began to understand what was happening, we tried to explain the situation to some of the parents. We wanted to put the children under twenty-four-hour-a-day observation. Needless to say, the parents refused. And why wouldn't they? There was nothing wrong with their children, nothing at all. It was impossible to make them understand what the problem was."

"So you began *stealing* the children?" Sally asked.

"Not at first. We simply kept track of them. You know how—you discovered our tracking system. But two years ago it became obvious to us that *all* the children were going to die. One way or another, the parents were going to lose them. So we took them, hoping that we could eventually discover how the burn-out phenomenon was triggered. So far, we haven't succeeded. But at least now we seem to know the source of the problem." He paused. "Wiseman."

"No," Sally objected. "It wasn't Dr. Wiseman. It couldn't have been. When he found out what was happening, he killed himself."

"Because he thought he'd been used, or because he knew he'd been caught?" Randolph countered.

"What are you saying?"

"Did you know that Arthur Wiseman was something of an expert in genetics?"

Sally looked puzzled, and Mark Malone frowned. "Even *I* didn't know that," he said.

"I don't see what—" Sally began, but Randolph interrupted her.

"If these children were somehow made the victims of some form of recombinant DNA, and apparently they were, it happened in Arthur Wiseman's office. He told Malone about a salve he used, which he claimed he got from PharMax. PharMax has never heard of it. It seems to me that Wiseman must have devised it himself."

"But why?" Sally flared. "Why would he do it?"

"Science," Randolph told her. "There are people in the world, Mrs. Montgomery, for whom research and experimentation exist for their own sake. They feel no responsibility for whatever they might create. For them, creation and discovery are fulfillment in themselves. Such people have no thoughts about the final results of what they are doing, no concern about any possible moral issues. Knowledge is to be sought, and used. If you *can* do something, you *must* do it. And if Wiseman found a way to alter the human form, the temptation to do so must have been overwhelming. It probably wasn't until this morning that the consequences of what he'd done became clear to him. And so he buried the evidence. There's nothing in the computer anymore, Mrs. Montgomery. No records of which children bear the GT-active factor, no records of which women were treated with Wiseman's compound. Nothing." He sank into a chair and shook his head. "I'm not sure we can ever rebuild those records."

Sally lay still, trying to sort it all out. Was he telling her the truth?

He wasn't. Deep inside, Sally was sure that he was lying to her, or, if not lying, then telling her only a part of the truth. After all, she reflected, he had admitted to having kidnaped Randy Corliss.

Had he also, somehow, killed Randy's parents and Carl Bronski?

Again, she wasn't certain. Of one thing, though, she was very sure.

What she had found out, or thought she had found out, had been taken away from her. There was no way she could get it back again. It was all probably still there, buried somewhere in the memory bank of a computer, but so deeply buried and expertly covered that she would never be able to dig it up.

And if she tried, she would very likely be killed.

And I, Sally thought silently to herself, am not going to be killed. I am going to tell this man whatever he wants to hear, and I am going to stay alive and raise my son.

My son.

Jason. Was he dying? Or was that, too, a lie? For that question, only time itself would provide an answer.

Sally pulled herself into a sitting position and carefully smoothed the sheets over her torso. Then she made herself meet Paul Randolph's eyes.

"Thank you," she said softly. "Thank you for coming here and telling me all this. You can't know what it's been like. It's been a nightmare."

"One that's over now, Mrs. Montgomery." He paused. "Except for the children."

"Yes," Sally breathed. "Except for the children. What can we do?"

Randolph made a helpless gesture. "I wish I could tell you. Watch them. Love them. Try to make their lives as happy as you can. And hope."

"Hope?" Sally asked. "Hope for what? You said none of them has lived to reach the age of ten."

"And so they haven't, Mrs. Montgomery. But we know practically nothing about this. Maybe some of them will live. Maybe your son, maybe Randy Corliss. All we can do is watch and hope."

"Randy Corliss." Sally repeated the name, then looked to Steve. "What's going to happen to him?"

Steve shrugged. "I don't know. He probably has relatives—"

"I want him."

"Sally—"

"Steve, I want us to take care of him. I—well, I feel as though he almost belongs to us now. The way he is, and Jason. Oh, Steve, we've got to take care of him. We owe it to Lucy and Jim."

"Sally, we've got to think about this—"

"No, Steve. We've got to do it. And if you don't want to, then I'll do it alone." Her voice suddenly dropped to a whisper. "Besides, it's only going to be for a little while."

Steve swallowed hard, knowing he wouldn't refuse Sally's request. And yet, even as he gave in, he began to wonder what was going to happen to him when each of the boys died. Would it be as it had been with Julie?

He had to talk to Sally about it, and he had to talk to her alone. He glanced up at Mark Malone, and the young doctor, reading the look, signaled to Paul Randolph. "I think we'd better leave these two alone for a while, Mr. Randolph."

Paul Randolph rose. "Of course," he said gently. He moved to offer his hand to Steve, but the gesture was refused. "I'm sorry," he said. "I'm sorry to have had to tell you all this, but sooner or later, it had to come out." Then, with Malone following him, he left the room.

As soon as they were alone, Sally's eyes locked onto Steve's.

"He's lying," she said. "He's lying about everything."

"Sally—"

She ignored his interruption. "It's over, Steve. I've lost. There's nothing I can do except take care of those boys and pretend nothing's wrong. Otherwise they'll kill me. Just like they killed Lucy and Jim and Carl."

"And what about me?" Steve asked.

Sally avoided his eyes. "I don't know, Steve. I don't expect you to believe me. I know what Randolph said sounded reasonable. But I simply do not believe him."

"Then we'll do it your way," Steve said. He sat down on the bed and gathered Sally into his arms. "Whatever happens from here on out, we'll do it your way." He drew her closer and felt her body stiffen. Then suddenly Sally relaxed. Her arms slid around Steve's neck.

"Hold me," she whispered. "Oh, please, just hold me for a minute."

They clung to each other, wondering what pain the future held for them, and how they would cope with it.

Whatever it was, they would face it together.

Mark Malone led Paul Randolph into his office and closed the door behind him.

"They didn't buy it," he said. "At least she didn't."

"No," Randolph replied. "She didn't. But I let her know that she'll never prove a thing, and I gave her Wiseman. There'll be just enough doubt in her mind to keep her quiet."

"Until Jason dies."

For the first time that day, Paul Randolph smiled.

"That's the most beautiful part of it," he said. "Hamlin doesn't think Jason Montgomery or Randy Corliss is going to die. It looks like the project's a success, Mark."

Mark Malone opened the bottom drawer of his desk and pulled out the thick stack of printouts that Sally had gleaned from the computer. He handed them to Randolph, his expression serious.

"You and Hamlin might be interested in seeing just how far Sally'd gotten," he said. "Next time, I think you'd better make sure *no one* can trace you." Then his face brightened, and he reached into the drawer once more, this time bringing out the bottle of Cognac he'd bought on the day the God Project had begun. For ten long years he'd been the project's watchdog. Today he was its savior. He broke the seal and poured them each a generous shot.

"Here's to the future," he said. "And all the wonderful creatures man is about to become."

EPILOGUE
Three Years Later

Sally Montgomery faced her reflection in the mirror with resignation. Her eyes seemed to have sunk deep within their sockets, and her hair, only three years ago a deep and luxuriant brown, had faded to a lifeless gray. Around her eyes, crow's feet had taken hold and her forehead was creased with worry. And yet, even as she examined the deterioration, she felt no urge to fight it, but only a sense of relief that for her, the pain might soon be over.

It was The Boys who had done it to her.

She no longer thought of Jason as her son, nor of Randy Corliss as her foster son. To her, they had become The Boys. Strange, alien beings she neither knew nor trusted.

It had not been that way at first. At first they had been her children, both of them, with Randy Corliss filling the void in her life that had been left when Julie died. Even now she could remember the flood of emotion that had nearly overwhelmed her when she had gone to see Randy in his room at Eastbury Community Hospital.

He had lain still in bed, his eyes wide, his face expressionless. An image had flashed through her mind of pictures she had seen of children rescued from the concentration camps after World War II, their bodies emaciated, their hair fallen out from starvation, their eyes vacant, bodies and minds numbed by years of unspeakable abuse.

But Randy's skin had been ruddy that day, and the lack of hair had given his head an oddly inhuman appearance. And in his eyes, instead of the look of pain and sorrow that Sally had expected, there had been curiosity, and a certain strange detachment.

"They're dead, aren't they?" he had asked. "Mom and Dad got killed in the fire, didn't they?"

"Yes," she had said, sitting by his bed and taking his hand in hers. "I'm sorry. I'm so sorry, Randy."

"What's going to happen to me?"

At the time, Sally had attributed the question, and the lack of response to his parents' deaths, to shock. She had explained to him that she and Steve were going to take care of him, and that he and Jason would be like brothers now.

Randy had smiled, then gone to sleep.

That had been the beginning.

The next day, she and Steve had taken Randy home and begun the wait. Every moment of every day and night they kept the vigil, waiting for the moment when Jason or Randy would suddenly, with no warning whatever, stop breathing and die.

But it hadn't happened. First the days, then the weeks and months, had slipped by and the boys grew and appeared to thrive. Slowly, imperceptibly, Sally and Steve began to let their guard down. Instead of watching for the boys' deaths, they began planning for their lives. After the end of the first year, when Randy turned eleven, and Jason was just past ten, they took them to Mark Malone for their monthly examination. When he was done with the boys, Dr. Malone spoke to Steve and Sally in his office.

"They're remarkable in every way," he said. "They're both large for their age and unusually well developed. It seems almost as if the GT-active factor, as well as protecting them, allows them to mature more quickly than normal children."

"What does that mean?" Sally asked. "I mean, for them?"

"I'm not sure," Malone admitted. "It could mean nothing, but it could be a first sign of premature aging. It could be that while they'll live very healthy lives, they'll live short lives, even if the burn-out syndrome is never triggered. But that's just speculation," he assured them. "Frankly, with these boys, there's no way of telling what might happen. All we can do is wait and see."

The waiting had gone on for two more years. During those years the boys had grown closer and closer, their personalities taking on each other's traits, until both Sally and Steve had unconsciously fallen into the habit of speaking to them as if they were a single unit. What was told to one would be passed on to the other. The blame for things gone wrong that was assigned to one was assumed by the other. What Randy did, Jason did, and vice versa.

They had no friends, being sufficient unto themselves, but Sally and Steve were never sure whether it was merely that the boys had no need for outside stimulation or whether such stimulation had become unavailable to them.

There had been incidents.

The worst of them had been what Sally had come to think of as The Circus.

It had occurred after the Barnum & Bailey extravaganza had played in Boston, and all the children of the neighborhood had decided to duplicate the show. Most of them, in the end, had decided that being a clown was the better part of valor, but Jason and Randy, though not invited to participate, had provided the thrills.

Their slack-rope act had not bothered Sally, for she had watched them prepare it, worried at first that they might hurt themselves, but impressed in the end that they had had the foresight to learn the trick of balancing on a rope at a low level. Only when they had become confident of themselves had they begun raising the rope, until eventually both of them were able to walk it with ease at a height of ten feet.

She had not watched them rehearse the knife-throwing act, nor had she seen it. But she had heard about it.

The Circus had taken place in the Connors' backyard, and the last act had been Jason and Randy. In turn, each of the boys had stood against the wall of the Connors' garage, while the other threw six steak knives at him. First Jason had stood against the wall, while Randy hurled the evil-looking blades.

One by one, the blades had struck the garage, inches from the target, their handles quivering as their blades dug into the wood siding. When all six knives were surrounding him, Jason had stepped forward, taken a bow, then pulled the knives from the wall.

Then Randy took his place against the wall, his feet spread wide apart, his arms stretched out.

Jason stood ten feet away and aimed the first of the six knives. It whirled through the air and struck the wall between Randy's legs.

The second knife buried itself in the wall next to his left ear.

The third knife struck next to his right ear.

By now the children in the audience were screaming and cheering so loudly that Kay Connors had looked out the window to see what was happening.

She was in time to see the last three knives whirl, in quick succession, through the air.

Two of them struck Randy Corliss's hands, pinning them to the wall.

The third buried itself in Randy's stomach.

The happy cheering turned into terrified screams. Frozen in horror, Mrs. Connors stared woodenly through the window.

She watched Jason calmly go to Randy and yank loose the two knives that were pinning his hands. And then she watched as Randy himself, his face wreathed in happy smiles, pulled the third knife from his own belly.

An hour later, as she listened to Kay Connors relate the story, Sally had tried to remain calm.

"I still don't know how they did it," Kay had said when she was finished telling the tale. Her face was still pale from her fright, and her hands were trembling slightly. "And I don't want to know. But I'll tell you right now, Sally, I don't want those boys at my house again. They scared me nearly to death, and I don't even want to think about how the other children felt. The girls were all crying, and some of the boys too. I know Jason and Randy thought it was a joke, but it wasn't funny."

Sally, of course, had immediately realized that it had not been a trick at all. Jason had simply hurled the knives into his friend, and Randy, far from being seriously injured, had healed within minutes. By the time the screaming children had been sorted out and Kay Connors had gotten to Randy, there hadn't been even so much as a scar left to betray the secret of the "trick."

Four days later, two five-year-old boys had tried to duplicate the trick. One of them had nearly bled to death, but the other one was unhurt, apparently the beneficiary of the flip of the coin that had determined which of the two would be the first target. Sally had suspected differently. Though she could no longer be certain, she thought she remembered the name of the uninjured boy, Tony Phelps, from the list of children in Group Twenty-one.

It was after that incident that Sally had begun to wonder about the boys. They had listened to her quietly while she talked to them, first about the "stunt" they had pulled, which she knew had not been a stunt at all, then about the little boy who had almost died.

"But everybody's going to die," was Randy's only comment.

"Besides," Jason had added, "people who can get hurt shouldn't play our games. They should just do whatever we tell them to do."

"Do what you tell them?" Sally echoed. "Why should people do what you tell them?"

Jason had met her eyes. "Because we're special," he said. "We're special, and that makes us better than other people."

Sally had tried to explain to them that their inability to be hurt, or even to feel pain, did not make them better than other people. If anything, it meant that they had to be particularly careful of other people, because they might accidentally do something that would hurt someone else. The boys had only looked at each other and shrugged.

"We don't do anything by accident," Jason had said.

And so the wondering had begun, and, once more, the watching had begun. And slowly, Sally had come to realize that there was more to The Boys than the GT-active factor. There was a coldness about them, and an ever-increasing sense of their own superiority that was at first disturbing and eventually frightening.

Now Jason was twelve and Randy was thirteen, but they looked five years older.

And they did what they wanted, when they wanted.

Last night, very late, Sally had talked to Steve about them.

"They're not human," she had finished. "They're not human and they're dangerous."

Steve, who had listened quietly for over an hour, had shifted uneasily in his chair, "What do you suggest we do?" he asked.

Sally had swallowed, unsure whether she would be able to voice the idea that had been growing steadily in her mind for several months now. But it had to be voiced. It had to be brought out in the open and discussed. If it wasn't, she would surely lose her mind.

"I think we have to kill them."

Steve Montgomery had stared at his wife. As the import of what she had just said began to register on part of his mind, another part seemed to shift gears, to step back, as if unwilling even to accept the words Sally had uttered.

What's happened to her, that part of his mind had wondered. What's happened to the woman I married? Sally, over the last three years, had become almost a stranger to him. He had seen the changes in her face, but more than that, he had felt the changes in her spirit. In many ways she seemed more like a hunted animal than anything else.

Hunted, or haunted?

And yet, he had slowly come to realize, what he now saw in his wife was a reflection of what he felt himself. He, too, had come to regard the boys as something apart from himself, something he could only barely comprehend, but was afraid of.

What, he had often wondered, would they grow up to be, if they grew up at all?

At first he had dismissed the question, but then, as time had moved on, and the boys had not died, he had forced himself to face it.

And the only answer he had come up with, time and time again, was that whatever they grew up to be, it would not be human.

And so he, too, had come to feel haunted. Haunted by the feeling that he was raising a new species of man, indistinguishable from other men, but different. Cold, unfeeling, impervious to pain.

Impervious to pain, and therefore impervious to suffering. How many of them were there, and what would they do when the time came, as it inevitably would, when they realized their powers? Steve Montgomery, like his wife, didn't know.

"All right," he had said last night.

Sally had stared at him, momentarily shaken by the ease with which he had apparently accepted her idea. "Is that all you have to say? Just all right?"

Steve had nodded. "Three years ago, when we talked to Paul Randolph, I found out that you'd been right about the children all along. And I made up my mind about something that day. I decided that from that moment on, where the children were concerned, I'd go along with any decision you made. But I've watched those boys too, Sally. Whatever they are, they aren't human. Randy Corliss is not our child, and never has been. And neither is Jason. I'm not sure what they are, but I know what they're not." Then he repeated the words once again: "They're not human."

And so, earlier today, Sally had gone alone to see Mark Malone, and quietly explained to him what she wanted to do. He had listened to her, and for a long time after she had finished, had sat silently, apparently thinking.

"I need some time, Sally," he'd said at last. "I need some time to think about this."

"How much time?" Sally had asked. "This isn't something I've just made up my mind to, Mark. I've been thinking about it for a long time. The boys are growing up, and I'm afraid of them."

"Have you thought of sending them away to school?"

"Of course I have," Sally replied bitterly. "I've thought of everything, and in the end I always come down to the same thought. They're some kind of monsters, Mark, and they have to be destroyed. It's not myself I'm afraid for—it's everybody. Can't you understand that?"

And Mark, to her relief, had nodded his head. "But I'll still have to think about it," he'd told her. "I'm a doctor. My training is to save lives, not end them."

"I know," Sally whispered unhappily. "Believe me, I wish I could have done this without even talking to you. But I need your help. I—well, I'm afraid I haven't the slightest idea of how to"—she faltered, then made herself finish the sentence—"how to kill them."

Mark had led her to the door. "Let me call you in a couple of hours, Sally. I'll have to think about this thing, and I won't promise you anything. In fact, I wish you hadn't come here today."

And so she had come home. Now she sat in front of her mirror, staring at her strange reflection, recognizing her image, but not understanding the person she had become.

But it didn't matter. Nothing about her own life mattered anymore, not as long as The Boys were alive. Only after they were dead would she worry about herself again. And yet, what if there was no way to kill them? What then?

And then the phone rang.

"It's Mark, Sally. There's something called succinylcholine chloride. If you'll come down to my office, I'll explain it to you."

Late that night, Randy and Jason came downstairs to say good night to Sally and Steve. Sally accepted a kiss from each of them, and then, as they started up the stairs, called to them.

"I almost forgot. Dr. Malone called me today and gave me some medicine for you. He wanted you to have it just before you went to bed."

The boys looked at each other curiously. This was something new. Medicine? Neither of them had ever needed medicine before.

"What's it for?" Randy asked.

"I'm not sure," Sally replied, praying that there would be no trembling in her voice. "It's just some kind of a shot."

"I don't want it," Jason said. His face set into a stubborn expression that both Sally and Steve had come to know too well.

Steve rose from his chair. "You're going to have it, son," he said, keeping his voice carefully under control.

Jason glanced toward Randy, and as Steve moved toward the foot of the stairs, he could feel the boys sizing him up, weighing their combined bulk against his own strength. He started up the stairs. The two boys watched him warily, and Steve braced himself against a possible attack. But then, as he approached the boys, Randy spoke.

"Fuck it, Jason. What the hell can it do to us?"

It can kill you, Steve thought with sudden detachment. Sally had told him about the chemical Mark Malone had given her. It was called succinylcholine chloride, and its effect would be to attack their nervous systems, paralyzing them to the point where they would be unable to breathe. In the few minutes it would take the GT-active factor to overcome the damage, they would be deprived of air and suffocated. Yes, he thought once again, it can kill you.

But the boys had already turned the whole thing into a joke, and while Sally prepared the hypodermic needles, Steve followed them into their room, where they undressed and slid into their beds. Randy grinned at Jason. "You ever had a shot?"

"Not since I was a little kid. But I've had blood tests."

"So have I. That week I was at the Academy, they took tests all the time. You can't even feel it."

"Who's afraid of feeling it?" Jason laughed. "It just pisses me off that Dr. Malone thinks something's wrong with us."

"What does he know?" Randy sneered. And then Sally came in, carrying two needles. Jason looked at them, frowning.

"What is it?"

"Succinylcholine chloride," Sally replied. "Five hundred milligrams for each of you. Which of you wants to be first?"

The boys glanced at each other and shrugged. "I'll go first," Randy offered.

"All right." Sally took his arm and rolled up the left sleeve of his pajama top. The injection, Malone had told her, was to go directly into muscle. The upper arm muscle would be fastest, but any muscle would do. Holding the needle in her right hand, she grasped his arm with her left.

And suddenly she lost her nerve.

Over Randy's head, her eyes met Steve's. "I—I can't do it," she whispered. "I just can't do it."

Steve shook his head. "Don't look at me," he said quietly. "I can't do it either."

And suddenly the boys were laughing at them. "Let me have the needle, Aunt Sally," Randy said. "I'll do it myself. It's no big deal."

"We'll do it together," Jason offered. "On three, we'll each give ourselves a shot in the leg. Okay?"

Silently, feeling as though she were in some kind of a dream, Sally gave each of the boys one of the needles. Then, as she and Steve looked on, they rolled up the legs of their pajamas, and, after Jason had counted to three, jabbed the needles into their legs, and pressed the plungers down. The liquid in the cylinders disappeared into the muscle of their thighs. When it was over, they pulled the needles out of their flesh, and looked at Sally, their eyes filled with contempt.

"Satisfied?" Jason asked.

Sally nodded and took the empty needles from her son. "Now go to bed," she said, her voice choking with all the emotions she had held so carefully in check ever since she had reached her decision. "Go to bed, and go to sleep."

She tucked them in and then did something she hadn't done for a long time. She leaned over and kissed each of them on the forehead. A moment later, leaving the lights on, she and Steve slipped out of the room.

When they were alone, Jason suddenly felt a strange sensation in his body.

"Randy?" he said.

"Hunh?"

There was an odd strangling sound to Randy's voice. Jason tried to sit up to look at his friend.

He couldn't.

All he could do, and even that was a struggle, was roll over and stare across at the other bed. Randy was lying on his back, his eyes wide open, struggling to breathe.

"Wha—what's wrong?" Jason managed to ask. "What—what did they give us?"

"Don't know," Randy gasped. "Can't—can't breathe."

And then, as the full force of the lethal dose of poison struck him, Jason fell back on his pillow, and slipped into unconsciousness.

Downstairs, Sally sat desolately on the sofa, trying to accept what she had just done.

"It was the right thing to do," she said over and over again. "It was the right thing to do and I had to do it." Her tears overflowed and ran down her cheeks. "But, oh, God, Steve, I'll never be able to live with it. Never."

Steve nodded unhappily. "I keep telling myself they weren't human," he whispered. "But I guess I still don't believe it. Randy, maybe. But Jason? God, Sally, he was our son."

"He wasn't," Sally said, her voice rising. "He wasn't our son. He was something else, and he had to die. He *had* to, Steve. But what's going to happen to us now?"

Steve looked up and Sally felt a sudden calmness emanating from him. "We'll be charged," she heard him say, his voice sounding as if it were coming from a great distance away. "We'll be charged with the murder of our own son and our foster son. And no one will believe it wasn't murder, Sally."

"And they'll be right," Sally cried. Her hands clenched together and she twisted them in her lap as if she were fighting some physical pain that was threatening to overwhelm her. "Oh, God, Steve, they'll be right."

And then, in a moment of silence, they heard a sound from upstairs.

They heard a door open. There were footsteps.

A moment later Jason and Randy came slowly down the stairs and stepped into the living room, where they stood quietly facing Jason's parents.

And, since they were his parents, it was Jason who spoke.

"You can't kill us," he said softly, his eyes sparkling evilly. "Dr. Malone knows that. That's why he gave you that stuff. It was just another experiment. But don't ever try to kill us again, Mother. Because if you do, we will destroy you. Without even thinking about it, we will kill you."

Then, in perfect unison, they turned, and went back up the stairs.

ABOUT THE AUTHOR

JOHN SAUL won instant acclaim for his first novel, *Suffer The Children,* a million-copy bestseller. He has since written numerous bestsellers, including *The Homing, Guardian, Shadows, Creature, Darkness* and the three novels contained in his previous Wings Books collection, *Hellfire, The Unwanted* and *Sleepwalk,* each a frightening tale of supernatural and psychological terror. John Saul lives in Seattle, Washington, where he is at work on his next novel.